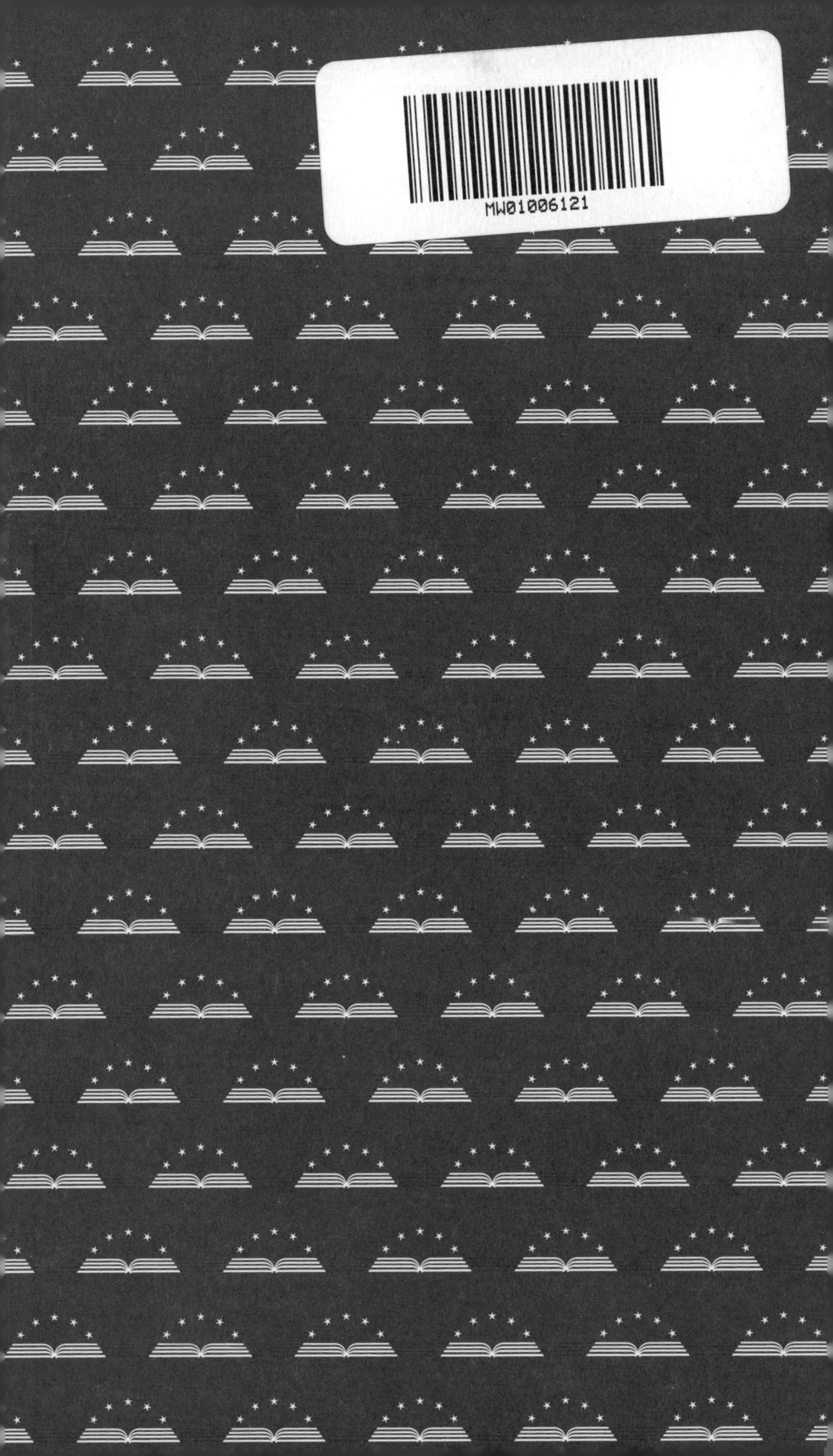
MW01006121

JOAN DIDION

Joan Didion

THE 1980s & 90s

Salvador
Democracy
Miami
After Henry
The Last Thing He Wanted

David L. Ulin, *editor*

THE LIBRARY OF AMERICA

JOAN DIDION: THE 1980s & 90s

Published in the United States by Library of America.
Visit our website at www.loa.org.

This paper exceeds the requirements of
ANSI/NISO Z39.48–1992 (Permanence of Paper).

Distributed to the trade in the United States
by Penguin Random House Inc.
and in Canada by Penguin Random House Canada Ltd.

Library of Congress Control Number: 2020941489
ISBN 978–1–59853–683–6

First Printing
The Library of America—341

Manufactured in the United States of America

Joan Didion: The 1980s & 90s
is published with support from

David Bruce Smith

and other friends of Library of America

Contents

SALVADOR

I am indebted for general background particularly to Thomas P. Anderson's *Matanza: El Salvador's Communist Revolt of 1932* (University of Nebraska Press: Lincoln, 1971) and *The War of the Dispossessed: Honduras and El Salvador, 1969* (University of Nebraska Press: Lincoln, 1981); to David Browning's *El Salvador: Landscape and Society* (Clarendon Press: Oxford, 1971); and to the officers and staff of the United States embassy in San Salvador. I am indebted most of all to my husband, John Gregory Dunne, who was with me in El Salvador and whose notes on, memories about, and interpretations of events there enlarged and informed my own perception of the place.

This book is for
Robert Silvers
and for
Christopher Dickey

"All Europe contributed to the making of Kurtz; and by-and-by I learned that, most appropriately, the International Society for the Suppression of Savage Customs had intrusted him with the making of a report, for its future guidance. And he had written it, too. I've seen it. I've read it. It was eloquent, vibrating with eloquence. . . . 'By the simple exercise of our will we can exert a power for good practically unbounded,' etc. etc. From that point he soared and took me with him. The peroration was magnificent, although difficult to remember, you know. It gave me the notion of an exotic Immensity ruled by an august Benevolence. It made me tingle with enthusiasm. This was the unbounded power of eloquence—of words—of burning noble words. There were no practical hints to interrupt the magic current of phrases, unless a kind of note at the foot of the last page, scrawled evidently much later, in an unsteady hand, may be regarded as the exposition of a method. It was very simple, and at the end of that moving appeal to every altruistic sentiment it blazed at you, luminous and terrifying, like a flash of lightning in a serene sky: 'Exterminate all the brutes!'"

—Joseph Conrad,
Heart of Darkness

THE THREE-YEAR-OLD El Salvador International Airport is glassy and white and splendidly isolated, conceived during the waning of the Molina "National Transformation" as convenient less to the capital (San Salvador is forty miles away, until recently a drive of several hours) than to a central hallucination of the Molina and Romero regimes, the projected beach resorts, the Hyatt, the Pacific Paradise, tennis, golf, water-skiing, condos, *Costa del Sol*; the visionary invention of a tourist industry in yet another republic where the leading natural cause of death is gastrointestinal infection. In the general absence of tourists these hotels have since been abandoned, ghost resorts on the empty Pacific beaches, and to land at this airport built to service them is to plunge directly into a state in which no ground is solid, no depth of field reliable, no perception so definite that it might not dissolve into its reverse.

The only logic is that of acquiescence. Immigration is negotiated in a thicket of automatic weapons, but by whose authority the weapons are brandished (Army or National Guard or National Police or Customs Police or Treasury Police or one of a continuing proliferation of other shadowy and overlapping forces) is a blurred point. Eye contact is avoided. Documents are scrutinized upside down. Once clear of the airport, on the new highway that slices through green hills rendered phosphorescent by the cloud cover of the tropical rainy season, one sees mainly underfed cattle and mongrel dogs and armored vehicles, vans and trucks and Cherokee Chiefs fitted with reinforced steel and bulletproof Plexiglas an inch thick. Such vehicles are a fixed feature of local life, and are popularly associated with disappearance and death. There was the Cherokee Chief seen following the Dutch television crew killed in Chalatenango province in March of 1982. There was the red Toyota three-quarter-ton pickup sighted near the van driven by the four American Catholic workers on the night they were killed in 1980. There were, in the late spring and summer of 1982, the three Toyota panel trucks, one yellow, one blue, and one green, none bearing plates, reported present at each of the mass detentions (a "detention" is another fixed feature of local life, and often precedes a "disappearance") in the Amatepec district of San Salvador. These are the details—the models and colors of armored vehicles, the makes and calibers of weapons, the particular methods of dismemberment and decapitation used in particular instances—on which the visitor to Salvador learns immediately to concentrate, to the exclusion of past or future concerns, as in a prolonged amnesiac fugue.

Terror is the given of the place. Black-and-white police cars cruise in pairs, each with the barrel of a rifle extruding from an open window. Roadblocks materialize at random, soldiers fanning out from trucks and taking positions, fingers always on triggers, safeties clicking on and off. Aim is taken as if to pass the time. Every morning *El Diario de Hoy* and *La Prensa Gráfica* carry cautionary stories. "*Una madre y sus dos hijos fueron asesinados con arma cortante (corvo) por ocho sujetos desconocidos el lunes en la noche*": A mother and her two sons hacked to death in their beds by eight *desconocidos*, unknown men. The same morning's paper: the unidentified body of a young man, strangled, found on the shoulder of a road. Same morning, different story: the unidentified bodies of three young men, found on another road, their faces partially destroyed by bayonets, one face carved to represent a cross.

It is largely from these reports in the newspapers that the United States embassy compiles its body counts, which are transmitted to Washington in a weekly dispatch referred to by embassy people as "the grim-gram." These counts are presented in a kind of tortured code that fails to obscure what is taken for granted in El Salvador, that government forces do most of the killing. In a January 15, 1982 memo to Washington, for example, the embassy issued a "guarded" breakdown on its count of 6,909 "reported" political murders between September 16, 1980 and September 15, 1981. Of these 6,909, according to the memo, 922 were "believed committed by security forces," 952 "believed committed by leftist terrorists," 136 "believed committed by rightist terrorists," and 4,889 "committed by unknown assailants," the famous *desconocidos* favored by those San Salvador newspapers still publishing. (The figures actually add up not to 6,909 but to 6,899, leaving ten in a kind of official limbo.) The memo continued:

> "The uncertainty involved here can be seen in the fact that responsibility cannot be fixed in the majority of cases. We note, however, that it is generally believed in El Salvador that a large number of the unexplained killings are carried out by the security forces, officially or unofficially. The Embassy is aware of dramatic claims that have been made by one interest group or another in which the security forces figure as the primary agents of murder here. El Salvador's tangled web of attack and vengeance, traditional criminal violence and political mayhem make this an impossible charge to sustain. In saying this, however, we make no attempt to lighten the responsibility for the deaths of many hundreds, and perhaps thousands, which can be attributed to the security forces. . . ."

The body count kept by what is generally referred to in San Salvador as "the Human Rights Commission" is higher than the embassy's, and documented periodically by a photographer who goes out looking for bodies. These bodies he photographs are often broken into unnatural positions, and the faces to which the bodies are attached (when they are attached) are equally unnatural, sometimes unrecognizable as human faces, obliterated by acid or beaten to a mash of misplaced ears and teeth or slashed ear to ear and invaded by insects. "*Encontrado en Antiguo Cuscatlán el día 25 de Marzo 1982: camison de dormir celeste*," the typed caption reads on one photograph: found in Antiguo Cuscatlán March 25, 1982 wearing a sky-blue nightshirt. The captions are laconic. Found in Soyapango May 21, 1982. Found in Mejicanos June 11, 1982. Found at El Playón May 30, 1982, white shirt, purple pants, black shoes.

The photograph accompanying that last caption shows a body with no eyes, because the vultures got to it before the photographer did. There is a special kind of practical information that the visitor to El Salvador acquires immediately, the way visitors to other places acquire information about the currency rates, the hours for the museums. In El Salvador one learns that vultures go first for the soft tissue, for the eyes, the exposed genitalia, the open mouth. One learns that an open mouth can be used to make a specific point, can be stuffed with something emblematic; stuffed, say, with a penis, or, if the point has to do with land title, stuffed with some of the dirt in question. One learns that hair deteriorates less rapidly than flesh, and that a skull surrounded by a perfect corona of hair is a not uncommon sight in the body dumps.

All forensic photographs induce in the viewer a certain protective numbness, but dissociation is more difficult here. In the first place these are not, technically, "forensic" photographs, since the evidence they document will never be presented in a court of law. In the second place the disfigurement is too routine. The locations are too near, the dates too recent. There is the presence of the relatives of the disappeared: the women who sit every day in this cramped office on the grounds of the archdiocese, waiting to look at the spiral-bound photo albums in which the photographs are kept. These albums have plastic covers bearing soft-focus color photographs of young Americans in dating situations (strolling through autumn foliage on one album, recumbent in a field of daisies on another), and the women, looking for the bodies of their husbands and brothers and sisters and children, pass them from hand to hand without comment or expression.

> "One of the more shadowy elements of the violent scene here [is] the death squad. Existence of these groups has long been disputed, but not by many Salvadorans. . . . Who constitutes the death squads is yet another difficult question. We do not believe that these squads exist as permanent formations but rather as ad hoc vigilante groups that coalesce according to perceived need. Membership is also uncertain, but in addition to civilians we believe that both on- and off-duty members of the security forces are participants. This was unofficially confirmed by right-wing spokesman Maj. Roberto D'Aubuisson who stated in an interview in early 1981 that security force members utilize the guise of the death squad when a potentially embarrassing or odious task needs to be performed."
>
> —*From the confidential but later declassified January 15, 1982 memo previously cited, drafted for the State Department by the political section at the embassy in San Salvador.*

The dead and pieces of the dead turn up in El Salvador everywhere, every day, as taken for granted as in a nightmare, or a horror movie. Vultures of course suggest the presence of a body. A knot of children on the street suggests the presence of a body. Bodies turn up in the brush of vacant lots, in the garbage thrown down ravines in the richest districts, in public rest rooms, in bus stations. Some are dropped in Lake Ilopango, a few miles east of the city, and wash up near the lakeside cottages and clubs frequented by what remains in San Salvador of the sporting bourgeoisie. Some still turn up at El Playón, the lunar lava field of rotting human flesh visible at one time or another on every television screen in America but characterized in June of 1982 in the *El Salvador News Gazette*, an English-language weekly edited by an American named Mario Rosenthal, as an "uncorroborated story . . . dredged up from the files of leftist propaganda." Others turn up at Puerta del Diablo, above Parque Balboa, a national *Turicentro* described as recently as the April–July 1982 issue of *Aboard TACA*, the magazine provided passengers on the national airline of El Salvador, as "offering excellent subjects for color photography."

I drove up to Puerta del Diablo one morning in June of 1982, past the Casa Presidencial and the camouflaged watch towers and heavy concentrations of troops and arms south of town, on up a narrow road narrowed further by landslides and deep crevices in the roadbed, a drive so insistently premonitory that after a while I began to hope that I would pass Puerta del Diablo without knowing it, just miss it, write it off, turn around and go back. There was however no way of missing it. Puerta del Diablo is a "view site" in an older and distinctly literary tradition, nature as lesson, an immense cleft rock through which half of El Salvador seems framed, a site so romantic and "mystical," so theatrically sacrificial in aspect, that it might be a cosmic parody of nineteenth-century landscape painting. The place presents itself as pathetic fallacy: the sky "broods," the stones "weep," a constant seepage of water weighting the ferns and moss. The foliage is thick and slick with moisture. The only sound is a steady buzz, I believe of cicadas.

Body dumps are seen in El Salvador as a kind of visitors' must-do, difficult but worth the detour. "Of course you have seen El Playón," an aide to President Alvaro Magaña said to me one day, and proceeded to discuss the site geologically, as evidence of the country's geothermal resources. He made no mention of the bodies. I was unsure if he was sounding me out or simply found the geothermal aspect of overriding interest. One difference between El Playón and Puerta del Diablo is that most bodies at El Playón appear to have been killed somewhere else, and then dumped; at Puerta del Diablo the executions are believed to occur in place, at the top, and the bodies thrown over. Sometimes reporters will speak of wanting to spend the night at Puerta del Diablo, in order to document the actual execution, but at the time I was in Salvador no one had.

The aftermath, the daylight aspect, is well documented. "Nothing fresh today, I hear," an embassy officer said when I mentioned that I had visited Puerta del Diablo. "Were there any on top?" someone else asked. "There were supposed to have been three on top yesterday." The point about whether or not there had been any on top was that usually it was necessary to go down to see bodies. The way down is hard. Slabs of stone, slippery with moss, are set into the vertiginous cliff, and it is down this cliff that one begins the descent to the bodies, or what is left of the bodies, pecked and maggoty masses of flesh, bone, hair. On some days there have been helicopters circling, tracking those making the descent. Other days there have been militia at the top, in the clearing where the road seems to run out, but on the morning I was there the only people on top were a man and a woman and three small children, who played in the wet grass while the woman started and stopped a Toyota pickup. She appeared to be learning how to drive. She drove forward and then back toward the edge, apparently following the man's signals, over and over again.

We did not speak, and it was only later, down the mountain and back in the land of the provisionally living, that it occurred to me that there was a definite question about why a man and a woman might choose a well-known body dump for a driving lesson. This was one of a number of occasions, during the two weeks my husband and I spent in El Salvador, on which I came to understand, in a way I had not understood before, the exact mechanism of terror.

Whenever I had nothing better to do in San Salvador I would walk up in the leafy stillness of the San Benito and Escalón districts, where the hush at midday is broken only by the occasional crackle of a walkie-talkie, the click of metal moving on a weapon. I recall a day in San Benito when I opened my bag to check an address, and heard the clicking of metal on metal all up and down the street. On the whole no one walks up here, and pools of blossoms lie undisturbed on the sidewalks. Most of the houses in San Benito are more recent than those in Escalón, less idiosyncratic and probably smarter, but the most striking architectural features in both districts are not the houses but their walls, walls built upon walls, walls stripped of the usual copa de oro and bougainvillea, walls that reflect successive generations of violence: the original stone, the additional five or six or ten feet of brick, and finally the barbed wire, sometimes concertina, sometimes electrified; walls with watch towers, gun ports, closed-circuit television cameras, walls now reaching twenty and thirty feet.

San Benito and Escalón appear on the embassy security maps as districts of relatively few "incidents," but they remain districts in which a certain oppressive uneasiness prevails. In the first place there are always "incidents"—detentions and deaths and disappearances—in the *barrancas*, the ravines lined with shanties that fall down behind the houses with the walls and the guards and the walkie-talkies; one day in Escalón I was introduced to a woman who kept the lean-to that served as a grocery in a *barranca* just above the Hotel Sheraton. She was sticking prices on bars of Camay and Johnson's baby soap, stopping occasionally to sell a plastic bag or two filled with crushed ice and Coca-Cola, and all the while she talked in a low voice about her fear, about her eighteen-year-old son, about the boys who had been taken out and shot on successive nights recently in a neighboring *barranca*.

In the second place there is, in Escalón, the presence of the Sheraton itself, a hotel that has figured rather too prominently in certain local stories involving the disappearance and death of Americans. The Sheraton always seems brighter and more mildly festive than either the Camino Real or the Presidente, with children in the pool and flowers and pretty women in pastel dresses, but there are usually several bulletproofed Cherokee Chiefs in the parking area, and the men drinking in the lobby often carry the little zippered purses that in San Salvador suggest not passports or credit cards but Browning 9-mm. pistols.

It was at the Sheraton that one of the few American *desaparecidos*, a young free-lance writer named John Sullivan, was last seen, in December of 1980. It was also at the Sheraton, after eleven on the evening of January 3, 1981, that the two American advisers on agrarian reform, Michael Hammer and Mark Pearlman, were killed, along with the Salvadoran director of the Institute for Agrarian Transformation, José Rodolfo Viera. The three were drinking coffee in a dining room off the lobby, and whoever killed them used an Ingram MAC-10, without sound suppressor, and then walked out through the lobby, unapprehended. The Sheraton has even turned up in the investigation into the December 1980 deaths of the four American churchwomen, Sisters Ita Ford and Maura Clarke, the two Maryknoll nuns; Sister Dorothy Kazel, the Ursuline nun; and Jean Donovan, the lay volunteer. In *Justice in El Salvador: A Case Study*, prepared and released in July of 1982 in New York by the Lawyers' Committee for International Human Rights, there appears this note:

> "On December 19, 1980, the [Duarte government's] Special Investigative Commission reported that 'a red Toyota ¾-ton pickup was seen leaving (the crime scene) at about 11:00 P.M. on December 2' and that 'a red splotch on the burned van' of the churchwomen was being checked to determine whether the paint splotch 'could be the result of a collision between that van and the red Toyota pickup.' By February 1981, the Maryknoll Sisters' Office of Social Concerns, which has been actively monitoring the investigation, received word from a source which it considered reliable that the FBI had matched the red splotch on the burned van with a red Toyota pickup belonging to the Sheraton hotel in San Salvador. . . . Subsequent to the FBI's alleged matching of the paint splotch and a Sheraton truck, the State Department has claimed, in a communication with the families of the churchwomen, that 'the FBI could not determine the source of the paint scraping.'"

There is also mention in this study of a young Salvadoran businessman named Hans Christ (his father was a German who arrived in El Salvador at the end of World War II), a part owner of the Sheraton. Hans Christ lives now in Miami, and that his name should have even come up in the Maryknoll investigation made many people uncomfortable, because it was Hans Christ, along with his brother-in-law, Ricardo Sol Meza, who, in April of 1981, was first charged with the murders of Michael Hammer and Mark Pearlman and José Rodolfo Viera at the Sheraton. These charges were later dropped, and were followed by a series of other charges, arrests, releases, expressions of "dismay" and "incredulity" from the American embassy, and even, in the fall of 1982, confessions to the killings from two former National Guard corporals, who testified that Hans Christ had led them through the lobby and pointed out the victims. Hans Christ and Ricardo Sol Meza have said that the dropped case against them was a government frame-up, and that they were only having drinks at the Sheraton the night of the killings, with a National Guard intelligence officer. It was logical for Hans Christ and Ricardo Sol Meza to have drinks at the Sheraton because they both had interests in the hotel, and Ricardo Sol Meza had just opened a roller disco, since closed, off the lobby into which the killers walked that night. The killers were described by witnesses as well dressed, their faces covered. The room from which they walked was at the time I was in San Salvador no longer a restaurant, but the marks left by the bullets were still visible, on the wall facing the door.

Whenever I had occasion to visit the Sheraton I was apprehensive, and this apprehension came to color the entire Escalón district for me, even its lower reaches, where there were people and movies and restaurants. I recall being struck by it on the canopied porch of a restaurant near the Mexican embassy, on an evening when rain or sabotage or habit had blacked out the city and I became abruptly aware, in the light cast by a passing car, of two human shadows, silhouettes illuminated by the headlights and then invisible again. One shadow sat behind the smoked glass windows of a Cherokee Chief parked at the curb in front of the restaurant; the other crouched between the pumps at the Esso station next door, carrying a rifle. It seemed to me unencouraging that my husband and I were the only people seated on the porch. In the absence of the headlights the candle on our table provided the only light, and I fought the impulse to blow it out. We continued talking, carefully. Nothing came of this, but I did not forget the sensation of having been in a single instant demoralized, undone, humiliated by fear, which is what I meant when I said that I came to understand in El Salvador the mechanism of terror.

"3/3/81: Roberto D'Aubuisson, a former Salvadoran army intelligence officer, holds a press conference and says that before the U.S. presidential election he had been in touch with a number of Reagan advisers and those contacts have continued. The armed forces should ask the junta to resign, D'Aubuisson says. He refuses to name a date for the action, but says 'March is, I think, a very interesting month.' He also calls for the abandonment of the economic reforms. D'Aubuisson had been accused of plotting to overthrow the government on two previous occasions. Observers speculate that since D'Aubuisson is able to hold the news conference and pass freely between Salvador and Guatemala, he must enjoy considerable support among some sections of the army. . . . 3/4/81: In San Salvador, the U.S. embassy is fired upon; no one is injured. Chargé d'Affaires Frederic Chapin says, 'This incident has all the hallmarks of a D'Aubuisson operation. Let me state to you that we oppose coups and we have no intention of being intimidated.'"

—*From the "Chronology of Events Related to Salvadoran Situation" prepared periodically by the United States embassy in San Salvador.*

"Since the Exodus from Egypt, historians have written of those who sacrificed and struggled for freedom: the stand at Thermopylae, the revolt of Spartacus, the storming of the Bastille, the Warsaw uprising in World War II. More recently we have seen evidence of this same human impulse in one of the developing nations in Central America. For months and months the world news media covered the fighting in El Salvador. Day after day, we were treated to stories and film slanted toward the brave freedom fighters battling oppressive government forces in behalf of the silent, suffering people of that tortured country. Then one day those silent suffering people were offered a chance to vote to choose the kind of government they wanted. Suddenly the freedom fighters in the hills were exposed for what they really are: Cuban-backed guerrillas. . . . On election day the people of El Salvador, an unprecedented [1.5 million] of them, braved ambush and gunfire, trudging miles to vote for freedom."

—*President Reagan, in his June 8, 1982 speech before both houses of the British Parliament, referring to the March 28, 1982 election which resulted in the ascension of Roberto D'Aubuisson to the presidency of the Constituent Assembly.*

From whence he shall come to judge the quick and the dead. I happened to read President Reagan's speech one evening in San Salvador when President Reagan was in fact on television, with Doris Day, in *The Winning Team*, a 1952 Warner Brothers picture about the baseball pitcher Grover Cleveland Alexander. I reached the stand at Thermopylae at about the time that *el salvador del Salvador* began stringing cranberries and singing "Old St. Nicholas" with Miss Day. "*Muy bonita*," he said when she tried out a rocking chair in her wedding dress. "*Feliz Navidad*," they cried, and, in accented English, "*Play ball!*"

As it happened "play ball" was a phrase I had come to associate in El Salvador with Roberto D'Aubuisson and his followers in the Nationalist Republican Alliance, or ARENA. "It's a process of letting certain people know they're going to have to play ball," embassy people would say, and: "You take a guy who's young, and everything 'young' implies, you send him signals, he plays ball, then we play ball." American diction in this situation tends toward the studied casual, the can-do, as if sheer cool and Bailey bridges could shape the place up. Elliott Abrams told *The New York Times* in July of 1982 that punishment within the Salvadoran military could be "a very important sign that you can't do this stuff any more," meaning kill the citizens. "If you clean up your act, all things are possible," is the way Jeremiah O'Leary, a special assistant to U.S. national security adviser William Clark, described the American diplomatic effort in an interview given *The Los Angeles Times* just after the March 28, 1982 election. He was speculating on how Ambassador Deane Hinton might be dealing with D'Aubuisson. "I kind of picture him saying, 'Goddamnit, Bobbie, you've got a problem and . . . if you're what everyone said you are, you're going to make it hard for everybody.'"

Roberto D'Aubuisson is a chain smoker, as were many of the people I met in El Salvador, perhaps because it is a country in which the possibility of achieving a death related to smoking remains remote. I never met Major D'Aubuisson, but I was always interested in the adjectives used to describe him. "Pathological" was the adjective, modifying "killer," used by former ambassador Robert E. White (it was White who refused D'Aubuisson a visa, after which, according to the embassy's "Chronology of Events" for June 30, 1980, "D'Aubuisson manages to enter the U.S. illegally and spends two days in Washington holding press conferences and attending luncheons before turning himself in to immigration authorities"), but "pathological" is not a word one heard in-country, where meaning tends to be transmitted in code.

In-country one heard "young" (the "and everything 'young' implies" part was usually left tacit), even "immature"; "impetuous," "impulsive," "impatient," "nervous," "volatile," "high-strung," "kind of coiled-up," and, most frequently, "intense," or just "tense." Offhand it struck me that Roberto D'Aubuisson had some reason to be tense, in that General José Guillermo García, who had remained a main player through several changes of government, might logically perceive him as the wild card who could queer everybody's ability to refer to his election as a vote for freedom. As I write this I realize that I have fallen into the Salvadoran mindset, which turns on plot, and, since half the players at any given point in the game are in exile, on the phrase "in touch with."

"I've known D'Aubuisson a long time," I was told by Alvaro Magaña, the banker the Army made, over D'Aubuisson's rather frenzied objections ("We stopped that one on the one-yard line," Deane Hinton told me about D'Aubuisson's play to block Magaña), provisional president of El Salvador. We were sitting in his office upstairs at the Casa Presidencial, an airy and spacious building in the tropical colonial style, and he was drinking cup after Limoges cup of black coffee, smoking one cigarette with each, carefully, an unwilling actor who intended to survive the accident of being cast in this production. "Since

Molina was president. I used to come here to see Molina, D'Aubuisson would be here, he was a young man in military intelligence, I'd see him here." He gazed toward the corridor that opened onto the interior courtyard, with cannas, oleander, a fountain not in operation. "When we're alone now I try to talk to him. I do talk to him, he's coming for lunch today. He never calls me Alvaro, it's always *usted, Señor, Doctor.* I call him Roberto. I say, Roberto, don't do this, don't do that, you know."

Magaña studied in the United States, at Chicago, and his four oldest children are now in the United States, one son at Vanderbilt, a son and a daughter at Santa Clara, and another daughter near Santa Clara, at Notre Dame in Belmont. He is connected by money, education, and temperament to oligarchal families. All the players here are densely connected: Magaña's sister, who lives in California, is the best friend of Nora Ungo, the wife of Guillermo Ungo, and Ungo spoke to Magaña's sister in August of 1982 when he was in California raising money for the FMLN–FDR, which is what the opposition to the Salvadoran government was called this year. The membership and even the initials of this opposition tend to the fluid, but the broad strokes are these: the FMLN–FDR is the coalition between the Revolutionary Democratic Front (FDR) and the five guerrilla groups joined together in the Farabundo Martí National Liberation Front (FMLN). These five groups are the Salvadoran Communist Party (PCS), the Popular Forces of Liberation (FPL), the Revolutionary Party of Central American Workers (PRTC), the People's Revolutionary Army (ERP), and the Armed Forces of National Resistance (FARN). Within each of these groups, there are further factions, and sometimes even further initials, as in the PRS and LP-28 of the ERP.

During the time that D'Aubuisson was trying to stop Magaña's appointment as provisional president, members of ARENA, which is supported heavily by other oligarchal elements, passed out leaflets referring to Magaña, predictably, as a communist, and, more interestingly, as "the little Jew." The manipulation of anti-Semitism is an undercurrent in Salvadoran life that is not much discussed and probably worth some study, since it refers to a tension within the oligarchy itself, the tension between those families who solidified their holdings in the mid-nineteenth century and those later families, some of them Jewish, who arrived in El Salvador and entrenched themselves around 1900. I recall asking a well-off Salvadoran about the numbers of his acquaintances within the oligarchy who have removed themselves and their money to Miami. "Mostly the Jews," he said.

"In San Salvador
in the year 1965
the best sellers
of the three most important
book stores
were:
The Protocols of the Elders of Zion;
a few books by
diarrhetic Somerset Maugham;
a book of disagreeably
obvious poems
by a lady with a European name
who nonetheless writes in Spanish about our
country
and a collection of
Reader's Digest condensed novels."

—*"San Salvador" by Roque Dalton, translated by Edward Baker.*

The late Roque Dalton García was born into the Salvadoran bourgeoisie in 1935, spent some years in Havana, came home in 1973 to jon the ERP, or the People's Revolutionary Army, and, in 1975, was executed, on charges that he was a CIA agent, by his own comrades. The actual executioner was said to be Joaquín Villalobos, who is now about thirty years old, commander of the ERP, and a key figure in the FMLN, which, as the Mexican writer Gabriel Zaid pointed out in the winter 1982 issue of *Dissent*, has as one of its support groups the Roque Dalton Cultural Brigade. The Dalton execution is frequently cited by people who want to stress that "the other side kills people too, you know," an argument common mainly among those, like the State Department, with a stake in whatever government is current in El Salvador, since, if it is taken for granted in Salvador that the government kills, it is also taken for granted that the other side kills; that everyone has killed, everyone kills now, and, if the history of the place suggests any pattern, everyone will continue to kill.

"Don't say I said this, but there are no issues here," I was told by a high-placed Salvadoran. "There are only ambitions." He meant of course not that there were no ideas in conflict but that the conflicting ideas were held exclusively by people he knew, that, whatever the outcome of any fighting or negotiation or coup or countercoup, the Casa Presidencial would ultimately be occupied not by *campesinos* and Maryknolls but by the already entitled, by a Guillermo Ungo or a Joaquín Villalobos or even by Roque Dalton's son, Juan José Dalton, or by Juan José Dalton's comrade in the FPL, José Antonio Morales Carbonell, the guerrilla son of José Antonio Morales Ehrlich, a former member of the Duarte junta who had himself been in exile during the Romero regime. In an open letter written shortly before his arrest in San Salvador in June 1980, José Antonio Morales Carbonell had charged his father with an insufficient appreciation of "Yankee imperialism." José Antonio Morales Carbonell and Juan José Dalton tried together to enter the United States in the summer of 1982, for a speaking engagement in San Francisco, but were refused visas by the American embassy in Mexico City.

Whatever the issues were that had divided Morales Carbonell and his father and Roque Dalton and Joaquín Villalobos, the prominent Salvadoran to whom I was talking seemed to be saying, they were issues that fell somewhere outside the lines normally drawn to indicate "left" and "right." That this man saw *la situación* as only one more realignment of power among the entitled, a conflict of "ambitions" rather than "issues," was, I recognized, what many people would call a conventional bourgeois view of civil conflict, and offered no solutions, but the people with solutions to offer were mainly somewhere else, in Mexico or Panama or Washington.

The place brings everything into question. One afternoon when I had run out of the Halazone tablets I dropped every night in a pitcher of tap water (a demented *gringa* gesture, I knew even then, in a country where everyone not born there was at least mildly ill, including the nurse at the American embassy), I walked across the street from the Camino Real to the Metrocenter, which is referred to locally as "Central America's Largest Shopping Mall." I found no Halazone at the Metrocenter but became absorbed in making notes about the mall itself, about the Muzak playing "I Left My Heart in San Francisco" and "American Pie" (". . . *singing this will be the day that I die* . . .") although the record store featured a cassette called *Classics of Paraguay*, about the *pâté de foie gras* for sale in the supermarket, about the guard who did the weapons check on everyone who entered the supermarket, about the young matrons in tight Sergio Valente jeans, trailing maids and babies behind them and buying towels, big beach towels printed with maps of Manhattan that featured Bloomingdale's; about the number of things for sale that seemed to suggest a fashion for "smart drinking," to evoke modish cocktail hours. There were bottles of Stolichnaya vodka packaged with glasses and mixer, there were ice buckets, there were bar carts of every conceivable design, displayed with sample bottles.

This was a shopping center that embodied the future for which El Salvador was presumably being saved, and I wrote it down dutifully, this being the kind of "color" I knew how to interpret, the kind of inductive irony, the detail that was supposed to illuminate the story. As I wrote it down I realized that I was no longer much interested in this kind of irony, that this was a story that would not be illuminated by such details, that this was a story that would perhaps not be illuminated at all, that this was perhaps even less a "story" than a true *noche obscura*. As I waited to cross back over the Boulevard de los Heroes to the Camino Real I noticed soldiers herding a young civilian into a van, their guns at the boy's back, and I walked straight ahead, not wanting to see anything at all.

"12/11/81: El Salvador's Atlacatl Battalion begins a 6-day offensive sweep against guerrilla strongholds in Morazán."

—*From the U.S. Embassy "Chronology of Events."*

"The department of Morazán, one of the country's most embattled areas, was the scene of another armed forces operation in December, the fourth in Morazán during 1981. . . . The hamlet of Mozote was completely wiped out. For this reason, the several massacres which occurred in the same area at the same time are collectively known as the 'Mozote massacre.' The apparent sole survivor from Mozote, Rufina Amaya, thirty-eight years old, escaped by hiding behind trees near the house where she and the other women had been imprisoned. She has testified that on Friday, December 11, troops arrived and began taking people from their homes at about 5 in the morning. . . . At noon, the men were blindfolded and killed in the town's center. Among them was Amaya's husband, who was nearly blind. In the early afternoon the young women were taken to the hills nearby, where they were raped, then killed and burned. The old women were taken next and shot. . . . From her hiding place, Amaya heard soldiers discuss choking the children to death; subsequently she heard the children calling for help, but no shots. Among the children murdered were three of Amaya's, all under ten years of age. . . . It should be stressed that the villagers in the area had been warned of the impending military operation by the FMLN and some did leave. Those who chose to stay, such as the evangelical Protestants and others, considered themselves neutral in the conflict and friendly with the army. According to Rufina Amaya, 'Because we knew the Army people, we felt safe.' Her husband, she said, had been on good terms with the local military and even had what she called 'a military safe-conduct.' Amaya and other survivors [of the nine hamlets in which the killing took place] accused the Atlacatl Battalion of a major role in the killing of civilians in the Mozote area."

> —*From the July 20, 1982 Supplement to the "Report on Human Rights in El Salvador" prepared by Americas Watch Committee and the American Civil Liberties Union.*

At the time I was in El Salvador, six months after the events referred to as the Mozote massacre and a month or so before President Reagan's July 1982 certification that sufficient progress was being made in specified areas ("human rights," and "land reform," and "the initiation of a democratic political process," phrases so remote *in situ* as to render them hallucinatory) to qualify El Salvador for continuing aid, a major offensive was taking place in Morazán, up in the mean hill country between the garrison town of San Francisco Gotera and the Honduran border. This June 1982 fighting was referred to by both sides as the heaviest of the war to date, but actual information, on this as on all subjects in San Salvador, was hard to come by.

Reports drifted back. The Atlacatl, which was trained by American advisers in 1981, was definitely up there again, as were two other battalions, the Atonal, trained, like the Atlacatl, by Americans in El Salvador, and the Ramón Belloso, just back from training at Fort Bragg. Every morning COPREFA, the press office at the Ministry of Defense, reported many FMLN casualties but few government. Every afternoon Radio Venceremos, the clandestine guerrilla radio station, reported many government casualties but few FMLN. The only way to get any sense of what was happening was to go up there, but Morazán was hard to reach: a key bridge between San Salvador and the eastern half of the country, the Puente de Oro on the Río Lempa, had been dynamited by the FMLN in October 1981, and to reach San Francisco Gotera it was now necessary either to cross the Lempa on a railroad bridge or to fly, which meant going out to the military airport, Ilopango, and trying to get one of the seven-passenger prop planes that the Gutierrez Flying Service operated between Ilopango and a grassy field outside San Miguel. At San Miguel one could sometimes get a taxi willing to go on up to San Francisco Gotera, or a bus, the problem with a bus being that even a roadblock that ended well (no one killed or detained) could take hours, while every passenger was questioned. Between San Miguel and Gotera, moreover, there was a further problem, another blown bridge, this one on the Río Seco, which was *seco* enough in the dry months but often impassable in the wet.

June was wet. The Río Seco seemed doubtful. Everything about the day ahead, on the morning I started for Gotera, seemed doubtful, and that I set out on such a venture with a real lightening of the spirit suggests to me now how powerfully I wanted to get out of San Salvador, to spend a day free of its ambiguous tension, its overcast, its mood of wary somnambulism. It was only a trip of perhaps eighty miles, but getting there took most of the morning. There was, first of all, the wait on the runway at Ilopango while the pilot tried to get the engines to catch. "*Cinco minutos*," he kept saying, and, as a wrench was produced, "*Momentito*." Thunderclouds were massing on the mountains to the east. Rain spattered the fuselage. The plane was full, seven paying passengers at ninety-five *colones* the round trip, and we watched the tinkering without comment until one and finally both of the engines turned over.

Once in the air I was struck, as always in Salvador, by the miniature aspect of the country, an entire republic smaller than some California counties (smaller than San Diego County, smaller than Kern or Inyo, smaller by two-and-a-half times than San Bernardino), the very circumstance that has encouraged the illusion that the place can be managed, salvaged, a kind of pilot project, like TVA. There below us in a twenty-five-minute flight lay half the country, a landscape already densely green from the rains that had begun in May, intensely cultivated, deceptively rich, the coffee spreading down every ravine, the volcanic ranges looming abruptly and then receding. I watched the slopes of the mountains for signs of fighting but saw none. I watched for the hydroelectric works on the Lempa but saw only the blown bridge.

There were four of us on the flight that morning who wanted to go on to Gotera, my husband and I and Christopher Dickey from *The Washington Post* and Joseph Harmes from *Newsweek*, and when the plane set down on the grass strip outside San Miguel a deal was struck with a taxi driver willing to take us at least to the Río Seco. We shared the taxi as far as San Miguel with a local woman who, although she and I sat on a single bucket seat, did not speak, only stared straight ahead, clutching her bag with one hand and trying with the other to keep her skirt pulled down over her black lace slip. When she got out at San Miguel there remained in the taxi a trace of her perfume, Arpège.

In San Miguel the streets showed the marks of January's fighting, and many structures were boarded up, abandoned. There had been a passable motel in San Miguel, but the owners had managed to leave the country. There had been a passable place to eat in San Miguel, but no more. Occasional troop trucks hurtled past, presumably returning empty from the front, and we all made note of them, dutifully. The heat rose. Sweat from my hand kept blurring my tally of empty troop trucks, and I copied it on a clean page, painstakingly, as if it mattered.

The heat up here was drier than that in the capital, harsher, dustier, and by now we were resigned to it, resigned to the jolting of the taxi, resigned to the frequent occasions on which we were required to stop, get out, present our identification (carefully, reaching slowly into an outer pocket, every move calculated not to startle the soldiers, many of whom seemed barely pubescent, with the M-16s), and wait while the taxi was searched. Some of the younger soldiers wore crucifixes wrapped with bright yarn, the pink and green of the yarn stained now with dust and sweat. The taxi driver was perhaps twenty years older than most of these soldiers, a stocky, well-settled citizen wearing expensive sunglasses, but at each roadblock, in a motion so abbreviated as to be almost imperceptible, he would touch each of the two rosaries that hung from the rearview mirror and cross himself.

By the time we reached the Río Seco the question of whether or not we could cross it seemed insignificant, another minor distraction in a day that had begun at six and was now, before nine, already less a day than a way of being alive. We would try, the driver announced, to ford the river, which appeared that day to be running shallow and relatively fast over an unpredictable bed of sand and mud. We stood for a while on the bank and watched a man with an earthmover and winch try again and again to hook up his equipment to a truck that had foundered midstream. Small boys dove repeatedly with hooks, and repeatedly surfaced, unsuccessful. It did not seem entirely promising, but there it was, and there, in due time, we were: in the river, first following the sandbar in a wide crescent, then off the bar, stuck, the engine dead. The taxi rocked gently in the current. The water bubbled inch by inch through the floorboards. There were women bathing naked in the shallows, and they paid no attention to the earthmover, the small boys, the half-submerged taxi, the *gringos* inside it. As we waited for our turn with the earthmover it occurred to me that fording the river in the morning meant only that we were going to have to ford it again in the afternoon, when the earthmover might or might not be around, but this was thinking ahead, and out of synch with the day at hand.

When I think now of that day in Gotera I think mainly of waiting, hanging around, waiting outside the *cuartel* ("COMANDO," the signs read on the gates, and "BOINAS VERDES," with a green beret) and waiting outside the church and waiting outside the Cine Morazán, where the posters promised *Fright* and *The Abominable Snowman* and the open lobby was lined with .50-caliber machine guns and 120-mm. mobile mortars. There were soldiers billeted in the Cine Morazán, and a few of them kicked a soccer ball, idly, among the mortars. Others joked among themselves at the corner, outside the saloon, and flirted with the women selling Coca-Cola in the stalls between the Cine Morazán and the parish house. The parish house and the church and the stalls and the saloon and the Cine Morazán and the *cuartel* all faced one another, across what was less a square than a dusty widening in the road, an arrangement that lent Gotera a certain proscenium aspect. Any event at all—the arrival of an armored personnel carrier, say, or a funeral procession outside the church—tended to metamorphose instantly into an opera, with all players onstage: the Soldiers of the Garrison, the Young Ladies of the Town, the Vendors, the Priests, the Mourners, and, since we were onstage as well, a dissonant and provocative element, the *norteamericanos*, in *norteamericano* costume, old Abercrombie khakis here, Adidas sneakers there, a Lone Star Beer cap.

We stood in the sun and tried to avoid adverse attention. We drank Coca-Cola and made surreptitious notes. We looked for the priests in the parish office but found only the receptionist, a dwarf. We presented our credentials again and again at the *cuartel*, trying to see the colonel who could give us permission to go up the few kilometers to where the fighting was, but the colonel was out, the colonel would be back, the colonel was delayed. The young officer in charge during the colonel's absence could not give us permission, but he had graduated from the Escuela Militar in one of the classes trained in the spring of 1982 at Fort Benning ("Mar-vel-*ous!*" was his impression of Fort Benning) and seemed at least amenable to us as Americans. Possibly there would be a patrol going up. Possibly we could join it.

In the end no patrol went up and the colonel never came back (the reason the colonel never came back is that he was killed that afternoon, in a helicopter crash near the Honduran border, but we did not learn this in Gotera) and nothing came of the day but overheard rumors, indefinite observations, fragments of information that might or might not fit into a pattern we did not perceive. One of the six A-37B Dragonfly attack jets that the United States had delivered just that week to Ilopango screamed low overhead, then disappeared. A company of soldiers burst through the *cuartel* gates and double-timed to the river, but when we caught up they were only bathing, shedding their uniforms and splashing in the shallow water. On the bluff above the river work was being completed on a helipad that was said to cover two mass graves of dead soldiers, but the graves were no longer apparent. The taxi driver heard, from the soldiers with whom he talked while he waited (talked and played cards and ate tortillas and sardines and listened to rock-and-roll on the taxi radio), that two whole companies were missing in action, lost or dead somewhere in the hills, but this was received information, and equivocal.

In some ways the least equivocal fact of the day was the single body we had seen that morning on the road between the Río Seco and Gotera, near San Carlos, the naked corpse of a man about thirty with a clean bullet-hole drilled neatly between his eyes. He could have been stripped by whoever killed him or, since this was a country in which clothes were too valuable to leave on the dead, by someone who happened past: there was no way of telling. In any case his genitals had been covered with a leafy branch, presumably by the *campesinos* who were even then digging a grave. A *subversivo*, the driver thought, because there was no family in evidence (to be related to someone killed in El Salvador is a prima facie death warrant, and families tend to vanish), but all anyone in Gotera seemed to know was that there had been another body at precisely that place the morning before, and five others before that. One of the priests in Gotera had happened to see the body the morning before, but when he drove past San Carlos later in the day the body had been buried. It was agreed that someone was trying to make a point. The point was unclear.

We spent an hour or so that day with the priests, or with two of them, both Irish, and two of the nuns, one Irish and one American, all of whom lived together in the parish house facing the *cuartel* in a situation that remains in my mind as the one actual instance I have witnessed of grace not simply under pressure but under siege. Except for the American, Sister Phyllis, who had arrived only a few months before, they had all been in Gotera a long time, twelve years, nine years, long enough to have established among themselves a grave companionableness, a courtesy and good humor that made the courtyard porch where we sat with them seem civilization's last stand in Morazán, which in certain ways it was.

The light on the porch was cool and aqueous, filtered through ferns and hibiscus, and there were old wicker rockers and a map of PARROQUIA SAN FRANCISCO GOTERA and a wooden table with a typewriter, a can of Planter's Mixed Nuts, copies of *Lives of the Saints: Illustrated* and *The Rules of the Secular Franciscan Order*. In the shadows beyond the table was a battered refrigerator from which, after a while, one of the priests got bottles of Pilsener beer, and we sat in the sedative half-light and drank the cold beer and talked in a desultory way about nothing in particular, about the situation, but no solutions.

These were not people much given to solutions, to abstracts: their lives were grounded in the specific. There had been the funeral that morning of a parishioner who had died in the night of cerebral hemorrhage. There had been the two children who died that week, of diarrhea, dehydration, in the squatter camps outside town where some 12,000 refugees were then gathered, many of them ill. There was no medicine in the camps. There was no water anywhere, and had been none since around the time of the election, when the tank that supplied Gotera with water had been dynamited. Five or six weeks after the tank was blown the rains had begun, which was bad in one way, because the rain washed out the latrines at the camps, but good in another, because at the parish house they were no longer dependent entirely on water from the river, soupy with bacteria and amoebae and worms. "We have the roof water now," Sister Jean, the Irish nun, said. "Much cleaner. It's greenish yellow, the river water, we only use it for the toilets."

There had been, they agreed, fewer dead around since the election, fewer bodies, they thought, than in the capital, but as they began reminding one another of this body or that there still seemed to have been quite a few. They spoke of these bodies in the matter-of-fact way that they might have spoken, in another kind of parish, of confirmation candidates, or cases of croup. There had been the few up the road, the two at Yoloaiquin. Of course there had been the forty-eight near Barrios, but Barrios was in April. "A *guardia* was killed last Wednesday," one of them recalled.

"Thursday."

"Was it Thursday then, Jerry?"

"A sniper."

"That's what I thought. A sniper."

We left the parish house that day only because rain seemed about to fall, and it was clear that the Río Seco had to be crossed now or perhaps not for days. The priests kept a guest book, and I thought as I signed it that I would definitely come back to this porch, come back with antibiotics and Scotch and time to spend, but I did not get back, and some weeks after I left El Salvador I heard in a third-hand way that the parish house had been at least temporarily abandoned, that the priests, who had been under threats and pressure from the garrison, had somehow been forced to leave Gotera. I recalled that on the day before I left El Salvador Deane Hinton had asked me, when I mentioned Gotera, if I had seen the priests, and had expressed concern for their situation. He was particularly concerned about the American, Sister Phyllis (an American nun in a parish under siege in a part of the country even then under attack from American A-37Bs was nothing the American embassy needed in those last delicate weeks before certification), and had at some point expressed this concern to the *comandante* at the garrison. The *comandante*, he said, had been surprised to learn the nationalities of the nuns and priests; he had thought them French, because the word used to describe them was always "Franciscan." This was one of those occasional windows that open onto the heart of El Salvador and then close, a glimpse of the impenetrable interior.

At the time I was in El Salvador the hostilities at hand were referred to by those reporters still in the country as "the number-four war," after Beirut, Iran-Iraq, and the aftermath of the Falklands. So many reporters had in fact abandoned the Hotel Camino Real in San Salvador (gone home for a while, or gone to the Intercontinental in Managua, or gone to whatever hotels they frequented in Guatemala and Panama and Tegucigalpa) that the dining room had discontinued its breakfast buffet, a fact often remarked upon: no breakfast buffet meant no action, little bang-bang, a period of editorial indifference in which stories were filed and held, and film rarely made the network news. "Get an NBC crew up from the Falklands, we might get the buffet back," they would say, and, "It hots up a little, we could have the midnight movies." It seemed that when the networks arrived in force they brought movies down, and showed them at midnight on their video recorders, *Apocalypse Now*, and Woody Allen's *Bananas.*

Meanwhile only the regulars were there. "Are you going out today?" they would say to one another at breakfast, and, "This might not be a bad day to look around." The Avis counter in the bar supplied signs reading "PRENSA INTERNACIONAL" with every car and van, and modified its insurance agreements with a typed clause excluding damage incurred by terrorists. The American embassy delivered translated transcripts of Radio Venceremos, prepared by the CIA in Panama. The COPREFA office at the Ministry of Defense sent over "urgent" notices, taped to the front desk, announcing events specifically devised, in those weeks before certification, for the American press: the ceremonial transfer of land titles, and the ritual display of "defectors," terrified-looking men who were reported in *La Prensa Gráfica* to have "abandoned the ranks of subversion, weary of so many lies and false promises."

A handful of reporters continued to cover these events, particularly if they were staged in provincial garrisons and offered the possibility of action en route, but action was less than certain, and the situation less accessible than it had seemed in the days of the breakfast buffet. The American advisers would talk to no one, although occasionally a reporter could find a few drinking at the Sheraton on Saturday night and initiate a little general conversation. (That the American advisers were still billeted at the Sheraton struck me as somewhat perverse, particularly because I knew that the embassy had moved its visiting AID people to a guarded house in San Benito. "Frankly, I'd rather stay at the Sheraton," an AID man had told me. "But since the two union guys got killed at the Sheraton, they want us here.") The era in which the guerrillas could be found just by going out on the highway had largely ended; the only certain way to spend time with them now was to cross into their territory from Honduras, through contact with the leadership in Mexico. This was a process that tended to discourage day-tripping, and in any case it was no longer a war in which the dateline "SOMEWHERE BEHIND GUERRILLA LINES, EL SALVADOR" was presumed automatically to illuminate much at all.

Everyone had already spent time, too, with the available government players, most of whom had grown so practiced in the process that their interviews were now performances, less apt to be reported than reviewed, and analyzed for subtle changes in delivery. Roberto D'Aubuisson had even taken part, wittingly or unwittingly, in an actual performance: a scene shot by a Danish film crew on location in Haiti and El Salvador for a movie about a foreign correspondent, in which the actor playing the correspondent "interviewed" D'Aubuisson, on camera, in his office. This Danish crew treated the Camino Real not only as a normal location hotel (the star, for example, was the only person I ever saw swim in the Camino Real pool) but also as a story element, on one occasion shooting a scene in the bar, which lent daily life during their stay a peculiar extra color. They left San Salvador without making it entirely clear whether or not they had ever told D'Aubuisson it was just a movie.

AT TWENTY-TWO minutes past midnight on Saturday June 19, 1982, there was a major earthquake in El Salvador, one that collapsed shacks and set off landslides and injured several hundred people but killed only about a dozen (I say "about" a dozen because figures on this, as on everything else in Salvador, varied), surprisingly few for an earthquake of this one's apparent intensity (Cal Tech registered it at 7.0 on the Richter scale, Berkeley at 7.4) and length, thirty-seven seconds. For the several hours that preceded the earthquake I had been seized by the kind of amorphous bad mood that my grandmother believed an adjunct of what is called in California "earthquake weather," a sultriness, a stillness, an unnatural light; the jitters. In fact there was no particular prescience about my bad mood, since it is always earthquake weather in San Salvador, and the jitters are endemic.

I recall having come back to the Camino Real about ten-thirty that Friday night, after dinner in a Mexican restaurant on the Paseo Escalón with a Salvadoran painter named Victor Barriere, who had said, when we met at a party a few days before, that he was interested in talking to Americans because they so often came and went with no understanding of the country and its history. Victor Barriere could offer, he explained, a special perspective on the country and its history, because he was a grandson of the late General Maximiliano Hernández Martínez, the dictator of El Salvador between 1931 and 1944 and the author of what Salvadorans still call *la matanza*, the massacre, or "killing," those weeks in 1932 when the government killed uncountable thousands of citizens, a lesson. ("Uncountable" because estimates of those killed vary from six or seven thousand to thirty thousand. Even higher figures are heard in Salvador, but, as Thomas P. Anderson pointed out in *Matanza: El Salvador's Communist Revolt of 1932*, "Salvadorans, like medieval people, tend to use numbers like fifty thousand simply to indicate a great number—statistics are not their strong point.")

As it happened I had been interested for some years in General Martínez, the spirit of whose regime would seem to have informed Gabriel García Márquez's *The Autumn of the Patriarch.* This original patriarch, who was murdered in exile in Honduras in 1966, was a rather sinister visionary who entrenched the military in Salvadoran life, was said to have held séances in the Casa Presidencial, and conducted both the country's and his own affairs along lines dictated by eccentric insights, which he sometimes shared by radio with the remaining citizens:

> "It is good that children go barefoot. That way they can better receive the beneficial effluvia of the planet, the vibrations of the earth. Plants and animals don't use shoes."
>
> "Biologists have discovered only five senses. But in reality there are ten. Hunger, thirst, procreation, urination, and bowel movements are the senses not included in the lists of biologists."

I had first come across this side of General Martínez in the United States Government Printing Office's *Area Handbook for El Salvador*, a generally straightforward volume ("designed to be useful to military and other personnel who need a convenient compilation of basic facts") in which, somewhere between the basic facts about General Martínez's program for building schools and the basic facts about General Martínez's program for increasing exports, there appears this sentence: "He kept bottles of colored water that he dispensed as cures for almost any disease, including cancer and heart trouble, and relied on complex magical formulas for the solution of national problems." This sentence springs from the *Area Handbook for El Salvador* as if printed in neon, and is followed by one even more arresting: "During an epidemic of smallpox in the capital, he attempted to halt its spread by stringing the city with a web of colored lights."

Not a night passed in San Salvador when I did not imagine it strung with those colored lights, and I asked Victor Barriere what it had been like to grow up as the grandson of General Martínez. Victor Barriere had studied for a while in the United States, at the San Diego campus of the University of California, and he spoke perfect unaccented English, with the slightly formal constructions of the foreign speaker, in a fluted, melodic voice that seemed always to suggest a higher reasonableness. The general had been, he said, sometimes misunderstood. Very strong men often were. Certain excesses had been inevitable. Someone had to take charge. "It was sometimes strange going to school with boys whose fathers my grandfather had ordered shot," he allowed, but he remembered his grandfather mainly as a "forceful" man, a man "capable of inspiring great loyalty," a theosophist from whom it had been possible to learn an appreciation of "the classics," "a sense of history," "the Germans." The Germans especially had influenced Victor Barriere's sense of history. "When you've read Schopenhauer, Nietzsche, what's happened here, what's happening here, well . . ."

Victor Barriere had shrugged, and the subject changed, although only fractionally, since El Salvador is one of those places in the world where there is just one subject, the situation, the *problema*, its various facets presented over and over again, as on a stereopticon. One turn, and the facet was former ambassador Robert White: "A real jerk." Another, the murder in March of 1980 of Archbishop Oscar Arnulfo Romero: "A real bigot." At first I thought he meant whoever stood outside an open door of the chapel in which the Archbishop was saying mass and drilled him through the heart with a .22-caliber dumdum bullet, but he did not: "Listening to that man on the radio every Sunday," he said, "was like listening to Adolf Hitler or Benito Mussolini." In any case: "We don't really know who killed him, do we? It could have been the right . . ." He drew the words out, *cantabile*. "Or . . . it could have been the left. We have to ask ourselves, who gained? Think about it, Joan."

I said nothing. I wanted only for dinner to end. Victor Barriere had brought a friend along, a young man from Chalatenango whom he was teaching to paint, and the friend brightened visibly when we stood up. He was eighteen years old and spoke no English and had sat through the dinner in polite misery. "He can't even speak Spanish properly," Victor Barriere said, in front of him. "However. If he were cutting cane in Chalatenango, he'd be taken by the Army and killed. If he were out on the street here he'd be killed. So. He comes every day to my studio, he learns to be a primitive painter, and I keep him from getting killed. It's better for him, don't you agree?"

I said that I agreed. The two of them were going back to the house Victor Barriere shared with his mother, a diminutive woman he addressed as "Mommy," the daughter of General Martínez, and after I dropped them there it occurred to me that this was the first time in my life that I had been in the presence of obvious "material" and felt no professional exhilaration at all, only personal dread. One of the most active death squads now operating in El Salvador calls itself the Maximiliano Hernández Martínez Brigade, but I had not asked the grandson about that.

In spite of or perhaps because of the fact that San Salvador had been for more than two years under an almost constant state of siege, a city in which arbitrary detention had been legalized (Revolutionary Governing Junta Decree 507), curfew violations had been known to end in death, and many people did not leave their houses after dark, a certain limited frivolity still obtained. When I got back to the Camino Real after dinner with Victor Barriere that Friday night there was for example a private party at the pool, with live music, dancing, an actual conga line.

There were also a number of people in the bar, many of them watching, on television monitors, "Señorita El Salvador 1982," the selection of El Salvador's entry in "Señorita Universo 1982," scheduled for July 1982 in Lima. Something about "Señorita Universo" struck a familiar note, and then I recalled that the Miss Universe contest itself had been held in San Salvador in 1975, and had ended in what might have been considered a predictable way, with student protests about the money the government was spending on the contest, and the government's predictable response, which was to shoot some of the students on the street and disappear others. (*Desaparecer*, or "disappear," is in Spanish both an intransitive and a transitive verb, and this flexibility has been adopted by those speaking English in El Salvador, as in *John Sullivan was disappeared from the Sheraton; the government disappeared the students*, there being no equivalent situation, and so no equivalent word, in English-speaking cultures.)

No mention of "Señorita Universo 1975" dampened "Señorita El Salvador 1982," which, by the time I got upstairs, had reached the point when each of the finalists was asked to pick a question from a basket and answer it. The questions had to do with the hopes and dreams of the contestants, and the answers ran to "*Dios*," "*Paz*," "El Salvador." A local entertainer wearing a white dinner jacket and a claret-colored bow tie sang "The Impossible Dream," in Spanish. The judges began their deliberations, and the moment of decision arrived: Señorita El Salvador 1982 would be Señorita San Vicente, Miss Jeannette Marroquín, who was several inches taller than the other finalists, and more *gringa*-looking. The four runners-up reacted, on the whole, with rather less grace than is the custom on these occasions, and it occurred to me that this was a contest in which winning meant more than a scholarship or a screen test or a new wardrobe; winning here could mean the difference between life and casual death, a provisional safe-conduct not only for the winner but for her entire family.

> "God damn it, he cut inaugural ribbons, he showed himself large as life in public taking on the risks of power as he had never done in more peaceful times, what the hell, he played endless games of dominoes with my lifetime friend General Rodrigo de Aguilar and my old friend the minister of health who were the only ones who . . . dared ask him to receive in a special audience the beauty queen of the poor, an incredible creature from that miserable wallow we call the dogfight district. . . . I'll not only receive her in a special audience but I'll dance the first waltz with her, by God, have them write it up in the newspapers, he ordered, this kind of crap makes a big hit with the poor. Yet, the night after the audience, he commented with a certain bitterness to General Rodrigo de Aguilar that the queen of the poor wasn't even worth dancing with, that she was as common as so many other slum Manuela Sánchezes with her nymph's dress of muslin petticoats and the gilt crown with artificial jewels and a rose in her hand under the watchful eye of a mother who looked after her as if she were made of gold, so he gave her everything she wanted which was only electricity and running water for the dogfight district. . . ."

That is Gabriel García Márquez, *The Autumn of the Patriarch*. On this evening that began with the grandson of General Maximiliano Hernández Martínez and progressed to "Señorita El Salvador 1982" and ended, at 12:22 A.M., with the earthquake, I began to see Gabriel García Márquez in a new light, as a social realist.

There were a number of metaphors to be found in this earthquake, not the least of them being that the one major building to suffer extensive damage happened also to be the major building most specifically and elaborately designed to withstand earthquakes, the American embassy. When this embassy was built, in 1965, the idea was that it would remain fluid under stress, its deep pilings shifting and sliding on Teflon pads, but over the past few years, as shelling the embassy came to be a favorite way of expressing dissatisfaction on all sides, the structure became so fortified—the steel exterior walls, the wet sandbags around the gun emplacements on the roof, the bomb shelter dug out underneath—as to render it rigid. The ceiling fell in Deane Hinton's office that night. Pipes burst on the third floor, flooding everything below. The elevator was disabled, the commissary a sea of shattered glass.

The Hotel Camino Real, on the other hand, which would appear to have been thrown together in the insouciant tradition of most tropical construction, did a considerable amount of rolling (I recall crouching under a door frame in my room on the seventh floor and watching, through the window, the San Salvador volcano appear to rock from left to right), but when the wrenching stopped and candles were found and everyone got downstairs nothing was broken, not even the glasses behind the bar. There was no electricity, but there was often no electricity. There were sporadic bursts of machine-gun fire on the street (this had made getting downstairs more problematic than it might have been, since the emergency stairway was exposed to the street), but sporadic bursts of machine-gun fire on the street were not entirely unusual in San Salvador. ("Sometimes it happens when it rains," someone from the embassy had told me about this phenomenon. "They get excited.") On the whole it was business as usual at the Camino Real, particularly in the discothèque off the lobby, where, by the time I got downstairs, an emergency generator seemed already to have been activated, waiters in black cowboy hats darted about the dance floor carrying drinks, and dancing continued, to Jerry Lee Lewis's "Great Balls of Fire."

Actual information was hard to come by in El Salvador, perhaps because this is not a culture in which a high value is placed on the definite. The only hard facts on the earthquake, for example, arrived at the Camino Real that night from New York, on the AP wire, which reported the Cal Tech reading of 7.0 Richter on an earthquake centered in the Pacific some sixty miles south of San Salvador. Over the next few days, as damage reports appeared in the local papers, the figure varied. One day the earthquake had been a 7.0 Richter, another day a 6.8. By Tuesday it was again a 7 in *La Prensa Gráfica*, but on a different scale altogether, not the Richter but the Modified Mercalli.

All numbers in El Salvador tended to materialize and vanish and rematerialize in a different form, as if numbers denoted only the "use" of numbers, an intention, a wish, a recognition that someone, somewhere, for whatever reason, needed to hear the ineffable expressed as a number. At any given time in El Salvador a great deal of what goes on is considered ineffable, and the use of numbers in this context tends to frustrate people who try to understand them literally, rather than as propositions to be floated, "heard," "mentioned." There was the case of the March 28, 1982 election, about which there continued into that summer the rather scholastic argument first posed by *Central American Studies*, the publication of the Jesuit university in San Salvador: Had it taken an average of 2.5 minutes to cast a vote, or less? Could each ballot box hold 500 ballots, or more? The numbers were eerily Salvadoran. There were said to be 1.3 million people eligible to vote on March 28, but 1.5 million people were said to have voted. These 1.5 million people were said, in turn, to represent not 115 percent of the 1.3 million eligible voters but 80 percent (or, on another float, "62–68 percent") of the eligible voters, who accordingly no longer numbered 1.3 million, but a larger number. In any case no one really knew how many eligible voters there were in El Salvador, or even how many people. In any case it had seemed necessary to provide a number. In any case the election was over, a success, *la solución pacífica*.

Similarly, there was the question of how much money had left the country for Miami since 1979: Deane Hinton, in March of 1982, estimated $740 million. The Salvadoran minister of planning estimated, the same month, twice that. I recall asking President Magaña, when he happened to say that he had gone to lunch every Tuesday for the past ten years with the officers of the Central Reserve Bank of El Salvador, which reviews the very export and import transactions through which money traditionally leaves troubled countries, how much he thought was gone. "You hear figures mentioned," he said. I asked what figures he heard mentioned at these Tuesday lunches. "The figure they mentioned is six hundred million," he said. He watched as I wrote that down, *600,000,000, central bank El Salvador*. "The figure the Federal Reserve in New York mentioned," he added, "is one thousand million." He watched as I wrote that down too, *1,000,000,000, Fed NY*. "Those people don't want to stay for life in Miami," he said then, but this did not entirely address the question, nor was it meant to.

Not only numbers but names are understood locally to have only a situational meaning, and the change of a name is meant to be accepted as a change in the nature of the thing named. ORDEN, for example, the paramilitary organization formally founded in 1968 to function, along classic patronage lines, as the government's eyes and ears in the countryside, no longer exists as ORDEN, or the Organización Democrática Nacionalista, but as the Frente Democrática Nacionalista, a transubstantiation noted only cryptically in the State Department's official "justification" for the January 28, 1982 certification: "The Salvadoran government, since the overthrow of General Romero, has taken explicit actions to end human rights abuses. The paramilitary organization 'ORDEN' has been outlawed, *although some of its former members may still be active*." (Italics added.)

This tactic of solving a problem by changing its name is by no means limited to the government. The small office on the archdiocese grounds where the scrapbooks of the dead are kept is still called, by virtually everyone in San Salvador, "the Human Rights Commission" (Comisión de los Derechos Humanos), but in fact both the Human Rights Commission and Socorro Jurídico, the archdiocesan legal aid office, were ordered in the spring of 1982 to vacate the church property, and, in the local way, did so: everything pretty much stayed in place, but the scrapbooks of the dead were thereafter kept, officially, in the "Oficina de Tutela Legal" of the "Comisión Arquidiocesana de Justicia y Paz." (This "Human Rights Commission," in any case, is not to be confused with the Salvadoran government's "Commission on Human Rights," the formation of which was announced the day before a scheduled meeting between President Magaña and Ronald Reagan. This official *comisión* is a seven-member panel notable for its inclusion of Colonel Carlos Reynaldo López Nuila, the director of the National Police.) This renaming was referred to as a "reorganization," which is one of many words in El Salvador that tend to signal the presence of the ineffable.

Other such words are "improvement," "perfection" (reforms are never abandoned or ignored, only "perfected" or "improved"), and that favorite from other fronts, "pacification." Language has always been used a little differently in this part of the world (an apparent statement of fact often expresses something only wished for, or something that might be true, a story, as in García Márquez's *many years later, as he faced the firing squad, Colonel Aureliano Buendía was to remember that distant afternoon when his father took him to discover ice*), but "improvement" and "perfection" and "pacification" derive from another tradition. Language as it is now used in El Salvador is the language of advertising, of persuasion, the product being one or another of the *soluciones* crafted in Washington or Panama or Mexico, which is part of the place's pervasive obscenity.

This language is shared by Salvadorans and Americans, as if a linguistic deal had been cut. "Perhaps the most striking measure of progress [in El Salvador]," Assistant Secretary of State Thomas Enders was able to say in August of 1982 in a speech at the Commonwealth Club in San Francisco, "is the transformation of the military from an institution dedicated to the status quo to one that spearheads land reform and supports constitutional democracy." Thomas Enders was able to say this precisely because the Salvadoran minister of defense, General

José Guillermo García, had so superior a dedication to his own status quo that he played the American card as Roberto D'Aubuisson did not, played the game, played ball, understood the importance to Americans of symbolic action: the importance of letting the Americans have their land reform program, the importance of letting the Americans pretend that while "democracy in El Salvador" may remain "a slender reed" (that was Elliott Abrams in *The New York Times*), the situation is one in which "progress" is measurable ("the minister of defense has ordered that all violations of citizens' rights be stopped immediately," the State Department noted on the occasion of the July 1982 certification, a happy ending); the importance of giving the Americans an acceptable president, Alvaro Magaña, and of pretending that this acceptable president was in fact commander-in-chief of the armed forces, *el generalísimo* as *la solución*.

La solución changed with the market. Pacification, although those places pacified turned out to be in need of repeated pacification, was *la solución*. The use of the word "negotiations," however abstract that use may have been, was *la solución*. The election, although it ended with the ascension of a man, Roberto D'Aubuisson, essentially hostile to American policy, was *la solución* for Americans. The land reform program, grounded as it was in political rather than economic reality, was *la solución* as symbol. "It has not been a total economic success," Peter Askin, the AID director working with the government on the program, told *The New York Times* in August 1981, "but up to this point it has been a political success. I'm firm on that. There does seem to be a direct correlation between the agrarian reforms and the peasants not having become more radicalized." The land reform program, in other words, was based on the principle of buying off, buying time, giving a little to gain a lot, *minifundismo* in support of *latifundismo*, which, in a country where the left had no interest in keeping the peasants less "radicalized" and the right remained unconvinced that these peasants could not simply be eliminated, rendered it a program about which only Americans could be truly enthusiastic, less a "reform" than an exercise in public relations.

Even *la verdad*, the truth, was a degenerated phrase in El Salvador: on my first evening in the country I was asked by a

Salvadoran woman at an embassy party what I hoped to find out in El Salvador. I said that ideally I hoped to find out *la verdad*, and she beamed approvingly. Other journalists, she said, did not want *la verdad*. She called over two friends, who also approved: no one told *la verdad*. If I wrote *la verdad* it would be good for El Salvador. I realized that I had stumbled into a code, that these women used *la verdad* as it was used on the bumper stickers favored that spring and summer by ARENA people. "Journalists, Tell the Truth!" the bumper stickers warned in Spanish, and they meant the truth according to Roberto D'Aubuisson.

In the absence of information (and the presence, often, of disinformation) even the most apparently straightforward event takes on, in El Salvador, elusive shadows, like a fragment of retrieved legend. On the afternoon that I was in San Francisco Gotera trying to see the commander of the garrison there, this *comandante*, Colonel Salvador Beltrán Luna, was killed, or was generally believed to have been killed, in the crash of a Hughes 500-D helicopter. The crash of a helicopter in a war zone would seem to lend itself to only a limited number of interpretations (the helicopter was shot down, or the helicopter suffered mechanical failure, are the two that come to mind), but the crash of this particular helicopter became, like everything else in Salvador, an occasion of rumor, doubt, suspicion, conflicting reports, and finally a kind of listless uneasiness.

The crash occurred either near the Honduran border in Morazán or, the speculation went, actually in Honduras. There were or were not four people aboard the helicopter: the pilot, a bodyguard, Colonel Beltrán Luna, and the assistant secretary of defense, Colonel Francisco Adolfo Castillo. At first all four were dead. A day later only three were dead: Radio Venceremos broadcast news of Colonel Castillo (followed a few days later by a voice resembling that of Colonel Castillo), not dead but a prisoner, or said to be a prisoner, or perhaps only claiming to be a prisoner. A day or so later another of the dead materialized, or appeared to: the pilot was, it seemed, neither dead nor a prisoner but hospitalized, incommunicado.

Questions about what actually happened to (or on, or after the crash of, or after the clandestine landing of) this helicopter provided table talk for days (one morning the newspapers emphasized that the Hughes 500-D had been *comprado en Guatemala*, bought in Guatemala, a detail so solid in this otherwise vaporous story that it suggested rumors yet unheard, intrigues yet unimagined), and remained unresolved at the time I left. At one point I asked President Magaña, who had talked to the pilot, what had happened. "They don't say," he said. Was Colonel Castillo a prisoner? "I read that in the paper, yes." Was Colonel Beltrán Luna dead? "I have that impression." Was the bodyguard dead? "Well, the pilot said he saw someone lying on the ground, either dead or unconscious, he doesn't know, but he believes it may have been Castillo's security man, yes." Where exactly had the helicopter crashed? "I didn't ask him." I looked at President Magaña, and he shrugged. "This is very delicate," he said. "I have a problem there. I'm supposed to be the commander-in-chief, so if I ask him, he should tell me. But he might say he's not going to tell me, then I would have to arrest him. So I don't ask." This is in many ways the standard development of a story in El Salvador, and is also illustrative of the position of the provisional president of El Salvador.

News of the outside world drifted in only fitfully, and in peculiar details. *La Prensa Gráfica* carried a regular column of news from San Francisco, California, and I recall reading in this column one morning that a man identified as a former president of the Bohemian Club had died, at age seventy-two, at his home in Tiburon. Most days *The Miami Herald* came in at some point, and sporadically *The New York Times* or *The Washington Post*, but there would be days when nothing came in at all, and I would find myself rifling back sports sections of *The Miami Herald* for installments of *Chrissie: My Own Story*, by Chris Evert Lloyd with Neil Amdur, or haunting the paperback stand at the hotel, where the collection ran mainly to romances and specialty items, like *The World's Best Dirty Jokes*, a volume in which all the jokes seemed to begin: "A midget went into a whorehouse . . ."

In fact the only news I wanted from outside increasingly turned out to be that which had originated in El Salvador: all other information seemed beside the point, the point being here, now, the situation, the *problema*, what did they mean the Hughes 500-D was *comprado en Guatemala*, was the Río Seco passable, were there or were there not American advisers on patrol in Usulután, who was going out, where were the roadblocks, were they burning cars today. In this context the rest of the world tended to recede, and word from the United States seemed profoundly remote, even inexplicable. I recall one morning picking up this message, from my secretary in Los Angeles: "JDD: Alessandra Stanley from *Time*, 213/273-1530. They heard you were in El Salvador and wanted some input from you for the cover story they're preparing on the women's movement. Ms. Stanley wanted their correspondent in Central America to contact you—I said that you could not be reached but would be calling me. She wanted you to call: Jay Cocks 212/841-2633." I studied this message for a long time, and tried to imagine the scenario in which a *Time* stringer in El Salvador received, by Telex from Jay Cocks in New York, a request to do an interview on the women's movement with someone who happened to be at the Camino Real Hotel. This was not a scenario that played, and I realized then that El Salvador was as inconceivable to Jay Cocks in the high keep of the Time-Life Building in New York as this message was to me in El Salvador.

I WAS TOLD in the summer of 1982 by both Alvaro Magaña and Guillermo Ungo that although each of course knew the other they were of "different generations." Magaña was fifty-six. Ungo was fifty-one. Five years is a generation in El Salvador, it being a place in which not only the rest of the world but time itself tends to contract to the here and now. History is *la matanza*, and then current events, which recede even as they happen: General José Guillermo García was in the summer of 1982 widely perceived as a fixture of long standing, an immovable object through several governments and shifts in the national temperament, a survivor. In context he was a survivor, but the context was just three years, since the Majano coup. All events earlier than the Majano coup had by then vanished into uncertain memory, and the coup itself, which took place on October 15, 1979, was seen as so distant that there was common talk of the next *juventud militar*, of the cyclical readiness for rebellion of what was always referred to as "the new generation" of young officers. "We think in five-year horizons," the economic officer at the American embassy told me one day. "Anything beyond that is evolution." He was talking about not having what he called "the luxury of the long view," but there is a real sense in which the five-year horizons of the American embassy constitute the longest view taken in El Salvador, either forward or back.

One reason no one looks back is that the view could only dispirit: this is a national history peculiarly resistant to heroic interpretation. There is no *libertador* to particularly remember. Public statues in San Salvador tend toward representations of abstracts, the Winged Liberty downtown, the *Salvador del Mundo* at the junction of Avenida Roosevelt and Paseo Escalón and the Santa Tecla highway; the expressionist spirit straining upward, outsized hands thrust toward the sky, at the Monument of the Revolution up by the Hotel Presidente. If the country's history as a republic seems devoid of shared purpose or unifying event, a record of insensate ambitions and their accidental consequences, its three centuries as a colony seem blanker still: Spanish colonial life was centered in Colombia and Panama to the south and Guatemala to the north, and Salvador lay between, a neglected frontier of the Captaincy General of Guatemala from 1525 until 1821, the year Guatemala declared its independence from Spain. So attenuated was El Salvador's sense of itself in its moment of independence that it petitioned the United States for admission to the union as a state. The United States declined.

In fact El Salvador had always been a frontier, even before the Spaniards arrived. The great Mesoamerican cultures penetrated this far south only shallowly. The great South American cultures thrust this far north only sporadically. There is a sense in which the place remains marked by the meanness and discontinuity of all frontier history, by a certain frontier proximity to the cultural zero. Some aspects of the local culture were imposed. Others were borrowed. An instructive moment: at an exhibition of native crafts in Nahuizalco, near Sonsonate, it was explained to me that a traditional native craft was the making of wicker furniture, but that little of this furniture was now seen because it was hard to obtain wicker in the traditional way. I asked what the traditional way of obtaining wicker had been. The traditional way of obtaining wicker, it turned out, had been to import it from Guatemala.

In fact there were a number of instructive elements about this day I spent in Nahuizalco, a hot Sunday in June. The event for which I had driven down from San Salvador was not merely a craft exhibit but the opening of a festival that would last several days, the sixth annual Feria Artesanal de Nahuizalco, sponsored by the Casa de la Cultura program of the Ministry of Education as part of its effort to encourage indigenous culture. Since public policy in El Salvador has veered unerringly toward the elimination of the indigenous population, this official celebration of its culture seemed an undertaking of some ambiguity, particularly in Nahuizalco: the uprising that led to the 1932 *matanza* began and ended among the Indian workers on the coffee *fincas* in this part of the country, and Nahuizalco and the other Indian villages around Sonsonate lost an entire generation to the *matanza*. By the early sixties estimates of the remaining Indian population in all of El Salvador ranged only between four and sixteen percent; the rest of the population was classified as *ladino*, a cultural rather than an ethnic designation, denoting only Hispanization, including both acculturated Indians and *mestizos*, and rejected by those upper-class members of the population who preferred to emphasize their Spanish ancestry.

Nineteen thirty-two was a year around Nahuizalco when Indians were tied by their thumbs and shot against church walls, shot on the road and left for the dogs, shot and bayoneted into the mass graves they themselves had dug. Indian dress was abandoned by the survivors. Nahuatl, the Indian language, was no longer spoken in public. In many ways race remains the ineffable element at the heart of this particular darkness: even as he conducted the *matanza*, General Maximiliano Hernández Martínez was dismissed, by many of the very oligarchs whose interests he was protecting by killing Indians, as "the little Indian." On this hot Sunday fifty years later the celebrants of Nahuizalco's indigenous culture would arrange themselves, by noon, into two distinct camps, the *ladinos* sitting in the shade of the schoolyard, the Indians squatting in the brutal sun outside. In the schoolyard there were trees, and tables, where the Queen of the Fair, who had a wicker crown and European features, sat with the local *guardia*, each of whom had an automatic weapon, a sidearm, and a bayonet. The *guardia* drank beer and played with their weapons. The Queen of the Fair studied her oxblood-red fingernails. It took twenty centavos to enter the schoolyard, and a certain cultural confidence.

There had been Indian dances that morning. There had been music. There had been the "blessing of the market": the statue of San Juan Bautista carried, on a platform trimmed with wilted gladioli, from the church to the market, the school, the homes of the bedridden. To the extent that Catholic mythology has been over four centuries successfully incorporated into local Indian life, this blessing of the market was at least part of the "actual" indigenous culture, but the dances and the music derived from other traditions. There was a Suprema Beer sound truck parked in front of the Casa de la Cultura office on the plaza, and the music that blared all day from its loudspeakers was "Roll Out the Barrel," "La Cucaracha," "Everybody Salsa."

The provenance of the dances was more complicated. They were Indian, but they were less remembered than recreated, and as such derived not from local culture but from a learned idea of local culture, an official imposition made particularly ugly by the cultural impotence of the participants. The women, awkward and uncomfortable in an approximation of native costume, moved with difficulty into the dusty street and performed a listless and unpracticed dance with baskets. Whatever men could be found (mainly little boys and old men, since those young men still alive in places like Nahuizalco try not to be noticed) had been dressed in "warrior" costume: headdresses of crinkled foil, swords of cardboard and wood. Their hair was lank, their walk furtive. Some of them wore sunglasses. The others averted their eyes. Their role in the fair involved stamping and lunging and brandishing their cardboard weapons, a display of warrior *machismo*, and the extent to which each of them had been unmanned—unmanned not only by history but by a factor less abstract, unmanned by the real weapons in the schoolyard, by the G-3 assault rifles with which the *guardia* played while they drank beer with the Queen of the Fair—rendered this display deeply obscene.

I had begun before long to despise the day, the dirt, the blazing sun, the pervasive smell of rotting meat, the absence of even the most rudimentary skill in the handicrafts on exhibit (there were sewn items, for example, but they were sewn by machine of sleazy fabric, and the simplest seams were crooked), the brutalizing music from the sound truck, the tedium; had begun most of all to despise the fair itself, which seemed contrived, pernicious, a kind of official opiate, an attempt to recreate or perpetuate a way of life neither economically nor socially viable. There was no pleasure in this day. There was a great deal of joyless milling. There was some shade in the plaza, from trees plastered with ARENA posters, but nowhere to sit. There was a fountain painted bright blue inside, but the dirty water was surrounded by barbed wire, and the sign read: "SE PROHIBE SENTARSE AQUI," no sitting allowed.

I stood for a while and watched the fountain. I bought a John Deere cap for seven *colones* and stood in the sun and watched the little ferris wheel, and the merry-go-round, but there seemed to be no children with the money or will to ride them, and after a while I crossed the plaza and went into the church, avoiding the bits of masonry which still fell from the bell tower damaged that week in the earthquake and its aftershocks. In the church a mass baptism was taking place: thirty or forty infants and older babies, and probably a few hundred mothers and grandmothers and aunts and godmothers. The altar was decorated with asters in condensed milk cans. The babies fretted, and several of the mothers produced bags of Fritos to quiet them. A piece of falling masonry bounced off a scaffold in the back of the church, but no one looked back. In this church full of women and babies there were only four men present. The reason for this may have been cultural, or may have had to do with the time and the place, and the G-3s in the schoolyard.

During the week before I flew down to El Salvador a Salvadoran woman who works for my husband and me in Los Angeles gave me repeated instructions about what we must and must not do. We must not go out at night. We must stay off the street whenever possible. We must never ride in buses or taxis, never leave the capital, never imagine that our passports would protect us. We must not even consider the hotel a safe place: people were killed in hotels. She spoke with considerable vehemence, because two of her brothers had been killed in Salvador in August of 1981, in their beds. The throats of both brothers had been slashed. Her father had been cut but stayed alive. Her mother had been beaten. Twelve of her other relatives, aunts and uncles and cousins, had been taken from their houses one night the same August, and their bodies had been found some time later, in a ditch. I assured her that we would remember, we would be careful, we would in fact be so careful that we would probably (trying for a light touch) spend all our time in church.

She became still more agitated, and I realized that I had spoken as a *norteamericana*: churches had not been to this woman the neutral ground they had been to me. I must remember: Archbishop Romero killed saying mass in the chapel of the Divine Providence Hospital in San Salvador. I must remember: more than thirty people killed at Archbishop Romero's funeral in the Metropolitan Cathedral in San Salvador. I must remember: more than twenty people killed before that on the steps of the Metropolitan Cathedral. CBS had filmed it. It had been on television, the bodies jerking, those still alive crawling over the dead as they tried to get out of range. I must understand: the Church was dangerous.

I told her that I understood, that I knew all that, and I did, abstractly, but the specific meaning of the Church she knew eluded me until I was actually there, at the Metropolitan Cathedral in San Salvador, one afternoon when rain sluiced down its corrugated plastic windows and puddled around the supports of the Sony and Phillips billboards near the steps. The effect of the Metropolitan Cathedral is immediate, and entirely literary. This is the cathedral that the late Archbishop Oscar Arnulfo Romero refused to finish, on the premise that the work of the Church took precedence over its display, and the high walls of raw concrete bristle with structural rods, rusting now, staining the concrete, sticking out at wrenched and violent angles. The wiring is exposed. Fluorescent tubes hang askew. The great high altar is backed by warped plyboard. The cross on the altar is of bare incandescent bulbs, but the bulbs, that afternoon, were unlit: there was in fact no light at all on the main altar, no light on the cross, no light on the globe of the world that showed the northern American continent in gray and the southern in white; no light on the dove above the globe, *Salvador del Mundo*. In this vast brutalist space that was the cathedral, the unlit altar seemed to offer a single ineluctable message: at this time and in this place the light of the world could be construed as out, off, extinguished.

In many ways the Metropolitan Cathedral is an authentic piece of political art, a statement for El Salvador as *Guernica* was for Spain. It is quite devoid of sentimental relief. There are no decorative or architectural references to familiar parables, in fact no stories at all, not even the Stations of the Cross. On the afternoon I was there the flowers laid on the altar were dead. There were no traces of normal parish activity. The doors were open to the barricaded main steps, and down the steps there was a spill of red paint, lest anyone forget the blood shed there. Here and there on the cheap linoleum inside the cathedral there was what seemed to be actual blood, dried in spots, the kind of spots dropped by a slow hemorrhage, or by a woman who does not know or does not care that she is menstruating.

There were several women in the cathedral during the hour

or so I spent there, a young woman with a baby, an older woman in house slippers, a few others, all in black. One of the women walked the aisles as if by compulsion, up and down, across and back, crooning loudly as she walked. Another knelt without moving at the tomb of Archbishop Romero in the right transept. "LOOR A MONSENOR ROMERO," the crude needlepoint tapestry by the tomb read, "Praise to Monsignor Romero from the Mothers of the Imprisoned, the Disappeared, and the Murdered," the *Comité de Madres y Familiares de Presos, Desaparecidos, y Asesinados Politicos de El Salvador.*

The tomb itself was covered with offerings and petitions, notes decorated with motifs cut from greeting cards and cartoons. I recall one with figures cut from a Bugs Bunny strip, and another with a pencil drawing of a baby in a crib. The baby in this drawing seemed to be receiving medication or fluid or blood intravenously, through the IV line shown on its wrist. I studied the notes for a while and then went back and looked again at the unlit altar, and at the red paint on the main steps, from which it was possible to see the guardsmen on the balcony of the National Palace hunching back to avoid the rain. Many Salvadorans are offended by the Metropolitan Cathedral, which is as it should be, because the place remains perhaps the only unambiguous political statement in El Salvador, a metaphorical bomb in the ultimate power station.

> ". . . I had nothing more to do in San Salvador. I had given a lecture on the topic that had occurred to me on the train to Tapachula: Little-known Books by Famous American Authors—*Pudd'nhead Wilson*, *The Devil's Dictionary*, *The Wild Palms.* I had looked at the university; and no one could explain why there was a mural of Marx, Engels, and Lenin in the university of this right-wing dictatorship."
>
> —Paul Theroux, *The Old Patagonian Express.*

The university Paul Theroux visited in San Salvador was the National University of El Salvador. This visit (and, given the context, this extraordinary lecture) took place in the late seventies, a period when the National University was actually open. In 1972 the Molina government had closed it, forcibly, with tanks and artillery and planes, and had kept it closed until 1974. In 1980 the Duarte government again moved troops onto the campus, which then had an enrollment of about 30,000, leaving fifty dead and offices and laboratories systematically smashed. By the time I visited El Salvador a few classes were being held in storefronts around San Salvador, but no one other than an occasional reporter had been allowed to enter the campus since the day the troops came in. Those reporters allowed to look had described walls still splashed with the spray-painted slogans left by the students, floors littered with tangled computer tape and with copies of what the National Guardsmen in charge characterized as *subversivo* pamphlets, for example a reprint of an article on inherited enzyme deficiency from *The New England Journal of Medicine.*

In some ways the closing of the National University seemed another of those Salvadoran situations in which no one came out well, and everyone was made to bleed a little, not excluding the National Guardsmen left behind to have their ignorance exposed by *gringo* reporters. The Jesuit university, UCA, or La Universidad Centroamericana José Simeón Cañas, had emerged as the most important intellectual force in the country, but the Jesuits had been so widely identified with the left that some local scholars would not attend lectures or seminars held on the UCA campus. (Those Jesuits still in El Salvador had in fact been under a categorical threat of death from the White Warriors Union since 1977. The Carter administration forced President Romero to protect the Jesuits, and on the day the killing was to have begun, July 22, 1977, the National Police are said to have sat outside the Jesuit residence in San Salvador on their motorcycles, with UZIs.) In any case UCA could manage an enrollment of only about 5,000. The scientific disciplines, which never had a particularly tenacious hold locally, had largely vanished from local life.

Meanwhile many people spoke of the National University in the present tense, as if it still existed, or as if its closing were a routine event on some long-term academic calendar. I recall talking one day to a former member of the faculty at the National University, a woman who had not seen her office since the morning she noticed the troops massing outside and left it. She lost her books and her research and the uncompleted manuscript of the book she was then writing, but she described this serenely, and seemed to find no immediate contradiction in losing her work to the Ministry of Defense and the work she did later with the Ministry of Education. The campus of the National University is said to be growing over, which is one way contradictions get erased in the tropics.

I was invited one morning to a gathering of Salvadoran writers, a kind of informal coffee hour arranged by the American embassy. For some days there had been a question about where to hold this *café literario*, since there seemed to be no single location that was not considered off-limits by at least one of the guests, and at one point the ambassador's residence was put forth as the most neutral setting. On the day before the event it was finally decided that UCA was the more appropriate place ("and just never mind," as one of the embassy people put it, that some people would not go to UCA), and at ten the next morning we gathered there in a large conference room and drank coffee and talked, at first in platitudes, and then more urgently.

These are some of the sentences spoken to me that morning: *It's not possible to speak of intellectual life in El Salvador. Every day we lose more. We are regressing constantly. Intellectual life is drying up. You are looking at the intellectual life of El Salvador. Here. In this room. We are the only survivors. Some of the others are out of the country, others are not writing because they are engaged in political activity. Some have been disappeared, many of the teachers have been disappeared. Teaching is very dangerous, if a student misinterprets what a teacher says, then the teacher may be arrested. Some are in exile, the rest are dead. Los muertos, you know? We are the only ones left. There is no one after us, no young ones. It is all over, you know?* At noon there was an exchange of books and *curricula vitae*. The cultural attaché from the embassy said that she, for one, would like to see this *café literario* close on a hopeful note, and someone provided one: it was a hopeful note that *norteamericanos* and *centroamericanos* could have such a meeting. This is what passed for a hopeful note in San Salvador in the summer of 1982.

THE AMBASSADOR of the United States of America in El Salvador, Deane Hinton, received on his desk every morning in the summer of 1982 a list of the American military personnel in-country that day. The number on this list, I was told, was never to exceed 55. Some days there were as few as 35. If the number got up to 55, and it was thought essential to bring in someone else, then a trade was made: the incoming American was juggled against an outgoing American, one normally stationed in Salvador but shunted down to Panama for as long as necessary to maintain the magic number.

Everything to do with the United States Military Group, or MILGP, was treated by the embassy as a kind of magic, a totemic presence circumscribed by potent taboos. The American A-37Bs presented to El Salvador in June of that year were actually flown up from Panama not by Americans but by Salvadorans trained at the United States Southern Air Command in Panama for this express purpose. American advisers could participate in patrols for training purposes but could not participate in patrols in combat situations. When both CBS and *The New York Times*, one day that June, reported having seen two or three American advisers in what the reporters construed as a combat situation in Usulután province, Colonel John D. Waghelstein, the MILGP commander, was called back from playing tennis in Panama (his wife had met him in Panama, there being no dependents allowed in El Salvador) in order, as he put it, "to deal with the press."

I happened to arrive for lunch at the ambassador's residence just as Colonel Waghelstein reported in from Panama that day, and the two of them, along with the embassy public affairs officer, walked to the far end of the swimming pool to discuss the day's problem out of my hearing. Colonel Waghelstein is massively built, crew-cut, tight-lipped, and very tanned, almost a cartoon of the American military presence, and the notion that he had come up from Panama to deal with the press was novel and interesting, in that he had made, during his tour in El Salvador, a pretty terse point of not dealing with the press. Some months later in Los Angeles I saw an NBC documentary in which I noticed the special effort Colonel Waghelstein had made in this case. American advisers had actually been made available to NBC, which in turn adopted a chiding tone toward CBS for the June "advisers in action" story. The total effect was mixed, however, since even as the advisers complained on camera about how "very few people" asked them what they did and about how some reporters "spend all their time with the other side," the camera angles seemed such that no adviser's face was distinctly seen. There were other points in this NBC documentary when I thought I recognized a certain official hand, for example the mention of the "sometimes cruel customs" of the Pipil Indians in El Salvador. The custom in question was that of flaying one another alive, a piece of pre-Columbian lore often tendered by embassy people as evidence that from a human-rights point of view, the trend locally is up, or at any rate holding.

Colonel Waghelstein stayed at the ambassador's that day only long enough for a drink (a Bloody Mary, which he nursed morosely), and, after he left, the ambassador and the public affairs officer and my husband and I sat down to lunch on the covered terrace. We watched a lime-throated bird in the garden. We watched the ambassador's English sheep dog bound across the lawn at the sound of shots, rifle practice at the Escuela Militar beyond the wall and down the hill. "Only time we had any quiet up here," the ambassador said in his high Montana twang, "was when we sent the whole school up to Benning." The shots rang out again. The sheep dog barked. "*Quieto*," the houseman crooned.

I have thought since about this lunch a great deal. The wine was chilled and poured into crystal glasses. The fish was served on porcelain plates that bore the American eagle. The sheep dog and the crystal and the American eagle together had on me a certain anesthetic effect, temporarily deadening that receptivity to the sinister that afflicts everyone in Salvador, and I experienced for a moment the official American delusion, the illusion of plausibility, the sense that the American undertaking in El Salvador might turn out to be, from the right angle, in the right light, just another difficult but possible mission in another troubled but possible country.

Deane Hinton is an interesting man. Before he replaced

Robert White in San Salvador he had served in Europe, South America, and Africa. He had been married twice, once to an American, who bore him five children before their divorce, and once to a Chilean, who had died not long before, leaving him the stepfather of her five children by an earlier marriage. At the time I met him he had just announced his engagement to a Salvadoran named Patricia de Lopez. Someone who is about to marry a third time, who thinks of himself as the father of ten, and who has spent much of his career in chancey posts —Mombasa, Kinshasa, Santiago, San Salvador—is apt to be someone who believes in the possible.

His predecessor, Robert White, was relieved of the San Salvador embassy in February 1981, in what White later characterized as a purge, by the new Reagan people, of the State Department's entire Latin American section. This circumstance made Deane Hinton seem, to many in the United States, the bearer of the administration's big stick in El Salvador, but what Deane Hinton actually said about El Salvador differed from what Robert White said about El Salvador more in style than in substance. Deane Hinton believed, as Robert White believed, that the situation in El Salvador was bad, terrible, squalid beyond anyone's power to understand it without experiencing it. Deane Hinton also believed, as Robert White believed to a point, that the situation would be, in the absence of one or another American effort, still worse.

Deane Hinton believes in doing what he can. He had gotten arrests on the deaths of the four American churchwomen. He had even ("by yelling some more," he said) gotten the government to announce these arrests, no small accomplishment, since El Salvador was a country in which the "announcement" of an arrest did not necessarily follow the arrest itself. In the case of the murders of Michael Hammer and Mark Pearlman and José Rodolfo Viera at the Sheraton, for example, it was not the government but the American embassy which announced at least two of the various successive arrests, those of the former guardsmen Abel Campos and Rodolfo Orellana Osorio. This embassy "announcement" was reported by the American press on September 15, 1982, and was followed immediately by another announcement: on September 16, 1982, "a police spokesman" in San Salvador announced not the arrest but the "release" of the same suspects, after what was described as a month in custody.

To persist in so distinctly fluid a situation required a personality of considerable resistance. Deane Hinton was even then working on getting new arrests in the Sheraton murders. He was even then working on getting trials in the murders of the four American women, a trial being another step that did not, in El Salvador, necessarily follow an arrest. There had been progress. There had been the election, a potent symbol for many Americans and perhaps even for some Salvadorans, although the symbolic content of the event showed up rather better in translation than on the scene. "There was some shooting in the morning," I recall being told by a parish priest about election day in his district, "but it quieted down around nine A.M. The army had a truck going around to go out and vote—*Tu Voto Es La Solución*, you know—so they went out and voted. They wanted that stamp on their identity cards to show they voted. The stamp was the proof of their good will. Whether or not they actually wanted to vote is hard to say. I guess you'd have to say they were more scared of the army than of the guerrillas, so they voted."

Four months after the fact, in *The New York Times Magazine*, former ambassador Robert White wrote about the election: "Nothing is more symbolic of our current predicament in El Salvador than the Administration's bizarre attempt to recast D'Aubuisson in a more favorable light." Even the fact that the election had resulted in what White called "political disaster" could be presented, with a turn of the mirror, positively: one man's political disaster could be another's democratic turbulence, the birth pangs of what Assistant Secretary of State Thomas Enders persisted in calling "nascent democratic institutions." "The new Salvadoran democracy," Enders was saying five months after the election, not long after Justice of the Peace Gonzalo Alonso García, the twentieth prominent Christian Democrat to be kidnapped or killed since the election, had been dragged from his house in San Cayetano Itepeque by fifteen armed men, "is doing what it is supposed to do—bringing a broad spectrum of forces and factions into a functioning democratic system."

In other words even the determination to eradicate the

opposition could be interpreted as evidence that the model worked. There was still, moreover, a certain obeisance to the land reform program, the lustrous intricacies of which were understood by so few that almost any interpretation could be construed as possible. "About 207, 207 always applied only to 1979, that is what no one understands," I had been told by President Magaña when I tried at one point to get straight the actual status of Decree 207, the legislation meant to implement the "Land-to-the-Tiller" program by providing that title to all land farmed by tenants be transferred immediately to those tenants. "There is no one more conservative than a small farmer," Peter Shiras, a former consultant to the Inter-American Development Bank, had quoted an AID official as saying about 207. "We're going to be breeding capitalists like rabbits."

Decree 207 had been the source of considerable confusion and infighting during the weeks preceding my arrival in El Salvador, suspended but not suspended, on and off and on again, but I had not before heard anyone describe it, as President Magaña seemed to be describing it, as a proposition wound up to self-destruct. Did he mean, I asked carefully, that Decree 207, implementing Land-to-the-Tiller, applied only to 1979 because no landowner, in practice, would work against his own interests by allowing tenants on his land after 207 took effect? "Right!" President Magaña had said, as if to a slow student. "Exactly! This is what no one understands. There were no new rental contracts in 1980 or 1981. No one would rent out land under 207, they would have to be crazy to do that."

What he said was obvious, but out of line with the rhetoric, and this conversation with President Magaña about Land-to-the-Tiller, which I had heard described through the spring as a centerpiece of United States policy in El Salvador, had been one of many occasions when the American effort in El Salvador seemed based on auto-suggestion, a dreamwork devised to obscure any intelligence that might trouble the dreamer. This impression persisted, and I was struck, a few months later, by the suggestion in the report on El Salvador released by the Permanent Select Committee on Intelligence of the House of Representatives (*U.S. Intelligence Performance in Central America: Achievements and Selected Instances of Concern*) that the intelligence was itself a dreamwork, tending to support policy, the report read, "rather than inform it," providing "reinforcement more than illumination," "'ammunition' rather than analysis."

A certain tendency to this kind of dreamwork, to improving upon rather than illuminating the situation, may have been inevitable, since the unimproved situation in El Salvador was such that to consider it was to consider moral extinction. "This time they won't get away with it," Robert White was reported to have said as he watched the bodies of the four American women dragged from their common grave, but they did, and White was brought home. This is a country that cracks Americans, and Deane Hinton gave the sense of a man determined not to crack. There on the terrace of the official residence on Avenida La Capilla in the San Benito district it was all logical. One step followed another, progress was slow. We were Americans, we would not be demoralized. It was not until late in the lunch, at a point between the salad and the profiteroles, that it occurred to me that we were talking exclusively about the appearances of things, about how the situation might be made to look better, about trying to get the Salvadoran government to "appear" to do what the American government needed done in order to make it "appear" that the American aid was justified.

It was sometimes necessary to stop Roberto D'Aubuisson "on the one-yard line" (Deane Hinton's phrase about the ARENA attempt to commandeer the presidency) because Roberto D'Aubuisson made a negative appearance in the United States, made things, as Jeremiah O'Leary, the assistant to national security adviser William Clark, had imagined Hinton advising D'Aubuisson after the election, "hard for everybody." What made a positive appearance in the United States, and things easier for everybody, were elections, and the announcement of arrests in cases involving murdered Americans, and ceremonies in which tractable *campesinos* were awarded land titles by army officers, and the Treasury Police sat on the platform, and the president came, by helicopter. "Our land reform program," Leonel Gómez, who had worked with the murdered José Rodolfo Viera in the Salvadoran Institute of Agrarian Transformation, noted in *Food Monitor*, "gave them an opportunity to build up points for the next U.S. AID grant." By "them" Leonel Gómez meant not his compatriots but Americans, meant the American Institute for Free Labor Development, meant Roy Prosterman, the architect of the Land-to-the-Tiller programs in both El Salvador and Vietnam.

In this light the American effort had a distinctly circular aspect (the aid was the card with which we got the Salvadorans to do it our way, and appearing to do it our way was the card with which the Salvadorans got the aid), and the question of why the effort was being made went unanswered. It was possible to talk about Cuba and Nicaragua, and by extension the Soviet Union, and national security, but this seemed only to justify a momentum already underway: no one could doubt that Cuba and Nicaragua had at various points supported the armed opposition to the Salvadoran government, but neither could anyone be surprised by this, or, given what could be known about the players, be unequivocally convinced that American interests lay on one side or another of what even Deane Hinton referred to as a civil war.

It was certainly possible to describe some members of the opposition, as Deane Hinton had, as "out-and-out Marxists," but it was equally possible to describe other members of the opposition, as the embassy had at the inception of the FDR in April of 1980, as "a broad-based coalition of moderate and center-left groups." The right in El Salvador never made this distinction: to the right, anyone in the opposition was a communist, along with most of the American press, the Catholic Church, and, as time went by, all Salvadoran citizens not of the right. In other words there remained a certain ambiguity about political terms as they were understood in the United States and in El Salvador, where "left" may mean, in the beginning, only a resistance to seeing one's family killed or disappeared. That it comes eventually to mean something else may be, to the extent that the United States has supported the increasing polarization in El Salvador, the Procrustean bed we made ourselves.

It was a situation in which American interests would seem to have been best served by attempting to isolate the "out-and-out Marxists" while supporting the "broad-based coalition of moderate and center-left groups," discouraging the one by encouraging the other, co-opting the opposition; but American policy, by accepting the invention of "communism," as defined by the right in El Salvador, as a daemonic element to be opposed at even the most draconic cost, had in fact achieved the reverse. "We believe in gringos," Hugh Barrera, an ARENA contender for the presidency, told Laurie Becklund of *The Los Angeles Times* when she asked in April of 1982 if ARENA did not fear losing American aid by trying to shut the Christian Democrats out of the government. "Congress would not risk losing a whole country over one party. That would be turning against a U.S. ally and encouraging Soviet intervention here. It would not be intelligent." In other words "anti-communism" was seen, correctly, as the bait the United States would always take.

That we had been drawn, both by a misapprehension of the local rhetoric and by the manipulation of our own rhetorical weaknesses, into a game we did not understand, a play of power in a political tropic alien to us, seemed apparent, and yet there we remained. In this light all arguments tended to trail off. Pros and cons seemed equally off the point. At the heart of the American effort there was something of the familiar ineffable, as if it were taking place not in El Salvador but in a mirage of El Salvador, the mirage of a society not unlike our own but "sick," a temporarily fevered republic in which the antibodies of democracy needed only to be encouraged, in which words had stable meanings north and south ("election," say, and "Marxist") and in which there existed, waiting to be tapped by our support, some latent good will. A few days before I arrived in El Salvador there appeared in *Diario de Hoy* a full-page advertisement placed by leaders of the Women's Crusade for Peace and Work. This advertisement accused the United States, in the person of its ambassador, Deane Hinton, of "blackmailing us with your miserable aid, which only keeps us subjugated in underdevelopment so that powerful countries like yours can continue exploiting our few riches and having us under your boot." The Women's Crusade for Peace and Work is an organization of the right, with links to ARENA, which may suggest how latent that good will remains.

This "blackmail" motif, and its arresting assumption that trying to keep Salvadorans from killing one another constituted a new and particularly crushing imperialism, began turning up more and more frequently. By October of 1982 advertisements were appearing in the San Salvador papers alleging that the blackmail was resulting in a "betrayal" of El Salvador by the military, who were seen as "lackeys" of the United States. At a San Salvador Chamber of Commerce meeting in late October, Deane Hinton said that "in the first two weeks of this month at least sixty-eight human beings were murdered in El Salvador under circumstances which are familiar to everyone here," stressed that American aid was dependent upon "progress" in this area, and fielded some fifty written questions, largely hostile, one of which read, "Are you trying to blackmail us?"

I was read this speech over the telephone by an embassy officer, who described it as "the ambassador's strongest statement yet." I was puzzled by this, since the ambassador had made most of the same points, at a somewhat lower pitch, in a speech on February 11, 1982; it was hard to discern a substantive advance between, in February, "If there is one issue which could force our Congress to withdraw or seriously reduce its support for El Salvador, it is the issue of human rights," and, in October: "If not, the United States—in spite of our other interests, in spite of our commitment to the struggle against communism, could be forced to deny assistance to El Salvador." In fact the speeches seemed almost cyclical, seasonal events keyed to the particular rhythm of the six-month certification process; midway in the certification cycle things appear "bad," and are then made, at least rhetorically, to appear "better," "improvement" being the key to certification.

I mentioned the February speech on the telephone, but the embassy officer to whom I was speaking did not see the similarity; this was, he said, a "stronger" statement, and would be "front-page" in both *The Washington Post* and *The Los Angeles Times.* In fact the story did appear on the front pages of both *The Washington Post* and *The Los Angeles Times*, suggesting that every six months the news is born anew in El Salvador.

Whenever I hear someone speak now of one or another *solución* for El Salvador I think of particular Americans who have spent time there, each in his or her own way inexorably altered by the fact of having been in a certain place at a certain time.

Some of these Americans have since moved on and others remain in Salvador, but, like survivors of a common natural disaster, they are equally marked by the place.

> "There are a lot of options that aren't playable. We could come in militarily and shape the place up. That's an option, but it's not playable, because of public opinion. If it weren't for public opinion, however, El Salvador would be the ideal laboratory for a full-scale military operation. It's small. It's self-contained. There are hemispheric cultural similarities."
>
> —*A United States embassy officer in San Salvador.*

> "June 15th was not only a great day for El Salvador, receiving \$5 million in additional U.S. aid for the private sector and a fleet of fighter planes and their corresponding observation units, but also a great day for me. Ray Bonner [of *The New York Times*] actually spoke to me at Ilopango airport and took my hand and shook it when I offered it to him. . . . Also, another correspondent pulled me aside and said that if I was such a punctilious journalist why the hell had I written something about him that wasn't true. Here I made no attempt to defend myself but only quoted my source. Later we talked and ironed out some wrinkles. It is a great day when journalists with opposing points of view can get together and learn something from each other, after all, we are all on the same side. I even wrote a note to Robert E. White (which he ignored) not long ago after he protested that I had not published his Letter to the Editor (which I had) suggesting that we be friendly enemies. The only enemy is totalitarianism, in any guise: communistic, socialistic, capitalistic or militaristic. Man is unique because he has free will and the capacity to choose. When this is suppressed he is no longer a man but an animal. That is why I say that despite differing points of view, we are none of us enemies."
>
> —*Mario Rosenthal, editor of the* El Salvador News Gazette, *in his June 14–20, 1982 column, "A Great Day."*

"You would have had the last interview with an obscure Salvadoran."

—An American reporter to whom I had mentioned that I had been trying to see Colonel Salvador Beltrán Luna on the day he died in a helicopter crash.

"It's not as bad as it could be. I was talking to the political risk people at one of the New York banks and in 1980 they gave El Salvador only a ten percent chance of as much stability in 1982 as we have now. So you see."

—The same embassy officer.

"Normally I wouldn't have a guard at my level, but there were death threats against my predecessor, he was on a list. I'm living in his old house. In fact something kind of peculiar happened today. Someone telephoned and wanted to know, very urgent, how to reach the Salvadoran woman with whom my predecessor lived. This person on the phone claimed that the woman's family needed to reach her, a death, or illness, and she had left no address. This might have been true and it might not have been true. Naturally I gave no information."

—Another embassy officer.

"AMBASSADOR WHITE: My embassy also sent in several months earlier these captured documents. There is no doubt about the provenance of these documents as they were handed to me directly by Colonel Adolfo Majano, then a member of the junta. They were taken when they captured ex-Major D'Aubuisson and a number of other officers who were conspiring against the Government of El Salvador.
SENATOR ZORINSKY: . . . Please continue, Mr. Ambassador.
AMBASSADOR WHITE: I would be glad to give you copies of these documents for your record. In these documents there are over a hundred names of people who are participating, both within the Salvadoran military as active conspirers against the Government, and also the names of people living in the United States and in Guatemala

City who are actively funding the death squads. I gave this document, in Spanish, to three of the most skilled political analysts I know in El Salvador without orienting them in any way. I just asked them to read this and tell me what conclusions they came up with. All three of them came up with the conclusion that there is, within this document, evidence that is compelling, if not 100 percent conclusive, that D'Aubuisson and his group are responsible for the murder of Archbishop Romero.

SENATOR CRANSTON: What did you say? Responsible for whose murder?

AMBASSADOR WHITE: Archbishop Romero . . ."

—*From the record of hearings before the Committee on Foreign Relations, U.S. Senate, April 9, 1981, two months after Robert White left San Salvador.*

Of all these Americans I suppose I think especially of Robert White, for his is the authentic American voice afflicted by El Salvador: *You will find one of the pages with Monday underlined and with quotation marks*, he said that April day in 1981 about his documents, which were duly admitted into the record and, as the report of the House Permanent Select Committee on Intelligence later concluded, ignored by the CIA; he talked about Operation Pineapple, and blood sugar, and 257 Roberts guns, about addresses in Miami, about Starlight scopes; about *documents handed to him directly by Colonel Majano*, about *compelling if not conclusive evidence* of activities that continued to fall upon the ears of his auditors as signals from space, unthinkable, inconceivable, dim impulses from a black hole. In the serene light of Washington that spring day in 1981, two months out of San Salvador, Robert White's distance from the place was already lengthening: in San Salvador he might have wondered, the final turn of the mirror, *what Colonel Majano had to gain by handing him the documents.*

That the texture of life in such a situation is essentially untranslatable became clear to me only recently, when I tried to describe to a friend in Los Angeles an incident that occurred some days before I left El Salvador. I had gone with my husband and another American to the San Salvador morgue, which, unlike most morgues in the United States, is easily accessible, through an open door on the ground floor around the back of the court building. We had been too late that morning to see the day's bodies (there is not much emphasis on embalming in El Salvador, or for that matter on identification, and bodies are dispatched fast for disposal), but the man in charge had opened his log to show us the morning's entries, seven bodies, all male, none identified, none believed older than twenty-five. Six had been certified dead by *arma de fuego*, firearms, and the seventh, who had also been shot, of shock. The slab on which the bodies had been received had already been washed down, and water stood on the floor. There were many flies, and an electric fan.

The other American with whom my husband and I had gone to the morgue that morning was a newspaper reporter, and since only seven unidentified bodies bearing evidence of *arma de fuego* did not in San Salvador in the summer of 1982 constitute a newspaper story worth pursuing, we left. Outside in the parking lot there were a number of wrecked or impounded cars, many of them shot up, upholstery chewed by bullets, windshield shattered, thick pastes of congealed blood on pearlized hoods, but this was also unremarkable, and it was not until we walked back around the building to the reporter's rented car that each of us began to sense the potentially remarkable.

Surrounding the car were three men in uniform, two on the sidewalk and the third, who was very young, sitting on his motorcycle in such a way as to block our leaving. A second motorcycle had been pulled up directly behind the car, and the space in front was occupied. The three had been joking among themselves, but the laughter stopped as we got into the car. The reporter turned the ignition on, and waited. No one moved. The two men on the sidewalk did not meet our eyes. The boy on the motorcycle stared directly, and caressed the G-3 propped between his thighs. The reporter asked in Spanish if one of the motorcycles could be moved so that we could get out. The men on the sidewalk said nothing, but smiled enigmatically. The boy only continued staring, and began twirling the flash suppressor on the barrel of his G-3.

This was a kind of impasse. It seemed clear that if we tried to leave and scraped either motorcycle the situation would deteriorate. It also seemed clear that if we did not try to leave the situation would deteriorate. I studied my hands. The reporter gunned the motor, forced the car up onto the curb far enough to provide a minimum space in which to maneuver, and managed to back out clean. Nothing more happened, and what did happen had been a common enough kind of incident in El Salvador, a pointless confrontation with aimless authority, but I have heard of no *solución* that precisely addresses this local vocation for terror.

Any situation can turn to terror. The most ordinary errand can go bad. Among Americans in El Salvador there is an endemic apprehension of danger in the apparently benign. I recall being told by a network anchor man that one night in his hotel room (it was at the time of the election, and because the Camino Real was full he had been put up at the Sheraton) he took the mattress off the bed and shoved it against the window. He happened to have with him several bulletproof vests that he had brought from New York for the camera crew, and before going to the Sheraton lobby he put one on. Managers of American companies in El Salvador (Texas Instruments is still there, and Cargill, and some others) are replaced every several months, and their presence is kept secret. Some companies bury their managers in a number-two or number-three post. American embassy officers are driven in armored and unmarked vans (no eagle, no seal, no CD plates) by Salvadoran drivers and Salvadoran guards, because, I was told, "if someone gets blown away, obviously the State Department would prefer it done by a local security man, then you don't get headlines saying 'American Shoots Salvadoran Citizen.'" These local security men carry automatic weapons on their laps.

In such a climate the fact of being in El Salvador comes to seem a sentence of indeterminate length, and the prospect of leaving doubtful. On the night before I was due to leave I did not sleep, lay awake and listened to the music drifting up from a party at the Camino Real pool, heard the band play "Malaguena" at three and at four and again at five A.M., when the party seemed to end and light broke and I could get up. I was picked up to go to the airport that morning by one of the embassy vans, and a few blocks from the hotel I was seized by the conviction that this was not the most direct way to the airport, that this was not an embassy guard sitting in front with the Remington on his lap; that this was someone else. That the van turned out in fact to be the embassy van, detouring into San Benito to pick up an AID official, failed to relax me: once at the airport I sat without moving and averted my eyes from the soldiers patrolling the empty departure lounges.

When the nine A.M. TACA flight to Miami was announced I boarded without looking back, and sat rigid until the plane left the ground. I did not fasten my seat belt. I did not lean back. The plane stopped that morning at Belize, setting down on the runway lined with abandoned pillboxes and rusting camouflaged tanks to pick up what seemed to be every floater on two continents, wildcatters, collectors of information, the fantasts of the hemisphere. Even a team of student missionaries got on at Belize, sallow children from the piney woods of Georgia and Alabama who had been teaching the people of Belize, as the team member who settled down next to me explained, to know Jesus as their personal savior.

He was perhaps twenty, with three hundred years of American hill stock in his features, and as soon as the plane left Belize he began filling out a questionnaire on his experience there, laboriously printing out the phrases, *in obedience to God, opportunity to renew commitment, most rewarding part of my experience, most disheartening part.* Somewhere over the Keys I asked him what the most disheartening part of his experience had been. The most disheartening part of his experience, he said, had been seeing people leave the Crusade as empty as they came. The most rewarding part of his experience had been renewing his commitment to bring the Good News of Jesus as personal savior to all these different places. The different places to which he was committed to bring the Good News were New Zealand, Iceland, Finland, Colorado, and El Salvador. This was *la solución* not from Washington or Panama or Mexico but from Belize, and the piney woods of Georgia. This flight from San Salvador to Belize to Miami took place at the end of June 1982. In the week that I am completing this report, at the end of October 1982, the offices in the Hotel Camino Real in San Salvador of the Associated Press, United Press International, United Press International Television News, NBC News, CBS News, and ABC News were raided and searched by members of the El Salvador National Police carrying submachine guns;

fifteen leaders of legally recognized political and labor groups opposing the government of El Salvador were disappeared in San Salvador; Deane Hinton said that he was "reasonably certain" that these disappearances had not been conducted under Salvadoran government orders; the Salvadoran Ministry of Defense announced that eight of the fifteen disappeared citizens were in fact in government custody; and the State Department announced that the Reagan administration believed that it had "turned the corner" in its campaign for political stability in Central America.

DEMOCRACY

This book is for Dominique and Quintana.
It is also for Elsie Giorgi.

ONE

I

THE LIGHT at dawn during those Pacific tests was something to see.

Something to behold.

Something that could almost make you think you saw God, he said.

He said to her.

Jack Lovett said to Inez Victor.

Inez Victor who was born Inez Christian.

He said: the sky was this pink no painter could approximate, one of the detonation theorists used to try, a pretty fair Sunday painter, he never got it. Just never captured it, never came close. The sky was this pink and the air was wet from the night rain, soft and wet and smelling like flowers, smelling like those flowers you used to pin in your hair when you drove out to Schofield, gardenias, the air in the morning smelled like gardenias, never mind there were not too many flowers around those shot islands.

They were just atolls, most of them.

Sand spits, actually.

Two Quonsets and one of those landing strips they roll down, you know, the matting, just roll it down like a goddamn bathmat.

It was kind of a Swiss Family Robinson deal down there, really. None of the observers would fly down until the technical guys had the shot set up, that's all I was, an observer. Along for the ride. There for the show. You know me. Sometimes we'd get down there and the weather could go off and we'd wait days, just sit around cracking coconuts, there was one particular event at Johnston where it took three weeks to satisfy the weather people.

Wonder Woman Two, that shot was.

I remember I told you I was in Manila.

I remember I brought you some little souvenir from Manila, actually I bought it on Johnston off a reconnaissance pilot who'd flown in from Clark.

Three weeks sitting around goddamn Johnston Island waiting for the weather and then no yield to speak of.

Meanwhile we lived in the water.

Caught lobsters and boiled them on the beach.

Played gin and slapped mosquitoes.

Couldn't walk. No place to walk. Couldn't write anything down, the point of the pen would go right through the paper, one thing you got to understand down there was why not much got written down on those islands.

What you could do was, you could talk. You got to hear everybody's personal life story down there, believe me, you're sitting on an island a mile and a half long and most of that is the landing strip.

Those technical guys, some of them had been down there three months.

Got pretty raunchy, believe me.

Then the weather people would give the go and bingo, no more stories. Everybody would climb on a transport around three A.M. and go out a few miles and watch for first light.

Watch for pink sky.

And then the shot, naturally.

Nevada, the Aleutians, those events were another situation altogether.

Nobody had very pleasurable feelings about Nevada, although some humorous things did happen there at Mercury, like the time a Livermore device fizzled and the Los Alamos photographers started snapping away at that Livermore tower —still standing, you understand, a two-meg gadget and the tower's still standing, which was the humorous part—and laughing like hell. The Aleutians were just dog duty, ass end of the universe, they give the world an enema they stick it in at Amchitka. Those shots up there did a job because by then they were using computers instead of analog for the diagnostics, but you would never recall an Aleutian event with any nostalgia whatsoever, nothing even humorous, you got a lot of congressmen up there with believe it or not their wives and daughters, big deal for the civilians but zero interest, zip, none.

He said to her.

Jack Lovett said to Inez Victor (who was born Inez Christian) in the spring of 1975.

But those events in the Pacific, Jack Lovett said.

Those shots around 1952, 1953.

Christ they were sweet.

You were still a little kid in high school when I was going down there, you were pinning flowers in your hair and driving out to Schofield, crazy little girl with island fever, I should have been put in jail. I'm surprised your Uncle Dwight didn't show up out there with a warrant. I'm surprised the whole goddamn Christian Company wasn't turned out for the lynching.

Water under the bridge.

Long time ago.

You've been around the world a little bit since.

You did all right.

You filled your dance card, you saw the show.

Interesting times.

I told you when I saw you in Jakarta in 1969, you and I had the knack for interesting times.

Jesus Christ, Jakarta.

Ass end of the universe, southern tier.

But I'll tell you one thing about Jakarta in 1969, Jakarta in 1969 beat Bien Hoa in 1969.

"Listen, Inez, get it while you can," Jack Lovett said to Inez Victor in the spring of 1975.

"Listen, Inez, use it or lose it."

"Listen, Inez, *un regard d'adieu*, we used to say in Saigon, last look through the door."

"Oh shit, Inez," Jack Lovett said one night in the spring of 1975, one night outside Honolulu in the spring of 1975, one night in the spring of 1975 when the C-130s and the C-141s were already shuttling between Honolulu and Anderson and Clark and Saigon all night long, thirty-minute turnaround at Tan Son Nhut, touching down and loading and taxiing out on flight idle, bringing out the dependents, bringing out the dealers, bringing out the money, bringing out the pet dogs and the sponsored bar girls and the porcelain elephants: "Oh shit, Inez," Jack Lovett said to Inez Victor, "Harry Victor's wife."

Last look through more than one door.

This is a hard story to tell.

2

CALL ME the author.

Let the reader be introduced to Joan Didion, upon whose character and doings much will depend of whatever interest these pages may have, as she sits at her writing table in her own room in her own house on Welbeck Street.

So Trollope might begin this novel.

I have no unequivocal way of beginning it, although I do have certain things in mind. I have for example these lines from a poem by Wallace Stevens:

> The palm at the end of the mind,
> Beyond the last thought, rises
> In the bronze distance,
> A gold-feathered bird
> Sings in the palm, without human meaning,
> Without human feeling, a foreign song.

Consider that.

I have: "Colors, moisture, heat, enough blue in the air," Inez Victor's fullest explanation of why she stayed on in Kuala Lumpur. Consider that too. I have those pink dawns of which Jack Lovett spoke. I have the dream, recurrent, in which my entire field of vision fills with rainbow, in which I open a door onto a growth of tropical green (I believe this to be a banana grove, the big glossy fronds heavy with rain, but since no bananas are seen on the palms symbolists may relax) and watch the spectrum separate into pure color. Consider any of these things long enough and you will see that they tend to deny the relevance not only of personality but of narrative, which makes them less than ideal images with which to begin a novel, but we go with what we have.

Cards on the table.

I began thinking about Inez Victor and Jack Lovett at a point in my life when I lacked certainty, lacked even that minimum level of ego which all writers recognize as essential to the writing of novels, lacked conviction, lacked patience with the past and interest in memory; lacked faith even in my own technique. A poignant (to me) assignment I came across recently in a textbook for students of composition: "*Didion begins with a rather ironic reference to her immediate reason to write this piece. Try using this ploy as the opening of an essay; you may want to copy the ironic-but-earnest tone of Didion, or you might try making your essay witty. Consider the broader question of the effect of setting: how does Didion use the scene as a rhetorical base? She returns again and again to different details of the scene: where and how and to what effect? Consider, too, Didion's own involvement in the setting: an atmosphere results. How?*"

Water under the bridge.

As Jack Lovett would say.

Water under the bridge and dynamite it behind you.

So I have no leper who comes to the door every morning at seven.

No Tropical Belt Coal Company, no unequivocal lone figure on the crest of the immutable hill.

In fact no immutable hill: as the granddaughter of a geologist I learned early to anticipate the absolute mutability of hills and waterfalls and even islands. When a hill slumps into the ocean I see the order in it. When a 5.2 on the Richter scale wrenches the writing table in my own room in my own house in my own particular Welbeck Street I keep on typing. A hill is a transitional accommodation to stress, and ego may be a similar accommodation. A waterfall is a self-correcting maladjustment of stream to structure, and so, for all I know, is technique. The very island to which Inez Victor returned in the spring of 1975—Oahu, an emergent post-erosional land mass along the Hawaiian Ridge—is a temporary feature, and every rainfall or tremor along the Pacific plates alters its shape and shortens its tenure as Crossroads of the Pacific. In this light it is difficult to maintain definite convictions about what happened down there in the spring of 1975, or before.

In fact I have already abandoned a great deal of what happened before.

Abandoned most of the stories that still dominate table talk down in that part of the world where Inez Victor was born and to which she returned in 1975.

Abandoned for example all stories about definite cases of typhoid contracted on sea voyages lasting the first ten months of 1856.

Abandoned all accounts of iridescence observed on the night sea off the Canaries, of guano rocks sighted southeast of the Falklands, of the billiards room at the old Hotel Estrella del Mar on the Chilean coast, of a particular boiled-beef lunch eaten on Tristan da Cunha in 1859; and of certain legendary poker games played on the Isthmus of Panama in 1860, with the losses and winnings (in gold) of every player.

Abandoned the bereaved widower who drowned himself at landfall.

Scuttled the festivities marking the completion of the first major irrigation ditch on the Nuannu ranch.

Jettisoned in fact those very stories with which most people I know in those islands confirm their place in the larger scheme, their foothold against the swell of the sea, the erosion of the reefs and the drowning of the valley systems and the glittering shallows left when islands vanish. Would it have been Inez Victor's grandmother Cissy or Cissy's best friend Tita Dowdell who wore the Highland Lassie costume to the Children's Ball at the palace in 1892? If Cissy went as the Highland Lassie and Tita Dowdell as the Spanish Dancer (Inez's grandfather definitely went as one of the Peasant Children of All Nationalities, that much was documented, that much Inez and her sister Janet knew from the photograph that hung on the landing of the house on Manoa Road), then how did the Highland Lassie costume end up with the Palace Restoration Committee on loan from Tita Dowdell's daughter-in-law? On the subject of Tita Dowdell's daughter-in-law, did her flat silver come to her through her father's and Inez and Janet's grandfather's mutual Aunt Tru? Was it likely that Aunt Tru's fire opal from the Great Barrier Reef (surrounded by diamond chips) would have been lost down a drain at the Outrigger Canoe Club if Janet or Inez or even their cousin Alice Campbell had been wearing it instead of Tita Dowdell's daughter-in-law? Where were the calabashes Alice Campbell's father got from Judge Thayer? Who had Leilani Thayer's koa settee? When Inez and Janet's mother left Honolulu on the reconditioned *Lurline* and never came back, did she or did she not have the right to take Tru's yellow diamond? These are all important questions down there, suggestive details in the setting, but the setting is for another novel.

3

"IMAGINE MY mother dancing," that novel began, in the first person. The first person was Inez, and was later abandoned in favor of the third:

"Inez imagined her mother dancing.

"Inez remembered her mother dancing.

"Brown-and-white spectator shoes, very smart. High-heeled sandals made of white silk twine, very beautiful. White gardenias in her hair on the beach at Lanikai. A white silk blouse with silver sequins shaped like stars. Shaped like new moons. Shaped like snowflakes. The sentimental things of life as time went by. Dancing under the camouflage net on the lawn at Kaneohe. Blue moon on the Nuannu ranch. Saw her standing alone. She smiled as she danced.

"Inez remembered no such thing.

"Inez remembered the shoes and the sequins like snowflakes but she only imagined her mother dancing, to make clear to herself that the story was one of romantic outline. You will notice that the daughters in romantic stories always remember their mothers dancing, or about to leave for the dance: these dance-bound mothers materialize in the darkened nursery (never a bedroom in these stories, always a 'nursery,' on the English model) in a cloud of perfume, a burst of light off a diamond hair clip. They glance in the mirror. They smile. They do not linger, for this is one of those moments in which the interests of mothers are seen to diverge sharply from the wishes of daughters. These mothers get on with it. These mothers lean for a kiss and leave for the dance. Inez and Janet's mother left, but not for the dance. Inez and Janet's mother left for San Francisco, on the *Lurline*, reconditioned. I specify 'reconditioned' because that was how Carol Christian's departure was characterized for Inez and Janet, as a sudden but compelling opportunity to make the first postwar crossing on the reconditioned *Lurline*. 'Just slightly irresistible,' was the way Carol Christian put it exactly."

What I had there was a study in provincial manners, in the acute tyrannies of class and privilege by which people assert themselves against the tropics; Honolulu during World War Two, martial law, submariners and fliers and a certain investor from Hong Kong with whom Carol Christian was said to drink brandy and Coca-Cola, a local scandal. I was interested more in Carol Christian than in her daughters, interested in the stubborn loneliness she had perfected during her marriage to Paul Christian, interested in her position as an outsider in the islands and in her compensatory yearning to be "talented," not talented at anything in particular but just talented, a state of social grace denied her by the Christians. Carol Christian arrived in Honolulu as a bride in 1934. By 1946 she was sometimes moved so profoundly by the urge for company that she would keep Inez and Janet home from school on the pretext of teaching them how to do their nails. She read novels out loud to them on the beach at Lanikai, popular novels she checked out from the lending library at the drugstore in Kailua. "'The random years were at an end,'" she would read, her voice rising to signal a dramatic effect, and then she would invent a flourish of her own: "'Now, they could harvest them.' Look there, *random harvest*, that explains the title, very poetic, a happy ending, *n'est-ce pas*?"

She was attracted to French phrases but knew only the several she had memorized during the semester of junior college in Stockton, California, that constituted her higher education. She was also attracted to happy endings, and located them for Inez and Janet wherever she could: in the Coke float that followed the skinned knee, in the rainbow after the rain, in magazine stories about furlough weddings and fortuitously misdelivered Dear John letters and, not least, in her own romance, which she dated from the day she left Stockton and got a job modeling at I. Magnin in San Francisco. "Eighteen years old and dressed to kill in a Chanel suit, the real McCoy," she would say to Inez and Janet. Eighteen years old and dressed to kill in a Mainbocher evening pajama, the genuine article. Eighteen years old and dressed to kill in a Patou tea gown, white satin cut on the bias, talk about drop dead, bare to *here* in back. The bias-cut Patou tea gown figured large in Carol

Christian's stories because this was the dress in which she had been sneaking a cigarette on the I. Magnin employees' floor when Paul Christian stepped off the elevator by mistake (another fortuitous misdelivery) and brushed the shadows away, brought her happiest day, one look at him and she had found a world completely new, the sole peculiarity being that the world was an island in the middle of the Pacific and Paul Christian was rarely there. "When a man stays away from a woman it means he wants to keep their love alive," Carol Christian advised Inez and Janet. She had an entire codex of these signals men and women supposedly sent to one another (when a woman blew smoke at a man it meant she was definitely interested, and when a man told a woman her dress was too revealing it meant he adored her), dreamy axioms she had heard or read or invented as a schoolgirl of romantic tendency and to which she clung in the face of considerable contrary evidence. That she had miscalculated when she married Paul Christian was a conclusion she seemed incapable of drawing. She made a love-knot of what she imagined to be her first gray hair and mailed it to him in Cuernavaca. "*Mon cher* Paul," she wrote on the card to which she pinned the love-knot. Inez watched her tie the hair but did not see the card for some years, loose in one of the boxes of shed belongings that Paul Christian would periodically ship express collect from wherever he was to Inez and Janet. "Who do you f—— to get off this island? (Just kidding of course) XXXX, C."

She left dark red lipstick marks on her cigarettes, smoked barely at all and then crushed out in coffee cups and Coke bottles and in the sand. She sat for hours at her dressing table, which was covered with the little paper parasols that came in drinks, yellow, turquoise, shocking pink, tissue parasols like a swarm of brittle butterflies. She sat at this dressing table and shaved her legs. She sat at this dressing table and smoothed Vaseline into her eyebrows. She sat at this dressing table and instructed her daughters in what she construed to be the language of love, a course she had notably failed. For a year or two after Carol Christian left Honolulu Janet would sit on the beach at Lanikai and sift the sand looking for cigarettes stained with her mother's lipstick. She kept the few she found in a shoebox, along with the tissue parasols from Carol Christian's dressing table and the postcards from San Francisco and Carmel and Lake Tahoe.

Of the daughters I was at first more interested in Janet, who was the younger, than in Inez. I was interested in the mark the mother had left on Janet, in Janet's defensive veneer of provincial gentility, her startling and avid preoccupation with other people's sexual arrangements; in her mercantile approach to emotional transactions, and her condescension to anyone less marketable than she perceived herself to be. As an adolescent Janet had always condescended, for example, to Inez, and became bewildered and rather sulky when it worked out, in her view, so well for Inez and so disappointingly for herself. I was interested in how Janet's husband Dick Ziegler made a modest fortune in Hong Kong housing and lost it in the development of windward Oahu. I was interested in Inez and Janet's grandmother, the late Sybil "Cissy" Christian, a woman remembered in Honolulu for the vehement whims and irritations that passed in that part of the world as opinions, as well as for the dispatch with which she had divested herself of her daughter-in-law. *Aloha oe.* "I believe your mother wants to go to night clubs," Cissy Christian said to Inez and Janet by way of explaining Carol Christian's departure. "But she's coming back," Janet said. "Now and then," Cissy Christian said. This conversation took place at lunch at the Pacific Club, one hour after Inez and Janet and their uncle Dwight saw the reconditioned *Lurline* sail. Janet bolted from the table. "Happy now?" Dwight Christian asked his mother. "Somebody had to do it," Cissy Christian said. "Not necessarily before lunch," Dwight Christian said.

I saw it as a family in which the colonial impulse had marked every member. I was interested in Inez and Janet's father, Paul Christian, and in the way in which he had reinvented himself as a romantic outcast, a remittance man of the Pacific. "He's going to end up a goddamn cargo cult," Paul Christian's brother Dwight once said about him. I was interested not only in Paul but in Dwight Christian, in his construction contracts at Long Binh and Cam Ranh Bay, his claim to have played every Robert Trent Jones golf course in the world with the exception of the Royal in Rabat; the particular way in which he used Wendell Omura to squeeze Dick Ziegler out of windward

Oahu and coincidentally out of the container business. "Let me give you a little piece of advice," Dwight Christian said when Paul Christian took up Dick Ziegler's side in this matter. "'Life can only be understood backwards, but it must be lived forwards.' Kierkegaard." Dwight Christian had an actual file of such quotations, most of them torn from the "Thoughts on the Business of Life" page in *Forbes* and given to a secretary to be typed out on three-by-five index cards. The cards were his hedge against a profound shyness. "Recently I ran across a thought from Racine," he would say on those occasions when he was called upon to chair a stockholders' meeting or to keynote the Kickoff Dinner for Punahou School Annual Giving or to have his picture taken, wearing a silk suit tailored in Hong Kong and an aluminum hard hat stencilled "D.C.," knee-deep in silica sand in the hold of a dry-bulk carrier.

That particular photograph appeared in *Business Week*, at the time Dwight Christian was trying (unsuccessfully, it turned out) to take over British Leyland.

I also had two photographs from *Fortune*, one showing Dwight Christian riding a crane over a cane field and the other showing him astride an eighteen-thousand-ton concrete dolos, with a Pan American Cargo Clipper overhead.

In fact I had a number of photographs of the Christians: in that prosperous and self-absorbed colony the Christians were sufficiently good-looking and sufficiently confident and, at least at the time Inez was growing up, sufficiently innocent not to mind getting their pictures in the paper. I had Cissy Christian smoking a cigarette in a white jade holder as she presented the Christian Prize in Sugar Chemistry at the University of Hawaii in 1938. I had Dwight and Ruthie Christian tea-dancing at the Alexander Young Hotel in 1940. I had Carol Christian second-from-the-left in a group of young Honolulu matrons who met every Tuesday in 1942 to drink daiquiris and eat chicken salad and roll bandages for the Red Cross. In this photograph Carol Christian is wearing a Red Cross uniform, but in fact she was invited to join this group only twice, both times by Ruthie Christian. "Spend time around that crowd and you see how the green comes out," she said when it became clear that she would not be included on a regular basis. "You see how the green comes out" was something Carol Christian said often. She said it whenever she divined a note of rejection or criticism or even suspended judgment in someone's response to her, or, by extension, to Inez or Janet. She seemed to believe herself the object of considerable "envy," a word Inez tried to avoid in later life, and perhaps she was.

"I detect just the slightest tinge of lime."

"Positively chartreuse."

"You find out fast enough who your friends are."

In fact it would have been hard to say who Carol Christian's friends were, since she had no friends at all who were not primarily Paul Christian's friends or Cissy Christian's friends or Dwight and Ruthie Christian's friends. "Seems like a nice enough gal," one of Paul Christian's cousins said about her when she had lived in Honolulu for ten years. "Of course I haven't known her that long."

I had, curiously, only two photographs of Paul Christian, and neither suggested the apparent confidence and innocence with which his mother and his brother and even his wife met the camera. The first showed Paul Christian playing backgammon with John Huston in Cuernavaca in 1948. Paul Christian was barefoot and dark from the sun in this snapshot, which would have been taken at roughly the time arrangements were being made for his wife to leave Honolulu on the reconditioned *Lurline.* The second photograph was taken as Paul Christian left the Honolulu YMCA in handcuffs on March 25, 1975, some hours after he fired the shots that resulted in the immediate death of Wendell Omura and the eventual death of Janet Christian Ziegler. In this photograph Paul Christian was again barefoot, and had his cuffed hands raised above his head in a posture of theatrical submission, even crucifixion; a posture so arresting, so peculiarly suggestive, that the photograph was carried in newspapers in parts of the world where there could have been no interest in the Christians or in Wendell Omura or even in Harry Victor. In most parts of the United States there was of course an interest in Harry Victor. VICTOR FAMILY TOUCHED BY ISLAND TRAGEDY, the caption read in the New York *Times.*

You see the shards of the novel I am no longer writing, the island, the family, the situation. I lost patience with it. I lost nerve. Still: there is a certain hour between afternoon and evening when the sun strikes horizontally between the trees and that island and that situation are all I see. Some days at this time one aspect of the situation will seem to me to yield the point, other days another. I see Inez Christian Victor in the spring of 1975 walking on the narrow beach behind Janet's house, the last sun ahead of her, refracted in the spray off Black Point. I see Jack Lovett watching her, a man in his sixties in a custom-made seersucker suit, his tie loosened but his bearing correct, military, suggestive of disciplines practiced for the sake of discipline; a man who is now, as he watches Inez Victor steady herself on the rocks down where the water meets the sea wall, smoking one of the five cigarettes he allows himself daily. I see Inez turn and walk back toward him, the sun behind her now, the water washing the rough coral sand over her bare feet.

I see Jack Lovett waiting for her.

I have not told you much about Jack Lovett.

Most often these days I find that my notes are about Jack Lovett, about those custom-made seersucker suits he wore, about the wide range of his interests and acquaintances and of the people to whom he routinely spoke (embassy drivers, oil riggers, airline stewardesses, assistant professors of English literature traveling on Fulbright fellowships, tropical agronomists traveling under the auspices of the Rockefeller Foundation, desk clerks and ticket agents and salesmen of rice converters and coco dryers and Dutch pesticides and German pharmaceuticals) in Manila and in Jakarta and around the Malacca Strait.

About his view of information as an end in itself.

About his access to airplanes.

About the way he could put together an observation here and a conversation there and gauge when the time had come to lay hands on a 727 or a C-46.

About the way he waited for Inez.

I have been keeping notes for some time now about the way Jack Lovett waited for Inez Victor.

4

FIRST LOOKS are widely believed instructive. The first glimpse of someone across a room, the first view of the big house on the rise, the first meeting between the protagonists: these are considered obligatory scenes, and are meant to be remembered later, recalled to a conclusive point, recalled not only by novelists but by survivors of accidents and by witnesses to murders; recalled in fact by anyone at all forced to resort to the narrative method.

I wonder.

The first time I ever saw Jack Lovett was in a *Vogue* photographer's studio on West 40th Street, where he had come to see Inez. Under different auspices and to different ends Inez Victor and I were both working for *Vogue* that year, 1960, and although she was in the fashion department and I was upstairs in the afterthought cubicle that constituted the feature department we occasionally had reason (when a playwright was to be photographed as part of a fashion layout, say, or an actress was to actually model the merchandise) to do a sitting together. I recall coming late to the studio on this particular morning and finding Inez already there, sitting at a wooden table apparently oblivious to the reflector propped against her knee, to Chubby Checker on the stereo at eighty decibels, and to the model for the sitting, a fading beauty named Kiki Watt, who was having a comb-out and trying to tell Inez about some "Stanley" they both seemed to know.

"The doorbell rings at midnight, who else," Kiki screamed through the music. "Stanley."

Inez said nothing. The table at which she sat was covered with take-out bags from the delicatessen downstairs, one of which was leaking coffee, but Inez seemed not to notice. Her attention was entirely fixed on the man who sat across the table, a stranger, considerably older than we were and notably uncomfortable in the rather louche camaraderie of the studio. I had not met Harry Victor but I doubted the man was Inez's husband. I recall thinking he could be her father.

"Somebody strike the music," Kiki screamed. "Now. You

can hear me. So. I said I had this sitting at dawn, but you know Stanley, Stanley had to have a drink. Naturally."

"Naturally." Inez looked at me. "This is Jack Lovett. He just got off a plane."

Jack Lovett stood up, trying to acknowledge me without looking at Kiki, who had dropped her wrapper and was working pieces of cotton into her brassiere.

"'This place is a pigsty,' Stanley announces halfway through his drink." Kiki sat on the table between Inez and Jack Lovett and began rummaging through the take-out bags. "'The maid didn't come,' I say. 'I don't suppose you own a vacuum,' Stanley says, ho hum, sarcasm, so interesting. 'Actually no,' I say. 'I don't own a vacuum.' As a matter of fact I don't, I mean I did but Gus pawned it with my jewelry. 'Listen,' Stanley says. 'As soon as Daisy leaves for Maine I'll bring over our vacuum. For the summer,' he says. Believe it?"

"Absolutely," Inez said. She took a doughnut from one of the take-out bags and held it out to Jack Lovett. Jack Lovett shook his head.

"Stanley left, I thought about it, I wanted to kill myself, you know?"

"Absolutely." Inez took a bite from the doughnut, then dropped it back into the bag.

"Wanted to take every red I had in the apartment, you know why?"

"Because you didn't want to use Daisy's vacuum," Inez said, and then she looked at me. "He has two hours in New York and he came to see me."

She turned back to Jack Lovett and smiled.

I had known Inez Victor for perhaps a year but I had never before seen her smile that way.

"He can't stay," she said then. "Because he's running a little coup somewhere. I just bet."

There it is, the first look.

The instructiveness of the moment remains moot.

Actually I know a lot about Jack Lovett.

Some men (fewer women) are solitary, unattached to any particular place or institution, most comfortable not exactly alone but in the presence of strangers. They are comfortable for example on airplanes. They buckle in, establish certain ground rules with the cabin crew (to be woken or not woken, extra ice or none, a reading light that works and a move after Singapore to the bulkhead seat); stake out blankets, pillows, territory. They are solaced by the menus with the Dong Kingman water colors on the cover, by the soothing repetition of the meal (*Rôti au Vol, Legumes Garnis*) at arbitrary intervals during flights that run eleven, twelve, twenty-two hours. A flight of fewer than eight hours is a hop, a trip these men barely recognize. On the ground they seem easy only in hotel lobbies and transit lounges, in the Express Check-Ins and Clipper Clubs of the world, sealed environments in which they always remember the names of the attendants who make the drinks and arrange the connecting flights. Such men also recognize one another, and exchange desultory recollections of other travels, absent travelers.

"That joint venture in Dakar," one hears them say.

"Frank was in Dakar."

"I saw Frank in Hong Kong Friday, he'd come down out of China."

"Frank and I were in a meeting in Surabaya with this gentleman who didn't speak a word of English. He sat through this meeting nodding and smiling, you know, a regular buddha, and then he spoke the only English words I ever heard him speak. 'Six hundred million sterling,' he said."

"They all speak sterling."

"Frank takes it in stride, a real player, looks at his watch and stands up. 'You decide you want to talk a reasonable number,' Frank says to the buddha, in English you understand, 'you can reach me tonight at the Hilton.' No change of expression from the buddha. The buddha thinks Frank's going to sweat out this call in Jakarta. 'In Manila,' Frank says then. 'The Hilton in Manila.'"

They recall other Franks, other meetings, Hiltons around the world. They are reserved, wary, only professionally affable. Their responses seem pragmatic but are often peculiarly abstract, based on systems they alone understand. They view other people as wild cards, useful in the hand but dangerous in the deck, and they gravitate to occupations in which they can deal their own hand, play their own system, their own information. All information is seen as useful. Inaccurate information is in itself accurate information about the informant.

I said that Jack Lovett was one of those men for whom information was an end in itself.

He was also a man for whom the accidental did not figure.

Many people are intolerant of the accidental, but this was something more: Jack Lovett did not believe that accidents happen. In Jack Lovett's system all behavior was purposeful, and the purpose could be divined by whoever attracted the best information and read it most correctly. A Laotian village indicated on one map and omitted on another suggested not a reconnaissance oversight but a population annihilated, *x* number of men, women, and children lined up one morning between the maps and bulldozed into a common ditch. A shipment of laser mirrors from Long Beach to a firm in Hong Kong that did no laser work suggested not a wrong invoice but transshipment, reexport, the diversion of technology to unfriendly actors. All nations, to Jack Lovett, were "actors," specifically "state actors" ("non-state actors" were the real wild cards here, but in Jack Lovett's extensive experience the average non-state actor was less interested in laser mirrors than in M-16s, AK-47s, FN-FALs, the everyday implements of short-view power, and when the inductive leap to the long view was made it would probably be straight to weapons-grade uranium), and he viewed such actors abstractly, as friendly or unfriendly, committed or uncommitted; as assemblies of armaments on a large board. Asia was ten thousand tanks here, three hundred Phantoms there. The heart of Africa was an enrichment facility.

5

THE WOMAN to whom Jack Lovett was married from 1945 until 1952 described his occupation, whenever during the course of their marriage she applied for a charge account or filled out the forms for a new gynecologist or telephone or gas connection, as "army officer." In fact Carla Lovett made a convincing army wife, a druggist's daughter from San Jose who was comfortable shopping at the commissary and spending large parts of her day at the officers' club swimming pool, indifferent to her surroundings, passive in bad climates. Fort Hood and Georgetown and Manila and Schofield Barracks were the same to Carla Lovett, particularly after a drink or two.

The woman to whom Jack Lovett was married from 1962 until 1964 was a Honolulu divorcee named Betty Bennett, a woman who lived only a few doors from Janet and Dick Ziegler on Kahala beach and with whom Janet Ziegler occasionally played bridge and discussed shopping trips to the mainland. Betty Bennett had received the Kahala house as part of the settlement from her first husband, and continued to live in it during and after her marriage to Jack Lovett, an eighteen-month crossed connection that left little impression on either of them. When Betty Bennett filed for her divorce from Jack Lovett (I say "her" divorce reflexively, I suppose because Betty Bennett was a woman who applied the possessive pronoun reflexively, as in "my house," "my 450-SL," "my wedding lunch") she described his occupation as "aircraft executive." According to Jack Lovett's visa applications in 1975 he was a businessman. According to Jack Lovett's business cards in 1975 he was a consultant in international development.

According to Jack Lovett himself he was someone who had "various irons in the fire."

Someone who kept "the usual balls in the air."

Someone who did "a little business here and there."

Someone who did what he could.

Anyone who did any reporting at all during the middle and late sixties and early seventies was apt to have run into Jack Lovett. He was a good contact. He knew a lot of things. After I finished my first novel and left *Vogue* and started reporting I actually ran into him quite a bit, most often in Honolulu but occasionally in one or another transit lounge or American embassy, and perhaps because he identified me as a friend of Inez Victor's he seemed to exempt me from his instinctive distrust of reporters. I am not saying that he ever told me anything he did not want me to know. I am saying only that we talked, and once in a while we even talked about Inez Victor. I recall one such conversation in 1971 in Honolulu and another in 1973, on a Garuda 727 that had jammed its landing gear and was in the process of dumping its fuel over the South China Sea. Jack Lovett told me for example that he considered Inez "one of the most noble" women he had ever met. I remember this specifically because the word "noble" seemed from another era, and as such surprising, and mildly amusing.

He never told me exactly what it was he did, nor would I have asked. Exactly what Jack Lovett did was tacitly understood by most people who knew him, but not discussed. Had he been listed in *Who's Who*, which he was not, even the most casual reader of his entry could have pieced together a certain pattern, discerned the traces of what intelligence people call "interest." Such an entry would have revealed odd overlapping dates, unusual posts at unusual times. There would have been the assignment to Vientiane, the missions to Haiti, Quebec, Rawalpindi. There would have been the associations with companies providing air courier service, air cargo service, aircraft parts; companies with telephone numbers that began "800" and addresses that were post-office boxes in Miami, Honolulu, Palo Alto. There would have been blank spots. The military career would have seemed erratic, off track.

Finally, such an entry would have been starred, indicating that the subject had supplied no information, for Jack Lovett supplied information only when he saw the chance, however remote, of getting information in return. When he registered at a hotel he gave as his address one or another of those post-office boxes in Miami, Honolulu, Palo Alto. The apartment he kept in Honolulu, a one-bedroom rental near Ala Moana in a building inhabited mostly by call girls, was leased in the name "Mid-Pacific Development." It was possible to see this tendency to obscure even the most inconsequential information as a professional reflex, but it was also possible to see it as something more basic, a temperamental secretiveness, a reticence that had not so much derived from Jack Lovett's occupation as led him to it. I recall a story I heard in 1973 or 1974 from a UPI photographer who had run into Jack Lovett in a Hong Kong restaurant, an upstairs place in the Wanchai district where the customers kept their bottles in a cupboard above the cash register. Jack Lovett's bottle was on his table, a quart of Johnnie Walker Black, but the name taped on the label, in his own handwriting, was "J. LOCKHART." "You don't want your name on too many bottles around town," Jack Lovett reportedly said when the photographer mentioned the tape on the label. This was a man who for more than twenty years had maintained a grave attraction to a woman whose every move was photographed.

In this context I always see Inez Victor as she looked on a piece of WNBC film showing a party on the St. Regis Roof given by the governor of New York; some kind of afternoon party, a wedding or a christening or an anniversary, nominally private but heavily covered by the press. On this piece of film, which was made and first shown on March 18, 1975, one week exactly before Paul Christian fired the shots that set this series of events in motion, Inez Victor can be seen dancing with Harry Victor. She is wearing a navy-blue silk dress and a shiny dark straw hat with red cherries. "Marvelous," she is heard to say repeatedly on the clip.

"Marvelous day."

"You look marvelous."

"Marvelous to be here."

"Clear space for the senator," a young man in a dark suit and a rep tie keeps saying. There are several such young men in the background, all carrying clipboards. This one seems only marginally aware of Inez Victor, and his clipboard collides a number of times with her quilted shoulder bag. "Senator Victor is here as the governor's guest, give him some room *please*."

"—Taking a more active role," a young woman with a microphone repeats.

"—Senator here as the governor's guest, *please* no interviews, that's all, that's it, hold it."

The band segues into "Isn't It Romantic."

"Hold two elevators," another of the young men says.

"I'm just a private citizen," Harry Victor says.

"Marvelous," Inez Victor says.

I first saw this clip not when it was first shown but some months later, at the time Jack Lovett was in the news, when, for the two or three days it took the story of their connection to develop and play out, Inez Victor could be seen dancing on the St. Regis Roof perhaps half a dozen times between five P.M. and midnight.

6

LET ME establish Inez Victor.

Born, as you know, Inez Christian in the Territory of Hawaii on the first day of January, 1935.

Known locally as Dwight Christian's niece.

Cissy Christian's granddaughter.

Paul Christian's daughter, of course, but Paul Christian was usually in Cuernavaca or Tangier or sailing a 12.9-meter Trintella-class ketch through the Marquesas and did not get mentioned as often as his mother and his brother. Carol Christian's daughter as well, but Carol Christian had materialized from the mainland and vanished back to the mainland, a kind of famous story in that part of the world, a novel in her own right, but not the one I have in mind.

Harry Victor's wife.

Oh shit, Inez, Jack Lovett said.

Harry Victor's wife.

He said it on the late March evening in 1975 when he and Inez sat in an empty off-limits bar across the bridge from Schofield Barracks and watched the evacuation on television of one or another capital in Southeast Asia. Conflicting reports, the anchorman said. Rapidly deteriorating situation. Scenes of panic and confusion. Down the tubes, the bartender said. Bye-bye Da Nang. On the screen above the bar the helicopter lifted again and again off the roof of the American mission and Jack Lovett watched without speaking and after a while he asked the bartender to turn off the sound and plug in the jukebox. No dancing, the bartender said. I'm already off fucking limits. You're not off limits from dancing, Jack Lovett said. You're off from fencing Sansui amps to an undercover. The bartender turned down the sound and plugged in the jukebox. Jack Lovett said nothing to Inez, only looked at her for a long time and then stood up and took her hand.

The Mamas and the Papas sang "Dream a Little Dream of Me."

The helicopter lifted again off the roof of the American mission.

In this bar across the bridge from Schofield Barracks Inez did not say "marvelous" as she danced. She did not say "marvelous day" as she danced. She did not say "you look marvelous," or "marvelous to be here." She did not say anything at all as she danced, did not even dance as you or I or the agency that regulated dancing in bars might have defined dancing. She only stood with her back against the jukebox and her arms around Jack Lovett. Her hair was loose and tangled from the drive out to Schofield and the graying streak at her left temple, the streak she usually brushed under, was exposed. Her eyes were closed against the flicker from the television screen.

"Fucking Arvin finally shooting each other," the bartender said.

"Oh shit, Inez," Jack Lovett said. "Harry Victor's wife."

7

BY THE spring of 1975 Inez Victor had in fact been Harry Victor's wife for twenty years.

Through Harry Victor's two years with the Justice Department, through the appearance in *The New York Times Magazine* of "Justice for Whom?—A Young Lawyer Wants Out," by Harry Victor and R.W. Dillon.

Through the Neighborhood Legal Coalition that Harry Victor and Billy Dillon organized out of the storefront in East Harlem. Through the publication of *The View from the Street: Root Causes, Radical Solutions and a Modest Proposal*, by Harry Victor, Based on Studies Conducted by Harry Victor with R.W. Dillon.

Through the marches in Mississippi and in the San Joaquin Valley, through Harry Victor's successful campaigns for Congress in 1964 and 1966 and 1968, through the sit-ins at Harvard and at the Pentagon and at Dow Chemical plants in Michigan and Pennsylvania and West Virginia.

Through Harry Victor's appointment in 1969 to fill out the last three years of a Senate term left vacant by the death of the incumbent.

Through Connie Willis and through Frances Landau ("Inez, I'm asking you nice, behave, girls like that come with the life," Billy Dillon said to Inez about Connie Willis and Frances Landau), through the major fundraising in California ("Inez, I'm asking you nice, put on your tap shoes, it's big green on the barrelhead," Billy Dillon said to Inez about California), through the speaking tours and the ad hoc committees and the fact-finding missions to Jakarta and Santiago and Managua and Phnom Penh; through the failed bid for a presidential nomination in 1972 and through the mistimed angling for a good embassy (this was one occasion when Jakarta and Santiago and Managua and Phnom Penh did not spring to Harry Victor's lips) that occurred in the wreckage of that campaign.

Through the mill.

Through the wars.

Through the final run to daylight: through the maneuvering

of all the above elements into a safe place on the field, into a score, into that amorphous but inspired convergence of rhetoric and celebrity known as the Alliance for Democratic Institutions.

Inez Victor had been there.

Because Inez Victor had been there many people believed that they knew her: not "most" people, since the demographics of Harry Victor's phantom constituency were based on comfort and its concomitant uneasiness, but most people of a type, most people who read certain newspapers and bought certain magazines, most people who knew what kind of girls came with the life, most people who knew where there was big green on the barrelhead, most people who were apt to have noticed Inez buying printed sheets on sale in Bloomingdale's basement or picking up stemmed strawberries at Gristede's or waiting for one of her and Harry Victor's twin children, the girl Jessie or the boy Adlai, in front of the Dalton School.

These were people who all knew exactly what Inez Victor did with the stemmed strawberries she picked up at Gristede's (passed them in a silver bowl at her famous New Year's Eve parties on Central Park West, according to *Vogue*); what Inez Victor did with the printed sheets she bought on sale in Bloomingdale's basement (cut them into round tablecloths for her famous Fourth of July parties in Amagansett, according to *W*); and what Inez Victor had paid for the Ungaro khaki shirtwaists she wore during the 1968 convention, the 1968 Chicago convention during which Harry Victor was photographed for *Life* getting tear-gassed in Grant Park.

These were people who all knew someone who knew someone who knew that on the night in 1972 when Harry Victor conceded the California primary before the polls closed Inez Victor flew back to New York on the press plane and sang "It's All Over Now, Baby Blue" with an ABC cameraman and the photographer from *Rolling Stone*.

These people had all seen Inez, via telephoto lens, drying Jessie's fine blond hair by the swimming pool at the house in Amagansett. These people had all seen Inez, in the *Daily News*, leaving Lenox Hill Hospital with Adlai on the occasion of his first automobile accident. These people had all seen photograph after photograph of the studied clutter in the library of the apartment on Central Park West, the Canton jars packed with marking pencils, the stacks of *Le Monde* and *Foreign Affairs* and *The Harvard Business Review*, the legal pads, the several telephones, the framed snapshots of Harry Victor eating barbecue with Eleanor Roosevelt and of Harry Victor crossing a police line with Coretta King and of Harry Victor playing on the beach at Amagansett with Jessie and with Adlai and with Frances Landau's Russian wolfhound.

These people had taken their toll.

By which I mean to suggest that Inez Victor had come to view most occasions as photo opportunities.

By which I mean to suggest that Inez Victor had developed certain mannerisms peculiar to people in the public eye: a way of fixing her gaze in the middle distance, a habit of smoothing her face in repose by pressing up on her temples with her middle fingers; a noticeably frequent blink, as if the photographers' strobes had triggered a continuing flash on her retina.

By which I mean to suggest that Inez Victor had lost certain details.

I recall being present one morning in a suite in the Hotel Doral in Miami, amid the debris of Harry Victor's 1972 campaign for the nomination, when a feature writer from the Associated Press asked Inez what she believed to be the "major cost" of public life.

"Memory, mainly," Inez said.

"Memory," the woman from the Associated Press repeated.

"Memory, yes. Is what I would call the major cost. Definitely." The suite in the Doral that morning was a set being struck. On a sofa that two workmen were pushing back against a wall Billy Dillon was trying to talk on the telephone. In the foyer a sound man from one of the networks was packing up equipment left the night before. "I believe I can speak for Inez when I say that we're looking forward to a period of being just plain Mr. and Mrs. Victor," Harry had said the night before on all three networks. Inez stood up now and began looking for a clean ashtray on a room-service table covered with half-filled glasses. "Something like shock treatment," she added.

"You mean you've had shock treatment."

"No. I mean you lose track. *As if* you'd had shock treatment."

"I see. 'Lose track' of what exactly?"

"Of what happened."

"I see."

"Of what you said. And didn't say."

"I see. Yes. During the campaign."

"Well, no. During your—" Inez looked at me for help. I pretended to be absorbed in the Miami *Herald.* Inez emptied a dirty ashtray into the lid of a film can and sat down again. "During your whole life."

"You mentioned shock treatment. You haven't personally—"

"I said no. Didn't I say no? I said 'as if.' I said 'something like.' I meant you drop fuel. You jettison cargo. Eject the crew. You *lose track.*"

There was a silence. Billy Dillon cradled the telephone against his shoulder and mimed a backhand volley. "It's a game, Inez, it's tennis," Billy Dillon always said to Inez about interviews. It was a routine between them. I had seen him do it that morning, when Inez said that since I had come especially to see her she did not want to do the AP interview. "Sure you do," Billy Dillon had said. "It's only going to last *x* minutes. Finite time. For those *x* minutes you're here to play. You're going to place the ball"—here Billy Dillon had paused, and executed a shadow serve—"inside the lines. The major cost of public life is privacy, Inez, that's an easy shot. The hardest part about Washington life is finding a sitter for the Gridiron Dinner. The fun part about Washington life is taking friends from home to the Senate cafeteria for navy-bean soup. You've tried the recipe at home but it never tastes the same. Yes, you do collect recipes. Yes, you do worry about the rising cost of feeding a family. Ninety-nine per cent of the people you know in Washington are basically concerned with the rising cost of feeding a family. Schools. Mortgages. Programs. You've always viewed victory as a mandate not for a man but for his programs. Now: you view defeat with mixed emotions. Why: because you've learned to treasure the private moments."

"*Private moments,*" Billy Dillon mouthed silently in the suite at the Hotel Doral.

Inez looked deliberately away from Billy Dillon.

"Here's an example." She lit a match, watched it burn, and

blew it out. "You looked up the clips on me before you came here."

"I did a little homework, yes." The woman's finger hovered over the stop button on her tape recorder. Now it was she who looked to me for help. I looked out the window. "Naturally. That's my business. We all do."

"That's my point."

"I'm afraid I don't quite—"

"Things that might or might not be true get repeated in the clips until you can't tell the difference."

"But that's why I'm here. I'm not writing a piece from the clips. I'm writing a piece based on what you tell me."

"You might as well write it from the clips," Inez said. Her voice was reasonable. "Because I've lost track. Which is what I said in the first place."

INEZ VICTOR CLAIMS SHE IS OFTEN MISQUOTED, is the way that went out on the Associated Press wire. "Somebody up there likes you, it doesn't say INEZ VICTOR DENIES SHOCK TREATMENT," Billy Dillon said when he read it.

8

I HAVE never been sure what Inez thought about how her days were passed during those years she spent in Washington and New York. The idea of "expressing" herself seems not to have occurred to her. She held the occasional job but pursued no particular work. Even the details of running a household did not engage her unduly. Her houses were professionally kept and, for all the framed snapshots and studied clutter, entirely impersonal, expressive not of some individual style but only of the conventions then current among the people she saw. Nothing of the remote world in which she had grown up intruded on the world in which she later found herself: the Christians, like many island families, had surrounded themselves with the mementos of their accomplishments, with water colors and painted tea cups and evidence of languages mastered and instruments played, framed recital programs and letters of commendation and the souvenirs of wedding trips and horse shows and trips to China, and it was the absence of any such jetsam that was eccentric in Inez's houses, as if she had buckled her seat belt and the island had dematerialized beneath her.

Of course there were rumors about her. She liked painters, and usually had a table or two of them at her big parties, and a predictable number of people said that she had had an affair with this one or that one or all of them. According to Inez she never had. I know for a fact that she never had what was called a "problem about drinking," another rumor, but the story that she did persisted, partly because Harry Victor did so little to discourage it. At a crowded restaurant in the East Fifties for example Harry Victor was heard asking Inez if she intended to drink her dinner. In that piece of WNBC film shot on the St. Regis Roof, another example, Harry Victor is seen taking a glass of champagne from Inez's hand and passing it out of camera range.

Inez remained indifferent. She seemed to dwell as little on the rest of her life as she did on her jobs, which she tried and abandoned like seasonal clothes. When Harry Victor was in the

Justice Department Inez worked, until the twins were born, in a docent capacity at the National Gallery. When Harry Victor left the Justice Department and came up to New York Inez turned up at *Vogue*, and was given one of those jobs that fashion magazines then kept for well-connected young women in unsettled circumstances, women who needed a place to pass the time between houses or marriages or lunches. Later she did a year at Parke-Bernet. She served on the usual boards, benefit committees, commissions for the preservation of wilderness and the enhancement of opportunity; when it became clear that Harry Victor would be making the run for the nomination and that Inez would need what Billy Dillon called a special interest, she insisted, unexpectedly and with considerable vehemence, that she wanted to work with refugees, but it was decided that refugees were an often controversial and therefore inappropriate special interest.

Instead, because Inez was conventionally interested in and by that time moderately knowledgeable about painting, she was named a consultant for the collection of paintings that hung in American embassies and residences around the world. In theory the wives of new ambassadors would bring Inez the measurements, furnished by the State Department, of the walls they needed to fill, and Inez would offer advice on which paintings best suited not only the wall space but the mood of the post. "Well, for example, I wouldn't necessarily think of sending a Sargent to Zaire," she explained to an interviewer, but she was hard put to say why. In any case only two new ambassadors were named during Inez's tenure as consultant, which made this special interest less than entirely absorbing. As for wanting to work with refugees, she finally did, in Kuala Lumpur, and it occurred to me when I saw her there that Inez Victor had herself been a kind of refugee. She had the protective instincts of a successful refugee. She never looked back.

9

OR AT least almost never.

I know of one occasion on which Inez Victor did in fact try to look back.

A try, an actual effort.

This effort was, for Inez, uncharacteristically systematic, and took place on the redwood deck of the borrowed house in which Harry and Inez Victor stayed the spring he lectured at Berkeley, between the 1972 campaign and the final funding of the Alliance for Democratic Institutions. It had begun with a quarrel after a faculty dinner in Harry's honor. "I've always tried to talk up to the American people," Harry had said when a physicist at the table questioned his approach to one or another energy program, and it had seemed to Inez that a dispirited pall fell over what had been, given the circumstances, a lively and pleasant evening.

"Not down," Harry had added. "You talk down to the American people at your peril."

The physicist had pressed his point, which was technical, and abstruse.

"Either Jefferson was right or he wasn't," Harry had said. "I happen to believe he was."

In fact Inez had heard Harry say this a number of times before, usually when he had no facts at hand, and she might never have remarked on it had Harry not mentioned the physicist on the drive home.

"Hadn't done his homework," Harry had said. "Those guys get their Nobels and start coasting."

Inez, who was driving, said nothing.

"Unless there's something behind us I don't know about," Harry said as she turned into San Luis Road, "you might try lightening up the foot on the gas pedal."

"Unless you're running for something I don't know about," Inez heard herself say, "you might try lightening up the rhetoric at the dinner table."

There had been a silence.

"That wasn't necessary," Harry said finally, his voice at first stiff and hurt, and then, marshalling for second strike: "I don't really care if you take out your quite palpable unhappiness on me, but I'm glad the children are in New York."

"Away from my quite palpable unhappiness I suppose you mean."

"On the money."

They had gone to bed in silence, and, the next morning, after Harry left for the campus without speaking, Inez took her coffee and a package of cigarettes out into the sun on the redwood deck and sat down to consider the phrase "quite palpable unhappiness." It did not seem to her that she was palpably unhappy, but neither did it seem that she was palpably happy. "Happiness" and "unhappiness" did not even seem to be cards in the hand she normally played, and there on the deck in the thin morning sunlight she resolved to reconstruct the details of occasions on which she recalled being happy. As she considered such occasions she was struck by their insignificance, their absence of application to the main events of her life. In retrospect she seemed to have been most happy in borrowed houses, and at lunch.

She recalled being extremely happy eating lunch by herself in a hotel room in Chicago, once when snow was drifting on the window ledges. There was a lunch in Paris that she remembered in detail: a late lunch with Harry and the twins at Pré Catelan in the rain. She remembered rain streaming down the big windows, rain blowing in the trees, the branches brushing the glass and the warm light inside. She remembered Jessie crowing with delight and pointing imperiously at a poodle seated on a gilt chair across the room. She remembered Harry unbuttoning Adlai's wet sweater, kissing Jessie's wet hair, pouring them each a half glass of white wine.

There was an entire day in Hong Kong that she managed to reconstruct, a day she had spent alone with Jessie in a borrowed house overlooking Repulse Bay. She and Harry had dropped Adlai in Honolulu with Janet and Dick Ziegler and they had bundled Jessie onto a plane to Hong Kong and when they landed at dawn they learned that Harry was expected in Saigon for a situation briefing. Harry had flown immediately down to Saigon and Inez had waited with Jessie in this house that belonged to the chief of the *Time* bureau in Hong Kong. The potted begonias outside that house had made Inez happy and the parched lawn made her happy and the particular cast of the sun on the sea made her happy and it even made her happy that the *Time* bureau chief had mentioned, as he gave her the keys at the airport, that baby cobras had recently been seen in the garden. This introduction of baby cobras into the day had lent Inez a sense of transcendent usefulness, a reason to carry Jessie wherever Jessie wanted to go. She had carried Jessie from the porch to the swing in the garden. She had carried Jessie from the swing in the garden to the bench from which they could watch the sun on the sea. She had carried Jessie even from the house to the government car that returned at sundown to take them to the hotel where Harry was due at midnight.

There in the sun on the redwood deck on San Luis Road Inez began to think of Berkeley as another place in which she might later remember being extremely happy, another borrowed house, and she resolved to keep this in mind, but by June of that year, back in New York, she was already losing the details. That was the June during which Adlai had the accident (the second accident, the bad one, the accident in which the fifteen-year-old from Denver lost her left eye and the function of one kidney), and it was also the June, 1973, during which Inez found Jessie on the floor of her bedroom with the disposable needle and the glassine envelope in her Snoopy wastebasket.

"Let me die and get it over with," Jessie said. "Let me be in the ground and go to sleep."

The doctor came in a sweat suit.

"I got a D in history," Jessie said. "Nobody sits with me at lunch. Don't tell Daddy."

"I'm right here," Harry said.

"Daddy's right here," Inez said.

"Don't tell Daddy," Jessie said.

"It might be useful to talk about therapy," the doctor said.

"It might also be useful to assign some narcs to the Dalton School," Harry said. "No. Strike that. Don't quote me."

"This is a stressful time," the doctor said.

The first therapist the doctor recommended was a young woman attached to a clinic on East 61st Street that specialized in the treatment of what the therapist called adolescent substance abuse. "It might be useful to talk about you," the therapist said. "Your own life, how you perceive it."

Inez remembered that the therapist was wearing a silver ankh.

She remembered that she could see Jessie through a glass partition, chewing on a strand of her long blond hair, bent over the Minnesota Multiphasic Personality Inventory.

"My life isn't really the problem at hand," she remembered saying. "Is it?"

The therapist smiled.

Inez lit a cigarette.

It occurred to her that if she just walked into the next room and took Jessie by the hand and got her on a plane somewhere, still wearing her Dalton School sweat shirt, the whole thing might blow over. They could go meet Adlai in Colorado Springs. Adlai had gone back to Colorado Springs the day before, for summer session at the school where he was trying to accumulate enough units to get into a college accredited for draft deferment. They could go meet Harry in Ann Arbor. Harry had left for Ann Arbor that morning, to deliver his lecture on the uses and misuses of civil disobedience. "I can't get through to her," Harry had said before he left for Ann Arbor. "Adlai may be a fuck-up, but I can talk to Adlai. I talk to her, I'm talking to a UFO."

"Adlai," Inez had said, "happens to believe that he can satisfy his American History requirement with a three-unit course called History of American Film."

"Very good, Inez. Broad, but good."

"Broad, but true. In addition to which. Moreover. I asked Adlai to make a point of going to the hospital to see Cynthia. Here's what he said."

"Cynthia who?" Harry said.

"Cynthia who he almost killed in the accident. 'She's definitely on the agenda.' Is what he said."

"At least he said something. All you'd get from her is the stare."

"You always say *her*. Her name is Jessie."

"*I know her goddamn name.*"

Strike Ann Arbor.

Harry would be sitting around in his shirtsleeves expressing admiration ("Admiration, Christ no, what I feel when I see you guys is a kind of *awe*") for the most socially responsible generation ever to hit American campuses.

Strike Colorado Springs.

Adlai already had his agenda.

Jessie looked up from the Minnesota Multiphasic Personality Inventory and smiled fleetingly at the glass partition.

"The 'problem at hand,' as you put it, is substance habituation." The therapist opened a drawer and extracted an ashtray and slid it across the desk toward Inez. She was still smiling. "I notice you smoke."

"I do, yes." Inez crushed out the cigarette and stood up. Jessie's complexion was clear and her hair was like honey and there was no way of telling that beneath the sleeves of the Dalton School sweatshirt there were needle tracks visible on her smooth tanned arms. "I also drink coffee."

The therapist's expression did not change.

Let me die and get it over with.

Let me be in the ground and go to sleep.

Don't tell Daddy.

Inez picked up her jacket.

On the other side of the glass partition Jessie took a pocket mirror from her shoulder bag and began lining her eyes with the IBM testing pencil.

"What I don't do is shoot heroin," Inez said.

The second therapist believed that the answer lay in a closer examination of the sibling gestalt. The third employed a technique incorporating elements of aversion therapy. At the clinic in Seattle to which Jessie was finally sent in the fall of 1974, a private facility specializing in the treatment of what the fourth therapist called adolescent chemical dependency, the staff referred to the patients as clients, maintained them on methadone, and obtained for them part-time jobs "suited to the character structure and particular skills of the individual client." Jessie's job was as a waitress in a place on Puget Sound called King Crab's Castle. "Pretty cinchy," Jessie said on the telephone, "if you can keep the pickled beet slice from running into the crab louis."

The bright effort in Jessie's voice had constricted Inez's throat.

"It's all experience," Inez said finally, and Jessie giggled.

"Really," Jessie said, emphasizing the word to suggest agreement. She was not yet eighteen.

10

OTHER COSTS.

Inez had stopped staying alone in the apartment on Central Park West after the superintendent told a reporter from *Newsday* that he had let himself in to drain a radiator and Mrs. Victor had asked him to fix her a double vodka. She took fingernail scissors and scratched the label off empty prescription bottles before she threw them in the trash. She stopped patronizing a bookstore on Madison Avenue after she noticed the names, addresses, and delivery instructions for all the customers, including herself ("doorman—Lloyd, maid lvs at 4") in an open account book by the cash register. She would not allow letters that came unsolicited from strangers to be opened inside the apartment, or packages that came from anyone. She had spoken to Billy Dillon about the possibility of suing *People* for including Adlai's accidents in an article on the problems of celebrity children, and also of enjoining *Who's Who* to delete mention of herself and Jessie and Adlai from Harry Victor's entry. "I don't quite see the significance, Inez," Billy Dillon had said. "Since I see your name in the paper two, three times a week minimum."

"The significance is," Inez said, "that some stranger might be sitting in a library somewhere reading *Who's Who*."

"Consider this stranger your bread and butter, an interested citizen," Billy Dillon said, but Inez never could. Strangers remembered. Strangers suffered disappointments, and became confused. A stranger might suffer a disappointment too deep to be lanced by a talk with *Newsday*, and become confused. Life outside camera range, life as it was lived by (Inez imagined then) her father and her Uncle Dwight and her sister Janet, had become for Inez only a remote idea, something she knew about but did not entirely comprehend. She did not for example comprehend how her father could give her telephone number to strangers he met on airplanes, and then call to remonstrate with her when he heard she had been short on the telephone. "I think you might have spared ten minutes," Paul Christian had said on one such call. "This young man you hung up on happens to have a quite interesting grassy-knoll slant on Sal Mineo's murder, he very much wanted Harry to hear it." She did not for example comprehend what moved Dwight to send her a clipping of every story in the Honolulu *Advertiser* in which her or Harry's name appeared. These clippings came in bundles, with Dwight's card attached. "Nice going," he sometimes pencilled on the card. Nor did she comprehend how Janet could have agreed, during the 1972 campaign, to be interviewed on *CBS Reports* about her and Inez's childhood. This particular *CBS Reports* had been devoted to capsule biographies of the candidates' wives and Inez had watched it with Harry and Billy Dillon in the library of the apartment on Central Park West. There had been a clip of Harry talking about Inez's very special loyalty and there had been a clip of Billy Dillon talking about Inez's very special feeling for the arts and there had been a clip of the headmaster at the Dalton School talking about the very special interest Inez took in education, but Janet's appearance on the program was a surprise.

"I wouldn't say 'privileged,' no," Janet had said on camera. She had seemed to be sitting barefoot on a catamaran in front of her beach house. "No. Off the mark. Not 'privileged.' I'd just call it a marvelous simple way of life that you might describe as gone with the wind."

"I hope nobody twigs she's talking about World War Two," Billy Dillon said.

"Of course everybody had their marvelous Chinese amah then," Janet was saying on camera. Her voice was high and breathy and nervous. The camera angle had changed to show Koko Head. Inez picked up a legal pad and began writing. "And then Nezzie and I had—oh, I suppose a sort of governess, a French governess, she was from Neuilly, needless to say Mademoiselle spoke flawless French, I remember Nezzie used to drive her wild by speaking pidgin."

"'Mademoiselle,'" Billy Dillon said.

Inez did not look up from the legal pad.

"'Mademoiselle,'" Billy Dillon repeated, "and 'Nezzie.'"

"I was never called 'Nezzie.'"

"You are now," Billy Dillon said.

"They pan left," Harry Victor said, "they could pick up Janet's private-property-no-trespassing-no-beach-access sign." He reached under the table to pick up the telephone. "Also her Mercedes. This should be Mort."

"Ask Mort how he thinks the governess from Neuilly tests out," Billy Dillon said. "Possibly Janet could make Mademoiselle available to do some coffees in West Virginia."

Inez said nothing.

She had never been called Nezzie.

She had never spoken pidgin.

The governess from Neuilly had not been a governess at all but the French wife of a transport pilot at Hickam who rented the studio over Cissy Christian's garage for a period of six months between the Leyte Gulf and the end of the war.

Janet was telling *CBS Reports* how she and Inez had been taught to store table linens between sheets of blue tissue paper.

Harry was on his evening conference call with Mort Goldman at MIT and Perry Young at Harvard and the petrochemical people at Stanford.

No Nezzie.

No pidgin.

No governess from Neuilly.

"That tip about the blue tissue paper goes straight to the hearts and minds," Billy Dillon said.

"Mort still sees solar as negative policy, Billy, maybe you better pick up," Harry Victor said.

"Tell Mort we just kiss it," Billy Dillon said. "Broad strokes only. Selected venues." He watched as Inez tore the top sheet from the legal pad on which she had been writing. "Strictly for the blue-tissue-paper crowd."

1) Shining Star, Inez had written on the piece of paper.

2) Twinkling Star

3) Morning Star

4) Evening Star

5) Southern Star

6) North Star

7) Celestial Star

8) Meridian Star

9) Day Star

10) ? ? ?

"Hey," Billy Dillon said. "Inez. If you're drafting a cable to Janet, tell her we're retiring her number."

"Mort's raising a subtle point here, Billy," Harry Victor said. "Pick up a phone."

Inez crumpled the piece of paper and threw it into the fire. On the day Carol Christian left for good on the *Lurline* Janet had not stopped crying until she was taken from the Pacific Club to the pediatrician's office and sedated, but Inez never did cry. *Aloha oe.* I am talking here about a woman who believed that grace would descend on those she loved and peace upon her household on the day she remembered the names of all ten Star Ferry boats that crossed between Hong Kong and Kowloon. She could never get the tenth. The tenth should have been *Night Star*, but was not. During the 1972 campaign and even later I thought of Inez Victor's capacity for passive detachment as an affectation born of boredom, the frivolous habit of an essentially idle mind. After the events which occurred in the spring and summer of 1975 I thought of it differently. I thought of it as the essential mechanism for living a life in which the major cost was memory. Drop fuel. Jettison cargo. Eject crew.

11

In the spring of 1975, during the closing days of what Jack Lovett called "the assistance effort" in Vietnam, I happened to be teaching at Berkeley, lecturing on the same short-term basis on which Harry Victor had lectured there between the 1972 campaign and the final funding of the Alliance for Democratic Institutions; living alone in a room at the Faculty Club and meeting a dozen or so students in the English Department to discuss the idea of democracy in the work of certain post-industrial writers. I spent my classroom time pointing out similarities in style, and presumably in ideas of democracy (the hypothesis being that the way a writer constructed a sentence reflected the way that writer thought), between George Orwell and Ernest Hemingway, Henry Adams and Norman Mailer. "The hills opposite us were grey and wrinkled like the skins of elephants" and "this war was a racket like all other wars" were both George Orwell, but were also an echo of Ernest Hemingway. "Probably no child, born in the year, held better cards than he" and "he began to feel the forty-foot dynamo as a moral force, much as the early Christians felt the Cross" were both Henry Adams, but struck a note that would reverberate in Norman Mailer.

What did this tell us, I asked my class.

Consider the role of the writer in a post-industrial society.

Consider the political implications of both the reliance on and the distrust of abstract words, consider the social organization implicit in the use of the autobiographical third person.

Consider, too, Didion's own involvement in the setting: an atmosphere results. How? It so happened that I had been an undergraduate at Berkeley, which meant that twenty years before in the same room or one like it (high transoms and golden oak moldings and cigarette scars on the floor, sixty years of undergraduate yearnings not excluding my own) I had considered the same questions or ones like them. In 1955 on this campus I had first noticed the quickening of time. In 1975 time was no longer just quickening but collapsing, falling in on itself, the way a disintegrating star contracts into a black hole, and at the scene of all I had left unlearned I could summon up only fragments of poems, misremembered. Apologies to A.E. Housman, T.S. Eliot, Delmore Schwartz:

Of my three-score years and ten
These twenty would not come again.
Black wing, brown wing, hover over
Twenty years and the spring is over.
This was the school in which we learned
That time was the fire in which we burned.

Sentimental sojourn.

Less time left for those visions and revisions.

In this rather febrile mood I seemed able to concentrate only on reading newspapers, specifically on reading the dispatches from Southeast Asia, finding in those falling capitals a graphic instance of the black hole effect. I said "falling." Many of the students to whom I spoke said "being liberated." "The establishment press has been giving us some joyous news," one said, and when next we spoke I modified "falling" to "closing down."

Every morning I walked from the Faculty Club to a newsstand off Telegraph Avenue to get the San Francisco *Chronicle*, the Los Angeles *Times*, and the New York *Times*. Every afternoon I got the same dispatches, under new headlines and with updated leads, in the San Francisco *Examiner*, the Oakland *Tribune*, and the Berkeley *Gazette*. Tank battalions vanished between editions. Three hundred fixed-wing aircraft disappeared in the new lead on a story about the president playing golf at the El Dorado Country Club in Palm Desert, California.

I would skim the stories on policy and fix instead on details: the cost of a visa to leave Cambodia in the weeks before Phnom Penh closed was five hundred dollars American. The colors of the landing lights for the helicopters on the roof of the American embassy in Saigon were red, white, and blue. The code names for the American evacuations of Cambodia and Vietnam respectively were EAGLE PULL and FREQUENT WIND. The amount of cash burned in the courtyard of the DAO in Saigon before the last helicopter left was three-and-a-half million dollars American and eighty-five million piastres. The code name for this operation was MONEY BURN. The number of Vietnamese soldiers who managed to get aboard the last American 727 to leave Da Nang was three hundred and thirty. The number of Vietnamese soldiers to drop from the wheel wells of the 727 was one. The 727 was operated by World Airways. The name of the pilot was Ken Healy.

I read such reports over and over again, pinned in the repetitions and dislocations of the breaking story as if in the beam of a runaway train, but I read only those stories that seemed to touch, however peripherally, on Southeast Asia. All other news receded, went unmarked and unread, and, if the first afternoon story about Paul Christian killing Wendell Omura had not been headlined CONGRESSIONAL FOE OF VIET CONFLICT SHOT IN HONOLULU, I might never have read it at all. Janet Ziegler was not mentioned that first afternoon but she was all over the morning editions and so, photographs in the *Chronicle* and a separate sidebar in the New York *Times*, VICTOR FAMILY TOUCHED BY ISLAND TRAGEDY, were Inez and Harry Victor.

That was March 26, 1975.

A Wednesday morning.

I tried to call Inez Victor in New York but Inez was already gone.

12

SEE IT this way.

See the sun rise that Wednesday morning in 1975 the way Jack Lovett saw it.

From the operations room at the Honolulu airport.

The warm rain down on the runways.

The smell of jet fuel.

The military charters, Jack Lovett's excuse for being in the operations room at the airport, C-130s, DC-8s, already coming in from Saigon all night long now, clustered around the service hangars.

The first light breaking on the sea, throwing into relief two islands (first one and then, exactly ninety seconds later, the second, two discrete land masses visible on the southeastern horizon only during those two or three minutes each day when the sun rises behind them.

The regularly scheduled Pan American 747 from Kennedy via LAX banking over the milky shallows and touching down, on time, the big wheels spraying up water from the tarmac, the slight skidding, the shudder as the engines cut down.

Five-thirty-seven A.M.

The ground crew in thin yellow slickers.

The steps wheeled into place.

The passenger service representative waiting at the bottom of the steps, carrying an umbrella, a passenger manifest in a protective vinyl envelope and, over his left arm, one plumeria lei.

The woman for whom both the passenger service representative and Jack Lovett are watching (Jack Lovett's excuse for being in the operations room at the airport is not the same as Jack Lovett's reason for being in the operations room at the airport) will be the next-to-last passenger off the plane. She is a woman at that age (a few months over forty in her case) when it is possible to look very good at certain times of day (Sunday lunch in the summertime is a good time of day for such women, particularly if they wear straw hats that shade their eyes and silk shirts that cover their elbows and if they resist the inclination to another glass of white wine after lunch) and not so good at other times of day. Five-thirty-seven A.M. is not a good time of day for this woman about to deplane the Pan American 747. She is bare-legged, pale despite one of those year-round suntans common among American women of some means, and she is wearing sling-heeled pumps, one of which has loosened and slipped down on her heel. Her dark hair, clearly brushed by habit to minimize the graying streak at her left temple, is dry and lustreless from the night spent on the airplane. She is wearing no makeup. She is wearing dark glasses. She is wearing a short knitted skirt and jacket, with a cotton jersey beneath the jacket, and at the moment she steps from the cabin of the plane into the moist warmth of the rainy tropical morning she takes off the jacket and leans to adjust the heel strap of her shoe. As the passenger service representative starts up the steps with the umbrella she straightens and glances back, apparently confused.

The man behind her on the steps, the man whose name appears on the manifest as DILLON, R.W., leans toward her and murmurs briefly.

She looks up, smiles at the passenger service representative, and leans forward, docile, while he attempts to simultaneously shield her with the umbrella and place the plumeria lei on her shoulders.

Aloha, he would be saying.

So kind.

Tragic circumstances.

Anything we as a company or I personally can do.

Facilitate arrangements.

When the senator arrives.

So kind.

As the passenger service representative speaks to the man listed on the manifest as DILLON, R.W., clearly a consultation about cars, baggage, facilitating arrangements, when the senator arrives, the woman stands slightly apart, still smiling dutifully. She has stepped beyond the protection of the umbrella and the rain runs down her face and hair. Absently she fingers the flowers of the lei, lifts them to her face, presses the petals against her cheek and crushes them. She will still be wearing the short knitted skirt and the crushed lei when she sees, two hours later, through a glass window in the third-floor intensive care unit at Queen's Medical Center, the unconscious body of her sister Janet.

This scene is my leper at the door, my Tropical Belt Coal Company, my lone figure on the crest of the immutable hill.

Inez Victor at 5:47 A.M. on the morning of March 26, 1975, crushing her lei in the rain on the runway.

Jack Lovett watching her.

"Get her in out of the goddamn rain," Jack Lovett said to no one in particular.

TWO

I

ON THE occasion when Dwight Christian seemed to me most explicitly himself he was smoking a long Havana cigar and gazing with evident satisfaction at the steam rising off the lighted swimming pool behind the house on Manoa Road. The rising steam and the underwater lights combined to produce an unearthly glow on the surface of the pool, bubbling luridly around the filter outflow; since the air that evening was warm the water temperature must have been, to give off steam, over one hundred. I recall asking Dwight Christian how (meaning why) he happened to keep the pool so hot. "No trick to heat a pool," Dwight Christian said, as if I had congratulated him. In fact Dwight Christian tended to interpret anything said to him by a woman as congratulation. "Trick is to cool one down."

It had not occurred to me, I said, that a swimming pool might need cooling down.

"Haven't spent time in the Gulf, I see." Dwight Christian rocked on his heels. "In the Gulf you have to cool them down, we developed the technology at Dhahran. Pioneered it for Aramco. Cost-efficient. Used it there and in Dubai. Had to. Otherwise we'd have sizzled our personnel."

A certain dreaminess entered his gaze for an instant, an involuntary softening at the evocation of Dhahran, Dubai, cost-efficient technology for Aramco, and then, quite abruptly, he made a harsh guttural noise, apparently intended as the sound of sizzling personnel, and laughed.

That was Dwight Christian.

"Visited DWIGHT and Ruthie (Mills College '33) CHRISTIAN at their very gracious island outpost, he has changed the least of our classmates over the years and is still Top Pineapple on the hospitality front," as an item I saw recently in the Stanford alumni notes had it.

On the occasion when Harry Victor seemed to me most explicitly himself he was patronizing the governments of western Europe at a dinner table on Tregunter Road in London. "Sooner or later they all show up with their shopping lists," he said, over *rijstaffel* on blue willow plates and the weak Scotch and soda he was nursing through dinner. He had arrived at dinner that evening not with Inez but with a young woman he identified repeatedly as "a grandniece of the first Jew on the Supreme Court of the United States." The young woman was Frances Landau. Frances Landau listened to everything Harry Victor said with studied attention, breaking her gaze only to provide glosses for the less attentive, her slightly hyperthyroid face sharp in the candlelight and her voice intense, definite, an insistent echo of every opinion she had ever heard expressed.

"What they want, in other words," Frances Landau said. "From the United States."

"Which is usually nuclear fuel," Harry Victor said, picking up a dessert spoon and studying the marking. He seemed to find Frances Landau's rapt interpolation suddenly wearing. He was not an insensitive man but he had the obtuse confidence, the implacable ethnocentricity, of many people who have spent time in Washington. "I slept last night on a carrier in the Indian Ocean," he had said several times before dinner. The implication seemed to be that he had slept on the carrier so that London might sleep free, and I was struck by the extent to which he seemed to perceive the Indian Ocean, the carrier, and even himself as abstracts, incorporeal extensions of policy.

"Nuclear fuel to start up their breeders," he added now, and then, quite inexplicably to the other guests, he launched as if by reflex into the lines from an Auden poem that he had been incorporating that year into all his public utterances: "'I and the public know what all schoolchildren learn. Those to whom evil is done do evil in return.' W.H. Auden. But I don't have to tell you that." He paused. "The English poet."

That was Harry Victor.

My point is this: I can remember a moment in which Harry Victor seemed to present himself precisely as he was and I can remember a moment in which Dwight Christian seemed to present himself precisely as he was and I can remember such moments about most people I have known, so ingrained by now is the impulse to define the personality, show the character, but I have no memory of any one moment in which either Inez Victor or Jack Lovett seemed to spring out, defined. They were equally evanescent, in some way emotionally invisible; unattached, wary to the point of opacity, and finally elusive. They seemed not to belong anywhere at all, except, oddly, together.

They had met in Honolulu during the winter of 1952. I can define exactly how winter comes to Honolulu: a kona wind comes up and the season changes. *Kona* means leeward, and this particular wind comes off the leeward side of the island, muddying the reef, littering the beaches with orange peels and prophylactics and bits of Styrofoam cups, knocking blossoms from the plumeria trees and dry fronds from the palms. The sea goes milky. Termites swarm on wooden roofs. The temperature has changed only slightly, but only tourists swim. At the edge of the known world there is only water, water as a definite presence, water as the end to which even the island will eventually come, and a certain restlessness prevails. Men like Dwight Christian watch the steam rise off their swimming pools and place more frequent calls to project sites in Taipei, Penang, Jedda. Women like Ruthie Christian take their furs out of storage, furs handed down from mother to daughter virtually unworn, the guard hairs still intact, and imagine trips to the mainland. It is during these days and nights when sheets of rain obscure the horizon and the surf rises on the north shore that the utter isolation of the place seems most profound, and it was on such a night, in 1952, that Jack Lovett first saw Inez Christian, and discerned in the grain of her predictable longings and adolescent vanities an eccentricity, a secretiveness, an emotional solitude to match his own. I see now.

I learned some of this from him.

January 1, 1952.

Intermission at the ballet, one of those third-string touring companies that afford the women and children and dutiful providers of small cities an annual look at "Afternoon of a Faun" and the Grand Pas de Deux from the "Nutcracker"; an occasion, a benefit, a reason to dress up after the general fretfulness of the season and the specific lassitude of the holiday and stand outside beneath an improvised canopy drinking champagne from paper cups. Subdued greetings. Attenuated attention. Cissy Christian smoking a cigarette in her white jade holder.

Inez, wearing dark glasses (wearing dark glasses because, after four hours of sleep, a fight with Janet, and telephone calls from Carol Christian in San Francisco and Paul Christian in Suva, she had spent most of the day crying in her room: one last throe of her adolescence), pinning and repinning a gardenia in her damp hair. This is our niece, Inez, Dwight Christian said. Inez, Major Lovett. Jack. Inez, Mrs. Lovett. Carla. A breath of air, a cigarette. This champagne is lukewarm. One glass won't hurt you, Inez, it's your birthday. Inez's birthday. Inez is seventeen. Inez's evening, really. Inez is our balletomane.

"Why are you wearing sunglasses," Jack Lovett said.

Inez Christian, startled, touched her glasses as if to remove them and then, looking at Jack Lovett, brushed her hair back instead, loosening the pins that held the gardenia.

Inez Christian smiled.

The gardenia fell to the wet grass.

"I used to know all the generals at Schofield," Cissy Christian said. "Great fun out there. Then."

"I'm sure." Jack Lovett did not take his eyes from Inez.

"Great polo players, some of them," Cissy Christian said. "I don't suppose you get much chance to play."

"I don't play," Jack Lovett said.

Inez Christian closed her eyes.

Carla Lovett drained her paper cup and crushed it in her hand.

"Inez is seventeen," Dwight Christian repeated.

"I think I want a real drink," Carla Lovett said.

During the days which immediately followed this meeting the image of Inez Christian was never entirely absent from Jack Lovett's mind, less a conscious presence than a shadow on the scan, an undertone. He would think of Inez Christian when he was just waking, or just going to sleep. He would summon up Inez Christian during lulls in the waning argument he and Carla Lovett were conducting that winter over when or how or why she would leave him. His interest in Inez was not, as he saw it, initially sexual: even at this most listless stage of his marriage he remained compelled by Carla, by Carla's very lethargy, and could still be actively aroused by watching her brush out her hair or pull on a shirt or kick off the huaraches she wore instead of slippers.

What Jack Lovett believed he saw in Inez Christian was something else. The picture he had was of Inez listening to something he was telling her, listening gravely, and then giving him her hand. In this picture she was wearing the gardenia in her hair and the white dress she had worn to the ballet, the only dress in which he had ever seen her, and the two of them were alone. In this picture the two of them were in fact the only people on earth.

"Pretty goddamn romantic."

As Jack Lovett said to me on the Garuda 727 with the jammed landing gear.

He remembered that her fingernails were blunt and unpolished.

He remembered a scar on her left wrist, and how he had wondered briefly if she had done it deliberately. He thought not.

It had occurred to him that he might never see her again (given his situation, given her situation, given the island and the fact that from her point of view he was a stranger on it) but one Saturday night in February he found her, literally, in the middle of a canefield; stopped to avoid hitting a stalled Buick on the narrow road between Ewa and Schofield and there she was, Inez Christian, age seventeen, flooding the big Buick engine while her date, a boy in a pink Oxford-cloth shirt, crouched in the cane vomiting.

They had been drinking beer, Inez Christian said, at a carnival in Wahiawa. There had been these soldiers, a bottle of rum, an argument over how many plush dogs had been won at the shooting gallery, the MPs had come and now this had happened.

The boy's name was Bobby Strudler.

Immediately she amended this: Robert Strudler.

The Buick belonged to Robert Strudler's father, she believed that the correct thing to do was to push the Buick onto a cane road and come out in daylight with a tow.

"The 'correct thing,'" Jack Lovett said. "You're a regular Miss Manners."

Inez Christian ignored this. Robert Strudler's father could arrange the tow.

She herself could arrange the tow.

In daylight.

Her feet were bare and she spoke even more precisely, as if to counter any suggestion that she might herself be drunk, and it was not until later, sitting in the front seat of Jack Lovett's car on the drive into town, Robert Strudler asleep in the back with his arms around the prize plush dogs, that Inez Christian gave any indication that she remembered him.

"I don't care about your wife," she said. She sat very straight and kept her eyes on the highway as she spoke. "So it's up to you. More or less."

She smelled of beer and popcorn and Nivea cream. The next time they met she had with her a key to the house on the Nuannu ranch. They had met a number of times before he told her that Carla Lovett had in fact already left him, had slept until noon on the last day of January and then, in an uncharacteristic seizure of hormonal energy, packed her huaraches and her shorty nightgowns and her Glenn Miller records and picked up a flight to Travis, and when he did tell her she only shrugged.

"It doesn't change anything," she said. "In point of fact."

In point of fact it did not, and it struck Jack Lovett then that what he had first read in Inez Christian as an extreme recklessness could also be construed as an extreme practicality, a temperamental refusal to deal with the merely problematic. The clandestine nature of their meetings was never questioned. The absence of any foreseeable future to these meetings was questioned only once, and that once by him.

"Will you remember doing this," Jack Lovett said.

"I suppose," Inez Christian said.

Her refusal to engage in even this most unspecific and pro forma speculation had interested him, even nettled him, and he had found himself persisting: "You'll go off to college and marry some squash player and forget we ever did any of it."

She had said nothing.

"You'll go your way and I'll go mine. That about it?"

"I suppose we'll run into each other," Inez Christian said. "Here or there."

By September of 1953, when Inez Christian left Honolulu for the first of the four years she had agreed to spend studying art history at Sarah Lawrence, Jack Lovett was in Thailand, setting up what later became the Air Asia operation. By May of 1955, when Inez Christian walked out of a dance class at Sarah

Lawrence on a Tuesday afternoon and got in Harry Victor's car and drove down to New York to marry him at City Hall, with a jersey practice skirt tied over her leotard and a bunch of daisies for a bouquet, Jack Lovett was already in Saigon, setting up lines of access to what in 1955 he was not yet calling the assistance effort. In 1955 he was still calling it the insurgency problem, but even then he saw its possibilities. He saw it as useful. I believe many people did, while it lasted. "NOT A SQUASH PLAYER," Inez Christian wrote across the wedding announcement she eventually mailed to his address in Honolulu, but it was six months before he got it.

It occurs to me that for Harry Victor to have driven up to Sarah Lawrence on a Tuesday afternoon in May and picked up Inez Christian in her leotard and married her at City Hall could be understood as impulsive, perhaps the only thing Harry Victor ever did that might be interpreted as a spring fancy, but this interpretation would be misleading. There were practical factors involved. Harry Victor was due to start work in Washington the following Monday, and Inez Christian was two months pregnant.

The afternoon of the wedding was warm and bright.

Billy Dillon was the witness.

After the ceremony Inez and Harry Victor and Billy Dillon and a girl Billy Dillon knew that year rode the ferry to Staten Island and back, had dinner at Luchow's, and went uptown to hear Mabel Mercer at the RSVP.

In the spring of the year, Mabel Mercer sang, and *this will be my shining hour.*

Two months to the day after the wedding Inez miscarried, but by then Harry was learning the ropes at Justice and Inez had decorated the apartment in Georgetown (white walls, Harvard chairs, lithographs) and they were giving dinner parties, administrative assistants and *suprêmes de volaille à l'estragon* at the Danish teak table in the living room. When Jack Lovett finally got Inez's announcement he sent her a wedding present he had won in a poker game in Saigon, a silver cigarette box engraved *Résidence du Gouverneur Général de l'Indo-Chine.*

2

In fact they did run into each other.

Here or there.

Often enough, during those twenty-some years during which Inez Victor and Jack Lovett refrained from touching each other, refrained from exhibiting undue pleasure in each other's presence or untoward interest in each other's activities, refrained most specifically from even being alone together, to keep the idea of it quick.

Quick, alive.

Something to think about late at night.

Something private.

She always looked for him.

She did not really expect to see him but she never got off a plane in certain parts of the world without wondering where he was, how he was, what he might be doing.

And once in a while he was there.

For example in Jakarta in 1969.

I learned this from her.

Official CODEL Mission, Dependents and Guests Accompanying, Inquiry into Status Human Rights in Developing (USAID Recipient) Nations.

One of many occasions on which Harry Victor descended on one tropic capital or another and set about obtaining official assurance that human rights remained inviolate in the developing (USAID Recipient) nation at hand.

One of several occasions, during those years after Harry Victor first got himself elected to Congress, on which Inez Victor got off the plane in one tropic capital or another and was met by Jack Lovett.

Temporarily attached to the embassy.

On special assignment to the military.

Performing an advisory function to the private sector.

"Just what we need here, a congressman," Inez remembered Jack Lovett saying that night in the customs shed at the Jakarta airport. The customs shed had been crowded and steamy and it had occurred to Inez that there were too many Americans in it. There was Inez, there was Harry, there were Jessie and Adlai. There was Billy Dillon. There was Frances Landau, in the same meticulously pressed fatigues and French aviator glasses she had worn the year before in Havana. There was Janet, dressed entirely in pink, pink sandals, a pink straw hat, a pink linen dress with rickrack. "I thought pink was the navy blue of the Indies," Janet had said in the Cathay Pacific lounge at Hong Kong.

"India," Inez had said. "Not the Indies. India."

"India, the Indies, whatever. Same look, *n'est-ce pas*?"

"Possibly to you," Frances Landau said.

"What is that supposed to mean?"

"It means I don't quite see why you decided to get yourself up like an English royal touring the colonies."

Janet had assessed Frances Landau's fatigues, washed and pressed to a silvery patina, loose and seductive against Frances Landau's translucent skin.

"Because I didn't bring my combat gear," Janet had said then.

Inez did not remember exactly why Janet had been along (some domestic crisis, a ragged season with Dick Ziegler or a pique with Dwight Christian, a barrage of urgent telephone calls and a pro forma invitation), nor did she remember exactly under what pretext Frances Landau had been along (legislative assistant, official photographer, drafter of one preliminary report or another, the use of Bahasa Indonesian in elementary education on Sumatra, the effects of civil disturbance on the infrastructure left on Java by the Dutch), but there they had been, in the customs shed of the Jakarta airport, along with nineteen pieces of luggage and two book bags and two tennis rackets and the boogie boards that Janet had insisted on bringing from Honolulu as presents for Jessie and Adlai. Jack Lovett had picked up the tennis rackets and handed them to the embassy driver. "A tennis paradise here, you don't mind the ballboys carry submachine guns."

"Let's get it clear at the outset, I don't want this visit tainted," Harry Victor had said.

"No embassy orchestration," Billy Dillon said.

"No debriefing," Harry Victor said.

"No reporting," Billy Dillon said.

"I want it understood," Harry Victor said, "I'm promising unconditional confidentiality."

"Harry wants it understood," Billy Dillon said, "he's not representing the embassy."

Jack Lovett opened the door of one of the embassy cars double-parked outside the customs shed. "You're parading through town some night in one of these Detroit boats with the CD 12 plates and a van blocks you off, you just explain all that to the guys who jump out. You just tell them. They can stop waving their Uzis. You're one American who doesn't represent the embassy. That'll impress them. They'll back right off."

"There's a point that should be made here," Frances Landau said.

"Trust you to make it," Janet said.

Frances Landau ignored Janet. "Harry. Billy. See if you don't agree. The point—"

"They'll lay down their Uzis and back off saluting," Jack Lovett said.

"This sounds like something Frances will be dressed for," Janet said.

"—Point I want to make is this," Frances Landau said. "Congressman Victor isn't interested in confrontation."

"That's something else he can tell them." Jack Lovett was looking at Inez. "Any points you want to make? Anything you want understood? Mrs. Victor?"

"About this friend of Inez's," Frances Landau had said later that night at the hotel.

Inez was lying on the bed in the suite that had finally been found for her and Harry and the twins. There had been a mix-up about whether they were to stay at the hotel or at the ambassador's residence and when Harry had insisted on the hotel the bags had to be retrieved from the residence. "We always put Codels at the residence," the junior political officer had kept saying. "This Codel doesn't represent the embassy," Jack Lovett had said, and the extra rooms had been arranged at the desk of the Hotel Borobudur and Jack Lovett had left and the junior political officer was waiting downstairs for the bags with a walkie-talkie and one of the ten autographed paperback copies of *The View from the Street: Root Causes, Radical Solutions and a Modest Proposal* that Frances Landau had thought to bring in her carry-on bag.

"Which friend of Inez's exactly," Inez said.

"Jack whatever his name is."

"Lovett." Janet was examining the curtains. "His name is Jack Lovett. This is just possibly the ugliest print I have ever seen."

"Batik," Frances Landau said. "A national craft. Lovett then."

"Frances is so instructive," Janet said. "Batik. A national craft. There is batik and there is batik, Frances. For your information."

Frances Landau emptied an ice tray into a plastic bucket. "What does he do?"

Inez stood up. "I believe he's setting up an export-credit program, Frances." She glanced at Billy Dillon. "Operating independently of Pertamina."

"AID funding," Billy Dillon said. "Exploring avenues. Et cetera."

"So he said." Frances Landau dropped three of the ice cubes into a glass. "In those words."

"I thought he was in the aircraft business," Janet said. "Inez? Wasn't he? When he was married to Betty Bennett? I'd be just a little leery of those ice cubes if I were you, Frances. Ice cubes are not a national craft."

"Really, the aircraft business," Frances Landau said. "Boeing? Douglas? What aircraft business?"

"I wouldn't develop this any further, Frances," Harry Victor said.

"I'd definitely let it lie," Billy Dillon said. "In country."

"It's not that clear cut," Harry Victor said.

"But this is ludicrous," Frances Landau said.

"Not black and white," Harry Victor said.

"Pretty gray, actually," Billy Dillon said. "In country."

"But this is everything I despise." Frances Landau looked at Harry Victor. "Everything you despise."

Inez looked at Billy Dillon.

Billy Dillon shrugged.

"Harry, if you could hear yourself. 'Not that clear cut.' 'Not black and white.' That's not the Harry Victor I—"

Frances Landau broke off.

There was a silence.

"The four of you are really fun company," Janet said.

"This conversation," Frances Landau said, "is making me quite ill."

"That or the ice cubes," Janet said.

When Inez remembered that week in Jakarta in 1969 she remembered mainly the cloud cover that hung low over the city and trapped the fumes of sewage and automobile exhaust and rotting vegetation as in a fetid greenhouse. She remembered the cloud cover and she remembered lightning flickering on the horizon before dawn and she remembered rain washing wild orchids into the milky waste ditches.

She remembered the rumors.

There had been new rumors every day.

The newspapers, censored, managed to report these rumors by carrying stories in which they deplored the spreading of rumors, or, as the newspapers put it, the propagation of falsehoods detrimental to public security. In order to deplore the falsehoods it was of course necessary to detail them, which was the trick. Among the falsehoods deplored one day was a rumor that an American tourist had been killed in the rioting at Surabaya, the rioting at Surabaya being only another rumor, deplored the previous day. There was a further rumor that the *Straits Times* in Singapore was reporting not only an American tourist but also a German businessman killed, and rioting in Solo as well as in Surabaya, but even the existence of the *Straits Times* report was impossible to confirm because the *Straits Times* was said to have been confiscated at customs. The rumor that the *Straits Times* had been confiscated at customs was itself impossible to confirm, another falsehood detrimental to public security, but there was no *Straits Times* in Jakarta for the rest of that week.

Inez remembered Harry giving a press conference and telling the wire reporters who showed up that the rioting in Surabaya reflected the normal turbulence of a nascent democracy.

Inez remembered Billy Dillon negotiating with the wire reporters to move Harry's press conference out in time for Friday deadlines at the New York *Times* and the Washington *Post.* "I made him available, now do me a favor," Billy Dillon said. "I don't want him on the wire so late he makes the papers Sunday afternoon, you see my point."

Inez remembered Jack Lovett asking Billy Dillon if he wanted the rioting rescheduled for the Los Angeles *Times*.

Inez remembered:

The reception for Harry at the university the night before the grenade exploded in the embassy commissary. She remembered Harry saying over and over again that Americans were learning major lessons in Southeast Asia. She remembered Jack Lovett saying finally that he could think of only one lesson Americans were learning in Southeast Asia. What was that, someone said. Harry did not say it, Harry was too careful to have said it. Billy Dillon was too careful to have said it. Frances Landau or Janet must have said it. What was that, Frances Landau or Janet said, and Jack Lovett clipped a cigar before he answered.

"A tripped Claymore mine explodes straight up," Jack Lovett said.

There had been bare light bulbs blazing over a table set with trays of sweetened pomegranate juice, little gold chairs set in rows, some kind of trouble outside: troops appearing at the doors and the occasional crack of a rifle shot, the congressman says, the congressman believes, major lessons for Americans in Southeast Asia.

"Let's move it out," Jack Lovett said.

"Goddamnit I'm not through," Harry Victor said.

"I believe some human rights are being violated on the verandah," Jack Lovett said.

Harry had turned back to the director of the Islamic Union.

Janet's hand had hovered over the sweetened pomegranate juice as if she expected it to metamorphose into a vodka martini.

Inez had watched Jack Lovett. She had never before seen Jack Lovett show dislike or irritation. Dislike and irritation were two of many emotions that Jack Lovett made a point of not showing, but he was showing them now.

"You people really interest me," Jack Lovett said. He said it to Billy Dillon but he was looking at Harry. "You don't actually see what's happening in front of you. You don't see it unless you read it. You have to read it in the New York *Times*, then you start talking about it. Give a speech. Call for an investigation. Maybe you can come down here in a year or two, investigate what's happening tonight."

"You don't understand," Inez had said.

"I understand he trots around the course wearing blinders, Inez."

Inez remembered:

Jack Lovett coming to get them in the coffee shop of the Borobudur the next morning, after the grenade was lobbed into the embassy commissary. The ambassador, he said, had a bungalow at Puncak. In the mountains. Inez and Janet and the children were to wait up there. Until the situation crystallized. A few hours, not far, above Bogor, a kind of resort, he would take them up.

"A hill station," Janet said. "Divine."

"Don't call it a hill station," Frances Landau said. "'Hill station' is an imperialist term."

"Let's save the politics until we get up there," Jack Lovett said.

"I don't want to go," Frances Landau said.

"Nobody gives a rat's ass if you go or don't go," Jack Lovett said. "You're not a priority dependent."

"Isn't this a little alarmist," Harry Victor said. Harry was cracking a boiled egg. Jack Lovett watched him spoon out the egg before he answered.

"This was a swell choice for a family vacation," Jack Lovett said then. "A regular Waikiki. I wonder why the charters aren't onto it. I also wonder if you know what it would cost us to get a congressman's kid back."

Jack Lovett's voice was pleasant, and so was Harry's.

"Ah," Harry said. "No. Not unless it's been in the New York *Times*."

Inez remembered:

The green lawn around the ambassador's bungalow at Puncak, the gardenia hedges.

The faded chintz slipcovers in the bungalow at Puncak, the English primroses, the tangles of bamboo and orchids in the ravine.

The mists blowing in at Puncak.

Standing with Jack Lovett on the green lawn at Puncak with

the mists blowing in over the cracked concrete of the empty swimming pool, over the ravine, over the tangles of bamboo and orchids, over the English primroses.

Standing with Jack Lovett.

Inez remembered that.

Inez also remembered that the only person killed when the grenade exploded in the embassy commissary was an Indonesian driver from the motor pool. The news had come in on the radio at Puncak while Inez and Jack Lovett sat in the dark on the porch waiting for word that it was safe to take the children back down to Jakarta. There had been fireflies, Inez remembered, and a whine of mosquitoes. Jessie and Adlai were inside the bungalow trying to get Singapore television and Janet was inside the bungalow trying to teach the houseman how to make coconut milk punches. The telephones were out. The radio transmission was mainly static. According to the radio other Indonesian and American personnel had sustained minor injuries but the area around the embassy was secure. The ambassador was interviewed and expressed his conviction that the bombing of the embassy commissary was an isolated incident and did not reflect the mood of the country. Harry was interviewed and expressed his conviction that this isolated incident reflected only the normal turbulence of a nascent democracy.

Jack Lovett had switched off the radio.

For a while there had been only the whining of the mosquitoes.

Jack Lovett's arm was thrown over the back of his chair and in the light that came from inside the bungalow Inez could see the fine light hair on the back of his wrist. The hair was neither blond nor gray but was lighter than Jack Lovett's skin. "You don't understand him," Inez said finally.

"Oh yes I do," Jack Lovett said. "He's a congressman."

Inez said nothing.

The hair on the back of Jack Lovett's wrist was translucent, almost transparent, no color at all.

"Which means he's a radio actor," Jack Lovett said. "A civilian."

Inez could hear Janet talking to the houseman inside the bungalow. "I said coconut milk," Janet kept saying. "Not goat milk. I think you thought I said goat milk. I think you misunderstood."

Inez did not move.

"Who is Frances," Jack Lovett said.

Inez did not answer immediately. Inez had accepted early on exactly what Billy Dillon had told her: girls like Frances came with the life. Frances came with the life the way fundraisers came with the life. Sometimes fundraisers were large and in a hotel and sometimes fundraisers were small and at someone's house and sometimes the appeal was specific and sometimes the appeal was general but they were all the same. There was always the momentary drop in the noise level when Harry came in and there were always the young men who talked to Inez as a way of ingratiating themselves with Harry and there were always these very pretty women of a type who were excited by public life. There was always a Frances Landau or a Connie Willis. Frances Landau was a rich girl and Connie Willis was a singer but they were just alike. They listened to Harry the same way. They had the same way of deprecating their own claims to be heard.

It's just a means to an end, Frances said about her money.

I just do two lines of coke and scream, Connie said about her singing.

If there were neither a Frances nor a Connie there would be a Meredith or a Brooke or a Binky or a Lacey. Inez considered trying to explain this to Jack Lovett but decided against it. She knew about certain things that came with her life and Jack Lovett knew about certain things that came with his life and none of these things had any application to this moment on this porch. Jack Lovett reached for his seersucker jacket and put it on and Inez watched him. She could hear Janet telling Jessie and Adlai about the goat milk in the coconut milk punches. "It's part of the exaggerated politeness these people have," Janet said. "They'll never admit they didn't understand you. That would imply you didn't speak clearly, a no-no."

"Either that or he didn't have any coconut milk," Jack Lovett said.

Frances did not have any application to this moment on this porch and neither did Janet.

Inez closed her eyes.

"We should go back down," she said finally. "I think we should go back down."

"I bet you think that would be the 'correct thing,'" Jack Lovett said. "Don't you. Miss Manners."

Inez sat perfectly still. Through the open door she could see Janet coming toward the porch.

Jack Lovett stood up. "We've still got it," he said. "Don't we."

"Got what," Janet said as she came outside.

"Nothing," Inez said.

"Plenty of nothing," Jack Lovett said.

Janet looked from Jack Lovett to Inez.

Inez thought that Janet would tell her story about the coconut milk punches but Janet did not. "Don't you dare run off together and leave me in Jakarta with Frances," Janet said.

That was 1969. Inez Victor saw Jack Lovett only twice again between 1969 and 1975, once at a large party in Washington and once at Cissy Christian's funeral in Honolulu. For some months after the evening on the porch of the bungalow at Puncak it had seemed to Inez that she might actually leave Harry Victor, might at least separate herself from him in a provisional way—rent a small studio, say, or make a discreet point of not going down to Washington, and of being at Amagansett when he was in New York—and for a while she did, but only between campaigns.

Surely you remember Inez Victor campaigning.

Inez Victor smiling at a lunch counter in Manchester, New Hampshire, her fork poised over a plate of scrambled eggs and toast.

Inez Victor smiling at the dedication of a community center in Madison, Wisconsin, her eyes tearing in the bright sun because it had been decided that she looked insufficiently congenial in sunglasses.

Inez Victor speaking her famous Spanish at a street festival in East Harlem. *Buenos días*, Inez Victor said on this and other such occasions. *Yo estoy muy contenta a estar aquí hoy con mi esposo.* In twenty-eight states and at least four languages Inez Victor said that she was very happy to be here today with her husband. In twenty-eight states she also said, usually in English but in Spanish for *La Opinión* in Los Angeles and for *La Prensa* in Miami, that the period during which she and her husband were separated had been an important time of renewal and rededication for each of them (*vida nueva*, she said for *La Opinión*, which was not quite right but since the reporter was only humoring Inez by conducting the interview in Spanish he got the drift) and had left their marriage stronger than ever. Oh shit, Inez, Jack Lovett said to Inez Victor in Wahiawa on the thirtieth of March, 1975. Harry Victor's wife.

3

AERIALISTS KNOW that to look down is to fall.

Writers know it too.

Look down and that prolonged spell of suspended judgment in which a novel is written snaps, and recovery requires that we practice magic. We keep our attention fixed on the wire, plan long walks, solitary evenings, measured drinks at sundown and careful meals at careful hours. We avoid addressing the thing directly during the less propitious times of day. We straighten our offices, arrange and rearrange certain objects, talismans, props. Here are a few of the props I have rearranged this morning.

Object (1): An old copy of *Who's Who*, open to Harry Victor's entry.

Object (2): A framed cover from the April 21, 1975, issue of *Newsweek*, a black-and-white photograph showing the American ambassador to Cambodia, John Gunther Dean, leaving Phnom Penh with the flag under his arm. The cover legend reads "GETTING OUT." There are several men visible in the background of this photograph, one of whom I believe to be (the background is indistinct) Jack Lovett. This photograph would have been taken during the period when Inez Victor was waiting for Jack Lovett in Hong Kong.

Objects (3) and (4): two faded Kodacolor snapshots, taken by me, both showing broken rainbows on the lawn of the house I was renting in Honolulu the year I began making notes about this situation.

Other totems: a crystal paperweight to throw color on the wall, not unlike the broken rainbows on the lawn (dense, springy Bermuda grass, I remember it spiky under my bare feet) outside that rented house in Honolulu. A map of Oahu, with an X marking the general location of the same house, in the Kahala district, and red push-pins to indicate the locations of Dwight and Ruthie Christian's house on Manoa Road and Janet and Dick Ziegler's house on Kahala Avenue. A postcard I bought the morning I flew up from Singapore to see Inez Victor in Kuala Lumpur, showing what was then the new Kuala

Lumpur International Airport at Subang. In this view of the Kuala Lumpur International Airport there are no airplanes visible but there is, suspended from the observation deck of the terminal, a banner reading "WELCOME PARTICIPANTS OF THE THIRD WORLD CUP HOCKEY." The morning I bought this postcard was one of several mornings, not too many, four or five mornings over a period of some years, when I believed I held this novel in my hand.

A few notes about those years.

The year I rented the house in Honolulu was 1975, in the summer, when everyone except Janet was still alive and the thing had not yet congealed into a story on which the principals could decline comment. In the summer of 1975 each of the major and minor players still had a stake in his or her own version of recent events, and I spent the summer collecting and collating these versions, many of them conflicting, most of them self-serving; an essentially reportorial technique. The year I flew up to Kuala Lumpur to see Inez Victor was also 1975, after Christmas. I remember specifically that it was after Christmas because Inez devoted much of our first meeting to removing the silver tinsel from an artificial Christmas tree in the administrative office of the refugee camp where she then worked. She removed the tinsel one strand at a time, smoothing the silver foil with her thumbnail and laying the strands one by one in a shallow box, and as she did this she talked, in a low and largely uninflected voice, about certain problems Harry Victor was then having with the Alliance for Democratic Institutions. The Alliance for Democratic Institutions had originally been funded, Inez said, by people who wanted to keep current the particular framework of ideas, the particular political dynamic, that Harry Victor had come to represent (she said "Harry Victor," not "Harry," as if the public persona were an entity distinct from the "Harry" she later described as having telephoned her every night for the past week), but there had recently been an ideological rift between certain of the major donors, and this internal dissension was threatening the survival of the Alliance *per se.*

Inez smoothed another strand of tinsel and laid it in the box. The walls of the office were covered with charts showing the flow of refugees through the camp (or rather the flow of refugees into the camp, since many came but few left) and through an open door I could see an Indian doctor in the next room preparing to examine one of several small children. All of the children had bright rashes on their cheeks, and the little boy on the examining table, a child about four wearing an oversized sweatshirt printed OHIO WESLEYAN, intermittently cried and coughed, a harsh tubercular hack that cut through the sound of Inez's voice.

The Alliance *qua* Alliance.

Add to that the predictable difficulties of mobilizing broad-based support in the absence of the war.

Add further the usual IRS attempts to reverse the Alliance's tax-exempt status.

Add finally a definite perception that the idea of Harry Victor as once and future candidate had lost a certain momentum. Momentum was all in the perception of momentum. Any perception of momentum would naturally have suffered because of everything that happened.

I recall seizing on "everything that happened," thinking to guide Inez away from the Alliance for Democratic Institutions, but Inez could not, that first afternoon, be deflected. When the momentum goes, she said, by then plucking the last broken bits of tinsel from the artificial needles, the money goes with it.

The child on the examining table let out a piercing wail.

The Indian doctor spoke sharply in French and withdrew a hypodermic syringe.

Inez never looked up, and it struck me that I had been watching a virtually impenetrable performance. It was possible to construe this performance as not quite attached, but it was equally possible to construe it as deliberate, a studied attempt to deflect any idea I might have that Inez Victor would ever talk about how she left Honolulu with Jack Lovett.

4

I AM resisting narrative here.

Two documents that apply.

I was given a copy of the first by Billy Dillon in August of 1975, not in Honolulu but in New York, during the several days I spent there and on Martha's Vineyard talking to him and to Harry Victor.

> UNIT ARRIVED AT LOCATION 7:32 AM 25 MARCH 1975. AT LOCATION BUT EXTERIOR TO RESIDENCE, OFFICERS NOTED AUTOMATIC GATE IN "OPEN" POSITION, AUTOMATIC SPRINKLERS IN OPERATION, AUTOMATIC POOL CLEANER IN OPERATION. OFFICERS NOTED TWO VEHICLES IN DRIVEWAY: ONE 1975 FORD LTD SEDAN (COLOR BLACK) BEARING HDMV PLATE "OYL-644" WITH US GOVERNMENT STICKER AND ONE 1974 MERCEDES 230-SL (COLOR LT. TAN) BEARING HDMV PLATE "JANET."
>
> OFFICERS ENTERED RESIDENCE VIA OPEN DOOR, NOTED NO EVIDENCE OF DISARRAY OR STRUGGLE, AND PROCEEDED ONTO LANAI, THEREBY LOCATING FEMALE VICTIM LATER IDENTIFIED AS JANET CHRISTIAN ZIEGLER LYING FACE-DOWN ON CARPET. FEMALE VICTIM WAS POSITIONED ON CARPET NEAR LAVA-ROCK WALL LEADING TO SHALLOW POOL IN WHICH OFFICERS OBSERVED ASSORTED PLANTINGS AND KOI-TYPE FISH. FEMALE VICTIM WAS CLOTHED IN LT. TAN SLACKS, WHITE BLOUSE, LT. TAN WINDBREAKER TYPE JACKET, NO STOCKINGS AND LOAFER STYLE SHOES. A LEATHER SHOULDER STYLE PURSE POSITIONED ON LEDGE OF LAVA-ROCK POOL CONTAINED FEMALE VICTIM'S IDENTIFICATION, ASSORTED CREDIT CARDS, ASSORTED PERSONAL ITEMS, AND $94 CASH AND WAS APPARENTLY UNDISTURBED.
>
> OFFICERS NOTED MALE VICTIM LATER IDENTIFIED AS WENDELL JUSTICE OMURA LYING ON BACK NEAR SOFA WITH APPARENT GUNSHOT WOUND UPPER ABDOMEN. MALE VICTIM WAS CLOTHED IN LT. TAN SLACKS, ALOHA

TYPE SHIRT, COTTON SPORTS JACKET, WHITE SOCKS AND SNEAKER STYLE SHOES.

MALE VICTIM EXHIBITED NO PULSE RATE OR RESPIRATORY ACTIVITY.

FEMALE VICTIM EXHIBITED LOW PULSE RATE AND UNEVEN RESPIRATORY ACTIVITY.

AMBULANCE UNIT AND FIRE DEPARTMENT INHALATOR SQUAD ARRIVED CONCURRENTLY AT 7:56 AM, ALSO CONCURRENT WITH ARRIVAL OF MRS. ROSE L. HAYAKAWA, 1173 21ST AVENUE, WHO IDENTIFIED SELF AS REGULAR PART-TIME HOUSEKEEPER AND STATED SHE LAST SAW FEMALE VICTIM PRECEDING DAY AT 1 PM WHEN FEMALE VICTIM APPEARED IN GOOD HEALTH AND SPIRITS. MRS. ROSE L. HAYAKAWA STATED THAT SHE WAS FAMILIAR WITH MALE VICTIM ONLY AS SPEAKER AT RECENT NISEI DAY BANQUET HONORING ALL-OAHU HIGH-SCHOOL ATHLETES OF JAPANESE DESCENT INCLUDING INFORMANT'S SON DANIEL M. HAYAKAWA, SAME ADDRESS (NOT PRESENT AT LOCATION).

AMBULANCE CARRYING FEMALE VICTIM DISPATCHED TO QUEEN'S MEDICAL CENTER AT 8:04 AM.

APPARENT BLOODSTAINS REVEALED BY REMOVAL FEMALE VICTIM ALTERED SIGNIFICANTLY WHEN MRS. ROSE L. HAYAKAWA ATTEMPTED TO APPLY COLD WATER TO CARPET. OFFICERS PERSUADED MRS. ROSE L. HAYAKAWA TO TERMINATE THIS ATTEMPT.

MALE VICTIM PRONOUNCED DEAD AT LOCATION AND RESUSCITATION ATTEMPT TERMINATED AFTER ARRIVAL DEPUTY MEDICAL EXAMINER FLOYD LIU, M.D., AT 8:25 AM. REMOVAL OF BODY PENDING ARRIVAL INVESTIGATING OFFICERS AND OTHER MEDICAL EXAMINERS AT APPROXIMATELY 9 AM.

COPY TO: CORONER

COPY TO: HOMICIDE.

I was shown the second document, a cable transmitted from Honolulu on October 2, 1975, by its recipient, Inez Victor, when I saw her that December in Kuala Lumpur.

VICTORY STOP THINKING OF YOU IN OUR HOUR OF TRIUMPH STOP (SIGNATURE) DWIGHT.

Despite the signature this cable had been sent, Inez said, not by Dwight Christian but by her father, Paul Christian, on the morning he was formally committed in Honolulu to a state facility for the care and treatment of the insane.

5

It was Billy Dillon who told Inez.

In the kitchen of the house at Amagansett.

To which he had driven, two hours in the rain on the Long Island Expressway and another hour on the Montauk Highway, flooding in the tunnel first shot out of the barrel and then construction on the L.I.E., no picnic, no day at the races, directly after he took the call from Dick Ziegler.

Dick Ziegler had called the office and tried to reach Harry.

Dick Ziegler was not yet on the scene, Dick Ziegler had been on Guam for two days trying to run an environmental-impact report around the Agana-Mariana Planning Commission.

Janet was not dead.

It was important to remember that Janet was not dead. Janet had been gravely injured, yes, in fact Janet was on life support at Queen's Medical Center, but Janet was not dead.

Wendell Omura was dead.

Inez must remember Wendell Omura, Inez would have met Wendell Omura in Washington, Wendell Omura was one of those Nisei who came out of the 442nd and went to law school on the G.I. Bill and spent the next twenty years cutting deals on a plane between Washington and his district. Silver Star. D.S.C. Real scrappy guy, had a triple bypass at Walter Reed a few years back, a week out of the hospital this spade tries to mug him, Omura decks the kid. The kind of guy who walks away from the Arno Line and a triple bypass, not to mention the spade, he probably didn't anticipate buying the farm on Janet's lanai.

Eating a danish.

Go for broke, see where it gets you.

The details were a little cloudy.

Don't ask, number one, how Wendell Omura happens to be on Janet's lanai.

Don't ask, number two, how Paul Christian happens to be seen leaving Janet's house with a .357 Magnum tucked in his beach roll.

The paper boy saw him.

The paper boy happened to recognize Paul Christian because Janet's paper boy is also Paul Christian's paper boy. Don't ask how the paper boy happened to recognize the .357 Magnum, maybe the paper boy is also a merc. There we are. Paul Christian has definitely been placed on the scene, but nobody can locate Paul Christian.

Paul Christian was the cloudy part.

Paul Christian was a fucking typhoon, you ask Billy Dillon.

Inez remembered listening to all this without speaking.

"I left word in Florida for Harry to call as soon as he checks in," Billy Dillon said. "Of course it's on the wire, but Harry might not hear the radio."

Inez lit a cigarette, and smoked it, leaning on the kitchen counter, looking out at the rain falling on the gray afternoon sea. Harry was on his way to Bal Harbour to speak at a Teamster meeting. Adlai was with Harry, earning credit for what the alternative college in Boston that had finally admitted him called an internship in public affairs. Jessie, at this hour in Seattle, would be just punching in at King Crab's Castle, punching in and putting on her apron and lining up the crab-cups-to-go, shredded lettuce, three fingers crab leg, King Crab's Special Sauce and lemon wedge on the side. Inez knew Jessie's exact routine at King Crab's Castle because Inez had spent Christmas with Jessie in Seattle. Jessie had cut her hair, gained ten pounds, and seemed, on methadone, generally cheerful.

"I was kind of thinking about going somewhere and getting a job," Jessie had said when Inez asked if she had given any thought to going back to school, possibly a class or two at NYU to start. "I understand there are some pretty cinchy jobs in Vietnam."

Inez had stared at her.

Jessie's information about the jobs in Vietnam was sketchy but she supposed that they involved "cooking for a construction crew, first aid, stuff like that."

Inez had tried to think about how best to phrase an objection.

"I got the idea from this guy I know who works for Boeing, he hangs out at the Castle, you don't know him."

Inez had said in as neutral a voice as she could manage that she did not think Vietnam a good place to look for a job.

Jessie had shrugged.

"How's the junkie," Adlai had said when Inez walked back into the apartment on Central Park West a few days after Christmas.

"That's unnecessary," Harry had said.

Inez had not mentioned the jobs in Vietnam to either Harry or Adlai.

"Dick calls, he's still on Guam," Billy Dillon said. He had found a chicken leg in the refrigerator and was eating it. "He says he 'thinks' he can get a flight up to Honolulu tonight. I say what's to 'think' about, he says Air Micronesia's on strike and Pan Am and TW are booked but he's 'working on' a reservation. He's 'working on' a fucking reservation. A major operator, your brother-in-law. I said Dick, get your ass over to Anderson, the last I heard the Strategic Air Command still had a route to Honolulu. 'What do I say,' Dick says. 'Tell them your father-in-law offed a congressman.' 'Wait a minute, fella,' Dick says. 'Not so speedy.' He says, get this, direct quote, 'there's considerable feeling we can contain this to an accident.'"

Inez said nothing.

"It's Snow White and the Seven Loons down there. 'Contain this to an accident.' 'Considerable feeling.' Where's this 'considerable feeling' he's talking about? On Guam? I try to tell him, 'Dick, no go,' and Dick says 'why.' 'Why,' he says. A member of the Congress has been killed, Dick's own wife has been shot, his father-in-law's been fingered, his father-in-law who is also lest we forget the father-in-law of somebody who ran for president, and Dick's talking 'containment.' 'Dick,' I said, 'take it on faith, this one's a hang-out.'"

Inez said nothing. She had located a telephone number chalked on the blackboard above the telephone and begun to dial it.

"We're on the midnight Pan Am out of Kennedy. There's an hour on the ground at LAX which puts us down around dawn in Honolulu. I told Dick we wouldn't—"

Billy Dillon broke off. He was watching Inez dial.

"Inez," he said finally. "I can't help noticing you're dialing Seattle. I sincerely hope you're not calling Jessie. Just yet."

"Of course I am. I want to tell her."

"You don't think we've got enough loose balls on the table already? You don't think Jessie could wait until we line up at least one shot?"

"She'll read about it."

"Not unless it makes *Tiger Beat*."

"Don't say that. *Hello?*" Inez's voice was suddenly bright. "This is Inez Victor. Jessica Victor's mother. Jessie's mom, yes. I'm calling from New York. Amagansett, actually—"

"Oh good," Billy Dillon said. "Doing fine. Amagansett to King Crab."

"Jessie? Darling? Can you hear me? No, it's a little gray. Raining, actually. Listen. I—"

Inez suddenly thrust the receiver toward Billy Dillon.

"Never open with the weather," Billy Dillon said as he took the receiver. "Jessie? Jessie honey? Uncle William here. Your mother and I are flying down to Honolulu tonight, we wanted to put you in the picture, you got a minute? Well just tell the crab cups to stand easy, Jess, OK?"

"Oh shit," Billy Dillon said on the telephone in the Pan American lounge at the Los Angeles airport, when Dick Ziegler told him that Paul Christian had called the police from the Honolulu YMCA and demanded that they come get him. "Oh Jesus fucking Christ shit, I better let Harry know." By that time Harry Victor had already spoken to the Teamsters in Bal Harbour and was on his way to a breakfast meeting in Houston. Billy Dillon had hung up on Dick Ziegler and tried three numbers in Florida and five in Texas but Harry was somewhere in between and there was no time to wait because the flight was reboarding. "Oh shit," Billy Dillon kept saying all the way down the Pacific, laying out hand after hand of solitaire in the empty lounge upstairs. Inez lay on the curved banquette and watched him. Inez had watched Billy Dillon playing solitaire on a lot of planes. "Why not trot out the smile and move easily through the cabin," he would say at some point in each flight, and the next day Inez would appear that way in the clips, the candidate's wife, "moving easily through the cabin," "deflecting questions with a smile."

"I have to admit I wasn't factoring in your father," Billy Dillon said now. "I knew he was a nutty, but I thought he was a nutty strictly on his own case. In fact I thought he was still looking for himself in Tangier. Or Sardinia. Or wherever the fuck he was when he used to fire off the letters to *Time* demanding Harry's impeachment."

"Tunis," Inez said. "He was in Tunis. He moved back to Honolulu last year. A mystic told him that Janet needed him. I told you. Listen. Do you remember before the Illinois primary when you and Harry and I were taken through the Cook County morgue?"

"Twenty-eight appearances in two days in Chicago and those clowns on advance commit us to a shake-hands with the coroner, very definitely I remember. Some metaphor. What about it."

"There was a noise in the autopsy room like an electric saw."

"Right."

"What was it?"

"It was an electric saw." Billy Dillon shuffled and cut the cards. "Don't dwell on it."

Inez said nothing.

"Don't anticipate. This one isn't going to improve, you try to look down the line. Think more like Jessie for once. I tell Jessie Janet's been shot, Janet's in a coma, we're not too sure what's going to happen, you know what Jessie says? Jessie says 'I guess whatever happens it's in her karma.'"

Inez said nothing.

"In . . . her . . . karma." Billy Dillon laid out another hand of solitaire. "That's the consensus from King Crab. Hey. Inez. Don't cry. Get some sleep."

"Watch the booze," Billy Dillon said about three A.M., and, a little later, to the stewardess who came upstairs and sat down beside him, "I'm only going to say this once, sweetheart, we don't want company." When first light came and the plane started its descent Billy Dillon reached across the table and took Inez's hand and held it. Inez had told Billy Dillon in Amagansett that there was no need for anyone to fly down with her but flying down with Inez was for Billy Dillon a reflex, part of managing a situation for Harry, and he held Inez's hand all the way to touchdown, which occurred at 5:37 A.M. Hawaiian Standard Time, March 26, 1975, on a runway swept by soft warm rain.

6

I WAS trained to distrust other people's versions, but we go with what we have.

We triangulate the coverage.

Handicap for bias.

Figure in leanings, predilections, the special circumstances which change the spectrum in which any given observer will see a situation.

Consider what filter is on the lens. So to speak. What follows is essentially through Billy Dillon's filter.

"This is a bitch," Billy Dillon remembered Dick Ziegler saying over and over. Dick Ziegler was still wearing the wrinkled cotton suit in which he had flown in from Guam and he was sitting on the floor in Dwight and Ruthie Christian's living room spreading shrimp paste on a cracker, covering the entire surface, beveling the edges.

Billy Dillon remembered the cracker particularly.

Billy Dillon could not recall ever before seeing a cracker given this level of attention.

"A real bitch. This whole deal. She was perfectly fine when I left for Guam."

"Why wouldn't she have been," Inez said.

Dick Ziegler did not look up. "She was going up to San Francisco Friday. To see the boys. Chris and Timmy were coming up from school, she had it all planned."

"I mean it's not a lingering illness," Inez said. "Getting shot."

"Inez," Dwight Christian said. "See if this doesn't beat any martini you get in New York."

"You don't exhibit symptoms," Inez said.

"Inez," Billy Dillon said.

"I add one drop of glycerine," Dwight Christian said. "Old Oriental trick."

"She'd already made a dinner reservation," Dick Ziegler said. "For the three of them. At Trader's."

"You don't lose your appetite either," Inez said.

"Inez," Billy Dillon repeated.

"I heard you the first time," Inez said.

"What's the trouble here," Dick Ziegler said.

"About Wendell Omura," Inez said.

"Ruthie's on top of that." Dwight Christian seemed to have slipped into an executive mode. "Flowers to the undertaker. Something to the house. Deepest condolences. Tragic accident, distinguished service. Et cetera. Ruthie?"

"Millie's doing her crab thing." Ruthie began spreading crackers with the shrimp paste. "To send to the house."

"That's not just what I meant," Inez said.

"I hardly knew the guy, frankly," Dick Ziegler said. "On a personal basis."

"Somebody must have known him," Inez said. "On a personal basis."

Dwight Christian cleared his throat. "Adlai still a big Mets fan, Inez?"

Inez looked at Billy Dillon.

Billy Dillon stood up. "I think what Inez means—"

"Jessie still so horse crazy?" Ruthie Christian said.

"Horse crazy," Billy Dillon repeated. "Yes. She is. You could say that. Now. If I read Inez correctly—amend this if I'm off base, Inez—Inez is still just a little unclear about—"

Billy Dillon trailed off.

Now Ruthie Christian was arranging the spread crackers to resemble a chrysanthemum.

"This is a delicate area," Billy Dillon said finally.

Inez put down her glass. "Inez is still just a little unclear about what Wendell Omura was doing on Janet and Dick's lanai at seven in the morning," she said. "Number one. Number two—"

"Tell Jessie we've got a new Arabian at the ranch," Dwight Christian said. "Pereira blue mare, dynamite."

"—Two, Inez is still just a little unclear about what Daddy was doing on Janet and Dick's lanai with a Magnum."

"Your father wasn't seen on the lanai," Dick Ziegler said. "He was seen leaving the house. Let's keep our facts straight."

"Dick," Inez said. "He *said* he was on the lanai. He *said* he fired the Magnum. You know that."

There was a silence.

"You should get Inez to show you the ranch, Billy." Ruthie

Christian did not look up. "Ask Millie to pack you a lunch, make a day of it."

"Number three," Inez said, "although less crucial, Inez is still just a little unclear about what Daddy was doing at the YMCA."

"If you drove around by the windward side you could see Dick's new project," Ruthie Christian said. "Sea Ranch? Sea Mountain? Whatever he calls it."

"He calls it Sea Meadow," Dwight Christian said. "Which suggests its drawback."

"Let's not get started on that," Dick Ziegler said.

"Goddamn swamp, as it stands."

"So was downtown Honolulu, Dwight. As it stood."

"Sea Meadow. I call that real truth-in-labeling. Good grazing for shrimp."

"Prime acreage, Dwight. As you know."

"Prime swamp. Excuse me. *Sacred* prime swamp. Turns out Dick's bought himself an old kahuna burial ground. Strictly *kapu* to developers."

"*Kapu* my ass. *Kapu* only after you started playing footsie with Wendell Omura."

"Speaking of Wendell Omura," Inez said.

"If you went around the windward side you could also stop at Lanikai." Ruthie Christian seemed oblivious, intent on her cracker chrysanthemum. "Give Billy a taste of how we really live down here."

"I think he's getting one now," Inez said.

Dwight Christian extracted the lemon peel from his martini and studied it.

Dick Ziegler gazed at the ceiling.

"Let's start by stipulating that Daddy was on the lanai," Inez said.

"Inez," Dwight Christian said. "I have thirty-two lawyers on salary. In house. If I wanted to hear somebody talk like a lawyer, I could call one up, ask him over. Give him a drink. Speaking of which—"

Dwight Christian held out his glass.

"Dwight's point as I see it is this," Ruthie Christian said. She filled Dwight Christian's glass from the shaker on the table, raised it to her lips and made a moue of distaste. "Why air family linen?"

"Exactly," Dwight Christian said. "Why accentuate the goddamn negative?"

"*Kapu* my ass," Dick Ziegler said.

Since Billy Dillon's filter tends to the comic his memory may be broad. What he said some months later about this first evening in Honolulu was that it had given him a "new angle" on the crisis-management techniques of the American business class. "They do it with crackers," he said. "Old Occidental trick. All the sharks know it." In his original account of that evening and of the four days that followed Billy Dillon failed to mention Jack Lovett, which was his own trick.

7

I ALSO have Inez's account.

Inez's account does not exactly conflict with Billy Dillon's account but neither does it exactly coincide. Inez's version of that first evening in Honolulu has less to do with those members of her family who were present than with those who were notably not.

Less to do with Dick Ziegler, say, than with Janet.

Less to do with Dwight and Ruthie Christian than with Paul Christian, and even Carol.

In Inez's version for example she at least got it straight about Paul Christian's room at the YMCA.

The room at the YMCA should have been an early warning, even Dick Ziegler and Dwight Christian could agree on that.

Surely one of them had told Inez before about her father's room at the YMCA.

His famous single room at the Y.

Paul Christian had taken this room when he came back from Tunis. He had never to anyone's knowledge spent an actual night there but he frequently mentioned it. "Back to my single room at the Y," he would say as he left the dinner table at Dwight and Ruthie's or at Dick and Janet's or at one or another house in Honolulu, and at least one or two of the other guests would rise, predictably, with urgent offers: a gate cottage here, a separate entrance there, the beach shack, the children's wing, absurd to leave it empty. Open the place up, give it some use. Doing us the favor, really. By way of assent Paul Christian would shrug and turn up his palms. "I'm afraid everyone knows my position," he would murmur, yielding.

Paul Christian had spoken often that year of his "position."

Surely Inez had heard her father speak of his position.

He conceived his position as "down," or "on the bottom," the passive victim of fortune's turn and his family's self-absorption ("Dwight's on top now, he can't appreciate my position," he said to a number of people, including Dick Ziegler), and, some months before, he had obtained the use of a house so situated—within sight both of Janet and Dick's house on Kahala Avenue and of the golf course on which Dwight Christian played every morning at dawn—as to exactly satisfy this conception.

"The irony is that I can watch Dwight teeing off while I'm making my instant coffee," he would sometimes say.

"The irony is that I can see Janet giving orders to her gardeners while I'm eating my little lunch of canned tuna," he would say at other times.

It was a location that ideally suited the prolonged mood of self-reflection in which Paul Christian arrived back from Tunis, and, during January and February, he had seemed to find less and less reason to leave the borrowed house. He had told several people that he was writing his autobiography. He had told others that he was gathering together certain papers that would constitute an indictment of the family's history in the islands, what he called "the goods on the Christians, let the chips fall where they may." He had declined invitations from those very hostesses (widows, divorcees, women from San Francisco who leased houses on Diamond Head and sat out behind them in white gauze caftans) at whose tables he was considered a vital ornament.

"I'm in no position to reciprocate," he would say if pressed, and at least one woman to whom he said this had told Ruthie Christian that Paul had made her feel ashamed, as if her very invitation had been presumptuous, an attempt to exploit the glamour of an impoverished noble. He had declined the dinner dance that Dwight and Ruthie Christian gave every February on the eve of the Hawaiian Open. He had declined at least two invitations that came complete with plane tickets (the first to a houseparty in Pebble Beach during the Crosby Pro-Am, the second to a masked ball at a new resort south of Acapulco), explaining that his sense of propriety would not allow him to accept first-class plane tickets when his position was such that he was reduced to eating canned tuna.

"Frankly, Daddy, everybody's a little puzzled by this 'canned tuna' business," Janet had apparently said one day in February.

"I'm sure I don't know why. Since 'everybody' isn't reduced to eating it."

"But I mean neither are you. Dwight says—"

"I'm sure it must be embarrassing for Dwight."

Janet had tried another approach.

"Daddy, maybe it's the 'canned' part. I mean what other kind of tuna is there?"

"Fresh. As you know. But that's not the point, is it."

"What is the point?"

"I'd rather you and Dwight didn't discuss my affairs, frankly. I'm surprised."

Tears of frustration would spring to Janet's eyes during these exchanges. "Canned tuna," she had said finally, "isn't even cheap."

"Maybe you could suggest something cheaper," Paul Christian had said. "For your father."

That was when Paul Christian had stopped speaking to Janet.

"Send him a whole tuna," Dwight Christian had advised when Janet reported this development. "Have it delivered. Packed in ice. Half a ton of bluefin. Goddamn, I'll do it myself."

Paul Christian had stopped speaking to Dwight a month before, after stopping by his office to say that the annual dinner dance on the eve of the Hawaiian Open seemed, from his point of view, a vulgar extravagance.

"'Vulgar,'" Dwight Christian had repeated.

"Vulgar, yes. From my point of view."

"Why don't you say from the point of view of a Cambodian orphan?"

"I don't understand."

"I could see the point of view of a Cambodian orphan. I could appreciate this orphan's position on dinner dances in Honolulu. I might not agree wholeheartedly but I could respect it, I could—"

"You could what?"

As Dwight Christian explained it to Inez he had realized in that instant that this particular encounter was no-win. This particular encounter had been no-win from the time Paul Christian hit on the strategy of coming not to the house but to the office. He had come unannounced, in the middle of the day, and had been cooling his heels in the reception room like some kind of drill-bit salesman when Dwight Christian came back from lunch.

"Your brother's been waiting almost an hour," the receptionist had said, and Dwight had read reproach in her voice.

As tactics went this one had been minor but effective, a step up from turning down invitations on the ground that they could not be reciprocated, and its impact on Dwight Christian had been hard to articulate. Dwight Christian did not believe that he had mentioned it even to Ruthie. In fact he had pushed it from his mind. It had seemed absurd. In that instant in the office Dwight Christian had realized that Paul Christian was no longer presenting himself as the casual victim of his family's self-absorption. He was now presenting himself as the deliberate victim of his family's malice.

"I could buy the orphan's point of view," Dwight Christian had said finally. "I can't buy yours."

"Revealing choice of words."

Dwight Christian said nothing.

"Always trying to 'buy,' aren't you, Dwight?"

Dwight Christian squared the papers on his desk before he spoke. "Ruthie will miss you," he said then.

"I'm sure you can get one of your Oriental friends to fill out the table," Paul Christian said.

Later that day the receptionist had mentioned to the most senior of Dwight Christian's secretaries, who in due course mentioned it to him, that she found it "a little sad" that Mr. Christian's brother had to live at the YMCA.

That was January.

At first Dwight Christian said February but Ruthie corrected him: it would have been January because the invitations to the dance had just gone out.

The dance itself was February.

The Open was February.

In February there had been the dance and the Open and the falling-out with Janet over the canned tuna. In February there had also been the Chriscorp annual meeting, at which Paul Christian had embarrassed everyone, most especially (according to Ruthie) himself, by introducing a resolution that called for the company to "explain itself." Of course the newspapers had got hold of it. "Unspecified allegations flowed from one dissident family member but the votes were overwhelmingly with management at Chriscorp's annual meeting yesterday," the Honolulu *Advertiser* had read. "DISGRUNTLED

CHRISTIAN SEEKS DISCLOSURE," was the headline in the *Star-Bulletin*.

The Chriscorp meeting was the fifteenth of February.

On the first of March Paul Christian had surfaced a second time in the *Advertiser*, with a letter to the editor demanding the "retraction" of a photograph showing Janet presenting an Outdoor Circle Environmental Protection Award for Special Effort in Blocking Development to Rep. Wendell Omura (D–Hawaii). Paul Christian's objection to the photograph did not appear to be based on the fact that the development Wendell Omura was then blocking was Dick Ziegler's. His complaint was more general, and ended with the phrase "lest we forget."

"I'm not sure they could actually 'retract' a photograph, Paul," Ruthie Christian had said when he called, at an hour when he knew Dwight to be on the golf course, to ask if she had seen the letter.

"I just want Janet to know," Paul Christian had said, "that in my eyes she's hit bottom."

He had said the same thing to Dick Ziegler. "An insult to you," he had added on that call. "How dare she."

"I respect your point," Dick Ziegler had said carefully, "but I wonder if the *Advertiser* was the appropriate place to make it."

"They've gone too far, Dickie."

After the letter to the *Advertiser* Paul Christian had begun calling Dick Ziegler several times a day with one or another cryptic assurance. "Our day's coming," he would say, or "tough times, Dickie, hang in there." Since it had been for Dick Ziegler a year of certain difficulties, certain reverses, certain differences with Dwight Christian (Dwight Christian's refusal to break ground for the mall that was to have been the linch-pin of the windward development was just one example) and certain strains with Janet (Janet's way of lining up with Dwight on the postponement of the windward mall had not helped matters), he could see in a general way that these calls from his father-in-law were intended as expressions of support.

Still, Dick Ziegler said to Inez, the calls troubled him.

He had found them in some way excessive.

He had found them peculiar.

"I may not be the most insightful guy in the world when it

comes to human psychology," Dick Ziegler said, "but I think your dad went off the deep end."

"Fruit salad," Dwight Christian said.

"That's hindsight," Ruthie Christian said.

"What the hell does that mean?" Dwight Christian had stopped drinking martinis and lapsed into a profound irritability. "Of course it's hindsight. Jesus Christ. 'Hindsight.'"

"Janet loves you, Inez," Dick Ziegler said. "Don't ever forget that. Janet loves you."

8

DURING THE time I spent talking to Inez Victor in Kuala Lumpur she returned again and again to that first day in Honolulu. This account was not sequential. For example she told me initially, perhaps because I had told her what Billy Dillon said about the crackers, about talking to Dwight and Ruthie Christian and to Dick Ziegler, but it had been late in the day when she talked to Dwight and Ruthie Christian and to Dick Ziegler.

First there had been the hospital.

She and Billy Dillon had gone directly from the airport to the hospital but Janet was being prepared for an emergency procedure to drain fluid from her brain and Inez had been able to see her only through the glass window of the intensive care unit.

They had gone then to the jail.

"I suppose Dwight'll be breaking out the champagne tonight," Paul Christian had said in the lawyers' room at the jail.

Inez had looked at Billy Dillon. "Why," she said finally.

"You know." Paul Christian smiled. He seemed relaxed, even buoyant, tilting back his wooden chair and propping his bare heels on the Formica table in the lawyers' room. His pants were rolled above his tanned ankles. His blue prison shirt was knotted jauntily at the waist. "You'll be there. I'm here. You can celebrate. Why not."

"Don't."

"Don't what? Actually I'm glad you're here." Paul Christian was still smiling. "I've been wondering what happened to Leilani Thayer's koa settee."

Inez considered this. "I have it in Amagansett," she said finally. "About Janet—"

"Strange, I didn't notice it when I visited you."

"You visited me in New York. The settee is in Amagansett. Daddy—"

"Not that I saw much of your apartment. The way I was rushed off to that so-called party."

Inez closed her eyes. Paul Christian had stopped in New

York without notice in 1972, on his way back to Honolulu with someone he had met on Sardinia, an actor who introduced himself only as "Mark." *I can't fathom what you were thinking,* Paul Christian had written later to Inez, *when I brought a good friend to visit you and instead of welcoming the opportunity to know him better you dragged me off (altogether ignoring Mark's offer to do a paella, by the way, which believe me did not go unremarked upon) to what was undoubtedly the worst party I've ever been to where nobody made the slightest effort to communicate whatsoever . . .*

"Actually that wasn't a party," Inez heard herself saying.

"Inez," Billy Dillon said. "Wrong train."

"Not by any standard of mine," Paul Christian said. "No. It was certainly not a party."

"It wasn't meant to be. It was a fundraiser. You remember, Harry spoke."

"I do remember. I listened. Mr.—is it Diller? Dillman?"

"Dillon," Billy Dillon said. "On Track Two."

"Mr. Dillman here will testify to the fact that I listened. When your husband spoke. I also remember that not a soul I spoke to had any opinion whatsoever about what your husband said."

"You were talking to the Secret Service."

"Whoever. They all wore brown shoes. I'm surprised you have Leilani's settee. Since you never really knew her."

Billy Dillon looked at Inez. "Pass."

"Everyone called her 'Kanaka' when we were at Cal," Paul Christian said. "Kanaka Thayer."

Inez said nothing.

"She was a Pi Phi."

Inez said nothing.

"Leilani and I were like brother and sister. Parties night and day. Leilani singing scat. I was meant to marry her. Not your mother." He hummed a few bars of "The Darktown Strutters' Ball," then broke off. "I was considered something of a catch, believe it or not. Ironic, isn't it?"

Inez unfastened her watch and examined the face.

"My life might have been very different. If I'd married Leilani Thayer."

Inez corrected her watch from New York to Honolulu time.

"That settee always reminded me."

"I want you to have it," Inez said carefully.

"That's very generous of you, but no. No, thank you."

"I could have it shipped down."

"Of course you 'could.' I know you 'could.' That's hardly the point, you 'could,' is it?"

Inez waited.

"I'm through with all that," Paul Christian said.

Billy Dillon opened his briefcase. "You mean because you're here."

"That whole life," Paul Christian said. "The mission fucking children and their pathetic little sticks of bad furniture. Those mean little screens they squabble over. That precious settee you're so proud of. That's all bullshit, really. Third-rate. Pathetic. If you want to know the truth."

Billy Dillon took a legal pad from his briefcase. "I wonder if we could run through a few specifics here. Just a few details that might help establish—"

"And if you don't know what this did to me, Inez, making me beg for that settee—"

"—Establish a chronology—"

"—Humiliating me when I'm down—"

"—Times, movements—"

"—Then I'm sorry, Inez, I don't care to discuss it."

During the next half hour Billy Dillon had managed to elicit the following information. Some time between 6:45 and 7:10 the previous morning, from a position midway between the koi pool and the exterior door on Janet's lanai, Paul Christian had fired five rounds from the Smith & Wesson .357 Magnum he was carrying in his beach roll. He had then replaced the Magnum in the beach roll and made one call, not identifying himself, giving the police emergency operator Janet's address.

He had been aware that Wendell Omura was on the floor, yes.

He had also been aware that Janet was on the floor.

Yes.

It would be quite impossible for either Inez or Mr. Dillman to understand how he felt about it.

When he left Janet's house he went not to the borrowed house in which he had been living but directly downtown to the YMCA. He had swum fifty laps in the YMCA pool, thirty backstroke and twenty Australian crawl.

"Be sure you put down 'crawl,'" he said. "I believe they call it 'freestyle' now but I'm sorry, I don't."

"'Crawl,'" Billy Dillon said. "Yes."

After swimming Paul Christian had breakfasted on tea and yoghurt in the YMCA cafeteria. There had been "a little incident" with the cashier.

"What kind of incident," Billy Dillon said.

"Somebody says 'have a nice day' to me, I always say 'sorry, I've made other plans,' that usually puts them in their place, but not this fellow. 'You're quite a comedian,' this fellow says. Well, I just looked at him."

"That was the incident," Billy Dillon said.

"Someone speaks impertinently, you're better off not answering."

"I see," Billy Dillon said.

Paul Christian had gone then to his room, and spent the rest of the day packing the few belongings he kept there. He attached to each box a list of its contents. He made a master list indicating the disposition of each box. He wrote several letters, including one to Janet in which he explained that he "stood by his actions," and, early that evening, just before calling the police and identifying himself, left these letters and instructions for their delivery with the night clerk downstairs. There had been "a little incident" with the night clerk.

"He spoke impertinently," Billy Dillon said.

"Completely out of line. As were the police."

"The police were out of line."

"They treated me like a common criminal."

"Which you're not."

"Which I most assuredly am not. I told them. Just what I told Janet. I told them I stood by my actions."

"You told the police you stood by your actions."

"Absolutely."

"Just as you told Janet."

"Exactly." Paul Christian looked at Inez. "You're being very quiet."

Inez said nothing.

"Am I to interpret your silence as disapproval?"

Inez said nothing.

"Now that I'm jailed like a common criminal you're going to administer the coup de grace? Step on me?" Paul Christian turned back to Billy Dillon. "Janet and I have always been close. Not this one."

There was a silence.

"You're going to miss Janet," Billy Dillon said.

Paul Christian looked at Inez again. "I should have known you'd be down for the celebration," he said.

After Paul Christian was taken from the room Inez lit a cigarette and put it out before either she or Billy Dillon spoke. Billy Dillon was making notes on his legal pad and did not look up. "How about it," he said finally.

"Quite frankly I don't like crazy people. They don't interest me."

"That's definitely one approach, Inez." Billy Dillon put the legal pad into his briefcase and closed it. "Forthright. Hard-edge. No fuzzy stuff. But I think the note we want to hit today is a little further toward the more-in-sorrow end of the scale. Your father is 'a sick man.' He has 'an illness like any other.' He 'needs treatment.'"

"He needs to be put away."

"That's what we're calling 'treatment,' Inez. We're calling it 'treatment' when we talk to the homicide guys and we're calling it 'treatment' when we talk to the shrinks and we're calling it 'treatment' when we talk to Frank Tawagata."

"I don't even know Frank Tawagata."

"You don't know the homicide guys, either, Inez. Just pretend we're spending the rest of the day on patrol. I'm on point." Billy Dillon looked at Inez. "You all right?"

"Yes."

"Then trot out the smile and move easily through the cabin, babe, OK?"

9

"I DON'T need to tell you, Frank, Harry appreciates what you did for him in Miami," Billy Dillon said at two o'clock that afternoon in Frank Tawagata's office. Billy Dillon and Inez had already seen the homicide detectives assigned to the investigation and they had already seen the psychiatrists assigned to examine Paul Christian and by then it was time to see Frank Tawagata. In fact Inez did know Frank Tawagata. She had met him at the 1972 convention. He had been a delegate. He was a lawyer, but his being a lawyer was not, Billy Dillon had said, the reason for seeing him. "This is a guy who truly believes, you want to get your grandma into heaven, you call in a marker at the courthouse," Billy Dillon had said. "Which is his strong point."

"You went to the wire for us in '72," Billy Dillon said now. "Harry knows that."

"Harry did one or two things for Wendell." Frank Tawagata did not look at Inez. "Anything I did for Harry I did for Wendell. Strictly."

"Harry knows that. Harry appreciates your position. Push comes to shove, you're on Wendell's team here. Which is why we're not pushing, Frank. You talk to Harry or me, you're talking *in camera*. Strictly."

"Strictly *in camera*," Frank Tawagata said, "I still can't help you."

"You can't, you can't. Just say the word."

"I just said it."

Inez watched Billy Dillon. She was tired. She had not eaten since breakfast the day before in Amagansett. She did not know what it was that Billy Dillon wanted from Frank Tawagata but she knew that he would get it. She could tell by the slight tensing of his shoulders, the total concentration with which he had given himself over to whatever it was he wanted.

"Wendell was a very well-liked guy," Billy Dillon said. "In the community. I know that."

"Very well-liked."

"Very respected family. The Omuras. Locally."

"Very respected."

"Not unlike the Christians. Ironic." Billy Dillon looked out the window. "One of the Omuras is even involved with Dwight Christian, isn't he? Via Wendell? Some kind of business deal? Some trade-off or another?"

Frank Tawagata had not answered immediately.

Billy Dillon was still looking out the window.

"I wouldn't call it a trade-off," Frank Tawagata said then.

"Of course you wouldn't, Frank. Neither would I."

There was a silence.

"Wasn't your wife an Omura?" Billy Dillon said. "Am I wrong on that?"

"No," Frank Tawagata said after a slight pause.

"Your wife wasn't an Omura?"

"I meant no, you're not wrong."

Billy Dillon smiled.

"So there would be a definite conflict," Frank Tawagata said, "if you were asking me to work on the defense."

"We're not talking 'defense,' Frank. We're talking a case that shouldn't see trial."

"I see."

"We're talking a sick man. Who needs help." Billy Dillon glanced at Inez. "Who needs treatment. And is going to get it."

"I see," Frank Tawagata said. "Yes."

"Look. Frank. All we need from you is a reading. A reading on where the markers are, what plays to expect. You know the community. You know the district attorney's office."

Frank Tawagata said nothing.

"I wouldn't think there was anybody shortsighted enough to see a career in playing this out in the media, but I don't know the office. For all I know, there's some guy over there operating in the bozo zone. Some guy who thinks he can make a name going to trial, embarrassing the Christians."

Frank Tawagata said nothing.

"Embarrassing Harry. Because face it, the guy to get is Harry."

"I would say 'was' Harry."

"Run that down for me."

"Harry's already been got, hasn't he? In '72?"

"Free shot, Frank. You deserve it. One of Wendell's cousins, isn't it? This deal with Dwight Christian?"

Frank Tawagata picked up a silver pen from his desk and poised it between his index fingers.

Inez watched Billy Dillon's shoulders. Killer mick, Harry always said about Billy Dillon, an accolade.

Billy Dillon leaned forward almost imperceptibly.

It occurred to Inez that the reason Harry was not himself a killer was that he lacked the concentration for it. Some part of his attention was always deflected back toward himself. A politician, Jack Lovett had said at Puncak. A radio actor.

"Didn't I see something about this in *Business Week*?" Billy Dillon said. "Just recently? Something about the container business? Is that right? One of Wendell's cousins?"

"One of Wendell's brothers." Frank Tawagata replaced the pen in its onyx holder before he spoke again. "My wife is a cousin."

"There you go," Billy Dillon said. "I love a town this size."

By three o'clock that afternoon it had been agreed, and could be duly reported to Harry Victor, that Frank Tawagata would sound out the district attorney's office on the most discreet and expeditious way to handle the eventual commitment to treatment of Paul Christian.

It had been agreed that Frank Tawagata would discuss the advisability of this disposition with certain key elements in the Nisei political community.

It had been agreed that Frank Tawagata would make his special understanding of both the district attorney's office and the community available to whatever lawyer was chosen to represent Paul Christian at what would ideally be mutually choreographed proceedings.

"You're not visualizing a criminal specialist," Frank Tawagata said.

"I'm visualizing a goddamn trust specialist," Billy Dillon said. "One of the old-line guys. One of those guys who's not too sure where the crapper is in the courthouse. I told you. We're not mounting a criminal defense here."

All that had been agreed upon and it had been agreed, above all, that no purpose would be served by further discussion of why Wendell Omura had introduced legislation hindering the development of Dick Ziegler's Sea Meadow, of how that legislation might have worked to benefit Dwight Christian, or of what interest Wendell Omura's brother might recently have gained in the Chriscorp Container Division.

"How exactly did you know that," Inez said when she and Billy Dillon left Frank Tawagata's office.

"Just what I said. *Business Week.* Something I read on the plane coming down."

"About Dwight?"

"Not specifically."

"About Dick?"

"About some Omura getting into containers. Two lines. A caption. That's all."

"You didn't even know it was Wendell Omura's brother?"

"I knew his name was Omura, didn't I?"

"Omura is a name like Smith."

"Inez, you don't get penalties for guessing," Billy Dillon said. "You know the moves."

IO

BY THE time Inez and Billy Dillon got back to Queen's Medical Center that first day in Honolulu it was almost four o'clock, and Janet's condition was unchanged. According to the resident in charge of the intensive care unit the patient was not showing the progress they would like to see. The patient's body temperature was oscillating. That the patient's body temperature was oscillating suggested considerable brainstem damage.

The patient was not technically dead, no.

The patient's electroencephalogram had not even flattened out yet.

Technical death would not occur until they had not one but three flat electroencephalograms, consecutive, spaced eight hours apart.

That was technical death, yes.

"Technical as opposed to what?" Inez said.

The resident seemed confused. "What we call technical death is death, as, well—"

"As opposed to actual death?"

"As opposed to, well, not death."

"Technical life? Is that what you mean?"

"It's not necessarily an either-or situation, Mrs. Victor."

"Life and death? Are not necessarily either-or?"

"Inez," Billy Dillon said.

"I want to get this straight. Is that what he's saying?"

"I'm saying there's a certain gray area, which may or may not be—"

Inez looked at Billy Dillon.

"He's saying she won't make it," Billy Dillon said.

"That's what I wanted to know."

Inez stood by the metal bed and watched Janet breathing on the respirator.

Billy Dillon waited a moment, then turned away.

"She called me," Inez said finally. "She called me last week and asked me if I remembered something. And I said I didn't. But I do."

When Inez talked to me in Kuala Lumpur about seeing Janet on the life-support systems she mentioned several times this telephone call from Janet, one of the midnight calls that Janet habitually made to New York or Amagansett or wherever Inez happened to be.

Do you remember, Janet always asked on these calls.

Do you remember the jade bat Cissy kept on the hall table. The ebony table in the hall. The ebony table Lowell Frazier said was maple veneer painted black. But you can't have forgotten Lowell Frazier, you have to remember Cissy going through the roof when Lowell and Daddy went to Fiji together. The time Daddy wanted to buy the hotel. Inez, the ten-room hotel. In Suva. After Mother left. Or was it before? You must remember. Concentrate. Now that I have you. I'm frankly amazed you picked up the telephone, usually you're out. I'm watching an absolutely paradisiacal sunset, how about you?

"It's midnight here," Inez had said on this last call from Janet.

"I dialed, and you picked up. Amazing. Usually I get your service. Now. Concentrate. I've been thinking about Mother. Do you remember Mother crying upstairs at my wedding?"

"No," Inez had said, but she did.

On the day Janet married Dick Ziegler at Lanikai Carol Christian had started drinking champagne at breakfast. She had a job booking celebrities on a radio interview show in San Francisco that year, and by noon she was placing calls to entertainers at Waikiki hotels asking them to make what she called guest appearances at Janet's wedding.

As you may or may not remember I'm the mother of the bride, Carol Christian said by way of greeting people at the reception.

I'd pace my drinks if I were you, Paul Christian had said.

I should worry, I should care, Carol Christian sang with the combo that played for dancing on the deck a Chriscorp crew had just that morning laid on the beach.

Your mother's been getting up a party for the Rose Bowl, Harry Victor said.

Carol's a real pistol, Dwight Christian said.

I should marry a millionaire.

It was when Janet went upstairs to change out of her white batiste wedding dress that Carol Christian began to cry. Not to blame your Uncle Dwight, she kept repeating, sitting on the bed in which she had fifteen years before taken naps with Inez and Janet. Our best interests at heart. Not his fault. Your grandmother. Cissy. Really. Too much. Anyhow, anyhoo. All's well that ends in bed. Old San Francisco saying. I got my marvelous interesting career, *which* I never would have had, and you got—

Inez, heavily pregnant that year, sat on the bed and tried to comfort her mother.

We got married, Janet prompted.

Forget married, Carol Christian said. You got horses. Convertibles when the time came. Tennis lessons.

I couldn't have paid for stringing your rackets if I'd taken you with me.

Let alone the lessons.

Forget the little white dresses.

Never mind the cashmere sweater sets and the gold bracelets and the camel's-hair coats.

I beg to differ, Janet Christian, Mrs. Ziegler, you did so have a camel's-hair coat.

You wore it when you came up for Easter in 1950.

Mon cher Paul: Who do you f——— to get off this island? (Just kidding of course) XXXX, C.

Neither Inez nor Janet had spoken. The windows were all open in the bedroom and the sounds of the party drifted upstairs in the fading light. Down on the beach the bridesmaids were playing volleyball in their gingham dresses. The combo was playing a medley from *My Fair Lady*. Brother Harry, Inez heard Dick Ziegler say directly below the bedroom windows. Let the man build you a real drink.

Where's Inez, Harry Victor said. I don't want Inez exhausted.

Enough of the bubbly, time for the hard stuff, Dick Ziegler said.

Excuse me but I'm looking for my wife, Harry Victor said.

Whoa man, excuse me, Dick Ziegler said. I doubt very much she's lost.

Upstairs in the darkening bedroom Janet had taken off her stephanotis lei and placed it on their mother's shoulders.

I should worry, I should care.

I should marry a millionaire.

Inez did remember that.

Inez also remembered that when she and Janet were fourteen and twelve Janet had studied snapshots of Carol Christian and cut her hair the same way.

Inez also remembered that when she and Janet were fifteen and thirteen Janet had propped the postcards from San Francisco and Lake Tahoe and Carmel against her study lamp and practiced Carol Christian's handwriting.

"Partners in a surprisingly contemporary marriage in which each granted the other freedom to pursue wide-ranging interests," was how Billy Dillon had solved the enigma of Paul and Carol Christian for Harry Victor's campaign biography. The writer had not been able to get it right and Billy Dillon had himself devised this slant.

Aloha oe.

I believe your mother wants to go to night clubs.

Nineteen days after Janet's wedding Carol Christian had been dead, killed in the crash of a Piper Apache near Reno, and there in the third-floor intensive care unit at Queen's Medical Center Janet was about to be dead. Janet had asked Inez to remember and Inez had pretended that she did not remember and now Janet had moved into the certain gray area between either and or.

Aloha oe.

Inez had touched Janet's hand, then turned away.

The click of her heels on the hospital floor struck her as unsynchronized with her walk.

The sound of her voice when she thanked the resident struck her as disembodied, inappropriate.

Outside the hospital rain still fell, and traffic was backed up on the Lunalilo Freeway. On the car radio there was an update on Janet's guarded condition at Queen's Medical Center, and on the numbers of congressmen and other public officials who had sent wires and taped messages expressing their sympathy and deep concern about the death of Wendell Omura. Among the taped messages was one from Harry, expressing not only his sympathy and deep concern but his conviction that this occasion of sadness for all Americans could be an occasion of resolve as well (Inez recognized Billy Dillon's style in the balanced "occasions"), resolve to overcome the divisions and differences tragically brought to mind today by this incident in the distant Pacific.

"Not so distant you could resist a free radio spot," Inez said to Billy Dillon.

At five o'clock that afternoon, when Inez and Billy Dillon arrived at Dwight and Ruthie Christian's house, the first thing Inez noticed was a photograph on the hall table of Janet, a photograph taken the day Janet married Dick Ziegler, Janet barefoot on the beach at Lanikai in her white batiste wedding dress. The photograph did not belong on the hall table, which was why Inez noticed it. The photograph had always been on Ruthie Christian's dressing table, and now it was here, its silver frame recently polished, the table on which it sat recently cleared of car keys and scarves and lacquer boxes and malachite frogs. The photograph was an offering, a propitiatory message to an indefinite providence, and the message it confirmed was that Janet was available to be dead.

"I called St. Andrew's this morning and told Chip Kinsolving what we want," Dwight Christian was saying in the living room. "When the time comes. Just the regular service, in and out, the ashes to ashes business. And maybe a couple of what do you call them, psalms. Not the one about the Lord is my goddamn shepherd. Specifically told him that. Dick? Isn't that what you want?"

"Don't anticipate," Dick Ziegler said. "How do I know what I want. She's not dead."

"Passive crap, the Lord is my shepherd," Dwight Christian said. "No sheep in this family."

"I'll tell you what I want," Inez heard herself say as she walked down the few steps into the living room. She was remotely aware, as if through Demerol, of the vehemence in her voice. "I want you to put that picture back where it belongs."

At this moment when Inez Victor walked into the living room of the house on Manoa Road she was still wearing the short knitted skirt and the cotton jersey and the plumeria lei in which she had left the airport ten hours before.

She had not yet slept.

She had not yet eaten.

She had not yet seen Jack Lovett, although Jack Lovett had seen her.

Get her in out of the goddamn rain, Jack Lovett had said.

11

THIS MUCH is now known about how Jack Lovett had spent the several months which preceded Inez Victor's arrival in Honolulu: he had spent those months shuttling between Saigon and Hong Kong and Honolulu. There had been innumerable details, loose ends, arrangements to be made. There had been exit paperwork to be fixed. There had been cash to be transferred. There had been end-user certificates to be altered for certain arms shipments, entry visas to be bought, negotiations to be opened and contacts to be made and houses to be located for displaced Vietnamese officers and officials (even this most minor detail was delicate, in those months when everyone knew the war was ending but everyone pretended that it was not, and Jack Lovett handled such purchases himself, with cash and the mention of overseas associates); the whole skein of threads necessary to transfer the phantom business predicated on the perpetuation of the assistance effort. That there is money to be made in time of war is something we all understand abstractly. Fewer of us understand war itself as a specifically commercial enterprise, but Jack Lovett did, not abstractly but viscerally, and his overriding concern during the months before Inez Victor reentered the field of his direct vision (she had always been there in his peripheral vision, a fitful shadow, the image that came forward when he was alone in a hotel room or at 35,000 feet) had been to insure the covert survival of certain business interests. On the morning Jack Lovett watched Inez arrive at the Honolulu airport, for example, he also watched the arrival and clearance from Saigon and immediate transshipment to Geneva via Vancouver of a certain amount of gold bullion, crated and palleted as "household effects." When he later mentioned this gold bullion to Inez he described it as "a favor I did someone." Jack Lovett did many people many favors during the spring of 1975, and many people did Jack Lovett favors in return.

As a reader you are ahead of the narrative here.

As a reader you already know that Inez Victor and Jack

Lovett left Honolulu together that spring. One reason you know it is because I said so, early on. Had I not said so you would have known it anyway: you would have guessed it, most readers being rather quicker than most narratives, or perhaps you would even have remembered it, from the stories that appeared in the newspapers and on television when Jack Lovett's operation was falling apart.

You might even have seen the film clip I mentioned.

Inez Victor dancing on the St. Regis Roof.

Nonetheless.

I could still do Inez Victor's four remaining days in Honolulu step by step, could proceed from the living room of the house on Manoa Road into the dining room and tell you exactly what happened that first night in Honolulu when Inez and Billy Dillon and Dick Ziegler and Dwight and Ruthie Christian finally sat down to dinner.

I could give you Jack Lovett walking unannounced into the dining room, through the French doors that opened onto the swimming pool.

I could give you Inez looking up and seeing him there.

"Goddamn photographers camped on the front lawn," Dwight Christian would say. "Jack. You know Inez. You know Janet's husband. Dick. You know Billy here?"

"We were both in Jakarta a few years back." Jack Lovett would be speaking to Dwight Christian but looking at Inez. "Inez was there. Inez was in Jakarta with Janet."

"Inez was also in Jakarta with her husband." Billy Dillon's voice would be pleasant. "And her two children."

"The reason the vultures are on the lawn is this," Dwight Christian would say. "Janet's not cutting it."

"Don't talk about Janet 'not cutting it,'" Dick Ziegler would say. "Don't sit there eating chicken pot pie and talk about Janet 'not cutting it.'"

"A change of subject," Dwight Christian would say. "For Dick. While I finish my chicken pot pie. Jack. What would you say if I told you Chriscorp was bidding a complete overhaul at Cam Ranh Bay?"

"I'd say Chriscorp must be bidding it for Ho Chi Minh." Jack Lovett would still look only at Inez. "How are you."

Inez would say nothing, her eyes on Jack Lovett.

"Do you want to go somewhere," Jack Lovett would say, his voice low and perfectly level.

A silence would fall over the table.

Inez would pick up her fork and immediately lay it down.

"Millie has dessert," Ruthie Christian would say, faintly.

"Inez," Billy Dillon would say.

Jack Lovett would look away from Inez and at Billy Dillon. "Here it is," he would say in the same low level voice. "I don't have time to play it out."

Well, there you are.

I could definitely do that.

I know the conventions and how to observe them, how to fill in the canvas I have already stretched; know how to tell you what he said and she said and know above all, since the heart of narrative is a certain calculated ellipsis, a tacit contract between writer and reader to surprise and be surprised, how not to tell you what you do not yet want to know. I appreciate the role played by specificity in this kind of narrative: not just the chicken pot pie and not just the weather either (I happen to like weather, but weather is easy), not just the way the clouds massed on the Koolau Range the next morning and not just the clatter of the palms in the afternoon trades behind Janet's house (anyone can do palms in the afternoon trades) when Inez went to get the dress in which Janet was buried.

I mean more than weather.

I mean specificity of character, of milieu, of the apparently insignificant detail.

The fact that when Harry and Adlai Victor arrived in Honolulu on the morning of March 28, Good Friday morning, the morning Janet's body was delivered to the coroner for autopsy, they were traveling on the Warner Communications G-2. The frequent occasions over the long Easter weekend before Janet's funeral on which Adlai found opportunity to mention the Warner Communications G-2. The delicacy of reasoning behind the decision that Harry and Adlai, but not Inez, should call on Wendell Omura's widow. The bickering over the arrangements for Janet's funeral (Dick Ziegler did after all want the Lord as Janet's shepherd, if only because Dwight Christian did not), and the way in which Ruthie Christian treated the interval between Janet's death and Janet's funeral as a particularly bracing exercise in quartermastering. The little flare-up when Inez advised Dick Ziegler that he could not delegate to Ruthie the task of calling Chris and Timmy at school to tell them their mother was dead.

"Frankly, Inez, when it comes to handling kids, I don't consider you the last word," Dick Ziegler said. "Considering Jessie."

"Never mind Jessie," Inez said. "Make the call."

The little difficulty Saturday morning when Chris and Timmy flew in from school and the airport dogs picked up marijuana in one of their duffels. The exact text of the letter Paul Christian drafted to the *Advertiser* about the "outrage" of not being allowed to attend Janet's funeral. The exact location of the arcade in Waianae where Jack Lovett took Inez to meet the radar specialist who was said to have seen Jessie.

Jessie.

Jessie is the crazy eight in this narrative.

I plan to address Jessie presently, but I wanted to issue this warning first: like Jack Lovett and (as it turned out) Inez Victor, I no longer have time for the playing out.

Call that a travel advisory.

A narrative alert.

12

THE FIRST electroencephalogram to show the entirely flat line indicating that Janet had lost all measurable brain activity was completed shortly before six o'clock on Wednesday evening, March 26, not long after Inez and Billy Dillon arrived at the house on Manoa Road. This electroencephalogram was read by the chief neurologist on Janet's case at roughly the time Inez and Billy Dillon and Dick Ziegler and Dwight and Ruthie Christian sat down to the chicken pot pie. The neurologist notified the homicide detectives that the first flat reading had been obtained, called the house on Manoa Road in an effort to reach Dick Ziegler, got a busy signal, and left the hospital, leaving an order with the resident on duty in the unit to keep trying Dick Ziegler. Ten minutes later a felony knifing came up from emergency and the resident overlooked the order to call Dick Ziegler.

This poses one of those questions that have to do only with perceived motive: would it have significantly affected what happened had the call come from the hospital before Inez got up from the dinner table and walked through the living room and out the front door with Jack Lovett? I think not, but a call from the hospital could at least have been construed as the "reason" Inez left the table.

A reason other than Jack Lovett.

A reason they could all pretend to accept.

As it was they could pretend only that Inez was overwrought. Ruthie Christian was the first to locate this note. "She's just overwrought," Ruthie Christian said, and Billy Dillon picked it up: "Overwrought," he repeated. "Absolutely. Naturally. She's overwrought."

As it was Inez just left.

"You could probably take off the lei," Jack Lovett said when they were sitting in his car outside the house on Manoa Road. Most of the reporters on the lawn seemed to have gone. There had been a single cameraman left on the steps when Inez and Jack Lovett came out of the house and he had perfunctorily run some film and then retreated. Jack Lovett had twice turned the ignition on and twice turned it off.

Inez took the crushed lei from around her neck and dropped it on the seat between them.

"I don't know where I thought we'd go," Jack Lovett said. "Frankly."

Inez looked at Jack Lovett and then she began to laugh.

"Hell, Inez. How was I to know you'd come?"

"You've had twenty years. To think where we'd go."

"Well sure. Stop laughing. I used to think I could always take you to Saigon. Drink citron pressé and watch the tennis. Scratch that. You want to go to the hospital?"

"Pretend we did go to Saigon. Pretend we did it all. Imagine it. It's all in the mind anyway."

"Not entirely," Jack Lovett said.

Inez looked at him, then away. The cameraman on the steps lit a cigarette and immediately flicked it across the lawn. He picked up his minicam and started toward the car. Inez picked up the lei and dropped it again. "Are we going to the hospital or not," she said finally.

Which was how Inez Victor and Jack Lovett happened to walk together into the third-floor intensive care unit at Queen's Medical Center when, as the older of the two homicide detectives put it, Janet's clock was already running.

"But I don't quite understand this," Inez kept saying to the resident and the two homicide detectives. The homicide detectives were at the hospital only to get a statement from one of the nurses and they wanted no part of Inez's interrogation of the resident. "You got a flat reading at six o'clock. Isn't that what you said?"

"Correct."

"And you need three. Eight hours apart. Isn't that what you told me? This afternoon? About technical death?"

"Also correct." The resident's face was flushed with irritation. "At least eight hours apart."

"Then why are you telling me you scheduled the second electroencephalogram for nine tomorrow morning?"

"At *least* eight hours apart. At least."

"Never mind 'at least.' You could do it at two this morning."

"That wouldn't be normal procedure."

Inez looked at the homicide detectives.

The homicide detectives looked away.

Inez looked at Jack Lovett.

Jack Lovett shrugged.

"Do it at two," Inez said. "Or she goes someplace where they will do it at two."

"Move the patient, you could confuse the cause of death." The resident looked at the detectives for corroboration. "Cloud it. Legally."

"I don't give a fuck about the cause of death," Inez said.

There was a silence.

"I'd say do it at two," the older of the two homicide detectives said.

"I notice you're still getting what you want," Jack Lovett said to Inez.

They did it at two and again at ten in the morning and each time it was flat but the chief neurologist, after consultation with the homicide detectives and the hospital lawyers, said that a fourth flat reading would make everyone more comfortable. A fourth flat reading would guarantee that removal of support could not be argued as cause of death. A fourth flat reading would be something everyone could live with.

"Everybody except Janet," Inez said, but she said it only to Jack Lovett.

Eight hours later they did it again and again it was flat and at 7:40 P.M. on Thursday, March 27, Janet Christian Ziegler was pronounced dead. During most of the almost twenty-four hours preceding this pronouncement Inez had waited on a large sofa in an empty surgical waiting room. During much of this time Jack Lovett was with her. Of whatever Jack Lovett said to Inez during those almost twenty-four hours she could distinctly remember later only a story he told her about a woman who cooked for him in Saigon in 1970. This woman had tried, over a period of some months, to poison selected dinner guests with oleander leaves. She had minced the leaves into certain soup bowls, very fine, a chiffonade of hemotoxins. Although none of these guests died at least two, a Reuters correspondent and an AID analyst, fell ill, but the cook was not suspected until her son-in-law, who believed himself cuckolded by the woman's daughter, came to Jack Lovett with the story.

"What was the point," Inez said.

"Whose point?"

"The cook's." Inez was drinking a bottle of beer that Jack Lovett had brought to the hospital. "What was the cook's motive?"

"Her motive." Jack Lovett seemed not interested in this part of the story. "Turned out she was just deluded. A strictly personal deal. Disappointing, actually. At first I thought I was onto something."

Inez had finished the beer and studied Jack Lovett's face. She considered asking him what he had thought he was onto but decided against it. After this little incident with the cook he had given up on housekeeping, he said. After this little incident with the cook he had gone back to staying at the Duc. Whenever he had to be in Saigon.

"You liked it there," Inez said. The beer had relaxed her and she was beginning to fall asleep, holding Jack Lovett's hand. "You loved it. Didn't you."

"Some days were better than others, I guess." Jack Lovett let go of Inez's hand and laid his jacket over her bare legs. "Oh sure," he said then. "It was kind of the place to be."

Occasionally during that night and day Dick Ziegler came to the hospital, but on the whole he seemed relieved to leave the details of the watch to Inez. "Janet doesn't even know we're here," Dick Ziegler said each time he came to the hospital.

"I'm not here for Janet," Inez said finally, but Dick Ziegler ignored her.

"Doesn't even know we're here," he repeated.

Quite often during that night and day Billy Dillon came to the hospital. "Naturally you're overwrought," Billy Dillon said each time he came to the hospital. "Which is why I'm not taking this seriously. Ask me what I think about what Inez is doing, I'd say no comment. She's overwrought."

"Listen," Billy Dillon said the last time he came to the hospital. "We're picking up incoming on the King Crab flank. Harry takes the Warner's plane to Seattle to pick up Jessie for the funeral, Jessie informs Harry she doesn't go to funerals."

Inez had looked at Billy Dillon.

"Well?" Billy Dillon said.

"Well what?"

"What should I tell Harry?"

"Tell him he should have advanced it better," Inez Victor said.

13

I SHOULD tell you something about Jessie Victor that very few people understood. Harry Victor for example never understood it. Inez understood it only dimly. Here it is: Jessie never thought of herself as a problem. She never considered her use of heroin an act of rebellion, or a way of life, or even a bad habit of particular remark; she considered it a consumer decision. Jessie Victor used heroin simply because she preferred heroin to coffee, aspirin, and cigarettes, as well as to movies, records, cosmetics, clothes, and lunch. She had been subjected repeatedly to the usual tests, and each battery showed her to be anxious, highly motivated, more intelligent than Adlai, and not given to falsification. Perhaps because she lacked the bent for falsification she did not have a notable sense of humor. What she did have was a certain incandescent inscrutability, a kind of luminous gravity, and it was always startling to hear her dismiss someone, in that grave low voice that thrilled Inez as sharply when Jessie was eighteen as it had when Jessie was two, as "an asshole." "You asshole" was what Jessie called Adlai, the night he and Harry Victor arrived in Seattle to pick her up for Janet's funeral and Jessie declined to go. Jessie did agree to have dinner with them, while the Warner Communications G-2 was being refueled, but dinner had gone badly.

"The crux of it is finding a way to transfer anti-war sentiment to a multiple-issue program," Adlai had said at dinner. He was telling Harry Victor about an article he proposed to write for the op-ed page of the New York *Times*. "It's something we've been tossing back and forth in Cambridge."

"Interesting," Harry Victor said. "Let me vet it. What do you think, Jess?"

"I think he shouldn't say 'Cambridge,'" Jessie said.

"Possibly you were nodding out when I went up there," Adlai said, "but Cambridge happens to be where I go to school."

"Maybe so," Jessie said, "but you don't happen to go to Harvard."

"OK, guys. You both fouled." Harry Victor turned to Adlai. "I could sound somebody out at the *Times.* If you're serious."

"I'm serious. It's time. Bring my generation into the dialogue, if you see my point."

"You asshole," Jessie said.

"Well," Harry Victor said after Adlai had left the table. "How are things otherwise?"

"I'm ready to leave."

"You said you weren't going. You have a principle. You don't go to funerals. This is a new principle on me, but never mind, you made your case. I accept it. As a principle."

"I don't mean leave for Janet's funeral. I mean actually leave. Period. This place. Seattle."

"You haven't finished the program."

"The program," Jessie said, "is for assholes."

"Just a minute," Harry said.

"I did the detox, I'm clean, I don't see the point."

"What do you mean you did the detox, the game plan here wasn't detox, it was methadone."

"I don't like methadone."

"Why not?"

"Because," Jessie had said patiently, "it doesn't make me feel good."

"It makes you feel bad?"

"It doesn't make me feel bad, no." Jessie had given this question her full attention. "It just doesn't make me feel good."

There had been a silence.

"What is it you want to do exactly?" Harry had said then.

"I want—" Jessie was studying a piece of bread that she seemed to have rolled into a ball. "To get on with my regular life. Make some headway, you know?"

"That's fine. Good news. Admirable."

"Get into my career."

"Which is what exactly?"

Jessie was breaking the ball of bread into little pellets.

"Don't misread me, Jessie. This is all admirable. My only point is that you need a program." Harry Victor found himself warming to the idea of the projected program. "A plan. Two plans, actually. Which dovetail. A long-range plan and a short-term plan. What's your long-range plan?"

"I'm not running for Congress," Jessie said. "If that's what you mean."

There seemed to Harry so plaintive a note in this that he let it go. "Well then. All right. How about your immediate plan?"

Jessie picked up another piece of bread.

Something in Harry Victor snapped. He had been trying for the past hour to avoid any contemplation of why Inez had walked out of Dwight Christian's house the night before with Jack Lovett. Billy Dillon had told him. "You have to think she's overwrought," Billy Dillon had said. "I have to think she's got loony timing," Harry Victor had said. Early on in this dinner he had tried out the overwrought angle on Jessie and Adlai. "I wouldn't be surprised if your mother were a little overwrought," he had said. Adlai had put down the menu and said that he wanted a shrimp cocktail and the New York stripper, medium bloody, sour cream and chives on the spud. Jessie had put down the menu and stared at him, he imagined fishily, from under the straw tennis visor she had worn to dinner.

Jessie had stared at him fishily from under her tennis visor and Adlai had wanted the New York stripper medium bloody and Inez had walked out of Dwight Christian's house with Jack Lovett and now Jessie was tearing her bread into little chickenshit pellets.

"Could you do me a favor? Jessie? Could you either eat the bread or leave it alone?"

Jessie had put her hands in her lap.

"I'm still kind of working on the immediate plan part," she said after a while. "Actually."

In fact Jessie Victor did have an immediate plan that Thursday evening in Seattle, the same plan she had mentioned in its less immediate form to Inez at Christmas, the plan Inez had selectively neglected to mention when she described her visit with Jessie to Harry and Adlai: the plan, if the convergence of yearning and rumor and isolation on which Jessie was operating in Seattle could be called a plan, to get a job in Vietnam.

Inez had not mentioned this plan to Harry because she did not believe it within the range of the possible.

Jessie did not mention this plan to Harry because she did not believe it to be the kind of plan that Harry would understand.

I see Jessie's point of view here. Harry would have talked specifics. Harry would have asked Jessie if she had read a newspaper lately. Harry would not have understood that specifics made no difference to Jessie. Getting a job in Vietnam seemed to Jessie a first step that had actually presented itself, a chance to put herself at last in opportunity's way, and because she believed that whatever went on there was only politics and that politics was for assholes she would have remained undeflected, that March night in 1975, the same night as it happened that the American evacuation of Da Nang deteriorated into uncontrolled rioting, by anything she might have heard or seen or read in a newspaper.

If in fact Jessie ever read a newspaper.

Which seemed to both Inez and Harry Victor a doubtful proposition.

When word reached them in Honolulu on the following Sunday night, Easter Sunday night 1975, the night before Janet's funeral, that three hours after the Warner Communications G-2 left Seattle, bringing Harry and Adlai Victor down to Honolulu, Jessie had walked out of the clinic that specialized in the treatment of adolescent chemical dependency and talked her way onto a C-5A transport that landed seventeen-and-one-half hours later (refueling twice in flight) at Tan Son Nhut, Saigon. "Maybe she heard she could score there," Adlai said, and Inez slapped him.

14

SHE DID it with no passport (her passport was in her otherwise empty stash box in the apartment on Central Park West) and a joke press card that somebody from *Life* had made up for her during the 1972 campaign. This press card had failed to get Jessie Victor at age fifteen into the backstage area at Nassau Coliseum during a Pink Floyd concert but it got her at age eighteen onto the C-5A to Saigon. This seems astonishing now, but we forget how confused and febrile those few weeks in 1975 actually were, the "reassessments" and the "calculated gambles" and the infusions of supplemental aid giving way even as they were reported to the lurid phantasmagoria of air lifts and marines on the roof and stranded personnel and tarmacs littered with shoes and broken toys. In the immediate glamour of the revealed crisis many things happened that could not have happened a few months earlier or a few weeks later, and what happened to Jessie Victor was one of them. Clearly an American girl who landed at Tan Son Nhut should have been detained there, but Jessie Victor was not. Clearly an American girl who landed at Tan Son Nhut with no passport should not have been stamped through immigration on the basis of a New York driver's license, but Jessie Victor was. Clearly an American girl with no passport, a New York driver's license and a straw tennis visor should not have been able to walk out of the littered makeshift terminal at Tan Son Nhut and, observed by several people who did nothing to stop her, get on a bus to Cholon, but Jessie Victor had done just that. Or so it appeared.

By the time Jack Lovett arrived at the house on Manoa Road that Easter Sunday night with the story about the American girl who appeared to be Jessie, the blond American girl who had left a New York driver's license at Tan Son Nhut in lieu of a visa, Inez and Harry Victor were speaking to each other only in the presence of other people.

They had been civil at the required meals but avoided the optional.

They had slept in the same room but not the same bed.

"You're overwrought," Harry had said on Friday night. "You're under a strain."

"Actually I'm not in the least overwrought," Inez had said. "I'm sad. Sad is different from overwrought."

"Why not just have another drink," Harry had said. "For a change."

By Saturday morning the argument was smoldering one more time on the remote steppes of the 1972 campaign. By Saturday evening it had jumped the break and was burning uncontained. "Do you know what I particularly couldn't stand," Inez had said. "I particularly couldn't stand it at Miami when you said you were the voice of a generation that had taken fire on the battlefields of Vietnam and Chicago."

"I'm amazed you were sober enough to notice. At Miami."

"I'd drop that theme if I were you. I think you've gotten about all the mileage you're going to get out of that."

"Out of what?"

"Harry Victor's Burden. I was sober enough to notice you didn't start speaking for this generation until after the second caucus. You were only the voice of a generation that had taken fire on the battlefields of Vietnam and Chicago after you knew you didn't have the numbers. In addition to which. Moreover. Actually that was never your generation. Actually you were older."

There had been a silence.

"Let me take a leap forward here," Harry had said. "Speaking of 'older.'"

Inez had waited.

"I don't think you chose a particularly appropriate way to observe your sister's death. Maybe I'm wrong."

Inez had looked out the window for a long time before she spoke. "Add it up, you and I didn't have such a bad time," she said finally. "Net."

"I'm supposed to notice the past tense. Is that it?"

Inez did not turn from the window. It was dark. She had lived in the north so long that she always forgot how fast the light went. She had gone late that afternoon to pick up the dress in which Dick Ziegler wanted Janet buried and the light had gone while she was still on Janet's beach. "You pick a dress," Dick Ziegler had said. "You go. I can't look in her closet."

After Inez found a dress she had sat on Janet's bed and called Jack Lovett on Janet's antique telephone. Jack Lovett had told her to wait on Janet's beach. "Listen," Inez had said when she saw him. "That pink dress she wore in Jakarta is in her closet. She has fourteen pink dresses. I counted them. Fourteen." She had been talking through tears. "Fourteen pink dresses all hanging next to each other. Didn't anybody ever tell her? She didn't look good in pink?" There on the beach with Jack Lovett in the last light of the day Inez had cried for the first time that week, but back in the house on Manoa Road with Harry she had felt herself sealed off again, her damage control mechanism still intact.

"I think I deserve a little better than a change of tense," Harry said.

"Don't dramatize," Inez said.

Or she did not.

She had either said "Don't dramatize" to Harry that Saturday evening or she had said "I love him" to Harry that Saturday evening. It seemed more likely that she had said "Don't dramatize" but she had wanted to say "I love him" and she did not remember which. She did remember that the actual words "Jack Lovett" remained unsaid by either of them until Sunday night.

"Your friend Lovett's downstairs," Harry had said then.

"Jack," Inez said, but Harry had left the room.

Jack Lovett repeated the details of the story about the American girl at Tan Son Nhut twice, once for Inez and Harry and Billy Dillon and again when Dwight Christian and Adlai came in. The details sounded even less probable in the second telling. The C-5A, the press card. The tennis visor. The bus to Cholon.

"I see," Harry kept saying. "Yes."

Jack Lovett had first heard Jessie's name that Sunday morning from one of the people to whom he regularly talked on the flight line at Tan Son Nhut. It had taken five further calls and the rest of the day to locate the New York driver's license that had been left at immigration in lieu of a visa.

"I see," Harry said. "Yes. Then you haven't actually seen this license."

"How could I have seen the license, Harry? The license is in Saigon."

Inez watched Jack Lovett unfold an envelope covered with scratched notes. Lovett. Jack. Your friend Lovett.

"Jessica Christian Victor?" Jack Lovett was squinting at his notes. "Born February 23, 1957?"

Harry did not look at Inez.

"Hair blond, eyes gray? Height five-four? Weight one-hundred-ten?" Jack Lovett folded the envelope and put it in his coat pocket. "The address was yours."

"But you didn't write it down."

Jack Lovett looked at Harry. "Because I knew it, Harry. 135 Central Park West."

There was a silence.

"Her weight was up when she got her license," Inez said finally. "She only weighs a hundred and three."

"The fact that somebody had Jessie's license doesn't necessarily mean it was Jessie," Harry said.

"Not necessarily," Jack Lovett said. "No."

"I mean Jesus Christ," Harry said. "Every kid in the country's got a tennis visor."

"What about a tennis visor?" Inez said.

"She was wearing one," Adlai said. "At dinner. In Seattle."

"Never mind the fucking tennis visor." Harry picked up the telephone. "You got the Seattle number, Billy?"

Billy Dillon took a small flat leather notebook from his pocket and opened it.

"I have it," Inez said.

"So does Billy." Harry drummed his fingers on the table as Billy Dillon dialed. "This is Harry Victor," he said after a moment. "I'd like to speak to Jessie."

Inez looked at Jack Lovett.

Jack Lovett was studying his envelope again.

"I see," Harry said. "Yes. Of course."

"Shit," Billy Dillon said.

"There's a kid who flew in this morning from Tan Son Nhut," Jack Lovett said. "A radar specialist who's been working Air America Operations."

"Her aunt, yes," Harry said. "No, I have it. Thank you."

He replaced the receiver. He still did not look at Inez. "Your move," he said after a while.

"This kid is supposed to have seen her," Jack Lovett said.

"Did he or didn't he?" Harry said.

"I don't know, Harry." Jack Lovett's voice was even. "I haven't talked to him yet."

"Then it's not relevant," Harry said.

"She only weighs a hundred and three," Inez repeated.

"That's the second time you've said that," Harry said. "It's about as relevant as this radar specialist of Lovett's. It doesn't mean anything."

"I'll tell you what it means," Dwight Christian said. "It means she'll fit right in."

Harry stared at Dwight Christian, then looked at Billy Dillon.

"Welcome to hard times, pal," Billy Dillon said. "Try mentioning Sea Meadow."

"In fact she'll outweigh nine-tenths of them," Dwight Christian said. "Nine-tenths of the citizenry of Saigon."

"I knew you could dress that up." Billy Dillon looked at Harry. "You want to make a pass through State? Usual channels?"

"Usual channels, Mickey Mouse," Dwight Christian said. "Call the White House. Get them to light a fire under the embassy. Lay on some pressure. Demand her release."

"Her release from what?" Harry said.

"From the citizenry of Saigon," Billy Dillon said. "Follow the ball."

There was a silence.

"I may not phrase things as elegantly as you two, but I do know what I want." Dwight Christian's voice had turned hard and measured. "I want her out of there. Harry?"

"It's not quite that simple, Dwight."

"Not if you're from Washington," Dwight Christian said. "I suppose not. Since I'm not from Washington, I don't quite see what the problem is."

"Dwight," Inez said. "The problem—"

"I had a foreman taken hostage on the Iguassú Falls project, I didn't phrase things so elegantly there, either, not being from Washington, but I goddamn well got him out."

"—The problem, Dwight, is that nobody took Jessie hostage."

Dwight Christian looked at Inez.

"She just went," Inez said.

"I know that, sweetheart." The hardness had gone out of Dwight Christian's voice. "I just want somebody to tell me why."

Which was when Adlai said maybe she heard she could score there.

Which was when Inez slapped Adlai.

Which was when Harry said keep your hands off my son.

But Dad, Adlai kept saying in the silence that followed. But Dad. Mom.

Aloha oe.

Billy Dillon once asked me if I thought Inez would have left that night had Jack Lovett not been there. Since human behavior seems to me essentially circumstantial I have not much feeling for this kind of question. The answer of course is no, but the answer is irrelevant, because Jack Lovett was there.

Jack Lovett was one of the circumstances that night.

Jack Lovett was there and Jessie was in Saigon, another of the circumstances that night.

Jessie was in Saigon and the radar specialist who was said to have seen her was to meet Jack Lovett at the Playboy Arcade in Waianae. This radar specialist who had or had not seen Jessie was meeting Jack Lovett in Waianae and an electrician who had worked on the installation of the research reactor at Dalat was meeting Jack Lovett in Wahiawa.

The research reactor at Dalat was a circumstance that night only in that it happened to be a card Jack Lovett was dealing that spring.

Jack Lovett did not see any immediate way to get the fuel out but he wanted to know, for future calculation, how much of this fuel was being left, in what condition, and for whom.

The research reactor at Dalat was a thread Jack Lovett had not yet tied in his attempt to transfer the phantom business predicated on the perpetuation of the assistance effort, which was why, on that Easter Sunday night in 1975, he took Inez first to meet the radar specialist at the Playboy Arcade in Waianae and then across Kolekole Pass to meet the electrician at the Happy Talk Lounge in Wahiawa.

The off-limits Happy Talk in Wahiawa.

The Happy Talk in Wahiawa across the bridge from Schofield Barracks.

Where Inez stood with her back against the jukebox and her arms around Jack Lovett.

Where The Mamas and the Papas sang "Dream a Little Dream of Me."

The radar specialist had been on the nod.

"I don't need the hassle," the radar specialist had said.

The electrician had already left the Happy Talk but had left a note with the bartender.

Da Nang going, that dude at Dalat definitely a wipe-out, the note read.

On the screen above the bar there were the helicopters. There were the helicopters lifting off the roof of the American mission and there were the helicopters vanishing into the fireball above the ammo dump and there were the helicopters ditching in the oil slick off the *Pioneer Contender*.

"Fucking Arvin finally shooting each other," the bartender said.

"Oh shit, Inez," Jack Lovett said. "Harry Victor's wife."

"Listen," Inez said. "It's too late for the correct thing. Forget the correct thing."

Which is how Jack Lovett and Inez Victor happened that Easter Sunday night in 1975 to take the Singapore Airlines flight that leaves Honolulu at 3:45 A.M. and at 9:40 A.M. one day later lands at Kai Tak, Hong Kong.

Recently when I took this flight I thought of Inez, who described it as an eleven-hour dawn.

Inez said she never closed her eyes.

Inez said she could still feel the cold of the window against her cheek.

Inez said the 3:45 A.M. flight from Honolulu to Hong Kong was exactly the way she hoped dying would be.

Dawn all the way.

Something to see, as Jack Lovett had said at the Happy Talk about another dawn in another year. Something to behold.

It occurs to me that Inez Victor's behavior the night she flew to Hong Kong may not have been so circumstantial after all.

She had to have a passport with her, didn't she?

What does that suggest?

You tell me.

THREE

I

THE DAY Jack Lovett flew down to Saigon the rain began in Hong Kong. The rain muddied the streets, stiffened the one pair of shoes Inez had with her, broke the blossoms from the bauhinia tree on the balcony of the apartment in which Jack Lovett had told her to wait and obscured the view of the Happy Valley track from the bedroom window. The rain reminded her of Honolulu. The rain and the obscured horizon and the breaking of the blossoms and the persistent smell of mildew in the small apartment all reminded her of Honolulu but it was colder in Hong Kong. She was always cold. Every morning after Jack Lovett left Inez would wake early in the slight chill and put on the galoshes and macintosh she had found in the otherwise empty closet and set out to walk. She developed a route. She would walk down Queen's Road and over behind the Anglican cathedral and up Garden Road to the American consulate, where she would sit in the reception room and read newspapers.

Quite often in the reception room of the American consulate on Garden Road Inez read about Harry Victor's relatives. In the *South China Morning Post* she read that Harry Victor's wife had not been present at the funeral of Harry Victor's sister-in-law, a private service in Honolulu after which Senator Victor declined to speak to reporters. In the Asian edition of the *International Herald-Tribune* she read that Harry Victor's father-in-law had required treatment at the Honolulu City and County Jail for superficial wounds inflicted during an apparent suicide attempt with a Bic razor. In the international editions of both *Time* and *Newsweek* she read that Harry Victor's daughter was ironically or mysteriously missing in Vietnam.

"Ironically" was the word used by *Time*, and "mysteriously" by *Newsweek*. Both *Time* and *Newsweek* used "missing," as did the *South China Morning Post*, the Asian editions of both the *Wall Street Journal* and the *International Herald-Tribune*, the *Straits Times*, and the pouched copies of the New York *Times* and the Washington *Post* that arrived at the consulate three days after publication. "Missing" did not seem to Inez to quite cover it. The pilots of downed fighters were said to be "missing," and correspondents last seen in ambush situations. "Missing" suggested some line of duty that did not quite encompass getting on a C-5A transport in Seattle and flying to Saigon to look for a job. Possibly that was the ironic part, or even the mysterious.

By the time Inez finished reading the papers it would be close to noon, and she would walk from the consulate on up Garden Road to what seemed to be a Chinese nursery school, with a terrace roofed in corrugated plastic under which the children played. She would stand in the rain and watch the children until, at the ping of a little bell, they formed a line and marched inside, and then she would take a taxi back to the apartment and hang the macintosh on the shower door to dry and set the galoshes behind the door. She had no idea to whom the galoshes and macintosh belonged. She had no idea to whom the apartment belonged.

"Somebody in Vientiane," Jack Lovett had said when she asked.

She presumed it was a woman because the galoshes and macintosh were small. She presumed the woman was an American because the only object in the medicine cabinet, a plastic bottle of aspirin tablets, was the house brand of a drugstore she knew to be in New York. She presumed that the American woman was a reporter because there was a standard Smith-Corona typewriter and a copy of *Modern English Usage* on the kitchen table, and a paperback copy of *Homage to Catalonia* in the drawer of the bed table. In Inez's experience all reporters had paperback copies of *Homage to Catalonia*, and kept them in the same place where they kept the matches and the candle and the notebook, for when the hotel was bombed. When she asked Jack Lovett if the person in Vientiane to whom the apartment belonged was in fact an American woman reporter he had shrugged.

"It doesn't matter," he said. "It's fine."

After that when Inez read the newspapers in the reception room of the American consulate she made a point of noticing the byline on any story originating in Vientiane, looking for a woman's name, but never found one.

The telephone in this apartment never rang. Jack Lovett got

his messages in Hong Kong at a small hotel off Connaught Road, and it was this number that Inez had given Adlai when she reached him in Honolulu the day she arrived. Because Harry had hung up mid-sentence when she called him from Wahiawa to say she was going to Hong Kong she made this call person-to-person to Adlai, but Harry had come on the line first.

"I happen to know you're in Hong Kong," Harry had said.

"Of course you happen to know I'm in Hong Kong," Inez had said. "I told you I was going."

"Will you speak to this party," the operator had kept saying. "Is this your party?"

"You hung up," Inez had said.

"No," Harry had said. "This is not her party."

"This doesn't have anything to do with you," Inez had said when Adlai finally picked up. "I just wanted to make sure you knew that."

"Dad told me." Adlai had made this sound slightly prosecutorial. "What does it have to do with?"

"Just not with you."

"What am I supposed to tell Dad?"

Inez had considered this. "Tell him hello," she said finally.

That had been Tuesday in Hong Kong and Monday in Honolulu.

It had been Wednesday the second of April in Hong Kong when Jack Lovett flew down to Saigon to look for Jessie.

Twice during that first week, the week of the rain, he had come back up to Hong Kong unexpectedly, once on an Air America transport with eighty-three third-country nationals who had been identified with American interests and once on a chartered Pan American 707 with the officers and cash reserves of the Saigon branches of the Bank of America, the First National City Bank, and the Chase Manhattan. The first time he came up it had been for only a few hours, which he spent placing calls from the telephone in the apartment, but the second time he had spent the night, and they had driven out to the Repulse Bay and taken a room overlooking the sea. They had ordered dinner in the room and slept and woke and slept again and whenever they were awake Jack Lovett had talked. He had seemed to regard the room at the Repulse Bay as neutral ground on which he could talk as he had not talked in the apartment that belonged to somebody in Vientiane. He talked all night. He talked to Inez but as if to himself. Certain words and phrases kept recurring.

Fixed-wing phase.

Tiger Ops.

Black flights.

Extraction.

Assets.

AID was without assets.

USIA was without assets.

By assets Jack Lovett had seemed to mean aircraft, aircraft and money. The Defense Attaché Office had assets. It was increasingly imperative to develop your own assets because without private assets no one could guarantee extraction. No one could guarantee extraction because they were living in a dream world down there. Amateur hour down there. Pencil pushers down there.

Each time Jack Lovett said "down there" he would glance toward the windows that opened on the water, as if "down there" were visible, nine hundred miles of South China Sea telescoped by the pressure of his obsession. Toward dawn he was talking about the lists they were making down there. They had finally decided to make a count of priority evacuees in case extraction was necessary.

In case.

Inez should note "in case."

"In case" was proof the inmates were running the bin.

Because the various agencies had been unable to agree on the count each agency was drawing up its own list. Some people said the lists would add up to a hundred-fifty-thousand priority evacuees, others said ten times that number. Nobody seemed in any rush to make it definite. They were talking about evacuating twenty years of American contacts, not to mention their own fat American asses, but they were still talking as if they had another twenty years to do it. Twenty years and the applause of the local population. An inter-agency task force had been appointed. To shake this down. The task force had met for dinner at the residence, met for goddamn dinner at the goddamn residence, add a little more lard to those asses, and by the time the cigars were passed they did not yet know whether they had a hundred-fifty-thousand priority evacuees or ten times that number but they did know what they needed.

They needed a wall map.

They needed a wall map of what they kept calling Metro Saigon.

This wall map had been requisitioned.

Through General Services.

They were getting their wall map any day now, and what they would do when they got it was this: they would make a population density plot. In other words they would plot, with little colored pins, the locations of a few types of people they might want to invite to the final extraction.

In case.

Strictly in case.

"Types" of people, right.

A little green pin for every holder of an embassy ration card.

A little yellow pin for every holder of a DAO liquor ration card.

A little red pin for every current member of the Cercle Sportif. Note "current." Behind on the dues, forget it.

The little white pins were the real stroke. Follow this. There was going to be an analysis of all taxi dispatch records for the period between the first of January and the first of April. Then there would be a little white pin placed on the map showing every location in Metro Saigon to which a taxi had been dispatched. Too bad for the guys who drove their own cars. Around Metro Saigon. Taken a cab, they'd be on the map. This map was going to be a genuine work of art. Anybody down there had any feeling for posterity, they'd get this map out and put it under glass at the State Department.

Pins intact.

Memento mori Metro Saigon.

By the time he stopped talking the room was light.

Inez sat on the edge of the bed and began brushing her hair.

"So what do you think," Jack Lovett said.

"I don't know."

Through the half-closed shutters Inez could see the early light on the water. It occurred to her for the first time that this was the same sea she had looked on with Jessie, the day there had been no baby cobras in the borrowed garden and Harry had been at the situation briefing in Saigon. Now there was about to be no more situation and Jessie was in Saigon and Jack Lovett was going back down to Saigon but Jack Lovett might not find her before it happened.

Nobody even knew what "it" was.

That was what he was telling her.

She brushed her hair harder. "I don't know how an evacuation is run."

"Not this way."

"She's not on anybody's list, is she." Inez found that she could not say Jessie's name. "She's not on the map."

Jack Lovett got up and opened the shutters wide. For a while the rain had stopped but now it was falling hard again, falling through the patchy sunlight, glistening on the palms outside the window and flooding the broken fountain in front of the hotel.

"Not unless she happened to join the Cercle Sportif," Jack Lovett said. "No." He closed the shutters again and turned back toward Inez. "Put down the hairbrush and look at me," he said. "Do you think I'd leave her there?"

"You might not find her."

"I always found you," Jack Lovett said. "I guess I can find your daughter."

2

In fact Jack Lovett did find Inez Victor's daughter.

In fact Jack Lovett found Inez Victor's daughter that very day, found her by what he called dumb luck, just got on the regular Air Vietnam flight from Hong Kong to Saigon and landed at Tan Son Nhut and half an hour later he was looking at Jessie Victor.

Jack Lovett called this dumb luck but you or I might not have had the same dumb luck.

You or I for example might not have struck up the connection with the helicopter maintenance instructor who happened to be one of the other two passengers on the Air Vietnam 707 to Saigon that day.

Jack Lovett did.

Jack Lovett struck up a connection with this helicopter maintenance instructor the same way he had struck up connections with all those embassy drivers and oil riggers and airline stewardesses and assistant professors of English literature traveling on Fulbright fellowships and tropical agronomists traveling under the auspices of the Rockefeller Foundation and desk clerks and ticket agents and salesmen of rice converters and coco dryers and Dutch pesticides and German pharmaceuticals.

By reflex.

The helicopter maintenance instructor who happened to be one of the two other passengers on the Air Vietnam 707 that day had last been in Saigon in 1973, when his contract was terminated. He had been in Los Angeles working for Hughes but now he was coming back to look for the wife and little girl he had left in 1973. The wife had been with her family in Pleiku and he had gotten a call from her saying that the little girl had been blinded on a C-130 during the evacuation south when a leaking hydraulic line overhead sprayed liquid into her face. The wife said Saigon was still safe but he thought it was time to come find her. He had the address she had given him but according to a buddy he had contacted this address did not check out. The helicopter maintenance instructor had seemed cheerful at the beginning of the flight but after two Seagram Sevens his mood had darkened.

What had she done to get on the C-130 in the first place?

Didn't everybody else walk out of Pleiku?

What about the fucking address?

Jack Lovett had offered him a ride into Saigon and the helicopter maintenance instructor had wanted to make one stop, to check the address with a bartender he used to know at the Legion club.

Which was where Jack Lovett found Jessie Victor.

Serving drinks and French fries at the American Legion club on the main road between Tan Son Nhut and Saigon.

Still wearing her tennis visor.

An *ao dai* and her tennis visor.

"Hey, no sweat, I'm staying," Jessie had said to Jack Lovett when he told her to sign off her shift and get in the car. "This dude who comes in has a friend at the embassy, he'll get the word when they pull the plug."

Jessie had insisted she was staying but Jack Lovett had said a few words to the bartender.

The words Jack Lovett said were Harry goddamn Victor's daughter.

"You know this plug you were talking about," Jack Lovett said then to Jessie. "I just pulled it."

3

"YOU'RE LOOKING for a guy in the woodwork, the Legion club is where you'd look," Jack Lovett said when he finally got through to Inez in Hong Kong. "Christ almighty. The Legion club. I covered Mimi's, I don't know how I missed the Legion club."

He was calling from the Duc.

He had left Jessie for the night at the apartment of a woman he referred to only as "B.J.," an intelligence analyst at the Defense Attaché Office.

B.J. would put Jessie up until he could get her out.

B.J. would take fine care of Jessie.

B.J. was even that night sounding out the air lift supervisor at Tiger Ops about the possibility of placing Jessie on a flight to Travis as an orphan escort. These orphans all had escorts, sure they did, that was the trick, the trick was to melt out as many nonessentials as possible without calling it an evacuation. They might or might not be orphans, these orphans, but they sure as hell had escorts. The whole goddamn DAO was trying to melt out with the orphans.

Which was what they didn't know at the Legion club.

Which was where you looked if you were looking for a guy in the woodwork.

"About these flights to Travis," Inez said.

"Looking, hell, look no further." Jack Lovett could not seem to get over the obviousness of finding Jessie at the Legion club. "This is it. This is the woodwork. American Legion Post No. 34. Through These Portals Pass America's Proudest Fighting Men, it says over the door to the can. Through those portals pass every AWOL and contract cowboy in Southeast Asia. Guys who came over with the Air Cav in '66. Guys who evacuated China in '49. Dudes. Dudes who think they've got a friend at the embassy."

"That was an orphan flight to Travis that crashed," Inez said. The connection was going and she had trouble hearing him. "Last week."

"There are other options," Jack Lovett said.

"Other options to crashing?"

"Other flights, Inez. Other kinds of flights. She's fine with B.J., there's no immediate problem. I'll check it out. I'll get her on a good flight."

Inez said nothing.

"Inez," Jack Lovett said. "This kid of yours is one of the world's great survivors. I take her kicking and screaming to B.J.'s, half an hour later they're splitting a bucket of Kentucky fried and comparing eye makeup. The lights go off, Jessie tells B.J. she knows where they could liberate a Signal Corps generator. 'Liberate' is what she says. She got here any earlier, she'd be running the rackets."

Inez said nothing. The connection was now crossed with another call, and she could hear laughter, and sharp bursts of Cantonese.

"She's as tough as you are," Jack Lovett said.

"That never stopped any plane from crashing," Inez said just before the line went to dial tone.

After Inez hung up she tried to call Harry at the apartment on Central Park West. Harry's private line rang busy and when she tried one of the other numbers Billy Dillon answered.

"This is pretty funny," Billy Dillon said when she told him about Jessie. "This is actually funny as hell."

"What's actually funny about it?"

"I don't know, Inez. You don't find it funny we're sending bar girls to Saigon, I can't help you. Hey. Inez. Do us all a favor? Tell Harry yourself?"

Inez had told Harry herself.

"I see," Harry said. "Yes."

There had been a silence.

"So," Inez said. "There it is."

"Serving drinks. Yes. I'll get hold of Adlai at school."

"What's he doing at school?"

"What do you mean, 'what's he doing at school'? You think Adlai should be serving drinks too?"

"I mean I thought he was doing this internship with you. I thought he didn't have to be back until May."

"He wanted to organize something," Harry said. "But that's not the point."

"Organize what?"

"Some kind of event."

"What kind of event?"

Harry had hesitated. "A vigil for the liberation of Saigon," he said finally.

Inez had said nothing.

"He's eighteen years old, Inez." Harry had sounded defensive. "He wanted to make a statement."

"I didn't say anything."

"Very eloquent. Your silence."

Inez said nothing.

"Jessie's tramping around Saigon, you're off with your war-lover, Adlai tries to make a statement and you've got nothing to say."

"I'm going to pretend you didn't say that."

"Fine then," Harry said. "Pretend what you want."

All that night Inez lay awake in the apartment that belonged to somebody in Vientiane and listened to the short-wave radio that Jack Lovett had left there. On the short-wave radio she could get Saigon and Bangkok. Jack Lovett had told her what to listen for. Jack Lovett had also told her that it was too soon to hear what he had told her to listen for but she listened anyway, whenever she could not sleep or wanted to hear a human voice.

"Mother wants you to call home," the American Service Radio announcer in Saigon would say when it was time for the final phase of the evacuation, and then a certain record would be played.

The record to be played was Bing Crosby singing "I'm Dreaming of a White Christmas."

"I could do better than that," Inez had said when Jack Lovett told her what to listen for. "I mean in the middle of April. Out of the blue in the middle of April. I could do considerably better than 'Mother wants you to call home' and 'I'm Dreaming of a White Christmas.'"

"What's your point," Jack Lovett said.

"It's not just the best secret signal I ever heard about."

"It's not going to be just the best evacuation you ever heard about either," Jack Lovett had said. "You want to get down to fine strokes."

Toward four in the morning Inez got up from the bed and

sat by the window and smoked a cigarette in the dark. The window was open and rain splashed on the balcony outside. Because it was still too soon to hear the American Service Radio announcer in Saigon say "Mother wants you to call home" Inez moved the dial back and forth and finally got what seemed to be a BBC correspondent interviewing former officials of the government of the Republic of Vietnam who had just been flown to Nakhon Phanom in Thailand.

"No more hopes from the American side," one of them said.

"The Americans would not come back again," another said. "*En un mot* bye-bye."

Their voices were pleasant and formal.

The transmission faded in and out.

As she listened to the rain and to the voices fading in and out from Nakhon Phanom Inez thought about Harry in New York and Adlai at school and Jessie at B.J.'s and it occurred to her that for the first time in almost twenty years she was not particularly interested in any of them.

Responsible for them in a limited way, yes, but not interested in them.

They were definitely connected to her but she could no longer grasp her own or their uniqueness, her own or their difference, genius, special claim. What difference did it make in the long run what she thought, or Harry thought, or Jessie or Adlai did? What difference did it make in the long run whether any one person got the word, called home, dreamed of a white Christmas? The world that night was full of people flying from place to place and fading in and out and there was no reason why she or Harry or Jessie or Adlai, or for that matter Jack Lovett or B.J. or the woman in Vientiane on whose balcony the rain now fell, should be exempted from the general movement.

Just because they believed they had a home to call.

Just because they were Americans.

No.

En un mot bye-bye.

FOUR

I

I SEE now that the state of rather eerie serenity in which I found Inez Victor in Kuala Lumpur had its genesis eight months before, during this period in Hong Kong when it came to her attention that her passport did not excuse her from what she characterized to me as "the long view." By "the long view" I believe she meant history, or more exactly the particular undertow of having and not having, the convulsions of a world largely unaffected by the individual efforts of anyone in it, that Inez's experience had tended to deny. She had spent her childhood immersed in the local conviction that the comfortable entrepreneurial life of an American colony in a tropic without rot represented a record of individual triumphs over a hostile environment. She had spent her adult life immersed in Harry Victor's conviction that he could be president.

This period in Hong Kong during which Inez ceased to claim the American exemption was defined by no special revelation, no instant of epiphany, no dramatic event. She had arrived in Hong Kong on the first day of April and she left it on the first day of May. During those four or five weeks mention of Janet and of Wendell Omura and of Janet's lanai gradually dropped out of even the Honolulu *Advertiser*, discarded copies of which Inez occasionally found in the lobbies of hotels frequented by flight crews.

Paul Christian was found incompetent to stand trial.

Adlai's vigil for the liberation of Saigon was edited into a vigil for "peace in Asia" and commended by the governor of Massachusetts as an instance of responsible campus expression, another situation managed by Billy Dillon.

The combat-loaded C-141 onto which Jack Lovett finally shoved Jessie (literally shoved, put his hands on her shoulders and pushed her through the hatch, because somewhere between Gate One and the loading ramp at Tan Son Nhut that evening Jessie realized that the flight Jack Lovett had told her they were meeting was her own, and tried to bolt) landed without incident at Agana, Guam, as did the commercial 747 on which Jessie sulked from Agana to Los Angeles.

Harry Victor met Jessie in customs.

He and Jessie had dinner at Chasen's.

Inez knew that Harry and Jessie had dinner at Chasen's because they called her in Hong Kong from their table, the front banquette inside the door. Jessie said that Jack Lovett had tricked her into going with him to Tan Son Nhut by saying that after he met this one flight they would go see the John Wayne movie playing at the Eden. Jessie said that she had not wanted to see the John Wayne movie in the first place but B.J. had gone back to the DAO after dinner which left nothing to do but see the John Wayne movie or sit there alone getting schitzy.

Jessie said that when she saw what was going down she asked Jack Lovett why she had to go on this flight and Jack Lovett had been rude.

Because I just shelled out a million piastres so you could, the fucker had said, and pushed her.

Hard.

She still had a bruise on her arm.

Forty-eight hours later.

"Tell the fucker I owe him a million piastres," Harry said when he came on the phone.

According to Inez Jessie landed in Los Angeles on the fifteenth of April.

According to Inez it was the twenty-eighth when she found she could no longer call Saigon; the twenty-ninth when American Service Radio in Saigon played "I'm Dreaming of a White Christmas" twice, played "The Stars and Stripes Forever" more times than Inez had counted, and stopped transmitting; and the first of May when Jack Lovett called her from Subic Bay and told her to meet him in Manila.

At one point I tried to work out a chronology for what Inez remembered of this period, and made the chart that still hangs on my office wall. The accuracy of this chart is problematic, not only because Inez kept no record of events as they happened but also because of the date line.

For example I have no idea whether Inez meant that the day Jessie landed in Los Angeles was the fifteenth in Los Angeles or the fifteenth in Hong Kong.

In either case the fifteenth seems doubtful, because Jack Lovett had been with Jessie in Saigon forty-eight hours before, promising her a John Wayne movie and bruising her arm, and many people believe Jack Lovett to have been in Phnom Penh for a period of some days (more than one day but fewer than five) between the time the American embassy closed there on the twelfth and the time the Khmer Rouge entered the city on the seventeenth. The report placing Jack Lovett in Phnom Penh after the embassy closed was one of the things that caused the speculation later, and eventually the investigation.

2

WHEN NOVELISTS speak of the unpredictability of human behavior they usually mean not unpredictability at all but a higher predictability, a more complex pattern discernible only after the fact. Examine the picture. Find the beast in the jungle, the figure in the carpet.

Context clues.

The reason why.

I have been examining this picture for some years now and still lack the reason why Inez Victor finally agreed to talk about what she "believed" had happened ("I believe we were in Jakarta," Inez would say, or "let's say it was May," as if even the most straightforward details of place and date were intrinsically unknowable, open to various readings) during the spring and summer of 1975.

At first she did not agree.

At first I talked to Billy Dillon and to Harry Victor and to Dwight Christian and even briefly to Jessie and to Adlai and to Dick Ziegler, each of whom, as I have suggested, had at least a limited stake in his or her own version of events, but Inez remained inaccessible. In the first place the very fact of where she and Jack Lovett seemed to be ruled out any pretense of casual access. I could call Dwight Christian and say that I just happened to be in Honolulu, but I could not call Inez and say that I just happened to be in Kuala Lumpur. No one "happens to be" in Kuala Lumpur, no one "passes through" en route somewhere else: Kuala Lumpur is en route nowhere, and for me to see Inez there implied premeditation, a definite purpose on my part and a definite decision on hers.

In the second place Inez seemed, that summer and fall after she left Honolulu with Jack Lovett, emotionally inaccessible. She seemed to have renounced whatever stake in the story she might have had, and erected the baffle of her achieved serenity between herself and what had happened. *It's the summer monsoon and quite sticky, you don't want to visit during the monsoon really but I'm sure Harry and Billy between them can sort out what you need to know. Excuse haste. Regards, Inez V.*

This was the response, scrawled on a postcard showing the lobby of the Hotel Equatorial in Kuala Lumpur, to the letter I wrote from Honolulu in July of 1975 asking Inez if she would see me. Since the "summer monsoon" in Kuala Lumpur is followed immediately by the "winter monsoon," which in turn lasts until the onset of the next "summer monsoon," Inez's response was even less equivocal than it might seem. In October, from Los Angeles, I wrote a second letter, and more or less promptly received a second postcard, again showing the lobby of the Hotel Equatorial, where incidentally Inez was not staying: *What you mention is all in the past and frankly I'd rather look ahead. In other words a visit would be unproductive. I.*

This card was postmarked the second of November and arrived in Los Angeles the fifteenth. Ten days later I received a third communication from Inez, a clipping of a book review, in which my name was mentioned in passing, from a month-old *International Herald-Tribune.* The note stapled to the clipping read *Sorry if my note seemed abrupt but you see my point I'm sure, Inez.* It was one week after that when Inez called my house in Los Angeles, having gone to some lengths to get the number, and asked me to come to Kuala Lumpur.

Actually she did not exactly "ask" me to come to Kuala Lumpur.

"When are you coming to K.L.," was what she said exactly.

I considered this.

"I wouldn't want to miss you," she said. "I could show you around."

At the time I thought that she had decided to talk to me only because Jack Lovett's name was just beginning to leak out of the various investigations into arms and currency and technology dealings on the part of certain former or perhaps even current overt and covert agents of the United States government. There had even been hints about narcotics dealings, which, although they made good copy and were played large in the early coverage (I recall the phrase "Golden Triangle" in many headlines, and a photograph of two blurred figures leaving a house on Victoria Peak, one identified as a "sometime Lovett business associate" and the other as a "known Hong Kong Triad opium lord"), remained just that, hints, rumors that would never be substantiated, but the other allegations were solid enough, and not actually surprising to anyone who had bothered to think about what Jack Lovett was doing in that part of the world.

There had been the affiliations with interlocking transport and air courier companies devoid of real assets. There had been the directorship of the bank in Vila that put the peculiarities of condominium government to such creative use. There had been all the special assignments and the special consultancies and the special relationships in a fluid world where the collection of information was indistinguishable from the use of information and where national and private interests (the interests of state and non-state actors, Jack Lovett would have said) did not collide but merged into a single pool of exchanged favors.

In order to understand what Jack Lovett did it was necessary only to understand how natural it was for him to do it, how at once entirely absorbing and supremely easy. There had always been that talent for putting the right people together, the right man at the Department of Defense, say, with the right man at Livermore or Los Alamos or Brookhaven, or, a more specific example with a more immediately calculable payout, the Director of Base Development for CINC-PAC/MACV with Dwight Christian.

There had always been something else as well.

There had been that emotional solitude, a detachment that extended to questions of national or political loyalty.

It would be inaccurate to call Jack Lovett disloyal, although I suppose some people did at the time.

It would be accurate only to say that he regarded the country on whose passport he traveled as an abstraction, a state actor, one of several to be factored into any given play.

In other words.

What Jack Lovett did was never black or white, and in the long run may even have been (since the principal gain to him was another abstraction, the pyramiding of further information) devoid of ethical content altogether, but since shades of gray tended not to reproduce in the newspapers the story was not looking good on a breaking basis. That Jack Lovett had reportedly made some elusive deals with the failed third force (or fourth force, or fifth force, this was a story on which the bottom kept dropping out) in Phnom Penh in those days after the embassy closed there did not look good. That the London dealer who was selling American arms abandoned in South Vietnam had received delivery from one of Jack Lovett's cargo services did not look good. It seemed clear to me that the connection with Inez would surface quite soon (as it did, the week I came back from Kuala Lumpur, when the WNBC tape of Inez dancing with Harry Victor on the St. Regis Roof temporarily obliterated my actual memory of Inez), and I assumed that Inez wanted to see me only because Jack Lovett wanted to see me. I assumed that Jack Lovett would find during my visit a way of putting out his own information. I assumed that Inez was acting for him.

In short I thought I was going to Kuala Lumpur as part of a defensive strategy that Inez might or might not understand.

This was, it turned out, too easy a reading of Inez Victor.

3

ONE THING she wanted to tell me was that Jack Lovett was dead.

That Jack Lovett had died on the nineteenth of August at approximately eleven o'clock in the evening in the shallow end of the fifty-meter swimming pool at the Hotel Borobudur in Jakarta.

After swimming his usual thirty laps.

That she had taken Jack Lovett's body to Honolulu and buried it on the twenty-first of August in the little graveyard at Schofield Barracks. Past where they buried the stillborn dependents. Beyond the Italian prisoners of war. Near a jacaranda tree, but the jacaranda had been out of bloom. When the jacaranda came into bloom and dropped its petals on the grass the pool of blue would just reach Jack Lovett's headstone. The grave was that close to the jacaranda. The colonel who had been her contact at Schofield had at first suggested another site but he had understood her objection. The colonel who had been her contact at Schofield had been extremely helpful.

Extremely cooperative.

Extremely kind really.

As had her original contact.

Mr. Soebadio. In Jakarta. Mr. Soebadio was the representative for Java of the bank in Vila and it turned out to be his telephone number that Jack Lovett had given her to call if any problem arose during the four or five days they were to be in Jakarta.

Jack Lovett had not given her Mr. Soebadio's name.

Only this telephone number.

To call. In case she was ill, or needed to reach him during the day, or he was in Solo or Surabaya and the rioting flared up again. In fact she had been thinking about this telephone number at the precise instant when she looked up and saw that Jack Lovett was lying face down in the very shallow end of the pool, the long stretch where the water was less than a foot deep and the little children with the Texas accents played all day.

It had been quite sudden.

She had watched him swimming toward the shallow end of the pool.

She had reached down to get him a towel.

She had thought at the exact moment of reaching for the towel about the telephone number he had given her, and wondered who would answer if she called it.

And then she had looked up.

There had been no one else at the pool that late. The last players had left the tennis courts, and the night lights had been turned off. Even the pool bar was shuttered, but there was a telephone on the outside wall, and it was from this telephone, twenty minutes later, that Inez called the number Jack Lovett had given her. She had sat on the edge of the pool with Jack Lovett's head in her lap until the Tamil doctor arrived. The Tamil doctor said that the twenty minutes she had spent giving Jack Lovett CPR had been beside the point. The Tamil doctor said that what happened had been instantaneous, circulatory, final. In the blood, he said, and simultaneously snapped his fingers and drew them across his throat, a short chop.

It was Mr. Soebadio who had brought the Tamil doctor to the pool.

It was Mr. Soebadio who worked Jack Lovett's arms into his seersucker jacket and carried him to the service area where his car was parked.

It was Mr. Soebadio who advised Inez to tell anyone who approached the car that Mr. Lovett was drunk and it was Mr. Soebadio who went back upstairs for her passport and it was Mr. Soebadio who suggested that certain possible difficulties in getting Mr. Lovett out of Indonesia could be circumvented by obtaining a small aircraft, what he called a good aircraft for clearance, which he happened to know how to do. He happened to know that there was a good aircraft for clearance on its way from Denpasar to Halim. He happened to know that the pilot, a good friend, would be willing to take Mrs. Victor and Mr. Lovett wherever Mrs. Victor wanted to go.

Within the limits imposed by the aircraft's range of course.

The aircraft being a seven-passenger Lear.

Halim to Manila, no problem.

Manila to Guam, no problem.

Honolulu, a definite problem, but with permission to refuel

on certain atolls unavailable to commercial aircraft Mr. Soebadio believed that he could solve it.

Say Kwajalein.

Say Johnston.

Guam to Kwajalein, thirteen hundred miles approximately, well within range.

Kwajalein to Johnston, say eighteen hundred, adjust for drag since the prevailing winds were westward, still within range.

Johnston to Honolulu, seven hundred seventeen precisely and no problem whatsoever.

Mr. Soebadio had a pocket calculator and he stood on the tarmac at Halim working out the ratios for weight and lift and ground distance and wind velocity while Inez watched the Tamil doctor and the pilot lift Jack Lovett onto the back passenger seats in the Lear and get him into a body bag. Before he zipped the body bag closed the Tamil doctor went through the pockets of Jack Lovett's seersucker jacket and handed the few cards he found to Mr. Soebadio. Mr. Soebadio glanced at the cards and dropped them into his own pocket, still intent on his calculator. Inez considered asking Mr. Soebadio for whatever had been in Jack Lovett's pockets but decided against it. Somebody dies, you'd just as soon he didn't have your card in his pocket, Jack Lovett had told her once. The zipper on the body bag caught on the lapel of the seersucker jacket and Mr. Soebadio helped the Tamil doctor work it loose. Another thing Inez decided not to ask Mr. Soebadio was where the body bag had come from.

The cotton dress she was wearing was soaked with pool water and cool against her skin.

She smelled the chlorine all night long.

At Manila she did not get out of the Lear.

At Guam she was half asleep but aware of the descent and the landing strobes and the American voices of the ground crew. The pilot checked into the operations room and brought back containers of coffee and a newspaper. WHERE AMERICA'S DAY BEGINS, the newspaper had worked into the eagle on its flag.

At Kwajalein she could see the missile emplacements from the air and was told on the ground that she did not have clearance to get out of the plane.

At Johnston she did get out, and walked by herself to the end of the long empty runway, where the asphalt met the lagoon. Jack Lovett had spent three weeks on Johnston. 1952. Waiting on the weather. Wonder Woman Two was the name of the shot. She remembered that. She even remembered him telling her he had been in Manila, and the souvenir he brought. A Filipino blouse. Starched white lace. The first summer she was married to Harry she had found it in a drawer and worn it at Rehoboth. The starched white lace against her bare skin had aroused both of them and later Harry had asked why she never wore the blouse again.

Souvenir of Manila.

Bought on Johnston from a reconnaissance pilot who had flown in from Clark.

She knew now.

She took off her sandals and waded into the lagoon and splashed the warm water on her face and soaked her bandana and then turned around and walked back to the Lear. While the pilot was talking to the mechanics about a minor circuit he believed to be malfunctioning Inez opened the body bag. She had intended to place the wet bandana in Jack Lovett's hands but when she saw that rigor had set in she closed the body bag again. She left the bandana inside. Souvenir of Johnston. It occurred to her that Johnston would have been the right place to bury him but no one on Johnston had been told about the body on the Lear and the arrangement had already been made between Mr. Soebadio and the colonel at Schofield and so she went on, and did it at Schofield.

Which was fine.

Johnston would have been the right place but Schofield was fine.

Once she got the other site.

The site near the jacaranda.

The first site the colonel had suggested had been too near the hedge. The hedge that concealed the graves of the executed soldiers. There were seven of them. To indicate that they died in disgrace they were buried facing away from the flag, behind the hedge. She happened to know about the hedge because Jack Lovett had shown it to her, not long after they met. In fact they had argued about it. She had thought it cruel and unusual to brand the dead. Forever and ever. He had thought that it was not cruel and unusual at all, that it was merely pointless. That it was sentimental to think it mattered which side of the hedge they buried you on.

She remembered exactly what he had said.

The sun still rises and you still don't see it, he had said.

Nevertheless.

All things being equal she did not want him buried anywhere near the hedge and the colonel had seen her point right away.

So it had worked out.

It had all been fine.

She had taken a commercial flight to Singapore that night and changed directly for Kuala Lumpur.

She had called no one.

We were sitting after dinner on the porch of the bungalow Inez was renting in Kuala Lumpur when she told me this. It was my first day there. All afternoon at the clinic she had talked about Harry Victor and the Alliance for Democratic Institutions, and when I asked at dinner where Jack Lovett was she had said only that he was not in Kuala Lumpur. After dinner we had sat on the porch without speaking for a while and then she had begun, abruptly.

"Something happened in August," she had said.

Somewhere between Guam and Kwajalein she had asked if I wanted tea, and had brought it out to the porch in a chipped teapot painted with a cartoon that suggested the bungalow's period: a cigar-smoking bulldog flanked by two rosebuds, one labeled "Lillibet" and the other "Margaret Rose." Inez was barefoot. Her hair was pulled back and she was wearing no makeup. There had been during the course of her account a sudden hard fall of rain, temporarily walling the porch with glassy sheets of water, and now after the rain termites swarmed around the light and dropped in our teacups, but Inez made no more note of the termites than she had of the rain or for that matter of the teapot. After she stopped talking we sat in silence a moment and then Inez poured me another cup of tea and flicked the termites from its surface with her fingernail. "What do you think about this," she said.

I said nothing.

Inez was watching me closely.

I thought about this precisely what Inez must have thought about this, but it was irrelevant. I thought there had been papers shredded all over the Pacific the night she was flying Jack Lovett's body from Jakarta to Schofield, but it was irrelevant. We were sitting in a swamp forest on the edge of Asia in a city that had barely existed a century before and existed now only as the flotsam of some territorial imperative and a woman who had once thought of living in the White House was flicking termites from her teacup and telling me about landing on a series of coral atolls in a seven-passenger plane with a man in a body bag.

An American in a body bag.

An American who, it was being said, had been doing business in situations where there were not supposed to be any Americans.

What did I think about this.

Finally I shrugged.

Inez watched me a moment longer, then shrugged herself.

"Anyway we were together," she said. "We were together all our lives. If you count thinking about it."

Inside the bungalow the telephone was ringing.

Inez made no move to answer it.

Instead she stood up and leaned on the wooden porch railing and looked out into the wet tangle of liana and casuarina that surrounded the bungalow. Through the growth I could see occasional headlight beams from the cars on Ampang Road. If I stood I could see the lights of the Hilton on the hill. The telephone had stopped ringing before Inez spoke again.

"Not that it matters," she said then. "I mean the sun still rises and he still won't see it. That was Harry calling."

4

JACK LOVETT had caught lobsters in the lagoon off Johnston in 1952. Inez had soaked her bandana in the lagoon off Johnston in 1975. Jessie and Adlai had played Marco Polo in the fifty-meter pool at the Borobudur in Jakarta in 1969. Jack Lovett had died in the fifty-meter pool at the Borobudur in Jakarta in 1975. In 1952 Inez and Jack Lovett had walked in the graveyard at Schofield Barracks. He had shown her the graves of the stillborn dependents, the Italian prisoners of war. He had shown her the hedge and the graves that faced away from the flag. The stillborn dependents and the Italian prisoners of war and the executed soldiers had all been there in 1952. Even the jacaranda would have been there in 1952.

During the five days I spent in Kuala Lumpur Inez mentioned such "correspondences," her word, a number of times, as if they were messages intended specifically for her, evidence of a narrative she had not suspected. She seemed to find these tenuous connections extraordinary. Given a life in which the major cost was memory I suppose they were.

By the time I got back to Los Angeles a congressional subpoena had been issued for Jack Lovett and the clip of Inez dancing on the St. Regis Roof had made its first network appearance. I have no idea why this particular clip was the single most repeated image of a life as exhaustively documented as Inez Victor's, but it was, and over those few days in January of 1976 this tape took on a life quite independent of the rather unexceptional moment it recorded, sometimes running for only a second or two, cut so short that it might have been only a still photograph; other times presenting itself as an extended playlet, reaching a dramatic curtain as the aide said "Hold two elevators" and Harry Victor said "I'm just a private citizen" and Inez said "Marvelous" and the band played "Isn't It Romantic."

I suppose one reason the tape was played again and again was simply that it remained the most recent film available on Inez Victor.

I suspect another reason was that the hat with the red cherries and "Just a private citizen" and "Marvelous" and "Isn't It Romantic" offered an irony accessible to even the most literal viewer.

Three weeks later a Washington *Post* reporter happened to discover in the Pentagon bureau of records that the reason Jack Lovett had not answered his congressional subpoena was that he had been dead since August, buried in fact on government property, and that the signature on the government forms authorizing his burial on government property was Inez Victor's.

That night the tape ran twice more, and then not again.

At any rate not again that I knew about, not even when NBC located Inez Victor at the refugee administration office in Kuala Lumpur and Inez Victor declined to be interviewed.

In March of 1976 Billy Dillon showed me the thirteen-word reply he got to a letter he had written Inez. He had resorted to writing the letter because calling Inez had been, he said, unsatisfactory.

"Raise anything substantive on the telephone," Billy Dillon said when he showed me Inez's reply, "Mother Teresa out there says she's wanted in the clinic. So I write. I give her the news, a little gossip, a long thought or two, I slip in one question. One. I ask if she can give me one fucking reason she's in goddamn K.L., and this is what I get. Thirteen words."

He handed me the sheet of lined paper on which, in Inez's characteristic scrawl, the thirteen words appeared: "*Colors, moisture, heat, enough blue in the air. Four fucking reasons. Love, Inez.*"

Colors, moisture, heat.

Enough blue in the air.

I told you the essence of that early on but not the context, which has been, you will note, the way I tried to stay on the wire in this novel of fitful glimpses. It has not been the novel I set out to write, nor am I exactly the person who set out to write it. Nor have I experienced the rush of narrative inevitability that usually propels a novel toward its end, the momentum that sets in as events overtake their shadows and the cards all fall in on one another and the options decrease to zero.

Perhaps because nothing in this situation encourages the basic narrative assumption, which is that the past is prologue to the present, the options remain open here.

Anything could happen.

As you may or may not know Billy Dillon has a new candidate, a congressman out of NASA who believes that his age and training put him on the right side of what he calls "the idea lag," and occasionally when Billy Dillon is in California to raise money I have dinner with him. In some ways I have replaced Inez as the woman Billy Dillon imagines he wishes he had married. Again as you may or may not know Harry Victor is in Brussels, special envoy to the Common Market. Adlai and Jessie are both well, Adlai in San Francisco, where he clerks for a federal judge on the Ninth Circuit; Jessie in Mexico City, where she is, curiously enough, writing a novel, and living with a *Newsweek* stringer who is trying to log in enough time in various troubled capitals to come back to New York and go on staff. When and if he does I suspect that Jessie will not come up with him, since her weakness is for troubled capitals. *Imagine my mother dancing*, I had hoped that Jessie's novel would begin, but according to a recent letter I had from her this particular novel is an historical romance about Maximilian and Carlota.

Inez of course is still in Kuala Lumpur.

She writes once a week to Jessie, somewhat less often to Adlai, and scarcely at all now to Harry. She sends an occasional postcard to Billy Dillon, and the odd clipping to me. One evening a week she teaches a course in American literature at the University of Malaysia and has dinner afterwards at the Lake Club, but most of her evenings as well as her days are spent on the administration of what are by now the dozen refugee camps around Kuala Lumpur.

A year ago when I was in London the *Guardian* ran a piece about Southeast Asian refugees, and Inez was quoted.

She said that although she still considered herself an American national (an odd locution, but there it was) she would be in Kuala Lumpur until the last refugee was dispatched.

Since Kuala Lumpur is not likely to dispatch its last refugee in Inez's or my lifetime I would guess she means to stay on, but I have been surprised before. When I read this piece in London I had a sudden sense of Inez and of the office in the camp and of how it feels to fly into that part of the world, of the dense greens and translucent blues and the shallows where islands once were, but so far I have not been back.

MIAMI

This book is for
Eduene Jerrett Didion
and
Frank Reese Didion

ONE

I

HAVANA VANITIES come to dust in Miami. On the August night in 1933 when General Gerardo Machado, then president of Cuba, flew out of Havana into exile, he took with him five revolvers, seven bags of gold, and five friends, still in their pajamas. Gerardo Machado is buried now in a marble crypt at Woodlawn Park Cemetery in Miami, Section Fourteen, the mausoleum. On the March night in 1952 when Carlos Prío Socarrás, who had helped depose Gerardo Machado in 1933 and had fifteen years later become president himself, flew out of Havana into exile, he took with him his foreign minister, his minister of the interior, his wife and his two small daughters. A photograph of the occasion shows Señora de Prío, quite beautiful, boarding the plane in what appears to be a raw silk suit, and a hat with black fishnet veiling. She wears gloves, and earrings. Her makeup is fresh. The husband and father, recently the president, wears dark glasses, and carries the younger child, María Elena, in his arms.

Carlos Prío is now buried himself at Woodlawn Park Cemetery in Miami, Section Three, not far from Gerardo Machado, in a grave marked by a six-foot marble stone on which the flag of Cuba waves in red, white and blue ceramic tile. CARLOS PRÍO SOCARRÁS 1903–1977, the stone reads, and directly below that, as if Carlos Prío Socarrás's main hedge against oblivion had been that period at the University of Havana when he was running actions against Gerardo Machado: MIEMBRO DEL DIRECTORIO ESTUDIANTIL UNIVERSITARIO 1930. Only then does the legend PRESIDENTE DE LA REPÚBLICA DE CUBA 1948–1952 appear, an anticlimax. Presidencies are short and the glamours of action long, there among the fallen frangipani and crepe myrtle blossoms at Woodlawn Park Cemetery in Miami. "They say that I was a terrible president of Cuba," Carlos Prío once said to Arthur M. Schlesinger, Jr., during a visit to the Kennedy White House some ten years into the quarter-century Miami epilogue to his four-year Havana presidency. "That may be true. But I was the best president Cuba ever had."

Many Havana epilogues have been played in Florida, and some prologues. Florida is that part of the Cuban stage where declamatory exits are made, and side deals. Florida is where the chorus waits to comment on the action, and sometimes to join it. The exiled José Martí raised money among the Cuban tobacco workers in Key West and Tampa, and in 1894 attempted to mount an invasionary expedition from north of Jacksonville. The exiled Fidel Castro Ruz came to Miami in 1955 for money to take the 26 Julio into the Sierra Maestra, and got it, from Carlos Prío. Fulgencio Batista had himself come back from Florida to take Havana away from Carlos Prío in 1952, but by 1958 Fidel Castro, with Carlos Prío's money, was taking it away from Fulgencio Batista, at which turn Carlos Prío's former prime minister tried to land a third force in Camagüey Province, the idea being to seize the moment from Fidel Castro, a notably failed undertaking encouraged by the Central Intelligence Agency and financed by Carlos Prío, at home in Miami Beach.

This is all instructive. In the continuing opera still called, even by Cubans who have now lived the largest part of their lives in this country, *el exilio*, the exile, meetings at private houses in Miami Beach are seen to have consequences. The actions of individuals are seen to affect events directly. Revolutions and counterrevolutions are framed in the private sector, and the state security apparatus exists exclusively to be enlisted by one or another private player. That this particular political style, indigenous to the Caribbean and to Central America, has now been naturalized in the United States is one reason why, on the flat coastal swamps of South Florida, where the palmettos once blew over the detritus of a dozen failed booms and the hotels were boarded up six months a year, there has evolved since the early New Year's morning in 1959 when Fulgencio Batista flew for the last time out of Havana (for this flight, to the Dominican Republic on an Aerovías Q DC-4, the women still wore the evening dresses in which they had gone to dinner) a settlement of considerable interest, not exactly an American city as American cities have until recently been understood but a tropical capital: long on rumor, short on memory, overbuilt on the chimera of runaway money and referring not to New York or Boston or Los Angeles or Atlanta but to Caracas and Mexico, to Havana and to Bogotá and to Paris and Madrid. Of American cities Miami has since 1959 connected only to Washington, which is the peculiarity of both places, and increasingly the warp.

In the passion of *el exilio* there are certain stations at which the converged, or colliding, fantasies of Miami and Washington appear in fixed relief. Resentments are recited, rosaries of broken promises. Occasions of error are recounted, imperfect understandings, instances in which the superimposition of Washington abstractions on Miami possibilities may or may not have been, in a word Washington came to prefer during the 1980s, flawed. On April 17, 1985, the twenty-fourth anniversary of the aborted invasion referred to by most Americans and even some Cubans as the Bay of Pigs, what seems in retrospect a particularly poignant progression of events was held in Miami to commemorate those losses suffered in 1961 at Playa Girón, on the southern coast of Matanzas Province, by the 2506 Brigade, the exile invasion force trained and supported—up to a point, the famous point, the midnight hour when John F. Kennedy sent down the decision to preserve deniability by withholding air cover—by the United States government.

The actual events of this 1985 anniversary were ritual, and as such differed only marginally from those of other years, say 1986, when Jeane Kirkpatrick would be present, to wave small souvenir flags, American and Cuban, and to speak of "how different the world would have been" had the brigade prevailed. By one minute past midnight on the morning of the 1985 anniversary, as in years before and after, some thirty members of the 2506, most of them men in their forties and fifties wearing camouflage fatigues and carrying AR-15 rifles, veterans of the invasion plus a few later recruits, had assembled at the Martyrs of Girón monument on Southwest Eighth Street in Miami and posted a color guard, to stand watch through the soft Florida night. A tape recording of "The Star Spangled Banner" had been played, and one of "La Bayamesa," the Cuban national anthem. *No temáis una muerte gloriosa*, the lyric of "La

Bayamesa" runs, striking the exact note of transcendent nationalism on which the occasion turned. *Do not fear a glorious death: To die for patria is to live.*

By late morning the police had cordoned off the weathered bungalow on Southwest Ninth Street which was meant to be the Casa, Museo y Biblioteca de la Brigada 2506 del Exilio Cubano, the projected repository for such splinters of the true cross as the 2506 flag presented to John F. Kennedy at the Orange Bowl, twenty months after the Bay of Pigs, when he promised to return the flag to the brigade "in a free Havana" and took it back to Washington, later expanding its symbolic content geometrically by consigning it to storage in what explicators of this parable usually refer to as a dusty basement. On the morning of the anniversary ground was being broken for the renovation of the bungalow, an occasion for Claude Pepper, fresh from the continuing debate in the House of Representatives over aid to the Nicaraguan contras, to characterize the landing at Girón as "one of the most heroic events in the history of the world" and for many of those present to voice what had become by that spring the most urgent concern of the exile community, the very concern which now lends the occasion its retrospective charge, that "the freedom fighters of the eighties" not be treated by the Reagan administration as the men of the 2506 had been treated, or believed that they had been treated, by the Kennedy administration.

Sometimes the word used to describe that treatment was "abandonment," and sometimes the word was "betrayal," but the meaning was the same, and the ardor behind the words cut across all class lines, not only that morning at the bungalow but later at the roll call at the monument and still later, at the Mass said that evening for the 2506 at the chapel on Biscayne Bay which is so situated as to face Cuba. There were men that morning in combat fatigues, but there were also men in navy-blue blazers, with the bright patch of the 2506 pinned discreetly to the pocket. There were National Rifle Association windbreakers and there were T-shirts featuring the American flag and the legend THESE COLORS DON'T RUN and there were crucifixes on bare skin and there were knife sheaths on belts slung so low that Jockey shorts showed, but there were also Brooks Brothers shirts, and rep ties, and briefcases of supple leather. There were men who would go later that day to offices in the new glass towers along Brickell Avenue, offices with Barcelona chairs and floor-to-ceiling views of the bay and the harbor and Miami Beach and Key Biscayne, and there were men whose only offices were the gun stores and the shooting ranges and the flying clubs out off Krome Avenue, where the West Dade subdivisions give way to the Everglades and only the sudden glitter of water reveals its encroaching presence and drugs get dropped and bodies dumped.

They have been construed since as political flotsam, these men of the 2506, uniformly hard cases, drifters among the more doubtful venues serviced by Southern Air Transport, but this is misleading. Some members of the 2506 had lived in Miami since before Fidel Castro entered Havana and some had arrived as recently as 1980, the year of the Mariel exodus. Some were American citizens and some never would be, but they were all Cuban first, and they proceeded equally from a kind of collective spell, an occult enchantment, from that febrile complex of resentments and revenges and idealizations and taboos which renders exile so potent an organizing principle. They shared not just Cuba as a birthplace but Cuba as a construct, the idea of birthright lost. They shared a definition of *patria* as indivisible from personal honor, and therefore of personal honor as that which had been betrayed and must be revenged. They shared, not only with one another but with virtually every other Cuban in Miami, a political matrix in which the very shape of history, its dialectic, its tendency, had traditionally presented itself as *la lucha*, the struggle.

For most of them as children there had of course been the formative story of *la lucha* against Spain, the central scenario of nineteenth-century Cuba. For some of their fathers there had been *la lucha* against Gerardo Machado and for some of them there had been *la lucha* against Fulgencio Batista and for all of them—for those who had fought originally with the 26 Julio and for those who had fought against it, for *barbudos* and *Batistianos* alike—there was now *la lucha* on the grand canvas of a quarter century, *la lucha* purified, *la lucha* in a preservative vacuum, *la lucha* not only against Fidel Castro but against his allies, and his agents, and all those who could conceivably be believed to have aided or encouraged him.

What constituted such aid or encouragement remained the great Jesuitical subject of *el exilio*, defined and redefined, distilled finally to that point at which a notably different angle obtained on certain events in the recent American past. The 1972 burglary at the Watergate headquarters of the Democratic National Committee, say, appeared from this angle as a patriotic mission, and the Cubans who were jailed for it as *mártires de la lucha*. Mariel appeared as a betrayal on the part of yet another administration, a deal with Fidel Castro, a decision by the Carter people to preserve the status quo in Cuba by siphoning off the momentum of what could have been, in the dreamtime of *el exilio*, where the betrayal which began with the Kennedy administration continued to the day at hand, a popular uprising. DOWN WITH THE KENNEDY-KHRUSHCHEV PACT was the legend, in Spanish, on one of the placards bobbing for attention in front of the minicams that day. ENOUGH TREASONS. On the back of another placard there was lettered a chant: CONTADORA / TRAIDORA / VENDA / PATRIA. That traitor who would back a political settlement in Central America, in other words, sold out his country, and so his honor.

In many ways the Bay of Pigs continued to offer Miami an ideal narrative, one in which the men of the 2506 were forever the valiant and betrayed and the United States was forever the seducer and betrayer and the blood of *los mártires* remained forever fresh. When the names of the 114 brigade members who died in Cuba were read off that day at the Playa Girón monument, the survivors had called out the responses in unison, the rhythm building, clenched fists thrust toward the sky: *Presente*, 114 times. The women, in silk dresses and high-heeled sandals, dabbed at their eyes behind dark glasses. "*Es triste*," one woman murmured, again and again, to no one in particular.

La tristeza de Miami. "We must attempt to strengthen the non-Batista democratic anti-Castro forces in exile," a Kennedy campaign statement had declared in 1960, and Miami had for a time believed John F. Kennedy a communicant in its faith. "We cannot have the United States walk away from one of the greatest moral challenges in postwar history," Ronald Reagan had declared two nights before this 1985 anniversary of the Bay of Pigs, at a Nicaraguan Refugee Fund benefit dinner in

Washington, and Miami once again believed an American president a communicant in its faith. Even the paper thimbles of sweet Cuban coffee distributed after the 2506 Mass that April evening in Miami, on the steps of the chapel which faces Cuba and has over its altar a sequined Virgin, a Virgin dressed for her *quince*, had the aspect of a secular communion, the body and blood of *patria*, *machismo*, *la lucha*, sentimental trinity. That *la lucha* had become, during the years since the Bay of Pigs, a matter of assassinations and bombings on the streets of American cities, of plots and counterplots and covert dealings involving American citizens and American institutions, of attitudes and actions which had shadowed the abrupt termination of two American presidencies and would eventually shadow the immobilization of a third, was a peculiarity left, that one evening, officially unexplored.

TWO

2

"THE GENERAL wildness, the eternal labyrinths of waters and marshes, interlocked and apparently never ending; the whole surrounded by interminable swamps. . . . Here I am then in the Floridas, thought I," John James Audubon wrote to the editor of *The Monthly American Journal of Geology and Natural Science* during the course of an 1831 foray in the territory then still called the Floridas. The place came first, and to touch down there is to begin to understand why at least six administrations now have found South Florida so fecund a colony. I never passed through security for a flight to Miami without experiencing a certain weightlessness, the heightened wariness of having left the developed world for a more fluid atmosphere, one in which the native distrust of extreme possibilities that tended to ground the temperate United States in an obeisance to democratic institutions seemed rooted, if at all, only shallowly. At the gate for such flights the preferred language was already Spanish. Delays were explained by weather in Panama. The very names of the scheduled destinations suggested a world in which many evangelical inclinations had historically been accommodated, many yearnings toward empire indulged. The Eastern 5:59 P.M. from New York/Kennedy to Miami and Panama and Santiago and Buenos Aires carried in its magazine racks, along with the usual pristine copies of *Golf* and *Ebony* and *U.S. News & World Report*, a monthly called *South: The Third World Magazine*, edited in London and tending to brisk backgrounders on coup rumors and capital flight.

In Miami itself this kind of news was considerably less peripheral than it might have seemed farther north, since to set foot in South Florida was already to be in a place where coup rumors and capital flight were precisely what put money on the street, and also what took it off. The charts on the wall in a Coral Gables investment office gave the time in Panama, San Salvador, Asunción. A chain of local gun shops advertised, as a "Father's Day Sale," the semiautomatic Intratec TEC-9, with extra ammo clip, case, and flash suppressor, reduced from $347.80 to $249.95 and available on layaway. I recall picking up the *Miami Herald* one morning in July of 1985 to read that the Howard Johnson's hotel near the Miami airport had been offering "guerrilla discounts," rooms at seventeen dollars a day under what an employee, when pressed by the *Herald* reporter, described as "a freedom fighters program" that was "supposed to be under wraps."

As in other parts of the world where the citizens shop for guerrilla discounts and bargains in semiautomatic weapons, there was in Miami an advanced interest in personal security. The security installations in certain residential neighborhoods could have been transplanted intact from Bogotá or San Salvador, and even modest householders had detailed information about perimeter defenses, areas of containment, motion monitors and closed-circuit television surveillance. Decorative grilles on doors and windows turned out to have a defensive intent. Break-ins were referred to by the Metro-Dade Police Department as "home invasions," a locution which tended to suggest a city under systematic siege. A firm specializing in security for the home and automobile offered to install bulletproof windows tested to withstand a 7.62mm NATO round of ammunition, for example one fired by an M60. A ten-page pamphlet found, along with $119,500 in small bills, in the Turnberry Isle apartment of an accused cocaine importer gave these tips for maintaining a secure profile: "Try to imitate an American in all his habits. Mow the lawn, wash the car, etc. . . . Have an occasional barbecue, inviting trusted relatives." The wary citizen could on other occasions, the pamphlet advised, "appear as the butler of the house. To any question, he can answer: the owners are traveling."

This assumption of extralegal needs dominated the advertisements for more expensive residential properties. The Previews brochure for a house on Star Island, built originally as the Miami Beach Yacht Club and converted to residential use in the 1920s by Hetty Green's son, emphasized, in the headline, not the house's twenty-one rooms, not its multiple pools, not even its 255 feet of bay frontage, but its "Unusual Security and Ready Access to the Ocean." Grove Isle, a luxury condominium complex with pieces by Isamu Noguchi and Alexander

Calder and Louise Nevelson in its sculpture garden, presented itself as "a bridge away from Coconut Grove," which meant, in the local code, that access was controlled, in this case by one of the "double security" systems favored in new Miami buildings, requiring that the permit acquired at the gate, or "perimeter," be surrendered at the second line of defense, the entrance to the building itself. A bridge, I was told by several people in Miami, was a good thing to have between oneself and the city, because it could be drawn up, or blocked, during times of unrest.

For a city even then being presented, in news reports and in magazine pieces and even in advertising and fashion promotions which had adopted their style from the television show "Miami Vice," as a rich and wicked pastel boomtown, Miami seemed, at the time I began spending time there, rather spectacularly depressed, again on the southern model. There were new condominiums largely unsold. There were new office towers largely unleased. There were certain signs of cutting and running among those investors who had misread the constant cash moving in and out of Miami as the kind of reliable American money they understood, and been left holding the notes. Helmsley-Spear, it was reported, had let an undeveloped piece on Biscayne Bay go into foreclosure, saving itself $3 million a year in taxes. Tishman Speyer had jettisoned plans for an $800-million medical complex in Broward County. WELL-HEELED INVESTORS RETURNING NORTH was a *Herald* headline in June of 1985. COSTLY CONDOS THREATENED WITH MASSIVE FORECLOSURES was a *Herald* headline in August of 1985. FORECLOSURES SOARING IN S. FLORIDA was a *Herald* headline in March of 1986.

The feel was that of a Latin capital, a year or two away from a new government. Space in shopping malls was unrented, or rented to the wrong tenants. There were too many shoe stores for an American city, and video arcades. There were also too many public works projects: a new mass transit system which did not effectively transport anyone, a projected "people mover" around the downtown area which would, it was said, salvage the new mass transit system. On my first visits to Miami the gleaming new Metrorail cars glided empty down to the

Dadeland Mall and back, ghost trains above the jammed traffic on the South Dixie Highway. When I returned a few months later service had already been cut back, and the billion-dollar Metrorail ran only until early evening.

A tropical entropy seemed to prevail, defeating grand schemes even as they were realized. Minor drug deals took place beneath the then unfinished people-mover tracks off Biscayne Boulevard, and plans were under way for yet another salvage operation, "Biscayne Centrum," a twenty-eight-acre sports arena and convention hall that could theoretically be reached by either Metrorail or people mover and offered the further advantage, since its projected site lay within the area sealed off during the 1982 Overtown riot, a district of generally apathetic but occasionally volatile poverty, of defoliating at least twenty-eight acres of potential trouble. ARENA FINANCING PLAN RELIES ON HOTEL GUESTS was a *Herald* headline one morning. S. FLORIDA HOTEL ROOMS GET EMPTIER was a *Herald* headline four months later. A business reporter for the *Herald* asked a local real-estate analyst when he thought South Florida would turn around. "Tell me when South America is going to turn around," the analyst said.

Meanwhile the construction cranes still hovered on the famous new skyline, which, floating as it did between a mangrove swamp and a barrier reef, had a kind of perilous attraction, like a mirage. I recall walking one October evening through the marble lobby of what was then the Pavillon Hotel, part of the massive new Miami Center which Pietro Belluschi had designed for a Virginia developer named Theodore Gould. There was in this vast travertine public space that evening one other person, a young Cuban woman in a short black dinner dress who seemed to be in charge of table arrangements for a gala not in evidence. I could hear my heels clicking on the marble. I could hear the young woman in the black taffeta dinner dress drumming her lacquered fingernails on the table at which she sat. It occurred to me that she and I might be the only people in the great empty skyline itself. Later that week control of the Pavillon, and of Miami Center, passed, the latest chapter in a short dolorous history of hearings and defaults and Chapter 11 filings, from Theodore Gould to the Bank of New York, and it was announced that the Inter-Continental chain would henceforth operate the hotel. The occupancy rate at the Pavillon was, at the time Inter-Continental assumed its management, 7 percent. Theodore Gould was said by the chairman of the Greater Miami Chamber of Commerce to have made "a very unique contribution to downtown Miami."

3

DURING THE spring when I began visiting Miami all of Florida was reported to be in drought, with dropping water tables and unfilled aquifers and SAVE WATER signs, but drought, in a part of the world which would be in its natural state a shelf of porous oolitic limestone covered most of the year by a shallow sheet flow of fresh water, proved relative. During this drought the city of Coral Gables continued, as it had every night since 1924, to empty and refill its Venetian Pool with fresh unchlorinated water, 820,000 gallons a day out of the water supply and into the storm sewer. There was less water than there might have been in the Biscayne Aquifer but there was water everywhere above it. There were rains so hard that windshield wipers stopped working and cars got swamped and stalled on I-95. There was water roiling and bubbling over the underwater lights in decorative pools. There was water sluicing off the six-story canted window at the Omni, a hotel from which it was possible to see, in the Third World way, both the slums of Overtown and those island houses with the Unusual Security and Ready Access to the Ocean, equally wet. Water plashed off banana palms, water puddled on flat roofs, water streamed down the CARNE U.S. GOOD & U.S. STANDARD signs on Flagler Street. Water rocked the impounded drug boats which lined the Miami River and water lapped against the causeways on the bay. I got used to the smell of incipient mildew in my clothes. I stuffed Kleenex in wet shoes and stopped expecting them to dry.

A certain liquidity suffused everything about the place. Causeways and bridges and even Brickell Avenue did not stay put but rose and fell, allowing the masts of ships to glide among the marble and glass facades of the unleased office buildings. The buildings themselves seemed to swim free against the sky: there had grown up in Miami during the recent money years an architecture which appeared to have slipped its moorings, a not inappropriate style for a terrain with only a provisional claim on being land at all. Surfaces were reflective, opalescent. Angles were oblique, intersecting to disorienting effect. The

Arquitectonica office, which produced the celebrated glass condominium on Brickell Avenue with the fifty-foot cube cut from its center, the frequently photographed "sky patio" in which there floated a palm tree, a Jacuzzi, and a lipstick-red spiral staircase, accompanied its elevations with crayon sketches, all moons and starry skies and airborne maidens, as in a Chagall. Skidmore, Owings and Merrill managed, in its Southeast Financial Center, the considerable feat of rendering fifty-five stories of polished gray granite incorporeal, a sky-blue illusion.

Nothing about Miami was exactly fixed, or hard. Hard consonants were missing from the local speech patterns, in English as well as in Spanish. Local money tended to move on hydraulic verbs: when it was not being washed it was being diverted, or channeled through Mexico, or turned off in Washington. Local stories tended to turn on underwater plot points, submerged snappers: on unsoundable extradition proceedings in the Bahamas, say, or fluid connections with the Banco Nacional de Colombia. I recall trying to touch the bottom of one such story in the *Herald*, about six hand grenades which had just been dug up in the bay-front backyard of a Biscayne Boulevard pawnbroker who had been killed in his own bed a few years before, shot at close range with a .25-caliber automatic pistol.

There were some other details on the surface of this story, for example the wife who fired the .25 caliber automatic pistol and the nineteen-year-old daughter who was up on federal weapons charges and the flight attendant who rented the garage apartment and said that the pawnbroker had collected "just basic things like rockets, just defused things," but the underwater narrative included, at last sounding, the Central Intelligence Agency (with which the pawnbroker was said to have been associated), the British intelligence agency MI6 (with which the pawnbroker was also said to have been associated), the late Anastasio Somoza Debayle (whose family the pawnbroker was said to have spirited into Miami shortly before the regime fell in Managua), the late shah of Iran (whose presence in Panama was said to have queered an arms deal about which the pawnbroker had been told), Dr. Josef Mengele (for whom the pawnbroker was said to be searching), and a Pompano Beach resident last seen cruising Miami in a cinnamon-colored Cadillac Sedan de Ville and looking to buy, he said for the Salvadoran insurgents, a million rounds of ammunition, thirteen thousand assault rifles, and "at least a couple" of jeep-mounted machine guns.

In this mood Miami seemed not a city at all but a tale, a romance of the tropics, a kind of waking dream in which any possibility could and would be accommodated. The most ordinary morning, say at the courthouse, could open onto the distinctly lurid. "I don't think he came out with me, that's all," I recall hearing someone say one day in an elevator at the Miami federal courthouse. His voice had kept rising. "What happened to all that stuff about how next time, he gets twenty keys, he could run wherever-it-is-Idaho, now he says he wouldn't know what to do with five keys, what is this shit?" His companion had shrugged. We had continued in silence to the main floor. Outside one courtroom that day a group of Colombians, the women in silk shirts and Chanel necklaces and Charles Jourdan suede pumps, the children in appliquéd dresses from Baby Dior, had been waiting for the decision in a pretrial detention hearing, one in which the government was contending that the two defendants, who between them lived in houses in which eighty-three kilos of cocaine and a million-three in cash had been found, failed to qualify as good bail risks.

"That doesn't make him a longtime drug dealer," one of the two defense lawyers, both of whom were Anglo and one of whom drove a Mercedes 380 SEL with the license plate DEFENSE, had argued about the million-three in cash. "That could be one transaction." Across the hall that day closing arguments were being heard in a boat case, a "boat case" being one in which a merchant or fishing vessel has been boarded and drugs seized and eight or ten Colombian crew members arrested, the kind of case in which pleas were typically entered so that one of the Colombians would get eighteen months and the others deported. There were never any women in Chanel necklaces around a boat case, and the lawyers (who were usually hired and paid for not by the defendants but by the unnamed owner of the "load," or shipment) tended to be Cuban. "You had the great argument, you got to give me some good ideas," one of the eight Cuban defense lawyers on this case joked with the prosecutor during a recess. "But you haven't heard my argument yet," another of the defense lawyers said. "The stuff about communism. Fabulous closing argument."

Just as any morning could turn lurid, any moment could turn final, again as in a dream. "I heard a loud, short noise and then there was just a plain moment of dullness," the witness to a shooting in a Miami Beach supermarket parking lot told the *Herald*. "There was no one around except me and two bagboys." I happened to be in the coroner's office one morning when autopsies were being performed on the bodies of two Mariels, shot and apparently pushed from a car on I-95 about nine the evening before, another plain moment of dullness. The story had been on television an hour or two after it happened: I had seen the crime site on the eleven o'clock news, and had not expected to see the victims in the morning. "When he came here in Mariel he stayed at our house but he didn't get along with my mom," a young girl was saying in the anteroom to one of the detectives working the case. "These two guys were killed together," the detective had pressed. "They probably knew each other."

"For sure," the young girl had said, agreeably. Inside the autopsy room the hands of the two young men were encased in the brown paper bags which indicated that the police had not yet taken what they needed for laboratory studies. Their flesh had the marbleized yellow look of the recently dead. There were other bodies in the room, in various stages of autopsy, and a young woman in a white coat taking eyes, for the eye bank. "Who are we going to start on next?" one of the assistant medical examiners was saying. "The fat guy? Let's do the fat guy."

It was even possible to enter the waking dream without leaving the house, just by reading the *Herald*. A Mariel named Jose "Coca-Cola" Yero gets arrested, with nine acquaintances, in a case involving 1,664 pounds of cocaine, a thirty-seven-foot Cigarette boat named *The Connection*, two Lamborghinis, a million-six in cash, a Mercedes 500 SEL with another $350,000 in cash in the trunk, one dozen Rolex watches color-coordinated to match Jose "Coca-Cola" Yero's wardrobe, and various houses in Dade and Palm Beach counties, a search of one of which turns up not just a photograph of Jose

"Coca-Cola" Yero face down in a pile of white powder but also a framed poster of Al Pacino as Tony Montana, the Mariel who appears at a dramatic moment in *Scarface* face down in a pile of white powder. "They got swept up in the fast lane," a Metro-Dade narcotics detective advises the *Herald*. "The fast lane is what put this whole group in jail." A young woman in South Palm Beach goes out to the parking lot of her parents' condominium and gets into her 1979 Pontiac Firebird, opens the T-top, starts the ignition and loses four toes when the bomb goes off. "She definitely knows someone is trying to kill her," the sheriff's investigator tells the *Herald*. "She knew they were coming, but she didn't know when."

Surfaces tended to dissolve here. Clear days ended less so. I recall an October Sunday when my husband and I were taken, by Gene Miller, a *Herald* editor who had won two Pulitzer Prizes for investigative reporting and who had access to season tickets exactly on the fifty-yard line at the Orange Bowl, to see the Miami Dolphins beat the Pittsburgh Steelers, 21–17. In the row below us the former Dolphin quarterback Earl Morrall signed autographs for the children who wriggled over seats to slip him their programs and steal surreptitious glances at his Super Bowl ring. A few rows back an Anglo teenager in sandals and shorts and a black T-shirt smoked a marijuana cigarette in full view of the Hispanic police officer behind him. Hot dogs were passed, and Coca-Cola spilled. Sony Watchmans were compared, for the definition on the instant replay. The NBC cameras dollied along the sidelines and the Dolphin cheerleaders kneeled on their white pom-poms and there was a good deal of talk about red dogging and weak secondaries and who would be seen and what would be eaten in New Orleans, come Super Bowl weekend.

The Miami on display in the Orange Bowl that Sunday afternoon would have seemed another Miami altogether, one with less weather and harder, more American surfaces, but by dinner we were slipping back into the tropical: in a virtually empty restaurant on top of a virtually empty condominium off Biscayne Boulevard, with six people at the table, one of whom was Gene Miller and one of whom was Martin Dardis, who as the chief investigator for the state attorney's office in Miami had led Carl Bernstein through the local angles on Watergate and who remained a walking data bank on CDs at the Biscayne Bank and on who called who on what payoff and on how to follow a money chain, we sat and we talked and we watched a storm break over Biscayne Bay. Sheets of warm rain washed down the big windows. Lightning began to fork somewhere around Bal Harbour. Gene Miller mentioned the Alberto Duque trial, then entering its fourth week at the federal courthouse, the biggest bank fraud case ever tried in the United States. Martin Dardis mentioned the ESM Government Securities collapse, just then breaking into a fraud case maybe bigger than the Duque.

The lightning was no longer forking now but illuminating the entire sky, flashing a dead strobe white, turning the bay fluorescent and the islands black, as if in negative. I sat and I listened to Gene Miller and Martin Dardis discuss these old and new turns in the underwater narrative and I watched the lightning backlight the islands. During the time I had spent in Miami many people had mentioned, always as something extraordinary, something I should have seen if I wanted to understand Miami, the *Surrounded Islands* project executed in Biscayne Bay in 1983 by the Bulgarian artist Christo. *Surrounded Islands*, which had involved surrounding eleven islands with two-hundred-foot petals, or skirts, of pink polypropylene fabric, had been mentioned both by people who were knowledgeable about conceptual art and by people who had not before heard and could not then recall the name of the man who had surrounded the islands. All had agreed. It seemed that the pink had shimmered in the water. It seemed that the pink had kept changing color, fading and reemerging with the movement of the water and the clouds and the sun and the night lights. It seemed that this period when the pink was in the water had for many people exactly defined, as the backlit islands and the fluorescent water and the voices at the table were that night defining for me, Miami.

4

ON MY first visits to Miami I was always being told that there were places I should not go. There were things I should and should not do. I should not walk the block and a half from the Omni to the *Herald* alone after dark. I should lock my car doors when I drove at night. If I hit a red light as I was about to enter I-95 I should not stop but look both ways, and accelerate. I should not drive through Liberty City, or walk around Overtown. If I had occasion to drive through what was called "the black Grove," those several dozen blocks of project housing which separated the expensive greenery of Coral Gables from the expensive greenery of Coconut Grove, I should rethink my route, avoid at all costs the territory of the disentitled, which in fact was hard to do, since Miami was a city, like so many to the south of it, in which it was possible to pass from walled enclaves to utter desolation while changing stations on the car radio.

In the end I went without incident to all of the places I had been told not to go, and did not or did do most of the things I had been told to do or not to do, but the subtext of what I had been told, that this was a city in which black people and white people viewed each other with some discontent, stayed with me, if only because the most dramatic recent season of that discontent, the spring of 1980, the season when certain disruptive events in Havana happened to coincide with a drama then being played out in a Florida courtroom, still figured so large in the local memory. Many people in Miami mentioned the spring of 1980 to me, speaking always of its "mood," which appeared to have been one of collective fever. In the spring of 1980 everyone had been, it was said, "nervous," or "tense." This tension had built, it was said, "to a point of just no return," or "to the breaking point." "It could drive you mad, just waiting for something to happen," one woman said. "The Cuban kids were all out leaning on their horns and the blacks were all out sitting on their porches," someone else said. "You knew it was going to happen but you didn't know when. And anyway it was going to happen. There was no doubt about that. It was like, well, a bad dream. When you try to wake up and you can't."

The Miami part of what happened that spring, the part people in Miami refer to as "McDuffie," had its proximate beginning early on the morning of December 17, 1979, when a thirty-three-year-old black insurance agent named Arthur McDuffie was said by police to have made a rolling stop at a red light, to have executed the maneuver called "popping a wheelie" on his borrowed Kawasaki motorcycle, and to have given the finger to a Dade County Public Safety Department officer parked nearby. The officer gave chase. By the time Arthur McDuffie was apprehended, eight minutes later, more than a dozen Dade County and city of Miami police units had converged on the scene.

Accounts of the next several minutes conflict. What is known is that at some point a rescue unit was called, for the victim of an "accident," and that four days later Arthur McDuffie died, without regaining consciousness, in Jackson Memorial Hospital. On March 31, 1980, four Dade County Public Safety Department officers, all four of them white, each charged with having played some role in the beating of Arthur McDuffie or in the subsequent attempt to make his injuries seem the result of a motorcycle accident, went on trial before an all-white jury in Tampa, where the case had been moved after a Miami judge granted a change of venue with these words: "This case is a time bomb. I don't want to see it go off in my courtroom or in this community."

The Havana part of what happened in the spring of 1980 was also a time bomb. There had been all that spring a dispute between Fidel Castro and the government of Peru over the disposition of a handful of disaffected Cubans who had claimed asylum at the Peruvian embassy in Havana. Castro wanted the Cubans turned out. Peru insisted that they be brought to Lima. It was April 4, four days after jury selection began in the McDuffie case in Tampa, when the Cuban government, as an apparently quixotic move in this dispute, bulldozed down the gates at the Peruvian embassy in Havana and set into motion, whether deliberately or inadvertently, that chain of events referred to as "Mariel," by which people in Miami mean not just the place and not just the boatlift and not just what many see as the "trick," the way in which Fidel Castro managed to take his own problem and make it Miami's, but the entire range of dislocations attendant upon the unloading of 125,000 refugees, 26,000 of them with prison records, onto an already volatile community.

The first Mariel refugees arrived in South Florida on April 21, 1980. By May 17, the day the McDuffie case went to the jury in Tampa, there were already some 57,000 Mariels camped under the bleachers at the Orange Bowl and in makeshift tent cities in the Orange Bowl parking area and on the public land under I-95, downtown, in the most visible and frequently traveled part of the city, in case it had escaped anybody's notice that the needs of the black community might not in the immediate future have Miami's full attention. May 17 was a Saturday. The temperature was in the mid-seventies. There was, in Miami, no rain in view.

There appears to have been an astonishing innocence about what happened that day. In another part of the country the judge in a trial as sensitive as the McDuffie trial might not have allowed the case to go to the jury on a clear Saturday morning, but the judge in Tampa did. In another part of the country the jury in such a case might not have brought in its verdicts, complete acquittal for all four defendants, in just two hours and forty-five minutes, which came down to something less than forty-two minutes per defendant, but the jury in Tampa did, in many ways predictably, for among the citizens of South Florida the urge to conciliate one another remained remarkably undeveloped. The president of the Orange Bowl Committee, which pretty much represents the established order in Miami, thought as recently as 1985, and said so, for attribution, that it was "not offensive" for the committee to entertain the participating college teams at the Indian Creek Country Club, which admitted no blacks or Jews as members but did allow them to visit the club as guests at private parties. "At the hospital where I work, the black doctors are intellectually fine and wonderful people, but they aren't able to handle the cosmopolitan aspects of circulating in society," a Miami surgeon said a few weeks later, also for attribution, to the *Herald* reporter who had asked him about restrictive policies at another local institution, the Bath Club, on Collins Avenue in Miami Beach.

Symbolic moves seemed to be missing here. A University of Miami study released the month of the 1968 Miami Riot had found it necessary to suggest that local black males resented being addressed by police as "boy," or "nigger." When a delegation of black citizens had asked the same year that a certain police officer be transferred, after conduct which had troubled the community, off his Liberty City beat, they were advised by the Miami chief of police that their complaint was "silly." Several weeks later it was reported that the officer in question and his partner had picked up a black seventeen-year-old, charged him with carrying a concealed knife, forced him to strip naked, and dangled him by his heels a hundred feet over the Miami River, from an unfinished span of the Dolphin Expressway.

During the twelve years between the 1968 Miami Riot and the Saturday in 1980 when the McDuffie case went to the jury, there had been, in Dade County, thirteen occasions on which the rage of some part of the black community went, for periods of time ranging from a few hours to a few days, out of control. This regular evidence of discontent notwithstanding, those gestures with which other troubled cities gradually learn to accommodate their citizens seemed not, in South Florida, to take hold. Blacks continued to be excluded for cause from juries in trials involving police officers accused of killing blacks. The juries in such cases continued to stay out two hours, and to bring in acquittals, on clear days, in the summer.

The McDuffie acquittals were on the Associated Press wire, that clear Saturday in 1980, by 2:42 P.M. The first police call reporting rioting in Liberty City came in at 6:02 P.M., from Miami Police Department Unit 621. By 9:44 P.M., when a call was placed to Tallahassee asking that the National Guard be sent in, there was rioting not only in Liberty City but in Overtown and in the black Grove and around the entire Metro Justice complex, where doctors and nurses answering emergency calls to Jackson Memorial Hospital were being stoned and beaten and the Metro Justice building itself was being torched. Four days later, when the 1980 Liberty City Riot, called that because Liberty City was where it had begun, had run its course, there were eighteen dead or fatally injured, eight of them whites who had driven down the wrong streets and been stoned or doused with gasoline and set afire or, in the case of one, a twenty-two-year-old Burdines warehouse loader on his way home from a day at the beach with his girlfriend and younger brother, dragged from the car to be beaten, kicked, struck not only with bottles and bricks and a twenty-three-pound chunk of concrete but also with a *Miami Herald* street dispenser, shot, stabbed with a screwdriver, run over by a green Cadillac and left, one ear cut off and lying on his chest and his tongue cut out, with a red rose in his mouth.

An instinct for self-preservation would have seemed at this point to encourage negotiations, or at least the appearance of negotiations, but few lessons get learned in tropical cities under attack from their own citizens. Lines only harden. Positions become more fixed, and privileges more fiercely defended. In December of 1982 another police killing of another black man occasioned another riot, the 1982 Overtown Riot, on the second night of which there happened to be held, in the ballroom of the Surf Club on Collins Avenue, which numbered among its 680 members no blacks and no Jews, one of the most expensive parties given that year in Miami, a debutante party at which actors performed the story of Little Red Riding Hood under two hundred freshly cut fir trees arranged to represent the Black Forest of Bavaria. In this case too the police officer in question, a Cuban, was eventually tried before an all-white jury, which again stayed out two hours and again brought in an acquittal. This verdict came in early one Thursday evening in March of 1984, and order was restored in Miami just after midnight on Saturday morning, which was applauded locally as progress, not even a riot.

There are between the street and the lobby levels of the Omni International Hotel on Biscayne Boulevard, one block east of the hundred-block area sealed off by police during the 1982 Overtown Riot, two levels of shops and movie theaters and carnival attractions: a mall, so designed that the teenagers, most of them black and most of them male, who hang out around the carousel in the evenings, waiting for a movie to break or for a turn at the Space Walk or at the Sea of Balls or just for something to happen, can look up to the Omni ballroom and lobby levels, but only with some ingenuity reach them, since a steel grille blocks the floating stairway after dark and armed security men patrol the elevator areas. The visible presence of this more or less forbidden upstairs lends the mall in the evening an unspecific atmosphere of incipient trouble, an uneasiness which has its equivalent in the hotel itself, where the insistent and rather sinister music from the carousel downstairs comes to suggest, particularly on those weekend nights when the mall is at its loosest and the hotel often given over to one or another of the lavish *quinces* or charity galas which fill the local Cuban calendar, a violent night world just underfoot, and perhaps not underfoot for long.

Not often does a social dynamic seem to present itself in a single tableau, but at the Omni in Miami one did, and during the time I spent there I came to see the hotel and its mall as the most theatrical possible illustration of how a native proletariat can be left behind in a city open to the convulsions of the Third World, something which had happened in the United States first and most dramatically in Miami but had been happening since in other parts of the country. Black Miami had of course been particularly unprepared to have the world move in. Its common experience was of the cracker South. Black assertiveness had been virtually nonexistent, black political organization absent. Into the 1960s, according to *The Miami Riot of 1980*, a study of the Liberty City Riot by Bruce Porter of Brooklyn College and Marvin Dunn of Florida International University, the latter a black candidate for mayor of Miami who lost in 1985 to a Cuban, Xavier Suarez, Miami blacks did not swim at Dade County beaches. When Miami blacks paid taxes at the Dade County Courthouse they did so at a separate window, and when Miami blacks shopped at Burdines, where they were allowed to buy although not to try on clothes, they did so without using the elevators.

This had been a familiar enough pattern throughout the South, but something else had happened here. Desegregation had not just come hard and late to South Florida but it had also coincided, as it had not in other parts of the South, with another disruption of the local status quo, the major Cuban influx, which meant that jobs and services which might have helped awaken an inchoate black community went instead to Cubans, who tended to be overtrained but willing. Havana bankers took jobs as inventory clerks at forty-five dollars a week. Havana newspaper publishers drove taxis. That these were the men in black tie who now danced with the women in the Chanel and Valentino evening dresses on the ballroom level of the Omni was an irony lost in its precise detail, although not in its broad outline, on the sons of the men who did not get jobs as inventory clerks or taxi drivers, the children downstairs, in the high-topped sneakers, fanning in packs through the dim avenues of the locked-up mall.

5

ON THE one hundred and fiftieth anniversary of the founding of Dade County, in February of 1986, the *Miami Herald* asked four prominent amateurs of local history to name "the ten people and the ten events that had the most impact on the county's history." Each of the four submitted his or her own list of "The Most Influential People in Dade's History," and among the names mentioned were Julia Tuttle ("pioneer businesswoman"), Henry Flagler ("brought the Florida East Coast Railway to Miami"), Alexander Orr, Jr. ("started the research that saved Miami's drinking water from salt"), Everest George Sewell ("publicized the city and fostered its deepwater seaport"), Carl Fisher ("creator of Miami Beach"), Hugh M. Anderson ("to whom we owe Biscayne Boulevard, Miami Shores, and more"), Charles H. Crandon ("father of Dade County's park system"), Glenn Curtiss ("developer and promoter of the area's aviation potential"), and James L. Knight ("whose creative management enabled the *Miami Herald* to become a force for good"), this last nominee the choice of a retired *Herald* editorial writer.

There were more names. There were John Pennekamp ("conceived Dade's metropolitan form of government and fathered the Everglades National Park") and Father Theodore Gibson ("inspirational spokesman for racial justice and social change"). There were Maurice Ferre ("mayor for twelve years") and Marjorie Stoneman Douglas ("indefatigable environmentalist") and Dr. Bowman F. Ashe ("first and longtime president of the University of Miami"). There was David Fairchild, who "popularized tropical plants and horticulture that have made the county a more attractive place to live." There was William A. Graham, "whose Miami Lakes is a model for real estate development," Miami Lakes being the area developed by William A. Graham and his brother, Senator Bob Graham, at the time of Dade's one hundred and fiftieth anniversary the governor of Florida, on three thousand acres their father had just west of the Opa-Locka Airport.

There was another Graham, Ernest R., the father of Bob and William A., nominated for his "experiments with sugarcane culture and dairying." There was another developer, John Collins, as in Collins Avenue, Miami Beach. There were, as a dual entry, Richard Fitzpatrick, who "owned four square miles between what is now Northeast 14th Street and Coconut Grove," and William F. English, who "platted the village of Miami." There was Dr. James M. Jackson, an early Miami physician. There was Napoleon Bonaparte Broward, the governor of Florida who initiated the draining of the Everglades. There appeared on three of the four lists the name of the developer of Coral Gables, George Merrick. There appeared on one of the four lists the name of the coach of the Miami Dolphins, Don Shula.

On none of these lists of "The Most Influential People in Dade's History" did the name Fidel Castro appear, nor for that matter did the name of any Cuban, although the presence of Cubans in Dade County did not go entirely unnoted by the *Herald* panel. When it came to naming the Ten Most Important "Events," as opposed to "People," all four panelists mentioned the arrival of the Cubans, but at slightly off angles ("Mariel Boatlift of 1980" was the way one panelist saw it), and as if this arrival had been just another of those isolated disasters or innovations which deflect the course of any growing community, on an approximate par with the other events mentioned, for example the Freeze of 1895, the Hurricane of 1926, the opening of the Dixie Highway, the establishment of Miami International Airport, and the adoption, in 1957, of the metropolitan form of government, "enabling the Dade County Commission to provide urban services to the increasingly populous unincorporated area."

This set of mind, in which the local Cuban community was seen as a civic challenge determinedly met, was not uncommon among Anglos to whom I talked in Miami, many of whom persisted in the related illusions that the city was small, manageable, prosperous in a predictable broad-based way, southern in a progressive sunbelt way, American, and belonged to them. In fact 43 percent of the population of Dade County was by that time "Hispanic," which meant mostly Cuban. Fifty-six percent of the population of Miami itself was Hispanic. The most visible new buildings on the Miami skyline, the Arquitectonica buildings along Brickell Avenue, were by a firm with a Cuban founder. There were Cubans in the board rooms of the major banks, Cubans in the clubs that did not admit Jews or blacks, and four Cubans in the most recent mayoralty campaign, two of whom, Raul Masvidal and Xavier Suarez, had beaten out the incumbent and all other candidates to meet in a runoff, and one of whom, Xavier Suarez, a thirty-six-year-old lawyer who had been brought from Cuba to the United States as a child, was by then mayor of Miami.

The entire tone of the city, the way people looked and talked and met one another, was Cuban. The very image the city had begun presenting of itself, what was then its newfound glamour, its "hotness" (hot colors, hot vice, shady dealings under the palm trees), was that of prerevolutionary Havana, as perceived by Americans. There was even in the way women dressed in Miami a definable Havana look, a more distinct emphasis on the hips and décolletage, more black, more veiling, a generalized flirtatiousness of style not then current in American cities. In the shoe departments at Burdines and Jordan Marsh there were more platform soles than there might have been in another American city, and fewer displays of the running-shoe ethic. I recall being struck, during an afternoon spent at La Liga Contra el Cancer, a prominent exile charity which raises money to help cancer patients, by the appearance of the volunteers who had met that day to stuff envelopes for a benefit. Their hair was sleek, of a slightly other period, immaculate page boys and French twists. They wore Bruno Magli pumps, and silk and linen dresses of considerable expense. There seemed to be a preference for strictest gray or black, but the effect remained lush, tropical, like a room full of perfectly groomed mangoes.

This was not, in other words, an invisible 56 percent of the population. Even the social notes in *Diario Las Americas* and in *El Herald*, the daily Spanish edition of the *Herald* written and edited for *el exilio*, suggested a dominant culture, one with money to spend and a notable willingness to spend it in public. La Liga Contra el Cancer alone sponsored, in a single year, two benefit dinner dances, one benefit ball, a benefit children's fashion show, a benefit telethon, a benefit exhibition of jewelry, a benefit presentation of Miss Universe contestants, and a benefit showing, with Saks Fifth Avenue and chicken *vol-au-vent*, of the Adolfo (as it happened, a Cuban) fall collection. One morning *El Herald* would bring news of the gala at the Pavillon of the Amigos Latinamericanos del Museo de Ciencia y Planetarium; another morning, of an upcoming event at the Big Five Club, a Miami club founded by former members of five fashionable clubs in prerevolutionary Havana: a *coctel*, or cocktail party, at which tables would be assigned for yet another gala, the annual "Baile Imperial de las Rosas" of the American Cancer Society, Hispanic Ladies Auxiliary. Some members of the community were honoring Miss America Latina with dinner dancing at the Doral. Some were being honored themselves, at the Spirit of Excellence Awards Dinner at the Omni. Some were said to be enjoying the skiing at Vail; others to prefer Bariloche, in Argentina. Some were reported unable to attend (but sending checks for) the gala at the Pavillon of the Amigos Latinamericanos del Museo de Ciencia y Planetarium because of a scheduling conflict, with *el coctel de* Paula Hawkins.

Fete followed fete, all high visibility. Almost any day it was possible to drive past the limestone arches and fountains which marked the boundaries of Coral Gables and see little girls being photographed in the tiaras and ruffled hoop skirts and maribou-trimmed illusion capes they would wear at their *quinces*, the elaborate fifteenth-birthday parties at which the community's female children came of official age. The favored facial expression for a *quince* photograph was a classic smolder. The favored backdrop was one suggesting Castilian grandeur, which was how the Coral Gables arches happened to figure. Since the idealization of the virgin implicit in the *quince* could exist only in the presence of its natural foil, *machismo*, there was often a brother around, or a boyfriend. There was also a mother, in dark glasses, not only to protect the symbolic virgin but to point out the better angle, the more aristocratic location. The *quinceañera* would pick up her hoop skirts and move as directed, often revealing the scuffed Jellies she had worn that day to school. A few weeks later there she would be, transformed in *Diario Las Americas*, one of the morning battalion of smoldering fifteen-year-olds, each with her arch, her fountain, her borrowed scenery, the gift if not exactly the intention of the late George Merrick, who built the arches when he developed Coral Gables.

Neither the photographs of the Cuban *quinceañeras* nor the notes about the *coctel* at the Big Five were apt to appear in the newspapers read by Miami Anglos, nor, for that matter, was much information at all about the daily life of the Cuban majority. When, in the fall of 1986, Florida International University offered an evening course called "Cuban Miami: A Guide for Non-Cubans," the *Herald* sent a staff writer, who covered the classes as if from a distant beat. "Already I have begun to make some sense out of a culture that, while it totally surrounds us, has remained inaccessible and alien to me," the *Herald* writer was reporting by the end of the first meeting, and, by the end of the fourth: "What I see day to day in Miami, moving through mostly Anglo corridors of the community, are just small bits and pieces of that other world, the tip of something much larger than I'd imagined. . . . We may frequent the restaurants here, or wander into the occasional festival. But mostly we try to ignore Cuban Miami, even as we rub up against this teeming, incomprehensible presence."

Only thirteen people, including the *Herald* writer, turned up for the first meeting of "Cuban Miami: A Guide for Non-Cubans" (two more appeared at the second meeting, along with a security guard, because of telephone threats prompted by what the *Herald* writer called "somebody's twisted sense of national pride"), an enrollment which tended to suggest a certain willingness among non-Cubans to let Cuban Miami remain just that, Cuban, the "incomprehensible presence." In fact there had come to exist in South Florida two parallel cultures, separate but not exactly equal, a key distinction being that only one of the two, the Cuban, exhibited even a remote interest in the activities of the other. "The American community is not really aware of what is happening in the Cuban community," an exile banker named Luis Botifoll said in a 1983 *Herald* Sunday magazine piece about ten prominent local Cubans. "We are clannish, but at least we know who is who in the American establishment. They do not." About another of the ten Cubans featured in this piece, Jorge Mas Canosa, the *Herald* had this to say: "He is an advisor to U.S. Senators, a confidant of federal bureaucrats, a lobbyist for anti-Castro U.S.

policies, a near unknown in Miami. When his political group sponsored a luncheon speech in Miami by Secretary of Defense Caspar Weinberger, almost none of the American business leaders attending had ever heard of their Cuban host."

The general direction of this piece, which appeared under the cover line "THE CUBANS: *They're ten of the most powerful men in Miami. Half the population doesn't know it*," was, as the *Herald* put it, "to challenge the widespread presumption that Miami's Cubans are not really Americans, that they are a foreign presence here, an exile community that is trying to turn South Florida into North Cuba. . . . The top ten are not separatists; they have achieved success in the most traditional ways. They are the solid, bedrock citizens, hard-working humanitarians who are role models for a community that seems determined to assimilate itself into American society."

This was interesting. It was written by one of the few Cubans then on the *Herald* staff, and yet it described, however unwittingly, the precise angle at which Miami Anglos and Miami Cubans were failing to connect: Miami Anglos were in fact interested in Cubans only to the extent that they could cast them as aspiring immigrants, "determined to assimilate," a "hard-working" minority not different in kind from other groups of resident aliens. (But had I met any Haitians, a number of Anglos asked when I said that I had been talking to Cubans.) Anglos (who were, significantly, referred to within the Cuban community as "Americans") spoke of cross-culturalization, and of what they believed to be a meaningful second-generation preference for hamburgers, and rock and roll. They spoke of "diversity," and of Miami's "Hispanic flavor," an approach in which 56 percent of the population was seen as decorative, like the Coral Gables arches.

Fixed as they were on this image of the melting pot, of immigrants fleeing a disruptive revolution to find a place in the American sun, Anglos did not on the whole understand that assimilation would be considered by most Cubans a doubtful goal at best. Nor did many Anglos understand that living in Florida was still at the deepest level construed by Cubans as a temporary condition, an accepted political option shaped by the continuing dream, if no longer the immediate expectation, of a vindicatory return. *El exilio* was for Cubans a ritual, a respected tradition. *La revolución* was also a ritual, a trope fixed in Cuban political rhetoric at least since José Martí, a concept broadly interpreted to mean reform, or progress, or even just change. Ramón Grau San Martín, the president of Cuba during the autumn of 1933 and again from 1944 until 1948, had presented himself as a revolutionary, as had his 1948 successor, Carlos Prío. Even Fulgencio Batista had entered Havana life calling for *la revolución*, and had later been accused of betraying it, even as Fidel Castro was now.

This was a process Cuban Miami understood, but Anglo Miami did not, remaining as it did arrestingly innocent of even the most general information about Cuba and Cubans. Miami Anglos, for example, still had trouble with Cuban names, and Cuban food. When the Cuban novelist Guillermo Cabrera Infante came from London to lecture at Miami-Dade Community College, he was referred to by several Anglo faculty members to whom I spoke as "Infante." Cuban food was widely seen not as a minute variation on that eaten throughout both the Caribbean and the Mediterranean but as "exotic," and full of garlic. A typical Thursday food section of the *Herald* included recipes for Broiled Lemon-Curry Cornish Game Hens, Chicken Tetrazzini, King Cake, Pimiento Cheese, Raisin Sauce for Ham, Sautéed Spiced Peaches, Shrimp Scampi, Easy Beefy Stir-Fry, and four ways to use dried beans ("Those cheap, humble beans that have long sustained the world's poor have become the trendy set's new pet"), none of them Cuban.

This was all consistent, and proceeded from the original construction, that of the exile as an immigration. There was no reason to be curious about Cuban food, because Cuban teenagers preferred hamburgers. There was no reason to get Cuban names right, because they were complicated, and would be simplified by the second generation, or even by the first. "Jorge L. Mas" was the way Jorge Más Canosa's business card read. "Raul Masvidal" was the way Raúl Masvidal y Jury ran for mayor of Miami. There was no reason to know about Cuban history, because history was what immigrants were fleeing. Even the revolution, the reason for the immigration, could be covered in a few broad strokes: "Batista," "Castro," "26 Julio," this last being the particular broad stroke that inspired the Miami Springs Holiday Inn, on July 26, 1985, the thirty-second anniversary of the day Fidel Castro attacked the Moncada Barracks and so launched his six-year struggle for power in Cuba, to run a bar special on Cuba Libres, thinking to attract local Cubans by commemorating their holiday. "It was a mistake," the manager said, besieged by outraged exiles. "The gentleman who did it is from Minnesota."

There was in fact no reason, in Miami as well as in Minnesota, to know anything at all about Cubans, since Miami Cubans were now, if not Americans, at least aspiring Americans, and worthy of Anglo attention to the exact extent that they were proving themselves, in the *Herald*'s words, "role models for a community that seems determined to assimilate itself into American society"; or, as Vice President George Bush put it in a 1986 Miami address to the Cuban American National Foundation, "the most eloquent testimony I know to the basic strength and success of America, as well as to the basic weakness and failure of Communism and Fidel Castro."

The use of this special lens, through which the exiles were seen as a tribute to the American system, a point scored in the battle of the ideologies, tended to be encouraged by those outside observers who dropped down from the northeast corridor for a look and a column or two. George Will, in *Newsweek*, saw Miami as "a new installment in the saga of America's absorptive capacity," and Southwest Eighth Street as the place where "these exemplary Americans," the seven Cubans who had been gotten together to brief him, "initiated a columnist to fried bananas and black-bean soup and other Cuban contributions to the tanginess of American life." George Gilder, in *The Wilson Quarterly*, drew pretty much the same lesson from Southwest Eighth Street, finding it "more effervescently thriving than its crushed prototype," by which he seemed to mean Havana. In fact Eighth Street was for George Gilder a street that seemed to "percolate with the forbidden commerce of the dying island to the south . . . the Refrescos Cawy, the Competidora and El Cuño cigarettes, the *guayaberas*, the Latin music pulsing from the storefronts, the pyramids of mangoes and tubers, gourds and plantains, the iced coconuts served with a straw, the new theaters showing the latest anti-Castro comedies."

There was nothing on this list, with the possible exception of the "anti-Castro comedies," that could not most days be found on Southwest Eighth Street, but the list was also a fantasy, and a particularly gringo fantasy, one in which Miami Cubans, who came from a culture which had represented western civilization in this hemisphere since before there was a United States of America, appeared exclusively as vendors of plantains, their native music "pulsing" behind them. There was in any such view of Miami Cubans an extraordinary element of condescension, and it was the very condescension shared by Miami Anglos, who were inclined to reduce the particular liveliness and sophistication of local Cuban life to a matter of shrines on the lawn and love potions in the *botánicas*, the primitive exotica of the tourist's Caribbean.

Cubans were perceived as most satisfactory when they appeared to most fully share the aspirations and manners of middle-class Americans, at the same time adding "color" to the city on appropriate occasions, for example at their *quinces* (the *quinces* were one aspect of Cuban life almost invariably mentioned by Anglos, who tended to present them as evidence of Cuban extravagance, *i.e.*, Cuban irresponsibility, or childishness), or on the day of the annual Calle Ocho Festival, when they could, according to the *Herald*, "samba" in the streets and stir up a paella for two thousand (10 cooks, 2,000 mussels, 220 pounds of lobster and 440 pounds of rice), using rowboat oars as spoons. Cubans were perceived as least satisfactory when they "acted clannish," "kept to themselves," "had their own ways," and, two frequent flash points, "spoke Spanish when they didn't need to" and "got political"; complaints, each of them, which suggested an Anglo view of what Cubans should be at significant odds with what Cubans were.

6

THIS QUESTION of language was curious. The sound of spoken Spanish was common in Miami, but it was also common in Los Angeles, and Houston, and even in the cities of the northeast. What was unusual about Spanish in Miami was not that it was so often spoken, but that it was so often heard: in, say, Los Angeles, Spanish remained a language only barely registered by the Anglo population, part of the ambient noise, the language spoken by the people who worked in the car wash and came to trim the trees and cleared the tables in restaurants. In Miami Spanish was spoken by the people who ate in the restaurants, the people who owned the cars and the trees, which made, on the socioauditory scale, a considerable difference. Exiles who felt isolated or declassed by language in New York or Los Angeles thrived in Miami. An entrepreneur who spoke no English could still, in Miami, buy, sell, negotiate, leverage assets, float bonds, and, if he were so inclined, attend galas twice a week, in black tie. "I have been after the *Herald* ten times to do a story about millionaires in Miami who do not speak more than two words in English," one prominent exile told me. "'Yes' and 'no.' Those are the two words. They come here with five dollars in their pockets and without speaking another word of English they are millionaires."

The truculence a millionaire who spoke only two words of English might provoke among the less resourceful native citizens of a nominally American city was predictable, and manifested itself rather directly. In 1980, the year of Mariel, Dade County voters had approved a referendum requiring that county business be conducted exclusively in English. Notwithstanding the fact that this legislation was necessarily amended to exclude emergency medical and certain other services, and notwithstanding even the fact that many local meetings continued to be conducted in that unbroken alternation of Spanish and English which had become the local patois ("I will be in Boston on Sunday and desafortunadamente yo tengo un compromiso en Boston que no puedo romper y yo no podré estar con Vds.," read the minutes of a 1984 Miami City

Commission meeting I had occasion to look up. "En espíritu, estaré, pero the other members of the commission I am sure are invited . . ."), the very existence of this referendum was seen by many as ground regained, a point made. By 1985 a St. Petersburg optometrist named Robert Melby was launching his third attempt in four years to have English declared the official language of the state of Florida, as it would be in 1986 of California. "I don't know why your legislators here are so, how should I put it?—spineless," Robert Melby complained about those South Florida politicians who knew how to count. "No one down here seems to want to run with the issue."

Even among those Anglos who distanced themselves from such efforts, Anglos who did not perceive themselves as economically or socially threatened by Cubans, there remained considerable uneasiness on the matter of language, perhaps because the inability or the disinclination to speak English tended to undermine their conviction that assimilation was an ideal universally shared by those who were to be assimilated. This uneasiness had for example shown up repeatedly during the 1985 mayoralty campaign, surfacing at odd but apparently irrepressible angles. The winner of that contest, Xavier Suarez, who was born in Cuba but educated in the United States, was reported in a wire service story to speak, an apparently unexpected accomplishment, "flawless English."

A less prominent Cuban candidate for mayor that year had unsettled reporters at a televised "meet the candidates" forum by answering in Spanish the questions they asked in English. "For all I or my dumbstruck colleagues knew," the *Herald* political editor complained in print after this event, "he was reciting his high school's alma mater or the ten Commandments over and over again. The only thing I understood was the occasional *Cubano vota Cubano* he tossed in." It was noted by another *Herald* columnist that of the leading candidates, only one, Raul Masvidal, had a listed telephone number, but: ". . . if you call Masvidal's 661-0259 number on Kiaora Street in Coconut Grove—during the day, anyway—you'd better speak Spanish. I spoke to two women there, and neither spoke enough English to answer the question of whether it was the candidate's number."

On the morning this last item came to my attention in the

Herald I studied it for some time. Raul Masvidal was at that time the chairman of the board of the Miami Savings Bank and the Miami Savings Corporation. He was a former chairman of the Biscayne Bank, and a minority stockholder in the M Bank, of which he had been a founder. He was a member of the Board of Regents for the state university system of Florida. He had paid $600,000 for the house on Kiaora Street in Coconut Grove, buying it specifically because he needed to be a Miami resident (Coconut Grove is part of the city of Miami) in order to run for mayor, and he had sold his previous house, in the incorporated city of Coral Gables, for $1,100,000. The Spanish words required to find out whether the number listed for the house on Kiaora Street was in fact the candidate's number would have been roughly these: "*Es la casa de Raúl Masvidal?*" The answer might have been "*Sí*," or the answer might have been "*No.*" It seemed to me that there must be very few people working on daily newspapers along the southern borders of the United States who would consider this exchange entirely out of reach, and fewer still who would not accept it as a commonplace of American domestic life that daytime telephone calls to middle-class urban households will frequently be answered by women who speak Spanish.

Something else was at work in this item, a real resistance, a balkiness, a coded version of the same message Dade County voters had sent when they decreed that their business be done only in English. WILL THE LAST AMERICAN TO LEAVE MIAMI PLEASE BRING THE FLAG, the famous bumper stickers had read the year of Mariel. "It was the last American stronghold in Dade County," the owner of Gator Kicks Longneck Saloon, out where Southwest Eighth Street runs into the Everglades, had said after he closed the place for good the night of Super Bowl Sunday, 1986. "Fortunately or unfortunately, I'm not alone in my inability," a *Herald* columnist named Charles Whited had written a week or so later, in a column about not speaking Spanish. "A good many Americans have left Miami because they want to live someplace where everybody speaks one language: theirs." In this context the call to the house on Kiaora Street in Coconut Grove which did or did not belong to Raul Masvidal appeared not as a statement of literal fact but as shorthand, a glove thrown down, a stand, a cry from the heart of a beleaguered raj.

7

ON THE whole the members of the beleaguered raj and the 56 percent of the population whose affairs they continued to believe they directed did not see politics on the same canvas, which tended to complicate the Anglo complaint about the way in which Cubans "got political."

> Every election in the city of Miami produces its share of rumors involving the *Herald*, and last Tuesday's mayoral runoff between Raul Masvidal and Xavier Suarez produced one that I think I'll have bronzed and hang on my office wall. It was *that* bizarre.
>
> Political Editor Tom Fiedler reported it in his column on Thursday. The previous day, Mr. Suarez was sworn in as mayor after readily defeating Mr. Masvidal, whom this newspaper had recommended, in the runoff. Tom wrote that "the rumor going around Little Havana is that the *Herald* really preferred Suarez the best and only used Masvidal as a feint. Follow this reasoning closely, now: because the newspaper knows that its endorsement actually hurts candidates in Little Havana, it endorsed Masvidal with the knowledge that Suarez would be the beneficiary of a backlash. Thus, according to this rationale, the *Herald* actually got what it wanted. Clever, huh?"
>
> I wish I knew where behind the looking glass the authors of these contortions reside. I'd like to meet them, really I would. Maybe if we chatted I could begin to understand the thought processes that make them see up as down, black as white, alpha as omega. Or maybe I simply would be left where I am now: scratching my head and chortling in baffled amusement.
>
> —Jim Hampton, Editor, the *Miami Herald*, November 17, 1985

Miami Anglos continued, as the editor of the *Herald* did, to regard the density and febrility of exile political life with "baffled amusement." They continued, as the editor of the *Herald* did, to find that life "bizarre." They thought of politics exactly the way most of their elected representatives thought of politics, not as the very structure of everything they did but as a specific and usually programmatic kind of activity: an election, a piece of legislation, the deals made and the trade-offs extracted during the course of the campaign or the legislative markup. Any more general notions tended to be amorphous, the detritus of a desultory education in the confident latitudes: politics were part of "civics," one of the "social studies," something taught with audiovisual aids and having as its goal the promotion of good citizenship.

Politics, in other words, remained a "subject," an assortment of maxims once learned and still available to be learned by those not blessed with American birth, which may have been why, on those infrequent occasions when the city's parallel communities contrived an opportunity to express their actual feelings about each other, Miami Anglos tended unveeringly toward the didactic. On March 7, 1986, a group called the South Florida Peace Coalition applied for and received a Miami police permit authorizing a demonstration, scheduled for a Saturday noon some two weeks later at the Torch of Friendship monument on Biscayne Boulevard, against American aid to the Nicaraguan contras. Since the cause of the Nicaraguan contras was one with which many Miami Cubans had come to identify their most febrile hopes and fears, the prospect of such a demonstration was not likely to go unremarked upon, nor did it: in due course, after what was apparently a general sounding of the alarm on local Cuban radio, a second police permit was applied for and issued, this one to Andres Nazario Sargen, the executive director of Alpha 66, one of the most venerable of the exile action groups and one which had regularly claimed, ever since what had appeared to be its original encouragement in 1962 by the CIA, to be running current actions against the government of Cuba.

This second permit authorized a counterdemonstration, intended not so much to show support for the contras, which in context went without saying, as to show opposition to those Anglos presumed to be working for hemispheric communism. "We took it as a challenge," Andres Nazario Sargen said of the original permit and its holders. "They know very well they are defending a communist regime, and that hurts the Cuban exile's sensibility." That the permits would allow the South Florida Peace Coalition demonstration and the Alpha 66 counterdemonstration to take place at exactly the same time and within a few yards of each other was a point defended by Miami police, the day before the scheduled events, as a "manpower" decision, a question of not wanting to "split resources." "With the number of police officers who will be there," a police spokesman was quoted as saying, "someone would have to be foolish to try anything."

This was not an assessment which suggested a particularly close reading, over the past twenty-five years, of either Alpha 66 or Andres Nazario Sargen, and I was not unduly surprised, on the Sunday morning after the fact, to find the front page of the *Herald* given over to double headlines (DEMONSTRATIONS TURN UGLY and VIOLENCE MARS PRO-CONTRA PROTEST) and a four-color photograph showing a number of exiles brandishing Cuban and American flags as they burned the placards abandoned by the routed South Florida Peace Coalition. It appeared that many eggs had been hurled, and some rocks. It appeared that at least one onion had been hurled, hitting the president of the Dade County Young Democrats, who later expressed his thoughts on the matter by describing himself as "an eleventh-generation American."

It appeared, moreover, that these missiles had been hurled in just one direction, that of the South Florida Peace Coalition demonstrators, a group of about two hundred which included, besides the president of the Dade County Young Democrats, some state and local legislators, some members of the American Friends Service Committee, a few people passing out leaflets bearing the name of the Revolutionary Communist Party, one schoolteacher who advised the *Herald* that she was there because "Americans need to reclaim Miami from these foreigners," and, the most inflammatory cut of all for the Alpha 66 demonstrators on the other side of the metal police barricades, at least one Cuban, a leader of the Antonio Maceo Brigade, a heretical exile group founded in the mid-seventies to sponsor student visits to Cuba.

From noon of that Saturday until about three, when a riot

squad was called and the South Florida Peace Coalition physically extracted from the fray, the police had apparently managed to keep the Alpha 66 demonstrators on the Alpha 66 side of the barricades. The two hundred Peace Coalition demonstrators had apparently spent those three hours listening to speeches and singing folk songs. The two thousand Alpha 66 demonstrators had apparently spent the three hours trying to rush the barricades, tangling with police, and shouting down the folksingers with chants of "*Comunismo no, Democracia sí*," and "*Rusia no, Reagan sí*." The mayor of Miami, Xavier Suarez, had apparently stayed on the Alpha 66 side of the barricades, at one point speaking from the back of a Mazda pickup, a technique he later described in a letter to the *Herald* as "mingling with the people and expressing my own philosophical agreement with their ideas—as well as my disagreement with the means by which some would implement those ideas," and also as "an effective way to control the crowd."

"Unfortunately, they have the right to be on the other side of the street" was what he apparently said at the time, from the back of the Mazda pickup. "I'm sure you've all looked clearly to see who is on that side, senators and representatives included, and surely some members of Marxist groups." This method of crowd control notwithstanding, nothing much seemed actually to have happened that Saturday afternoon at the Torch of Friendship (only one demonstrator had been arrested, only one required hospital treatment), but the fevers of the moment continued for some weeks to induce a certain exhortatory delirium in the pages of the *Herald*. Statements were framed, and letters to the editor written, mostly along the preceptive lines favored by the Anglo community.

"I was raised to believe that the right to peaceful dissent was vital to our freedoms," one such letter read, from a woman who noted that she had been present at the Peace Coalition demonstration but had "fortunately" been "spared the vocal vituperation—as it was totally in the Spanish language." "Apparently," she continued, "some in the Cuban community do not recognize my right. . . . Evidently, their definition of human rights is not the same as that of most native-born Americans. It is as simple as that. No, my Cuban brothers and sisters, this is not the American way. Shame!"

Voltaire was quoted, somewhat loosely ("'I disagree with what you say, but I will defend to the death your right to say it'"), and even Wendell Willkie, the inscription on whose grave marker ("'Because we are generous with our freedom, we share our rights with those who disagree with us'") was said to be "our American creed, as spelled out in the Constitution." One correspondent mentioned how "frightening" it was to realize "that although we live in a democracy that guarantees the right of free speech, when we exercise this right we can be physically attacked by a group of people whom we have given refuge here in our country."

The subtext here, that there were some people who belonged in Miami and other people who did not, became, as the letters mounted, increasingly explicit, taking on finally certain aspects of a crusade. "Perhaps," another correspondent suggested, taking the point a step further, "it is time for a change of venue to countries in which they may vent their spleen at risk only to the governments they oppose and themselves." A *Herald* columnist, Carl Hiaasen, put the matter even more flatly: "They have come to the wrong country," he wrote about those pro-contra demonstrators who had that Saturday afternoon attacked a young man named David Camp, "a carpenter and stagehand who was born here, and has always considered himself patriotic . . . They need to go someplace where they won't have to struggle so painfully with the concept of free speech, or the right to dissent. Someplace where the names of Paine and Jefferson have no meaning, where folks wouldn't know the Bill of Rights if it was stapled to their noses."

If this native reduction of politics to a Frank Capra movie was not an approach which provided much of a libretto for the tropical Ring of exile and conspiracy that had been Cuban political experience, neither had the Cubans arrived in Miami equipped with much instinctive feeling for the native way. Miami Cubans were not the heirs to a tradition in which undue effort had been spent defining the rights and responsibilities of "good citizens," nor to one in which loosely organized democracies on the American model were widely admired. They were the heirs instead to the Spanish Inquisition, and after that to a tradition of anti-Americanism so sturdy that it had often been for Cubans a motive force. "It is my duty," José Martí had written to a friend in May of 1895, a few days before he was killed on his white horse fighting for the independence of Cuba at Dos Ríos, "to prevent, through the independence of Cuba, the U.S.A. from spreading over the West Indies and falling with added weight upon other lands of Our America. All I have done up to now and shall do hereafter is to that end. . . . I know the Monster, because I have lived in its lair—and my weapon is only the slingshot of David."

From within this matrix, which was essentially autocratic, Miami Cubans looked at the merely accidental in American life and found a design, often sinister. They looked at what amounted to Anglo indifference (on the question, say, of which of two Cubans, neither of whom could be expected to recall the Hurricane of 1926 or the opening of the Dixie Highway, was to be mayor of Miami) and divined a conspiratorial intention. They looked at American civil rights and saw civil disorder. They had their own ideas about how order should be maintained, even in the lair of the Monster that was the United States. "All underaged children will not be allowed to leave their homes by themselves," one Cuban candidate in the 1985 Miami mayoralty campaign promised to ensure if elected. "They should always be accompanied by an adult, with parents or guardians being responsible for compliance with the law." Another Cuban candidate in the same election, General Manuel Benítez, who had been at one time chief of the Batista security forces, promised this: ". . . you can rest assured that within six months there will be no holdups, life in general will be protected and stores will be able to open their doors without fear of robberies or murders. . . . A powerful force of security guards, the county school personnel, teachers, professionals, retirees, Boy Scouts and church people will all take part in a program of citizen education and in the constant fight against evil and immorality."

"Unfortunately," as the winning candidate in that campaign, Mayor Xavier Suarez, had said of the Peace Coalition demonstrators at the Torch of Friendship, "they have the right to be on the other side of the street." That this was a right devised to benefit those who would subvert civil order was, for many Cubans, a given, because this was a community in which nothing could be inadvertent, nothing without its place in a larger, usually hostile, scheme. The logic was close, even claustrophobic. That the *Herald* should have run, on the 1985 anniversary of the Bay of Pigs, a story about Canadian and Italian tourists vacationing on what had been the invasion beaches (RESORT SELLS SUN, FUN—IN CUBA: TOPLESS BATHERS FROLIC AS HAVANA TRIES HAND AT TOURISM) was, in this view, not just a minor historical irony, not just an arguably insensitive attempt to find a news peg for a twenty-four-year-old annual story, but a calculated affront to the Cuban community, "a slap," I was repeatedly told, "in the face." That the *Herald* should have run, a few weeks before, a story suggesting a greater availability of consumer goods in Cuba (FREE MARKETS ALLOW HAVANA TO SPIFF UP) not only sealed the affront but indicated that it was systematic, directed by Washington and signaling a rapprochement between the Americans and Havana, the imminence of which was a fixed idea among Miami Cubans.

Fixed ideas about Americans seemed, among Miami Cubans, general. Americans, I was frequently told, never touched one another, nor did they argue. Americans did not share the attachment to family which characterized Cuban life. Americans did not share the attachment to *patria* which characterized Cuban life. Americans placed undue importance on being on time. Americans were undereducated. Americans, at one and the same time, acted exclusively in their own interests and failed to see their own interests, not only because they were undereducated but because they were by temperament "naive," a people who could live and die without ever understanding those nuances of conspiracy and allegiance on which, in the Cuban view, the world turned.

Americans, above all, lacked "passion," which was the central failing from which most of these other national peculiarities flowed. If I wanted evidence that Americans lacked passion, I was advised repeatedly, I had only to consider their failure to appreciate *la lucha.* If I wanted further evidence that Americans lacked passion, I had only to turn on a television set and watch Ted Koppel's "Nightline," a program on which, I was told a number of times, it was possible to observe Americans "with very opposing points of view" talking "completely without passion," "without any gestures at all," and "seemingly without any idea in the world of conspiring against each other, despite being totally opposed."

This repeated reference to "Nightline" was arresting. At the end of a day or an evening in Miami I would look through my notes and find the references underlined and boxed in my notebook, with arrows, and the notation, "Ch.: NIGHTLINE???" The mode of discourse favored by Ted Koppel (it was always, for reasons I never discerned, Ted Koppel, no one else) and his guests seemed in fact so consistent a source of novelty and derision among the Cubans to whom I spoke in Miami that I began to see these mentions of "Nightline" as more shorthand, the Cuban version of the Anglo telephone call to the house on Kiaora Street in Coconut Grove which did or did not belong to Raul Masvidal, another glove thrown down, another stand; the code which indicated that the speaker, like José Martí, knew the Monster, and did not mean to live easily in its lair.

"Let those who desire a secure homeland conquer it," José Martí also wrote. "Let those who do not conquer it live under the whip and in exile, watched over like wild animals, cast from one country to another, concealing the death of their souls with a beggar's smile from the scorn of free men." The humiliation of the continuing exile was what the Monster, lacking passion, did not understand. It was taken for granted in this continuing exile that the Monster, lacking passion or understanding, could be utilized. It was also taken for granted in this continuing exile that the Monster, lacking passion or understanding, could not be trusted. "We must attempt to strengthen the non-Batista democratic anti-Castro forces in exile," a John F. Kennedy campaign statement had declared in the course of working up an issue against Richard Nixon in 1960. "We cannot have the United States walk away from one of the greatest moral challenges in postwar history," Ronald Reagan had declared in the course of working up support for the Nicaraguan freedom fighters in 1985.

"We have seen that movie before," one prominent exile had said to me about the matter of the United States not, as Ronald Reagan had put it, walking away from the Nicaraguan freedom fighters. Here between the mangrove swamp and the barrier reef was an American city largely populated by people who believed that the United States had walked away before, had betrayed them at the Bay of Pigs and later, with consequences we have since seen. Here between the swamp and the reef was an American city populated by people who also believed that the United States would betray them again, in Honduras and in El Salvador and in Nicaragua, betray them at all the barricades of a phantom war they had once again taken not as the projection of another Washington abstraction but as their own struggle, *la lucha*, *la causa*, with consequences we have not yet seen.

THREE

8

"DON'T FORGET that we have a disposal problem" is what Arthur M. Schlesinger, Jr., tells us that Allen Dulles said on March 11, 1961, by way of warning John F. Kennedy about the possible consequences of aborting the projected Cuban invasion and cutting loose what the CIA knew to be a volatile and potentially vengeful asset, the 2506 Brigade. What John F. Kennedy was said to have said, four weeks later, to Arthur M. Schlesinger, Jr., is this: "If we have to get rid of these 800 men, it is much better to dump them in Cuba than in the United States, especially if that is where they want to go." This is dialogue recalled by someone without much ear for it, and the number of men involved in the invasion force was closer to fifteen hundred than to eight hundred, but the core of it, the "dump them in Cuba" construction, has an authentic ring, as does "disposal problem" itself. Over the years since the publication of *A Thousand Days* I had read the chapter in which these two lines appear several times, but only after I had spent time in Miami did I begin to see them as curtain lines, or as the cannon which the protagonist brings onstage in the first act so that it may be fired against him in the third.

"I would say that John F. Kennedy is still the number two most hated man in Miami," Raul Masvidal said to me one afternoon, not long after he had announced his candidacy for mayor, in a cool and immaculate office on the top floor of one of the Miami banks in which he has an interest. Raul Masvidal, who was born in Havana in 1942, would seem in many ways a model for what both Anglo Miami and the rest of the United States like to see as Cuban assimilation. He was named by both Cubans and non-Cubans in a 1983 *Miami Herald* poll as the most powerful Cuban in Miami. He received the endorsement of the *Herald* in his campaign to become mayor of Miami, the election he ultimately lost to Xavier Suarez. He was, at the time we spoke, one of two Cuban members (the other being Armando Codina, a Miami entrepreneur and member of the advisory board of the Southeast First National Bank) of

The Non-Group, an unofficial and extremely private organization which had been called the shadow government of South Florida and included among its thirty-eight members, who met once a month for dinner at one another's houses or clubs, the ownership or top management of Knight-Ridder, Eastern Airlines, Arvida Disney, Burdines, the Miami Dolphins, and the major banks and utilities.

"Castro is of course the number one most hated," Raul Masvidal added. "Then Kennedy. The entire Kennedy family." He opened and closed a leather folder, the only object on his marble desk, then aligned it with the polished edge of the marble. On the wall behind him hung a framed poster with the legend, in English, YOU HAVE NOT CONVERTED A MAN BECAUSE YOU HAVE SILENCED HIM, a sentiment so outside the thrust of local Cuban thinking that it lent the office an aspect of having been dressed exclusively for visits from what Cubans sometimes call, with a slight ironic edge, the mainstream population.

"Something I did which involved Ted Kennedy became very controversial here," Raul Masvidal said then. "Jorge asked me to contact Senator Kennedy." He was talking about Jorge Mas Canosa, the Miami engineering contractor (the "advisor to U.S. Senators," "confidant of federal bureaucrats," "lobbyist for anti-Castro U.S. policies" and "near unknown in Miami," as the *Herald* had described him a few years before) who had been, through the Washington office of the Cuban American National Foundation and its companion PAC, the National Coalition for a Free Cuba, instrumental in the lobbying for Radio Martí. "To see if we could get him to reverse his position on Radio Martí. We needed Kennedy to change his vote, to give that bill the famous luster. I did that. And the Cubans here took it as if it had been an attempt to make peace with the Kennedys."

The man who had been accused of attempting to make peace with the Kennedys arrived in this country in 1960, when he was eighteen. He enrolled at the University of Miami, then took two semesters off to train with the 2506 for the Bay of Pigs. After the 1962 Cuban missile crisis, which was then and is still perceived in Miami as another personal betrayal on the part of John F. Kennedy, Raul Masvidal again dropped out of the University of Miami, this time to join a unit of Cubans recruited by the United States Army for training at Fort Knox, Kentucky, part of what Theodore C. Sorensen, in *Kennedy*, recalled in rather soft focus as a "special arrangement" under which Bay of Pigs veterans "were quietly entering the American armed forces."

This seems to have been, even through the filter offered by diarists of the Kennedy administration, a gray area. Like other such ad hoc attempts to neutralize the 2506, the recruitment program involved, if not outright deception, a certain encouragement of self-deception, an apparent willingness to allow those Cubans who "were quietly entering the American armed forces" to do so under the misapprehension that the United States was in fact preparing to invade Cuba. Sentences appear to have been left unfinished, and hints dropped. Possibilities appear to have been floated, and not exclusively, as it has become the convention in this kind of situation to suggest, by some uncontrollable element in the field, some rogue agent. "President Kennedy came to the Orange Bowl and made us a promise," Jorge Mas Canosa, who is also a veteran of the 2506, repeated insistently to me one morning, his voice rising in the retelling of what has become for Miami a primal story. "December. Nineteen sixty-two. What he said turned out to be another—I won't say deception, let us call it a misconception—another misconception on the part of President Kennedy."

Jorge Mas Canosa had drawn the words "President" and "Kennedy" out, inflecting all syllables with equal emphasis. This was the same Jorge Mas Canosa who had enlisted Raul Masvidal in the effort to secure the luster of the Kennedy name for Radio Martí, the Jorge Mas Canosa who had founded the Cuban American National Foundation and was one of those funding its slick offices overlooking the Potomac in Georgetown; the Jorge Mas Canosa who had become so much a figure in Washington that it was sometimes hard to catch up with him in Miami. I had driven finally down the South Dixie Highway that morning to meet him at his main construction yard, the cramped office of which was decorated with a LONG LIVE FREE GRENADA poster and framed photographs of Jorge Mas Canosa with Ronald Reagan and Jorge Mas Canosa with Jeane Kirkpatrick and Jorge Mas Canosa with Paula Hawkins. "And at the Orange Bowl he was given the flag," Jorge Mas Canosa continued. "The flag the invasion forces had taken to Playa Girón. And he took this flag in his hands and he promised that he would return it to us in a free Havana. And he called on us to join the United States armed forces. To get training. And try again."

This particular effort to get the cannon offstage foundered, as many such efforts foundered, on the familiar shoal of Washington hubris. In this instance the hubris took the form of simultaneously underestimating the exiles' distrust of the United States and overestimating their capacity for self-deception, which, although considerable, was tempered always by a rather more extensive experience in the politics of conspiracy than the Kennedy administration's own. The exiles had not, once they put it together that the point of the exercise was to keep them occupied, served easily. Jorge Mas Canosa, who had been sent to Fort Benning, had stayed only long enough to finish OCS, then resigned his commission and returned to Miami. At Fort Knox, according to Raul Masvidal, there had been, "once it became evident that the United States and Russia had reached an agreement and the United States had no intention of invading Cuba," open rebellion.

"A lot of things happened," Raul Masvidal said. "For example we had a strike, which was unheard of for soldiers. One day we just decided we were going to remain in our barracks for a few days. They threatened us with all kinds of things. But at that point we didn't care much for the threats." A representative of the Kennedy White House had finally been dispatched to Fort Knox to try to resolve the situation, and a deal had been struck, a renegotiated "special arrangement," under which the exiles agreed to end their strike in return for an immediate transfer to Fort Jackson, South Carolina (they had found Kentucky, they said, too cold), and an almost immediate discharge. At this point Raul Masvidal went back to the University of Miami, to parking cars at the Everglades Hotel, and to the more fluid strategies of CIA/Miami, which was then running, through a front operation on the south campus of the University of Miami called Zenith Technological Services and code-named JM/WAVE, a kind of action about which everybody in Miami and nobody in Washington seemed to know.

"I guess during that period I was kind of a full-time student and part-time warrior," Raul Masvidal had recalled the afternoon we spoke. "In those days the CIA had these infiltration teams in the Florida Keys, and they ran sporadic missions to Cuba." These training camps in the Keys, which appear to have been simultaneously run by the CIA and, in what was after the Cuban missile crisis a further convolution of the disposal problem, periodically raided by the FBI, do not much figure in the literature of the Kennedy administration. Theodore C. Sorensen, in *Kennedy*, mentioned "a crackdown by Federal authorities on the publicity-seeking Cuban refugee groups who conducted hit-and-run raids on Cuban ports and shipping," further distancing the "publicity-seeking Cuban refugee groups" from the possessive plural of the White House by adding that they damaged "little other than our efforts to persuade the Soviets to leave." Arthur M. Schlesinger, Jr., elided this Miami action altogether in *A Thousand Days*, an essentially antihistorical work in which the entire matter of the Cuban exiles is seen to have resolved itself on an inspirational note in December of 1962, when Jacqueline Kennedy stood at the Orange Bowl before the Bay of Pigs veterans, 1,113 of whom had just returned from imprisonment in Cuba, and said, in Spanish, that she wanted her son to be "a man at least half as brave as the members of Brigade 2506." In his more complex reconsideration of the period, *Robert Kennedy and His Times*, Schlesinger did deal with the Miami action, but with so profound a queasiness as to suggest that the question of whether the United States government had or had not been involved with it ("But had CIA been up to its old tricks?") remained obscure, as if unknowable.

Such accounts seem, in Miami, where an impressive amount of the daily business of the city is carried on by men who speak casually of having run missions for the CIA, remote to the point of the delusional. According to reports published in 1975 and 1976 and prompted by hearings before the Church committee, the Senate Select Committee to Study Governmental Operations with Respect to Intelligence Operations, the CIA's JM/WAVE station on the University of Miami campus was by 1962 the largest CIA installation, outside Langley, in the world, and one of the largest employers in the state of Florida.

There were said to have been at JM/WAVE headquarters between 300 and 400 case officers from the CIA's clandestine services branch. Each case officer was said to have run between four and ten Cuban "principal agents," who were referred to in code as "amots." Each principal agent was said to have run in turn between ten and thirty "regular agents," again mainly exiles.

The arithmetic here is impressive. Even the minimum figures, 300 case officers each running 4 principal agents who in turn ran 10 regular agents, yield 12,000 regular agents. The maximum figures yield 120,000 regular agents, each of whom might be presumed to have contacts of his own. There were, all operating under the JM/WAVE umbrella, flotillas of small boats. There were mother ships, disguised as merchant vessels, what an unidentified CIA source described to the *Herald* as "the third largest navy in the western hemisphere." There was the CIA's Miami airline, Southern Air Transport, acquired in 1960 and subsequently financed through its holding company, Actus Technology Inc., and through another CIA holding company, the Pacific Corporation, with more than $16.7 million in loans from the CIA's Air America and an additional $6.6 million from the Manufacturers Hanover Trust Company. There were hundreds of pieces of Miami real estate, residential bungalows maintained as safe houses, waterfront properties maintained as safe harbors. There were, besides the phantom "Zenith Technological Services" that was JM/WAVE headquarters itself, fifty-four other front businesses, providing employment and cover and various services required by JM/WAVE operations. There were CIA boat shops. There were CIA gun shops. There were CIA travel agencies and there were CIA real-estate agencies and there were CIA detective agencies.

Anyone who spent any time at all on the street in Miami during the early 1960s, then, was likely to have had dealings with the CIA, to have known what actions were being run, to have known who was running them, and for whom. Among Cubans of his generation in Miami, Raul Masvidal was perhaps most unusual in that he did not actually run the missions himself. "I was more an assistant to the person who was running the program," he had said the day we talked. "Helping with the logistics. Making sure the people got fed and had the necessary weapons. It was a frustrating time, because you could see the pattern right away. The pattern was for a decline in activity toward Castro. We were just being kept busy. For two reasons. One reason was that it provided a certain amount of intelligence in which the CIA was interested."

Raul Masvidal is wary, almost impassive. He speaks carefully, in the even cadences of American management, the cadences of someone who received a degree in international business at Thunderbird, the American Graduate School of International Management in Arizona, and had been by the time he was thirty a vice president of Citibank in New York and Madrid, and this was one of the few occasions during our conversation when he allowed emotion to enter his voice. "The other reason," he said, "was that it was supposed to keep people in Miami thinking that something was being done. The fact that there were a few Cubans running around Miami saying that they were being trained, that they were running missions—well, it kept up a few hopes." Raul Masvidal paused. "So I guess that was important to the CIA," he said then. "To try to keep people here from facing the very hard and very frustrating fact that they were not going home because their strongest and best ally had made a deal. Behind their backs."

Bottom soundings are hard to come by here. We are talking about 1963, the year which ended in the death of John F. Kennedy. It was a year described by Arthur M. Schlesinger, Jr., as one in which "the notion of invading Cuba had been dead for years" (since the notion of invading Cuba had demonstrably not been dead as recently as April of 1961, the "for years" is interesting on its face, and suggestive of the way in which Washington's perception of time expands and contracts with its agenda); a year in which, in the wake of the missile crisis and John F. Kennedy's 1962 agreement not to invade Cuba, the administration's anti-Castro policy had been "drastically modified" and in which the White House was in fact, as Schlesinger put it, "drifting toward accommodation." It was a year in which the official and well-publicized Washington policy toward Miami exile operations was one of unequivocal discouragement and even prosecution, a year of repeated exile arrests and weapons seizures; a year that was later described by the chief of station for JM/WAVE, in testimony before the Church committee, as one in which "the whole apparatus of government, Coast Guard, Customs, Immigration and Naturalization, FBI, CIA, were working together to try to keep these operations from going to Cuba." (The chief of station for JM/WAVE in 1963 happened to be Theodore Shackley, who left Miami in 1965, spent from 1966 until 1972 as political officer and chief of station in Vientiane and Saigon, and turned up in 1987 in the Tower Commission report, meeting on page B-3 in Hamburg with Manucher Ghorbanifar and with the former head of SAVAK counterespionage; discussing on page B-11 the hostage problem over lunch with Michael Ledeen.)

On the one hand "the whole apparatus of government" did seem to be "working together to try to keep these operations from going to Cuba," and on the other hand the whole apparatus of government seemed not to be doing this. There was still, it turned out, authorized CIA funding for such "autonomous operations" (a concept devised by Walt Whitman Rostow at the State Department) as the exile action group JURE, or Junta Revolucionaria Cubana, an "autonomous operation" being an operation, according to guidelines summarized in a CIA memorandum, with which the United States, "if ever charged with complicity," would deny having anything to do. "Autonomous operations" were, it turned out, part of the "track two" approach, which, whatever it meant in theory, meant for example in practice that JURE could, on "track two," request and receive explosives and grenades from the CIA even as, on track one, JURE was being investigated for possession of illegal firearms by the FBI and the INS.

"Track two" and "autonomous operations" were of course Washington phrases, phrases from the special vocabulary of Special Groups and Standing Groups and "guidelines" and "approaches," words from a language in which deniability was built into the grammar, and as such may or may not have had a different meaning, or any meaning, in 1963 in Miami, where deniability had become in many ways the very opposite of the point. In a CIA review of various attempts between 1960 and 1963 to assassinate Fidel Castro (which were "merely one aspect of the overall active effort to overthrow the regime," in other words not exactly a third track), an internal report prepared in 1967 by the Inspector General of the CIA and declassified in 1978 for release to the House Select Committee on Assassinations, there appears, on the matter of Washington language, this instructive reflection:

> . . . There is a third point, which was not directly made by any of those we interviewed, but which emerges clearly from the interviews and from reviews of files. The point is that of frequent resort to synecdoche—the mention of a part when the whole is to be understood, or vice versa. Thus, we encounter repeated references to phrases such as "disposing of Castro," which may be read in the narrow, literal sense of assassinating him, when it is intended that it be read in the broader, figurative sense of dislodging the Castro regime. Reversing the coin, we find people speaking vaguely of "doing something about Castro" when it is clear that what they have specifically in mind is killing him. In a situation wherein those speaking may not have actually meant what they seemed to say or may not have said what they actually meant, they should not be surprised if their oral shorthand is interpreted differently than was intended.

In the superimposition of the Washington dreamwork on that of Miami there has always been room, in other words, for everyone to believe what they need to believe. Arthur M. Schlesinger, Jr., in *Robert Kennedy and His Times*, finally went so far as to conclude that the CIA had during 1963 in Miami continued to wage what he still preferred to call "its private war against Castro," or had "evidently" done so, "despite," as he put it, in a clause that suggests the particular angle of deflection in the superimposition, "the lack of Special Group authorization." Asked at a press conference in May of 1963 whether either the CIA or the White House was supporting exile paramilitary operations, John F. Kennedy said this: "We may well be . . . well, none that I am familiar with . . . I don't think as of today that we are." What James Angleton, who was then chief of counterintelligence for the CIA, was later quoted as having said about the year 1963 in Miami, and about what the CIA was or was not doing, with or without Special Group authorization, was this: "The concept of Miami was correct. In a Latino area, it made sense to have a base in Miami for Latin American problems, as an extension of the desk. If it had been self-contained, then it would have had the quality of being a foreign base of sorts. It was a novel idea. But it got out of hand, it became a power unto itself. And when the target diminishes, it's very difficult for a bureaucracy to adjust. What do you do with your personnel? We owed a deep obligation to the men in Miami."

In Washington in 1962, according to a footnote in *Robert Kennedy and His Times*, "the regular Special Group—[Maxwell] Taylor, McGeorge Bundy, Alexis Johnson, [Roswell] Gilpatric, [Lyman] Lemnitzer and [John] McCone—would meet at two o'clock every Thursday afternoon. When its business was finished, Robert Kennedy would arrive, and it would expand into the Special Group (CI). At the end of the day, Cuba would become the subject, and the group, with most of the same people, would metamorphose into Special Group (Augmented)." That was the context in which those people with the most immediate interest in the policy of the United States toward Cuba appear, during the years of the Kennedy administration, to have been talking in Washington. This was the context in which those people with the same interest during the same years appear, according to testimony later given before the Church committee by the 1963 chief of station for JM/WAVE, to have been talking in Miami: "'Assassination' was part of the ambience of that time . . . nobody could be involved in Cuban operations without having had some sort of discussion at some time with some Cuban who said . . . the way to create a revolution is to shoot Fidel and Raúl . . . so the fact that somebody would talk about assassination just wasn't anything really out of the ordinary at that time."

What John F. Kennedy actually said when he held the 2506 flag in his hands at the Orange Bowl on December 29, 1962, was this: "I can assure you that this flag will be returned to this brigade in a free Havana." How Theodore C. Sorensen described this was as "a supposed Kennedy promise for a second invasion." How Arthur M. Schlesinger, Jr., described it was as "a promise," but one "not in the script," a promise made "in the emotion of the day." What Jorge Mas Canosa said about it, that morning in the office with the LONG LIVE FREE GRENADA poster and the framed photographs of figures from yet another administration, the office in the construction yard forty minutes down the South Dixie Highway, a forty-minute drive down a flat swamp of motor home rentals and discount waterbed sales and boat repairs and bird and reptile sales and Midas Mufflers and Radio Shacks, was this: "I remember that later some people here made a joke about President Kennedy and that promise." Jorge Mas Canosa had again drawn out the syllables, *Pres-ee-dent Ken-ned-ee*, and I listened closely, because, during a considerable amount of time spent listening to exiles in Miami talk about the promise John F. Kennedy made at the Orange Bowl, I had not before heard anything approaching a joke. "The joke," Jorge Mas Canosa said, "was that the 'Free Havana' he meant was a bar by that name here in Miami."

9

TO SPEND time in Miami is to acquire a certain fluency in cognitive dissonance. What Allen Dulles called the disposal problem is what Miami calls *la lucha*. One man's loose cannon is another's freedom fighter, or, in the local phrase, man of action, or man of valor. "This is a thing for men of valor, not for weaklings like you," an exile named Miriam Arocena had told the *Miami Herald* reporter who tried to interview her after the arrest of her husband, Eduardo Arocena, who was finally convicted, in a series of trials which ended a few days before the Bay of Pigs twenty-fourth anniversary observances at the 2506 bungalow and at the Martyrs of Girón monument and at the chapel which faces Cuba, of seventy-one federal counts connected with bombings in New York and Miami and with the 1980 assassination in New York of Félix García Rodríguez, an attaché at the Cuban mission to the United Nations, as well as with the attempted assassination the same year of Raúl Roa Kouri, at that time the Cuban ambassador to the United Nations.

The Florida bombings in question had taken place, between 1979 and 1983, at the Mexican consulate in Miami, at the Venezuelan consulate in Miami, and at various Miami businesses rumored in the exile community to have had dealings with, or sympathy for, or perhaps merely indifference toward, the current government of Cuba. None of these bombings had caused deaths or mutilations, although bombings which did had become commonplace enough in Miami during the 1970s to create a market for devices designed to flick the ignition in a parked car by remote signal, enabling the intended victim to watch what might have been his own incineration from across the street, an interested bystander.

Many of the bombings mentioned in the government's case against Eduardo Arocena involved what the FBI called his signature, a pocket-watch timer with a floral backpiece. All had been claimed, in communiqués to local Spanish radio stations and newspapers, by Omega 7, which was by the time of these Arocena trials perhaps the most extensively prosecuted and so the most widely known of all the exile action groups operating out of Miami and New Jersey, where there had been since the beginning of the exile a small but significant exile concentration. Omega 7, the leader of which used the code name "Omar," was said by the FBI to have been involved in not only the machine-gunning in Queens of Felíx García Rodríguez and the attempted car-bombing in Manhattan of Raúl Roa Kouri (whose driver had discovered the bag of plastique under the car, which was parked at 12 East Eighty-first Street) but also in the 1979 murder in Union City, New Jersey, of Eulalio José Negrin, an exile who supported the normalization of relations between the United States and Cuba and so was killed by a fusillade of semiautomatic fire as he got into a car with his thirteen-year-old son.

Omega 7 had claimed, in New York, the 1979 TWA terminal bombing at Kennedy airport. Omega 7 had claimed the 1978 Avery Fisher Hall bombing at Lincoln Center. Omega 7 had claimed, in Manhattan alone, the 1975 and 1977 bombings of the Venezuelan Mission to the United Nations on East Fifty-first Street, the 1976 and 1978 bombings at the Cuban Mission to the United Nations on East Sixty-seventh Street, the two 1979 bombings of the relocated Cuban Mission to the United Nations on Lexington Avenue, the 1979 bombing of the Soviet Mission to the United Nations on East Sixty-seventh Street, the 1978 bombing of the office of *El Diario–La Prensa* on Hudson Street, the 1980 bombing of the Soviet Union's Aeroflot ticket office on Fifth Avenue, and, by way of protesting the inclusion of Cuban boxers on the card at Madison Square Garden, the 1978 bombing of the adjacent Gerry Cosby Sporting Goods store at 2 Penn Plaza.

The issue in dispute, then, during the three trials that made up *United States of America* v. *Eduardo Arocena*, the first in New York and the second and third in Miami, was not whether Omega 7 had committed the acts mentioned in the indictments, but whether Eduardo Arocena was in fact its leader, "Omar." The government continued to maintain, with considerable success, that he was. Eduardo Arocena continued to maintain that he was not, notwithstanding the fact that he had in 1982 talked at some length to the FBI, in a room at the Ramada Inn near the Miami airport, about Omega 7 actions; had declared during his New York trial that he "unconditionally supported" those actions; and had advised the second of his Miami juries that they had in him "the most confirmed terrorist of all," one who would never repent. "*Padre*, forgive them," Eduardo Arocena had said when this jury handed down its verdicts of guilty on all counts. "For they know not what they do." Miriam Arocena, a small intense woman who strained forward in her seat during testimony and moved to crouch protectively behind her husband whenever the lawyers were conferring with the judge, had called the trial a "comedy," "a farce the government of the United States is carrying out in order to benefit Fidel Castro."

Early in the course of this third Arocena trial I had spent some time at the federal courthouse in downtown Miami, watching the federal prosecutors enter their physical evidence, the wigs and the hairpieces and the glue and the Samsonite attaché cases ("Contents—one pair black gloves, one cheesecloth Handi Wipe rag," or "Contents—one .38-caliber revolver") seized at the bungalow on Southwest Seventh Street in which Eduardo Arocena had been apprehended: an entire modus operandi for the hypothetical Omar, conjured up from the brassbound trunks which the prosecution hauled into court every morning. There was the Browning 9mm pistol. There was the sales receipt for the Browning, as well as for the .25-caliber Beretta Jetfire, the AR-15, and the UZI. There were the timers and there were the firecracker fuses. There were the Eveready Energizer alkaline batteries. There was the target list, with the names and the locations of offending businesses, some of them underscored: *Réplica* magazine, Padron Cigars, Almacén El Español, Ebenezer Trading Agency, a half dozen others. All that was missing finally was the explosive material itself, the stuff, the dynamite or the plastique, but the defendant, according to the government, had already advised the FBI that the military plastique called C-4 could be readily obtained on the street in Miami.

This was all engrossing, not least because it was curiously artless, devoid of much instinct for the clandestine, the wigs and the hairpieces notwithstanding. The sales receipts for the Browning and for the Beretta and for the AR-15 and for the UZI were in the defendant's own name. The target list bore on its upper-left-hand corner the notation TARGETS, suggesting an indifference to discovery which tended to undermine the government's exhaustive cataloging of that which had been discovered. A man who buys a Browning and a Beretta and an AR-15 and an UZI under his own name does not have as his first interest the successful evasion of American justice. A man who compiles a target list under the heading TARGETS may in fact have a first interest best served by disclosure, the inclination toward public statement natural to someone who sees himself as engaged not in a crime but a crusade. HEROES DE OMEGA 7, as the Omega 7 stencils were lettered. The stencils were Exhibit 3036, recovered by the FBI from a self-storage locker on Southwest Seventy-second Street. LA VERDAD ES NUESTROS.

There was flickering all through this presentation of the government's evidence a certain stubborn irritability, a sense of crossed purposes, crossed wires, of cultures not exactly colliding but glancing off one another, at unpromising angles. Eduardo Arocena's attorney, a rather rumpled Cuban who had adopted as his general strategy the argument that this trial was taking place at all only because the United States had caved in to what he called "the international community," looked on with genial contempt. The government attorneys, young and well-pressed, rummaged doggedly through their trunks, property masters for what had become in Miami, after some years of trials in which the defense talked about the international community and the prosecution about cheesecloth Handi Wipe rags, a kind of local puppet theater, to which the audience continued to respond in ways novel to those unfamiliar with the form.

This was a theater in which the defendant was always cast as the hero and martyr, not at all because the audience believed him wrongly accused, innocent of whatever charges had been trumped up against him, but precisely because the audience believed him to be guilty. The applause, in other words, was for the action, not for the actor. "Anybody who fights communism has my sympathy," the head of the 2506 Brigade told the *Miami Herald* at the time of Eduardo Arocena's arrest. "The best communist is a dead communist. If that is his way to fight, I won't condemn him." Andres Nazario Sargen of Alpha 66 had said this: "He is a person who chose that path for the liberation of Cuba. We have to respect his position but we think our methods are more effective."

Nor was this response confined exclusively to those members of the audience who, like the men of the 2506 or Alpha 66, might be expected to exhibit a certain institutional tolerance toward bombing as a political tactic. "It's like asking the Palestinian people about Arafat," the news director of WQBA, the Miami radio station that calls itself *La Cubanísima*, had said to the *Herald* about Eduardo Arocena. "He may be a terrorist, but to the Palestinian people he's not thought of that way." All *el exilio* stood by its men of action. When, for example, after Eduardo Arocena's arrest in July of 1983, a fund for his defense was organized within the exile community, one of the contributors was Xavier Suarez, who was that year running a losing campaign for the post to which he was later elected, mayor of Miami. Xavier Suarez was brought to this country as a child, in 1960. He is a graduate of Villanova. He is a graduate of Harvard Law. He has a master's degree in public policy from the John F. Kennedy School of Government at Harvard. He said about Eduardo Arocena that he preferred to think of him not as a terrorist, but a freedom fighter.

Sometimes (when, say, Xavier Suarez says that he prefers to think of Eduardo Arocena not as a terrorist but a freedom fighter, or when, say, Xavier Suarez stands on the back of a Mazda pickup and speaks of the right to be on the other side of the street as unfortunate) words are believed in Miami to be without consequence. Other times they are not. Among the bombs which Omega 7 was credited with having left around Miami in January of 1983, a period of considerable industry for Omega 7, was one at the office of *Réplica*, a Spanish-language weekly largely devoted to soft news and entertainment gossip (CATHY LEE CROSBY: EL SEXO ES MUY IMPORTANTE PARA ELLA is a not atypical photo caption) and edited by an exile named Max Lesnik. Max Lesnik was, in the period after Fidel Castro's 1953 attack on the Moncada Barracks, a youth leader in the Cuban People's Party, the party founded by Eduardo Chibás and known as the "Ortodoxo" party. Opposed to Batista, Max Lesnik was also opposed to Castro, on the grounds that he and his 26 Julio were destructive to the anti-Batista movement.

During the time Castro was in the Sierra Maestra, Max Lesnik was working underground in Havana against Batista, not with the 26 Julio but with the Segundo Frente del Escambray, and it was he, in the waning days of 1958, who interested the CIA in the last-ditch attempt to bring Carlos Prío back from Miami as Batista's successor. He made his final break with Castro, and with Cuba, in 1961.

This demonstrable lack of enthusiasm for Fidel Castro notwithstanding, Max Lesnik was considered, by some people in Miami, insufficiently anti-Castro, principally because he, or *Réplica*, had a history of using what were seen to be the wrong words. "Negotiation," for example, was a wrong word, and so, in this context, was "political," as in "a political approach." A political approach implied give-and-take, even compromise, an unthinkable construct in a community organized exclusively around the principle of implacable resistance, and it was the occasional discussion of such an approach in the pages of *Réplica* that had caused *Réplica* to be underscored on Eduardo Arocena's target list, and five bombs to have been left at the *Réplica* office between 1981 and 1984.

Some of *Réplica*'s trouble on this point dated from 1974, when a contributor named Luciano Nieves suggested that the way to bring Fidel Castro down might be "politically," by working with Cubans within Cuba in an effort to force elections and the acceptance of a legal opposition. Someone who did not agree with Luciano Nieves broke a chair over his head in the Versailles, a Cuban restaurant on Southwest Eighth Street where many of the more visible figures in *el exilio* turn up late in the evening. Several other people who did not agree with Luciano Nieves conspired to try, in November of 1974, to assassinate him, a count on which three members of an action group called the Pragmatistas were later tried and convicted, but Luciano Nieves, and *Réplica*, persisted.

In February of 1975, two days after *Réplica* published his declaration that he would return to Cuba to participate in any election Fidel Castro should call, Luciano Nieves was shot and killed, in the parking lot of Variety Children's Hospital in Miami, an event construed locally as his own fault. "I'm glad I never finally came out publicly in favor of peaceful coexistence with Castro," an unidentified professor at what was then Miami-Dade Junior College was quoted as having said a few days later in the *Miami News*, in a story headlined INTELLECTUALS FEARFUL AFTER CUBAN KILLING. "Now, I'll be more than careful not to. Cubans are apparently very sensitive to that." The incident in the parking lot of Variety Children's Hospital was mentioned to me by a number of people during the time I spent in Miami, always to this corrective point.

10

THE BOMB Eduardo Arocena was believed to have left at the *Réplica* office in January of 1983 did not, as it happened, go off, but another bomb credited that month to Omega 7 did, this one at a factory on Flagler Street owned by an exiled cigar manufacturer named Orlando Padron. Orlando Padron's treason, as it was viewed by many, had been to visit Havana in 1978 (he was said to have been photographed handing Fidel Castro a Padron cigar) as a member of the "Committee of 75," a participant in what was called the *diálogo*, or dialogue, a word with the same reverberations as "political."

The *diálogo* began as an essay into private diplomacy on the part of a prominent exile banker, Bernardo Benes, whose somewhat visionary notion it was that the exiles themselves, with the tacit cooperation of the Carter administration, could, in what was to become a series of visits to Havana, open a continuing discussion with the Cuban government. Secretary of State Cyrus Vance was approached. The National Security Council and the CIA and the FBI were consulted. The visits to Havana took place, and resulted in two concessions, one an agreement by the Cuban government to release certain political prisoners, some thirty-six hundred in all, the other an agreement allowing exiles who wished to visit relatives in Cuba to do so on seven-day package tours.

Such agreements might have seemed, outside Miami, unexceptionable. Such agreements might even have seemed, outside Miami, to serve the interests of the exile community, but to think this would be to miss the drift of the exile style. Americans, it is often said in Miami, will act always in their own interests, an indictment. Miami Cubans, by implicit contrast, take their stand on a higher ground, *la lucha* as a sacred abstraction, and any talk about "interests," or for that matter "agreements," remains alien to the local temperament, which is absolutist, and sacrificial, on the Spanish model.

Which is to say on the Cuban model. ". . . I feel my belief in sacrifice and struggle getting stronger," Fidel Castro wrote from his prison cell on the Isle of Pines on December 19, 1953.

"I despise the kind of existence that clings to the miserly trifles of comfort and self-interest. I think that a man should not live beyond the age when he begins to deteriorate, when the flame that lighted the brightest moment of his life has weakened . . ." In exile as well as in situ, this is the preferred Cuban self-perception, the same idealization of gesture and intention which led, in the months and years after the *diálogo*, to bombings and assassinations and to public occasions of excoriation and recantation, to accusations and humiliations which broke some and estranged many; an unloosing of fratricidal furies from which *el exilio* did not entirely recover.

Bernardo Benes, the architect of the *diálogo* and its principal surviving victim, arrived at the Miami airport, alone, on November 11, 1960, a day he recalls as the bleakest of his life. He recalls believing that the exile would last at most nine months. He recalls himself as unprepared in every way to accept the exile as an immigration, and yet, like many of the early exiles, a significant number of whom had been educated to move in the necessarily international commercial life of prerevolutionary Havana, Bernardo Benes apparently managed to maintain the notion of Florida as a kind of colonial opportunity, an India to be tapped, and in this spirit he prospered, first as an officer of a Miami savings and loan, Washington Federal, and then as a local entrepreneur. He was, for example, the first exile to own a major automobile dealership in Miami. He was among the first exiles to start a bank in Miami, the Continental. He was also, and this continued to be, in the culturally resistant world of *el exilio*, a more ambiguous distinction, the first exile to travel what has been in provincial American cities a traditional road to assimilation, the visible doing of approved works, the act of making oneself available for this steering committee, for that kickoff dinner.

"I am frank," Bernardo Benes said when I talked to him one morning at his house on Biscayne Bay. "I do not beat around the bush. Until 1977, 1978, I was The Cuban in Miami. This goes back to when I was still at Washington Federal, I was chief of all the branches, I was the contact for Latin America. So sometimes I was working twenty hours a day to make the time, but believe me, I did. There was nothing important happening in Miami that I wasn't involved with. I was the guerrilla in the establishment, the first person to bring other Cubans into the picture." Bernardo Benes paused. "I and I and I and I," he said finally. "And then came the big change in my life. I was no longer the first token Cuban in Miami. I was the Capitán Dreyfus of Miami."

We were sitting at the kitchen counter, drinking the caffeine and sugar infusion that is Cuban coffee, and as Bernardo Benes began to talk about the *diálogo* and its aftermath he glanced repeatedly at his wife, a strikingly attractive woman who was clearing the breakfast dishes with the brisk, definite movements of someone who has only a limited enthusiasm for the discussion at hand. The *diálogo*, Bernardo Benes said, had come about by "pure chance." There had been, he said, a family vacation in Panama. There had been in Panama, he said, a telephone call from a friend, an entreaty to have lunch with two officers of the Cuban government. This lunch in Panama, he said, had been "the beginning of the end."

There was about this account a certain foretold quality, a collapsing of sequence, as in a dream, or an accident report taken from the sole survivor. Somewhere after the beginning there had been the meetings in Washington with Cyrus Vance and the involvement of the FBI and the CIA and the National Security Council. Somewhere before the end there had been the meetings in Havana with Fidel Castro, 14 meetings, 120 hours during which the first exile to own a major automobile dealership in Miami talked one on one with the number one most hated man in Miami.

The end itself, what Bernardo Benes called the castigation, the casting out, had of course been in Miami, and it had begun, as many such scourgings have begun in Miami, with the long invective exhortations of those Spanish-language radio stations on which *el exilio* depends not only for news but for the daily dissemination of rumor and denunciation. Bernardo Benes was said on the radio to be a communist. Bernardo Benes was said to be a Castro agent. Bernardo Benes was said to be at best a *tonto útil*, or *idiota útil*, a useful fool, which is what exiles call one another when they wish to step back from the precipice of the legally actionable.

"This is Miami," Bernardo Benes said about the radio

attacks. "Pure Miami. A million Cubans are blackmailed, totally controlled, by three radio stations. I feel sorry for the Cuban community in Miami. Because they have imposed on themselves, by way of the Right, the same condition that Castro has imposed on Cuba. Total intolerance. And ours is worse. Because it is entirely voluntary."

Bernardo Benes again glanced at his wife, who stood now against the kitchen sink, her arms folded. "My bank was picketed for three weeks." He shrugged. "Every morning when I walked in, twenty or thirty people would be screaming whatever they could think to call me. Carrying signs. Telling people to close their accounts. If I went to a restaurant with my wife, people would come to the table and call me names. But maybe the worst was something I learned only a few months ago. My children never told me at the time, my wife never told me, they knew what I was going through. Here is what I just learned: my children's friends were never allowed to come to our house. Because their parents were afraid. All the parents were afraid their children might be at our house when the bomb went off."

This would not have been a frivolous fear. The *diálogo* took place in the fall of 1978. In April of 1979 a twenty-six-year-old participant in the *diálogo* named Carlos Muñiz Varela was murdered in San Juan, Puerto Rico, by a group calling itself "Comando Cero." In November of 1979 there was the murder in Union City of another participant in the *diálogo*, Eulalio José Negrin, the one who was stepping into his car with his son when two men in ski masks appeared and the fusillade started. The October 1978 bombing at *El Diario–La Prensa* in New York was connected to the *diálogo*: the newspaper had run an editorial in favor of the arrangement allowing exiles to visit Cuba. The March 1979 bombing at Kennedy airport (the bomb was in a suitcase about to be loaded into the hold of an L-1011, TWA #17, due to leave for Los Angeles twelve minutes later with more than 150 people already aboard) was connected to the *diálogo*: TWA had provided equipment for some charters to Cuba.

The scars *el exilio* inflicts upon its own do not entirely heal, nor are they meant to. Seven years after the *diálogo*, when Bernardo Benes's daughter was shopping at Burdines and presented her father's credit card, the saleswoman, a Cuban, looked at the name, handed back the card, and walked away. Bernardo Benes himself sold his business interests, and is no longer so visible a presence around Miami. "You move on," he said. "For example something has happened in my life at age fifty. I have become hedonistic. I lost twenty-five pounds, I joined a sauna, and in my garage you will find a new convertible. Which I drive around Miami. With the top down."

Bernardo Benes and I spoke, that morning in the pleasant house on Biscayne Bay, for an hour or so. From the windows of that house it was possible to look across the bay at the Miami skyline, at buildings through which Bernardo Benes had moved as someone entitled. Mrs. Benes spoke only once, to interrupt her husband with a protective burst of vehement Spanish. "No Cubans will read what she writes," Bernardo Benes said in English. "You will be surprised," his wife said in English. "Anything I say can be printed, that's the price of being married to me, I'm a tough cookie," Bernardo Benes said in English. "All right," his wife said, in English, and she walked away. "You just make your life insurance more."

11

SOME EXILES in Miami will now allow that Bernardo Benes was perhaps a sacrificial victim, the available if accidental symbol of a polarization within the exile which had actually begun some years before, and had brought into question the very molecular code of the community, its opposition to Fidel Castro. There were at the time of the *diálogo*, and are still, certain exiles, most of them brought to the United States as children, fewer of them living now in Miami than in New York and Washington, who were not in fact opposed to Fidel Castro. Neither were many of them exactly pro-Castro, except to the extent that they believed that there was still in progress in Cuba a revolutionary process, and that this process, under the direction of Fidel Castro or not under the direction of Fidel Castro, should continue. *Somos Cubanos*, the editors of *Areíto*, published as a quarterly by the Círculo de Cultura Cubana in New York, had declared in their first issue, in April 1974. "While recognizing that the revolutionary process has implied sacrifices, sufferings and errors," the *Areíto* manifesto had continued, "we maintain that Cuba in 1958 needed measures capable of radically transforming its political, social and economic structures. We understand that that process has established the basis for a more just and egalitarian society, and that it has irreversibly taken root in Cuban society."

The editors of *Areíto* had put the name of the Havana poet Roberto Fernández Retamar on their masthead, and also that of Gabriel García Márquez. In 1984, for the tenth anniversary issue, they had reprinted the 1974 manifesto, and added: "Solidarity with the Cuban revolution was and is a position based on principle for our Editorial Board. . . . The ten years that have passed took us on a return trip to Cuba, to confront for ourselves in its entirety the complexity of that society, and by that token, to rid ourselves of the romantic notions which were typical of our group at that time. . . . Because of that, today we assume our position with more firmness and awareness of its consequences." *Areíto* contributors thought of themselves less as exiles than as "Cubans outside Cuba," and of exile Miami, in the words of this tenth anniversary issue, as "the deformed foetus of Meyer Lansky, the Cuban lumpen bourgeoisie and the North American security state."

The *Grupo Areíto*, as *Areíto*'s editors and contributors came to call themselves, had perhaps never represented more than a very small number of exiles, but these few were young, articulate, and determined to be heard. There had been members of the *Areíto* group involved in the Washington lobby originally called the Cuban-American Committee for the Normalization of Relations with Cuba, not to be confused with its polar opposite, the Cuban American National Foundation. There had been members of the *Areíto* group involved with Bernardo Benes in those visits to Cuba which constituted the *diálogo*. (Carlos Muñiz Varela, the member of the Committee of 75 who had been assassinated in 1979 in San Juan, Puerto Rico, was a founder of *Areíto*.) There had been members of the *Areíto* group involved in the inception of the Antonio Maceo Brigade, which was organized along the lines of the largely Anglo Venceremos Brigade and offered working sojourns in Cuba to, in the words of its 1978 statement of purpose, "any young Cuban who (1) left Cuba by family decision, (2) has not participated in counterrevolutionary activities and would not support violence against the revolution, and (3) defines him or herself as opposed to the blockade and in favor of the normalization of relations between the United States and Cuba."

These children of *el exilio* who had taken to talking about the deformed foetus of the North American security state and to writing articles with such titles as "Introduction to the Sandinista Documentary Cinema" were not, in other words, pursuing a course which was likely to slip the attention of exile Miami, nor did it. There were bombings. There were death threats. Members of the Antonio Maceo Brigade were referred to as *traidores*, traitors, and the brigade itself as a demonic strategy by which Fidel Castro hoped to divide the exile along generational lines. *Areíto* was said in Miami to be directly funded by the Cuban government, a charge its editors dismissed as a slander, in fact a *cantinela*, the kind of repeated refrain that set the teeth on edge. "It's very difficult for people like us, who maintain a position like we do, to live in Miami," an *Areíto* board member named Marifeli Pérez-Stable told the *Miami*

Herald in 1983, by way of explaining why she lived in New York. "Everybody knows everything, and it makes it difficult for those who are fingered as having a pro-Castro position to do something as simple as going to the market."

Marifeli Pérez-Stable was in 1983, when she spoke to the *Herald*, thirty-four. Lourdes Casal, a founder of *Areíto* and for many people its personification, was in 1981, when she died in Havana, forty-two. *Areíto* was published not at all during 1985 or 1986. Time passes and heat goes, although less reliably in Miami, where, at the "First Annual Festival of Hispanic Theatre" in May of 1986, all scheduled performances of a one-act play by a New York playwright and former *Areíto* contributor named Dolores Prida were, after several days of radio alarms and a bomb threat, canceled.

The play itself, *Coser y Cantar*, described by the *Herald* theater reviewer as "pleasant if flawed," a "modest piece" about an Hispanic woman living in New York and her Anglo alter ego (the latter wants to make lists and march at the United Nations, the former to read *Vanidades* and shop for sausage at Casa Moneo), seemed not to be the question here. The question seemed to be Dolores Prida's past, which included connections with *Areíto* and with the *diálogo* and with the Cuban-American Committee, three strikes against her in a city where even one proved allegiance to what was referred to locally as "the so-called Cuban 'revolution.'" Dolores Prida was said by the news director of WQBA–*La Cubanísima* to be "an enemy of the exiles." That Dolores Prida should even think of visiting Miami was said by Metro-Dade commissioner George Valdes to be "a Castroite and communist plan . . . a tactic of the Cuban government to divide us and make us look bad."

Nonetheless, at the height of her local celebrity, Dolores Prida did visit Miami, where, as part of a conference at Miami-Dade Community College on "The Future of Hispanic Theatre in Miami: Goals and Constraints," she supervised a previously unscheduled reading of *Coser y Cantar*, the audience for which had been frisked by Miami police with hand-held metal detectors. Dolores Prida told the *Herald* that the word "communist" was used so loosely in Miami that she did not know what it meant. "If you're progressive," Dolores Prida said, "you're a communist." Dolores Prida told the *Herald* that the only card she carried was American Express. Dolores Prida, who was at the time of this dispute forty-three years old, also told the *Herald* that the only city other than Miami in which she had ever been afraid to express herself, the only other place "where people look over their shoulder to see if they can say what they were going to say," was Havana.

In many ways these midlife survivors of what had been a student movement seem familiar to us. We have met, if not them, their American-born counterparts, people who at one time thought and in many cases still think along lines they might or might not call, as the *Areíto* group often called itself, "progressive." These were exiles who, to at least some extent, thought of America's interests as their own, and of America's issues as their own; who seemed to fall, in a way that Miami exiles often did not, within the American experience. They experienced for example the Vietnam War, and the movement against it, as their own, in a way that many Miami exiles, some of whom told me that they had avoided the draft not because they opposed the war but because they had been at the time engaged in a war which meant more to them, did not. They experienced the social changes of the sixties and seventies in a way that many Miami exiles did not, and they had been in some cases confused and torn by those changes, which seemed to be, in a light way, part of what Dolores Prida's play was about.

In other words they were Americans, yet they were not. *Somos Cubanos.* They remained Cubans, and they remained outside Cuba, and as Cubans outside Cuba but estranged from *el exilio* they came to occupy a particularly hermetic vacuum, one in which, as in *el exilio* itself, positions were defined and redefined and schisms were divined and dissected and a great deal of what went on floated somewhere in a diaspora of its own. I recall a 1984 issue of *Areíto* in which several pages were given over to the analysis of a schism between the *Areíto* group and the generally like-minded Institute of Cuban Studies, and of what ideological error had caused the Institute of Cuban Studies not only to suggest that the late Lourdes Casal had "deviated from the canons of socialist realism" but to misrepresent her position on the relationship between the intellectual and the Cuban revolutionary process, a position made clear for example in her later refinement of her original 1972 statement on the case of the poet Heberto Padilla. These were questions which seemed at a significant tonal remove from those then being asked in New York or New Haven or Boston or Berkeley, although not, curiously enough, from those then being asked in Miami.

On January 9, 1961, at a time when the Cuban revolution was two years under way and the 2506 Brigade was training in Guatemala for the April invasion, the United States Department of State granted to a Miami priest, Monsignor Bryan O. Walsh, the authority to grant a visa waiver to any Cuban child between the ages of six and sixteen who wished to enter the United States under the guardianship of the Catholic diocese of Miami. According to *Catholicism in South Florida: 1868–1968*, by Michael J. McNally, a Miami priest and professor of church history at St. Vincent de Paul Seminary in Boynton Beach, such waivers were issued, between January of 1961 and September of 1963, to 14,156 children, each of whom was sent alone, by parents or guardians still living in Cuba, to live in special camps established and operated by the Unaccompanied Children's Program of the Diocese of Miami.

There were, in all, six such camps, the last of which did not close until the middle of 1981. The reason that these camps were established and the Unaccompanied Children's Program was initiated, Father McNally tells us, was that, by the end of 1960, "rumors were rife" that Fidel Castro planned to send Cuban children to work on Soviet farms, and that, during 1961, "rumors spread" that Fidel Castro had still another plan, "to have children ages three to ten live in state-run dormitories, seeing their parents for only two days a month." It was "to avoid these two possibilities" that parents dispatched their children to Miami and the Unaccompanied Children's Program, which was also known, according to Father McNally, as "Operation Pedro Pan."

No spread rumor goes unrewarded. In *Contra Viento y Marea*, edited by Lourdes Casal and published in 1978 by Casa de las Américas in Havana, there appear a number of descriptions, under the joint byline *Grupo Areíto*, of camp life as it was experienced by those who lived it. These members of the *Areíto* group who arrived in the United States as wards of Operation Pedro Pan characterized this experience, in *Contra Viento y Marea*, as "perhaps the most enduring" of their lives. They described the camps as the "prehistory" of their radicalization, the places in which they first formulated, however inchoately, the only analysis which seemed to them to explain the "lunacy," the "political troglodytism," the "traumatic experience," of having been banished by their parents to live in a barracks in a foreign country. The speakers in this part of *Contra Viento y Marea* are both those who spent time in the camps as children and those who worked in them as adults:

> It was said that Monsignor Walsh . . . had practically unlimited authority to issue visa waivers to children in order to "save them from communism." This episode in our recent history can be seen in retrospect as a period of near-delirium, based as it was on the insistent propaganda that the revolutionary government would strip parents of their authority and send their children to Russia. . . .
>
> The first time I began to see through and reevaluate a few things was when I was working at Opa-Locka, one of the camps where they brought the children who came alone from Cuba. Opa-Locka was managed by the Jesuits. Again and again I asked myself what had motivated these parents to send their children alone to the United States. . . .
>
> Sometimes we would give little talks to the American Legion Auxiliary ladies, who were fascinated to see these white Cubans who knew how to eat with knives and forks . . . but most of all they wanted to hear the horrible story of how and why we were there: the incredible and sad tale of how communism, in order to destroy parental authority, had been going to put us on boats bound for Russia. . . . We would sing Cuban songs and the old ladies would go home crying.
>
> It must be said that the Americans were using the Cubans: the mass emigration, the children who came alone . . . The departure of the children was used largely as a propaganda ploy. What came out of the camps would be a wounded generation. . . .

These accounts, however colored, are suggestive. The parents in Cuba had been, as the children put it together, the victims of *una estafa*, a trick, a deceit, since the distinction between being banished to camps in the USSR and banished to camps in the United States lacked, for the children, significance. The nuns in the camps, who had advised their charges that one day they would appreciate this distinction, were, as the children saw it, equally the victims of *una estafa*. The children themselves, some of whom had later become these Cubans outside Cuba but estranged from *el exilio*, these middle-aged scholars and writers whose visits to Miami necessitated metal detectors, had been, as they saw it then and saw it still, "used" by the government of the United States, "utilized" by the government of the United States, "manipulated" by the government of the United States, made by the government of the United States the victims of a "propaganda ploy"; a way of talking about the government of the United States, as it happened, indistinguishable from what was said every day in exile Miami.

12

"THE MIAMI exiles are not anti-communist," an exile named Carlos M. Luis said one night at dinner. It was about eleven o'clock, the preferred hour for dinner in those exile houses where Spanish manners still prevailed, and there were at the table nine people, eight Cubans and me. There had been before Carlos Luis spoke a good deal of spirited argument. There had been a mounting rhythm of declamation and interruption. Now there was a silence. "The Miami exiles are not anti-communist," Carlos Luis repeated. "I believe this. Anti-communism is not their motivation."

Carlos Luis was the director of the Museo Cubano de Arte y Cultura in Miami, an interesting and complicated man who had entered exile with his wife in 1962, deciding to move to New York after the cultural restructuring which began in Cuba with the confiscation of Orlando Jiménez Leal's documentary film *P.M.*, or *Pasado Meridiano*, and led eventually to Fidel Castro's declaration that there was no art, or would be no art, outside the revolution. "The *P.M.* affair," as it was called in Miami, had plunged Havana into a spiral of confrontation and flagellation not unlike that which later characterized *el exilio*, and was for many a kind of turning point.

It was the *P.M.* affair, involving as it did the banning of a film showing "decadent" nightlife in Havana, which more or less codified such repressive moves as the official persecution of homosexuals later examined by Orlando Jiménez Leal and the Academy Award–winning cinematographer Nestor Almendros, by then both in exile, in *Mauvaise Conduite.* It was the *P.M.* affair which had in fact gotten Nestor Almendros, at the time a young filmmaker who had written admiringly about *P.M.*, fired from his job at *Bohemia*, the Havana weekly which had by then closed itself down and been restaffed by people closer to the direction in which the regime seemed to be moving. And it was the *P.M.* affair which had caused a number of Cuban artists and intellectuals to doubt that there would be room within this revolution for whatever it was that they might have valued above the revolution; to conclude that, as

Carlos Luis put it, "it was time to leave, there was no more for me in staying."

"The first group left because they were Batistianos," Carlos Luis said now, reaching for a bottle of wine. "The second group left because they were losing their property." Carlos Luis paused, and poured an inch of wine into his glass. "Then," he said, "the people started coming who were unhappy because they couldn't get toothpaste."

"You mean these exiles were anti-Castro but not necessarily anti-communist," our host, an exile, said, as if to clarify the point not for himself but for me.

"Anti-Castro, yes," Carlos Luis had shrugged. "Anti-Castro it goes without saying."

That the wish to see Fidel Castro removed from power in Cuba did not in itself constitute a political philosophy was a point rather more appreciated in *el exilio*, which had as its legacy a tradition of considerable political sophistication, than in Washington, which tended to accept the issue as an idea, and so to see Cuban exiles as refugees not just from Castro but from politics. In fact exile life in Miami was dense with political distinctions, none of them exactly in the American grain. Miami was for example the only American city I had ever visited in which it was not unusual to hear one citizen describe the position of another as "Falangist," or as "essentially Nasserite." There were in Miami exiles who defined themselves as communists, anti-Castro. There were in Miami a significant number of exile socialists, also anti-Castro, but agreed on only this single issue. There were in Miami two prominent groups of exile anarchists, many still in their twenties, all anti-Castro, and divided from one another, I was told, by "personality differences," "personality differences" being the explanation Cubans tend to offer for anything from a dinner-table argument to a coup.

This urge toward the staking out of increasingly recondite positions, traditional to exile life in Europe and in Latin America, remained, in South Florida, exotic, a nervous urban brilliance not entirely apprehended by local Anglos, who continued to think of exiles as occupying a fixed place on the political spectrum, one usually described as "right-wing," or "ultra-conservative." It was true enough that there were a number of exiles in Miami who believed the most effective extant political leaders in the hemisphere (aside from Fidel Castro, to whom diabolic powers were attributed) to be General Augusto Pinochet of Chile and General Alfredo Stroessner of Paraguay. In fact those two names were heard with some frequency even in the conversation of exiles who did not share this belief, usually turning up in the "as" construction, in which the speaker thinks to disarm the listener by declaring himself "every bit as hostile to the Pinochet government," or "just as unalterably opposed to General Stroessner," as to Fidel Castro. It was also true enough that there were a number of Cubans in Miami, most notably those tobacco growers who between the fall of Fulgencio Batista and the fall of Anastasio Somoza had managed to maintain their operations in Nicaragua, who supported the military leadership of the Nicaraguan contras not in spite of but precisely because of whatever association that leadership had with the Somoza militia.

Still, "right-wing," on the American spectrum, where political positions were understood as marginally different approaches to what was seen as a shared goal, seemed not to apply. This was something different, a view of politics as so central to the human condition that there may be no applicable words in the political vocabulary of most Americans. Virtually every sentient member of the Miami exile community was on any given day engaged in what was called an "ideological confrontation" with some other member of the Miami exile community, over points which were passionately debated at meals and on the radio and in the *periodiquitos*, the throwaway newspapers which appeared every week on Southwest Eighth Street. Everything was read. I was asked one day by several different people if I had seen a certain piece that morning, by a writer whose name I did not recognize. The piece, it turned out, had appeared not in the *Miami Herald* or the *Miami News*, not in *El Herald* or *Diario Las Americas*, not in any of the *periodiquitos* and not even in *The New York Times*, but in *El Tiempo*, one day late from Bogotá. Analysis was close, and overcharged. Obscure points were "clarified," and immediately "answered." The whole of exile Miami could engage itself in the morning deconstruction of, say, something said by Roberto Fernández Retamar in Havana as reported by *El País* in Madrid and "answered" on the radio in Miami.

I talked one evening to Agustin Tamargo, an exile whose radio broadcasts with such prominent exiles as the novelist Guillermo Cabrera Infante and the poet Heberto Padilla and the legendary 26 Julio *comandante* Huber Matos, what Agustin Tamargo called "all the revolutionary people," had tended over the years to attract whatever excess animus happened to be loose in the community. "I come from a different place on the political spectrum than most of the other radio commentators here," Agustin Tamargo said. "There are many Batista people in Miami. They call me a communist because I wrote in *Bohemia*, which was to them a leftist-Marxist paper. Actually it was maybe center."

Agustin Tamargo entered exile in 1960, the year *Bohemia*, which had been perhaps the most influential voice of the anti-Batista movement, suspended its own publication with the declaration "this is a revolution betrayed." After he left Havana he was managing editor of *Bohemia*-in-exile, which was published first in New York, with what Agustin Tamargo believes to have been CIA money, and then in Caracas, with what he calls "different business partners, completely separated from American interests," the entire question of "American interests" remaining in Miami an enduring preoccupation. I recall one visit when everyone to whom I spoke seemed engaged in either an attack on or a defense of the exiled writer and former political prisoner Carlos Alberto Montaner, who had written a column from Madrid which some found, because it seemed to them to suggest that Fidel Castro could be tolerated to the extent that he could be separated from Soviet interests, insufficiently separated from American interests. I was advised by one exile that "Montaner thinks about Fidel exactly the way Reagan thinks about Fidel," not, since even those exiles who voted in large numbers for Ronald Reagan in 1980 and 1984 did so despite their conviction that he was bent on making a secret deal with Fidel Castro, an endorsement.

There seemed in fact very few weeks in Miami when, on the informal network the community used to talk to itself, one or another exile spokesman was not being excoriated on or defended against this charge of being insufficiently separated from American interests. One week it was said that the poet Jorge Valls, because he had left Cuba after twenty years in prison and suggested on the radio in Miami that there should be "an interchange of ideas" between the United States and Havana, was insufficiently separated from American interests. Another week it was said that Armando Valladares, whose *Contra Toda Esperanza*, an account of the twenty-two years he had spent imprisoned by Fidel Castro, appeared in this country as *Against All Hope*, was, because he had received support from the National Endowment for Democracy, insufficiently separated from American interests. "There's nothing wrong with American money," Agustin Tamargo had said the evening we talked, by way of amending an impassioned indictment of another exile who was, he believed, getting it. "Or Chinese money or any other kind. I will take it if they give it to me. But only to do what I want to do. Not what they want me to do. There is the difference."

In Miami, where he was at the time we met doing a nightly broadcast for WOCN-Union Radio about which there was controversy even within the station itself, Agustin Tamargo was regarded as an eccentric and even a quixotic figure, which seemed to be how he construed his role. "Fifty thousand people listen to me every night," he said. "And every night I say Franco was a killer. Every night I say Pinochet is an assassin. Most of the other Cuban commentators here never say anything about Pinochet. This is a program on which people say every kind of thing about the Cuban past. We say that maybe things before the revolution were not so golden as people here like to think. And still they listen. Which suggests to me that maybe the exile is not so one-sided as the communists say it is."

We were sitting that evening in an office at WOCN-Union Radio on Flagler Street, and outside in the reception room there was an armed security guard who would later walk Agustin Tamargo to his car, Miami being a city in which people who express their opinions on the radio every night tend, particularly since 1976, when a commentator named Emilio Milian got his legs blown off in the WQBA-*La Cubanísima* parking lot, to put a little thought into the walk to the car. "Listen to me," Agustin Tamargo said. "You do see a change here. A few years ago no one in exile would admit that any kind of solution to the Cuban situation could come from inside. They wouldn't hear of it. Now they admit it. They admit that a rebellion inside Cuba could lead to a military solution, a coup." Agustin Tamargo had shrugged. "That's a real advance. A few years ago here, you said that, you got killed. Immediately."

Emilio Milian lost his legs because he suggested in a series of editorials on WQBA–*La Cubanísima* that it was counterproductive for exiles to continue bombing and assassinating one another on the streets of Miami. That this was an exceptionable opinion in an American city in 1976 was hard for some Americans to entirely appreciate, just as it was hard for some Americans, accustomed as they were to the official abhorrence of political violence, to appreciate the extent to which many people in Miami regarded such violence as an inevitable and even a necessary thread in the social fabric. The Miami City Commission in 1982 voted a ten-thousand dollar grant to Alpha 66, which was, however venerable, however fixed an element on the Miami landscape, a serious action group, one of the twenty exile groups believed by the House Select Committee on Assassinations in 1978 to have had "the motivation, capability and resources" to have assassinated President John F. Kennedy, and one of the two, according to the committee's report, about which there were as well "indications of a possible connection with figures named in the Kennedy assassination, specifically with Lee Harvey Oswald." At a 1983 meeting, the same Miami City Commission proclaimed March twenty-fifth "Dr. Orlando Bosch Day," in recognition of the Miami pediatrician who was then imprisoned at Cuartel San Carlos in Caracas on charges of planning the bombing in 1976 of a Cubana DC-8 off Barbados, killing all seventy-three passengers, including twenty-four members of the Cuban national fencing team.

The case of Orlando Bosch was interesting. He had been, before he moved to Miami in July of 1960, the chief of the 26 Julio for Las Villas Province. During his first month in Miami he had helped to launch the insurgent group called the MIRR, the Movimiento Insurreccional de Recuperación Revolucionaria, which became known that August, when four Castro army officers and a hundred of their men deserted their posts and took up arms in the Las Villas mountains. Over the next several years in Miami, Orlando Bosch was arrested repeatedly on charges connected with MIRR activity, but was, until 1968, repeatedly acquitted. In 1968 he was finally convicted on a federal charge, that of shelling a Polish freighter in the Port of Miami, was sentenced to ten years and paroled after four. In 1974, back in Miami and subpoenaed for questioning in the assassination of an exile leader, Orlando Bosch had broken parole by fleeing the country.

There were, in all, four Cuban exiles charged by Venezuela in the 1976 Cubana bombing. Two were accused of actually placing the bomb on the plane and the other two, one of whom was Dr. Bosch and the other of whom was a 2506 member named Luis Posada Carriles, of planning or arranging this placement. Not least because Luis Posada Carriles happened to be a former operations chief of the Venezuelan secret police, DISIP, the Cubana case was a sensitive one for Venezuela, and, after a decade of what appeared to many to be stalling actions, Orlando Bosch was in 1986 acquitted by a Venezuelan judge, who noted that at the time the plane actually fell from the sky "citizen Orlando Bosch was not in the company" of the two men accused of placing the bomb, both of whom were convicted. In the case of the fourth defendant, Luis Posada Carriles, there was no final disposition, since he had the year before escaped from the penitentiary in San Juan de Los Morros (aided, it was reported, by $28,600 in payoffs), some sixty miles southwest of Caracas, and appeared to have next surfaced in the Escalón district of San Salvador, living in a rented house and working on the covert contra supply operation at Ilopango air base under the name "Ramon Medina."

The name "Ramon Medina" began coming up in late 1986, at the time the first details of the contra supply network organized by Lieutenant Colonel Oliver North and Major General Richard V. Secord were becoming known, and there was some speculation that his job at Ilopango had been arranged by Felix Rodriguez, also known as Max Gomez, who in turn had been recommended as an adviser to the Salvadoran armed forces by the office of Vice President George Bush. "We have been asked if Mr. Bush knew or knows Ramon Medina," a spokesman for Vice President George Bush said. "The answer is no. The same answer holds for Ramon Posada or any other names or aliases." Some weeks later, in Miami, an exhibition of Orlando Bosch's paintings was held, some sixty oils, priced at $25 to $500 and listed under such titles as *The Southern Coast of Cuba* and *Nightfall in the Tropics.* Tea sandwiches were served, and wine. The president of the Committee to Free Orlando Bosch pointed out that the paintings had certain common motifs, that doors kept turning up, and roads, and bodies of water; that the painter was "always looking for the way to freedom." (Luis Posada Carriles' oils, of Venezuelan landscapes, had been exhibited in Miami a year before.) Orlando Bosch himself was still in jail in Caracas, waiting for yet another obstacle to be negotiated, the confirmation of his acquittal. He was also still, from the point of view of the United States, a fugitive terrorist, someone who, if he tried to reenter the United States, faced immediate arrest on his parole violation.

That the governing body of an American city should have declared a "day" in honor of someone with so clouded a history might have in most parts of the United States profoundly disturbed the citizens of that city, but Miami was a community in which, as the *Herald* had pointed out in 1985, a significant percentage of the population continued to see Orlando Bosch as a hero. "You are mistaken when you say that 'many exiles believe that Bosch is a hero,'" a letter to *El Herald* complained on this point. "Not just 'many,' as you say, but ALL Cuban exiles believe Dr. Bosch to be so decent a man, so Rambo-like a hero, that, even supposing there were any truth to the allegations about that communist plane crash many years ago, Dr. Bosch would only have been trying to pay back in kind those enemies of this country who, every day, all over the world, are bombing and killing and maiming innocent citizens, including elderly tourists in their wheelchairs." This note of *machismo* was often struck when people mentioned Orlando Bosch. "Most people talk more than they act," an exile named Cosme Barros told the *Herald* after the acquittal in Caracas. "Bosch has acted more than he has talked." "He is how every man should be," an exile named Norma Garcia told the same reporter. "If we had more men like him, today Cuba would be free."

The case of Orlando Bosch and Luis Posada Carriles and the bombing of the Cubana DC-8 had always been complicated, as most stories in this part of the world turned out to be, by more than just one sensitive connection. There had been, besides the line from Luis Posada Carriles to the Venezuelan secret police, visible lines from both Luis Posada Carriles and Orlando Bosch to the government of the United States. According to a 1977 CIA document obtained by the *Miami Herald*, Luis Posada Carriles, who was later called Ramon Medina, had received CIA demolition and weapons training before the Bay of Pigs, had formally joined the CIA in 1965, had worked briefly in Guatemala and then moved on to Venezuela and DISIP, finally resigning as DISIP operations chief in 1974. Throughout this period, according to the 1977 document quoted by the *Herald*, Luis Posada Carriles had remained on the CIA payroll.

Orlando Bosch himself, according to staff interviews conducted by and to CIA and FBI memos released to the 1978 House Select Committee on Assassinations, had been under contract to the CIA during the early 1960s, running, with Evelio Duque of the Ejército Cubano Anticomunista, a camp in Homestead, the last Florida town before the Keys. Orlando Bosch told the House committee staff members who interviewed him in Cuartel San Carlos that he had soon begun to see this Homestead camp as, in the committee's words, "an exercise in futility." He had begun to suspect that such CIA-sponsored camps were, again in the committee's words, "merely a means of keeping the exiles busy." His CIA contact had, he said, "privately and unofficially" confirmed this suspicion.

This was a peculiar climate in South Florida, and had been so since 1960. Signals seemed to get mixed. Transmissions seemed to jam. Some atmospheric anomaly seemed to create trick mirrors, in which those people (or personnel, or assets) who were to be kept busy (or disposed of) and those people who could be strategically deployed (or used) appeared to be one and the same, their image changing with the light, and the distant agenda, in Washington. Sometimes even those people who were to be kept busy (or strategically deployed) and those people who were running the distant agenda appeared to be one and the same, or so it might have seemed to anyone looking in the mirror when the images spoke. "You have to fight violence with violence," Orlando Bosch was quoted as saying in the *Miami News* in 1978. "At times you cannot avoid hurting innocent people." The same year, 1978, Richard Helms, who had been directing CIA operations from Washington during the time Orlando Bosch was running the camp in Homestead, said this to the House Select Committee on Assassinations: "I would like to point out something since we are so deeply into this. When one government is trying to upset another government and the operation is successful, people get killed."

13

IN 1985 and 1986 it was said in exile Miami that the coup, the coup in Cuba, the "solution from inside," the "military solution" Agustin Tamargo had mentioned the night we spoke in his office at WOCN-Union Radio, would take place in three, maybe four years. In 1985 and 1986 it was also said in exile Miami that the coup would not take place. In 1985 and 1986 it was also said in exile Miami that the coup, were the coup allowed to take place, which it would not be, would occur along anti-Soviet lines, and could begin among certain officers from the one Cuban military school to which there had been assigned no Soviet trainers. Still, this coup would never take place. The reason this coup would never take place, it was said by various people to whom I spoke in exile Miami in 1985 and 1986, was because "the United States wants a Cuba it can control," because "a coup would mean a new situation," and because "in the changed situation after the coup they would hate the United States even more than the communists do."

The coup which the United States would never allow to take place had in fact by the 1980s largely supplanted, as an exile plot point, the invasion which the United States had never allowed to take place, and was for the time being, until something more concrete came along (the narrative bones for this something, the projected abandonment of the Nicaraguan contras, were of course already in place), the main story line for what *el exilio* continued to see as its betrayal, its utilization, its manipulation, by the government of the United States. A rather unsettling number of exiles to whom I spoke cited, as evidence of Washington's continuing betrayal, the Omega 7 prosecutions. Others cited the Reagan administration's attempts to deport the so-called "Mariel excludables," those refugees whose criminal records would normally be grounds, under American immigration policy, for deportation or exclusion. Many, including Agustin Tamargo, cited Radio Martí, about which there had been, it seemed, considerable controversy within the exile community. "Radio Martí is a department of the Voice of America," Agustin Tamargo had said the evening we met in his office at WOCN-Union Radio. "Which is a guarantee to me that when the American government makes its deal with Fidel Castro, Radio Martí will say amen."

I had then been in Miami only a short time, and had not before been exposed to this local view of Radio Martí as yet another way in which the government of the United States was deceiving the exile community. I said to Agustin Tamargo that I did not quite understand. I said that I, and I believed many other Americans, including several to whom I had talked in Washington who had been involved with the issue as it passed through Congress, had tended to think of Radio Martí as something the Miami exile community specifically wanted. I said that I had in fact met Miami exiles, for example Jorge Mas Canosa, who had gone to some lengths to see the Radio Martí legislation enacted.

"Rich people," Agustin Tamargo said.

I allowed that this was possibly true.

"The same rich people who are Republicans. Listen. I hate communists, but I hate some of these exiles more." Agustin Tamargo was on this subject a dog with a bone. "They are why we are here all these years. If a man like Che Guevara were on our side, we would have been back in Cuba long ago. However. Instead of Che Guevara, we have Mas Canosa. I'm sorry. I mention him only because he is one of the richest."

This was one of those leaps to the ad hominem toward which exile conversation seemed ever to tend. I had known that there was within the community a certain resistance to the leadership claims of Jorge Mas Canosa and the other supporters of the Cuban American National Foundation. I had also known that resistance derived in part from the well-publicized conviction of the Cuban American National Foundation, a group somewhat more attuned than the average Miami exile to the pitch at which an American congressman is apt to lose eye contact, that exile aims could best be achieved by working within the American political system; that, in other words, the time had passed for running raids on Cuba and shelling Soviet-bloc ships in the Port of Miami. Still, even ad hominem, even given the fact that Jorge Mas Canosa and the Cuban American National Foundation had been largely responsible for Radio Martí, the point about Radio Martí as proof of American perfidy remained obscure to me, and I had looked for help to another exile who had joined us that evening, a young man named Daniel Morcate.

"I disagree with Agustin strongly on Radio Martí," Daniel Morcate had said, and then, deferentially: "But then the whole exile community is divided. On that question." Daniel Morcate, whose wife Gina was a writer and an assistant to Carlos Luis at the Museo Cubano de Arte y Cultura, had left Cuba at fourteen, in 1971. He had spent four years in Madrid and lived since (except for one year, 1979, when he returned to Madrid to work for Carlos Alberto Montaner) in Miami, where he was, at the time we met, working for WOCN-Union Radio and teaching philosophy at St. Thomas University, an institution founded in Miami by Augustinian brothers formerly affiliated with Villanueva University in Havana. He was among those younger exiles who defined themselves as philosophical anarchists. He had stressed that evening that he was "not a man of action," but that, at certain times and under certain conditions, he supported the idea of action. He was, he had said, "a man of words," and he chose them carefully.

As this might suggest, Daniel Morcate's position on Radio Martí and the Cuban American National Foundation (which was to say, I was beginning to see, his position on working within the American system) was subtle, even tortured. His own concerns about Radio Martí had been sufficient to keep him from accepting one of the Radio Martí jobs which had been passed around Miami as a particularly exotic form of patronage, and he differed from those of his contemporaries who did work in Washington, both for Radio Martí and for the Cuban American National Foundation, on several key points. Despite the fact that he was not, as he had said, a man of action, Daniel Morcate did believe, as the Cuban American National Foundation pointedly did not believe, that now was as good a time as any for running physical actions against the government of Cuba. He also believed that groups running such actions should seek support not only from the United States but from other nations.

Still, given these exceptions and under certain limited conditions, he agreed in principle with such Washington exiles of his generation as Ramon Mestre at Radio Martí and Frank

Calzón, who was at that time director of the Cuban American National Foundation, that it was possible for exiles to coexist with and even to influence the government of the United States. "I think that many goals of the United States government are very legitimate," Daniel Morcate said. "Many Cubans do. And so they believe that they can use the United States government without compromising their own ideals. This is what many people in the Cuban American National Foundation believe."

"They believe in publicity," Agustin Tamargo had said, interrupting.

"I happen to think that someone like Frank Calzón is a deep-rooted nationalist," Daniel Morcate had insisted. "I believe that he thinks he is utilizing the United States government." He had paused, and shrugged. "Of course the United States government thinks the same about him."

Agustin Tamargo had been patient. "Look. Radio Martí is an instrument of American foreign policy." He had ticked off the points on his fingers. "The American government decides that it is going to coexist with Castro and the next day we will have a long story on Radio Martí about our cooperation with the United States government. We have no say in this. In the Reagan administration more than ever. The Reagan administration has one goal in Cuba. Which is to separate Castro from Moscow. Not to overthrow Castro. They put in jail anybody here who says he wants to overthrow Castro. They put in jail the Omega 7. We have been taught to throw bombs, taught to work with every kind of *desgraciado*, and then they throw us in jail. We have no choice in the matter. There is absolutely nothing going on now. There is no bombing, there is no fighting in the customs line, there is no tax, there is no terrorism, there is *nothing*."

I supposed that what Agustin Tamargo meant by "no tax" was that there was no community effort, as there had been on occasion in the past, to finance actions against Cuba by collecting from each exile a part of his or her earnings. I did not know what he meant by "no fighting in the customs line," nor, because he seemed at that moment almost mute with disgust, did I ask.

"Nothing," Agustin Tamargo had repeated finally. "Under Reagan."

That there was in Miami under the Reagan administration "nothing" going on was something said to me by many exiles, virtually all of whom spoke as if this "nothing," by which they seemed to mean the absence of more or less daily threats of domestic terror, might be only a temporary suspension, an intermission of uncertain duration in an otherwise familiar production. There was in Miami a general sense that the Reagan administration, largely by the way in which it had managed to convince some exiles that its commitment to "freedom fighters" extended to them, had to some extent co-opted exile action. There was also in Miami a general sense that this was on the Reagan administration's part just another trick of another mirror, another camp in Homestead, say, another interim occupation for Luis Posada Carriles or his manifold doubles, and as such could end predictably. Some exiles spoke with considerable foreboding about what they saw as the community's misplaced wish to believe in the historically doubtful notion that its interests would in the long run coincide with those of Washington. Some exiles suggested that this wish to believe, or rather this willing suspension of disbelief, had not in the past been and was by no means now an open ticket, that there would once again come a point when exile and Washington interests would be seen to diverge, and diverge dramatically.

These exiles saw, when and if this happened, a rekindling of certain familiar frustrations, the unloosing of furies still only provisionally contained; saw, in other words, built into the mirror trick, yet another narrative on which to hang the betrayal, the utilization, the manipulation of *el exilio* by the government of the United States. "I wouldn't be surprised to see some Cubans attempting to re-create political violence in the United States," Daniel Morcate had said the evening we met in Agustin Tamargo's office at WOCN-Union Radio. He had been talking about what he saw as the Reagan administration's reluctance to directly confront Fidel Castro. "There is a very clear danger here that nobody is pointing out. I wouldn't be surprised if other Omega *Siete* groups were emerging."

I had asked Raul Masvidal, the day I saw him in the cool office with the poster that read YOU HAVE NOT CONVERTED A MAN BECAUSE YOU HAVE SILENCED HIM, if he believed that a perceived divergence of exile and Washington interests, a perception in Miami that promises were once again being broken, could bring about a resurgence of the kind of action which had characterized the exile until recently. Raul Masvidal had looked at me, and shrugged. "That kind of action is here today," he had said. I had asked the same question of Luis Lauredo, who was then the president of Raul Masvidal's Miami Savings Bank and was, as the president of Cuban-American Democrats, perhaps the most visible and active member of that 35 percent of the Dade County Cuban electorate who were registered Democrats.

Luis Lauredo had nodded, and then shook his head, as if the question did not bear contemplation. "I was talking about this last night," he said finally. "With some of the Republicans." We had been sitting across from each other at lunch that day, and I had watched Luis Lauredo fillet a fish before he continued. "We had a kind of gathering," he said then. "And I said to them, 'listen, when it happens, I'll cover your backs.' Because they are going to lose all credibility. It's like a Greek tragedy. That's the way it's going to be. When it happens."

"Those radio guys who attacked me are just looking for ratings," Carlos Luis said one day when I had met him at the Museo Cubano and we had gone around to get something to eat and a coffee, just out of the rain, in the courtyard of the Malaga restaurant on Eighth Street. "Which is why I never answered them. I did a program with Agustin Tamargo, which was good, but I never answered the attacks."

The rain that day had been blowing the bits of colored glass and mirror strung from the tree in the Malaga courtyard and splashing from the eaves overhanging our table and we had been talking in a general way about action of the Left and action of the Right and Carlos Luis had said that he had come to wonder if silence was not the only moral political response. He had a few weeks before, on the twenty-fifth anniversary of the death of Albert Camus, published in *El Herald* a reflection on Camus which had this as its subtext, and it was to this subtext that the "radio guys" had been responding, there apparently being in Miami no subject so remote or abstruse as to rule out its becoming the focus for several hours of invective on AM radio.

"In any event that's the way things are here," Carlos Luis said. "It's very confusing. The guy who attacked me to begin with was totally incapable of discussing Camus's position. Which was a very tragic one. Because the choices Camus had in front of him were not choices at all. Making a choice between terrorism of the Right and terrorism of the Left was incomprehensible to him. Maybe he was right. As time goes by I think that men who were unable to make choices were more right than those who made them. Because there are no clean choices."

Carlos Luis drummed his fingers absently on the wet metal table. It was possible to walk from the Malaga to the bungalow on Seventh Street where Eduardo Arocena had been arrested with the Beretta and the Browning and the AR-15 and the UZI and the target list. It was also possible to walk from the Malaga to the parking lot where Emilio Milian had lost his legs for suggesting on WQBA–*La Cubanísima* that exiles might be working against their own interests by continuing to bomb and assassinate one another on the streets of Miami. On my way to the Museo Cubano de Arte y Cultura that morning I had noticed in a storefront window this poster: ¡NICARAGUA HOY, CUBA MAÑANA! SUPPORT THE FREEDOM FIGHTERS FUND. COMANDO SATURNINO BELTRAN. FREEDOM FIGHTERS FUND, P.O. BOX 661571, MIAMI SPRINGS FL 33266. JEFATURA MILITAR BRIGADA 2506, P.O. BOX 4086, HIALEAH FL 33014.

This was a year and a half before the Southern Air Transport C-123K carrying Eugene Hasenfus crashed inside Nicaragua. There was between the day of Ronald Reagan's first inauguration and the day the C-123K crashed inside Nicaragua "nothing" going on, but of course there was also "something" going on, something peculiar to the early 1980s in Miami but suggestive of the early 1960s in Miami, something in which certain familiar words and phrases once again figured. It was again possible to hear in Miami about "training," and about air charters and altered manifests and pilots hired for onetime flights from Miami to "somewhere" in Central America. It was again possible to hear in Washington about two-track strategies, about back channels and alternative avenues, about what Robert C. McFarlane, at that time the Reagan administration's National Security Affairs adviser, described variously in the *Washington Post* in 1985 as "a continuity of policy," "a national interest in keeping in touch with what was going on"; a matter of "not breaking faith with the freedom fighters," which in turn came down to "making it clear that the United States believes in what they are doing."

What exactly was involved in making it clear that the United States believed in what the freedom fighters were doing was still, at that time in Miami, the spring of 1985, hard to know in detail, but it was already clear that some of the details were known to some Cubans. There were Cubans around Miami who would later say, about how they happened to end up fighting with the Nicaraguan contras, that they had been during the spring of 1985 "trained" at a camp in the Everglades operated by the Jefatura Militar Brigada 2506. There were Cubans around Miami who would later say, about how they happened to join the Nicaraguan contras, that they had been during the spring of 1985 "recruited" at the little park on Eighth Street a few blocks west of the Malaga. Nothing was happening but certain familiar expectations were being raised, and to speak of choices between terrorism of the Left and terrorism of the Right did not seem, in the courtyard of the Malaga on Eighth Street in Miami during the spring of 1985, an entirely speculative exercise. "There are no choices at all," Carlos Luis said then.

14

WHEN I think now about mirror tricks and what might or might not be built into them, about the ways in which frustrations can be kindled and furies unloosed, I think of Guillermo Novo, called Bill Novo. Guillermo Novo was known to FBI agents and federal prosecutors and the various personnel who made up "terrorist task forces" on the eastern seaboard of the United States as one of the Novo brothers, Ignacio and Guillermo, two exiles who first came to national attention in 1964, when they fired a dud bazooka shell at the United Nations during a speech by Che Guevara. There were certain farcical elements here (the embattled brothers bobbing in a small boat, the shell plopping harmlessly into the East River), and, in a period when Hispanics were seen by many Americans as intrinsically funny, an accent joke, this incident was generally treated tolerantly, a comic footnote to the news. As time went by, however, the names of the Novo brothers began turning up in less comic footnotes, for example this one, on page 93 of volume X of the report made by the House Select Committee on Assassinations on its 1978 investigation of the assassination of John F. Kennedy:

> (67) Immunized executive session testimony of Marita Lorenz, May 31, 1978. Hearings before the House Select Committee on Assassinations. Lorenz, who had publicly claimed she was once Castro's mistress (*Miami News*, June 15, 1976), told the committee she was present at a September 1963 meeting in Orlando Bosch's Miami home during which Lee Harvey Oswald, Frank Sturgis, Pedro Diaz Lanz, and Bosch made plans to go to Dallas. . . . She further testified that around November 15, 1963, she, Jerry Patrick Hemming, the Novo brothers, Pedro Diaz Lanz, Sturgis, Bosch, and Oswald traveled in a two-car caravan to Dallas and stayed in a motel where they were contacted by Jack Ruby. There were several rifles and scopes in the motel room . . .

> Lorenz said she returned to Miami around November 19 or 20. . . . The committee found no evidence to support Lorenz's allegation.

Guillermo Novo himself was among those convicted, in a 1979 trial which rested on the demonstration of connections between the Cuban defendants and DINA, the Chilean secret police, of the assassination in Washington of the former Chilean diplomat Orlando Letelier and of the Institute for Policy Studies researcher who happened to be with him when his car blew up, Ronni Moffitt. This conviction was overturned on appeal (the appellate court ruled that the testimony of two jailhouse informants had been improperly admitted), and in a 1981 retrial, after the federal prosecutors turned down a deal in which the defense offered a plea of guilty on the lesser charge of conspiracy, plus what Guillermo Novo's attorney called "a sweetener," a "guarantee" by Guillermo Novo "to stop all violence by Cuban exiles in the United States," Guillermo Novo was acquitted.

I happened to meet Guillermo Novo in 1985, one Monday morning when I was waiting for someone in the reception room at WRHC–Cadena Azul, Miami, a station the call letters of which stood for Radio Havana Cuba. There was about this meeting nothing of either moment or consequence. A man who introduced himself as "Bill Novo" just appeared beside me, and we exchanged minor biography for a few minutes. He said that he had noticed me reading a letter framed on the wall of the reception room. He said that he was the sales manager for WRHC, and had lived in Miami only three years. He said that he had however lived in the United States since 1954, mostly in New York and New Jersey. He was a small sharp-featured man in a white tropical suit, who in fact spoke English with an accent which suggested New Jersey, and he had a way of materializing and dematerializing sideways, of appearing from and then sidling back into an inner office, which was where he retreated after he gave me his business card, the exchange of cards remaining a more or less fixed ritual in Cuban Miami. GUILLERMO NOVO SAMPOL, the card read. *Gerente de Ventas, WRHC–Cadena Azul.*

That it was possible on a Monday morning in Miami to

have so desultory an encounter with one of the Novo brothers seemed to me, perhaps because I was not yet accustomed to a rhythm in which dealings with DINA and unsupported allegations about Dallas motel rooms could be incorporated into the American business day, remarkable, and later that week I asked an exile acquaintance who was familiar with WRHC if the Guillermo Novo who was the sales manager there was in fact the Guillermo Novo who had been tried in the Letelier assassination. There had been, my acquaintance demurred, "a final acquittal on the Letelier count." But it was, I persisted, the same man. My acquaintance had shrugged impatiently, not as if he thought it best not mentioned, but as if he did not quite see the interest. "Bill Novo has been a man of action," he said. "Yes. Of course."

To be a man of action in Miami was to receive encouragement from many quarters. On the wall of the reception room at WRHC–Cadena Azul, Miami, where the sales manager was Guillermo Novo and an occasional commentator was Fidel and Raúl Castro's estranged sister Juanita and the host of the most popular talk show was Felipe Rivero, whose family had from 1832 until 1960 published the powerful *Diario de la Marina* in Havana and who would in 1986, after a controversy fueled by his insistence that the Holocaust had not occurred but had been fabricated "to defame and divide the German people," move from WRHC to WOCN, there hung in 1985 a framed letter, the letter Guillermo Novo had mentioned when he first materialized that Monday morning. This letter, which was dated October 1983 and signed by the President of the United States, read:

> I learned from Becky Dunlop [presumably Becky Norton Dunlop, a White House aide who later followed Edwin Meese to the Justice Department] about the outstanding work being done at WRHC. Many of your listeners have also been in touch, praising your news coverage and your editorials. Your talented staff deserves special commendation for keeping your listeners well-informed.
>
> I've been particularly pleased, of course, that you have been translating and airing a Spanish version of my weekly

> talks. This is important because your signal reaches the people of Cuba, whose rigidly controlled government media suppress any news Castro and his communist henchmen do not want them to know. WRHC is performing a great service for all its listeners. Keep up the good work, and God bless you.
>
> [signed] RONALD REAGAN

At the time I first noticed it on the WRHC wall, and attracted Guillermo Novo's attention by reading it, this letter interested me because I had the week before been looking back through the administration's arguments for Radio Martí, none of which, built as they were on the figure of beaming light into utter darkness, had alluded to these weekly talks which the people of Cuba appeared to be getting on WRHC–Cadena Azul, Miami. Later the letter interested me because I had begun reading back through the weekly radio talks themselves, and had come across one from 1978 in which Ronald Reagan, not yet president, had expressed his doubt that either the Pinochet government or the indicted "Cuban anti-Castro exiles," one of whom had been Guillermo Novo, had anything to do with the Letelier assassination.

Ronald Reagan had wondered instead ("I don't know the answer, but it is a question worth asking . . .") if Orlando Letelier's "connections with Marxists and far-left causes" might not have set him up for assassination, caused him to be, as the script for this talk put it, "murdered by his own masters." Here was the scenario: "Alive," Ronald Reagan had reasoned in 1978, Orlando Letelier "could be compromised; dead he could become a martyr. And the left didn't lose a minute in making him one." Actually this version of the Letelier assassination had first been advanced by Senator Jesse Helms (R–N.C.), who had advised his colleagues on the Senate floor that it was not "plausible" to suspect the Pinochet government in the Letelier case, because terrorism was "most often an organized tool of the left," but the Reagan reworking was interesting on its own, a way of speaking, later to become familiar, in which events could be revised as they happened into illustrations of ideology.

"There was no blacklist of Hollywood," Ronald Reagan told Robert Scheer of the *Los Angeles Times* during the 1980 campaign. "The blacklist in Hollywood, if there was one, was provided by the communists." "I'm going to voice a suspicion now that I've never said aloud before," Ronald Reagan told thirty-six high-school students in Washington in 1983 about death squads in El Salvador. "I wonder if all of this is right wing, or if those guerrilla forces have not realized that by infiltrating into the city of San Salvador and places like that, they can get away with these violent acts, helping to try and bring down the government, and the right wing will be blamed for it." "New intelligence shows," Ronald Reagan told his Saturday radio listeners in March of 1986, by way of explaining why he was asking Congress to provide "the Nicaraguan freedom fighters" with what he called "the means to fight back," that "Tomás Borge, the communist interior minister, is engaging in a brutal campaign to bring the freedom fighters into discredit. You see, Borge's communist operatives dress in freedom fighter uniforms, go into the countryside and murder and mutilate ordinary Nicaraguans."

Such stories were what David Gergen, when he was the White House communications director, had once called "a folk art," the President's way of "trying to tell us how society works." Other members of the White House staff had characterized these stories as the President's "notions," casting them in the genial framework of random avuncular musings, but they were something more than that. In the first place they were never random, but systematic, and rather energetically so. The stories were told to a single point. The language in which the stories were told was not that of political argument but of advertising ("New intelligence shows . . ." and "Now it has been learned . . ." and, a construction that got my attention in a 1984 address to the National Religious Broadcasters, "Medical science doctors confirm . . ."), of the sales pitch.

This was not just a vulgarity of diction. When someone speaks of Orlando Letelier as "murdered by his own masters," or of the WRHC signal reaching a people denied information by "Castro and his communist henchmen," or of the "freedom fighter uniforms" in which the "communist operatives" of the "communist interior minister" disguise themselves, that person is not arguing a case, but counting instead on the willingness of the listener to enter what Hannah Arendt called, in a discussion of propaganda, "the gruesome quiet of an entirely imaginary world." On the morning I met Guillermo Novo in the reception room at WRHC–Cadena Azul I copied the framed commendation from the White House into my notebook, and later typed it out and pinned it to my own office wall, an aide-mémoire to the distance between what is said in the high ether of Washington, which is about the making of those gestures and the sending of those messages and the drafting of those positions which will serve to maintain that imaginary world, about two-track strategies and alternative avenues and Special Groups (Augmented), about "not breaking faith" and "making it clear," and what is heard on the ground in Miami, which is about consequences.

In many ways Miami remains our most graphic lesson in consequences. "I can assure you that this flag will be returned to this brigade in a free Havana," John F. Kennedy said at the Orange Bowl in 1962 (the "supposed promise," the promise "not in the script," the promise "made in the emotion of the day"), meaning it as an abstraction, the rhetorical expression of a collective wish; a kind of poetry, which of course makes nothing happen. "We will not permit the Soviets and their henchmen in Havana to deprive others of their freedom," Ronald Reagan said at the Dade County Auditorium in 1983 (2,500 people inside, 60,000 outside, 12 standing ovations and a *pollo asado* lunch at La Esquina de Tejas with Jorge Mas Canosa and 203 other provisional loyalists), and then Ronald Reagan, the first American president since John F. Kennedy to visit Miami in search of Cuban support, added this: "Someday, Cuba itself will be free."

This was of course just more poetry, another rhetorical expression of the same collective wish, but Ronald Reagan, like John F. Kennedy before him, was speaking here to people whose historical experience has not been that poetry makes nothing happen. On one of the first evenings I spent in Miami I sat at midnight over *carne con papas* in an art-filled condominium in one of the Arquitectonica buildings on Brickell Avenue and listened to several exiles talk about the relationship of what was said in Washington to what was done in Miami. These exiles were all well-educated. They were well-read, well-traveled, comfortable citizens of a larger world than that of either Miami or Washington, with well-cut blazers and French dresses and interests in New York and Madrid and Mexico. Yet what was said that evening in the expensive condominium overlooking Biscayne Bay proceeded from an almost primitive helplessness, a regressive fury at having been, as these exiles saw it, repeatedly used and repeatedly betrayed by the government of the United States. "Let me tell you something," one of them said. "They talk about 'Cuban terrorists.' The guys they call 'Cuban terrorists' are the guys they trained."

This was not, then, the general exile complaint about a government which might have taken up their struggle but had not. This was something more specific, a complaint that the government in question had in fact taken up *la lucha*, but for its own purposes, and, in what these exiles saw as a pattern of deceit stretching back through six administrations, to its own ends. The pattern, as they saw it, was one in which the government of the United States had repeatedly encouraged or supported exile action and then, when policy shifted and such action became an embarrassment, a discordant note in whatever message Washington was sending that month or that year, had discarded the exiles involved, had sometimes not only discarded them but, since the nature of *la lucha* was essentially illegal, turned them in, set them up for prosecution; positioned them, as it were, for the fall.

They mentioned, as many exiles did, the Omega 7 prosecutions. They mentioned, as many exiles did, the Cuban burglars at the Watergate, who were told, because so many exiles had come by that time to distrust the CIA, that the assignment at hand was not just CIA, but straight from the White House. They mentioned the case of Jose Elias de la Torriente, a respected exile leader who had been, in the late 1960s, recruited by the CIA to lend his name and his prestige to what was set forth as a new plan to overthrow Fidel Castro, the "Work Plan for Liberation," or the Torriente Plan.

Money had once again been raised, and expectations. The entire attention of *el exilio* had for a time been focused on the Torriente Plan, a diversion of energy which, as years passed and nothing happened, suggested to many that what the plan may have been from its inception was just another ad hoc solution to the disposal problem, another mirror trick. Jose Elias de la Torriente had been called, by a frustrated community once again left with nowhere to go, a traitor. Jose Elias de la Torriente had been called a CIA stooge. Jose Elias de la Torriente had finally been, at age seventy, as he sat in his house in Coral Gables watching *The Robe* on television about nine o'clock on the evening of Good Friday, 1974, assassinated, shot through the venetian blind on a window by someone, presumably an exile, who claimed the kill in the name "Zero."

This had, in the telling at the dinner table, the sense of a situation played out to its Aristotelian end, of that inexorable Caribbean progress from cause to effect which I later came to see as central to the way Miami thought about itself. Miami stories tended to have endings. The cannon onstage tended to be fired. One of those who spoke most ardently that evening was a quite beautiful young woman in a white jersey dress, a lawyer, active in Democratic politics in Miami. This dinner in the condominium overlooking Biscayne Bay took place in March of 1985, and the woman in the white jersey dress was María Elena Prío Durán, the child who flew into exile in March of 1952 with her father's foreign minister, her father's minister of the interior, her father, her sister, and her mother, the equally beautiful woman in the hat with the fishnet veiling.

I recall watching María Elena Prío Durán that night as she pushed back her hair and reached across the table for a cigarette. This, like the lunch in the Malaga courtyard when Carlos Luis had talked about Albert Camus and the choice between terror of the Right and terror of the Left, was a long time before the C-123K carrying Eugene Hasenfus fell from the sky inside Nicaragua. This was a long time before Eugene Hasenfus mentioned the names of the 2506 members already in place at Ilopango. NICARAGUA HOY, CUBA MAÑANA. Let me tell you about Cuban terrorists, another of the exiles at dinner that night, a prominent Miami architect named Raúl Rodríguez, was saying at the end of the table. Cuba never grew plastique. Cuba grew tobacco. Cuba grew sugarcane. Cuba never grew C-4. María Elena Prío Durán lit the cigarette and immediately crushed it out. C-4, Raúl Rodríguez said, and he slammed his palm down on the white tablecloth as he said it, grew here.

FOUR

15

EARLY ON the morning of April 19, 1961, when it was clear in Washington that the invasion then underway at Playa Girón had failed, President John F. Kennedy dispatched Adolf A. Berle of the State Department and Arthur M. Schlesinger, Jr., of the White House staff to Miami, to meet with what had been until a few hours before the projected provisional government for a post-Castro Cuba, the Cuban Revolutionary Council, the members of which were being kept temporarily incommunicado in a CIA barracks at the Opa-Locka Airport. "A couple of hours into our meeting with the Kennedy people, I got the feeling that we were being taken for a ride," one member of the council later told the exile sociologist José Llanes, who quoted but did not name him in *Cuban Americans: Masters of Survival*. "The *comierda* [Llanes translates this as "shit face"] they sent me was only worried about the political popularity of their man." In *A Thousand Days*, Arthur M. Schlesinger, Jr., described his and Adolf Berle's thoughts during the same meeting: "Our hearts sank as we walked out for a moment into the dazzling sun. How could we notify the Cubans that there was no hope, that their sons were abandoned for captivity or death—and at the same time dissuade them from public denunciation of the CIA and the United States government?"

What is interesting here is how closely these two views of the meeting at the Opa-Locka Airport, the Miami and the Washington, appear to coincide. The problem that April morning for Schlesinger and Berle, Schlesinger seems himself to suggest, was one of presentation, of damage control, which is another way of saying that they were worried about the political popularity of their man. The solution, as they devised it, was to take the exiles for a literal ride: to fly them immediately to Washington and give them an afternoon audience in the Oval Office, a meeting at which the members of the Cuban Revolutionary Council (several of whom had sons or brothers on the beachhead that day) would sit by the fireplace and hear the President speak of the responsibilities of leadership, of the struggle against communism on its many fronts and of his own commitment to the "eventual" freedom of Cuba; a meeting which in fact took place, and at which, according to Schlesinger, the President spoke "slowly and thoughtfully" ("I had never seen the President more impressive"), and the members of the Cuban Revolutionary Council had been, "in spite of themselves," "deeply moved." Here, the Washington and the Miami views no longer coincide: the recitative of seduction and betrayal from which Miami took its particular tone was in a key Washington failed then to hear, and does still.

On April 10, 1984, midway through yet another administration during which it was periodically suggested that the struggle against communism on its many fronts included a commitment to the eventual freedom of Cuba, an unexceptional Tuesday morning during a week in which *The New York Times* reported that the mining of Nicaraguan harbors had "rekindled doubts in Congress and among some officials in the Reagan administration about the extensive use of covert activities to advance United States interests in Central America," Ronald Reagan, the fortieth President of the United States, was presented to be photographed in the following Washington settings: greeting President Salvador Jorge Blanco of the Dominican Republic on the South Grounds of the White House (10:00 A.M.), conferring with President Salvador Jorge Blanco of the Dominican Republic in the Oval Office of the White House (10:30 A.M.), and placing a telephone call from the Oval Office to the *Challenger* space shuttle, an event covered only by a pool camera crew but piped live into the press briefing room in the West Wing of the White House:

THE PRESIDENT: Hello, Bob—these calls—

ASTRONAUT CRIPPEN: Good afternoon, Mr. President. Thank you very much for speaking with us.

THE PRESIDENT: Well, these calls between the two of us are becoming a habit. I promise you, though, I won't reverse the charges. Over.

ASTRONAUT CRIPPEN: I don't think I can afford them, Mr. President. (*Laughter.*)

THE PRESIDENT: Well, once again, I'm calling to congratulate you and the rest of the crew aboard the *Challenger* there on an historic mission. The retrieval of the Solar Max satellite this morning was just great. And you and the crew demonstrated once again just how versatile the space shuttle is and what we can accomplish by having a team in space and on the ground. I know you'll agree that those folks at the Goddard Space Flight Center did a fantastic job maneuvering the satellite for you. And, Terry, I guess you made one long reach for man this morning when you snapped that satellite with the fifty-foot robot arms. And George and Jim, you've done fine work as well. The pictures sent back of you working in space are spectacular. They're also a little scary for those of us who are sitting comfortably anchored to the earth. But, Bob, I understand that satellite you have on board would cost us about two hundred million dollars to build at today's prices, so if you can't fix it up there, would you mind bringing it back? Over.

ASTRONAUT CRIPPEN: Well, we—we're going to do our best to repair it tomorrow, sir, and if, for some reason, that is unsuccessful, which we don't think it will be, we will be able to return it. We certainly concur with all of your remarks. The *Challenger* and its sister ships are magnificent flying machines and I think that they can make a significant road into space in regard to repair and servicing of satellites. And we believe this is the initial step. I would also like to concur with your remarks regarding the people up at Goddard who managed to put this satellite back in a configuration that we could retrieve it after the little problem we ran into the other day. Those people and the people in Houston and everybody that worked on it truly made this recovery possible. It is a team effort all the way. It so happens we get to do the fun part.

THE PRESIDENT: Well, let me tell you, you're all a team that has made all Americans very proud of what you're doing up there, and what the future bodes for all of us with regard to this opening up of that great frontier of

> space. And, seriously, I just want to again say how proud we all are of all of you, and congratulations to you all. Have a safe mission, a safe trip home, and God bless all of you. I'll sign out and let you get on with your chores.

There was at first a silence in the West Wing briefing room. "Sign off," someone said then. "Not 'sign out,' '*sign off*.'"

"'And, seriously'?" someone else said. "What does that mean, 'And, seriously'?"

This telephone call between the Oval Office and space lasted four minutes, between 12:01 P.M. and 12:05 P.M., and was followed immediately in the briefing room by a report on the meeting between President Reagan and President Salvador Jorge Blanco of the Dominican Republic, or rather on that part of the meeting which had taken place after the pool camera crew left the Oval Office. This report was delivered by Assistant Secretary of State for Inter-American Affairs Langhorne Motley ("This briefing is on background and is attributable to 'a senior Administration official,'" a voice on the loudspeaker had advised before Langhorne Motley appeared), who said that the meeting between the two presidents, dealing with how best to oppose those who were "destabilizing" and "working against the forces of democracy" in Central America, had in fact ended when the pool camera crew was escorted back into the Oval Office to light the phone call to the astronauts.

On this unexceptional Tuesday midway through his administration the President of the United States was lit and photographed as well in the Old Executive Office Building at a ceremony marking Fair Housing Month (1:30 P.M.); in the Rose Garden signing H.R. 4072, the Agricultural Programs Adjustments Act of 1984 (3:45 P.M.); in the Oval Office signing H.R. 4206, an amendment to the Internal Revenue Code (4:30 P.M.); in the Oval Office greeting the board of directors of the Electronics Industries Association (4:45 P.M.), and, later, in three State Dinner situations: descending the Grand Staircase at 7:45 P.M., toasting President Jorge Blanco in the State Dining Room at 9:15 P.M., and, at 10:35 P.M., addressing his guests, including Wayne Newton and his date, Brooke Shields and her mother, Oscar de la Renta, Pilar Crespi and Tommy Lasorda, in the East Room. Of the day's events, some had been open to the White House press corps at large; others limited to the camera crews and a few pool print reporters, who duly submitted their reports for distribution by the White House press office:

> POOL REPORT, Reagan and Fair Housing: The ceremony was attended by representatives of civil rights and fair housing groups, builders and realtors who cooperated with HUD to make sure fair housing law works. The room was half full. Secretary Pierce presented several awards. One celebrity present, Phyllis Hyman, Celebrities for Fair Housing. She is a Broadway musical star. The President stood under a sign:
>
> Fair Housing
> I support it
> President Reagan supports it
> All America Needs It.
>
> He spoke for about five minutes.
>
> —*Vic Ostrowidzki*
> *Hearst Newspapers.*
>
> POOL REPORT, Meeting with President Jorge Blanco in the Oval Office: The two presidents sat side by side, exchanging pleasantries. When we were brought in, President Jorge Blanco was in the process of telling President Reagan about his prior visit to the U.S. and that this trip was "an extension of that visit." At one point, President Reagan said "when you were speaking this morning the planes were coming over. They are a big problem at the time they take off. They come every three minutes apart. There is a great deal of public sentiment about that." We never found out what that "sentiment" is because the President suddenly looked up, saw us staring at him expectantly and stopped in mid-sentence. To a question "Are you going to discuss the mining of ports?" Reagan responded "no questions at photo opportunity" and L. Speakes shouted, "lights out."
>
> —*Vic Ostrowidzki*
> *Hearst Newspapers.*

"Almost everything we do is determined by whether we think it will get on the network news shows in the evening," Larry Speakes, at that time the chief White House spokesman, was quoted as saying in an Associated Press story later that week. "We obviously would like to highlight the positive story of the day for the President," Michael Deaver, then White House deputy chief of staff, said in the same story, which was about his efforts to get the President photographed in more "spontaneous" settings, for example making a surprise visit to Monticello and eating a hot dog in the Baltimore Orioles' dugout. "I think you have to give credit to Mike Deaver and to Bill Henkel, our chief advance man, for setting the scene at the demilitarized zone in South Korea last December," David Gergen had said not long before, to *The New York Times*, when asked for highlights of his three-year tenure as White House director of communications. "The pictures said as much as anything the President could say." He was talking about those still photographs and pieces of film which had shown the President, in the course of a visit to South Korea, at the 38th parallel, with field glasses and battle helmet. "Audiences," David Gergen had added, "will listen to you more if they see the President in an interesting setting. Their memory of the event will be more vivid. We spend a fair amount of time thinking about that."

In Washington, then, midway through the Reagan administration, it was taken for granted that the White House schedule should be keyed to the daily network feeds. It was taken for granted that the efforts of the White House staff should be directed toward the setting of interesting scenes. It was taken for granted that the overriding preoccupation of the White House staff (the subject of a senior staff meeting every morning, an additional meeting every Wednesday, a meeting on foreign coverage every Thursday, and a "brainstorming" lunch at Blair House every Friday) should be the invention of what had come to be called "talking points," the production of "guidance"; the creation and strategic management of what David Gergen had characterized as "the story line we are trying to develop that week or that month."

The story's protagonist, the President himself, was said, even then, to be "detached," or "disengaged from the decision-making process," a condition presented, in the accepted cipher, as an asset in itself: here was a protagonist who "delegated authority," who "refused to get mired in details," attractive managerial skills that suggested a superior purchase on the larger picture. Patrick Buchanan reported that the President had "mastered the art of compartmentalization." Morton Kondracke wondered when "Mr. Reagan's opponents would stop underestimating him and would begin to realize that he has to be pretty smart—even if his intellect does not work like an academic's—and that he has to have a grasp of the large issues confronting the country, even if he has a disconcerting way of not bothering with the details."

"You don't need to know who's playing on the White House tennis court to be a good president," James Baker had liked to say when he was chief of staff. "A president has many roles," White House aides frequently advised reporters, a construct sufficiently supple, even silky, to cover any missed cue, dropped stitch, irreconcilable contradiction or frank looniness that came to light. "I don't have any problem with a reporter or a news person who says the President is uninformed on this issue or that issue," David Gergen had said in the course of a 1984 discussion sponsored by the American Enterprise Institute. "I don't think any of us would challenge that. I do have a problem with the singular focus on this, as if that's the only standard by which we ought to judge a president. What we learned in the last administration was how little having an encyclopedic grasp of all the facts has to do with governing."

Such professed faith in the mystery of "governing," in the ineffable contract that was said to exist between the President and the people (often so called), was only part of what was taken for granted, midway through the Reagan administration. It was also taken for granted that the presidency had been redefined as an essentially passive role, that of "communicator," or "leader," which had been redefined in turn to mean that person whose simple presence before a camera was believed to command support for the policy proposed. It was taken for granted that the key to understanding the policy could be found in the shifts of position and ambition among the President's men. It was taken for granted that the President himself was, if not exactly absent when Larry Speakes ordered lights out, something less than entirely present, the condition expressed even then by the code word "incurious." It was taken for granted, above all, that the reporters and camera operators and still photographers and sound technicians and lighting technicians and producers and electricians and on-camera correspondents showed up at the White House because the President did, and it was also taken for granted, the more innovative construction, that the President showed up at the White House because the reporters and camera operators and still photographers and sound technicians and lighting technicians and producers and electricians and on-camera correspondents did.

In Washington midway through the Reagan administration many things were taken for granted, I learned during time spent there during two consecutive springs, that were not necessarily taken for granted in less abstract venues. I recall talking about the administration's Central American policy, one afternoon in 1984, to David Gergen, and being struck not exactly by what he said but by the way in which he said it, by the terms in which he described what he called the "several stages" of "the same basic policy." The terms David Gergen used that afternoon were exclusively those of presentation. He spoke first of "the very hard line taken in the spring of 1981," a time for "a lot of focus, a lot of attention." He spoke of a period, later the same spring, when "it wasn't looking good, so we kind of moved it back." He spoke of a later period, in 1982, "when some people in the administration thought it could become serious," a time when "we thought we should start laying the groundwork, building some public support for what we might have to do"; a time, then, for moving it not "back" but forward. "I would say this continued to the end of 1983," David Gergen had said finally that afternoon in 1984, his voice trailing off and perhaps his attention: this was to him a familiar chronology, and like many people whose business was the art of the possible he appeared to have only a limited interest in even the most recent past. "Then some people began to see it as a negative issue, and to ask why do we want to make Central America front and center again, so there was an effort to pull it back."

David Gergen had worked in the White House during three administrations, and acquired during the course of them an entire vocabulary of unattributable nods and acquiescent silences, a diction that tended to evaporate like smoke, but the subtext of what he was saying on this spring afternoon in 1984 seemed clear, and to suggest a view of the government of the United States, from someone who had labored at its exact heart for nine of the preceding thirteen years, not substantively different from the view of the government of the United States held by those Cubans to whom I later talked in Miami: the government of the United States was in this view one for which other parts of the world, in this instance Central America, existed only as "issues." In some seasons, during some administrations and in the course of some campaigns, Central America had seemed a useful issue, one to which "focus" and "attention" could profitably be drawn. In other seasons it had seemed a "negative" issue, one which failed to meet, for whatever reason, the test of "looking good."

In all seasons, however, it remained a potentially valuable asset in this business of the art of the possible, and not just an ordinary special-interest, domestic asset, but a national security card, a jeopardy chip, a marker that carried with it the glamour of possible military action, the ultimate interesting setting. As such, it would ideally remain on the board, sometimes available to be moved "back," sometimes available to be moved (whenever the moment seemed to call for a show of determination and resolution, a demonstration, say, of standing tall) "front and center." That each move left a certain residue on the board was what some people in Washington had called their disposal problem, and some people in Miami their betrayal.

16

THERE WERE in Washington during the Reagan administration a small but significant number of people for whom the commitment to American involvement in Central America did not exist exclusively as an issue, a marker to be moved sometimes front, sometimes back. These were people for whom the commitment to American involvement in Central America was always front, in fact "the" front, the battleground on which, as Ronald Reagan had put it in his second inaugural address and on many occasions before and after, "human freedom" was "on the march." These were people who had believed early on and even formulated what was eventually known as the Reagan Doctrine, people committed to the idea that "rollback," or the reversal of Soviet power which had been part of the rhetoric of the American Right since at least the Eisenhower administration, could now be achieved by supporting guerrilla resistance movements around the world; people who believed that, in the words of *A New Inter-American Policy for the Eighties*, a fifty-three-page policy proposal issued in the summer of 1980 by the Council for Inter-American Security, "containment of the Soviet Union is not enough. Detente is dead. Survival demands a new U.S. foreign policy. America must seize the initiative or perish. For World War III is almost over."

A New Inter-American Policy for the Eighties, usually referred to, because the discussions from which it derived took place in New Mexico, as the Santa Fe statement or the Santa Fe document, was a curious piece of work, less often talked about in this country than in Managua and Havana, where it was generally regarded, according to Edward Cody in the *Washington Post* and Christopher Dickey in *With the Contras*, as a blueprint to Reagan administration intentions in the hemisphere. In fact what seemed most striking about the Santa Fe document was not that it was read in, but that it might have been written in, Managua or Havana. As a document prepared by Americans it seemed not quite authentic, perhaps a piece of "black propaganda," something put forth clandestinely by a foreign government but purporting to be, in the interests of encouraging anti-American sentiment, American. The grasp on the language was not exactly that of native English speakers. The tone of the preoccupations was not exactly that of the American foreign policy establishment:

> During the last several years, United States policy toward the other nations within the Western Hemisphere has been one of hoping for the best. Too often it has been a policy described by The Committee of Santa Fe as "anxious accommodation," as if we would prevent the political coloration of Latin America to red crimson by an American-prescribed tint of pale pink. Whatever the pedigree of American policy toward our immediate neighbors, it is not working. . . .
>
> The policies of the past decade regarding arms sales and security assistance are totally bankrupt and discredited at home and abroad. . . . Combining our arsenal of weaponry with the manpower of the Americas, we can create a free hemisphere of the Americas, that can withstand Soviet-Cuban aggression. . . .
>
> U.S. policy formation must insulate itself from propaganda appearing in the general and specialized media which is inspired by forces specifically hostile to the United States. . . .
>
> U.S. foreign policy must begin to counter (not react against) liberation theology as it is utilized in Latin America by the "liberation theology" clergy. . . .
>
> A campaign to capture the Ibero-American intellectual elite through the media of radio, television, books, articles and pamphlets, plus grants, fellowships and prizes must be initiated. For consideration and recognition are what most intellectuals crave, and such a program would attract them. The U.S. effort must reflect the true sentiments of the American people, not the narrow spectrum of New York and Hollywood. . . .
>
> Human rights, which is a culturally and politically relative concept . . . must be abandoned and replaced by a non-interventionist policy of political and ethical realism.

> The culturally and ethically relative nature of notions of human rights is clear from the fact that Argentines, Brazilians and Chileans find it repugnant that the United States, which legally sanctions the liquidation of more than 1,000,000 unborn children each year, exhibits moral outrage at the killing of a terrorist who bombs and machine-guns innocent citizens. What, they ask, about the human rights of the victims of left-wing terrorism? U.S. policy-makers must discard the illusion that anyone who picks up a Molotov cocktail in the name of human rights is human-righteous. . . .
>
> Havana must be held to account for its policies of aggression against its sister states in the Americas. Among those steps will be the establishment of a Radio Free Cuba, under open U.S. government sponsorship, which will beam objective information to the Cuban people that, among other things, details the costs of Havana's unholy alliance with Moscow. If propaganda fails, a war of national liberation against Castro must be launched.

The five authors of *A New Inter-American Policy for the Eighties*, who called themselves "The Committee of Santa Fe," were all well-known on the Right, regulars on the boards and letterheads of the various conservative lobbies and foundations around Washington. There was Lynn Francis Bouchey of the Council for Inter-American Security. There was David C. Jordan, a professor of government at the University of Virginia and the coauthor of *Nationalism in Contemporary Latin America*. There was Lieutenant General Gordon Sumner, Jr., at one time chairman of the Inter-American Defense Board and later, during the Reagan administration, special adviser to the assistant secretary of state for inter-American affairs. There was Roger Fontaine, formerly the director for Latin America at the Georgetown University Center for Strategic and International Studies and later, during the Reagan administration, a Latin American specialist at the National Security Council. There was, finally, Lewis Tambs, who had worked in Caracas and Maracaibo as a pipeline engineer for Creole Petroleum and was later, during the Reagan administration, appointed as ambassador first to Colombia, then to Costa Rica, where, as he eventually told both the Tower Commission and the select committees investigating arms shipments to the contras, he understood himself to have been charged with the task of opening a southern front for the Nicaraguan resistance.

According to these men and to that small but significant group of people who thought as they did, the people with whom they shared the boards and letterheads of the various conservative lobbies and foundations around Washington, the "crisis" facing the United States in Central America was "metaphysical." The war was "for the minds of mankind." What the Santa Fe document had called "ideo-politics" would "prevail." These were not people, as time passed and men like James Baker and Michael Deaver and David Gergen moved into the White House, men who understood that the distinction between a crisis and no crisis was one of "perception," or "setting the scene," particularly close to the center of power. They were all, in varying degrees, ideologues, people who had seized or been seized by an idea, and, as such, they were to the White House only sometimes useful.

Where they were useful, of course, was in voicing the concerns not only of the American Right but in some inchoate way of the President himself: with the Santa Fe document they had even managed, in the rather astonishing context of a foreign policy proposal, to drill through their own discussion of the Roldós Doctrine and the Rio Treaty and into that molten core where "New York" was the problem, and "Hollywood," and women who liquidated their unborn children, the very magma of resentment on which Ronald Reagan's appeal had seemed always to float. Where these conservative spokesmen were less useful, where they were in fact profoundly not useful, was in recognizing when the moment had come to move the war for the minds of mankind "back," or anywhere but "front"; in accepting a place in the wings when the stage was set for a different scene. They tended to lack an appreciation of the full script. They tended not to wait backstage without constant diversion, and it was precisely the contriving of such diversion which seemed to most fully engage, as time went by, the attention and energy of the Reagan White House.

Sometimes a diversion was referred to as "sending a signal." The White House Outreach Working Group on Central America, or, as it was sometimes called, "Operation Outreach," was a "signal," one of several efforts conceived during 1982 and 1983 when the White House decided that the time was right for, as David Gergen put it, "laying the groundwork," for "building some public support for what we might have to do"; for, in the words of an April 1982 National Security Planning Group document, addressing the "public affairs dimension of the Central American problem" through a "concerted public information effort." There was at first talk about something called "Project Truth." "Project Truth" melted almost immediately into the "Office of Public Diplomacy," which was set up in 1982, put under the direction of a former Miami city official named Otto Juan Reich (who was born in Havana, in 1945, but whose parents had emigrated to Cuba from Austria), and charged with a task which appeared in practice to consist largely of disseminating classified and sometimes "unevaluated" information ("unevaluated" information was that which had not been and in some cases could not be corroborated) tending to support administration contentions about Nicaragua and El Salvador.

The Office of Public Diplomacy, although at the time of its inception controlled by the White House and the National Security Council, was technically under the aegis of the State Department. At the White House itself there was the "Office of Public Liaison" (the word "public," in this administration even more than in others, tended to suggest a sell in progress), and it was out of this "Office of Public Liaison," then under the direction of Faith Ryan Whittlesey, that the White House Outreach Working Group on Central America emerged. The idea was, on its face, straightforward enough: a series of regular briefings, open to the public, at which the administration could "tell its story" about Central America, "make the case" for its interests there. "We hadn't in a systematic way communicated the facts to people who were perfectly willing to do more themselves to support the President but just didn't have access to the information," Faith Ryan Whittlesey told the *Los Angeles Times* not long after the Outreach Working Group began meeting, every Wednesday afternoon at two-thirty, in Room

450 of the Old Executive Office Building. "All the people need is information. They know what to do with it."

The briefings themselves were somewhat less straightforward. For one thing they were not, or the first forty-five of them were not, open to the public at all: they were not open, most specifically, to reporters, the very people who might have been expected to carry the information to a larger number of Americans than were apt to arrange their Wednesday afternoons to include a two-hour session in Room 450 of the Old Executive Office Building. Even after the Outreach briefings had finally been opened to the press, in April of 1984, the White House Office of Public Liaison seemed notably uninterested in talking to reporters: I recall one week in Washington during which, from Monday through Friday, I placed repeated calls to Faith Ryan Whittlesey's office, each time giving my affiliation (I had been asked by a magazine to write a piece about the Reagan administration, and given a kind of introduction to the White House by the magazine's Washington editor), detailing my interest in discussing the Outreach program, and expressing my hope that either Mrs. Whittlesey or someone else in the White House Office of Public Liaison could find a moment to return my call.

Neither Mrs. Whittlesey nor anyone else in the White House Office of Public Liaison did find such a moment, not any day that week or ever, which did not at the time unduly surprise me: it had been my experience that people who worked for the government in Washington were apt to regard anyone who did not work for the government in Washington as a supplicant, a citizen to whom the rightful order must constantly be made clear, and that one of the several ways of asserting this rightful order was by not returning telephone calls. In other words I thought of these unreturned calls to Faith Ryan Whittlesey as unspecific, evidence only of an attitude that came with the particular autointoxication of the territory. Not until later, after I had managed to attend a few Outreach meetings, febrile afternoons in 1984 and 1985 during which the United States was seen to be waging the war for the minds of mankind not only against the Sandinistas in Nicaragua and the FMLN in El Salvador and the Castro government in Cuba and the Machel government in Mozambique but also against its own

Congress, against its own State Department, against some members (James Baker, Michael Deaver) of its own executive branch, and, most pointedly, against its own press, did it occur to me that this particular series of unreturned telephone calls may well have been specific; that there was in the White House Outreach Working Group on Central America an inherent peculiarity perhaps best left, from the White House point of view, undiscussed.

This peculiarity was at first hard to assimilate. It did not exactly derive from the actual briefings, most of which seemed, however casually inflammatory, however apt to veer vertiginously out of Central America and into Mozambique and Angola and denunciations of Chester Crocker on the African desk at the State Department, standard enough. There was Francis X. Gannon, then adviser to Alejandro Orfila at the Organization of American States, on "Central America: A Democratic Perspective." ("Somebody at OAS said about the Kissinger Commission, 'What should we send them?' And I said, 'Send them a map.'") There was General Alexander M. Haig, Jr., on "The Imperatives of Central America in Perspective" ("My opinion of what is happening in Central America is this: the jury is still out"), a raconteur's version of American foreign policy during which General Haig referred to one of its principals with doubtful bonhomie ("So Henry had one of those Germanic tantrums of his . . ."), to another by a doubtful diminutive ("I again will not make any apologies for recounting the fact that I was opposed to covert action in 1981, as Jeannie Kirkpatrick will tell you . . ."), and to himself in the third person, as "Al Haig," or just "Haig."

Some briefings got a little closer to the peculiarity. I recall one particularly heady Outreach meeting, in 1985, at which one of the speakers was a fantast named Jack Wheeler, who liked to say that *Izvestia* had described him as an "ideological gangster" ("When the Soviet Union calls me that, it means I'm starting to get under their skin") but was identified on the afternoon's program simply as "Philosopher, Traveler, and Founder of the Freedom Research Foundation." As it happened I had heard Jack Wheeler before, at a Conservative Political Action Conference session on "Rolling Back the Soviet Empire," where he had received a standing ovation after suggesting that copies of the Koran be smuggled into the Soviet Union to "stimulate an

Islamic revival" and the subsequent "death of a thousand cuts," and I was already familiar not only with many of his exploits but with his weird and rather punitive enthusiasm. Jack Wheeler had recently been with the *mujaheddin* in Afghanistan. He had recently been with Jonas Savimbi in Angola. He had recently been with the insurgents in Cambodia, and Mozambique. He knew of a clandestine radio operating in South Yemen. He saw the first stirrings of democratic liberation in Suriname. He had of course recently been with the contras in Nicaragua, and had, that afternoon in Room 450 of the Old Executive Office Building, brought a few slides to share.

"This is Charley." Jack Wheeler had chuckled as the first slide appeared on the screen. "Charley is a contra. He only looks like he's going to kill you. Actually he's a very nice guy. I told him he looked like Chuck Berry." The slide had changed, and there on the screen was Jack Wheeler himself, his arm around Enrique Bermúdez, the FDN comandante who had been until 1979 a colonel in the Somoza National Guard: "Enrique Bermúdez is convinced—he told me—that only the physical defeat of the Sandinistas will remove the cancer of Soviet-Cuban imperialism and Marxism from Central America." Another slide, this one of a full-breasted young woman carrying a rifle, another chuckle: "One thing that has got to be dispelled is this myth of hopelessness. The myth that they can't win, so why support them . . . I wouldn't mind having her fighting alongside of me."

On such afternoons the enemy was manifold, and often within. The "Red Empire" was of course the enemy. "Christian communists" were also the enemy. "Guilt-ridden masochistic liberals" were the enemy, and "the radical chic crowd that always roots for the other side," the "Beverly Hills liberals with their virulent hatred of America." I recall a briefing on the 1984 Salvadoran election in which "people like Tom Brokaw" were the enemy, people like Richard Meislin of *The New York Times* and Sam Dillon of the *Miami Herald*, people whose "sneer was showing," people who "did not need to be in El Salvador to write what they did"; people who were "treated well" (". . . although the bar at the Camino Real was closed for the day, they got back to it that night . . .") but persisted in following what the briefer of the day, a frequent speaker named Daniel James, who had been in the 1950s managing editor of *The New Leader* and whose distinctly polemical interest in Latin America had led him to the directorship of the Americas Coalition, one of several amorphous groups formed to support the administration's Central American policy, referred to as "the media party line."

"I'm saying 'party line' in quotes," Daniel James had added quickly. "Because I don't mean to imply that there's any kind of political party involved." This kind of parenthetical disclaimer was not uncommon in Room 450, where irony, or "saying in quotes," was often signaled by raising two fingers on each hand and wiggling them. "Party line" was in quotes, yet there were for Daniel James "just too many similarities" in stories filed from El Salvador. The American press, it seemed, had been "making up deeds of right-wing terror" in El Salvador. The American press, it seemed, had been refusing to "put tough questions to the guerrillas" in El Salvador. "What does that tell you?" Daniel James had asked that afternoon in 1984. "Is this responsible reporting? Or is it done with some kind of political motivation?"

The answer to such questions was, in Room 450, understood, since the meetings of the White House Outreach Working Group on Central America were attended almost exclusively by what might have seemed the already converted, by the convinced, by administration officials and by exiles from the countries in question and by native ideologues from both the heart and the distant fringes of the American Right; true believers who in many cases not only attended the briefings but on occasion gave them. I recall seeing Sam Dickens of the American Security Council, which had co-sponsored the lunch and press conference at which Roberto D'Aubuisson spoke during his illegal 1980 visit to Washington and which was already deeply committed to aiding the Nicaraguan contras. I recall seeing Lynn Francis Bouchey, one of the authors of the Santa Fe document and the chairman of the Council for Inter-American Security, which was equally committed. "Hear, hear," Lynn Francis Bouchey said when Jack Wheeler asked him if the situation in Mozambique did not remind him of the situation in Nicaragua.

This was not a group which would have appeared to need much instruction in administration policy in Central America.

This was not a group apt to raise those questions about Central America commonly raised in less special venues. In fact there was for many people in Room 450 just one question about Central America, which was why the United States was compelled to deal through surrogates there when it could be fighting its own war for the minds of mankind, and it was this question that the briefers addressed by tapping into the familiar refrain: the United States was forced to deal through surrogates because of the defeatists, because of the appeasers, because of the cowards and the useful fools and the traitors, because of what Jack Wheeler had called "that virulent hatred for America as a culture and as a nation and as a society" which was understood, by virtually everyone in the room, to infect the Congress, to infect the State Department, and above all to infect the media, which were, as Otto Juan Reich had said not long after he was appointed coordinator of public diplomacy, "being played like a violin by the Sandinistas."

There were some tricky points in this, although none that the briefers did not negotiate to the apparent satisfaction of most people in the room. The United States was forced to wage the war for the minds of mankind (or, as J. William Middendorf, U.S. ambassador to the OAS, was calling it, "the battle for the freedom of the western world") through surrogates, but in any case these surrogates could, if allowed to do so, win: "The only thing keeping the contras from victory is Congress," as Alexander M. Haig, Jr., had advised the group in Room 450. The war for the minds of mankind was being fought through surrogates only because the United States was thwarted in its wish to enter the war directly, but in any case the entry of the United States could not affect the outcome: "What is needed to shatter the myth of the inevitability of Marxist-Leninism is a genuine peasant rebellion from within a Soviet colony," as Jack Wheeler had advised the group in Room 450. "These heroic freedom fighters ask only for our help, they do not want us to fight for them."

An arresting amount of administration effort went into what might have seemed this marginal project. The weekly planning meetings for the Outreach program were attended not only by Faith Ryan Whittlesey and her aides at the Office of Public Liaison but also by representatives from the United States

Information Agency, from the Central Intelligence Agency, from the State Department and from the National Security Council. The National Security Council was often represented by the protean Colonel Oliver North (Colonel North was responsible as well for overseeing Otto Juan Reich's Office of Public Diplomacy at the State Department), who was, according to a *Washington Post* story in August of 1985, a "mainstay" of the Outreach project, not only in the planning meetings but also as a "briefer of choice" in Room 450 itself.

Some of the peculiarity inherent in the Outreach project seemed clear enough at the time. It was of course clear that the program had been designed principally, if not entirely, as a weekly audience between the administration and its most passionate, most potentially schismatic communicants; a bone thrown to those famously restless troops on the far frontiers of the faith. It was also clear that many people in Room 450 on these Wednesday afternoons had links to, or could be useful to, the private funding network then being quite publicly organized, in support of the Reagan Doctrine and the war for the minds of mankind, under the official direction of Major General John K. Singlaub and what was known even then to be the unofficial direction of some of the very administration officials who gave the briefings in Room 450.

Other things were less clear than they might have been. One thing that was less clear, in those high years of the Reagan administration when we had not yet begun to see just how the markers were being moved, was how many questions there might later be about what had been the ends and what the means, what the problem and what the solution; about what, among people who measured the consequences of what they said and did exclusively in terms of approval ratings affected and network news calibrated and pieces of legislation passed or not passed, had come first, the war for the minds of mankind or the private funding network or the need to make a move for those troops on the far frontiers. What was also less clear then, particularly in Washington, most abstract of cities, entirely absorbed by the messages it was sending itself, narcotized by its own action, rapt in the contemplation of its own markers and its own moves, was just how much residue was already on the board.

Steven Carr for example was residue. Jesus Garcia for example was residue. Steven Carr was, at twenty-six, a South Florida lowlife, a sometime Naples construction worker with the motto DEATH BEFORE DISHONOR and a flaming skull tattooed on his left biceps; a discharge from the Navy for alcohol abuse; and a grand-theft conviction for stealing two gold-and-diamond rings, valued at $578, given to his mother by his stepfather. "She only wore them on holidays, I thought she'd never notice they were gone," Steven Carr later said about the matter of his mother's rings. He did not speak Spanish. He had no interest in any side of the conflict in Nicaragua. Nonetheless, in March of 1985, according to the story he began telling after he had been arrested in Costa Rica on weapons charges and was awaiting trial at La Reforma prison in San José, Steven Carr had collected arms for the contras at various locations around Dade County, loaded them onto a chartered Convair 440 at Fort Lauderdale–Hollywood International Airport, accompanied this shipment to Ilopango airport in San Salvador, and witnessed the eventual delivery of the arms to a unit of 2506 veterans fighting with the contras from a base about three miles south of the Nicaraguan border.

This story later became familiar, but its significance at the time Steven Carr first told it, in the summer of 1985 to Juan Tamayo of the *Miami Herald*, was that he was the first person to publicly claim firsthand knowledge of all stages of a single shipment. By the summer of 1986, after Steven Carr had bonded out of La Reforma and was back in South Florida (the details of how he got there were disputed, but either did or did not involve American embassy officials in Panama and San José who either did or did not give him a plane ticket and instructions to "get the hell out of Dodge"), doing six months in the Collier County jail for violation of probation on the outstanding matter of his mother's rings, he was of course telling it as well to investigators from various congressional committees and from the U.S. attorney's office in Miami. This was the point, in August 1986, at which his lawyers asked that he be released early and placed, on the grounds that the story he was telling endangered his life, in a witness protection program. "I'm not too popular with a lot of people because I'm telling the truth,"

Steven Carr told the *Miami Herald* a few days before this petition was heard and denied. "I wouldn't feel very safe just walking the streets after all this is over."

Steven Carr was released from the Collier County jail, having served his full sentence, on November 20, 1986. Twenty-three days later, at two-thirty on the morning of December 13, 1986, Steven Carr collapsed outside the room he was renting in Panorama City, California (a room which, according to the woman from whom he had rented it, Jackie Scott, he rarely left, and in which he slept with the doors locked and the lights on), convulsed, and died, of an apparent cocaine overdose. "I'm sorry," Steven Carr had said when Jackie Scott, whose daughter had heard "a commotion" and woken her, found him lying in the driveway. Jackie Scott told the *Los Angeles Times* that she had not seen Steven Carr drinking or taking drugs that evening, nor could she shed any light on what he had said next: "I paranoided out—I ate it all."

Jesus Garcia was a former Dade County corrections officer who was, at the time he began telling his story early in 1986, doing time in Miami for illegal possession of a MAC-10 with silencer. Jesus Garcia, who had been born in the United States of Cuban parents and thought of himself as a patriot, talked about having collected arms for the contras during the spring of 1985, and also about the plan, which he said had been discussed in the cocktail lounge of the Howard Johnson's near the Miami airport in February of 1985, to assassinate the new American ambassador to Costa Rica, blow up the embassy there, and blame it on the Sandinistas. The idea, Jesus Garcia said, had been to give the United States the opportunity it needed to invade Nicaragua, and also to collect on a million-dollar contract the Colombian cocaine cartel was said to have out on the new American ambassador to Costa Rica, who had recently been the American ambassador to Colombia and had frequently spoken of what he called "narco-guerrillas."

There were in the story told by Jesus Garcia and in the story told by Steven Carr certain details that appeared to coincide. Both Jesus Garcia and Steven Carr mentioned the Howard Johnson's near the Miami airport, which happened also to be the Howard Johnson's with the seventeen-dollar-a-night "guerrilla discount." Both Jesus Garcia and Steven Carr mentioned meetings in Miami with an American named Bruce Jones, who was said to own a farm on the border between Costa Rica and Nicaragua. Both Jesus Garcia and Steven Carr mentioned Thomas Posey, the Alabama produce wholesaler who had founded the paramilitary group CMA, or Civilian Materiel Assistance, formerly Civilian Military Assistance. Both Jesus Garcia and Steven Carr mentioned Robert Owen, the young Stanford graduate who had gone to Washington to work on the staff of Senator Dan Quayle (R–Ind.), had then moved into public relations, at Gray and Company, had in January of 1985 founded the nonprofit Institute for Democracy, Education, and Assistance, or IDEA (which was by the fall of 1985 on a consultancy contract to the State Department's Nicaraguan Humanitarian Assistance Office), and had been, it was later revealed, carrying cash to and from Central America for Oliver North.

This was, as described, a small world, and one in which encounters seemed at once random and fated, as in the waking dream that was Miami itself. People in this world spoke of having "tripped into an organization." People saw freedom fighters on "Nightline," and then in Miami. People saw boxes in motel rooms, and concluded that the boxes contained C-4. People received telephone calls from strangers, and picked them up at the airport at three in the morning, and began looking for a private plane to fly to Central America. Some people just turned up out of the nowhere: Jesus Garcia happened to meet Thomas Posey because he was working the afternoon shift at the Dade County jail on the day Thomas Posey was booked for trying to take a .380 automatic pistol through the X-ray machine on Concourse G at the Miami airport. Some people turned up not exactly out of the nowhere but all over the map: Jesus Garcia said that he had seen Robert Owen in Miami, more specifically, as an assistant U.S. attorney in Miami put it, "at that Howard Johnson's when they were planning that stuff," by which the assistant U.S. attorney meant weapons flights. Steven Carr said that he had seen Robert Owen in Costa Rica, witnessing a weapons delivery at the base near the Nicaraguan border. Robert Owen, when he eventually appeared before the select committees, acknowledged that he had been present when such a delivery was made, but said that he never saw the actual unloading, and that his presence on the scene was, as the *Miami Herald* put it, "merely coincidental": another random but fated encounter.

There were no particularly novel elements in either the story told by Jesus Garcia or the story told by Steven Carr. They were Miami stories, fragments of the underwater narrative, and as such they were of a genre familiar in this country since at least the Bay of Pigs. Such stories had often been, like these, intrinsically impossible to corroborate. Such stories had often been of doubtful provenance, had been either leaked by prosecutors unable to make a case or elicited, like these, in jailhouse interviews, a circumstance which has traditionally tended, like a DEATH BEFORE DISHONOR tattoo, to work against the credibility of the teller. Any single Miami story, moreover, was hard to follow, and typically required a more extensive recall of other Miami stories than most people outside Miami could offer. Characters would frequently reappear. A convicted bomber named Hector Cornillot, a onetime member of Orlando Bosch's Cuban Power movement, turned out, for example, to have been during the spring of 1985 the night bookkeeper at the Howard Johnson's near the Miami airport. Motivation, often opaque in a first or a second appearance, might come clear only in a third, or a tenth.

Miami stories were low, and lurid, and so radically reliant on the inductive leap that they tended to attract advocates of an ideological or a paranoid bent, which was another reason they remained, for many people, easy to dismiss. Stories like these had been told to the Warren Commission in 1964, but many people had preferred to discuss what was then called the climate of violence, and the healing process. Stories like these had been told during the Watergate investigations in 1974, but the President had resigned, enabling the healing process, it was again said, to begin. Stories like these had been told to the Church committee in 1975 and 1976, and to the House Select Committee on Assassinations in 1977 and 1978, but many people had preferred to focus instead on the constitutional questions raised, not on the hypodermic syringe containing Black Leaf 40 with which the CIA was trying in November of 1963 to get Fidel Castro assassinated, not on Johnny Roselli in the oil drum in Biscayne Bay, not on that motel room in Dallas where Marita Lorenz claimed she had seen the rifles and the scopes and Frank Sturgis and Orlando Bosch and Jack Ruby and the Novo brothers, but on the separation of powers, and the proper role of congressional oversight. "The search for conspiracy," Anthony Lewis had written in *The New York Times* in September of 1975, "only increases the elements of morbidity and paranoia and fantasy in this country. It romanticizes crimes that are terrible because of their lack of purpose. It obscures our necessary understanding, all of us, that in this life there is often tragedy without reason."

This was not at the time an uncommon note, nor was it later. Particularly in Washington, where the logical consequences of any administration's imperial yearnings were thought to be voided when the voting levels were next pulled, the study of the underwater narrative, these stories about what people in Miami may or may not have done on the basis of what people in Washington had or had not said, was believed to serve no useful purpose. That the assassination of John F. Kennedy might or might not have been the specific consequence of his administration's own incursions into the tropic of morbidity and paranoia and fantasy (as early as 1964, two staff attorneys for the Warren Commission, W. David Slawson and William Coleman, had prepared a memorandum urging the commission to investigate the possibility that Lee Harvey Oswald had been acting for, or had been set up by, anti-Castro Cuban exiles) did not recommend, in this view, a closer study of the tropic. That there might or might not be, in the wreckage of the Reagan administration, certain consequences to that administration's similar incursions recommended only, in this view, that it was again time to focus on the mechanical model, time to talk about runaway agencies, arrogance in the executive branch, about constitutional crises and the nature of the presidency, about faults in the structure, flaws in the process; time to talk, above all, about 1988, when the levers would again be pulled and the consequences voided and any lingering morbidity dispelled by the enthusiasms, the energies, of the new team. "Dick Goodwin was handling Latin America and a dozen other problems," Arthur M. Schlesinger, Jr., once told us about the early months of the Kennedy administration, as suggestive a sentence as has perhaps been written about this tabula rasa effect in Washington life.

In the late summer of 1985, some months after the Outreach meeting in Room 450 of the Old Executive Office Building in Washington at which I had heard Jack Wheeler talk about the necessity for supporting freedom fighters around the world, I happened to receive a letter ("Dear Fellow American") from Major General John K. Singlaub, an invitation to the International Freedom Fighters Dinner to be held that September in the Crystal Ballroom of the Registry Hotel in Dallas. This letter was dated August 7, 1985, a date on which Steven Carr was already sitting in La Reforma prison in San José and on which Jesus Garcia was one day short of receiving a call from a twenty-nine-year-old stranger who identified himself as Allen Saum, who said that he was a major in the U.S. Marines and had been sent by the White House, who enlisted Jesus Garcia in a mission he described as "George Bush's baby," and who then telephoned the Miami office of the FBI and told them where they could pick up Jesus Garcia and his MAC-10. "He looked typical Ivy League, I thought he must be CIA," Jesus Garcia later said about "Allen Saum," who did not show up for Jesus Garcia's trial but did appear at a pretrial hearing, where he said that he took orders from a man he knew only as "Sam."

The letter from General Singlaub urged that any recipient unable to attend the Dallas dinner ($500 a plate) plan in any case to have his or her name listed on the International Freedom Fighters Commemorative Program ($50 a copy), which General Singlaub would, in turn, "personally present to President Reagan." Even the smallest donation, General Singlaub stressed, would go far toward keeping "freedom's light burning." The *mujaheddin* in Afghanistan, for example, who would be among the freedom fighters to benefit from the Dallas dinner (along with those in Angola, Laos, South Vietnam, Cambodia, Mozambique, Ethiopia, and of course Nicaragua), had not long before destroyed "approximately twenty-five per cent of the Afghan government's Soviet supplied air force" (or, according to General Singlaub, twenty MIGs, worth $100 million) with just "a few hundred dollars spent on plastic explosives."

I recall experiencing, as I read this sentence about the *mujaheddin* and the few hundred dollars spent on plastic explosives, the exact sense of expanding, or contracting, possibility that I had recently experienced during flights to Miami. Many apparently disparate elements seemed to be converging in the letter from General Singlaub, and the convergence was not one which discouraged that "search for conspiracy" deplored by Anthony Lewis a decade before. The narrative in which a few hundred dollars spent on plastic explosives could reverse history, which appeared to be the scenario on which General Singlaub and many of the people I had seen in Room 450 were operating, was the same narrative in which meetings at private houses in Miami Beach had been seen to overturn governments. This was that narrative in which the actions of individuals had been seen to affect events directly, in which revolutions and counterrevolutions had been framed in the private sector; that narrative in which the state security apparatus existed to be enlisted by one or another private player.

This was also the narrative in which words had tended to have consequences, and stories endings. NICARAGUA HOY, CUBA MAÑANA. When Jesus Garcia talked about meeting in the cocktail lounge of the Howard Johnson's near the Miami airport to discuss a plan to assassinate the American ambassador to Costa Rica, bomb the American embassy there, and blame it on the Sandinistas, the American ambassador he was talking about was Lewis Tambs, one of the authors of the Santa Fe document, the fifty-three pages which had articulated for many people in Washington the reasons for the exact American involvement in the politics of the Caribbean which this plan discussed in the cocktail lounge of the Howard Johnson's near the Miami airport was meant to ensure. Let me tell you about Cuban terrorists, Raúl Rodríguez had said at the midnight dinner in the Arquitectonica condominium overlooking Biscayne Bay. Cuba never grew plastique. Cuba grew tobacco, Cuba grew sugarcane. Cuba never grew C-4.

The air that evening in Miami had been warm and soft even at midnight, and the glass doors had been open onto the terrace overlooking the bay. The daughter of the fifteenth president of the Republic of Cuba, María Elena Prío Durán, whose father's grave at Woodlawn Park Cemetery in Miami lay within sight of the private crypt to which the body of another exiled president, Anastasio Somoza Debayle of Nicaragua, was flown forty-eight hours after his assassination in Asunción (no name on this crypt, no dates, no epitaph, only the monogram "AS" worked among the lilies on a stained-glass window, as if the occupant had negotiated himself out of history), had lit her cigarette and immediately put it out. When Raúl Rodríguez said that evening that C-4 grew here, he was talking about what it had cost to forget that decisions made in Washington had effects outside Washington; about the reverberative effect of certain ideas, and about their consequences. This dinner in Miami took place on March 26, 1985. The meetings in Miami described by Jesus Garcia had already taken place. The flights out of Miami described by Jesus Garcia and Steven Carr had already taken place. These meetings and these flights were the least of what had already taken place; of what was to take place; and also of what, in this world where stories have tended to have endings, has yet to take place. "As a matter of fact I was very definitely involved in the decisions about support to the freedom fighters," the fortieth President of the United States said more than two years later, on May 15, 1987. "My idea to begin with."

Notes

These notes are meant only as a guide, and reflect only the smallest part of those published sources on which I have drawn and to whose authors I owe thanks. Aside from published sources, I would like particularly to thank, among the many people who were helpful to me in Miami and in Washington, the editors and staff of the Miami Herald, *especially Madeleine Blais and John Katzenbach; Frank Calzón at the Cuban American National Foundation; Ernesto Betancourt at Radio Martí; Carlos Luis at the Museo Cubano de Arte y Cultura in Miami; Ricardo Pau-Llosa at Miami-Dade Community College in Miami; and Mr. and Mrs. George Stevens, Jr., in Washington. I would like also to thank, in New York, Robert Silvers, Michael Korda, Lois Wallace, Sophie Sorkin, and especially Rebecca Stowe, whose tireless willingness to research even the smallest point has made any error in this book entirely my own.*

CHAPTER 1, *pages 241 to 247*

I am indebted for much of the historical detail in this chapter to Hugh Thomas, *Cuba* (London: Eyre & Spottiswoode, 1971). The photograph of the Prío family leaving Havana appeared in *Cuba*, and before that in *Life*, March 24, 1952.

"They say that I was a terrible president . . .": *A Thousand Days* by Arthur M. Schlesinger, Jr. (Boston: Houghton Mifflin, 1965), p. 216.

An account of the attempt to land a third force in Camagüey Province appears in *The Winds of December* by John Dorschner and Roberto Fabricio (New York: Coward, McCann & Geoghegan, 1980). Dorschner and Fabricio also provide a detailed account of Fulgencio Batista's departure from Havana on January 1, 1959.

The Kennedy campaign statement mentioned on page 246 is discussed by Schlesinger in *A Thousand Days*, p. 72.

The Nicaraguan Refugee Fund dinner at which Ronald Reagan spoke was covered by both the *Miami Herald* and *The New York Times* on April 16, 1985.

CHAPTER 2, *pages 251 to 255*

The *Miami Herald* report mentioning "guerrilla discounts" was by Juan Tamayo and appeared July 21, 1985, under the headline, "Cuban exiles said to ship guns to rebels."

The pamphlet giving tips for maintaining a secure profile was reported by Brian Duffy in the *Miami Herald*, June 5, 1985, under the headine, "Smuggling guidebook offers 'how to' hints."

"Well-heeled investors returning north" appeared in the *Herald* on June 16, 1985. "Costly condos threatened with massive foreclosures" appeared August 2, 1985, and "Foreclosures soaring in S. Florida" on March 28, 1986. "Arena financing plan relies on hotel guests" appeared June 7, 1985, and "S. Florida hotel rooms get emptier" on October 19, 1985. The real-estate analyst quoted on page 254 was Mike Cannon, president of Appraisal and Real Estate Economics Associates, Inc., quoted by Dory Owens in "Wirth betting that office glut will end," *Miami Herald*, July 17, 1985.

Reports on Theodore Gould and Miami Center appeared in the *Miami Herald* on August 9 and October 11, 1985.

CHAPTER 3, *pages 256 to 261*

Reports by Brian Duffy and Nancy Ancrum on the cache of hand grenades and the pawnbroker appeared in the *Miami Herald* on October 25 and November 2, 1985. Debbie Sontag's report ("Former guard accidentally kills self in Beach supermarket lot") on the shooting in the Miami Beach parking lot appeared October 9, 1985. The arrest of Jose "Coca Cola" Yero was reported by Jeff Leen in the October 22, 1985, *Herald*. Charisse L. Grant's report on the young woman who was car-bombed in South Palm Beach ("Bomb victim feared for her life, cops say") appeared June 28, 1986.

CHAPTER 4, *pages 262 to 268*

Black tensions in Miami have been extensively covered since 1980 not only in the *Herald* but in *The New York Times* and the *Los Angeles Times*. For background see *The Miami Riot of 1980* by Bruce Porter and Marvin Dunn (Lexington, Mass.: D. C. Heath and Company—Lexington Books, 1984); "Overwhelmed in Miami" by John Katzenbach in *Police Magazine*, September 1980; "Under Siege in an Urban Ghetto" by Bruce Porter and Marvin Dunn in *Police Magazine*, July 1981; and "Open Wounds" by Madeleine Blais in the *Miami Herald*'s Sunday magazine, *Tropic*, May 12, 1985.

The quote from the president of the Orange Bowl committee appeared in "CRB 'slaps' OB for party at restrictive club," by Marc Fisher, *Miami Herald*, March 21, 1985. Membership policies at South Florida private clubs were covered in Marc Fisher's three-part report on private clubs, appearing in the *Herald* on April 7, 8, and 9, 1985. The Surf Club party on page 266 was mentioned in "Miami's Elite

Holds Fast to Tradition," April 4, 1985, part of a *Herald* series on "Society in South Florida."

For background on Mariel, see *The Cuban-American Experience: Culture, Images and Perspectives* by Thomas D. Boswell and James R. Curtis (Totowa, N.J.: Rowman & Allanheld, 1984); *Cuban Americans: Masters of Survival* by José Llanes (Cambridge, Mass.: Abt Books, 1982); and "The Cubans: A People Divided" and "The Cubans: A People Changed," two *Miami Herald* Special Reports published as supplements to the editions of December 11 and 18, 1983. This chapter also draws on a 1985 study by Helga Silva called "Children of Mariel: From Shock to Integration," provided to me by the Cuban American National Foundation in Washington, D.C.

CHAPTER 5, *pages 269 to 277*

"The Most Influential People in Dade's History" and "The Most Important Events in Dade's History" appeared in the *Miami Herald*, February 3, 1986. The population statistics on page 270 are those given for 1986 by the Miami Chamber of Commerce.

The *Herald* reports on "Cuban Miami: A Guide for Non-Cubans" appeared each Friday from October 10 to November 21, 1986. The *Herald* piece in which Luis Botifoll was quoted was by Guillermo Martinez and appeared in *Tropic* on January 16, 1983. The *Herald* food section mentioned was that for March 20, 1986. A note on the Miami Springs Holiday Inn and its 26 Julio bar special appeared in Fred Tasker's *Herald* column on July 26, 1985.

The address quoted by Vice President George Bush was delivered in Miami on May 20, 1986.

The column by George Will ("The First Contras") appeared in *Newsweek*, March 31, 1986. George Gilder's piece ("Making It") appeared in the Winter 1985 issue of *The Wilson Quarterly*. The "samba" report on the Calle Ocho Festival appeared in the *Herald*, March 10, 1986.

CHAPTER 6, *pages 278 to 280*

The lines quoted are from p. 34 of the transcript for a January 19, 1984, meeting of the Miami City Commission, and the speaker was Maurice Ferre, then mayor of Miami.

Robert Melby was quoted in the *Miami Herald*, March 21, 1985, in a report ("English proponent renews drive") by Andres Viglucci. The reference to Xavier Suarez's "flawless English" appeared in the *Los Angeles Times*, November 13, 1985, in a story ("Attorney Suarez Elected Mayor in Miami") credited to Times Wire Services. The

Herald political editor quoted was Tom Fiedler, and the quoted lines appeared in his column ("On the fringes of politics"), October 6, 1985. The quoted note about Raul Masvidal's unlisted telephone number appeared in Fred Tasker's *Herald* column on September 23, 1985. The closing of Gator Kicks Longneck Saloon (which was, incidentally, the bar for whose advertising Donna Rice was photographed, before she met Gary Hart, with the Confederate flag) was covered in the *Herald* ("Colorful country roadhouse closes" by Ivonne Rovira Kelly), February 8, 1986. The quoted column by Charles Whited appeared February 9, 1986.

CHAPTER 7, *pages 281 to 289*

Jim Hampton's column ("Voters' kiss of death? Kiss off!") appeared in the *Herald* November 17, 1985. The quotes from Andres Nazario Sargen and from police spokesmen on page 282–283 appeared in the *Herald*, March 21, 1986, in "Opposing rallies OKd at same site" by Andres Viglucci. The headlines and photograph mentioned on page 283 appeared March 23, 1986. Other sources on the Torch of Friendship demonstrations included "Suarez clarifies his stand on 'free speech'" by Justin Gillis, *Miami Herald*, April 5, 1986; the letters columns of the *Herald* for March 27 and 28, 1986 (a letter from Mayor Suarez appeared March 27); Charles Whited's *Herald* column ("Impeding right to free speech is undemocratic") for March 25, 1986; and Carl Hiaasen's *Herald* column ("Goons who hit man at rally aren't patriots") for March 26, 1986.

The José Martí letter quoted on page 286 was to Manuel Mercado and appears in volume I of *Obras Completas*. The translation here is Hugh Thomas's.

The mayoralty candidate with the plan to confine minors to their houses was Evelio Estrella, and his statement appeared in the *Miami News* (in the "Miami Mayoral Forum" series) on October 10, 1985. General Benítez's statement appeared in the same series October 8, 1985.

"Resort sells sun, fun—in Cuba" by Alfonso Chardy appeared in the *Herald*, April 17, 1985. "Free markets allow Havana to spiff up," also by Alfonso Chardy (whose ethnic background remained a source of some speculation in the Cuban community), appeared March 25, 1985.

The José Martí lines on page 288 are from volume III of *Obras Completas*, and also appear on p. 109 of *José Martí: Thoughts/Pensamientos* (New York: Eliseo Torres & Sons—Las Américas Publishing Co., 1980 and 1985), by Carlos Ripoll, whose translation this is.

For the Kennedy and Reagan quotes see notes on chapter 1.

CHAPTER 8, *pages 293 to 303*

Allen Dulles is quoted by Schlesinger in *A Thousand Days*, p. 242; John F. Kennedy on p. 257.

The poll mentioned on p. 293 appeared in *Tropic*, *Miami Herald*, January 16, 1983. The existence of The Non-Group was first reported by Celia W. Dugger in "The 38 who secretly guide Dade," *Miami Herald*, September 1, 1985.

The Theodore C. Sorensen quotes on pages 295 and 297 appear in his *Kennedy* (New York: Harper & Row, 1965), p. 722.

For background on JM/WAVE, see William R. Amlong, "How the CIA operated in Dade," *Miami Herald*, March 9, 1975; Taylor Branch and George Crile III, "The Kennedy Vendetta," *Harper's*, August 1975; *Portrait of a Cold Warrior* by Joseph Burkholder Smith (New York: G. P. Putnam's Sons, 1976); and *Investigation of the Assassination of President John F. Kennedy: Hearings before the Select Committee on Assassinations of the U.S. House of Representatives, 95th Congress* (Washington, D.C.: U.S. Government Printing Office, 1979), particularly volume X. CIA activities out of Miami during this period are also discussed in *The Investigation of the Assassination of President John F. Kennedy: Performance of the Intelligence Agencies*, which is book V of the *Final Report of the Select Committee to Study Governmental Operations with respect to Intelligence Activities, U.S. Senate, 94th Congress* (Washington, D.C.: U.S. Government Printing Office, 1976).

The December 1962 appearance of President and Mrs. Kennedy at the Orange Bowl is discussed by Sorensen in *Kennedy*, p. 308, and by Schlesinger in both *A Thousand Days*, p. 839, and *Robert Kennedy and His Times* (New York: Ballantine Books, 1979), p. 579. "But had CIA been up to its old tricks?" appears in *Robert Kennedy and His Times*, p. 586.

The financing of Southern Air Transport was reported by William R. Amlong in "CIA sold airline cheap," *Miami Herald*, March 10, 1975, and also by Martin Merzer in "Airline does job—quietly," *Miami Herald*, December 10, 1986.

The Schlesinger quotes on page 299 are from *Robert Kennedy and His Times*, p. 588. The Church commitee testimony quoted on page 300 was given on May 16, 1976, and quoted on p. 11 of book V, *The Investigation of the Assassination of President John F. Kennedy: Performance of the Intelligence Agencies.*

There is a section on JURE, and on "autonomous operations," beginning on p. 77 of volume X of the 1979 *Investigation of the Assassination of President John F. Kennedy: Hearings before the Select Committee on Assassinations of the U.S. House of Representatives.*

There is an account of the June 1963 Special Group meeting authorizing CIA supervision of exile actions within Cuba in the Church committee's 1975 *Interim Report: Alleged Assassination Plots Involving Foreign Leaders.*

The CIA internal report quoted appears on p. 126 of volume IV of the 1979 *Investigation of the Assassination of President John F. Kennedy: Hearings before the Select Committee on Assassinations of the U.S. House of Representatives.*

The Schlesinger quote on page 301 appears on p. 586 of *Robert Kennedy and His Times.* The Kennedy quote appears on p. 14 of volume X of the 1979 *Investigation of the Assassination of President John F. Kennedy: Hearings before the Select Committee on Assassinations of the U.S. House of Representatives.* James Angleton was quoted by Dick Russell, after a series of interviews which took place at the Army-Navy Club in Washington, in "Little Havana's Reign of Terror," *New Times,* October 29, 1976.

The footnote from *Robert Kennedy and His Times* appears on p. 513. The testimony before the Church committee mentioned on page 302 was given May 6, 1976, and quoted on p. 14, book V, *Final Report of the U.S. Senate Select Committee to Study Governmental Operations with respect to Intelligence Activities.*

The Kennedy quote on p. 302 appears in *A Thousand Days,* p. 839. The Sorensen quote appears in *Kennedy,* p. 722. The Schlesinger quote appears in *Robert Kennedy and His Times,* p. 579.

CHAPTER 9, *pages 304 to 310*

A report on the arrest of Eduardo Arocena ("Arocena 'Armory' Uncovered" by Jim McGee) appeared in the *Miami Herald,* July 24, 1983, and the quotes from Miriam Arocena, from the head of the 2506, from Andres Nazario Sargen, and from Tomas Garcia Fuste, the news director of WQBA, appeared in this piece. For Xavier Suarez and the Arocena defense fund, see Helga Silva and Guy Gugliotta, "'La Causa' binds exile community," *Miami Herald* Special Report, December 11, 1983. Omega 7 itself has been covered since the late 1970s in both the *Herald* and *The New York Times,* which published a particularly complete report ("'Highest Priority' Given by U.S. to Capture of Anti-Castro Group" by Robin Herman) on March 3, 1980.

For background on Max Lesnik, see Hugh Thomas, *Cuba*; John Dorschner and Roberto Fabricio, *The Winds of December*; and Helga Silva, "Those called 'soft' are often shunned," *Miami Herald* Special Report, December 11, 1983.

The incident with Luciano Nieves in the Versailles is mentioned by José Llanes in *Cuban Americans: Masters of Survival*, p. 127. According to the *Miami Herald* ("Killer asks for clemency," November 26, 1986), an exile named Valentin Hernandez was in 1978 convicted of the killing of Luciano Nieves and sentenced to twenty-five years without possibility of parole. Eight years later, when he petitioned the court for an early release, six thousand letters were received in support of his request, along with petitions describing him as "a political prisoner guilty of fighting against the oppression of communism."

CHAPTER 10, *pages 311 to 315*

The *diálogo*, and Orlando Padron and the cigar, are discussed by Barry Bearak, "Anti-Fidel Fervor Still Burns in Little Havana," *Los Angeles Times*, November 30, 1982. Also see David Vidal, "In Union City, the Memories of the Bay of Pigs Don't Die," *The New York Times*, December 21, 1979, and Jorge Fierro, "For the *Comunidad*, the Visit Is a Sad Show," *The New York Times*, January 20, 1980. Also: Max Azicri, "Un análisis pragmático del diálogo entre la Cuba del interior y la del exterior," *Areíto* IX, no. 36 (1984).

The quote from Fidel Castro appears on p. 67, *Diary of the Cuban Revolution* by Carlos Franqui (New York: The Viking Press, 1980).

For background on Carlos Muñiz Varela, see Luis Angel Torres, "Semblanza de Carlos Muñiz," *Areíto* IX, no. 36 (1984). The murder of Eulalio José Negrin was reported in *The New York Times*, November 26, 1979, "Cuban Refugee Leader Slain in Union City." The *El Diario–La Prensa* bombing was discussed by Robin Herman in the March 3, 1980, *New York Times* piece cited in the notes for Chapter 9. For the TWA bombing, see Robert D. McFadden, "Kennedy Bomb Hurts Four Workers in Baggage Area," *The New York Times*, March 26, 1979.

CHAPTER 11, *pages 316 to 322*

The translations of *Areíto*'s 1974 and 1984 statements of purpose are those provided by *Areíto*. The piece referring to exile Miami as "the deformed foetus . . ." appears in *Areíto* IX, no. 36 (1984) ("El Miami cubano" by Lourdes Argüelles and Gary MacEoin), and the translation is mine.

"Introduction to the Sandinista Documentary Cinema" (p. 317) appeared in *Areíto* X, no. 37 (1984). Marifeli Pérez-Stable was quoted by Helga Silva in "Those called soft . . . ," *Miami Herald* Special Report, December 11, 1983. For background on Lourdes Casal see *Areíto*

IX, no. 36 (1984). Dolores Prida and the controversy over *Coser y Cantar* were extensively covered in the *Miami Herald* during the first two weeks of May 1986.

The issue of *Areíto* referred to on page 319 is volume IX, no. 36, and the pieces referred to are "El Instituto de Estudios Cubanos o los estrechos límites del pluralismo" (Consejo de Dirección de Areíto) and "Sobre las relaciones entre el Instituto de Estudios Cubanos y Areíto: convergencias y divergencias" (María Cristina Herrera/Consejo de Dirección de Areíto).

For the Unaccompanied Children's Program, see Michael J. McNally's *Catholicism in South Florida: 1868–1968* (Gainesville: University of Florida Press, 1982). The extracts from *Contra Viento y Marea* were reprinted in *Areíto* (vol. IX, no. 36), and the translation is mine.

CHAPTER 12, *pages 323 to 332*

For "the *P.M.* affair," see *Area Handbook for Cuba*, Foreign Area Studies of The American University (Washington, D.C.: U.S. Government Printing Office, 1976), p. 330; *Family Portrait with Fidel* by Carlos Franqui (New York: Vintage Books, 1985), pp. 131–33; and *A Man with a Camera* by Nestor Almendros (New York: Farrar, Straus & Giroux, 1984), p. 139. For *Bohemia*, see Franqui, *Family Portrait*, and also Hugh Thomas, *Cuba*, p. 1292.

About the Jorge Valls controversy: see Liz Balmaseda and Jay Ducassi, "Hero in jail, freed poet provokes exile ire," *Miami Herald*, September 2, 1984. About Armando Valladares: Carl Gershman, president of the National Endowment for Democracy, stated to the Senate Foreign Relations Committee on March 29, 1985, that Endowment efforts "in the fields of education, culture and communications" included "assistance to a program organized by the distinguished Cuban writer and former political prisoner Armando Valladares to inform European public opinion about the human rights situation in Cuba."

For background on Dr. Orlando Bosch, see pp. 89–93, volume X of the 1979 *Investigation of the Assassination of President John F. Kennedy: Hearings before the Select Committee . . .* , cited in the notes for Chapter 8. For background on Luis Posada Carriles, see Tim Golden, "Sandinistas say escapee ran supplies," *Miami Herald*, October 16, 1986; Sam Dillon, "Fugitive may be contra supplier," *Miami Herald*, October 21, 1986; Sam Dillon and Guy Gugliotta, "How jail escapee joined rebels' supply network," *Miami Herald*, November 2, 1986 (the spokesman for George Bush mentioned on pages 329–330 is quoted in this report); and p. 44, volume X of the 1979 *Investigation of the Assassination of President John F. Kennedy . . .* , also cited for Chapter 8.

The president of the Committee to Free Orlando Bosch was quoted by Sandra Dibble, "Bosch's friends turn out to view exhibit of his artworks," *Miami Herald*, December 13, 1986. The letter in defense of Dr. Bosch appeared in *El Herald*, November 20, 1985; translation mine. Cosme Barros and Norma Garcia were quoted by Reinaldo Ramos, "To Miami Cubans, Bosch is folk hero," *Miami Herald*, July 27, 1986. The 1977 CIA document mentioned is discussed by Sam Dillon and Guy Gugliotta, "How jail escapee . . . ," cited above.

Orlando Bosch's CIA experience is discussed on p. 90, volume X of the 1979 *Investigation of the Assassination of President John F. Kennedy . . .* , cited above. The Richard Helms quote appears on p. 159 of volume IV, the same House Select Committee hearings.

CHAPTER 13, *pages 333 to 340*

Robert C. McFarlane was quoted by Joanne Omang in one of the first pieces to name Lieutenant Colonel Oliver North, "The White House's Nicaragua Middleman: A Marine Officer Implements Policy," *Washington Post National Weekly Edition*, August 26, 1985.

CHAPTER 14, *pages 341 to 348*

For Guillermo Novo and the Letelier case, see Taylor Branch and Eugene M. Propper, former assistant U.S. attorney for the District of Columbia, *Labyrinth* (New York: The Viking Press, 1982).

For Felipe Rivero and Cuban radio in Miami, see Fabiola Santiago, "When stations talk, listeners act" and "Some voices of Miami's Spanish-language radio," *Miami Herald*, June 22, 1986.

The Reagan radio talks about the death of Orlando Letelier are reprinted on pp. 521–23 of *On Reagan: The Man and His Presidency* by Ronnie Dugger (New York: McGraw-Hill, 1983). Jesse Helms was quoted by Taylor Branch and Eugene M. Propper in *Labyrinth*. Ronald Reagan on the blacklist was quoted by Robert Scheer on p. 259 of his *With Enough Shovels: Reagan, Bush & Nuclear War* (New York: Random House, 1982).

For Ronald Reagan on the Salvadoran death squads, see George Skelton, "Reagan Suspects Rebels of Death Squad Killings," *Los Angeles Times*, December 3, 1983. For Ronald Reagan on Sandinistas dressing up in freedom fighter uniforms, see "Nicaraguan killers really Sandinista agents," *Miami Herald*, March 16, 1986, and Rudy Abramson, "Sandinistas Kill in Contra Guise, Reagan Charges," *Los Angeles Times*, March 16, 1986.

Ronnie Dugger quotes David Gergen on pp. 463–64, *On Reagan*. For Ronald Reagan on "Medical science doctors confirm . . . ," see

Francis X. Clines, "Reagan Tells Broadcasters Aborted Fetuses Suffer Pain," *The New York Times*, January 31, 1984. Hannah Arendt's discussion of propaganda appears on pp. 341–364 of *The Origins of Totalitarianism* (New York: Harcourt Brace, the 1966 edition).

For Ronald Reagan's 1983 visit to Miami see George Skelton, "Reagan Vows to Defend Latin American Liberty," *Los Angeles Times*, May 21, 1983; Reginald Stuart, "Cubans in Miami Await Reagan's Visit Eagerly," *The New York Times*, May 20, 1983, and Helga Silva and Liz Balmaseda, "Superstar Wows Little Havana," *Miami Herald*, May 21, 1983.

CHAPTER 15, *pages 351 to 359*

"A couple of hours into our meeting . . .": see José Llanes, *Cuban Americans: Masters of Survival*, cited in the notes for Chapter 4, p. 74. "Our hearts sank . . ." and "I had never seen . . . ," see Schlesinger, *A Thousand Days*, pp. 283–284. For "rekindled doubts in Congress . . . ," see Philip Taubman, "Latin Debate Refocused," *New York Times*, April 9, 1984.

The Associated Press story quoting Larry Speakes and Michael Deaver (mentioned on page 356) was by Michael Putzel, and was on the wire April 12, 1984, for release April 15. David Gergen was quoted in *The New York Times* by Steven R. Weisman and Francis X. Clines in "Q. & A.: David R. Gergen—Key Presidential Buffer Looks Back," January 10, 1984. The quote from Morton Kondracke comes from his review of Robert Dallek's *Ronald Reagan: The Politics of Symbolism*, in *The New York Times Book Review*, March 4, 1984. The 1984 American Enterprise Institute discussion mentioned took place at the Mayflower Hotel in Washington on March 1, 1984, and was called "The Reagan Administration and the Press: What's the Problem?"

CHAPTER 16, *pages 360 to 378*

A New Inter-American Policy for the Eighties can be obtained in some libraries (Library of Congress Catalog Card No. 81–68443) or from the Council for Inter-American Security, 729 Eighth St., S.E., Washington, D.C. 20003. The Edward Cody piece mentioning the Santa Fe document is "Disappointment in Havana: No Thaw in U.S. Relations," *Washington Post National Weekly Edition*, June 17, 1985.

For the National Security Planning Group document mentioned on page 364, Project Truth, and the establishment of the Office of Public Diplomacy, see Alfonso Chardy, "Secrets leaked to harm Nicaragua, sources say," *Miami Herald*, October 13, 1986. Faith Ryan Whittlesey and Otto Juan Reich are quoted by Tim Golden, "Reagan

Countering Critics of Policies in Central America," *Los Angeles Times*, December 21, 1983.

For background on Jack Wheeler, see Paul Dean, "Adventurer Devotes Energy to Anti-Communist Causes," *Los Angeles Times*, August 1, 1985. The *Washington Post* story mentioned on page 370 is Joanne Omang's "The White House's Nicaragua Middleman . . . ," cited in the notes for Chapter 13.

For background on Steven Carr and Jesus Garcia, see Juan Tamayo, "Cuban exiles said to ship guns to rebels," *Miami Herald*, July 21, 1985; Lori Rozsa, "Contra mercenary wants new life," *Miami Herald*, August 10, 1986; Steven J. Hedges, "Witness claimed U.S. aided escape," *Miami Herald*, January 6, 1987; Alfonso Chardy, "Contra weapons probe may bring first prosecution," *Miami Herald*, July 13, 1986; Lynn O'Shaughnessy and Mark Henry, "Witness in Nicaragua Arms Trafficking Dies," *Los Angeles Times*, December 15, 1986; Sandra Dibble, "Contra supporter lands in jail," *Miami Herald*, August 4, 1986; Stephen J. Hedges, "Independent counsel may end Miami probe," *Miami Herald*, December 30, 1986; Alfonso Chardy, "Rebel guns may spur U.S. probe," *Miami Herald*, July 12, 1986; "Inquiry Reported into Contra Arms," *The New York Times*, April 11, 1986; Caitlin Randall, "5 await trial in 'sensitive' Costa Rican case," *Miami Herald*, April 23, 1986; and, on Robert Owen: Alfonso Chardy, "Idealism drew him into contra struggle," *Miami Herald*, June 8, 1986, and Tim Golden, "State Department adviser tied to misuse of rebel aid," *Miami Herald*, February 16, 1987.

The column by Anthony Lewis mentioned on page 375, "What Not to Do," appeared in *The New York Times*, September 25, 1975. The memorandum prepared by W. David Slawson and William Coleman is quoted at length on p. 5, volume X, of the 1979 *Investigation of the Assassination of President John F. Kennedy* . . . , cited in the notes for Chapter 8. The Schlesinger line quoted appears in *A Thousand Days*, p. 207.

AFTER HENRY

Acknowledgments

"In the Realm of the Fisher King," "Insider Baseball," Shooters Inc.," "Girl of the Golden West," and "Sentimental Journeys" appeared originally in *The New York Review of Books.* "Los Angeles Days," "Down at City Hall," "L.A. *Noir*," "Fire Season," "Times Mirror Square," and part of "Pacific Distances" appeared originally as "Letters from Los Angeles" in *The New Yorker.* Most of "Pacific Distances" and the introductory piece, "After Henry," appeared originally in *New West*, which later became *California* and eventually folded. I would like to thank my editors at all three magazines, Jon Carroll at *New West*, Robert Gottlieb at *The New Yorker*, and most especially, since he has put up with me over nineteen years and through many long and eccentric projects, Robert Silvers at *The New York Review.*

This book is dedicated to Henry Robbins
and to Bret Easton Ellis,
each of whom did time
with its publisher.

Contents

After Henry

IN THE summer of 1966 I was living in a borrowed house in Brentwood, and had a new baby. I had published one book, three years before. My husband was writing his first. Our daybook for those months shows no income at all for April, $305.06 for May, none for June, and, for July, $5.29, a dividend on our single capital asset, fifty shares of Transamerica stock left to me by my grandmother. This 1966 daybook shows laundry lists and appointments with pediatricians. It shows sixty christening presents received and sixty thank-you notes written, shows the summer sale at Saks and the attempt to retrieve a fifteen-dollar deposit from Southern Counties Gas, but it does not show the date in June on which we first met Henry Robbins.

This seems to me now a peculiar and poignant omission, and one that suggests the particular fractures that new babies and borrowed houses can cause in the moods of people who live largely by their wits. Henry Robbins was until that June night in 1966 an abstract to us, another New York editor, a stranger at Farrar, Straus & Giroux who had called or written and said that he was coming to California to see some writers. I thought so little of myself as a writer that summer that I was obscurely ashamed to go to dinner with still another editor, ashamed to sit down again and discuss this "work" I was not doing, but in the end I did go: in the end I put on a black silk dress and went with my husband to the Bistro in Beverly Hills and met Henry Robbins and began, right away, to laugh. The three of us laughed until two in the morning, when we were no longer at the Bistro but at the Daisy, listening over and over to "In the Midnight Hour" and "Softly As I Leave You" and to one another's funny, brilliant, enchanting voices, voices that transcended lost laundry and babysitters and prospects of $5.29, voices full of promise, *writers'* voices.

In short we got drunk together, and before the summer was out Henry Robbins had signed contracts with each of us, and, from that summer in 1966 until the summer of 1979, very few weeks passed during which one or the other of us did not talk to Henry Robbins about something which was amusing us or interesting us or worrying us, about our hopes and about our doubts, about work and love and money and gossip; about our news, good or bad. On the July morning in 1979 when we got word from New York that Henry Robbins had died on his way to work a few hours before, had fallen dead, age fifty-one, to the floor of the 14th Street subway station, there was only one person I wanted to talk to about it, and that one person was Henry.

"Childhood is the kingdom where nobody dies" is a line, from the poem by Edna St. Vincent Millay, that has stuck in my mind ever since I first read it, when I was in fact a child and nobody died. Of course people did die, but they were either very old or died unusual deaths, died while rafting on the Stanislaus or loading a shotgun or doing 95 drunk: death was construed as either a "blessing" or an exceptional case, the dramatic instance on which someone else's (never our own) story turned. Illness, in that kingdom where I and most people I knew lingered long past childhood, proved self-limiting. Fever of unknown etiology signaled only the indulgence of a week in bed. Chest pains, investigated, revealed hypochondria.

As time passed it occurred to many of us that our benign experience was less than general, that we had been to date blessed or charmed or plain lucky, players on a good roll, but by that time we were busy: caught up in days that seemed too full, too various, too crowded with friends and obligations and children, dinner parties and deadlines, commitments and overcommitments. "You can't imagine how it is when everyone you know is gone," someone I knew who was old would say to me, and I would nod, uncomprehending, yes I can, I can imagine; would even think, God forgive me, that there must be a certain peace in outliving all debts and claims, in being known to no one, floating free. I believed that days would be too full forever, too crowded with friends there was no time to see. I believed, by way of contemplating the future, that we would all be around for one another's funerals. I was wrong. I had failed to imagine, I had not understood. Here was the way it was going to be: I would be around for Henry's funeral, but he was not going to be around for mine.

The funeral was not actually a funeral but a memorial service, in the prevailing way, an occasion for all of us to meet on a tropical August New York morning in the auditorium of the Society for Ethical Culture at 64th and Central Park West. A truism about working with language is that other people's arrangements of words are always crowding in on one's actual experience, and this morning in New York was no exception. "Abide with me: do not go away" was a line I kept hearing, unspoken, all through the service; my husband was speaking, and half a dozen other writers and publishers who had been close to Henry Robbins—Wilfrid Sheed, Donald Barthelme, John Irving, Doris Grumbach; Robert Giroux from Farrar, Straus & Giroux; John Macrae from Dutton—but the undersongs I heard were fragments of a poem by Delmore Schwartz, dead thirteen years, the casualty of another New York summer. *Abide with me: do not go away*, and then:

> *Controlling our pace before we get old,*
> *Walking together on the receding road,*
> *Like Chaplin and his orphan sister.*

Five years before, Henry had left Farrar, Straus for Simon and Schuster, and I had gone with him. Two years after that he had left Simon and Schuster and gone to Dutton. This time I had not gone with him, had stayed where my contract was, and yet I remained Henry's orphan sister, Henry's writer. I remember that he worried from time to time about whether we had enough money, and that he would sometimes, with difficulty, ask us if we needed some. I remember that he did not like the title *Play It As It Lays* and I remember railing at him on the telephone from a hotel room in Chicago because my husband's novel *True Confessions* was not yet in the window at Kroch's & Brentano's and I remember a Halloween night in New York in 1970 when our children went trick-or-treating together in the building on West 86th Street in which Henry and his wife and their two children then lived. I remember that this apartment on West 86th Street had white curtains, and that on one hot summer evening we all sat there and ate chicken in tarragon aspic and watched the curtains lift and move in the air off the river and our world seemed one of considerable promise.

I remember arguing with Henry over the use of the second person in the second sentence of *A Book of Common Prayer*. I remember his actual hurt and outrage when any of us, any of his orphan sisters or brothers, got a bad review or a slighting word or even a letter that he imagined capable of marring our most inconsequential moment. I remember him flying to California because I wanted him to read the first 110 pages of *A Book of Common Prayer* and did not want to send them to New York. I remember him turning up in Berkeley one night when I needed him in 1975; I was to lecture that night, an occasion freighted by the fact that I was to lecture many members of the English department who had once lectured me, and I was, until Henry arrived, scared witless, the sacrificial star of my own exposure dream. I remember that he came first to the Faculty Club, where I was staying, and walked me down the campus to 2000 LSB, where I was to speak. I remember him telling me that it would go just fine. I remember believing him.

I always believed what Henry told me, except about two things, the title *Play It As It Lays* and the use of the second person in the second sentence of *A Book of Common Prayer*, believed him even when time and personalities and the difficulty of making a living by either editing books or writing them had complicated our relationship. What editors do for writers is mysterious, and does not, contrary to general belief, have much to do with titles and sentences and "changes." Nor, my railing notwithstanding, does it have much to do with the window at Kroch's & Brentano's in Chicago. The relationship between an editor and a writer is much subtler and deeper than that, at once so elusive and so radical that it seems almost parental: the editor, if the editor was Henry Robbins, was the person who gave the writer the idea of himself, the idea of herself, the image of self that enabled the writer to sit down alone and do it.

This is a tricky undertaking, and requires the editor not only to maintain a faith the writer shares only in intermittent flashes but also to like the writer, which is hard to do. Writers are only rarely likeable. They bring nothing to the party, leave their game at the typewriter. They fear their contribution to the general welfare to be evanescent, even doubtful, and, since the business of publishing is an only marginally profitable enterprise that increasingly attracts people who sense this marginality all too keenly, people who feel defensive or demeaned because they are not at the tables where the high rollers play (not managing mergers, not running motion picture studios, not even principal players in whatever larger concern holds the paper on the publishing house), it has become natural enough for a publisher or an editor to seize on the writer's fear, reinforce it, turn the writer into a necessary but finally unimportant accessory to the "real" world of publishing. Publishers and editors do not, in the real world, get on the night TWA to California to soothe a jumpy midlist writer. Publishers and editors in the real world have access to corporate G-3s, and prefer cruising the Galápagos with the raiders they have so far failed to become. A publisher or editor who has contempt for his own class position can find solace in transferring that contempt to the writer, who typically has no G-3 and can be seen as dependent on the publisher's largesse.

This was not a solace, nor for that matter a contempt, that Henry understood. The last time I saw him was two months before he fell to the floor of the 14th Street subway station, one night in Los Angeles when the annual meeting of the American Booksellers Association was winding to a close. He had come by the house on his way to a party and we talked him into skipping the party, staying for dinner. What he told me that night was indirect, and involved implicit allusions to other people and other commitments and everything that had happened among us since that summer night in 1966, but it came down to this: he wanted me to know that I could do it without him. That was a third thing Henry told me that I did not believe.

WASHINGTON

In the Realm of the Fisher King

PRESIDENT RONALD REAGAN, we were later told by his speechwriter Peggy Noonan, spent his off-camera time in the White House answering fifty letters a week, selected by the people who ran his mail operation, from citizens. He put the family pictures these citizens sent him in his pockets and desk drawers. When he did not have the zip code, he apologized to his secretary for not looking it up himself. He sharpened his own pencils, we were told by Helene von Damm, his secretary first in Sacramento and then in Washington, and he also got his own coffee.

In the post-Reagan rush to establish that we knew all along about this peculiarity in that particular White House, we forgot the actual peculiarity of the place, which had to do less with the absence at the center than with the amount of centrifugal energy this absence left spinning free at the edges. The Reagan White House was one in which great expectations were allowed into play. Ardor, of a kind that only rarely survives a fully occupied Oval Office, flourished unchecked. "You'd be in someone's home and on the way to the bathroom you'd pass the bedroom and see a big thick copy of Paul Johnson's *Modern Times* lying half open on the table by the bed," Peggy Noonan, who gave Ronald Reagan the boys of Pointe du Hoc and the *Challenger* crew slipping the surly bonds of earth and who gave George Bush the thousand points of light and the kinder, gentler nation, told us in *What I Saw at the Revolution: A Political Life in the Reagan Era.*

"Three months later you'd go back and it was still there," she wrote. "There were words. You had a notion instead of a thought and a dustup instead of a fight, you had a can-do attitude and you were in touch with the zeitgeist. No one had intentions they had an agenda and no one was wrong they were fundamentally wrong and you didn't work on something you broke your pick on it and it wasn't an agreement it was a done deal. All politics is local but more to the point all economics is micro. There were phrases: personnel is policy and ideas have consequences and ideas drive politics and it's a war of ideas

. . . and to do nothing is to endorse the status quo and roll back the Brezhnev Doctrine and there's no such thing as a free lunch, especially if you're dining with the press."

Peggy Noonan arrived in Washington in 1984, thirty-three years old, out of Brooklyn and Massapequa and Fairleigh Dickinson and CBS Radio, where she had written Dan Rather's five-minute commentaries. A few years later, when Rather told her that in lieu of a Christmas present he wanted to make a donation to her favorite charity, the charity she specified was The William J. Casey Fund for the Nicaraguan Resistance. She did not immediately, or for some months after, meet the man for whose every public utterance she and the other staff writers were responsible; at the time she checked into the White House, no speechwriter had spoken to Mr. Reagan in more than a year. "We wave to him," one said.

In the absence of an actual president, this resourceful child of a large Irish Catholic family sat in her office in the Old Executive Office Building and invented an ideal one: she read Vachel Lindsay (particularly "I brag and chant of Bryan Bryan Bryan / Candidate for President who sketched a silver Zion") and she read Franklin Delano Roosevelt (whom she pictured, again ideally, up in Dutchess County "sitting at a great table with all the chicks, eating a big spring lunch of beefy red tomatoes and potato salad and mayonnaise and deviled eggs on the old china with the flowers almost rubbed off") and she thought "this is how Reagan should sound." What Miss Noonan had expected Washington to be, she told us, was "Aaron Copland and 'Appalachian Spring'." What she found instead was a populist revolution trying to make itself, a crisis of raised expectations and lowered possibilities, the children of an expanded middle class determined to tear down the established order and what they saw as its repressive liberal orthodoxies: "There were libertarians whose girlfriends had just given birth to their sons, hoisting a Coors with social conservatives who walked into the party with a wife who bothered to be warm and a son who carried a Mason jar of something daddy grew in the backyard. There were Protestant fundamentalists hoping they wouldn't be dismissed by neocon intellectuals from Queens and neocons talking to fundamentalists thinking: I wonder if when they look at me they see what Annie Hall's grandmother saw when she looked down the table at Woody Allen."

She stayed at the White House until the spring of 1986, when she was more or less forced out by the refusal of Donald Regan, at that time chief of staff, to approve her promotion to head speechwriter. Regan thought her, according to Larry Speakes, who did not have a famous feel for the romance of the revolution, too "hard-line," too "dogmatic," too "right-wing," too much "Buchanan's protégée." On the occasion of her resignation she received a form letter from the president, signed with the auto-pen. Donald Regan said that there was no need for her to have what was referred to as "a good-bye moment," a farewell shake-hands with the president. On the day Donald Regan himself left the White House, Miss Noonan received this message, left on her answering machine by a friend at the White House: "Hey, Peggy, Don Regan didn't get his good-bye moment." By that time she was hearing the "true tone of Washington" less as "Appalachian Spring" than as something a little more raucous, "nearer," she said, "to Jefferson Starship and 'They Built This City on Rock and Roll'."

The White House she rendered was one of considerable febrility. Everyone, she told us, could quote Richard John Neuhaus on what was called the collapse of the dogmas of the secular enlightenment. Everyone could quote Michael Novak on what was called the collapse of the assumption that education is or should be "value-free." Everyone could quote George Gilder on what was called the humane nature of the free market. Everyone could quote Jean-François Revel on how democracies perish, and everyone could quote Jeane Kirkpatrick on authoritarian versus totalitarian governments, and everyone spoke of "the movement," as in "he's movement from way back," or "she's good, she's hard-core."

They talked about subverting the pragmatists, who believed that an issue could not be won without the *Washington Post* and the networks, by "going over the heads of the media to the people." They charged one another's zeal by firing off endless letters, memos, clippings. "Many thanks for Macedo's new monograph; his brand of judicial activism is more principled than Tribe's," such letters read. "If this gets into the hands of the Russians, it's curtains for the free world!" was the tone to take on the yellow Post-It attached to a clipping. "Soldier on!" was the way to sign off. Those PROF memos we later saw from Robert McFarlane to Lieutenant Colonel Oliver North ("Roger Ollie. Well done—if the world only knew how many times you have kept a semblance of integrity and gumption to US policy, they would make you Secretary of State. But they can't know and would complain if they did—such is the state of democracy in the late 20th century. . . . Bravo Zulu") do not seem, in this context, quite so unusual.

"Bureaucrats with soft hands adopted the clipped laconic style of John Ford characters," Miss Noonan noted. "A small man from NSC was asked at a meeting if he knew of someone who could work up a statement. Yes, he knew someone at State, a paid pen who's pushed some good paper." To be a moderate was to be a "squish," or a "weenie," or a "wuss." "He got rolled," they would say of someone who had lost the day, or, "He took a lickin' and kept on tickin'." They walked around the White House wearing ties ("slightly stained," according to Miss Noonan, "from the mayonnaise that fell from the sandwich that was wolfed down at the working lunch on judicial reform") embroidered with the code of the movement: eagles, flags, busts of Jefferson. Little gold Laffer curves identified the wearers as "free-market purists." Liberty bells stood for "judicial restraint."

The favored style here, like the favored foreign policy, seems to have been less military than paramilitary, a matter of talking tough. "That's not off my disk," Lieutenant Colonel Oliver North would snap by way of indicating that an idea was not his. "The fellas," as Miss Noonan called them, the sharp, the smooth, the inner circle and those who aspired to it, made a point of not using seat belts on Air Force One. The less smooth flaunted souvenirs of action on the far borders of the Reagan doctrine. "Jack Wheeler came back from Afghanistan with a Russian officer's belt slung over his shoulder," Miss Noonan recalls. "Grover Norquist came back from Africa rubbing his eyes from taking notes in a tent with Savimbi." Miss Noonan herself had lunch in the White House mess with a "Mujahadeen warrior" and his public relations man. "What is the condition of your troops in the field?" she asked. "We need help," he said. The Filipino steward approached, pad and pencil in hand. The mujahadeen leader looked up. "I will have meat," he said.

This is not a milieu in which one readily places Nancy Reagan, whose preferred style derived from the more structured, if equally rigorous, world from which she had come. The nature of this world was not very well understood. I recall being puzzled, on visits to Washington during the first year or two of the Reagan administration, by the tenacity of certain misapprehensions about the Reagans and the men generally regarded as their intimates, that small group of industrialists and entrepreneurs who had encouraged and financed, as a venture in risk capital, Ronald Reagan's appearances in both Sacramento and Washington. The president was above all, I was told repeatedly, a Californian, a Westerner, as were the acquaintances who made up his kitchen cabinet; it was the "Westernness" of these men that explained not only their rather intransigent views about America's mission in the world but also their apparent lack of interest in or identification with Americans for whom the trend was less reliably up. It was "Westernness," too, that could explain those affronts to the local style so discussed in Washington during the early years, the overwrought clothes and the borrowed jewelry and the Le Cirque hair and the wall-to-wall carpeting and the table settings. In style and substance alike, the Reagans and their friends were said to display what was first called "the California mentality," and then, as the administration got more settled and the social demonology of the exotic landscape more specific, "the California Club mentality."

I recall hearing about this "California Club mentality" at a dinner table in Georgetown, and responding with a certain atavistic outrage (I was from California, my own brother then lived during the week at the California Club); what seems curious in retrospect is that many of the men in question, including the president, had only a convenient connection with California in particular and the West in general. William Wilson was actually born in Los Angeles, and Earle Jorgenson in

San Francisco, but the late Justin Dart was born in Illinois, graduated from Northwestern, married a Walgreen heiress in Chicago, and did not move United Rexall, later Dart Industries, from Boston to Los Angeles until he was already its president. The late Alfred Bloomingdale was born in New York, graduated from Brown, and seeded the Diners Club with money from his family's New York store. What these men represented was not "the West" but what was for this century a relatively new kind of monied class in America, a group devoid of social responsibilities precisely because their ties to any one place had been so attenuated.

Ronald and Nancy Reagan had in fact lived most of their adult lives in California, but as part of the entertainment community, the members of which do not belong to the California Club. In 1964, when I first went to live in Los Angeles, and for some years later, life in the upper reaches of this community was, for women, quite rigidly organized. Women left the table after dessert, and had coffee upstairs, isolated in the bedroom or dressing room with demitasse cups and rock sugar ordered from London and cinnamon sticks in lieu of demitasse spoons. On the hostess's dressing table there were always very large bottles of Fracas and Gardenia and Tuberose. The dessert that preceded this retreat (a soufflé or mousse with raspberry sauce) was inflexibly served on Flora Danica plates, and was itself preceded by the ritual of the finger bowls and the doilies. I recall being repeatedly told a cautionary tale about what Joan Crawford had said to a young woman who removed her finger bowl but left the doily. The details of exactly what Joan Crawford had said and to whom and at whose table she had said it differed with the teller, but it was always Joan Crawford, and it always involved the doily; one of the reasons Mrs. Reagan ordered the famous new china was because, she told us in her own account of life in the Reagan White House, *My Turn*, the Johnson china had no finger bowls.

These subtropical evenings were not designed to invigorate. Large arrangements of flowers, ordered from David Jones, discouraged attempts at general conversation, ensuring that the table was turned on schedule. Expensive "resort" dresses and pajamas were worn, Pucci silks to the floor. When the women rejoined the men downstairs, trays of white crème de menthe were passed. Large parties were held in tents, with pink lights and chili from Chasen's. Lunch took place at the Bistro, and later at the Bistro Garden and at Jimmy's, which was owned by Jimmy Murphy, who everyone knew because he had worked for Kurt Niklas at the Bistro.

These forms were those of the local *ancien régime*, and as such had largely faded out by the late sixties, but can be examined in detail in the photographs Jean Howard took over the years and collected in *Jean Howard's Hollywood: A Photo Memoir*. Although neither Reagan appears in Miss Howard's book (the people she saw tended to be stars or powers or famously amusing, and the Reagans, who fell into hard times and television, were not locally thought to fill any of these slots), the photographs give a sense of the rigors of the place. What one notices in a photograph of the Joseph Cottens' 1955 Fourth of July lunch, the day Jennifer Jones led the conga line into the pool, is not the pool. There are people in the pool, yes, and even chairs, but most of the guests sit decorously on the lawn, wearing rep ties, silk dresses, high-heeled shoes. Mrs. Henry Hathaway, for a day in the sun at Anatole Litvak's beach house, wears a strapless dress of embroidered and scalloped organdy, and pearl earrings. Natalie Wood, lunching on Minna Wallis's lawn with Warren Beatty and George Cukor and the Hathaways and the Minnellis and the Axelrods, wears a black straw hat with a silk ribbon, a white dress, black and white beads, perfect full makeup, and her hair pinned back.

This was the world from which Nancy Reagan went in 1966 to Sacramento and in 1980 to Washington, and it is in many ways the world, although it was vanishing *in situ* even before Ronald Reagan was elected governor of California, she never left. *My Turn* did not document a life radically altered by later experience. Eight years in Sacramento left so little imprint on Mrs. Reagan that she described the house in which she lived there—a house located on 45th Street off M Street in a city laid out on a numerical and alphabetical grid running from 1st Street to 66th Street and from A Street to Y Street—as "an English-style country house in the suburbs."

She did not find it unusual that this house should have been bought for and rented to her and her husband (they paid $1,250 a month) by the same group of men who gave the State of California eleven acres on which to build Mrs. Reagan the "governor's mansion" she actually wanted and who later funded the million-dollar redecoration of the Reagan White House and who eventually bought the house on St. Cloud Road in Bel Air to which the Reagans moved when they left Washington (the street number of the St. Cloud house was 666, but the Reagans had it changed to 668, to avoid an association with the Beast in Revelations); she seemed to construe houses as part of her deal, like the housing provided to actors on location. Before the kitchen cabinet picked up Ronald Reagan's contract, the Reagans had lived in a house in Pacific Palisades remodeled by his then sponsor, General Electric.

This expectation on the part of the Reagans that other people would care for their needs struck many people, right away, as remarkable, and was usually characterized as a habit of the rich. But of course it is not a habit of the rich, and in any case the Reagans were not rich: they, and this expectation, were the products of studio Hollywood, a system in which performers performed, and in return were cared for. "I preferred the studio system to the anxiety of looking for work in New York," Mrs. Reagan told us in *My Turn.* During the eight years she lived in Washington, Mrs. Reagan said, she "never once set foot in a supermarket or in almost any other kind of store, with the exception of a card shop at 17th and K, where I used to buy my birthday cards," and carried money only when she went out for a manicure.

She was surprised to learn ("Nobody had told us") that she and her husband were expected to pay for their own food, dry cleaning, and toothpaste while in the White House. She seemed never to understand why it was imprudent of her to have accepted clothes from their makers when so many of them encouraged her to do so. Only Geoffrey Beene, whose clothes for Patricia Nixon and whose wedding dress for Lynda Bird Johnson were purchased through stores at retail prices, seemed to have resisted this impulse. "I don't quite understand how clothes can be 'on loan' to a woman," he told the *Los Angeles Times* in January of 1982, when the question of Mrs. Reagan's clothes was first raised. "I also think they'll run into a great deal of trouble deciding which of all these clothes are of museum quality. . . . They also claim she's helping to 'rescue' the American fashion industry. I didn't know it was in such dire straits."

The clothes were, as Mrs. Reagan seemed to construe it, "wardrobe"—a production expense, like the housing and the catering and the first-class travel and the furniture and paintings and cars that get taken home after the set is struck—and should rightly have gone on the studio budget. That the producers of this particular production—the men Mrs. Reagan called their "wealthier friends," their "very generous" friends—sometimes misunderstood their own role was understandable: Helene von Damm told us that only after William Wilson was warned that anyone with White House credentials was subject to a full-scale FBI investigation (Fred Fielding, the White House counsel, told him this) did he relinquish Suite 180 of the Executive Office Building, which he had commandeered the day after the inauguration in order to vet the appointment of the nominal, as opposed to the kitchen, cabinet.

"So began my stewardship," Edith Bolling Wilson wrote later about the stroke that paralyzed Woodrow Wilson in October of 1919, eighteen months before he left the White House. The stewardship Nancy Reagan shared first with James Baker and Ed Meese and Michael Deaver and then less easily with Donald Regan was, perhaps because each of its principals was working a different scenario and only one, James Baker, had anything approaching a full script, considerably more Byzantine than most. Baker, whose ultimate role in this White House was to preserve it for the established order, seems to have relied heavily on the tendency of opposing forces, let loose, to neutralize each other. "Usually in a big place there's only one person or group to be afraid of," Peggy Noonan observed. "But in the Reagan White House there were two, the chief of staff and his people and the First Lady and hers—a pincer formation that made everyone feel vulnerable." Miss Noonan showed us Mrs. Reagan moving through the corridors with her East Wing entourage, the members of which were said in the West Wing to be "not serious," readers of *W* and *Vogue*. Mrs. Reagan herself was variously referred to as "Evita," "Mommy," "The Missus," "The Hairdo with Anxiety." Miss Noonan dismissed her as not "a liberal or a leftist or a moderate or a détentist" but "a Galanoist, a wealthy well-dressed woman who followed the common wisdom of her class."

In fact Nancy Reagan was more interesting than that: it was precisely "her class" in which she had trouble believing. She was not an experienced woman. Her social skills, like those of many women trained in the insular life of the motion picture community, were strikingly undeveloped. She and Raisa Gorbachev had "little in common," and "completely different outlooks on the world." She and Betty Ford "were different people who came from different worlds." She seems to have been comfortable in the company of Michael Deaver, of Ted Graber (her decorator), and of only a few other people. She seems not to have had much sense about who goes with who. At a state dinner for José Napoleón Duarte of El Salvador, she seated herself between President Duarte and Ralph Lauren. She had limited social experience and apparently unlimited social anxiety. Helene von Damm complained that Mrs. Reagan would not consent, during the first presidential campaign, to letting the fund-raisers call on "her New York friends"; trying to put together a list for the New York dinner in November of 1979 at which Ronald Reagan was to announce his candidacy, Miss von Damm finally dispatched an emissary to extract a few names from Jerry Zipkin, who parted with them reluctantly, and then said, "Remember, don't use my name."

Perhaps Mrs. Reagan's most endearing quality was this little girl's fear of being left out, of not having the best friends and not going to the parties in the biggest houses. She collected slights. She took refuge in a kind of piss-elegance, a fanciness (the "English-style country house in the suburbs"), in using words like "inappropriate." It was "inappropriate, to say the least" for Geraldine Ferraro and her husband to leave the dais and go "down on the floor, working the crowd" at a 1984 Italian-American Federation dinner at which the candidates on both tickets were speaking. It was "uncalled for—and mean" when, at the time John Koehler had been named to replace Patrick Buchanan as director of communications and it was learned that Koehler had been a member of Hitler Youth, Donald Regan said "blame it on the East Wing."

Mrs. Gorbachev, as Mrs. Reagan saw it, "condescended" to her, and "expected to be deferred to." Mrs. Gorbachev accepted an invitation from Pamela Harriman before she answered one from Mrs. Reagan. The reason Ben Bradlee called Iran-contra "the most fun he'd had since Watergate" was just possibly because, she explained in *My Turn*, he resented her relationship with Katharine Graham. Betty Ford was given a box on the floor of the 1976 Republican National Convention, and Mrs. Reagan only a skybox. Mrs. Reagan was evenhanded: Maureen Reagan "may have been right" when she called this slight deliberate. When, on the second night of that convention, the band struck up "Tie a Yellow Ribbon Round the Ole Oak Tree" during an ovation for Mrs. Reagan, Mrs. Ford started dancing with Tony Orlando. Mrs. Reagan was magnanimous: "Some of our people saw this as a deliberate attempt to upstage me, but I never thought that was her intention."

Michael Deaver, in his version of more or less the same events, *Behind the Scenes*, gave us an arresting account of taking the Reagans, during the 1980 campaign, to an Episcopal church near the farm on which they were staying outside Middleburg, Virginia. After advancing the church and negotiating the subject of the sermon with the minister (Ezekiel and the bones rather than what Deaver called "reborn Christians," presumably Christian rebirth), he finally agreed that the Reagans would attend an eleven o'clock Sunday service. "We were not told," Deaver wrote, "and I did not anticipate, that the eleven o'clock service would also be holy communion," a ritual he characterized as "very foreign to the Reagans." He described "nervous glances," and "mildly frantic" whispers about what to do, since the Reagans' experience had been of Bel Air Presbyterian, "a proper Protestant church where trays are passed containing small glasses of grape juice and little squares of bread." The moment arrived: ". . . halfway down the aisle I felt Nancy clutch my arm. . . . '*Mike!*' she hissed. '*Are those people drinking out of the same cup?*'"

Here the incident takes on elements of "I Love Lucy." Deaver assures Mrs. Reagan that it will be acceptable to just dip the wafer in the chalice. Mrs. Reagan chances this, but manages somehow to drop the wafer in the wine. Ronald Reagan, cast here as Ricky Ricardo, is too deaf to hear Deaver's whispered instructions, and has been instructed by his wife to "do exactly as I do." He, too, drops the wafer in the wine, where it is left to float next to Mrs. Reagan's. "Nancy was relieved to leave the church," Deaver reports. "The president was chipper as he stepped into the sunlight, satisfied that the service had gone quite well."

I had read this account several times before I realized what so attracted me to it: here we had a perfect model of the Reagan White House. There was the aide who located the correct setting ("I did some quick scouting and found a beautiful Episcopal church"), who anticipated every conceivable problem and handled it adroitly (he had "a discreet chat with the minister," he "gently raised the question"), and yet who somehow missed, as in the visit to Bitburg, a key point. There was the wife, charged with protecting her husband's face to the world, a task requiring, she hinted in *My Turn*, considerable vigilance. This was a husband who could be "naive about people." He had for example "too much trust" in David Stockman. He had "given his word" to Helmut Kohl, and so felt "duty-bound to honor his commitment" to visit Bitburg. He was, Mrs. Reagan disclosed during a "Good Morning America" interview at the time *My Turn* was published, "the softest touch going" when it came to what she referred to as (another instance of somehow missing a key point) "the poor." Mrs. Reagan understood all this. She handled all this. And yet there she was outside Middleburg, Virginia, once again the victim of bad advance, confronted by the "foreign" communion table and rendered stiff with apprehension that a finger bowl might get removed without its doily.

And there, at the center of it all, was Ronald Reagan, insufficiently briefed (or, as they say in the White House, "badly served") on the wafer issue but moving ahead, stepping "into the sunlight" satisfied with his own and everyone else's performance, apparently oblivious of (or inured to, or indifferent to) the crises being managed in his presence and for his benefit.

What he had, and the aide and the wife did not have, was the story, the high concept, what Ed Meese used to call "the big picture," as in "he's a big-picture man." The big picture here was of the candidate going to church on Sunday morning; the details obsessing the wife and the aide—what church, what to do with the wafer—remained outside the frame.

From the beginning in California, the principal in this administration was operating on what might have seemed distinctly special information. He had "feelings" about things, for example about the Vietnam War. "I have a feeling that we are doing better in the war than the people have been told," he was quoted as having said in the *Los Angeles Times* on October 16, 1967. With the transforming power of the presidency, this special information that no one else understood—these big pictures, these high concepts—took on a magical quality, and some people in the White House came to believe that they had in their possession, sharpening his own pencils in the Oval Office, the Fisher King himself, the keeper of the grail, the source of that ineffable contact with the electorate that was in turn the source of the power.

There were times, we know now, when this White House had fairly well absented itself from the art of the possible. McFarlane flying to Teheran with the cake and the Bible and ten falsified Irish passports did not derive from our traditional executive tradition. The place was running instead on its own superstition, on the reading of bones, on the belief that a flicker of attention from the president during the presentation of a plan (the ideal presentation, Peggy Noonan explained, was one in which "the president was forced to look at a picture, read a short letter, or respond to a question") ensured the transfer of the magic to whatever was that week exciting the ardor of the children who wanted to make the revolution—to SDI, to the mujahadeen, to Jonas Savimbi, to the contras.

Miss Noonan recalled what she referred to as "the contra meetings," which turned on the magical notion that putting the president on display in the right setting (i.e., "going over the heads of the media to the people") was all that was needed to "inspire a commitment on the part of the American people."

They sat in those meetings and discussed having the president speak at the Orange Bowl in Miami on the anniversary of John F. Kennedy's Orange Bowl speech after the Bay of Pigs, never mind that the Kennedy Orange Bowl speech had become over the years in Miami the symbol of American betrayal. They sat in those meetings and discussed having the president go over the heads of his congressional opponents by speaking in Jim Wright's district near the Alamo: ". . . something like '*Blank* miles to the north of here is the Alamo,'" Miss Noonan wrote in her notebook, sketching out the ritual in which the magic would be transferred. "'. . . Where brave heroes *blank*, and where the commander of the garrison wrote during those terrible last days *blank* . . .'"

But the Fisher King was sketching another big picture, one he had had in mind since California. We have heard again and again that Mrs. Reagan turned the president away from the Evil Empire and toward the meetings with Gorbachev. (Later, on NBC "Nightly News," the San Francisco astrologer Joan Quigley claimed a role in influencing both Reagans on this point, explaining that she had "changed their Evil Empire attitude by briefing them on Gorbachev's horoscope.") Mrs. Reagan herself allowed that she "felt it was ridiculous for these two heavily armed superpowers to be sitting there and not talking to each other" and "did push Ronnie a little."

But how much pushing was actually needed remains in question. The Soviet Union appeared to Ronald Reagan as an abstraction, a place where people were helpless to resist "communism," the inanimate evil which, as he had put it in a 1951 speech to a Kiwanis convention and would continue to put it for the next three and a half decades, had "tried to invade our industry" and been "fought" and eventually "licked." This was a construct in which the actual citizens of the Soviet Union could be seen to have been, like the motion picture industry, "invaded"—in need only of liberation. The liberating force might be the appearance of a Shane-like character, someone to "lick" the evil, or it might be just the sweet light of reason. "A people free to choose will always choose peace," as President Reagan told students at Moscow State University in May of 1988.

In this sense he was dealing from an entirely abstract deck, and the opening to the East had been his card all along, his big picture, his story. And this is how it went: what he would like to do, he had told any number of people over the years (I recall first hearing it from George Will, who cautioned me not to tell it because conversations with presidents were privileged), was take the leader of the Soviet Union (who this leader would be was another of those details outside the frame) on a flight to Los Angeles. When the plane came in low over the middle-class subdivisions that stretch from the San Bernardino mountains to LAX, he would direct the leader of the Soviet Union to the window, and point out all the swimming pools below. "Those are the pools of the capitalists," the leader of the Soviet Union would say. "No," the leader of the free world would say. "Those are the pools of the workers." *Blank* years further on, when brave heroes *blanked*, and where the leader of the free world *blank*, accidental history took its course, but we have yet to pay for the ardor.

—1989

Insider Baseball

IT OCCURRED to me during the summer of 1988, in California and Atlanta and New Orleans, in the course of watching first the California primary and then the Democratic and Republican national conventions, that it had not been by accident that the people with whom I had preferred to spend time in high school had, on the whole, hung out in gas stations. They had not run for student body office. They had not gone to Yale or Swarthmore or DePauw, nor had they even applied. They had gotten drafted, gone through basic at Fort Ord. They had knocked up girls, and married them, had begun what they called the first night of the rest of their lives with a midnight drive to Carson City and a five-dollar ceremony performed by a justice still in his pajamas. They got jobs at the places that had laid off their uncles. They paid their bills or did not pay their bills, made down payments on tract houses, led lives on that social and economic edge referred to, in Washington and among those whose preferred locus is Washington, as "out there." They were never destined to be, in other words, communicants in what we have come to call, when we want to indicate the traditional ways in which power is exchanged and the status quo maintained in the United States, "the process."

"The process today gives everyone a chance to participate," Tom Hayden, by way of explaining "the difference" between 1968 and 1988, said to Bryant Gumbel on NBC at 7:50 A.M. on the day after Jesse Jackson spoke at the 1988 Democratic convention in Atlanta. This was, at a convention that had as its controlling principle the notably nonparticipatory idea of "unity," demonstrably not true, but people inside the process, constituting as they do a self-created and self-referring class, a new kind of managerial elite, tend to speak of the world not necessarily as it is but as they want people out there to believe it is. They tend to prefer the theoretical to the observable, and to dismiss that which might be learned empirically as "anecdotal." They tend to speak a language common in Washington but not specifically shared by the rest of us. They talk about "programs," and "policy," and how to "implement" them or it, about "trade-offs" and constituencies and positioning the candidate and distancing the candidate, about the "story," and how it will "play." They speak of a candidate's performance, by which they usually mean his skill at circumventing questions, not as citizens but as professional insiders, attuned to signals pitched beyond the range of normal hearing: "I hear he did all right this afternoon," they were saying to one another in the press section of the Louisiana Superdome in New Orleans on the evening in August of 1988 when Dan Quayle was or was not to be nominated for the vice presidency. "I hear he did OK with Brinkley." By the time the balloons fell that night the narrative had changed: "Quayle, zip," the professionals were saying as they brushed the confetti off their laptops.

These were people who spoke of the process as an end in itself, connected only nominally, and vestigially, to the electorate and its possible concerns. "She used to be an issues person but now she's involved in the process," a prominent conservative said to me in New Orleans by way of suggesting why an acquaintance who believed Jack Kemp was "speaking directly to what people out there want" had nonetheless backed George Bush. "Anything that brings the process closer to the people is all to the good," George Bush had declared in his 1987 autobiography, *Looking Forward*, accepting as given this relatively recent notion that the people and the process need not automatically be on convergent tracks.

When we talk about the process, then, we are talking, increasingly, not about "the democratic process," or the general mechanism affording the citizens of a state a voice in its affairs, but the reverse: a mechanism seen as so specialized that access to it is correctly limited to its own professionals, to those who manage policy and those who report on it, to those who run the polls and those who quote them, to those who ask and those who answer the questions on the Sunday shows, to the media consultants, to the columnists, to the issues advisers, to those who give the off-the-record breakfasts and to those who attend them; to that handful of insiders who invent, year in and year out, the narrative of public life. "I didn't realize you were a political junkie," Martin Kaplan, the former *Washington Post* reporter and Mondale speechwriter who was married to Susan Estrich, the manager of the Dukakis campaign, said when I mentioned that I planned to write about the campaign; the assumption here, that the narrative should be not just written only by its own specialists but also legible only to its own specialists, is why, finally, an American presidential campaign raises questions that go so vertiginously to the heart of the structure.

What strikes one most vividly about such a campaign is precisely its remoteness from the actual life of the country. The figures are well known, and suggest a national indifference usually construed, by those inside the process, as ignorance, or "apathy," in any case a defect not in themselves but in the clay they have been given to mold. Only slightly more than half of those eligible to vote in the United States did vote in the 1984 presidential election. An average 18.5 percent of what Nielsen Media Research calls the "television households" in the United States tuned into network coverage of the 1988 Republican convention in New Orleans, meaning 81.5 percent did not. An average 20.2 percent of these "television households" tuned into network coverage of the 1988 Democratic convention in Atlanta, meaning 79.8 percent did not. The decision to tune in or out ran along predictable lines: "The demography is good even if the households are low," a programming executive at Bozell, Jacobs, Kenyon & Eckhardt told the *New York Times* in July of 1988 about the agency's decision to buy "campaign event" time for Merrill Lynch on both CBS and CNN. "The ratings are about nine percent off 1984," an NBC marketing vice president allowed, again to the *New York Times*, "but the upscale target audience is there."

When I read this piece I recalled standing, the day before the California primary, in a dusty Central California schoolyard to which the leading Democratic candidate had come to speak one more time about what kind of president he wanted to be. The crowd was listless, restless. There were gray thunderclouds overhead. A little rain fell. "We welcome you to Silicon Valley," an official had said by way of greeting the candidate, but this was not in fact Silicon Valley: this was San Jose, and a part of San Jose particularly untouched by technological prosperity, a neighborhood in which the lowering of two-toned Impalas remained a central activity.

"I want to be a candidate who brings people together," the candidate was saying at the exact moment a man began shouldering his way past me and through a group of women with children in their arms. This was not a solid citizen, not a member of the upscale target audience. This was a man wearing a down vest and a camouflage hat, a man with a definite little glitter in his eyes, a member not of the 18.5 percent and not of the 20.2 percent but of the 81.5, the 79.8. "I've got to see the next president," he muttered repeatedly. "I've got something to tell him."

". . . Because that's what this party is all about," the candidate said.

"Where is he?" the man said, confused. "Who is he?"

"Get lost," someone said.

". . . Because that's what this country is all about," the candidate said.

Here we had the last true conflict of cultures in America, that between the empirical and the theoretical. On the empirical evidence this country was about two-toned Impalas and people with camouflage hats and a little glitter in their eyes, but this had not been, among people inclined to the theoretical, the preferred assessment. Nor had it even been, despite the fact that we had all stood together on the same dusty asphalt, under the same plane trees, the general assessment: this was how Joe Klein, writing a few weeks later in *New York* magazine, had described those last days before the California primary:

> Breezing across California on his way to the nomination last week, Michael Dukakis crossed a curious American threshold. . . . The crowds were larger, more excited now; they seemed to be searching for reasons to love him. They cheered eagerly, almost without provocation. People reached out to touch him—not to shake hands, just to touch him. . . . Dukakis seemed to be making an almost subliminal passage in the public mind: he was becoming presidential.

Those June days in 1988 during which Michael Dukakis did or did not cross a curious American threshold had in fact been instructive. The day that ended in the schoolyard in San Jose had at first seemed, given that it was the day before the California primary, underscheduled, pointless, three essentially meaningless events separated by plane flights. At Taft High School in Woodland Hills that morning there had been little girls waving red and gold pom-poms in front of the cameras; "Hold that tiger," the band had played. "Dream . . . maker," the choir had crooned. "Governor Dukakis . . . this is . . . Taft High," the student council president had said. "I understand that this is the first time a presidential candidate has come to Taft High," Governor Dukakis had said. "Is there any doubt . . . under those circumstances . . . who you should support?"

"Jackson," a group of Chicano boys on the back sidewalk shouted in unison.

"That's what it's all about," Governor Dukakis had said, and "health care," and "good teachers and good teaching."

This event had been abandoned, and another materialized: a lunchtime "rally," in a downtown San Diego office plaza through which many people were passing on their way to lunch, a borrowed crowd but a less than attentive one. The cameras focused on the balloons. The sound techs picked up "La Bamba." "We're going to take child-support enforcement seriously in this country," Governor Dukakis had said, and "tough drug enforcement here and abroad." "Tough choices," he had said, and "we're going to make teaching a valued profession in this country."

Nothing said in any venue that day had seemed to have much connection with anybody listening ("I want to work with you and with working people all over this country," the candidate had said in the San Diego office plaza, but people who work in offices in San Diego do not think of themselves as "working people"), and late that afternoon, on the bus to the San Jose airport, I had asked a reporter who had traveled through the spring with the various campaigns (among those who moved from plane to plane it was agreed, by June, that the Bush plane had the worst access to the candidate and the best food, that the Dukakis plane had average access and average food, and that the Jackson plane had full access and no time to eat) if the candidate's appearances that day did not seem a little off the point.

"Not really," the reporter said. "He covered three major markets."

Among those who traveled regularly with the campaigns, in other words, it was taken for granted that these "events" they were covering, and on which they were in fact filing, were not merely meaningless but deliberately so: occasions on which film could be shot and no mistakes made ("They hope he won't make any big mistakes," the NBC correspondent covering George Bush kept saying the evening of the September 25, 1988, debate at Wake Forest College, and, an hour and a half later, "He didn't make any big mistakes"), events designed only to provide settings for those unpaid television spots which in this case were appearing, even as we spoke, on the local news in California's three major media markets. "On the fishing trip, there was no way for the television crews to get videotapes out," the *Los Angeles Times* noted a few weeks later in a piece about how "poorly designed and executed events" had interfered with coverage of a Bush campaign "environmental" swing through the Pacific Northwest. "At the lumber mill, Bush's advance team arranged camera angles so poorly that in one setup only his legs could get on camera." A Bush adviser had been quoted: "There is no reason for camera angles not being provided for. We're going to sit down and talk about these things at length."

Any traveling campaign, then, was a set, moved at considerable expense from location to location. The employer of each reporter on the Dukakis plane the day before the California primary was billed, for a total flying time of under three hours, $1,129.51; the billing to each reporter who happened, on the morning during the Democratic convention in Atlanta when Michael Dukakis and Lloyd Bentsen met with Jesse Jackson, to ride along on the Dukakis bus from the Hyatt Regency to the World Congress Center, a distance of perhaps ten blocks, was $217.18. There was the hierarchy of the set: there were actors, there were directors, there were script supervisors, there were grips.

There was the isolation of the set, and the arrogance, the contempt for outsiders. I recall pink-cheeked young aides on the Dukakis campaign referring to themselves, innocent of irony and therefore of history, as "the best and the brightest."

On the morning after the Wake Forest debate, Michael Oreskes of the *New York Times* gave us this memorable account of Bush aides crossing the Wake Forest campus:

> The Bush campaign measured exactly how long it would take its spokesmen to walk briskly from the room in which they were watching the debate to the center where reporters were filing their articles. The answer was three and a half minutes—too long for Mr. Bush's strategists, Lee Atwater, Robert Teeter, and Mr. Darman. They ran the course instead as young aides cleared students and other onlookers from their path.

There was also the tedium of the set: the time spent waiting for the shots to be set up, the time spent waiting for the bus to join the motorcade, the time spent waiting for telephones on which to file, the time spent waiting for the Secret Service ("the agents," they were called on the traveling campaigns, never the Secret Service, just "the agents," or "this detail," or "this rotation") to sweep the plane.

It was a routine that encouraged a certain passivity. There was the plane, or the bus, and one got on it. There was the schedule, and one followed it. There was time to file, or there was not. "We should have had a page-one story," a *Boston Globe* reporter complained to the *Los Angeles Times* after the Bush campaign had failed to provide the advance text of a Seattle "environment" speech scheduled to end only twenty minutes before the departure of the plane for California. "There are times when you sit up and moan, 'Where is Michael Deaver when you need him?'" an ABC producer said to the *Times* on this point.

A final victory, for the staff and the press on a traveling campaign, would mean not a new production but only a new location: the particular setups and shots of the campaign day (the walk on the beach, the meet-and-greet at the housing project) would dissolve imperceptibly, isolation and arrogance and tedium intact, into the South Lawns, the Oval Office signings, the arrivals and departures of the administration day. There would still be the "young aides." There would still be "onlookers" to be cleared from the path. Another location, another stand-up: "We already shot a tarmac departure," they say on the campaign planes. "This schedule has two Rose Gardens," they say in the White House pressroom. Ronald Reagan, when asked by David Frost how his life in the Oval Office had differed from his expectations of it, said this: "—I was surprised at how familiar the whole routine was—the fact that the night before I would get a schedule telling me what I'm going to do all day the next day and so forth."

American reporters "like" covering a presidential campaign (it gets them out on the road, it has balloons, it has music, it is viewed as a big story, one that leads to the respect of one's peers, to the Sunday shows, to lecture fees and often to Washington), which is one reason why there has developed among those who do it so arresting an enthusiasm for overlooking the contradictions inherent in reporting that which occurs only in order to be reported. They are willing, in exchange for "access," to transmit the images their sources wish transmitted. They are even willing, in exchange for certain colorful details around which a "reconstruction" can be built (the "kitchen table" at which the Dukakis campaign conferred on the night Lloyd Bentsen was added to the 1988 Democratic ticket, the "slips of paper" on which key members of the 1988 Bush campaign, aboard Air Force Two on their way to New Orleans, wrote down their own guesses for vice president), to present these images not as a story the campaign wants told but as fact. This was *Time*, reporting from New Orleans on George Bush's reaction when Dan Quayle came under attack:

> Bush never wavered in support of the man he had lifted so high. "How's Danny doing?" he asked several times. But the Vice President never felt the compulsion to question Quayle face-to-face. The awkward investigation was left to Baker. Around noon, Quayle grew restive about answering further questions. "Let's go," he urged, but Baker pressed to know more. By early afternoon, the mood began to brighten in the Bush bunker. There were no new revelations: the media hurricane had for the moment blown out to sea.

This was Sandy Grady, reporting from Atlanta:

> Ten minutes before he was to face the biggest audience of his life, Michael Dukakis got a hug from his 84-year-old mother, Euterpe, who chided him, "You'd better be good, Michael." Dukakis grinned and said, "I'll do my best, Ma."

"Appeal to the media by exposing the [Bush campaign's] heavy-handed spin-doctoring," William Safire advised the Dukakis campaign on September 8, 1988. "We hate to be seen being manipulated."

"Periodically," the *New York Times* reported in March 1988, "Martin Plissner, the political editor of CBS News, and Susan Morrison, a television producer and former political aide, organize gatherings of the politically connected at their home in Washington. At such parties, they organize secret ballots asking the assembled experts who will win. . . . By November 1, 1987, the results of Mr. Dole's organizing efforts were apparent in a new Plissner-Morrison poll . . ." The symbiosis here was complete, and the only outsider was the increasingly hypothetical voter, who was seen as responsive not to actual issues but to their adroit presentation: "At the moment the Republican message is simpler and more clear than ours," the Democratic chairman for California, Peter Kelly, said to the *Los Angeles Times* on August 31, 1988, complaining, on the matter of what was called the Pledge of Allegiance issue, not that it was a false issue but that Bush had seized the initiative, or "the symbolism."

"Bush Gaining in Battle of TV Images," the *Washington Post* headlined a page-one story on September 10, 1988, and quoted Jeff Greenfield, the ABC News political reporter: "George Bush is almost always outdoors, coatless, sometimes with his sleeves rolled up, and looks ebullient and Happy Warrior–ish. Mike Dukakis is almost always indoors, with his jacket on, and almost always behind a lectern." The Bush campaign, according to that week's issue of *Newsweek*, was, because it had the superior gift for getting film shot in "dramatic settings—like Boston Harbor," winning "the all-important battle of the backdrops." A CBS producer covering the Dukakis campaign was quoted complaining about an occasion when Governor Dukakis, speaking to students on a California beach, had faced the students instead of the camera. "The only reason Dukakis was on the beach was to get his picture taken," the producer had said. "So you might as well see his face." Pictures, *Newsweek* had concluded, "often speak louder than words."

This "battle of the backdrops" story appeared on page twenty-four of the *Newsweek* dated September 12, 1988. On page twenty-three of the same issue there appeared, as illustrations for the lead National Affairs story ("Getting Down and Dirty: As the mud-slinging campaign moves into full gear, Bush stays on the offensive—and Dukakis calls back his main street-fighting man"), two half-page color photographs, one of each candidate, which seemed to address the very concerns expressed on page twenty-four and in the *Post*. The photograph of George Bush showed him indoors, with his jacket on, and behind a lectern. That of Michael Dukakis showed him outdoors, coatless, with his sleeves rolled up, looking ebullient, about to throw a baseball on an airport tarmac: something had been learned from Jeff Greenfield, or something had been told to Jeff Greenfield. "We talk to the press, and things take on a life of their own," Mark Siegel, a Democratic political consultant, said to Elizabeth Drew.

About this baseball on the tarmac. On the day that Michael Dukakis appeared at the high school in Woodland Hills and at the rally in San Diego and in the schoolyard in San Jose, there was, although it did not appear on the schedule, a fourth event, what was referred to among the television crews as a "tarmac arrival with ball tossing." This event had taken place in late morning, on the tarmac at the San Diego airport, just after the chartered 737 had rolled to a stop and the candidate had emerged. There had been a moment of hesitation. Then baseball mitts had been produced, and Jack Weeks, the traveling press secretary, had tossed a ball to the candidate. The candidate had tossed the ball back. The rest of us had stood in the sun and given this our full attention, undeflected even by the arrival of an Alaska Airlines 767: some forty adults standing on a tarmac watching a diminutive figure in shirtsleeves and a red tie toss a ball to his press secretary.

"Just a regular guy," one of the cameramen had said, his inflection that of the "union official" who confided, in an early Dukakis commercial aimed at blue-collar voters, that he had known "Mike" a long time, and backed him despite his not being "your shot-and-beer kind of guy."

"I'd say he was a regular guy," another cameraman had said. "Definitely."

"I'd sit around with him," the first cameraman said.

Kara Dukakis, one of the candidate's daughters, had at that moment emerged from the 737.

"You'd have a beer with him?"

Jack Weeks had tossed the ball to Kara Dukakis.

"I'd have a beer with him."

Kara Dukakis had tossed the ball to her father. Her father had caught the ball and tossed it back to her.

"OK," one of the cameramen had said. "We got the daughter. Nice. That's enough. Nice."

The CNN producer then on the Dukakis campaign told me, later in the day, that the first recorded ball tossing on the Dukakis campaign had been outside a bowling alley somewhere in Ohio. CNN had shot it. When the campaign realized that only one camera had it, they had restaged it.

"We have a lot of things like the ball tossing," the producer said. "We have the Greek dancing for example."

I asked if she still bothered to shoot it.

"I get it," she said, "but I don't call in anymore and say, 'Hey, hold it, I've got him dancing.'"

This sounded about right (the candidate might, after all, bean a citizen during the ball tossing, and CNN would need film), and not until I read Joe Klein's version of these days in California did it occur to me that this eerily contrived moment on the tarmac at San Diego could become, at least provisionally, history. "The Duke seemed downright jaunty," Joe Klein reported. "He tossed a baseball with aides. He was flagrantly multilingual. He danced Greek dances . . ." In the July 25, 1988, issue of *U.S. News & World Report*, Michael Kramer opened his cover story, "Is Dukakis Tough Enough?," with a more developed version of the ball tossing:

> The thermometer read 101 degrees, but the locals guessed 115 on the broiling airport tarmac in Phoenix. After all, it was under a noonday sun in the desert that Michael Dukakis was indulging his truly favorite campaign ritual—a game of catch with his aide Jack Weeks. "These days," he has said, "throwing the ball around when we land somewhere is about the only exercise I get." For 16 minutes, Dukakis shagged flies and threw strikes. Halfway through, he rolled up his sleeves, but he never loosened his tie. Finally, mercifully, it was over and time to pitch the obvious tongue-in-cheek question: "Governor, what does throwing a ball around in this heat say about your mental stability?" Without missing a beat, and without a trace of a smile, Dukakis echoed a sentiment he has articulated repeatedly in recent months: "What it means is that I'm tough."

Nor was this the last word. On July 31, 1988, in the *Washington Post*, David S. Broder, who had also been with the Dukakis campaign in Phoenix, gave us a third, and, by virtue of his seniority in the process, perhaps the official version of the ball tossing:

> Dukakis called out to Jack Weeks, the handsome, curly-haired Welshman who good-naturedly shepherds us wayward pressmen through the daily vagaries of the campaign schedule. Weeks dutifully produced two gloves and a baseball, and there on the tarmac, with its surface temperature just below the boiling point, the governor loosened up his arm and got the kinks out of his back by tossing a couple hundred 90-foot pegs to Weeks.

What we had in the tarmac arrival with ball tossing, then, was an understanding: a repeated moment witnessed by many people, all of whom believed it to be a setup and yet most of whom believed that only an outsider, only someone too "naive" to know the rules of the game, would so describe it.

2

The narrative is made up of many such understandings, tacit agreements, small and large, to overlook the observable in the interests of obtaining a dramatic story line. It was understood, for example, that the first night of the 1988 Republican National Convention in New Orleans should be for Ronald Reagan "the last hurrah." "Reagan Electrifies GOP" was the headline the next morning on page one of *New York Newsday*; in fact the Reagan appearance, which was rhetorically pitched not to a live audience but to the more intimate demands of the camera, was, inside the Superdome, barely registered. It was understood, similarly, that Michael Dukakis's acceptance speech on the last night of the 1988 Democratic National Convention in Atlanta should be the occasion on which his "passion," or "leadership," emerged. "Could the no-nonsense nominee reach within himself to discover the language of leadership?" *Time* had asked. "Could he go beyond the pedestrian promise of 'good jobs at good wages' to give voice to a new Democratic vision?"

The correct answer, since the forward flow of the narrative here demanded the appearance of a genuine contender (a contender who could be seventeen points "up," so that George Bush could be seventeen points "down," a position from which he could rise to "claim" his own convention), was yes: "The best speech of his life," David Broder reported. Sandy Grady found it "superb," evoking "Kennedyesque echoes" and showing "unexpected craft and fire." *Newsweek* had witnessed Michael Dukakis "electrifying the convention with his intensely personal acceptance speech." In fact the convention that evening had been electrified, not by the speech, which was the same series of nonsequential clauses Governor Dukakis had employed during the primary campaign ("My friends . . . son of immigrants . . . good jobs at good wages . . . make teaching a valued and honored profession . . . it's what the Democratic Party is all about"), but because the floor had been darkened, swept with laser beams, and flooded with "Coming to America," played at concert volume with the bass turned up.

It is understood that this invented narrative will turn on certain familiar elements. There is the continuing story line of the "horse race," the reliable daily drama of one candidate falling behind as another pulls ahead. There is the surprise of the new poll, the glamour of the one-on-one colloquy on the midnight plane, a plot point (the nation sleeps while the candidate and his confidant hammer out its fate) pioneered by Theodore H. White. There is the abiding if unexamined faith in the campaign as personal odyssey, and in the spiritual benefits accruing to those who undertake it. There is, in the presented history of the candidate, the crucible event, the day that "changed the life."

Robert Dole's life was understood to have changed when he was injured in Italy in 1945. George Bush's life is understood to have changed when he and his wife decided to "get out and make it on our own" (his words, or rather those of his speechwriter, Peggy Noonan, from the "lived the dream" acceptance speech at the 1988 convention, suggesting action, shirtsleeves, privilege cast aside) in west Texas. For Bruce Babbitt, "the dam just kind of broke" during a student summer in Bolivia. For Michael Dukakis, the dam was understood to have broken not during his student summer in Peru but after his 1978 defeat in Massachusetts; his tragic flaw, we read repeatedly during the 1988 campaign, was neither his evident sulkiness at losing that earlier election nor what many saw later as a rather dissociated self-satisfaction ("We're two people very proud of what we've done," he said on NBC in Atlanta, falling into a favorite speech pattern, "very proud of each other, actually . . . and very proud that a couple of guys named Dukakis and Jackson have come this far"), but the more attractive "hubris."

The narrative requires broad strokes. Michael Dukakis was physically small, and had associations with Harvard, which suggested that he could be cast as an "intellectual"; the "immigrant factor," on the other hand, could make him tough (as in "What it means is that I'm tough"), a "streetfighter." "He's cool, shrewd and still trying to prove he's tough," the July 25, 1988, cover of *U.S. News & World Report* said about Dukakis. "Toughness is what it's all about," one of his advisers was quoted as having said in the cover story. "People need to feel that a candidate is tough enough to be president. It is the threshold perception."

George Bush had presented a more tortured narrative problem. The tellers of the story had not understood, or had not responded to, the essential Bush style, which was complex, ironic, the diffident edge of the Northeastern elite. This was what was at first identified as "the wimp factor," which was replaced not by a more complicated view of the personality but by its reverse: George Bush was by late August no longer a "wimp" but someone who had "thrown it over," "struck out" to make his own way: no longer a product of the effete Northeast but someone who had thrived in Texas, and was therefore "tough enough to be president."

That George Bush might have thrived in Texas not in spite of being but precisely because he was a member of the Northeastern elite was a shading that had no part in the narrative: "He was considered back at the time one of the most charismatic people ever elected to public office in the history of Texas," Congressman Bill Archer of Houston said. "That charisma, people talked about it over and over again." People talked about it, probably, because Andover and Yale and the inheritable tax avoidance they suggested were, during the years George Bush lived in Texas, the exact ideals toward which the Houston and Dallas establishment aspired, but the narrative called for a less ambiguous version: "Lived in a little shotgun house, one room for the three of us," as Bush, or Peggy Noonan, had put it in the celebrated no-subject-pronoun cadences of the "lived the dream" acceptance speech. "Worked in the oil business, started my own. . . . Moved from the shotgun to a duplex apartment to a house. Lived the dream—high school football on Friday night, Little League, neighborhood barbecue . . . pushing into unknown territory with kids and a dog and a car . . ."

All stories, of course, depend for their popular interest upon the invention of personality, or "character," but in the political narrative, designed as it is to maintain the illusion of "consensus" by obscuring rather than addressing actual issues, this invention served a further purpose. It was by 1988 generally if unspecifically agreed that the United States faced certain social and economic realities that, if not intractable, did not entirely lend themselves to the kinds of policy fixes people who run for elected office, on whatever ticket, were likely to undertake.

We had not yet accommodated the industrialization of parts of the third world. We had not yet adjusted to the economic realignment of a world in which the United States was no longer the principal catalyst for change. "We really are in an age of transition," Brent Scowcroft, Bush's leading foreign policy adviser, told Robert Scheer of the *Los Angeles Times* in the fall of 1988, "from a postwar world where the Soviets were the enemy, where the United States was a superpower and trying to build up both its allies and its former enemies and help the third world transition to independence. That whole world and all of those things are coming to an end or have ended, and we are now entering a new and different world that will be complex and much less unambiguous than the old one."

What continued to dominate the rhetoric of the 1988 campaign, however, was not this awareness of a new and different world but nostalgia for an old one, and coded assurance that symptoms of ambiguity or change, of what George Bush called the "deterioration of values," would be summarily dealt with by increased social control. It was not by accident that the word "enforcement," devoid of any apparent awareness that it had been tried before, kept coming up in this campaign. A problem named seemed, for both campaigns, a problem solved. Michael Dukakis had promised, by way of achieving his goal of "no safe haven for dope dealers and drug profits anywhere on this earth," to "double the number" of Drug Enforcement Administration agents, not a promising approach. George Bush, for his part, had repeatedly promised the death penalty, and not only the Pledge of Allegiance but prayer, or "moments of silence," in the schools. "We've got to change this entire culture," he said in the Wake Forest debate; the polls indicated that the electorate wanted "change," and this wish for change had been translated, by both campaigns, into the wish for a "change back," a regression to the "gentler America" of which George Bush repeatedly spoke.

To the extent that there was a "difference" between the candidates, the difference lay in just where on the time scale this "gentler America" could be found. The Dukakis campaign was oriented to "programs," and the programs it proposed were similar to those that had worked (the encouragement of private sector involvement in low-cost housing, say) in the boom years following World War II. The Bush campaign was oriented to "values," and the values to which it referred were those not of a postwar but of a prewar America. In neither case did "ideas" play a part: "This election isn't about ideology, it's about competence," Michael Dukakis had said in Atlanta. "First and foremost, it's a choice between two persons," one of his senior advisers, Thomas Kiley, had told the *Wall Street Journal.* "What it all comes down to, after all the shouting and the cheers, is the man at the desk," George Bush had said in New Orleans. In other words, what it was "about," what it came "down to," what was wrong or right with America, was not a historical shift largely unaffected by the actions of individual citizens but "character," and if "character" could be seen to count, then every citizen—since everyone was a judge of character, an expert in the field of personality—could be seen to count. This notion, that the citizen's choice among determinedly centrist candidates makes a "difference," is in fact the narrative's most central element, and also its most fictive.

3

The Democratic National Convention of 1968, during which the process was put to a popular vote on the streets of Chicago and after which it was decided that what had occurred could not be allowed to recur, is generally agreed to have prompted the multiplication of primaries, and the concomitant coverage of those primaries, which led to the end of the national party convention as a more than ceremonial occasion. Early in 1987, as the primary campaigns got under way for the 1988 election, David S. Broder, in the *Washington Post*, offered this compelling analysis of the power these "reforms" in the nominating procedure had vested not in the party leadership, which is where this power of choice ultimately resides, but in "the existing communications system," by which he meant the press, or the medium through which the party leadership sells its choice:

> Once the campaign explodes to 18 states, as it will the day after New Hampshire, when the focus shifts to a superprimary across the nation, the existing communications system simply will not accommodate more than two or

> three candidates in each party. Neither the television networks, nor newspapers nor magazines, have the resources of people, space and time to describe and analyze the dynamics of two simultaneous half-national elections among Republicans and Democrats. That task is simply beyond us. Since we cannot reduce the number of states voting on Super Tuesday, we have to reduce the number of candidates treated as serious contenders. Those news judgments will be arbitrary—but not subject to appeal. Those who finish first or second in Iowa and New Hampshire will get tickets from the mass media to play in the next big round. Those who don't, won't. A minor exception may be made for the two reverends, Jesse L. Jackson and Marion G. (Pat) Robertson, who have their own church-based communications and support networks and are less dependent on mass-media attention. But no one else.

By the time the existing communications system set itself up in July and August of 1988 in Atlanta and New Orleans, the priorities were clear. "NOTICE NOTICE NOTICE," read the typed note given to some print reporters when they picked up their credentials in Atlanta. "Because the National Democratic Convention Committee permitted the electronic media to exceed specifications for their broadcast booths, your assigned seat's sight line to the podium and the convention floor was obliterated." The network skyboxes, in other words, had been built in front of the sections originally assigned to the periodical press. "This is a place that was chosen to be, for all intents and purposes, a large TV studio, to be able to project our message to the American people and a national audience," Paul Kirk, the chairman of the Democratic National Committee, said by way of explaining why the podium and the skyboxes had so reduced the size of the Omni Coliseum in Atlanta that some thousand delegates and alternates had been, on the evening Jesse Jackson spoke, locked out. Mayor Andrew Young of Atlanta apologized for the lockout, but said that it would be the same on nights to follow: "The one hundred and fifty million people in this country who are going to vote have got to be our major target." Still, convention delegates were seen to have a real role: "The folks in the hall are so important for how it looks," Lane Venardos, senior producer in charge of convention coverage for CBS News, said to the *New York Times* about the Republican convention. The delegates, in other words, could be seen as dress extras.

During those eight summer evenings in 1988, four in Atlanta and four in New Orleans, when roughly 80 percent of the television sets "out there" were tuned somewhere else, the entire attention of those inside the process was directed toward the invention of this story in which they themselves were the principal players, and for which they themselves were the principal audience. The great arenas in which the conventions were held became worlds all their own, constantly transmitting their own images back to themselves, connected by skywalks to interchangeable structures composed not of floors but of "levels," mysteriously separated by fountains and glass elevators and escalators that did not quite connect.

In the Louisiana Superdome in New Orleans as in the Omni Coliseum in Atlanta, the grids of lights blazed and dimmed hypnotically. Men with rifles patrolled the high catwalks. The nets packed with balloons swung gently overhead, poised for that instant known as the "money shot," the moment, or "window," when everything was working and no network had cut to a commercial. Minicams trawled the floor, fishing in Atlanta for Rob Lowe, in New Orleans for Donald Trump. In the NBC skybox Tom Brokaw floated over the floor, adjusting his tie, putting on his jacket, leaning to speak to John Chancellor. In the CNN skybox Mary Alice Williams sat bathed in white light, the blond madonna of the skyboxes. On the television screens in the press section the images reappeared, but from another angle: Tom Brokaw and Mary Alice Williams again, broadcasting not just above us but also to us, the circle closed.

At the end of prime time, when the skyboxes went dark, the action moved across the skywalks and into the levels, into the lobbies, into one or another Hyatt or Marriott or Hilton or Westin. In the portage from lobby to lobby, level to level, the same people kept materializing, in slightly altered roles. On a level of the Hyatt in Atlanta I saw Ann Lewis in her role as a Jackson adviser. On a level of the Hyatt in New Orleans I saw Ann Lewis in her role as a correspondent for *Ms.* Some pictures were vivid: "I've been around this process awhile, and one thing I've noticed, it's the people who write the checks who get treated as if they have a certain amount of power," I recall Nadine Hack, the chairman of Dukakis's New York Finance Council, saying in a suite at the Hyatt in Atlanta: here was a willowy woman with long blond hair standing barefoot on a table and trying to explain how to buy into the action. "The great thing about those evenings was you could even see Michael Harrington there," I recall Richard Viguerie saying to me at a party in New Orleans: here was the man who managed the action for the American right trying to explain the early 1960s, and evenings we had both spent on Washington Square.

There was in Atlanta in 1988, according to the Democratic National Committee, "twice the media presence" that there had been at the 1984 convention. There were in New Orleans "media workspaces" assigned not only to 117 newspapers and news services and to the American television and radio industry in full strength but to fifty-two foreign networks. On every corner one turned in New Orleans someone was doing a stand-up. There were telephone numbers to be called for quotes: "Republican State and Local Officials," or "Pat Robertson Campaign" or "Richard Wirthlin, Reagan's Pollster." Newspapers came with teams of thirty, forty, fifty. In every lobby there were stacks of fresh newspapers, the *Atlanta Constitution*, the *New Orleans Times-Picayune*, the *Washington Post*, the *Miami Herald*, the *Los Angeles Times.* In Atlanta these papers were collected in bins, and "recycled": made into thirty thousand posters, which were in turn distributed to the press in New Orleans.

This perfect recycling tended to present itself, in the narcosis of the event, as a model for the rest: like American political life itself, and like the printed and transmitted images on which that life depended, this was a world with no half-life. It was understood that what was said here would go on the wire and vanish. Garrison Keillor and his cute kids would vanish. Ann Richards and her peppery ripostes would vanish. Phyllis Schlafly and Olympia Snowe would vanish. All the opinions and all the rumors and all the housemaid Spanish spoken in both Atlanta and New Orleans would vanish, all the quotes would vanish, and all that would remain would be the huge arenas themselves, the arenas and the lobbies and the levels and the skywalks to which they connected, the incorporeal heart of the process itself, the agora, the symbolic marketplace in which the narrative was not only written but immediately, efficiently, entirely, consumed.

A certain time lag exists between this world of the arenas and the world as we know it. One evening in New York between the Democratic and Republican conventions I happened to go down to Lafayette Street, to the Public Theater, to look at clips from documentaries on which the English-born filmmaker Richard Leacock had worked during his fifty years in America. We saw folk singers in Virginia in 1941 and oil riggers in Louisiana in 1946 (this was *Louisiana Story*, which Leacock had shot for Robert Flaherty) and tent performers in the corn belt in 1954; we saw Eddy Sachs preparing for the Indianapolis 500 in 1960 and Piri Thomas in Spanish Harlem in 1961. We saw parades, we saw baton twirlers. We saw quints in South Dakota in 1963.

There on the screen at the Public Theater that evening were images and attitudes from an America that had largely vanished, and what was striking was this: these were the very images and attitudes on which "the campaign" was predicated. That "unknown territory" into which George Bush had pushed "with kids and a dog and a car" had existed in this vanished America, and long since been subdivided, cut up for those tract houses on which the people who were not part of the process had made down payments. Michael Dukakis's "snowblower," and both the amusing frugality and the admirable husbandry of resources it was meant to suggest, derived from some half-remembered idea of what citizens of this vanished America had laughed at and admired. "The Pledge" was an issue from that world. "A drug-free America" had perhaps seemed in that world an achievable ideal, as had "better schools." I recall listening in Atlanta to Dukakis's foreign policy expert, Madeleine

Albright, as she conjured up, in the course of arguing against a "no first use" minority plank in the Democratic platform, a scenario in which "Soviet forces overrun Europe" and the United States has, by promising no first use of nuclear weapons, crippled its ability to act: she was talking about a world that had not turned since 1948. What was at work here seemed on the one hand a grave, although in many ways a comfortable, miscalculation of what people in America might have as their deepest concerns in 1988; it seemed on the other hand just another understanding, another of those agreements to overlook the observable.

4

It was into this sedative fantasy of a fixable imperial America that Jesse Jackson rode, on a Trailways bus. "You've never heard a sense of panic sweep the party as it has in the past few days," David Garth had told the *New York Times* during those perilous spring weeks in 1988 when there seemed a real possibility that a black candidate with no experience in elected office, a candidate believed to be so profoundly unelectable that he could take the entire Democratic party down with him, might go to Atlanta with more delegates than any other Democratic candidate. "The party is up against an extraordinary endgame," the pollster Paul Maslin had said. "I don't know where this leaves us," Robert S. Strauss had said. One uncommitted superdelegate, the *New York Times* had reported, "said the Dukakis campaign had changed its message since Mr. Dukakis lost the Illinois primary. Mr. Dukakis is no longer the candidate of 'inevitability' but the candidate of order, he said. 'They're not doing the train's leaving the station and you better be on it routine anymore,' this official said. 'They're now saying that the station's about to be blown up by terrorists and we're the only ones who can defuse the bomb.'"

The threat, or the possibility, presented by Jesse Jackson, the "historic" (as people liked to say after it became certain he would not have the numbers) part of his candidacy, derived from something other than the fact that he was black, a circumstance that had before been and could again be compartmentalized.

For example: "Next week, when we launch our black radio buys, when we start doing our black media stuff, Jesse Jackson needs to be on the air in the black community on our behalf," Donna Brazile of the Dukakis campaign said to the *New York Times* on September 8, 1988, by way of emphasizing how much the Dukakis campaign "sought to make peace" with Jackson.

"Black," in other words, could be useful, and even a moral force, a way for white Americans to attain more perfect attitudes: "His color is an enormous plus. . . . How moving it is, and how important, to see a black candidate meet and overcome the racism that lurks in virtually all of us white Americans," Anthony Lewis had noted in a March 1988 column explaining why the notion that Jesse Jackson could win was nonetheless "a romantic delusion" of the kind that had "repeatedly undermined" the Democratic party. "You look at what Jesse Jackson has done, you have to wonder what a Tom Bradley of Los Angeles could have done, what an Andy Young of Atlanta could have done," I heard someone say on one of the Sunday shows after the Jackson campaign had entered its "historic" (or, in the candidate's word, its "endless") phase.

"Black," then, by itself and in the right context—the "right context" being a reasonable constituency composed exclusively of blacks and supportive liberal whites—could be accommodated by the process. Something less traditional, and also less manageable, was at work in the 1988 Jackson candidacy. I recall having dinner, the weekend before the California primary, at the Pebble Beach house of the chairman of a large American corporation. There were sixteen people at the table, all white, all well-off, all well dressed, all well educated, all socially conservative. During the course of the evening it came to my attention that six of the sixteen, or every one of the registered Democrats present, intended to vote on Tuesday for Jesse Jackson. Their reasons were unspecific, but definite. "I heard him, he didn't sound like a politician," one said. "He's talking about right now," another said. "You get outside the gate here, take a look around, you have to know we've got some problems, and he's talking about them."

What made the 1988 Jackson candidacy a bomb that had to be defused, then, was not that blacks were supporting a black candidate, but that significant numbers of whites were supporting—not only supporting but in many cases overcoming deep emotional and economic conflicts of their own in order to support—a candidate who was attractive to them not because of but in spite of the fact that he was black, a candidate whose most potent attraction was that he "didn't sound like a politician." "Character" seemed not to be, among these voters, the point-of-sale issue the narrative made it out to be: a number of white Jackson supporters to whom I talked would quite serenely describe their candidate as a "con man," or even as, in George Bush's word, a "hustler."

"And yet . . . ," they would say. What "and yet" turned out to mean, almost without variation, was that they were willing to walk off the edge of the known political map for a candidate who was running against, as he repeatedly said, "politics as usual," against what he called "consensualist centrist politics"; against what had come to be the very premise of the process, the notion that the winning of and the maintaining of public office warranted the invention of a public narrative based at no point on observable reality.

In other words they were not idealists, these white Jackson voters, but empiricists. By the time Jesse Jackson got to California, where he would eventually get 25 percent of the entire white vote and 49 percent of the total vote from voters between the demographically key ages of thirty to forty-four, the idealists had rallied behind the sole surviving alternative, who was, accordingly, just then being declared "presidential." In Los Angeles, during May and early June of 1988, those Democrats who had not fallen in line behind Dukakis were described as "self-indulgent," or as "immature"; they were even described, in a dispiriting phrase that prefigured the tenor of the campaign to come, as "issues wimps." I recall talking to a rich and politically well-connected Californian who had been, through the primary campaign there, virtually the only prominent Democrat on the famously liberal west side of Los Angeles who was backing Jackson. He said that he could afford "the luxury of being more interested in issues than in process," but that he would pay for it: "When I want something, I'll have a hard time getting people to pick up the phone. I recognize that. I made the choice."

On the June night in 1988 when Michael Dukakis was declared the winner of the California Democratic primary, and the bomb officially defused, there took place in the Crystal Room of the Biltmore Hotel in Los Angeles a "victory party" that was less a celebration than a ratification by the professionals, a ritual convergence of those California Democrats for whom the phones would continue to get picked up. Charles Manatt was there. John Emerson and Charles Palmer were there. John Van de Kamp was there. Leo McCarthy was there. Robert Shrum was there. All the custom-made suits and monogrammed shirts in Los Angeles that night were there, met in the wide corridors of the Biltmore in order to murmur assurances to one another. The ballroom in fact had been cordoned as if to repel late invaders, roped off in such a way that once the Secret Service, the traveling press, the local press, the visiting national press, the staff, and the candidate had assembled, there would be room for only a controllable handful of celebrants, over whom the cameras would dutifully pan.

In fact the actual "celebrants" that evening were not at the Biltmore at all, but a few blocks away at the Los Angeles Hilton, dancing under the mirrored ceiling of the ballroom in which the Jackson campaign had gathered, its energy level in defeat notably higher than that of other campaigns in victory. Jackson parties tended to spill out of ballrooms onto several levels of whatever hotel they were in, and to last until three or four in the morning: anyone who wanted to be at a Jackson party was welcome at a Jackson party, which was unusual among the campaigns, and tended to reinforce the populist spirit that had given this one its extraordinary animation.

Of that evening at the Los Angeles Hilton I recall a pretty woman in a gold lamé dress, dancing with a baby in her arms. I recall empty beer bottles, Corona and Excalibur and Budweiser, sitting among the loops of television cable. I recall the candidate himself, dancing on the stage, and, on this June evening when the long shot had not come in, this evening when the campaign was effectively over, giving the women in the traveling press the little parody wave they liked to give him, "the press chicks' wave," the stiff-armed palm movement they called "the Nancy Reagan wave"; then taking off his tie and throwing it into the crowd, like a rock star. This was of course a narrative of its own, but a relatively current one, and one that had, because it seemed at some point grounded in the recognizable, a powerful glamour for those estranged from the purposeful nostalgia of the traditional narrative.

In the end the predictable decision was made to go with the process, with predictable, if equivocal, results. On the last afternoon of the 1988 Republican convention in New Orleans I walked from the hotel in the Quarter where I was staying over to Camp Street. I wanted to see 544 Camp, a local point of interest not noted on the points-of-interest maps distributed at the convention but one that figures large in the literature of American conspiracy. "544 Camp Street" was the address stamped on the leaflets Lee Harvey Oswald was distributing around New Orleans between May and September of 1963, the "Fair Play for Cuba Committee" leaflets that, in the years after Lee Harvey Oswald assassinated John F. Kennedy, suggested to some that he had been acting for Fidel Castro and to others that he had been set up to appear to have been acting for Fidel Castro. Guy Banister had his detective agency at 544 Camp. David Ferrie and Jack Martin frequented the coffee shop on the ground floor at 544 Camp. The Cuban Revolutionary Council rented an office at 544 Camp. People had taken the American political narrative seriously at 544 Camp. They had argued about it, fallen out over it, had hit each other over the head with pistol butts over it.

In fact I never found 544 Camp, because there was no more such address: the small building had been bought and torn down in order to construct a new federal courthouse. Across the street in Lafayette Square that afternoon there had been a loudspeaker, and a young man on a makeshift platform talking about abortion, and unwanted babies being put down the Disposall and "clogging the main sewer drains of New Orleans," but no one except me had been there to listen. "Satan —you're the liar," the young woman with him on the platform had sung, lip-syncing a tape originally made, she told me, by a woman who sang with an Alabama traveling ministry, the Ministry of the Happy Hunters. "There's one thing you can't deny . . . you're the father of every lie . . ." The young woman had been wearing a black cape, and was made up to portray Satan, or Death, I was unclear which and it had not seemed a distinction worth pursuing.

Still, there were clouds off the Gulf that day and the air was wet and there was about the melancholy of Camp Street a certain sense of abandoned historic moment, heightened, quite soon, by something unusual: the New Orleans police began lining Camp Street, blocking every intersection from Canal Street west. I noticed a man in uniform on a roof. Before long there were Secret Service agents, with wires in their ears. The candidates, it seemed, would be traveling east on Camp Street on their way from the Republican National Committee Finance Committee Gala (Invitation Only) at the Convention Center to the Ohio Caucus Rally (Media Invited) at the Hilton. I stood for a while on Camp Street, on this corner that might be construed as one of those occasional accidental intersections where the remote narrative had collided with the actual life of the country, and waited until the motorcade itself, entirely and perfectly insulated, a mechanism dedicated like the process for which it stood only to the maintenance of itself, had passed, and then I walked to the Superdome. "I hear he did OK with Brinkley," they said that night in the Superdome, and, then, as the confetti fell, "Quayle, zip."

—1988

Shooters Inc.

In August of 1986, George Bush, traveling in his role as vice president of the United States and accompanied by his staff, the Secret Service, the traveling press, and a personal camera crew wearing baseball caps reading "Shooters, Inc." and working on a $10,000 retainer paid by a Bush PAC called the Fund for America's Future, spent several days in Israel and Jordan. The schedule in Israel included, according to reports in the *Los Angeles Times* and the *New York Times*, shoots at the Western Wall, at the Holocaust memorial, at David Ben-Gurion's tomb, and at thiry-two other locations chosen to produce campaign footage illustrating that George Bush was, as Marlin Fitzwater, at that time the vice-presidential press secretary, put it, "familiar with the issues." The Shooters, Inc. crew did not go on to Jordan (there was, an official explained to the *Los Angeles Times*, "nothing to be gained from showing him schmoozing with Arabs"), but the Bush advance team had nonetheless directed, in Amman, considerable attention toward improved visuals for the traveling press. The advance team had requested, for example, that the Jordanian army marching band change its uniforms from white to red; that the Jordanians, who did not have enough helicopters to transport the press, borrow some from the Israeli air force; that, in order to provide the color of live military action behind the vice president, the Jordanians stage maneuvers at a sensitive location overlooking Israel and the Golan Heights; that the Jordanians raise the American flag over their base there; that Bush be photographed looking through binoculars studying "enemy territory," a shot ultimately vetoed by the State Department since the "enemy territory" at hand was Israel; and, possibly the most arresting detail, that camels be present at every stop on the itinerary.

Some months later I happened to be in Amman, and mentioned reading about this Bush trip to several officials at the American embassy there. They could have, it was agreed, "cordially killed" the reporters in question, particularly Charles P. Wallace from the *Los Angeles Times*, but the reports themselves had been accurate. "You didn't hear this, but they didn't write half of it," one said.

This is in fact the kind of story we expect to hear about our elected officials. We not only expect them to use other nations as changeable scrims in the theater of domestic politics but encourage them to do so. After the April failure of the Bay of Pigs in 1961, John Kennedy's job approval rating was four points higher than it had been in March. After the 1965 intervention in the Dominican Republic, Lyndon Johnson's job approval rating rose six points. After the 1983 invasion of Grenada, Ronald Reagan's job approval rating rose four points, and what was that winter referred to in Washington as "Lebanon"—the sending of American Marines into Beirut, the killing of the 241, and the subsequent pullout—was, in the afterglow of this certified success in the Caribbean, largely forgotten. "Gemayel could fall tonight and it would be a two-day story," I recall David Gergen saying a few months later. In May of 1984, Francis X. Clines of the *New York Times* described the view taken by James Baker, who was routinely described during his years in the Reagan White House as "the ultimate pragmatist," a manager of almost supernatural executive ability: "In attempting action in Lebanon, Baker argues, President Reagan avoided another 'impotent' episode, such as the taking of American hostages in Iran, and in withdrawing the Marines, the President avoided another 'Vietnam' . . . 'Pulling the Marines out put the lie to the argument that the President's trigger-happy,' he [Baker] said." The "issue," in other words, was one of preserving faith in President Reagan at home, a task that, after the ultimate pragmatist left the White House, fell into the hands of the less adroit.

History is context. At a moment when the nation had seen control of its economy pass to its creditors and when the administration-elect had for political reasons severely limited its ability to regain that control, this extreme reliance on the efficacy of faith over works meant something different from what it might have meant in 1984 or 1980. On the night in New Orleans in August of 1988 when George Bush accepted the Republican nomination and spoke of his intention to "speak for freedom, stand for freedom, and be a patient friend to anyone, east or west, who will fight for freedom," the word "patient" was construed by some in the Louisiana Superdome as an abandonment of the Reagan Doctrine, a suggestion that a Bush administration would play a passive rather than an active role in any dreams of rollback. This overlooked the real nature of the Reagan Doctrine, the usefulness of which to the Reagan administration was exclusively political.

Administrations with little room to maneuver at home have historically looked for sideshows abroad, for the creation of what the pollsters call "a dramatic event," an external crisis, preferably one so remote that it remains an abstraction. On the evening of the November 1988 election and on several evenings that followed, I happened to sit at dinner next to men with considerable experience in the financial community. They were agreed that the foreign markets would allow the new Bush administration, which was seen to have limited its options by promising for political reasons not to raise taxes, only a limited time before calling in the markers; they disagreed only as to the length of that time and to the nature of the downturn. One thought perhaps two years, another six months. Some saw a "blowout" ("blowout" was a word used a good deal), others saw a gradual tightening, a transition to the era of limited expectations of which Jerry Brown had spoken when he was governor of California.

These men were, among themselves, uniformly pessimistic. They saw a situation in which the space available for domestic maneuvering had been reduced to zero. In this light it did not seem encouraging that George Bush, on the Thursday he left for his post-election Florida vacation, found time to meet not with those investors around the world who were sending him a message that week (the dollar was again dropping against the yen, against the mark, and against the pound; the Dow was dropping 78.47 points), not with the Germans, not with the Japanese, not even with anyone from the American financial community, but with representatives of the Afghan resistance. "Once in a while I think about those things, but not much," the president-elect told a CBS News crew which asked him, a few days later in Florida, about the falling market.

—1988

CALIFORNIA

Girl of the Golden West

THE DOMESTIC details spring to memory. Early on the evening of February 4, 1974, in her duplex apartment at 2603 Benvenue in Berkeley, Patricia Campbell Hearst, age nineteen, a student of art history at the University of California at Berkeley and a granddaughter of the late William Randolph Hearst, put on a blue terry-cloth bathrobe, heated a can of chicken-noodle soup and made tuna fish sandwiches for herself and her fiancé, Steven Weed; watched "Mission Impossible" and "The Magician" on television; cleaned up the dishes; sat down to study just as the doorbell rang; was abducted at gunpoint and held blindfolded, by three men and five women who called themselves the Symbionese Liberation Army, for the next fifty-seven days.

From the fifty-eighth day, on which she agreed to join her captors and was photographed in front of the SLA's cobra flag carrying a sawed-off M-1 carbine, until September 18, 1975, when she was arrested in San Francisco, Patricia Campbell Hearst participated actively in the robberies of the Hibernia Bank in San Francisco and the Crocker National Bank outside Sacramento; sprayed Crenshaw Boulevard in Los Angeles with a submachine gun to cover a comrade apprehended for shoplifting; and was party or witness to a number of less publicized thefts and several bombings, to which she would later refer as "actions," or "operations."

On trial in San Francisco for the Hibernia Bank operation she appeared in court wearing frosted-white nail polish, and demonstrated for the jury the bolt action necessary to chamber an M-1. On a psychiatric test administered while she was in custody she completed the sentence "Most men . . ." with the words ". . . are assholes." Seven years later she was living with the bodyguard she had married, their infant daughter, and two German shepherds "behind locked doors in a Spanish-style house equipped with the best electronic security system available," describing herself as "older and wiser," and dedicating her account of these events, *Every Secret Thing*, to "Mom and Dad."

It was a special kind of sentimental education, a public coming-of-age with an insistently literary cast to it, and it seemed at the time to offer a parable for the period. Certain of its images entered the national memory. We had Patricia Campbell Hearst in her first-communion dress, smiling, and we had Patricia Campbell Hearst in the Hibernia Bank surveillance stills, not smiling. We again had her smiling in the engagement picture, an unremarkably pretty girl in a simple dress on a sunny lawn, and we again had her not smiling in the "Tania" snapshot, the famous Polaroid with the M-1. We had her with her father and her sister Anne in a photograph taken at the Burlingame Country Club some months before the kidnapping: all three Hearsts smiling there, not only smiling but wearing leis, the father in maile and orchid leis, the daughters in pikake, that rarest and most expensive kind of lei, strand after strand of tiny Arabian jasmine buds strung like ivory beads.

We had the bank of microphones in front of the Hillsborough house whenever Randolph and Catherine Hearst ("Dad" and "Mom" in the first spectral messages from the absent daughter, "pig Hearsts" as the spring progressed) met the press, the potted flowers on the steps changing with the seasons, domestic upkeep intact in the face of crisis: azaleas, fuchsias, then cymbidium orchids massed for Easter. We had, early on, the ugly images of looting and smashed cameras and frozen turkey legs hurled through windows in West Oakland, the violent result of the Hearsts' first attempt to meet the SLA ransom demand, and we had, on television the same night, the news that William Knowland, the former United States senator from California and the most prominent member of the family that had run Oakland for half a century, had taken the pistol he was said to carry as protection against terrorists, positioned himself on a bank of the Russian River, and blown off the top of his head.

All of these pictures told a story, taught a dramatic lesson, carrying as they did the *frisson* of one another, the invitation to compare and contrast. The image of Patricia Campbell Hearst on the FBI "wanted" fliers was for example cropped from the image of the unremarkably pretty girl in the simple dress on the sunny lawn, schematic evidence that even a golden girl could be pinned in the beam of history. There was no actual connection between turkey legs thrown through windows in West Oakland and William Knowland lying facedown in the Russian River, but the paradigm was manifest, one California busy being born and another busy dying. Those cymbidiums on the Hearsts' doorstep in Hillsborough dissolved before our eyes into the image of a flaming palm tree in south-central Los Angeles (the model again was two Californias), the palm tree above the stucco bungalow in which Patricia Campbell Hearst was believed for a time to be burning to death on live television. (Actually Patricia Campbell Hearst was in yet a third California, a motel room at Disneyland, watching the palm tree burn as we all were, on television, and it was Donald DeFreeze, Nancy Ling Perry, Angela Atwood, Patricia Soltysik, Camilla Hall, and William Wolfe, one black escaped convict and five children of the white middle class, who were dying in the stucco bungalow.)

Not only the images but the voice told a story, the voice on the tapes, the depressed voice with the California inflection, the voice that trailed off, now almost inaudible, then a hint of whine, a schoolgirl's sarcasm, a voice every parent recognized: *Mom, Dad. I'm OK. I had a few scrapes and stuff, but they washed them up. . . . I just hope you'll do what they say, Dad. . . . If you can get the food thing organized before the nineteenth then that's OK. . . . Whatever you come up with is basically OK, it was never intended that you feed the whole state. . . . I am here because I am a member of a ruling-class family and I think you can begin to see the analogy. . . . People should stop acting like I'm dead, Mom should get out of her black dress, that doesn't help at all. . . . Mom, Dad . . . I don't believe you're doing all you can . . . Mom, Dad . . . I'm starting to think that no one is concerned about me anymore. . . .* And then: *Greetings to the people. This is Tania.*

Patricia Campbell Hearst's great-grandfather had arrived in California by foot in 1850, unschooled, unmarried, thirty years old with few graces and no prospects, a Missouri farmer's son who would spend his thirties scratching around El Dorado and Nevada and Sacramento counties looking for a stake. In 1859 he found one, and at his death in 1891 George Hearst could leave the schoolteacher he had married in 1862 a fortune taken from the ground, the continuing proceeds from the most productive mines of the period, the Ophir in Nevada, the Homestake in South Dakota, the Ontario in Utah, the Anaconda in Montana, the San Luis in Mexico. The widow, Phoebe Apperson Hearst, a tiny, strong-minded woman then only forty-eight years old, took this apparently artesian income and financed her only child in the publishing empire he wanted, underwrote a surprising amount of the campus where her great-granddaughter would be enrolled at the time she was kidnapped, and built for herself, on sixty-seven thousand acres on the McCloud River in Siskiyou County, the original Wyntoon, a quarried-lava castle of which its architect, Bernard Maybeck, said simply: "Here you can reach all that is within you."

The extent to which certain places dominate the California imagination is apprehended, even by Californians, only dimly. Deriving not only from the landscape but from the claiming of it, from the romance of emigration, the radical abandonment of established attachments, this imagination remains obdurately symbolic, tending to locate lessons in what the rest of the country perceives only as scenery. Yosemite, for example, remains what Kevin Starr has called "one of the primary California symbols, a fixed factor of identity for all those who sought a primarily Californian aesthetic." Both the community of and the coastline at Carmel have a symbolic meaning lost to the contemporary visitor, a lingering allusion to art as freedom, freedom as craft, the "bohemian" pantheism of the early twentieth century. The Golden Gate Bridge, referring as it does to both the infinite and technology, suggests, to the Californian, a quite complex representation of land's end, and also of its beginning.

Patricia Campbell Hearst told us in *Every Secret Thing* that the place the Hearsts called Wyntoon was "a mystical land," "fantastic, otherworldly," "even more than San Simeon," which was in turn "so emotionally moving that it is still beyond my powers of description." That first Maybeck castle on the McCloud River was seen by most Californians only in photographs, and yet, before it burned in 1933, to be replaced by a compound of rather more playful Julia Morgan chalets ("Cinderella House," "Angel House," "Brown Bear House"), Phoebe Hearst's gothic Wyntoon and her son's baroque San Simeon seemed between them to embody certain opposing impulses in the local consciousness: northern and southern, wilderness sanctified and wilderness banished, the aggrandizement of nature and the aggrandizement of self. Wyntoon had mists, and allusions to the infinite, great trunks of trees left to rot where they fell, a wild river, barbaric fireplaces. San Simeon, swimming in sunlight and the here and now, had two swimming pools, and a zoo.

It was a family in which the romantic impulse would seem to have dimmed. Patricia Campbell Hearst told us that she "grew up in an atmosphere of clear blue skies, bright sunshine, rambling open spaces, long green lawns, large comfortable houses, country clubs with swimming pools and tennis courts and riding horses." At the Convent of the Sacred Heart in Menlo Park she told a nun to "go to hell," and thought herself "quite courageous, although very stupid." At Santa Catalina in Monterey she and Patricia Tobin, whose family founded one of the banks the SLA would later rob, skipped Benediction, and received "a load of demerits." Her father taught her to shoot, duck hunting. Her mother did not allow her to wear jeans into San Francisco. These were inheritors who tended to keep their names out of the paper, to exhibit not much interest in the world at large ("Who the hell is this guy again?" Randolph Hearst asked Steven Weed when the latter suggested trying to approach the SLA through Regis Debray, and then, when told, said, "We need a goddamn South American revolutionary mixed up in this thing like a hole in the head"), and to regard most forms of distinction with the reflexive distrust of the country club.

Yet if the Hearsts were no longer a particularly arresting California family, they remained embedded in the symbolic content of the place, and for a Hearst to be kidnapped from Berkeley, the very citadel of Phoebe Hearst's aspiration, was California as opera. "My thoughts at this time were focused on the single issue of survival," the heiress to Wyntoon and

San Simeon told us about the fifty-seven days she spent in the closet. "Concerns over love and marriage, family life, friends, human relationships, my whole previous life, had really become, in SLA terms, bourgeois luxuries."

This abrupt sloughing of the past has, to the California ear, a distant echo, and the echo is of emigrant diaries. "Don't let this letter dishearten anybody, never take no cutoffs and hurry along as fast as you can," one of the surviving children of the Donner Party concluded her account of that crossing. "Don't worry about it," the author of *Every Secret Thing* reported having told herself in the closet after her first sexual encounter with a member of the SLA. "Don't examine your feelings. Never examine your feelings—they're no help at all." At the time Patricia Campbell Hearst was on trial in San Francisco, a number of psychiatrists were brought in to try to plumb what seemed to some an unsoundable depth in the narrative, that moment at which the victim binds over her fate to her captors. "She experienced what I call the death anxiety and the breaking point," Robert Jay Lifton, who was one of these psychiatrists, said. "Her external points of reference for maintenance of her personality had disappeared," Louis Jolyon West, another of the psychiatrists, said. Those were two ways of looking at it, and another was that Patricia Campbell Hearst had cut her losses and headed west, as her great-grandfather had before her.

The story she told in 1982 in *Every Secret Thing* was received, in the main, querulously, just as it had been when she told it during *The United States of America v. Patricia Campbell Hearst*, the 1976 proceeding during which she was tried for and convicted of the armed robbery of the Hibernia Bank (one count) and (the second count), the use of a weapon during the commission of a felony. Laconic, slightly ironic, resistant not only to the prosecution but to her own defense, Patricia Hearst was not, on trial in San Francisco, a conventionally ingratiating personality. "I don't know," I recall her saying over and over again during the few days I attended the trial. "I don't remember." "I suppose so." Had there not been, the prosecutor asked one day, telephones in the motels in which she had stayed when she drove across the country with Jack Scott? I recall Patricia Hearst looking at him as if she thought him deranged. I recall Randolph Hearst looking at the floor. I recall Catherine Hearst arranging a Galanos jacket over the back of her seat.

"Yes, I'm sure," their daughter said.

Where, the prosecutor asked, were these motels?

"One was . . . I think . . ." Patricia Hearst paused, and then: "Cheyenne? Wyoming?" She pronounced the names as if they were foreign, exotic, information registered and jettisoned. One of these motels had been in Nevada, the place from which the Hearst money originally came: the heiress pronounced the name *Nevahda*, like a foreigner.

In *Every Secret Thing* as at her trial, she seemed to project an emotional distance, a peculiar combination of passivity and pragmatic recklessness ("I had crossed over. And I would have to make the best of it . . . to live from day to day, to do whatever they said, to play my part, and to pray that I would survive") that many people found inexplicable and irritating. In 1982 as in 1976, she spoke only abstractly about *why*, but quite specifically about *how*. "I could not believe that I had actually fired that submachine gun," she said of the incident in which she shot up Crenshaw Boulevard, but here was how she did it: "I kept my finger pressed on the trigger until the entire clip of thirty shots had been fired. . . . I then reached for my own weapon, the semiautomatic carbine. I got off three more shots . . ."

And, after her book as after her trial, the questions raised were not exactly about her veracity but about her authenticity, her general intention, about whether she was, as the assistant prosecutor put it during the trial, "for real." This was necessarily a vain line of inquiry (whether or not she "loved" William Wolfe was the actual point on which the trial came to turn), and one that encouraged a curious rhetorical regression among the inquisitors. "Why did she choose to write this book?" Mark Starr asked about *Every Secret Thing* in *Newsweek*, and then answered himself: "Possibly she has inherited her family's journalistic sense of what will sell." "The rich get richer," Jane Alpert concluded in *New York* magazine. "Patty," Ted Morgan observed in the *New York Times Book Review*, "is now, thanks to the proceeds of her book, reverting to a more traditional family pursuit, capital formation."

These were dreamy notions of what a Hearst might do to turn a dollar, but they reflected a larger dissatisfaction, a conviction that the Hearst in question was telling less than the whole story, "leaving something out," although what the something might have been, given the doggedly detailed account offered in *Every Secret Thing*, would be hard to define. If "questions still linger," as they did for *Newsweek*, those questions were not about how to lace a bullet with cyanide: the way the SLA did it was to drill into the lead tip to a point just short of the gunpowder, dip the tiny hole in a mound of cyanide crystals, and seal it with paraffin. If *Every Secret Thing* "creates more puzzles than it solves," as it did for Jane Alpert, those questions were not about how to make a pipe bomb: the trick here was to pack enough gunpowder into the pipe for a big bang and still leave sufficient oxygen for ignition, a problem, as Patricia Hearst saw it, of "devising the proper proportions of gunpowder, length of pipe and toaster wire, minus Teko's precious toilet paper." "Teko," or Bill Harris, insisted on packing his bombs with toilet paper, and, when one of them failed to explode under a police car in the Mission District, reacted with "one of his worst temper tantrums." Many reporters later found Bill and Emily Harris the appealing defendants that Patricia Hearst never was, but *Every Secret Thing* presented a convincing case for their being, as the author put it, not only "unattractive" but, her most pejorative adjective, "incompetent."

As notes from the underground go, Patricia Hearst's were eccentric in detail. She told us that Bill Harris's favorite television program was "S.W.A.T." (one could, he said, "learn a lot about the pigs' tactics by watching these programs"); that Donald DeFreeze, or "Cinque," drank plum wine from half-gallon jugs and listened to the radio for allusions to the revolution in song lyrics; and that Nancy Ling Perry, who was usually cast by the press in the rather glamorous role of "former cheerleader and Goldwater Girl," was four feet eleven inches tall, and affected a black accent. Emily Harris trained herself to "live with deprivation" by chewing only half sticks of gum. Bill Harris bought a yarmulke, under the impression that this was the way, during the sojourn in the Catskills after the Los Angeles shootout, to visit Grossinger's unnoticed.

Life with these people had the distorted logic of dreams, and Patricia Hearst seems to have accepted it with the wary acquiescence of the dreamer. Any face could turn against her. Any move could prove lethal. "My sisters and I had been brought up to believe that we were responsible for what we did and could not blame our transgressions on something being wrong inside our heads. I had joined the SLA because if I didn't they would have killed me. And I remained with them because I truly believed that the FBI would kill me if they could, and if not, the SLA would." She had, as she put it, crossed over. She would, as she put it, make the best of it, and not "reach back to family or friends."

This was the point on which most people foundered, doubted her, found her least explicable, and it was also the point at which she was most specifically the child of a certain culture. Here is the single personal note in an emigrant diary kept by a relative of mine, William Kilgore, the journal of an overland crossing to Sacramento in 1850: "This is one of the trying mornings for me, as I now have to leave my family, or back out. Suffice it to say, we started." Suffice it to say. Don't examine your feelings, they're no help at all. Never take no cutoffs and hurry along as fast as you can. We need a goddamn South American revolutionary mixed up in this thing like a hole in the head. This was a California girl, and she was raised on a history that placed not much emphasis on *why*.

She was never an idealist, and this pleased no one. She was tainted by survival. She came back from the other side with a story no one wanted to hear, a dispiriting account of a situation in which delusion and incompetence were pitted against delusion and incompetence of another kind, and in the febrile rhythms of San Francisco in the midseventies it seemed a story devoid of high notes. The week her trial ended in 1976, the *San Francisco Bay Guardian* published an interview in which members of a collective called New Dawn expressed regret at her defection. "It's a question of your self-respect or your ass," one of them said. "If you choose your ass, you live with nothing." This idea that the SLA represented an idea worth defending (if only on the grounds that any idea must be better than none) was common enough at the time, although most people granted that the idea had gone awry. By March of 1977 another writer in the *Bay Guardian* was making a distinction between the "unbridled adventurism" of the SLA and the "discipline and skill" of the New World Liberation Front, whose "fifty-odd bombings without a casualty" made them a "definitely preferable alternative" to the SLA.

As it happened I had kept this issue of the *Bay Guardian*, dated March 31, 1977 (the *Bay Guardian* was not at the time a notably radical paper, by the way, but one that provided a fair guide to local tofu cookery and the mood of the community), and when I got it out to look at the piece on the SLA I noticed for the first time another piece: a long and favorable report on a San Francisco minister whose practice it was to "confront people and challenge their basic assumptions . . . as if he can't let the evil of the world pass him by, a characteristic he shares with other moral leaders." The minister, who was compared at one point to Cesar Chavez, was responsible, according to the writer, for a "mind-boggling" range of social service programs—food distribution, legal aid, drug rehabilitation, nursing homes, free Pap smears—as well as for a "twenty-seven-thousand-acre agricultural station." The agricultural station was in Guyana, and the minister of course was the Reverend Jim Jones, who eventually chose self-respect over his own and nine hundred other asses. This was another local opera, and one never spoiled by a protagonist who insisted on telling it her way.

—1982

Pacific Distances

A GOOD PART of any day in Los Angeles is spent driving, alone, through streets devoid of meaning to the driver, which is one reason the place exhilarates some people, and floods others with an amorphous unease. There is about these hours spent in transit a seductive unconnectedness. Conventional information is missing. Context clues are missing. In Culver City as in Echo Park as in East Los Angeles, there are the same pastel bungalows. There are the same leggy poinsettia and the same trees of pink and yellow hibiscus. There are the same laundromats, body shops, strip shopping malls, the same travel agencies offering bargain fares on LACSA and TACA. *San Salvador*, the signs promise, on Beverly Boulevard as on Pico as on Alvarado and Soto. *¡No más barata!* There is the same sound, that of the car radio, tuned in my case to KRLA, an AM station that identifies itself as "the heart and soul of rock and roll" and is given to dislocating programming concepts, for example doing the top hits ("Baby, It's You," "Break It to Me Gently," "The Lion Sleeps Tonight") of 1962. Another day, another KRLA concept: "The Day the Music Died," an exact radio recreation of the day in 1959, including news breaks (Detroit may market compacts), when the plane carrying Buddy Holly, Ritchie Valens, and the Big Bopper crashed near Clear Lake, Iowa. A few days later, KRLA reports a solid response on "The Day the Music Died," including "a call from Ritchie Valens's aunt."

Such tranced hours are, for many people who live in Los Angeles, the dead center of being there, but there is nothing in them to encourage the normal impulse toward "recognition," or narrative connection. Those glosses on the human comedy (the widow's heartbreak, the bad cop, the mother-and-child reunion) that lend dramatic structure to more traditional forms of urban life are hard to come by here. There are, in the pages of the Los Angeles newspapers, no Crack Queens, no Coma Moms or Terror Tots. Events may be lurid, but are rarely personalized. "Mother Apologizes to Her Child, Drives Both Off Cliff," a headline read in the *Los*

Angeles Times one morning in December 1988. (Stories like this are relegated in the *Times* either to the Metro Section or to page three, which used to be referred to as "the freak-death page," not its least freaky aspect being that quite arresting accounts of death by Clorox or by rattlesnake or by Dumpster tended to appear and then vanish, with no follow-up.) Here was the story, which had to do with a young woman who had lived with her daughter, Brooke, in a Redondo Beach condominium and was said by a neighbor to have "looked like she was a little down":

> A Redondo Beach woman apologized to her 7-year-old daughter, then apparently tried to take both their lives by driving over a cliff in the Malibu area Tuesday morning, authorities said. The mother, identified by the county coroner's office as Susan Sinclair, 29, was killed, but the child survived without serious injury. "I'm sorry I have to do this," the woman was quoted as telling the child just before she suddenly swerved off Malibu Canyon Road about 2½ miles north of Pacific Coast Highway.

"I'm sorry I have to do this." This was the last we heard of Susan and Brooke Sinclair. When I first moved to Los Angeles from New York, in 1964, I found this absence of narrative a deprivation. At the end of two years I realized (quite suddenly, alone one morning in the car) that I had come to find narrative sentimental. This remains a radical difference between the two cities, and also between the ways in which the residents of those cities view each other.

2

Our children remind us of how random our lives have been. I had occasion in 1979 to speak at my daughter's school in Los Angeles, and I stood there, apparently a grown woman, certainly a woman who had stood up any number of times and spoken to students around the country, and tried to confront a question that suddenly seemed to me almost impenetrable: How had I become a writer, how and why had I made the particular choices I had made in my life? I could see my daughter's friends in the back of the room, Claudia, Julie, Anna. I could see my daughter herself, flushed with embarrassment, afraid, she told me later, that her presence would make me forget what I meant to say.

I could tell them only that I had no more idea of how I had become a writer than I had had, at their age, of how I would become a writer. I could tell them only about the fall of 1954, when I was nineteen and a junior at Berkeley and one of perhaps a dozen students admitted to the late Mark Schorer's English 106A, a kind of "fiction workshop" that met for discussion three hours a week and required that each student produce, over the course of the semester, at least five short stories. No auditors were allowed. Voices were kept low. English 106A was widely regarded in the fall of 1954 as a kind of sacramental experience, an initiation into the grave world of real writers, and I remember each meeting of this class as an occasion of acute excitement and dread. I remember each other member of this class as older and wiser than I had hope of ever being (it had not yet struck me in any visceral way that being nineteen was not a long-term proposition, just as it had not yet struck Claudia and Julie and Anna and my daughter that they would recover from being thirteen), not only older and wiser but more experienced, more independent, more interesting, more possessed of an exotic past: marriages and the breaking up of marriages, money and the lack of it, sex and politics and the Adriatic seen at dawn: not only the stuff of grown-up life itself but, more poignantly to me at the time, the very stuff that might be transubstantiated into five short stories. I recall a Trotskyist, then in his forties. I recall a young woman who lived, with a barefoot man and a large white dog, in an attic lit only by candles. I recall classroom discussions that ranged over meetings with Paul and Jane Bowles, incidents involving Djuna Barnes, years spent in Paris, in Beverly Hills, in the Yucatán, on the Lower East Side of New York and on Repulse Bay and even on morphine. I had spent seventeen of my nineteen years more or less in Sacramento, and the other two in the Tri Delt house on Warring Street in Berkeley. I had never read Paul or Jane Bowles, let alone met them, and when, some fifteen years later at a friend's house in Santa Monica Canyon, I did meet Paul Bowles, I was immediately rendered as dumb and awestruck as I had been at nineteen in English 106A.

I suppose that what I really wanted to say that day at my daughter's school is that we never reach a point at which our lives lie before us as a clearly marked open road, never have and never should expect a map to the years ahead, never do close those circles that seem, at thirteen and fourteen and nineteen, so urgently in need of closing. I wanted to tell my daughter and her friends, but did not, about going back to the English department at Berkeley in the spring of 1975 as a Regents' Lecturer, a reversal of positions that should have been satisfying but proved unsettling, moved me profoundly, answered no questions but raised the same old ones. In Los Angeles in 1975 I had given every appearance of being well settled, grown-up, a woman in definite charge of her own work and of a certain kind of bourgeois household that made working possible. In Berkeley in 1975 I had unpacked my clothes and papers in a single room at the Faculty Club, walked once across campus, and regressed, immediately and helplessly, into the ghetto life of the student I had been twenty years before. I hoarded nuts and bits of chocolate in my desk drawer. I ate tacos for dinner (combination plates, *con arroz y frijoles*), wrapped myself in my bedspread and read until two A.M., smoked too many cigarettes and regretted, like a student, only their cost. I found myself making daily notes, as carefully as I had when I was an undergraduate, of expenses, and my room at the Faculty Club was littered with little scraps of envelopes:

$1.15, papers, etc.
$2.85, taco plate
$ .50, tips
$ .15, coffee

I fell not only into the habits but into the moods of the student day. Every morning I was hopeful, determined, energized by the campanile bells and by the smell of eucalyptus and by the day's projected accomplishments. On the way to breakfast I would walk briskly, breathe deeply, review my "plans" for the day: I would write five pages, return all calls, lunch on raisins and answer ten letters. I would at last read E. H. Gombrich. I would once and for all get the meaning of the word "structuralist." And yet every afternoon by four o'clock, the hour when I met my single class, I was once again dulled, glazed, sunk in an excess of carbohydrates and in my own mediocrity, in my failure—still, after twenty years!—to "live up to" the day's possibilities.

In certain ways nothing at all had changed in those twenty years. The clean light and fogs were exactly as I had remembered. The creek still ran clear among the shadows, the rhododendron still bloomed in the spring. On the bulletin boards in the English department there were still notices inviting the reader to apply to Mrs. Diggory Venn for information on the Radcliffe Publishing Procedures course. The less securely tenured members of the department still yearned for dramatic moves to Johns Hopkins. Anything specific was rendered immediately into a general principle. Anything concrete was rendered abstract. That the spring of 1975 was, outside Berkeley, a season of remarkably specific and operatically concrete events seemed, on the campus, another abstract, another illustration of a general tendency, an instance tending only to confirm or not confirm one or another idea of the world. The wire photos from Phnom Penh and Saigon seemed as deliberately composed as symbolist paintings. The question of whether one spoke of Saigon "falling" or of Saigon's "liberation" reduced the fact to a political attitude, a semantic question, another idea.

Days passed. I adopted a shapeless blazer and no makeup. I remember spending considerable time, that spring of 1975, trying to break the code that Telegraph Avenue seemed to present. There, just a block or two off the campus, the campus with its five thousand courses, its four million books, its five million manuscripts, the campus with its cool glades and clear creeks and lucid views, lay this mean wasteland of small venture capital, this unweeded garden in which everything cost more than it was worth. Coffee on Telegraph Avenue was served neither hot nor cold. Food was slopped lukewarm onto chipped plates. Pita bread was stale, curries were rank. Tatty "Indian" stores offered faded posters and shoddy silks. Bookstores featured sections on the occult. Drug buys were in progress up and down the street. The place was an illustration of some tropism toward disorder, and I seemed to understand it no better in 1975 than I had as an undergraduate.

I remember trying to discuss Telegraph Avenue with some

people from the English department, but they were discussing a paper we had heard on the plotting of *Vanity Fair*, *Middlemarch*, and *Bleak House*. I remember trying to discuss Telegraph Avenue with an old friend who had asked me to dinner, at a place far enough off campus to get a drink, but he was discussing Jane Alpert, Eldridge Cleaver, Daniel Ellsberg, Shana Alexander, a Modesto rancher of his acquaintance, Jules Feiffer, Herbert Gold, Herb Caen, Ed Janss, and the movement for independence in Micronesia. I remember thinking that I was still, after twenty years, out of step at Berkeley, the victim of a different drummer. I remember sitting in my office in Wheeler Hall one afternoon when someone, not a student, walked in off the street. He said that he was a writer, and I asked what he had written. "Nothing you'll ever dare to read," he said. He admired only Céline and Djuna Barnes. With the exception of Djuna Barnes, women could not write. It was possible that I could write but he did not know, he had not read me. "In any case," he added, sitting on the edge of my desk, "your time's gone, your fever's over." It had probably been a couple of decades, English 106A, since I last heard about Céline and Djuna Barnes and how women could not write, since I last encountered this particular brand of extraliterary machismo, and after my caller had left the office I locked the door and sat there a long time in the afternoon light. At nineteen I had wanted to write. At forty I still wanted to write, and nothing that had happened in the years between made me any more certain that I could.

3

Etcheverry Hall, half a block uphill from the north gate of the University of California at Berkeley, is one of those postwar classroom and office buildings that resemble parking structures and seem designed to suggest that nothing extraordinary has been or will be going on inside. On Etcheverry's east terrace, which is paved with pebbled concrete and bricks, a few students usually sit studying or sunbathing. There are benches, there is grass. There are shrubs and a small tree. There is a net for volleyball, and, on the day in late 1979 when I visited Etcheverry, someone had taken a piece of chalk and printed the word RADIATION on the concrete beneath the net, breaking the letters in a way that looked stenciled and official and scary. In fact it was here, directly below the volleyball court on Etcheverry's east terrace, that the Department of Nuclear Engineering's TRIGA Mark III nuclear reactor, light-water cooled and reflected, went critical, or achieved a sustained nuclear reaction, on August 10, 1966, and had been in continuous operation since. People who wanted to see the reactor dismantled said that it was dangerous, that it could emit deadly radiation and that it was perilously situated just forty yards west of the Hayward Fault. People who ran the reactor said that it was not dangerous, that any emission of measurable radioactivity was extremely unlikely and that "forty yards west of" the Hayward Fault was a descriptive phrase without intrinsic seismological significance. (This was an assessment with which seismologists agreed.) These differences of opinion represented a difference not only in the meaning of words but in cultures, a difference in images and probably in expectations.

Above the steel door to the reactor room in the basement of Etcheverry Hall was a sign that glowed either green or Roman violet, depending on whether what it said was SAFE ENTRY, which meant that the air lock between the reactor room and the corridor was closed and the radiation levels were normal and the level of pool water was normal, or UNSAFE ENTRY, which meant that at least one of these conditions, usually the first, had not been met. The sign on the steel door itself read only ROOM 1140 / EXCLUSION AREA / ENTRY LIST A, B, OR C / CHECK WITH RECEPTIONIST. On the day I visited Etcheverry I was issued a dosimeter to keep in my pocket, then shown the reactor by Tek Lim, at that time the reactor manager, and Lawrence Grossman, a professor of nuclear engineering. They explained that the Etcheverry TRIGA was a modification of the original TRIGA, which is an acronym for Training/Research/Isotopes/General Atomic, and was designed in 1956 by a team, including Edward Teller and Theodore Taylor and Freeman Dyson, that had set for itself the task of making a reactor so safe, in Freeman Dyson's words, "that it could be given to a bunch of high school children to play with, without any fear that they would get hurt."

They explained that the TRIGA operated at a much lower heat level than a power reactor, and was used primarily for "making things radioactive." Nutritionists, for example, used it to measure trace elements in diet. Archaeologists used it for dating. NASA used it for high-altitude pollution studies, and for a study on how weightlessness affects human calcium metabolism. Stanford was using it to study lithium in the brain. Physicists from the Lawrence Berkeley Laboratory, up the hill, had been coming down to use it for experiments in the development of a fusion, or "clean," reactor. A researcher from Ghana used it for a year, testing samples from African waterholes for the arsenic that could kill the animals.

The reactor was operating at one megawatt as we talked. All levels were normal. We were standing, with Harry Braun, the chief reactor operator, on the metal platform around the reactor pool, and I had trouble keeping my eyes from the core, the Cerenkov radiation around the fuel rods, the blue shimmer under twenty feet of clear water. There was a skimmer on the side of the pool, and a bath mat thrown over the railing. There was a fishing pole, and a rubber duck. Harry Braun uses the fishing rod to extract samples from the specimen rack around the core, and the rubber duck to monitor the water movement. "Or when the little children come on school tours," he added. "Sometimes they don't pay any attention until we put the duck in the pool."

I was ten years old when "the atomic age," as we called it then, came forcibly to the world's attention. At the time the verbs favored for use with "the atomic age" were "dawned" or "ushered in," both of which implied an upward trend to events. I recall being told that the device which ended World War II was "the size of a lemon" (this was not true) and that the University of California had helped build it (this was true). I recall listening all one Sunday afternoon to a special radio report called "The Quick and the Dead," three or four hours during which the people who had built and witnessed the bomb talked about the bomb's and (by extension) their own eerie and apparently unprecedented power, their abrupt elevation to that place from whence they had come to judge the quick and the dead, and I also recall, when summer was over and school started again, being taught to cover my eyes and my brain stem and crouch beneath my desk during atomic-bomb drills.

So unequivocal were these impressions that it never occurred to me that I would not sooner or later—most probably sooner, certainly before I ever grew up or got married or went to college—endure the moment of its happening: first the blinding white light, which appeared in my imagination as a negative photographic image, then the waves of heat, the sound, and, finally, death, instant or prolonged, depending inflexibly on where one was caught in the scale of concentric circles we all imagined pulsing out from ground zero. Some years later, when I was an undergraduate at Berkeley and had an apartment in an old shingled house a few doors from where Etcheverry now stands, I could look up the hill at night and see the lights at the Lawrence Berkeley Laboratory, at what was then called "the rad lab," at the cyclotron and the Bevatron, and I still expected to wake up one night and see those lights in negative, still expected the blinding white light, the heat wave, the logical conclusion.

After I graduated I moved to New York, and after some months or a year I realized that I was no longer anticipating the blinding flash, and that the expectation had probably been one of those ways in which children deal with mortality, learn to juggle the idea that life will end as surely as it began, to perform in the face of definite annihilation. And yet I know that for me, and I suspect for many of us, this single image —this blinding white light that meant death, this seductive reversal of the usual associations around "light" and "white" and "radiance"—became a metaphor that to some extent determined what I later thought and did. In my Modern Library copy of *The Education of Henry Adams*, a book I first read and scored at Berkeley in 1954, I see this passage, about the 1900 Paris Great Exposition, underlined:

> . . . to Adams the dynamo became a symbol of infinity. As he grew accustomed to the great gallery of machines, he began to feel the forty-foot dynamos as a moral force, much as the early Christians felt the Cross.

It had been, at the time I saw the TRIGA Mark III reactor in the basement of Etcheverry Hall, seventy-nine years since Henry Adams went to Paris to study Science as he had studied Mont-Saint-Michel and Chartres. It had been thirty-four years since Robert Oppenheimer saw the white light at Alamogordo. The "nuclear issue," as we called it, suggesting that the course of the world since the Industrial Revolution was provisional, open to revision, up for a vote, had been under discussion all those years, and yet something about the fact of the reactor still resisted interpretation: the intense blue in the pool water, the Cerenkov radiation around the fuel rods, the blue past all blue, the blue like light itself, the blue that is actually a shock wave in the water and is the exact blue of the glass at Chartres.

4

At the University of California's Lawrence Livermore Laboratory, a compound of heavily guarded structures in the rolling cattle and orchard country southeast of Oakland, badges had to be displayed not only at the gate but again and again, at various points within the compound, to television cameras mounted between two locked doors. These cameras registered not only the presence but the color of the badge. A red badge meant "No Clearance U.S. Citizen" and might or might not be issued with the white covering badge that meant "Visitor Must Be Escorted." A yellow badge meant "No Higher Than Confidential Access." A green badge banded in yellow indicated that access was to be considered top level but not exactly unlimited: "Does Need to Know Exist?" was, according to a sign in the Badge Office, LLL Building 310, the question to ask as the bearer moved from station to station among the mysteries of the compound.

The symbolic as well as the literal message of a badge at Livermore—or at Los Alamos, or at Sandia, or at any of the other major labs around the country—was that the government had an interest here, that big money was being spent, Big Physics done. Badges were the totems of the tribe, the family. This was the family that used to keep all the plutonium in the world in a cigar box outside Glenn Seaborg's office in Berkeley, the family that used to try different ways of turning on the early twenty-seven-and-one-half-inch Berkeley cyclotron so as not to blow out large sections of the East Bay power grid. "Very gently" was said to work best. I have a copy of a photograph that suggests the day-to-day life of this family with considerable poignance, a snapshot taken during the fifties, when Livermore was testing its atmospheric nuclear weapons in the Pacific. The snapshot shows a very young Livermore scientist, with a flattop haircut and an engaging smile, standing on the beach of an unidentified atoll on an unspecified day just preceding or just following (no clue in the caption) a test shot. He is holding a fishing rod, and, in the other hand, a queen triggerfish, according to the caption "just a few ounces short of a world record." He is wearing only swimming trunks, and his badge.

On the day in February 1980 when I drove down to Livermore from Berkeley the coast ranges were green from the winter rains. The acacia was out along the highway, a haze of chrome yellow in the window. Inside the compound itself, narcissus and daffodil shoots pressed through the asphalt walkways. I had driven down because I wanted to see Shiva, Livermore's twenty-beam laser, the $35 million tool that was then Livermore's main marker in the biggest Big Physics game then going, the attempt to create a controlled fusion reaction. An uncontrolled fusion reaction was easy, and was called a hydrogen bomb. A controlled fusion reaction was harder, so much harder that it was usually characterized as "the most difficult technological feat ever undertaken," but the eventual payoff of could be virtually limitless nuclear power produced at a fraction of the hazard of the fission plants then operating. The difficulty in a controlled fusion reaction was that it involved achieving a thermonuclear burn of 100 million degrees centigrade, or more than six times the heat of the interior of the sun, without exploding the container. That no one had ever done this was, for the family, the point.

Ideas about how to do it were intensely competitive. Some laboratories had concentrated on what was called the "magnetic bottle" approach, involving the magnetic confinement of plasma; others, on lasers, and the theoretical ability of laser beams to trigger controlled fusion by simultaneously heating and compressing tiny pellets of fuel. Livermore had at that time a magnetic-bottle project but was gambling most heavily on its lasers, on Shiva and on Shiva's then unfinished successor, Nova. This was a high-stakes game: the prizes would end up at those laboratories where the money was, and the money would go to those laboratories where the prizes seemed most likely. It was no accident that Livermore was visited by so many members of Congress, by officials of the Department of Defense and of the Department of Energy, and by not too many other people: friends in high places were essential to the family. The biography of Ernest O. Lawrence, the first of the Berkeley Nobel laureates and the man after whom the Lawrence Berkeley and the Lawrence Livermore laboratories were named, is instructive on this point: there were meetings at the Pacific Union Club, sojourns at Bohemian Grove and San Simeon, even "a short trip to Acapulco with Randy and Catherine Hearst." The Eniwetok tests during the fifties were typically preceded for Lawrence by stops in Honolulu, where, for example,

> . . . he was a guest of Admiral John E. Gingrich, a fine host. He reciprocated with a dinner for the admiral and several others at the Royal Hawaiian Hotel the night before departure for Eniwetok, a ten-hour flight from Honolulu. Eniwetok had much the atmosphere of a South Seas resort. A fine officers' club on the beach provided relaxation for congressmen and visitors. The tropical sea invited swimmers and scuba divers. There were no phones to interrupt conversations with interesting and important men . . . chairs had been placed on the beach when observers assembled at the club near dawn [to witness the shot]. Coffee and sandwiches were served, and dark glasses distributed . . .

On the day I visited Livermore the staff was still cleaning up after a January earthquake, a Richter 5.5 on the Mount Diablo–Greenville Fault. Acoustical tiles had fallen from the ceilings of the office buildings. Overhead light fixtures had plummeted onto desks, and wiring and insulation and air-conditioning ducts still hung wrenched from the ceilings. "You get damage in the office buildings because the office buildings are only built to local code," I was told by John Emmett, the physicist then in charge of the Livermore laser program. When the ceilings started falling that particular January, John Emmett had been talking to a visitor in his office. He had shown the visitor out, run back inside to see if anyone was trapped under the toppled bookshelves and cabinets, and then run over to the building that houses Shiva. The laser had been affected so slightly that all twenty beams were found, by the sixty-three microcomputers that constantly aligned and realigned the Shiva beams, to be within one-sixteenth of an inch of their original alignment. "We didn't anticipate any real damage and we didn't get any," John Emmett said. "That's the way the gadget is designed."

What John Emmett called "the gadget" was framed in an immaculate white steel scaffolding several stories high and roughly the size of a football field. This frame was astonishingly beautiful, a piece of pure theater, a kind of abstract set on which the actors wore white coats, green goggles, and hard hats. "You wear the goggles because even when we're not firing we've got some little beams bouncing around," John Emmett said. "The hard hat is because somebody's always dropping something." Within the frame, a single infrared laser beam was split into twenty beams, each of which was amplified and reamplified until, at the instant two or three times a day when all twenty beams hit target, they were carrying sixty times as much power as was produced in the entire (exclusive of this room) United States. The target under bombardment was a glass bead a fraction the size of a grain of salt. The entire shoot took one-half billionth of a second. John Emmett and the Livermore laser team had then achieved with Shiva controlled temperatures of 85 million degrees centigrade, or roughly five times the heat at the center of the sun, but not 100 million. They were gambling on Nova for 100 million, the prize.

I recall, that afternoon at Livermore, asking John Emmett what would happen if I looked at the invisible infrared beam without goggles. "It'll blow a hole in your retina," he said matter-of-factly. It seemed that he had burned out the retina of one of his own eyes with a laser when he was a graduate student at Stanford. I asked if the sight had come back. "All but one little spot," he said. *Give me a mind that is not bored, that does not whimper, whine or sigh / Don't let me worry overmuch about the fussy thing called I*: these are two lines from a popular "prayer," a late-twenties precursor to the "Desiderata" that

Ernest O. Lawrence kept framed on his desk until his death. The one little spot was not of interest to John Emmett. Making the laser work was.

5

Wintertime and springtime, Honolulu: in the winter there was the garbage strike, forty-two days during which the city lapsed into a profound and seductive tropicality. Trash drifted in the vines off the Lunalilo Freeway. The airport looked Central American, between governments. Green plastic bags of garbage mounded up on the streets, and orange peels and Tab cans thrown in the canals washed down to the sea and up to the tide line in front of our rented house on Kahala Avenue. A day goes this way: in the morning I rearrange our own green plastic mounds, pick up the orange peels and Tab cans from the tide line, and sit down to work at the wet bar in the living room, a U-shaped counter temporarily equipped with an IBM Selectric typewriter. I turn on the radio for news of a break in the garbage strike: I get a sig-alert for the Lunalilo, roadwork between the Wilder Avenue off-ramp and the Punahou overpass. I get the weather: mostly clear. Actually water is dropping in great glassy sheets on the windward side of the island, fifteen minutes across the Pali, but on leeward Oahu the sky is quicksilver, chiaroscuro, light and dark and sudden falls of rain and rainbow, mostly clear. Some time ago I stopped trying to explain to acquaintances on the mainland the ways in which the simplest routines of a day in Honolulu can please and interest me, but on these winter mornings I am reminded that they do. I keep an appointment with a dermatologist at Kapiolani-Children's Medical Center, and am pleased by the drive down Beretania Street in the rain. I stop for groceries at the Star Market in the Kahala Mall, and am pleased by the sprays of vanda orchids and the foot-long watercress and the little Manoa lettuces in the produce department. Some mornings I am even pleased by the garbage strike.

The undertone of every day in Honolulu, the one fact that colors every other, is the place's absolute remove from the rest of the world. Many American cities began remote, but only Honolulu is fated to remain so, and only in Honolulu do the attitudes and institutions born of extreme isolation continue to set the tone of daily life. The edge of the available world is sharply defined: one turns a corner or glances out an office window and there it is, blue sea. There is no cheap freedom to be gained by getting in a car and driving as far as one can go, since as far as one can go on the island of Oahu takes about an hour and fifteen minutes. "Getting away" involves actual travel, scheduled carriers, involves reservations and reconfirmations and the ambiguous experience of being strapped passive in a darkened cabin and exposed to unwanted images on a flickering screen; involves submission to other people's schedules and involves, most significantly, money.

I have rarely spent an evening at anyone's house in Honolulu when someone in the room was not just off or about to catch an airplane, and the extent to which ten-hour flights figure in the local imagination tends to reinforce the distinction between those who can afford them and those who cannot. More people probably travel in Honolulu than can actually afford to: one study showed recent trips to the mainland in almost 25 percent of Oahu households and recent trips to countries outside the United States in almost 10 percent. Very few of those trips are to Europe, very few to the east coast of the United States. Not only does it take longer to fly from Honolulu to New York than from Honolulu to Hong Kong (the actual air time is about the same, ten or eleven hours either way, but no carrier now flies nonstop from Honolulu to New York), but Hong Kong seems closer in spirit, as do Manila, Tokyo, Sydney. A druggist suggests that I stock up on a prescription over the counter the next time I am in Hong Kong. The daughter of a friend gets a reward for good grades, a sweet-sixteen weekend on the Great Barrier Reef. The far Pacific is home, or near home in mood and appearance (there are parts of Oahu that bear more resemblance to Southeast Asia than to anywhere in the mainland United States), and the truly foreign lies in the other direction: airline posters feature the New England foliage, the Statue of Liberty, exotic attractions from a distant culture, a culture in which most people in Honolulu have no roots at all and only a fitful interest. This leaning toward Asia makes Honolulu's relation to the rest of America oblique, and divergent at unexpected points, which is part of the place's great but often hidden eccentricity.

To buy a house anywhere on the island of Oahu in the spring of 1980 cost approximately what a similar property would have cost in Los Angeles. Three bedrooms and a bath-and-a-half in the tracts near Pearl Harbor were running over $100,000 ("$138,000" was a figure I kept noticing in advertisements, once under the headline "This Is Your Lucky Day"), although the occasional bungalow with one bath was offered in the nineties. At the top end of the scale (where "life is somehow bigger and disappointment blunted," as one advertisement put it), not quite two-thirds of an acre with a main house, guesthouse, gatehouse, and saltwater pool on the beach at Diamond Head was offered—"fee simple," which was how a piece of property available for actual sale was described in Honolulu—at $3,750,000.

"Fee simple" was a magical phrase in Honolulu, since one of the peculiarities of the local arrangement had been that not much property actually changed hands. The island of Oahu was, at its longest and widest points, forty-five miles long and thirty miles wide, a total land mass—much of it vertical, unbuildable, the sheer volcanic precipices of the Koolau and Waianae ranges —of 380,000 acres. Almost 15 percent of this land was owned by the federal government and an equal amount by the State of Hawaii. Of the remaining privately owned land, more than 70 percent was owned by major landholders, by holders of more than five thousand acres, most notably, on Oahu, by the Campbell Estate, the Damon Estate, Castle and Cooke, and, in the most densely populated areas of Honolulu, the Bishop Estate. The Bishop Estate owned a good part of Waikiki, and the Kahala and Waialae districts, and, farther out, Hawaii Kai, which was a Kaiser development but a Bishop holding. The purchaser of a house on Bishop land bought not title to the property itself but a "leasehold," a land lease, transferred from buyer to buyer, that might be within a few years of expiration or might be (the preferred situation) recently renegotiated, fixed for a long term. An advertisement in the spring of 1980 for a three-bedroom, two-bath, $230,000 house in Hawaii Kai emphasized its "long, low lease," as did an advertisement for a similar house in the Kahala district offered at $489,000. One Sunday that spring, the Dolman office, a big residential realtor in Honolulu, ran an advertisement in the *Star-Bulletin & Advertiser* featuring forty-seven listings, of which thirty-nine were leasehold. The Earl Thacker office, the same day, featured eighteen listings, ten of which were leasehold, including an oceanfront lease for a house on Kahala Avenue at $1,250,000.

This situation, in which a few owners held most of the land, was relatively unique in the developed world (under 30 percent of the private land in California was held by owners of more than five thousand acres, compared to the more than 70 percent of Oahu) and lent a rather feudal and capricious uncertainty, a note of cosmic transience, to what was in other places a straightforward transaction, a direct assertion of territory, the purchase of a place to live. In some areas the Bishop Estate had offered "conversions," or the opportunity to convert leasehold to fee-simple property at prices then averaging $5.62 a square foot. This was regarded as a kind of land reform, but it worked adversely on the householder who had already invested all he or she could afford in the leasehold. Someone I know whose Bishop lease came up recently was forced to sell the house in which she had lived for some years because she could afford neither the price of the conversion nor the raised payments of what would have been her new lease. I went with another friend in 1980 to look at a house on the "other," or non-oceanfront, side of Kahala Avenue, listed at $695,000. The Bishop lease was fixed for thirty years and graduated: $490 a month until 1989, $735 until 1999, and $979 until 2009. The woman showing the house suggested that a conversion might be obtained. No one could promise it, of course, nor could anyone say what price might be set, if indeed a price were set at all. It was true that nothing on Kahala Avenue itself had at that time been converted. It was also true that the Bishop Estate was talking about Kahala Avenue as a logical place for hotel development. Still, the woman and my friend seemed to agree, it was a pretty house, and a problematic stretch to 2009.

When I first began visiting Honolulu, in 1966, I read in a tourist guidebook that the conventional points of the compass —north, south, east, west—were never employed locally, that one gave directions by saying that a place was either *makai*, toward the sea, or *mauka*, toward the mountains, and, in the city, usually either "diamond head" or "ewa," depending on whether the place in question lay, from where one stood, toward Diamond Head or Ewa Plantation. The Royal Hawaiian Hotel, for example, was diamond head of Ewa, but ewa of Diamond Head. The Kahala Hilton Hotel, since it was situated between Diamond Head and Koko Head, was said to be koko head of Diamond Head, and diamond head of Koko Head. There was about this a resolute colorfulness that did not seem entirely plausible to me at the time, particularly since the federally funded signs on the Lunalilo Freeway read EAST and WEST, but as time passed I came to see not only the chimerical compass but the attitude it seemed to reflect as intrinsic to the local accommodation, a way of maintaining fluidity in the rigid structure and isolation of an island society.

This system of bearings is entirely relative (nothing is absolutely ewa, for instance; the Waianae coast is makaha of Ewa, or toward Makaha, and beyond Makaha the known world metamorphoses again), is used at all levels of Honolulu life, and is common even in courtrooms. I recall spending several days at a murder trial during which the HPD evidence specialist, a quite beautiful young woman who looked as if she had walked off "Hawaii Five-O," spoke of "picking up latents ewa of the sink." The police sergeant with whom she had fingerprinted the site said that he had "dusted the koko head bedroom and the koko head bathroom, also the ewa bedroom and the kitchen floor." The defendant was said to have placed his briefcase, during a visit to the victim's apartment, "toward the ewa-makai corner of the couch." This was a trial, incidentally, during which one of the witnesses, a young woman who had worked a number of call dates with the victim (the victim was a call girl who had been strangled with her own telephone cord in her apartment near Ala Moana), gave her occupation as "full-time student at the University of Hawaii, carrying sixteen units." Another witness, also a call girl, said, when asked her occupation, that she was engaged in "part-time construction."

The way to get to Ewa was to go beyond Pearl Harbor and down Fort Weaver Road, past the weathered frame building that was once the hospital for Ewa Plantation and past the Japanese graveyard, and turn right. (Going straight instead of turning right would take the driver directly to Ewa Beach, a different proposition. I remember being advised when I first visited Honolulu that if I left the keys in a car in Waikiki I could look for it stripped down in Ewa Beach.) There was no particular reason to go to Ewa, no shops, no businesses, no famous views, no place to eat or even walk far (walk, and you walked right into the cane and the KAPU, or KEEP OUT, signs of the Oahu Sugar Company); there was only the fact that the place was there, intact, operational, a plantation town from another period. There was a school, a post office, a grocery. There were cane tools for sale in the grocery, and the pint bottles of liquor were kept in the office, a kind of wire-mesh cage with a counter. There was the Immaculate Conception Roman Catholic Church, there was the Ewa Hongwanji Mission. On the telephone poles there were torn and rain-stained posters for some revolution past or future, some May Day, a rally, a caucus, a "Mao Tse-tung Memorial Meeting."

Ewa was a company town, and its identical frame houses were arranged down a single street, the street that led to the sugar mill. Just one house on this street stood out: a house built of the same frame as the others but not exactly a bungalow, a house transliterated from the New England style, a *haole* house, a manager's house, a house larger than any other house for miles around. A Honolulu psychiatrist once told me, when I asked if he saw any characteristic island syndrome, that, yes, among the children of the planter families, children raised among the memories of the island's colonial past, he did. These patients shared the conviction that they were being watched, being observed, and not living up to what was expected of them. In Ewa one understood how that conviction might take hold. In Ewa one watched the larger house.

On my desk I used to keep a clock on Honolulu time, and

around five o'clock by that clock I would sometimes think of Ewa. I would imagine driving through Ewa at that time of day, when the mill and the frame bungalows swim in the softened light like amber, and I would imagine driving on down through Ewa Beach and onto the tract of military housing at Iroquois Point, a place as rigidly structured and culturally isolated in one way as Ewa was in another. From the shoreline at Iroquois Point one looks across the curve of the coast at Waikiki, a circumstance so poignant, suggesting as it does each of the tensions in Honolulu life, that it stops discussion.

6

On the December morning in 1979 when I visited Kai Tak East, the Caritas transit camp for Vietnamese refugees near Kai Tak airport, Kowloon, Hong Kong, a woman of indeterminate age was crouched on the pavement near the washing pumps bleeding out a live chicken. She worked at the chicken's neck with a small paring knife, opening and reopening the cut and massaging the blood into a tin cup, and periodically she would let the bird run free. The chicken did not exactly run but stumbled, staggered, and finally lurched toward one of the trickles of milky waste water that drained the compound. A flock of small children with bright scarlet rashes on their cheeks giggled and staggered, mimicking the chicken. The woman retrieved the dying chicken and, with what began to seem an almost narcoleptic languor, resumed working the blood from the cut, stroking rhythmically along the matted and stained feathers of the chicken's neck. The chicken had been limp a long time before she finally laid it on the dusty pavement. The children, bored, drifted away. The woman still crouched beside her chicken in the thin December sunlight.

When I think of Hong Kong I remember a particular smell in close places, a smell I construed as jasmine and excrement and sesame oil in varying proportions, and at Kai Tak East, where there were too many people and too few places for them to sleep and cook and eat and wash, this smell pervaded even the wide and dusty exercise yard that was the center of the camp. The smell was in fact what I noticed first, the smell and the dustiness and a certain immediate sense of physical dislocation, a sense of people who had come empty-handed and been assigned odd articles of cast-off clothing, which they wore uneasily: a grave little girl in a faded but still garish metallic bolero, an old man in a Wellesley sweatshirt, a wizened woman in a preteen sweater embroidered with dancing cats. In December in Hong Kong the sun lacked real warmth, and the children in the yard seemed bundled in the unfamiliar fragments of other people's habits. Men talking rubbed their hands as if to generate heat. Women cooking warmed their hands over the electric woks. In the corrugated-metal barracks, each with tiers of 144 metal and plywood bunks on which whole families spread their clothes and eating utensils and straw sleeping mats, mothers and children sat huddled in thin blankets. Outside one barrack a little boy about four years old pressed me to take a taste from his rice bowl. Another urinated against the side of the building.

After a few hours at Kai Tak East the intrinsic inertia and tedium of the camp day became vivid. Conversations in one part of the yard gave way only to conversations in another part of the yard. Preparations for one meal melted into preparations for the next. At the time I was in Hong Kong there were some three hundred thousand Vietnamese refugees, the largest number of whom were "ethnic Chinese," or Vietnamese of Chinese ancestry, waiting to be processed in improvised camps in the various countries around the South China Sea, in Hong Kong and Thailand and Malaysia and Macao and Indonesia and the Philippines. More than nine thousand of these were at Kai Tak East, and another fifteen thousand at Kai Tak North, the adjoining Red Cross camp. The details of any given passage from Vietnam to Hong Kong differed, but, in the case of the ethnic Chinese, the journey seemed typically to have begun with the payment of gold and the covert collusion of Vietnamese officials and Chinese syndicates outside Vietnam. The question was shadowy. Refugees were a business in this part of the world. Once in Hong Kong, any refugee who claimed to be Vietnamese underwent, before assignment to Kai Tak East or Kai Tak North or one of the other transit camps in the colony, an initial processing and screening by the Hong Kong police, mostly to establish that he or she was not an illegal immigrant from China looking to be relocated instead of repatriated, or, as they said in Hong Kong, "sent north." Only after this initial screening did refugees receive the yellow photographic identification cards that let them pass freely through the transit camp gates. The Vietnamese at Kai Tak East came and went all day, going out to work and out to market and out just to get out, but the perimeter of the camp was marked by high chain-link fencing, and in some places by concertina wire. The gates were manned by private security officers. The yellow cards were scrutinized closely. "This way we know," a camp administrator told me, "that what we have here is a genuine case of refugee."

They were all waiting, these genuine cases of refugee, for the consular interview that might eventually mean a visa out, and the inert tension of life at Kai Tak East derived mainly from this aspect of waiting, of limbo, of suspended hopes and plans and relationships. Of the 11,573 Vietnamese who had passed through Kai Tak East since the camp opened, in June 1979, only some 2,000 had been, by December, relocated, the largest number of them to the United States and Canada. The rest waited, filled out forms, pretended fluency in languages they had barely heard spoken, and looked in vain for their names on the day's list of interviews. Every week or so a few more would be chosen to go, cut loose from the group and put on the truck and taken to the airport for a flight to a country they had never seen.

Six Vietnamese happened to be leaving Kai Tak East the day I was there, two sisters and their younger brother for Australia, and a father and his two sons for France. The three going to Australia were the oldest children of a family that had lost its home and business in the Cholon district of Saigon and been ordered to a "new economic zone," one of the supervised wastelands in the Vietnamese countryside where large numbers of ethnic Chinese were sent to live off the land and correct their thinking. The parents had paid gold, the equivalent of six ounces, to get these three children out of Saigon via Haiphong, and now the children hoped to earn enough money in Australia to get out their parents and younger siblings. The sisters, who were twenty-three and twenty-four, had no idea how long this would take or if it would be possible. They knew only that they were leaving Hong Kong with their brother on the evening Qantas. They were uncertain in what Australian city the evening Qantas landed, nor did it seem to matter.

I talked to the two girls for a while, and then to the man who was taking his sons to France. This man had paid the equivalent of twelve or thirteen ounces of gold to buy his family out of Hanoi. Because his wife and daughters had left Hanoi on a different day, and been assigned to a different Hong Kong camp, the family was to be, on this day, reunited for the first time in months. The wife and daughters would already be on the truck when it reached Kai Tak East. The truck would take them all to the airport and they would fly together to Nice, "*toute la famille.*" Toward noon, when the truck pulled up to the gate, the man rushed past the guards and leapt up to embrace a pretty woman. "*Ma femme!*" he cried out again and again to those of us watching from the yard. He pointed wildly, and maneuvered the woman and little girls into better view. "*Ma femme, mes filles!*"

I stood in the sun and waved until the truck left, then turned back to the yard. In many ways refugees had become an entrenched fact of Hong Kong life. "They've got to go, there's no room for them here," a young Frenchwoman, Saigon born, had said to me at dinner the night before. Beside me in the yard a man sat motionless while a young woman patiently picked the nits from his hair. Across the yard a group of men and women watched without expression as the administrator posted the names of those selected for the next day's consular interviews. A few days later the *South China Morning Post* carried reports from intelligence sources that hundreds of boats were being assembled in Vietnamese ports to carry out more ethnic Chinese. The headline read, "HK Alert to New Invasion." It was believed that weather would not be favorable for passage to Hong Kong until the advent of the summer monsoon. Almost a dozen years later, the British government, which had agreed to relinquish Hong Kong to the Chinese in 1997, reached an accord with the government of Vietnam providing for the forcible repatriation of Hong Kong's remaining Vietnamese refugees. The flights back to Vietnam began in the fall of 1991. Some Vietnamese were photographed crying and resisting as they were taken to the Hong Kong airport. Hong Kong authorities stressed that the guards escorting the refugees were unarmed.

—1979–1991

Los Angeles Days

DURING ONE of the summer weeks I spent in Los Angeles in 1988 there was a cluster of small earthquakes, the most noticeable of which, on the Garlock Fault, a major lateral-slip fracture that intersects the San Andreas in the Tehachapi range north of Los Angeles, occurred at six minutes after four on a Friday afternoon when I happened to be driving in Wilshire Boulevard from the beach. People brought up to believe that the phrase "terra firma" has real meaning often find it hard to understand the apparent equanimity with which earthquakes are accommodated in California, and tend to write it off as regional spaciness. In fact it is less equanimity than protective detachment, the useful adjustment commonly made in circumstances so unthinkable that psychic survival precludes preparation. I know very few people in California who actually set aside, as instructed, a week's supply of water and food. I know fewer still who could actually lay hands on the wrench required to turn off, as instructed, the main gas valve; the scenario in which this wrench will be needed is a catastrophe, and something in the human spirit rejects planning on a daily basis for catastrophe. I once interviewed, in the late sixties, someone who did prepare: a Pentecostal minister who had received a kind of heavenly earthquake advisory, and on its quite specific instructions was moving his congregation from Port Hueneme, north of Los Angeles, to Murfreesboro, Tennessee. A few months later, when a small earthquake was felt not in Port Hueneme but in Murfreesboro, an event so novel that it was reported nationally, I was, I recall, mildly gratified.

A certain fatalism comes into play. When the ground starts moving all bets are off. Quantification, which in this case takes the form of guessing where the movement at hand will rank on the Richter scale, remains a favored way of regaining the illusion of personal control, and people still crouched in the nearest doorjamb will reach for a telephone and try to call Caltech, in Pasadena, for a Richter reading. "Rock and roll," the D.J. said on my car radio that Friday afternoon at six minutes past four. "This console is definitely shaking . . . no word from Pasadena yet, is there?"

"I would say this is a three," the D.J.'s colleague said. "Definitely a three, maybe I would say a little higher than a three."

"Say an eight . . . just joking."

"It felt like a six where I was."

What it turned out to be was a five-two, followed by a dozen smaller aftershocks, and it had knocked out four of the six circuit breakers at the A. D. Edmonston pumping plant on the California Aqueduct, temporarily shutting down the flow of Northern California water over the Tehachapi range and cutting off half of Southern California's water supply for the weekend. This was all within the range not only of the predictable but of the normal. No one had been killed or seriously injured. There was plenty of water for the weekend in the system's four southern reservoirs, Pyramid, Castaic, Silverwood, and Perris lakes. A five-two earthquake is not, in California, where the movements people remember tend to have Richter numbers well over six, a major event, and the probability of earthquakes like this one had in fact been built into the Aqueduct: the decision to pump the water nineteen hundred feet over the Tehachapi was made precisely because the Aqueduct's engineers rejected the idea of tunneling through an area so geologically complex, periodically wrenched by opposing displacements along the San Andreas and the Garlock, that it has been called California's structural knot.

Still, this particular five-two, coming as it did when what Californians call "the Big One" was pretty much overdue (the Big One is the eight, the Big One is the seven in the wrong place or at the wrong time, the Big One could even be the six-five centered near downtown Los Angeles at nine on a weekday morning), made people a little uneasy. There was some concern through the weekend that this was not merely an ordinary five-two but a "foreshock," an earthquake prefiguring a larger event (the chances of this, according to Caltech seismologists, run about one in twenty), and by Sunday there was what seemed to many people a sinister amount of activity on other faults: a three-four just east of Ontario at twenty-two minutes past two in the afternoon, a three-six twenty-two minutes later at Lake Berryessa, and, four hours and one minute later, northeast of San Jose, a five-five on the Calaveras Fault. On Monday, there was a two-three in Playa del Rey and a three in Santa Barbara.

Had it not been for the five-two on Friday, very few people would have registered these little quakes (the Caltech seismological monitors in Southern California normally record from twenty to thirty earthquakes a day with magnitudes below three), and in the end nothing came of them, but this time people did register them, and they lent a certain moral gravity to the way the city happened to look that weekend, a temporal dimension to the hard white edges and empty golden light. At odd moments during the next few days people would suddenly clutch at tables, or walls. "Is it going," they would say, or "I think it's moving." They almost always said "it," and what they meant by "it" was not just the ground but the world as they knew it. I have lived all my life with the promise of the Big One, but when it starts going now even I get the jitters.

2

What is striking about Los Angeles after a period away is how well it works. The famous freeways work, the supermarkets work (a visit, say, to the Pacific Palisades Gelson's, where the aisles are wide and the shelves full and checkout is fast and free of attitude, remains the zazen of grocery shopping), the beaches work. The 1984 Olympics were not supposed to work, but they did (daily warnings of gridlock and urban misery gave way, during the first week, to a county-wide block party, with pink and aquamarine flags fluttering over empty streets and parking spaces for once available even in Westwood); not only worked but turned a profit, of almost $223 million, about which there was no scandal. Even the way houses are bought and sold seems to work more efficiently than it does in New York (for all practical purposes there are no exclusive listings in Los Angeles, and the various contingencies on which closing the deal depends are arbitrated not by lawyers but by an escrow company), something that came to my attention when my husband and I arranged to have our Los Angeles house shown for the first time to brokers at eleven o'clock one Saturday morning, went out to do a few errands, and came back at one to find that we had three offers, one of them for appreciably more than the asking price.

Selling a house in two hours was not, in 1988 in Los Angeles, an entirely unusual experience. Around February of 1988, midway through what most people call the winter but Californians call the spring ("winter" in California is widely construed as beginning and ending with the Christmas season, reflecting a local preference for the upside), at a time when residential real estate prices in New York were already plunging in response to the October 1987 stock market crash, there had in fact developed on the west side of Los Angeles a heightened enthusiasm for committing large sums of money to marginal improvements in one's domestic situation: to moving, say, from what was called in the listings a "convertible 3" in Santa Monica (three bedrooms, one of which might be converted into a study) to a self-explanatory "4 + lib" in Brentwood Park, or to acquiring what was described in the listings as an "H/F pool," meaning heated and filtered, or a "N/S tennis court," meaning the preferred placement on the lot, the north-south orientation believed to keep sun from the players' eyes.

By June of 1988 a kind of panic had set in, of a kind that occurs periodically in Southern California but had last occurred in 1979. Multiple offers were commonplace, and deals stalled because bank appraisers could not assess sales fast enough to keep up with the rising market. Residential real estate offices were routinely reporting "record months." People were buying one- and two-million-dollar houses as investments, to give their adolescent children what brokers referred to as "a base in the market," which was one reason why small houses on modest lots priced at a million-four were getting, the day they were listed, thirty and forty offers.

All this seemed to assume an infinitely upward trend, and to be one of those instances in which the preoccupations and apprehensions of people in Los Angeles, a city in many ways predicated on the ability to deal with the future at a rather existential remove, did not exactly coincide with those of the country at large. October 19, 1987, which had so immediately affected the New York market that asking prices on some apartments had in the next three or four months dropped as much as a million dollars, seemed, in Los Angeles, not to have happened. Those California brokers to whom I talked, if they mentioned the crash at all, tended to see it as a catalyst for good times, an event that had emphasized the "real" in real estate.

The *Los Angeles Times* had taken to running, every Sunday, a chat column devoted mainly to the buying and selling of houses: Ruth Ryon's "Hot Property," from which one could learn that the highest price paid for a house in Los Angeles to that date was $20.25 million (by Marvin Davis, to Kenny Rogers, for The Knoll in Beverly Hills); that the $2.5 million paid in 1986 for 668 St. Cloud Road in Bel Air (by Earle Jorgenson and Holmes Tuttle and some eighteen other friends of President and Mrs. Reagan, for whom the house was bought and who rent it with an option to buy) was strikingly under value, since even an unbuilt acre in the right part of Bel Air (the house bought by the Reagans' friends is definitely in the right part of Bel Air) will sell for $3 million; and that two houses in the Reagans' new neighborhood sold recently for $13.5 million and $14.75 million respectively. A typical "Hot Property" item ran this way:

> Newlyweds Tracey E. Bregman Recht, star of the daytime soap "The Young and the Restless," and her husband Ron Recht, a commercial real estate developer, just bought their first home, on 2.5 acres in a nifty neighborhood. They're just up the street from Merv Griffin's house (which I've heard is about to be listed at some astronomical price) and they're just down the street from Pickfair, now owned by Pia Zadora and her husband. The Rechts bought a house that was built in 1957 on San Ysidro Drive in Beverly Hills for an undisclosed price, believed to be several million dollars, and now they're fixing it up . . .

I spent some time, before this 1988 bull market broke, with two West Side brokers, Betty Budlong and Romelle Dunas of the Jon Douglas office, both of whom spoke about the going price of "anything at all" as a million dollars, and of "something decent" as two million dollars. "Right now I've got two clients in the price range of five to six hundred thousand dollars," Romelle Dunas said. "I sat all morning trying to think what I could show them today."

"I'd cancel the appointment," Betty Budlong said.

"I just sold their condo for four. I'm sick. The houses for five-fifty are smaller than their condo."

"I think you could still find something in Ocean Park," Betty Budlong said. "Ocean Park, Sunset Park, somewhere like that. Brentwood Glen, you know, over here, the Rattery tract . . . of course that's inching towards six."

"Inching toward six and you're living in the right lane of the San Diego Freeway," Romelle Dunas said.

"In seventeen hundred square feet," Betty Budlong said.

"If you're lucky. I saw one that was fifteen hundred square feet. I have a feeling when these people go out today they're not going to close on their condo."

Betty Budlong thought about this. "I think you should make a good friend of Sonny Fox," she said at last.

Sonny Fox was a Jon Douglas agent in Sherman Oaks, in the San Fernando Valley, only a twenty-minute drive from Beverly Hills on the San Diego Freeway but a twenty-minute drive toward which someone living on the West Side—even someone who would drive forty minutes to Malibu—was apt to display considerable sales resistance.

"In the Valley," Romelle Dunas said after a pause.

Betty Budlong shrugged. "In the Valley."

"People are afraid to get out of this market," Romelle Dunas said.

"They can't afford to get out," Betty Budlong said. "I know two people who in any other market would have sold their houses. One of them has accepted a job in Chicago, the other is in Washington for at least two years. They're both leasing their houses. Because until they're sure they're not coming back, they don't want to get out."

The notion that land will be worth more tomorrow than it is worth today has been a real part of the California experience, and remains deeply embedded in the California mentality, but this seemed extreme, and it occurred to me that the buying and selling of houses was perhaps one more area in which the local capacity for protective detachment had come into play, that people capable of compartmentalizing the Big One might be less inclined than others to worry about getting their money out of a 4 + lib, H/F pool. I asked if foreign buyers could be pushing up the market.

Betty Budlong thought not. "These are people who are moving, say, from a seven-fifty house to a million-dollar house."

I asked if the market could be affected by a defense cutback.

Betty Budlong thought not. "Most of the people who buy on the West Side are professionals, or in the entertainment industry. People who work at Hughes and Douglas, say, don't live in Brentwood or Santa Monica or Beverly Hills."

I asked Betty Budlong if she saw anything at all that could affect the market.

"Tight money could affect this market," Betty Budlong said. "For a while."

"Then it always goes higher," Romelle Dunas said.

"Which is why people can't afford to get out," Betty Budlong said.

"They couldn't get back in," Romelle Dunas said.

3

This entire question of houses and what they were worth (and what they should be worth, and what it meant when the roof over someone's head was also his or her major asset) was, during the spring and summer of 1988, understandably more on the local mind than it perhaps should have been, which was one reason why a certain house then under construction just west of the Los Angeles Country Club became the focus of considerable attention, and of emotions usually left dormant on the west side of Los Angeles. The house was that being built by the television producer ("Dynasty," "Loveboat," "Fantasy Island") Aaron Spelling and his wife Candy at the corner of Mapleton and Club View in Holmby Hills, on six acres the Spellings had bought in 1983, for $10,250,000, from Patrick Frawley, the chairman of Schick.

At the time of the purchase there was already a fairly impressive house on the property, a house once lived in by Bing Crosby, but the Spellings, who had become known for expansive domestic gestures (crossing the country in private railroad cars, for example, and importing snow to Beverly Hills for their children's Christmas parties), had decided that the Crosby/Frawley house was what is known locally as a teardown. The progress of the replacement, which was rising from the only residential site I have ever seen with a two-story contractor's office and a sign reading CONSTRUCTION AREA: HARD HATS REQUIRED, became over the next several months not just a form of popular entertainment but, among inhabitants of a city without much common experience, a unifying, even a political, idea.

At first the project was identified, on the kind of site sign usually reserved for office towers in progress, as "THE MANOR"; later "THE MANOR" was modified to what seemed, given the resemblance of the structure to a resort Hyatt, the slightly nutty discretion of "594 SOUTH MAPLETON DRIVE." It was said that the structure ("house" seemed not entirely to cover it) would have 56,500 square feet. It was said that the interior plan would include a bowling alley, and 560 square feet of extra closet space, balconied between the second and the attic floors. It was said, by the owner, that such was the mass of the steel frame construction that to break up the foundation alone would take a demolition crew six months, and cost from four to five million dollars.

Within a few months the site itself had become an established attraction, and evening drive-bys were enlivened by a skittish defensiveness on the part of the guards, who would switch on the perimeter floods and light up the steel girders and mounded earth like a prison yard. The *Los Angeles Times* and *Herald Examiner* published periodic reports on and rumors about the job ("Callers came out of the woodwork yesterday in the wake of our little tale about Candy Spelling having the foundation of her $45-million mansion-in-progress lowered because she didn't want to see the Robinson's department store sign from where her bed-to-be was to sit"), followed by curiously provocative corrections, or "denials," from Aaron Spelling. "The only time Candy sees the Robinson's sign is when she's shopping" was one correction that got everyone's attention, but in many ways the most compelling was this: "They say we have an Olympic-sized swimming pool. Not true. There's no gazebo, no guesthouse. . . . When people go out to dinner, unless they talk about their movies, they have nothing else to talk about, so they single out Candy."

In that single clause, "unless they talk about their movies," there was hidden a great local truth, and the inchoate heart of the matter: this house was, in the end, that of a television producer, and people who make movies did not, on the average evening, have dinner with people who make television. People who make television had most of the money, but people who make movies still had most of the status, and believed themselves the keepers of the community's unspoken code, of the rules, say, about what constituted excess on the housing front. This was a distinction usually left tacit, but the fact of the Spelling house was making people say things out loud. "There are people in this town worth hundreds of millions of dollars," Richard Zanuck, one of the most successful motion picture producers in the business, once said to my husband, "and they can't get a table at Chasen's." This was a man whose father had run a studio and who had himself run a studio, and his bewilderment was that of someone who had uncovered an anomaly in the wheeling of the stars.

4

When people in Los Angeles talk about "this town," they do not mean Los Angeles, nor do they exactly mean what many of them call "the community." "The community" is more narrowly defined, and generally confined to those inhabitants of this town who can be relied upon to sit at one another's tables on approved evenings (benefiting the American Film Institute, say) and to get one another's daughters into approved schools, say Westlake, in Holmby Hills, not far from the Spellings' house but on eleven acres rather than six. People in the community meet one another for lunch at Hillcrest, but do not, in the main, attend Friars' Club Roasts. People in the community sojourn with their children in Paris, and Aspen, and at the Kahala Hilton in Honolulu, but visit Las Vegas only on business. "The community" is made up of people who can, in other words, get a table at Chasen's.

"This town" is broader, and means just "the industry," which is the way people who make television and motion pictures refer, tellingly, to the environment in which they work. The extent to which the industry in question resembles conventional industries is often obscured by its unconventional product, which requires that its "workers" perform in unconventional ways, for which they are paid unconventional sums of money: some people do make big money writing and directing and producing and acting in television, and some people also make big money, although considerably less big, writing and directing and producing and acting in motion pictures.

Still, as in other entrepreneurial enterprises, it is not those who work on the line in this industry but those who manage it who make the biggest money of all, and who tend to have things their way, which is what the five-month 1988 Writers Guild of America strike, which had become by the time of its settlement in early August 1988 perhaps the most acrimonious union strike in recent industry history, was initially and finally about. It was not about what were inflexibly referred to by both union and management as "the so-called creative issues," nor was it exclusively about the complicated formulas and residuals that were the tokens on the board. It was about respect, and about whether the people who made the biggest money were or were not going to give a little to the people who made the less big money.

In other words, it was a class issue, which was hard for people outside the industry—who in the first place did not understand the essentially adversarial nature of the business (a good contract, it is understood in Hollywood, is one that ensures the other party's breach) and in the second place believed everybody involved to be overpaid—to entirely understand. "Whose side does one take in such a war—that of the writers with their scads of money, or that of the producers with their tons of money?" the *Washington Post*'s television reporter, Tom Shales, demanded (as it turned out, rhetorically) in a June 29, 1988, piece arguing that the writers were "more interested in strutting and swaggering than in reaching a settlement," that "a handful of hotheads" who failed to realize that "the salad days are over" were bringing down an industry beset by "dwindling" profits, and that the only effect of the strike was to crush "those in the lowest-paying jobs," for example a waitress, laid off when Universal shut down its commissary, who Tom

Shales perceived to be "not too thrilled with the writers and their grievances" when he saw her interviewed on a television newscast. (This was an example of what became known locally during the strike as "the little people argument," and referred to the traditional practice among struck companies of firing their nonunion hostages. When hard times come to Hollywood, the typing pool goes first, and is understood to symbolize the need of the studio to "cut back," or "slash costs.") "Just because the producers are richer doesn't mean the writers are right. Or righteous," Tom Shales concluded. "These guys haven't just seen too many Rambo movies, they've written too many Rambo movies."

This piece, which reflected with rather impressive fidelity the arguments then being made by the Alliance of Motion Picture and Television Producers, the negotiating body for management, was typical of most coverage of the strike, and also of what had become, by early summer of 1988, the prevailing mood around town. Writers have never been much admired in Hollywood. In an industry predicated on social fluidity, on the daily calibration and reassessment of status and power, screenwriters, who perform a function that remains only dimly understood even by the people who hire them, occupy a notably static place: even the most successful of them have no real power, and therefore no real status. "I can always get a writer," Ray Stark once told my husband, who had expressed a disinclination to join the team on a Stark picture for which he had been, Ray Stark had told him a few weeks before, "the only possible writer."

Writers (even the only possible writers), it is universally believed, can always be replaced, which is why they are so frequently referred to in the plural. Writers, it is believed by many, are even best replaced, hired serially, since they bring, in this view, only a limited amount of talent and energy to bear on what directors often call their "vision." A number of directors prefer to hire fresh writers—usually writers with whom they have previously worked—just before shooting: Sydney Pollack, no matter who wrote the picture he is directing, has the habit of hiring for the period just before and during production David Rayfiel or Elaine May or Kurt Luedtke. "I want it in the contract when David Rayfiel comes in," a writer I know once said when he and Pollack were talking about doing a picture together; this was a practical but unappreciated approach.

The previous writer on a picture is typically described as "exhausted," or "worn-out on this." What is meant by "this" is the task at hand, which is seen as narrow and technical, one color in the larger vision, a matter of taking notes from a producer or an actor or a director, and adding dialogue—something, it is understood, that the producer or actor or director could do without a writer, if only he or she had the time, if only he or she were not required to keep that larger vision in focus. "I've got the ideas," one frequently hears in the industry. "All I need is a writer."

Such "ideas," when explored, typically tend toward the general ("relationships between men and women," say, or "rebel without a cause in the west Valley"), and the necessity for paying a writer to render such ideas specific remains a source of considerable resentment. Writers are generally seen as balky, obstacles to the forward flow of the project. They take time. They want money. They are typically the first element on a picture, the people whose job it is to invent a world sufficiently compelling to interest actors and directors, and, as the first element, they are often unwilling to recognize the necessity for keeping the front money down, for cutting their fees in order to get a project going. "Everyone," they are told, is taking a cut ("everyone" in this instance generally means every one of the writers), yet they insist on "irresponsible" fees. A director who gets several million dollars a picture will often complain, quite bitterly, about being "held up" by the demands of his writers. "You're haggling over pennies," a director once complained to me.

This resentment surfaces most openly in contract negotiations ("We don't give points to writers," studio business-affairs lawyers will say in a negotiation, or, despite the fact that a writer has often delivered one or two drafts on the basis of a deal memo alone, "Our policy is no payment without a fully executed contract"), but in fact suffuses every aspect of life in the community. Writers do not get gross from dollar one, nor do they get the Thalberg Award, nor do they even determine when and where a meeting will take place: these are facts of local life known even to children. Writers who work regularly live comfortably, but not in the houses with the better N/S courts. Writers sometimes get to Paris on business, but rarely on the Concorde. Writers occasionally have lunch at Hillcrest, but only when their agents take them. Writers have at best a provisional relationship with the community in which they live, which is precisely what has made them, over the years, such convenient pariahs. "Fuck 'em, they're weaklings," as one director I know said about the Guild.

As the strike wore on, then, a certain natural irritation, even a bellicosity, was bound to surface when the subject of the writers (or, as some put it, "the writers and their so-called demands") came up, as was an impatience with the whole idea of collective bargaining. "If you're good enough, you can negotiate your own contract," I recall being told by one director. It was frequently suggested that the strike was supported only by those members of the Guild who were not full-time working writers: "A lot of them aren't writers," an Alliance spokesman told the *Los Angeles Times.* "They pay their one-hundred-dollar-a-year dues and get invitations to screenings." A television producer suggested to me that perhaps the answer was "another guild," one that would function, although he did not say this, as a sweetheart union. "A guild for working writers," he said. "That's a guild we could negotiate with."

I heard repeatedly during the strike that I, as a member of the Guild "but an intelligent person," had surely failed to understand what "the leadership" of the Guild was doing to me; when I said that I did understand it, that I had lost three pictures during the course of the strike and would continue to vote against a settlement until certain money issues had been resolved, I was advised that such intransigence would lead nowhere, because "the producers won't budge," because "they're united on this," because "they're going to just write off the Guild," and because, an antic note, "they're going to start hiring college kids—they're even going to start hiring journalists."

In this mounting enthusiasm to punish the industry's own writers by replacing them "even" with journalists ("Why not air traffic controllers?" said a writer to whom I mentioned this threat), certain facts about the strike receded early into the mists of claim and counterclaim. Many people preferred to believe that, as Tom Shales summarized it, the producers had "offered increases," and that the writers had "said they were not enough." In fact the producers had offered, on the key points in the negotiation, rollbacks on a residual payment structure established in 1985, when the WGA contract had been last negotiated. Many people preferred to believe, as Tom Shales seemed to believe, that it was the writers, not the producers, who were refusing to negotiate. In fact the strike had been, from the Alliance's "last and final offer" on March 6, 1988, until a federal mediator called both sides to meet on May 23, 1988, less a strike than a lockout, with the producers agreeing to attend only a single meeting, on April 8, which lasted twenty minutes before the Alliance negotiators walked out. "It looks like the writers are shooting the whole industry in the foot—and they're doing it willfully and stupidly," Grant Tinker, the television producer and former chairman of NBC, told the *Los Angeles Times* after the Guild rejected, by a vote of 2,789 to 933, the June version of the Alliance's series of "last and final" offers. "It's just pigheaded and stupid for the writers to have so badly misread what's going on here."

What was going on here was interesting. This had not been an industry unaccustomed to labor disputes, nor had it been one, plans to hire "journalists" notwithstanding, historically hospitable to outsiders. ("We don't go for strangers in Hollywood," Cecilia Brady said in *The Last Tycoon*; this remains the most succinct description I know of the picture business.) For reasons deep in the structure of the industry, writers' strikes have been a fixed feature of local life, and gains earned by the writers have traditionally been passed on to the other unions —who themselves strike only rarely—in a fairly inflexible ratio: for every dollar in residuals the Writers Guild gets, another dollar goes to the Directors Guild, three dollars go to the Screen Actors Guild, and eight or nine dollars go to IATSE, the principal craft union, which needs the higher take because its pension and health benefits, unlike those of the other unions, are funded entirely from residuals. "So when the WGA negotiates for a dollar increase in residuals, say, the studios don't think just a dollar, they think twelve or thirteen," a former Guild president told me. "The industry is a kind of family, and its members are interdependent."

Something new was at work, and it had to do with a changed

attitude among the top executives. I recall being told, quite early in this strike, by someone who had been a studio head of production and had bargained for management in previous strikes, that this strike would be different, and in many ways unpredictable. The problem, he said, was the absence at the bargaining table of "a Lew Wasserman, an Arthur Krim." Lew Wasserman, the chairman of MCA-Universal, it is said in the industry, was always looking for the solution; as he grew less active, Arthur Krim, at United Artists, and to a lesser extent Ted Ashley, at Warner Brothers, fulfilled this function, which was essentially that of the *consigliere*. "The guys who are running the studios now, they don't deal," he said. "Sid Sheinberg bargaining for Universal, Barry Diller for Fox, that's ridiculous. They won't even talk. As far as the Disney guys go, Eisner, Katzenberg, they play hardball, that's the way they run their operation."

Roger Fisher, the Williston Professor of Law at Harvard Law School and director of the Harvard Negotiation Project, suggested, in an analysis of the strike published in the *Los Angeles Times*, that what had been needed between management and labor in this case was "understanding, two-way communication, reliability, and acceptance," the very qualities that natural selection in the motion picture industry had tended to eliminate. It was in fact June of 1988, three months into the strike, before the people running the studios actually entered the negotiating sessions, which they referred to, significantly, as "downtime." "I talked to Diller, Mancuso, Daly," I was told by one of the two or three most powerful agents in the industry. He meant Barry Diller at Twentieth Century-Fox and Frank Mancuso at Paramount and Robert Daly at Warner Brothers. "I said look, you guys, you want this thing settled, you better indicate you're taking it seriously enough to put in the downtime yourselves. Sheinberg [Sidney Sheinberg of MCA-Universal] and Mancuso have kind of emerged as the point players for management, but you've got to remember, these guys are all prima donnas, they hate each other, so it was a big problem presenting a sufficiently united front to put somebody out there speaking for all of them."

In the context of an industry traditionally organized, like a mob family, around principles of discretion and unity, this notion of the executive as prima donna was a new phenomenon, and not one tending toward an appreciation of the "interdependence" of unions and management. It did not work toward the settlement of this strike that the main players on one side of the negotiations were themselves regarded as stars, the subjects of fan profiles, pieces often written by people who admired and wanted to work in the industry. Michael Eisner of Disney had been on the cover of *Time*. Sidney Sheinberg of Universal had been on the cover of *Manhattan, inc.* Executive foibles had been detailed (Jeffrey Katzenberg of Disney "guzzled" Diet Coke, and "sold his Porsche after he almost killed himself trying to shift gears and dial at the same time"), as had, and this presented a problem, company profits and executive compensation. Nineteen eighty-seven net profit for Warner Communications was up 76.6 percent over 1986. Nineteen eighty-seven net profit for Paramount was up 130 percent over 1986. CBS was up 21 percent, ABC 53 percent. The chairman and CEO of Columbia, Victor Kaufman, received in 1987 $826,154 in salary and an additional $1,506,142 in stock options and bonuses. Michael Eisner was said to have received, including options and bonuses, a figure that ranged from $23 million (this was Disney's own figure) to more than $80 million (this was what the number of shares involved in the stock options seemed to suggest), but was most often given as $63 million.

During a season when management was issuing white papers explaining the "new, colder realities facing the entertainment industry," this last figure in particular had an energizing effect on the local consciousness, and was frequently mentioned in relation to another figure, that for the combined total received in residual payments by all nine thousand members of the Writers Guild. This figure was $58 million, which, against Michael Eisner's $63, made it hard for many people to accept the notion that residual rollbacks were entirely imperative. Trust seemed lacking, as did a certain mutuality of interest. "We used to sit across the table from people we had personally worked with on movies," I was told by a writer who had sat in on negotiating sessions during this and past strikes. "These people aren't movie people. They think like their own business-affairs lawyers. You take somebody like Jeff Katzenberg, he has a very ideological position. He said the other night, 'I'm speaking as a dedicated capitalist. I own this screenplay. So why should I hand anybody else the right to have any say about it?'"

In June of 1988, three months into the strike, it was said around Los Angeles that the strike was essentially over, because the producers said it was over, and that the only problem remaining was to find a way for the Guild negotiators to save face—"a bone," as Jeffrey Katzenberg was said to be calling it, to throw the writers. "This has largely come down to a question of how Brian will look," I was told that month by someone close to management. He was talking about Brian Walton, the Guild's executive director and chief negotiator. "It's a presentation problem, a question of giving him something he can present to the membership, after fifteen weeks, as something approaching win-win." It was generally conceded that the producers, despite disavowals, were determined to break the union; even the disavowals, focusing as they did on the useful clerical work done by the Guild ("If the Guild didn't exist we'd have to invent it," Sidney Sheinberg said at one point), suggested that what the producers had in mind was less a union than a trade association. It was taken for granted that it was not the producers but the writers who, once the situation was correctly "presented," would give in. "Let's get this town back to work," people were saying, and "This strike has to end."

Still, this strike did not end. By late July, it was said around Los Angeles that the negotiations once again in progress were not really negotiations at all; that "they" were meeting only because a federal mediator had ordered them to meet, and that the time spent at the table was just that, time spent at a table, downtime. Twenty-one writers had announced their intention of working in spite of the strike, describing this decision as evidence of "the highest form of loyalty" to the Guild. "What's it for?" people were saying, and "This is lose-lose."

"Writers are children," Monroe Stahr had said almost half a century before, in *The Last Tycoon*, by way of explaining why his own negotiations with the Writers Guild had reached, after a year, a dead end. "They are not equipped for authority. There is no substitute for will. Sometimes you have to fake will when you don't feel it at all. . . . So I've had to take an attitude in this Guild matter." In the end, the attitude once again was taken and once again prevailed. "This strike has run out of gas," people began to say, and "This is ridiculous, this is enough," as if the writers were not only children but bad children, who had been humored too long. "We've gotten to the end of the road and hit a brick wall," the negotiator for the Alliance of Motion Picture and Television Producers, J. Nicholas Counter III, said on the Sunday afternoon of July 31, 1988, at a press conference called by the Alliance to announce that negotiations with the Writers Guild were at an end, "hopelessly" deadlocked. "I suggest it's time for Mr. Walton to look to himself for the answer as to why his guild is still on strike," Jeffrey Katzenberg said that afternoon to Aljean Harmetz of the *New York Times*. That evening, Jeffrey Katzenberg and the other executives of the major studios met with Kenneth Ziffren, a prominent local lawyer who represented several Guild members who, because they had television production companies, had a particular interest in ending the strike; the marginally different formulas suggested by Kenneth Ziffren seemed to many the bone they had been looking for: a way of solving "the presentation problem," of making the strike look, now that the writers understood that it had run out of gas, "like something approaching win-win." On the following Sunday, August 7, 1988, the Guild membership voted to end the strike, on essentially the same terms it had turned down in June.

During the five months of the dispute many people outside the industry had asked me what the strike was about, and I had heard myself talk about ancillary markets and about the history of pattern bargaining, about the "issues," but the dynamic of the strike, the particular momentum that kept several thousand people with not much in common voting for at least a while against what appeared to be their own best interests, had remained hard to explain. The amounts of money to be gained or lost had seemed, against the money lost during the course of the strike, insignificant. The "creative" issues, the provisions that touched on the right of the writer to have some say in the production, would have been, if won, unenforceable.

Yet I had been for the strike, and felt toward that handful of writers who had declared their intention to desert it, and by so doing encouraged the terms on which it would end, a coolness bordering on distaste, as if we had gone back forty years, and they had named names. "You need to have worked in the industry," I would say by way of explanation, or "You have to live there." Not until July of 1988, at the Democratic National Convention in Atlanta, did the emotional core of the strike come clear to me. I had gone to Atlanta in an extra-industry role, that of "reporter" (or, as we say in Hollywood, "journalist"), with credentials that gave me a seat in the Omni but access to only a rotating pass to go on the floor. I was waiting for this rotating pass one evening when I ran into a director I knew, Paul Mazursky. We talked for a moment, and I noticed that he, like all the other industry people I saw in Atlanta, had a top pass, one of the several all-access passes. In this case it was a floor pass, and, since I was working and he seemed not about to go on the floor, I asked if I might borrow it for half an hour.

He considered this.

He would, he said, "really like" to do this for me, but thought not. He seemed surprised that I had asked, and uncomfortable that I had breached the natural order of the community as we both knew it: directors and actors and producers, I should have understood, have floor passes. Writers do not, which is why they strike.

—1988

Down at City Hall

JUST INSIDE the main lobby of City Hall in Los Angeles there was for some time a curious shrine to Tom Bradley, the seventy-one-year-old black former police officer who was in April of 1989 elected to his fifth four-year term as mayor of Los Angeles. There was an Olympic flag, suspended behind glass and lit reverentially, its five interlocking rings worked in bright satin. There were, displayed in a kind of architectural niche, various other mementos of the 1984 Los Angeles Olympics, the event that remained the symbolic centerpiece not only of Tom Bradley's sixteen-year administration (arriving passengers at LAX, for example, were for some years after 1984 confronted on the down escalators by large pictures of Mayor Bradley and the somewhat unsettling legend "Welcome to Los Angeles XXIII Olympiad," as if the plane had touched down in a time warp), but of what Bradley's people liked to present as the city's ascension, under his guidance, to American capital of the Pacific rim.

And there was, behind a crimson silk rope, a sheet of glass on which a three-dimensional holographic image of Tom Bradley, telephone to ear, appeared and disappeared. If the viewer moved to the right, the mayor could be seen to smile; if the viewer moved to the left, the mayor turned grave, and lowered his head to study a paper. From certain angles the mayor vanished altogether, leaving only an eerie blue. It was this disappearing effect, mirroring as it did what many saw as a certain elusiveness about the mayor himself, that most often arrested the passing citizen. "That's the shot on the Jackson endorsement," I recall a television cameraman saying as we passed this dematerializing Tom Bradley one afternoon in June of 1988, a few days before the California presidential primary, on our way from a press conference during which the actual Tom Bradley had successfully, and quite characteristically, managed to appear with Jesse Jackson without in the least recommending him.

In fact it seemed the shot on the entire Bradley administration, the enduring electability of which was something many people in Los Angeles found hard to define, or even to talk about. "I don't think Tom Bradley is beatable," I was told not long before the 1989 mayoralty election by Zev Yaroslavsky, a Los Angeles City Council member who ran an abortive campaign against Bradley in 1985 and aborted a second campaign against him in January of 1989. "At least not by me. His personal popularity transcends the fact that he has been presiding over a city that in some aspects has been experiencing serious difficulties during his term in office. Most people agree that we've got this traffic, that air quality stinks, that they see a hundred and one things wrong with the quality of life. But nobody blames him for it."

In part because of this perceived ability to float free of his own administration and in part because of his presumed attractiveness to black voters, Tom Bradley was over the years repeatedly mentioned, usually in the same clause with Andrew Young, as a potential national figure, even a vice-presidential possibility. This persistent white fantasy to one side, Tom Bradley was never a charismatic, or even a particularly comfortable, candidate. His margin in the April 1989 election, for which a large majority of Los Angeles voters did not bother even to turn out, was surprisingly low. His votes never traveled outside Los Angeles. He twice tried, in 1982 and in 1986, to become governor of California, and was twice defeated by George Deukmejian, not himself noted for much sparkle as a candidate.

Bradley's strength in Los Angeles did not derive exclusively or even principally from the black community, which, in a city where the fastest-growing ethnic groups were Asian and Hispanic, constituted a decreasing percentage of the population and in any case had come to vote for Bradley, who was the first black ever elected to the Los Angeles City Council, grudgingly at best. One city official to whom I spoke during the 1989 campaign pointed out that when Bradley last ran for governor, there was a falling off in even those low-income black precincts in south-central Los Angeles that had previously been, however unenthusiastically, his territory. "He assumed south-central would be there for him," she said. "And so he didn't work it. And having been taken for granted, it wasn't there."

"He is probably less liked in south-central than other elected officials who represent south-central," another city official conceded. "I mean they view him as somebody who is maybe more interested in wining and dining Prince Andrew and Princess Sarah or whatever her name is than in dealing with the crumbling floor in the Nickerson Gardens gymnasium."

Nickerson Gardens was a housing project in Watts, where people may vote but tended not to bid on city contracts, tended not to exhibit interest in the precise location of proposed freeway exits, tended not to have projects that could be made "important" to the mayor because they were "important" to them; tended not, in other words, to require the kind of access that generates contributions to a campaign. Tom Bradley was an access politician in the traditional mold. "We would be rather disappointed if, having supported him, he were inaccessible to us," Eli Broad, a longtime Bradley supporter and the chairman of Kaufman & Broad, told the *Los Angeles Times* during the summer of 1988. "It's not really a quid pro quo. [But] there's no question that . . . if someone . . . wants money for the campaign, and if you want to talk to them six months later and don't hear from them, you just don't give any more."

Kaufman & Broad was at that time the largest builder of single-family houses in California, the developer and builder of such subdivisions as California Dawn ("From $108,990, 2, 3, and 4 Bedroom Homes"), California Esprit ("From the low $130,000s, 3 and 4 Bedroom Homes"), and California Gallery ("From $150,000, 3 and 4 Bedroom Homes"). California Dawn, California Esprit, and California Gallery were all in Palmdale, on the Mojave desert, an hour and a half northeast of Los Angeles. According to the final report of the Los Angeles 2000 Committee, a group appointed by Mayor Bradley to recommend a development strategy for the city, the Los Angeles Department of Airports was reviving a languishing plan to build an international airport on 17,750 acres the city happened to own six miles from the center of Palmdale.

The notion of building a Palmdale airport, first proposed in 1968 and more or less dormant since the midseventies, had met, over the years, considerable resistance, not the least of which derived from an almost total disinclination on the part of both carriers and passengers to go to Palmdale. But the possibilities were clear at the outset. There would be first of all the acquisition of the 17,750 acres (which would ultimately cost the city about $100 million to buy and to maintain), and the speculative boom that would accompany any such large-scale public acquisition. There would be the need for a highway project, estimated early on at another $100 million, to link Palmdale with the population. There could even be the eventual possibility of a $1.5 billion mountain tunnel, cutting the distance roughly in half. The construction of a monorail could be investigated. The creation of a foreign-trade zone could be studied. There would be the demand not only for housing (as in California Dawn, California Esprit, and California Gallery) but for schools, shopping centers, aircraft-related industry.

This hypothetical Palmdale International Airport, then, had survived as that ideal civic project, the one that just hangs in there, sometimes a threat, sometimes a promise, in either case a money machine. Here was the way the machine worked: with the encouragement of interested investors and an interested city government, the city would eventually reach Palmdale, and the Palmdale International Airport would reach critical mass, at which point many possibilities would be realized and many opportunities generated, both for development and for the access required to facilitate that development. This has been the history of Los Angeles.

Tom Bradley turned up in June of 1988 at a dinner dance honoring Eli Broad. He turned up in September of 1988 as a speaker at a party celebrating Kaufman & Broad's thirtieth anniversary. Bradley's most useful tool as a campaigner may well have been this practice of turning up wherever a supporter or potential supporter asked him to turn up, an impassive and slightly baffling stranger at bar mitzvahs and anniversary cocktail parties and backyard barbecues. "It is just something that I do because I enjoy it," Bradley told the *Los Angeles Times* in the summer of 1988 about another such event, a neighborhood barbecue at the South El Monte home of one of his planning commissioners. "I showed up and I tell you, you've never seen a happier couple in your life than that man and his wife. And the whole family was there. . . . As we were out in the front yard chatting or taking pictures, everybody who drove by was honking and waving. It was important to him. He enjoyed that. And I enjoyed his enjoyment. I get a pleasure out of that."

This fairly impenetrable style was often referred to locally as "low-keyed," or "conciliatory," which seemed in context to be code words for staying out of the way, not making waves, raising the money and granting the access the money is meant to secure. Tom Bradley was generally regarded as a pro-business, pro-development mayor, a supporter of the kinds of redevelopment and public works projects that tend, however problematical their ultimate public benefit, to suggest considerable opportunity to the kinds of people who are apt to support one or another political campaign. He was often credited with having built the downtown skyline, which translated roughly into having encouraged developers to think of downtown Los Angeles, which was until his tenure a rather somnolent financial district enlivened by the fact that it was also *el centro*, the commercial core of the Mexican and Central American communities, as bulldozable, a raw canvas to be rendered indistinguishable from Atlanta or Houston.

Bradley was redeveloping Watts. He was redeveloping Hollywood. He was redeveloping, in all, more than seven thousand acres around town. He was building—in a city so decentralized as to render conventional mass transit virtually useless and at a time when big transit projects had been largely discredited (one transportation economist had demonstrated that San Francisco's BART system must operate for 535 years before the energy presumably saved by its use catches up with the energy expended on its construction)—one of the world's most expensive mass-transit projects: $3.5 billion for the projected twenty miles of track, from downtown through Hollywood and over Cahuenga Pass to the San Fernando Valley, that would constitute the system's "first phase" and "second phase." This route was one that, according to the project's opponents, could serve at maximum use only 1.5 percent of the work force; most of that 1.5 percent, however, either lived or worked in the heart of the Hollywood Redevelopment. "You go out to where the houses stop and buy land," Bob Hope is supposed to have said when he was asked how he made so much money. This is, in Los Angeles, one way to make money, and the second is to buy land on which the houses have already been built, and get the city to redevelop it.

Metrorail and the Hollywood Redevelopment were of course big projects, major ways of creating opportunity. The true Bradley style was perhaps most apparent when the opportunities were small, for example in the proposal during the spring of 1989 to sell a thirty-five-year-old public housing project, Jordan Downs, to a private developer. Jordan Downs was in Watts, south-central. The price asked for Jordan Downs was reported to be around $10 million. The deal was to include a pledge by the prospective buyer to spend an additional $14 million renovating the project.

Now. When we talk about Jordan Downs we are talking about seven hundred rental units in a virtual war zone, an area where the median family income was $11,427 and even children carried AK-47s. Presented with a developer who wants to spend $24 million to take on the very kind of property that owners all over the country are trying, if not to torch, at least to abandon, the average urban citizen looks for subtext. The subtext in this instance was not hard to find: Jordan Downs was a forty-acre piece of property, only 15 percent of which was developed. This largely undeveloped property bordered both the Century Freeway, which was soon to be completed, and the Watts Redevelopment. In other words the property would very soon, if all went as planned, vastly increase in value, and 85 percent of it would be in hand, available either for resale or for development.

Nor was the developed 15 percent of the property, Jordan Downs itself, the problem it might have seemed at first glance. The project, it turned out, would have to be maintained as low-income rental housing for an estimated period of at most fifteen years, during which time the developer stood in any case to receive, from the federal Department of Housing and Urban Development and the city housing authority, a guaranteed subsidy of $420,000 a month plus federal tax credits estimated at $1.6 million a year. This was the kind of small perfect deal—nobody is actually hurt by it, unless the nobody happens to be a tenant at Jordan Downs, and unable to pay the rent required to make the property break even—that has traditionally been the mother's milk of urban politics. But many people believed

Los Angeles to be different, and in one significant aspect it was: the difference in Los Angeles was that very few of its citizens seemed to notice the small perfect deals, or, if they did notice, to much care.

It was believed for a while during 1988 in Los Angeles that Zev Yaroslavsky, who represented the largely west-side and affluent Fifth District in the Los Angeles City Council (the Fifth includes, in the basin, Beverly-Fairfax, Century City, Bel Air, Westwood, and part of West Los Angeles, and, in the San Fernando Valley, parts of Sherman Oaks, Van Nuys, and North Hollywood), could beat Bradley. It was, people said, "Zev's year." It was said to be "time for Zev." It was to be, Zev Yaroslavsky himself frequently said, "an election about who runs Los Angeles," meaning do a handful of developers run it or do the rest of the citizens run it. He had raised almost $2 million. He had gained the support of a number of local players who had previously backed Bradley, including Marc Nathanson, the chairman of Falcon Cable TV, and Barry Diller, the chairman of Twentieth Century-Fox. He had flat-out won what many saw as an exhibition game for the mayoralty race: a showdown, in November of 1988, between Armand Hammer's Occidental Petroleum Corporation, which had wanted since 1966 to begin drilling for oil on two acres it was holding across the Pacific Coast Highway from Will Rogers State Beach, and the many people who did not want—and had so far, through a series of legal maneuvers, managed to prevent—this drilling.

The showdown took the form of placing opposing propositions, one co-sponsored by Zev Yaroslavsky and the other by an Occidental front calling itself the Los Angeles Public and Coastal Protection Committee, before the voters on the November 8, 1988, ballot. The Los Angeles Public and Coastal Protection Committee had some notable talent prepared to labor on its behalf. It had the support of Mayor Bradley. It would have, by the eve of the election, the endorsement of the *Los Angeles Times*. It had not only Armand Hammer's own attorney, Arthur Groman, but also, and perhaps most importantly, Mickey Kantor, of Manatt, Phelps, Rothenberg, and Phillips, a law firm so deeply connected to Democratic power in California that most people believed Bradley to be backing the Occidental proposition not for Armand Hammer but for Manatt. It had Robert Shrum, of Doak & Shrum, who used to write speeches for Ted Kennedy but was now running campaigns in California. It had, above all, $7.3 million, $7.1 million of it provided directly by Occidental.

There was considerable opacity about this entire endeavor. In the first place, the wording of the Los Angeles Public and Coastal Protection Committee (or Occidental) proposition tended to equate a vote for drilling with a vote for more efficient crime fighting, for more intensive drug-busting, for better schools, and for the cleanup of toxic wastes, all of which were floated as part of Occidental's dedication to public and coastal protection. In the second place, the players themselves had kept changing sides. On the side of the antidrilling proposition there was of course its co-author, Zev Yaroslavsky, but Zev Yaroslavsky had backed Occidental when the drilling question came before the City Council in 1978. On the side of the Occidental proposition there was of course Tom Bradley, but Tom Bradley had first been elected mayor, in 1973, on an anti-Occidental platform, and in 1978 he had vetoed drilling on the Pacific Coast Highway site after the City Council approved it.

During the summer and fall of 1988, when the drilling and the antidrilling propositions were placed fairly insistently before the voters, there were seventeen operating oil fields around town, with tens of thousands of wells. There were more wells along the highways leading north and south. Oil was being pumped from the Beverly Hills High School campus. Oil was being pumped from the golf course at the Hillcrest Country Club. Oil was being pumped from the Twentieth Century-Fox lot. Off Carpinteria, south of Santa Barbara, oil was being pumped offshore, and even people who had expensive beach houses at Rincon del Mar had come to think of the rigs as not entirely unattractive features of the view—something a little mysterious out there in the mist, something a little Japanese on the horizon. In other words the drilling for and pumping of crude oil in Southern California had not historically carried much true political resonance, which made this battle of the propositions a largely symbolic, or "political," confrontation, not entirely about oil drilling. That Zev Yaroslavsky won it

—and won it spending only $2.8 million, some $4 million less than Occidental spent—seemed to many to suggest a certain discontent with the way things were going, a certain desire for change: the very desire for change on which Zev Yaroslavsky was planning, in the course of his campaign for the mayor's office, to run.

There was, early on, considerable interest in this promised mayoralty race between Tom Bradley and Zev Yaroslavsky. Some saw the contest, and this was the way the Bradley people liked to present it, as a long-awaited confrontation between the rest of the city (Bradley) and the West Side (Yaroslavsky), which was well-off, heavily Jewish, and the only part of the city that visitors to Los Angeles normally saw. This scenario had in fact been laid out in the drilling battle, during which Occidental, by way of Mickey Kantor and Robert Shrum, introduced the notion that a vote for Occidental was a vote against "a few selfish people who don't want their beach view obstructed," against "elitists," against, in other words, the West Side. "The euphemism they kept using here was that it was another ploy by the 'rich Westsiders' against the poor minorities and the blacks," I was told by a deputy to Councilman Marvin Braude, who had co-authored the antidrilling proposition with Zev Yaroslavsky and in whose district Occidental's Pacific Coast Highway property lay. "You always heard about 'rich Westsiders' in connection with anything we were doing. It was the euphemism for the Jews."

Others saw the race, and this was increasingly the way the Yaroslavsky people liked to frame it, as a confrontation between the forces of unrestricted growth (developers, the oil business, Bradley) and the proponents of controlled, or "slow," growth (environmentalists, the No Oil lobby, the West Side, Yaroslavsky). Neither version was long on nuance, and both tended to overlook facts that did not support the favored angles (Bradley had for years been the West Side's own candidate, for example, and Yaroslavsky had himself broken bread with a developer or two), but the two scenarios, Yaroslavsky's *Greed v. Slow Growth* and Bradley's *The People v. the West Side*, continued to provide, for that handful of people in Los Angeles who actually followed city politics, a kind of narrative line. The election would fall, as these people saw it, to whoever told his story best, to whoever had the best tellers, the best fixers.

Only a few people in Los Angeles were believed to be able to fix things, whether the things to be fixed, or arranged, or managed, were labor problems or city permits or elections. There was the master of them all, Paul Ziffren, whose practice as a lawyer had often been indistinguishable from the practice of politics, but he was by the time of this race less active than he had once been. There was his son Kenneth Ziffren, who settled the Writers Guild of America strike in the summer of 1988. There was, operating in a slightly different arena, Sidney Korshak, who settled the Delano grape strike against Schenley in 1966. There was almost anybody at the Manatt office. There was Joseph Cerrell, a political consultant about whom it had been said, "You want to get elected to the judicial, you call him, a campaign can run you fifty thousand dollars." There was Robert Shrum, who worked Alan Cranston's last campaign for the Senate and Representative Richard Gephardt's campaign in the 1988 presidential primaries. There were Michael Berman and Carl D'Agostino, of BAD Campaigns, Inc., who were considered direct mail (most of it negative) geniuses and were central to what was locally called "the Waxman-Berman machine," the Democratic and quite specifically Jewish political organization built by Michael Berman; his brother, Representative Howard Berman; Representative Henry Waxman; and Representative Mel Levine, who was positioning himself to run for Alan Cranston's Senate seat in 1992. It was Michael Berman who figured out how to send Howard Berman and Henry Waxman and Mel Levine to Congress in the first place. It was Michael Berman and Carl D'Agostino who continued to figure out how to elect Waxman-Berman candidates on the state and local levels.

These figures were not without a certain local glamour, and a considerable amount of the interest in this mayoralty race derived from the fact that Doak & Shrum—which, remember, had been part of Mickey Kantor's team on the Occidental proposition—was working for Bradley, while Berman and

D'Agostino, who had been hired by Yaroslavsky and Braude to run their antidrilling proposition, were backing Yaroslavsky. A mayoralty contest between Shrum and the Berman-D'Agostino firm, Bill Boyarsky wrote in the *Los Angeles Times*, could be "one of the great matchups of low-down campaigning"; in other words a chance, as I recall being told in June of 1988 by someone else, "for Berman and D'Agostino to knock off Doak & Shrum."

Then something happened, nobody was saying quite how. One Friday in August of 1988, a reporter at the *Los Angeles Times*, Kenneth Reich, got a phone call from a woman who refused to identify herself but said that she was sending him certain material prepared by BAD Campaigns, Inc. The material —delivered the following Monday with a typewritten and unsigned note reading, "You should be interested to see this. Government is bad enough without BAD"—consisted of three strategy memos addressed to Zev Yaroslavsky. One was dated March 29, 1988, another was dated May 4, 1988, and the third, headed "Things to Do," was undated.

Berman and D'Agostino acknowledged that the two dated documents were early drafts of memos prepared by their office, but denied having written the undated memo, which, accordingly, was never printed by the *Times*. The memos that were printed, which Yaroslavsky charged had been stolen from a three-ring binder belonging to one of his aides, had, however, an immediately electrifying effect, not because they said anything that most interested people in Los Angeles did not know or believe but because they violated the local social contract by saying it out loud, and in the vernacular. The memos printed in the *Times* read, in part:

> The reason why BAD thinks you [Yaroslavsky] can beat Bradley is: you've got fifty IQ-points on him (and that's no compliment). . . . Just because you are more slow-growth than Bradley does not mean you can take anti-growth voters for granted . . . many are racially tolerant people who are strongly pulled to Bradley because of his height, skin color, and calm demeanor. They like voting for him—they feel less guilty about how little they used to pay their household help. . . .

> Yaroslavsky's vision [should be that] there is no reason on this earth why some flitty restaurateur should be allowed to build a hotel at the corner of Beverly and La Cienega. . . . The Yaroslavsky vision says "there is no reason on earth why anyone should be building more places to shop in West L.A." . . . There is no reason for guilt-ridden liberals to vote out of office that fine, dignified "person of color" except that your Vision is total, unwavering and convincing. You want to hug every tree, stop every new building, end the traffic jams and clean up the Bay. . . .
>
> To beat Bradley, you must be intensely, thoroughly and totally committed to your vision of L.A. . . . It is the way you overcome the racial tug many Jews and non-Jewish liberals feel toward Bradley. It is also the way you overcome the possible Republican preference for the conservative black over the Jewish kid friendly with the Waxman-Berman machine. . . .
>
> Bradley can and will excite black voters to outvote the white electorate especially if there is a runoff where his mayoral office is seen as jeopardized by a perfidious Jew. . . .
>
> What we do know is that Jewish wealth in Los Angeles is endless. That almost every Jewish person who meets you will like you and that asking for $2,000 is not an unreasonable request to people who are both wealthy and like you. . . .
>
> The Yaroslavsky campaign becomes the United Jewish appeal. . . .

This was not, on the face of it, remarkable stuff. The language in the memos was widely described as "cynical," but of course it was not: it was just the working shorthand of people who might even be said, on the evidence of what they wrote down, to have an idealized view of the system, people who noticed the small perfect deals and did not approve of them, or at any rate assumed that there was an electorate out there that did not approve of them. This may have been an erroneous assumption, a strategic miscalculation, but the idea that some of Yaroslavsky's people might have miscalculated the electorate was not, for some people who had supported him and were now beginning to back away, the problem.

"Make a complete list of mainstream Jewish charities," the March 29 memo had advised. "Find a person in each charity to slip us a list with name, address and phone numbers of $1,000-and-above contributors. . . . Zev begins dialing for dollars. . . . Make a list of 50 contributors to Zev who have not participated to their ability and who belong to every Jewish country club in the L.A. area. . . . Make a list of every studio, Hollywood PR firm and 100 top show business personalities in Jewish Los Angeles. . . . You cannot let Bradley become the chichi, in, campaign against the pushy Jew. . . ."

It was this acknowledgment, even this insistence, that there were in Los Angeles not only Jewish voters but specifically Jewish interests, and Jewish money, that troubled many people, most particularly those very members of the West Side Jewish community on whose support the Yaroslavsky people were counting. What happened next was largely a matter of "perceptions," of a very few people talking among themselves, as they were used to talking whenever there was something to be decided, some candidate or cause to be backed or not backed. The word "divisive" started coming up again and again. It would be, people were saying, a "divisive" campaign, even a "disastrous" campaign, a campaign that would "pit the blacks against the Jews." There was, it was said, "already enough trouble," trouble that had been simmering, as these people saw it, since at least 1985, when Tom Bradley's Jewish supporters on the West Side had insisted that he denounce the Reverend Louis Farrakhan, and some black leaders had protested that Bradley should not be taking orders from the West Side. This issue of race, most people hastened to say, would never be raised by the candidates themselves. The problem would be, as Neil Sandberg of the American Jewish Committee put it to Bill Boyarsky of the *Los Angeles Times*, "undisciplined elements in both communities." The problem would be, in other words, the candidates' "people."

Discussions were held. Many telephone calls were made. In December of 1988, a letter was drafted and signed by some of the most politically active people on the West Side. This letter called on Zev Yaroslavsky to back off, not to run, not to proceed on a course that the signers construed as an invitation, if not to open ethnic conflict, at least to a breaking apart of the coalition between the black and Jewish communities that had given the West Side its recent power over the old-line Los Angeles establishment—the downtown and San Marino money base, which was what people in Los Angeles meant when they referred to the California Club. On the sixth of January, citing a private poll that showed Bradley to be running far ahead, Zev Yaroslavsky announced that he would not run. The BAD memos, he said, had "played absolutely no role" in his decision to withdraw. The "fear of a divisive campaign," he said, had "played no role on my part."

This "fear of a divisive campaign," and the attendant specter of the membership of the California Club invading City Hall, seemed on the face of it incorporeal, one of those received fears that sometimes overtake a community and redirect the course of its affairs. Still, the convergence of the BAD memos and the polarization implicit in the Occidental campaign had generated a considerable amount of what could only be described as class conflict. "Most of us have known for a long time that the environmentalists are . . . white, middle-class groups who have not really shown a lot of concern about the black community or black issues," Maxine Waters, who represented part of south-central in the California State Assembly and was probably the most effective and visible black politician in Southern California, told Bill Boyarsky when he talked to her, after the publication of the BAD memos, about the drilling issue. "Yet we have continued to give support. . . . I want to tell you I may very well support the oil drilling. I feel such a need to assert independence from this kind of crap, and I feel such a need for the black community not to be led on by someone else's agenda and not even knowing what the agenda was."

One afternoon in February of 1989 when I happened to be in City Hall seeing Zev Yaroslavsky and Marvin Braude, I asked what they made of the "divisive campaign" question. The apprehension, Yaroslavsky said, had been confined to "a very small group of people," whose concern, as he saw it, had been "fueled by my neighbors here in the mayor's office, who were trying to say we could have another Chicago, another Ed Koch."

"Some of it started before your candidacy," Marvin Braude said to him. "With the Farrakhan incident. That set the tone of it."

"Let me tell you," Zev Yaroslavsky said. "If there's any reason why I would have run, it would have been to disprove that notion. Because nothing so offends me—politically and personally—as the notion that I, simply because I'm white or Jewish, don't have the right to run against a fourth-term incumbent just because he happens to be black."

Zev Yaroslavsky, at that point, was mounting a campaign to save his own council seat. He had put the mayoral campaign behind him. Still, it rankled. "Nothing I was talking about had remotely to do with race," he said. "It never would have been an issue, unless Bradley brought it up. But I must say they made every effort to put everything we did into a racial context. They tried to make the Oxy oil initiative racial. They tried to make Proposition U—which was our first slow-growth initiative—racial. They pitted rich against poor, white against black, West Side against South Side—"

"It wasn't only Bradley," Marvin Braude said, interrupting. "It was the people who were using this for their own selfish purposes. It was the developers. It was Occidental."

"I think if the election had gone on . . ." Zev Yaroslavsky paused. "It doesn't matter. At this point it's speculative. But I think the mayor and his people, especially his people, were running a very risky strategy of trying to make race an issue. For their candidate's benefit."

During the week in February 1989 when I saw Zev Yaroslavsky and Marvin Braude, the *Los Angeles Times* Poll did a telephone sampling to determine local attitudes toward the city and its mayor. About 60 percent of those polled, the *Times* reported a few days later, under the headline "People Turn Pessimistic About Life in Los Angeles," believed that the "quality of life" in Los Angeles had deteriorated during the last fifteen years. About 50 percent said that within the past year they had considered leaving Los Angeles, mainly for San Diego. Sixty-seven percent of those polled, however, believed that Tom Bradley, who had been mayor during this period when the quality of life had so deteriorated that many of them were thinking of moving to San Diego, had done a good job.

This was not actually news. On the whole, life in Los Angeles, perhaps because it is a city so largely populated by people who are ready to drop everything and move to San Diego (just as they or their parents or their grandparents had dropped everything and moved to Los Angeles), seems not to encourage a conventional interest in its elected officials. "Nobody but the press corps and a few elites care anything about the day-to-day workings in city government" is the way this was put in one of the "cynical" BAD memos.

In fact there were maybe a hundred people in Los Angeles, aside from the handful of reporters assigned to the city desk, who followed City Hall. A significant number of the hundred were lawyers at Manatt. All of the hundred were people who understand access. Some of these people said that of course Zev Yaroslavsky would run again, in 1993, when he would be only forty-four and Tom Bradley would be seventy-five and presumably ready to step aside. Nineteen ninety-three, in this revised view, would be "Zev's year." Nineteen ninety-three would be "time for Zev." Others said that 1993 would be too late, that the entire question of whether or not Zev Yaroslavsky could hold together Tom Bradley's famous black-Jewish coalition would be, in a Los Angeles increasingly populated by Hispanics and Asians, irrelevant, history, moot. Nineteen ninety-three, these people said, would be the year for other people altogether, for more recent figures on the local political landscape, for people like Gloria Molina or Richard Alatorre, people like Mike Woo, people whose names would tell a different story, although not necessarily to a different hundred people.

—1989

L.A. Noir

AROUND DIVISION 47, Los Angeles Municipal Court, the downtown courtroom where, for eleven weeks during the spring and summer of 1989, a preliminary hearing was held to determine if the charges brought in the 1983 murder of a thirty-three-year-old road-show promoter named Roy Alexander Radin should be dismissed or if the defendants should be bound over to superior court for arraignment and trial, it was said that there were, "in the works," five movies, four books, and "countless" pieces about the case. Sometimes it was said that there were four movies and five books "in the works," or one movie and two books, or two movies and six books. There were, in any event, "big balls" in the air. "Everybody's working this one," a reporter covering the trial said one morning as we waited to get patted down at the entrance to the courtroom, a security measure prompted by a telephoned bomb threat and encouraged by the general wish of everyone involved to make this a noticeable case. "Major money."

This was curious. Murder cases are generally of interest to the extent that they suggest some anomaly or lesson in the world revealed, but there seemed neither anomalies nor lessons in the murder of Roy Radin, who was last seen alive getting into a limousine to go to dinner at a Beverly Hills restaurant, La Scala, and was next seen decomposed, in a canyon off Interstate 5. Among the defendants actually present for the preliminary hearing was Karen Delayne ("Lanie") Jacobs Greenberger, a fairly attractive hard case late of South Florida, where her husband was said to have been the number-two man in the cocaine operation run by Carlos Lehder, the only major Colombian drug figure to have been tried and convicted in the United States. (Lanie Greenberger herself was said to have done considerable business in this line, and to have had nearly a million dollars in cocaine and cash stolen from her Sherman Oaks house not long before Roy Radin disappeared.) The other defendants present were William Mentzer and Alex Marti, somewhat less attractive hard cases, late of Larry Flynt's security staff. (Larry Flynt is the publisher of *Hustler*, and one of the collateral artifacts that turned up in the Radin case was a million-dollar check Flynt had written in 1983 to the late Mitchell Livingston WerBell III, a former arms dealer who operated a counterterrorism school outside Atlanta and described himself as a retired lieutenant general in the Royal Free Afghan Army. The Los Angeles County Sheriff's Department said that Flynt had written the check to WerBell as payment on a contract to kill Frank Sinatra, Hugh Hefner, Bob Guccione, and Walter Annenberg. Larry Flynt's lawyer said that there had been no contract, and described the check, on which payment was stopped, as a dinner-party joke.) There was also an absent defendant, a third Flynt security man, fighting extradition from Maryland.

In other words this was a genre case, and the genre, L.A. *noir*, was familiar. There is a *noir* case every year or two in Los Angeles. There was for example the Wonderland case, which involved the 1981 bludgeoning to death of four people. The Wonderland case, so called because the bludgeoning took place in a house on Wonderland Avenue in Laurel Canyon, turned, like the Radin case, on a million-dollar cocaine theft, but featured even more deeply *noir* players, including a nightclub entrepreneur and convicted cocaine dealer named Adel Nasrallah, aka "Eddie Nash"; a pornographic-movie star, now dead of AIDS, named John C. Holmes, aka "Johnny Wadd"; and a young man named Scott Thorson, who was, at the time he first testified in the case, an inmate in the Los Angeles County Jail (Scott Thorson was, in the natural ecology of the criminal justice system, the star witness for the state in the Wonderland case), and who in 1982 sued Liberace on the grounds that he had been promised $100,000 a year for life in return for his services as Liberace's lover, driver, travel secretary, and animal trainer.

In this context there would have seemed nothing particularly novel about the Radin case. It was true that there were, floating around the edges of the story, several other unnatural deaths, for example that of Lanie Greenberger's husband, Larry Greenberger, aka "Vinnie De Angelo," who either shot himself or was shot in the head in September of 1988 on the front porch of his house in Okeechobee, Florida, but these deaths were essentially unsurprising. It was also true that the

Radin case offered not bad sidebar details. I was interested for example in how much security Larry Flynt apparently had patrolling Doheny Estates, where his house was, and Century City, where the *Hustler* offices were. I was interested in Dean Kahn, who ran the limousine service that provided the stretch Cadillac with smoked windows in which Roy Radin took, in the language of this particular revealed world, his last ride. I was interested in how Roy Radin, before he came to Los Angeles and decided to go to dinner at La Scala, had endeavored to make his way in the world by touring high school auditoriums with Tiny Tim, Frank Fontaine, and a corps of tap-dancing dwarfs.

Still, promoters of tap-dancing dwarfs who get done in by hard cases have not been, historically, the stuff of which five movies, four books, and countless pieces are made. The almost febrile interest in this case derived not from the principals but from what was essentially a cameo role, played by Robert Evans. Robert Evans had been head of production at Paramount during the golden period of *The Godfather* and *Love Story* and *Rosemary's Baby*, had moved on to produce independently such successful motion pictures as *Chinatown* and *Marathon Man*, and was, during what was generally agreed to be a dry spell in his career (he had recently made a forty-five-minute videotape on the life of John Paul II, and had announced that he was writing an autobiography, to be called *The Kid Stays in the Picture*), a district attorney's dream: a quite possibly desperate, quite famously risk-oriented, high-visibility figure with low-life connections.

It was the contention of the Los Angeles County District Attorney's office that Lanie Greenberger had hired her codefendants to kill Roy Radin after he refused to cut her in on his share of the profits from Robert Evans's 1984 picture *The Cotton Club*. It was claimed that Lanie Greenberger had introduced Roy Radin, who wanted to get into the movie business, to Robert Evans. It was claimed that Roy Radin had offered to find, in return for 45 percent of the profits from either one Evans picture (*The Cotton Club*) or three Evans pictures (*The Cotton Club*, *The Sicilian*, and *The Two Jakes*), "Puerto Rican investors" willing to put up either thirty-five or fifty million dollars.

Certain objections leap to the nonprosecutorial mind here (the "Puerto Rican investors" turned out to be one Puerto Rican banker with "connections," the money never actually materialized, Roy Radin therefore had no share of the profits, there were no profits in any case), but seem not to have figured in the state's case. The District Attorney's office was also hinting, if not quite contending, that Robert Evans himself had been in on the payoff of Radin's killers, and the DA's office had a protected witness (still another Flynt security man, this one receiving $3,000 a month from the Los Angeles County Sheriff's Department) who had agreed to say in court that one of the defendants, William Mentzer, told him that Lanie Greenberger and Robert Evans had, in the witness's words, "paid for the contract." Given the state's own logic, it was hard to know what Robert Evans might have thought to gain by putting out a contract on the goose with the $50 million egg, but the deputy district attorney on the case seemed unwilling to let go of this possibility, and had in fact told reporters that Robert Evans was "one of the people who we have not eliminated as a suspect."

Neither, on the other hand, was Robert Evans one of the people they had arrested, a circumstance suggesting certain lacunae in the case from the major-money point of view, and also from the district attorney's. Among people outside the criminal justice system, it was widely if vaguely assumed that Robert Evans was somehow "on trial" during the summer of 1989. "Evans Linked for First Time in Court to Radin's Murder," the headlines were telling them, and, in the past-tense obituary mode, "Evans' Success Came Early: Career Epitomized Hollywood Dream."

"Bob always had a premonition that his career would peak before he was fifty and fade downhill," Peter Bart, who had worked under Evans at Paramount, told the *Los Angeles Times*, again in the obituary mode. "He lived by it. He was haunted by it. . . . To those of us who knew him and knew what a good-spirited person he was, it's a terrible sadness." Here was a case described by the *Times* as "focused on the dark side of Hollywood deal making," a case offering "an unsparing look at the film capital's unsavory side," a case everyone was calling just Cotton Club, or even just Cotton, as in "'Cotton': Big Movie Deal's Sequel Is Murder."

Inside the system, the fact that no charge had been brought against the single person on the horizon who had a demonstrable connection with *The Cotton Club* was rendering Cotton Club, *qua* Cotton Club, increasingly problematic. Not only was Robert Evans not "on trial" in Division 47, but what was going on there was not even a "trial," only a preliminary hearing, intended to determine whether the state had sufficient evidence and cause to prosecute those charged, none of whom was Evans. Since 1978, when a California Supreme Court ruling provided criminal defendants the right to a preliminary hearing even after indictment by a grand jury, preliminary hearings have virtually replaced grand juries as a way of indicting felony suspects in California, and are one of the reasons that criminal cases in Los Angeles now tend to go on for years. The preliminary hearing alone in the McMartin child-abuse case lasted eighteen months.

On the days I dropped by Division 47, the judge, a young black woman with a shock of gray in her hair, seemed fretful, inattentive. The lawyers seemed weary. The bailiffs discussed their domestic arrangements on the telephone. When Lanie Greenberger entered the courtroom, not exactly walking but undulating forward on the balls of her feet, in a little half-time prance, no one bothered to look up. The courtroom had been full on the day Robert Evans appeared as the first witness for the prosecution and took the Fifth, but in the absence of Evans there were only a few reporters and the usual two or three retirees in the courtroom, perhaps a dozen people in all, reduced to interviewing each other and discussing alternative names for the Night Stalker case, which involved a man named Richard Ramirez who had been accused of thirteen murders and thirty other felonies committed in Los Angeles County during 1984 and 1985. One reporter was calling the Ramirez case, which was then in its sixth month of trial after nine weeks of preliminary hearings and six months of jury selection, Valley Intruder. Another had settled on Serial Killer. "I still slug it Night Stalker," a third said, and she turned to me. "Let me ask you," she said. "This is how hard up I am. Is there a story in your being here?"

The preliminary hearing in the Radin case had originally been scheduled for three weeks, and lasted eleven. On July 12, 1989, in Division 47, Judge Patti Jo McKay ruled not only that there was sufficient evidence to bind over Lanie Greenberger, Alex Marti, and William Mentzer for trial but also that the Radin murder may have been committed for financial gain, which meant that the defendants could receive, if convicted, penalties of death. "Mr. Radin was an obstacle to further negotiation involving *The Cotton Club*," the prosecuting attorney had argued in closing. "The deal could not go through until specific issues such as percentages were worked out. It was at that time that Mrs. Greenberger had the motive to murder Mr. Radin."

I was struck by this as a final argument, because it seemed to suggest an entire case based on the notion that an interest in an entirely hypothetical share of the entirely hypothetical profits from an entirely hypothetical motion picture (at the time Roy Radin was killed, *The Cotton Club* had an advertising poster but no shooting script and no money and no cast and no start date) was money in the bank. All that had stood between Lanie Greenberger and Fat City, as the prosecutor saw it, was boilerplate, a matter of seeing that "percentages were worked out."

The prosecution's certainty on this point puzzled me, and I asked an acquaintance in the picture business if he thought there had ever been money to be made from *The Cotton Club*. He seemed not to believe what I was asking. There had been "gross positions," he reminded me, participants with a piece of the gross rather than the net. There had been previous investors. There had been commitments already made on *The Cotton Club*, paper out all over town. There had been, above all, a $26 million budget going in (it eventually cost $47 million), and a production team not noted for thrift. "It had to make a hundred to a hundred forty million, depending on how much got stolen, before anybody saw gross," he said. "Net on this baby was dreamland. Which could have been figured out, with no loss of life, by a junior agent just out of the William Morris mailroom."

There was always in the Cotton Club case a certain dreamland aspect, a looniness that derived in part from the ardent if misplaced faith of everyone involved, from the belief in windfalls, in sudden changes of fortune (five movies and four books would change someone's fortune, a piece of *The Cotton Club* someone else's, a high-visibility case the district attorney's); in killings, both literal and figurative. In fact this kind of faith is not unusual in Los Angeles. In a city not only largely conceived as a series of real estate promotions but largely supported by a series of confidence games, a city even then afloat on motion pictures and junk bonds and the B-2 Stealth bomber, the conviction that something can be made of nothing may be one of the few narratives in which everyone participates. A belief in extreme possibilities colors daily life. Anyone might have woken up one morning and been discovered at Schwab's, or killed at Bob's Big Boy. "Luck is all around you," a silky voice says on the California State Lottery's Lotto commercials, against a background track of "Dream a Little Dream of Me." "Imagine winning millions . . . what would you do?"

During the summer of 1989 this shimmer of the possible still lay on Cotton Club, although there seemed, among those dreamers to whom I spoke in both the picture business and the criminal justice business, a certain impatience with the way the case was actually playing out. There was nobody in either business, including the detectives on the case, who could hear the words "Cotton Club" and not see a possible score, but the material was resistant. It still lacked a bankable element. There was a definite wish to move on, as they say in the picture business, to screenplay. The detectives were keeping in touch with motion picture producers, car phone to car phone, sketching in connecting lines not apparent in the courtroom. "This friend of mine in the sheriff's office laid it out for me three years ago," one producer told me. "The deal was, 'This is all about drugs, Bob Evans is involved, we're going to get him.' And so forth. He wanted me to have the story when and if the movie was done. He called me a week ago, from his car, wanted to know if I was going to move on it."

I heard a number of alternative scenarios. "The story is in this one cop who wouldn't let it go," I was told by a producer. "The story is in the peripheral characters," I was told by a detective I had reached by dialing his car phone. Another producer reported having run into Robert Evans's lawyer, Robert Shapiro, the evening before at Hillcrest Country Club, where the Thomas Hearns–Sugar Ray Leonard fight was being shown closed circuit from Caesars Palace in Las Vegas. "I asked how our boy was doing," he said, meaning Evans. "Shapiro says he's doing fine. Scotfree, he says. Here's the story. A soft guy from our world, just sitting up there in his sixteen-room house, keeps getting visits from these detectives. Big guys. Real hard guys. Apes. Waiting for him to crack."

Here we had the rough line for several quite different stories, but it would have been hard not to notice that each of them depended for its dramatic thrust on the presence of Robert Evans. I mentioned this one day to Marcia Morrissey, who—as co-counsel with the Miami trial lawyer Edward Shohat, who had defended Carlos Lehder—was representing Lanie Greenberger. "Naturally they all *want* him in," Marcia Morrissey said.

I asked if she thought the District Attorney's Office would manage to get him in.

Marcia Morrissey rolled her eyes. "That's what it's called, isn't it? I mean face it. It's called Cotton Club."

—1989

Fire Season

"I'VE SEEN fire and I've seen rain," I recall James Taylor singing over and over on the news radio station between updates on the 1978 Mandeville and Kanan fires, both of which started on October 23 of that year and could be seen burning toward each other, systematically wiping out large parts of Malibu and Pacific Palisades, from an upstairs window of my house in Brentwood. It was said that the Kanan fire was burning on a twenty-mile front and had already jumped the Pacific Coast Highway at Trancas Canyon. The stand in the Mandeville fire, it was said, would be made at Sunset Boulevard. I stood at the window and watched a house on a hill above Sunset implode, its oxygen sucked out by the force of the fire.

Some thirty-four thousand acres of Los Angeles County burned that week in 1978. More than eighty thousand acres had burned in 1968. Close to a hundred and thirty thousand acres had burned in 1970. Seventy-four-some thousand had burned in 1975, sixty-some thousand would burn in 1979. Forty-six thousand would burn in 1980, forty-five thousand in 1982. In the hills behind Malibu, where the moist air off the Pacific makes the brush grow fast, it takes about twelve years before a burn is ready to burn again. Inland, where the manzanita and sumac and chamise that make up the native brush in Southern California grow more slowly (the wild mustard that turns the hills a translucent yellow after rain is not native but exotic, introduced in the 1920s in an effort to reseed burns), regrowth takes from fifteen to twenty years. Since 1919, when the county began keeping records of its fires, some areas have burned eight times.

In other words there is nothing unusual about fires in Los Angeles, which is after all a desert city with only two distinct seasons, one beginning in January and lasting three or four months during which storms come in from the northern Pacific and it rains (often an inch every two or three hours, sometimes and in some places an inch a minute) and one lasting eight or nine months during which it burns, or gets ready to burn. Most years it is September or October before the Santa

Ana winds start blowing down through the passes and the relative humidity drops to figures like 7 or 6 or 3 percent and the bougainvillea starts rattling in the driveway and people start watching the horizon for smoke and tuning in to another of those extreme local possibilities, in this case that of imminent devastation. What was unusual in 1989, after two years of drought and a third year of less than average rainfall, was that it was ready to burn while the June fogs still lay on the coastline. On the first of May that year, months earlier than ever before, the California Department of Forestry had declared the start of fire season and begun hiring extras crews. By the last week in June there had already been more than two thousand brush and forest fires in California. Three hundred and twenty of them were burning that week alone.

One morning early that summer I drove out the San Bernardino Freeway to the headquarters of the Los Angeles County Fire Department, which was responsible not only for coordinating fire fighting and reseeding operations throughout the county but for sending, under the California Master Mutual Aid agreement, both equipment and strike teams to fires around the state. Los Angeles County sent strike teams to fight the 116,000-acre Wheeler fire in Ventura County in 1985. (The logistics of these big fires are essentially military. Within twelve hours of the first reports on the Wheeler fire, which eventually burned for two weeks and involved three thousand fire fighters flown in from around the country, a camp had materialized, equipped with kitchen, sanitation, transportation and medical facilities, a communications network, a "situation trailer," a "what if" trailer for long-range contingency planning, and a "pool coordinator," to get off-duty crews to and from the houses of residents who had offered the use of their swimming pools. "We simply superimposed a city on top of the incident," a camp spokesman said at the time.) Los Angeles County sent strike teams to fight the 100,000-acre Las Pilitas fire in San Luis Obispo County the same year. It sent specially trained people to act as "overhead" on, or to run, the crews of military personnel brought in from all over the United States to fight the Yellowstone fires in 1988.

On the June morning in 1989 when I visited the headquarters building in East Los Angeles, it was already generally agreed that, as one of the men to whom I spoke put it, "we pretty much know we're going to see some fires this year," with no probable break until January or February. (There is usually some November rain in Los Angeles, often enough to allow crews to gain control of a fire already burning, but only rarely does November rain put enough moisture into the brush to offset the Santa Ana winds that blow until the end of December.) There had been unusually early Santa Ana conditions, a week of temperatures over one hundred. The measurable moisture in the brush, a measurement the Fire Department calls the "fuel stick," was in some areas already down to single digits. The daily "burn index," which rates the probability of fire on a scale running from 0 to 200, was that morning showing figures of 45 for the Los Angeles basin, 41 for what is called the "high country," 125 for the Antelope Valley, and, for the Santa Clarita Valley, 192.

Anyone who has spent fire season in Los Angeles knows some of its special language—knows, for example, the difference between a fire that has been "controlled" and a fire that has so far been merely "contained" (a "contained" fire has been surrounded, usually by a trench half as wide as the brush is high, but is still burning out of control within this line and may well jump it), knows the difference between "full" and "partial" control ("partial" control means, if the wind changes, no control at all), knows about "backfiring" and about "making the stand" and about the difference between a Red Flag Alert (there will probably be a fire today) and a Red Flag Warning (there will probably be a Red Flag Alert within three days).

Still, "burn index" was new to me, and one of the headquarters foresters, Paul Rippens, tried that morning to explain it. "Let's take the Antelope Valley, up around Palmdale, Lancaster," he said. "For today, temperature's going to be ninety-six, humidity's going to be seventeen percent, wind speed's going to be fifteen miles per hour, and the fuel stick is six, which is getting pretty low."

"Six burns very well," another forester, John Haggenmiller, said. "If the fuel stick's up around twelve, it's pretty hard to get it to burn. That's the range that you have. Anything under six and it's ready to burn very well."

"So you correlate all that, you get an Antelope Valley

burn index today of one twenty-five, the adjective for which is 'high,'" Paul Rippens continued. "The adjectives we use are 'low,' 'moderate,' 'high,' 'very high,' and 'extreme.' One twenty-five is 'high.' High probability of fire. We had a hundred-plus-acre fire out there yesterday, about a four-hour fire. Divide the burn index by ten and you get the average flame length. So a burn index of one twenty-five is going to give you a twelve-and-a-half-foot flame length out there. If you've got a good fire burning, flame length has a lot to do with it."

"There's a possibility of a grass fire going through and not doing much damage at all," John Haggenmiller said. "Other cases, where the fuel has been allowed to build up—say you had a bug kill or a dieback, a lot of decadent fuel—you're going to get a flame length of thirty, forty feet. And it gets up into the crown of a tree and the whole thing goes down. That does a lot of damage."

Among the men to whom I spoke that morning there was a certain grudging admiration for what they called "the big hitters," the major fires, the ones people remember. "I'd say about ninety-five percent of our fires, we're able to hold down to under five acres," I was told by Captain Garry Oversby, who did community relations and education for the Fire Department. "It's the ones when we have extreme Santa Ana conditions, extreme weather—they get started, all we can do is try to hold the thing in check until the weather lays down a little bit for us. Times like that, we revert to what we call a defensive attack. Just basically go right along the edges of that fire until we can get a break. Reach a natural barrier. Or sometimes we make a stand several miles in advance of the fire—construct a line there, and then maybe set a backfire. Which will burn back toward the main fire and take out the vegetation, rob the main fire of its fuel."

They spoke of the way a true big hitter "moved," of the way it "pushed," of the way it could "spot," or throw embers and firebrands, a mile ahead of itself, rendering any kind of conventional firebreak useless; of the way a big hitter, once it got moving, would "outrun anybody." "You get the right weather conditions in Malibu, it's almost impossible to stop it," Paul Rippens said. He was talking about the fires that typically start somewhere in the brush off the Ventura Freeway and then burn twenty miles to the sea, the fires that roar over a ridge in a matter of seconds and make national news because they tend to take out, just before they hit the beach along Malibu, houses that belong to well-known people. Taking out houses is what the men at headquarters mean when they talk about "the urban interface."

"We can dump all our resources out there," Paul Rippens said, and he shrugged.

"You can pick up the flanks and channel it," John Haggenmiller said, "but until the wind stops or you run out of fuel, you can't do much else."

"You get into Malibu," Paul Rippens said, "you're looking at what we call two-story brush."

"You know the wind," John Haggenmiller said. "You're not going to change that phenomenon."

"You can dump everything you've got on that fire," Paul Rippens said. "It's still going to go to what we call the big blue break."

It occurred to me then that it had been eleven years since the October night in 1978 when I listened to James Taylor singing "Fire and Rain" between reports on how the Kanan fire had jumped the Pacific Coast Highway to go to the big blue break. On the twelve-year-average fire cycle that regulates life in Malibu, the Kanan burn, which happened to include a beach on which my husband and daughter and I had lived from 1971 until June of 1978, was coming due again. "Beautiful country burn again," I wrote in my notebook, a line from a Robinson Jeffers poem I remember at some point during every fire season, and I got up to leave.

A week or so later 3,700 acres burned in the hills west of the Antelope Valley. The flames reached sixty feet. The wind was gusting at forty miles an hour. There were 250 fire fighters on the ground, and they evacuated 1,500 residents, one of whom returned to find her house gone but managed to recover, according to the *Los Angeles Times*, "an undamaged American flag and a porcelain Nativity set handmade by her mother." A week after this Antelope Valley fire, 1,500 acres burned in the Puente Hills, above Whittier. The temperatures that day were in the high nineties, and the flames were as high as fifty feet. There were more than 970 fire fighters on the line. Two hundred and fifty families were evacuated. They took with them what people always take out of fires, mainly snapshots, mementos small enough to put in the car. "We won't have a stitch of clothing, but at least we'll have these," a woman about to leave the Puente Hills told the *Times* as she packed the snapshots into the trunk of her car.

People who live with fires think a great deal about what will happen "when," as the phrase goes in the instruction leaflets, "the fire comes." These leaflets, which are stuck up on refrigerator doors all over Los Angeles County, never say "if." When the fire comes there will be no water pressure. The roof one watered all the night before will go dry in seconds. Plastic trash cans must be filled with water and wet gunnysacks kept at hand, for smothering the sparks that blow ahead of the fire. The garden hoses must be connected and left where they can be seen. The cars must be placed in the garage, headed out. Whatever one wants most to save must be placed in the cars. The lights must be left on, so that the house can be seen in the smoke. I remember my daughter's Malibu kindergarten sending home on the first day of the fall semester a detailed contingency plan, with alternative sites where, depending on the direction of the wind when the fire came, the children would be taken to wait for their parents. The last-ditch site was the naval air station at Point Mugu, twenty miles up the coast.

"Dry winds and dust, hair full of knots," our Malibu child wrote when asked, in the fourth grade, for an "autumn" poem. "Gardens are dead, animals not fed. . . . People mumble as leaves crumble, fire ashes tumble." The rhythm here is not one that many people outside Los Angeles seem to hear. In the *New York Times* this morning I read a piece in which the way people in Los Angeles "persist" in living with fire was described as "denial." "Denial" is a word from a different lyric altogether. This will have been only the second fire season over twenty-five years during which I did not have a house somewhere in Los Angeles County, and the second during which I did not keep the snapshots in a box near the door, ready to go when the fire comes.

—1989

Times Mirror Square

HARRISON GRAY OTIS, the first successful editor and publisher of the *Los Angeles Times* and in many ways the prototypical Los Angeles citizen, would seem to have been one of those entrepreneurial drifters at once set loose and energized by the Civil War and the westward expansion. He was born in a log house in Ohio in 1837. He went to work as an apprentice printer at fourteen. He was a delegate at twenty-three to the Republican National Convention at which Abraham Lincoln was nominated for the presidency. He spent forty-nine months in the Ohio Infantry, was wounded at Antietam in 1862 and again in Virginia in 1864, and then parlayed his Army connections into government jobs, first as a journeyman printer at the Government Printing Office in Washington and then at the Patent Office. He made his first foray to Southern California in 1874, to investigate a goat-raising scheme that never materialized, and pronounced the place "the fattest land I was ever in." He drifted first to Santa Barbara, where he published a small daily without notable success (he and his wife and three children, he noted later, were reduced to living in the fattest land on "not enough to keep a rabbit alive"), and struck out then for Alaska, where he had lucked into a $10-a-day government sinecure as the special agent in charge of poaching and liquor control in the Seal Islands.

In 1882, already a forty-five-year-old man with a rather accidental past and unremarkable prospects, Harrison Gray Otis managed finally to seize the moment: he quit the government job, returned to Southern California, and put down $6,000, $5,000 of it borrowed, for a quarter interest in the four-page *Los Angeles Daily Times*, a failed paper started a few months before by a former editor of the *Sacramento Union* (the *Union*, for which Mark Twain was a correspondent, is the oldest California daily still publishing) and abandoned almost immediately to its creditors. "Small beginnings, but great oaks, etc.," Harrison Gray Otis later noted of his purchase. He seems to have known immediately what kind of Los Angeles he wanted, and what role a newspaper could play in getting it: "Los Angeles wants no dudes, loafers and paupers; people who have no means and trust to luck," the new citizen announced in an early editorial, already shedding his previous skin, his middle-aged skin, the skin of a person who had recently had no means and trusted to luck. Los Angeles, as he saw it, was all capital formation, no service. It needed, he said, no "cheap politicians, failures, bummers, scrubs, impecunious clerks, bookkeepers, lawyers, doctors. The market is overstaffed already. We need workers! Hustlers! Men of brains, brawn and guts! Men who have a little capital and a good deal of energy—first-class men!"

The extent to which Los Angeles was literally invented by the *Los Angeles Times* and by its owners, Harrison Gray Otis and his descendants in the Chandler family, remains hard for people in less recent parts of the country to fully apprehend. At the time Harrison Gray Otis bought his paper there were only some five thousand people living in Los Angeles. There was no navigable river. The Los Angeles River was capable of providing ditch water for a population of two or three hundred thousand, but there was little other ground water to speak of. Los Angeles has water today because Harrison Gray Otis and his son-in-law Harry Chandler wanted it, and fought a series of outright water wars to get it. "With this water problem out of the way, the growth of Los Angeles will leap forward as never before," the *Times* advised its readers in 1905, a few weeks before the initial vote to fund the aqueduct meant to bring water from the Owens River, 233 miles to the north. "Adjacent towns will soon be knocking on our doors for admission to secure the benefits to be derived from our never-failing supply of life-giving water, and Greater Los Angeles will become a magnificent reality." Any citizen voting against the aqueduct bonds, the *Times* warned on the day before the election, would be "placing himself in the attitude of an *enemy of the city*."

To oppose the Chandlers, in other words, was to oppose the perfection of Los Angeles, the expansion that was the city's imperial destiny. The false droughts and artful title transactions that brought Northern California water south are familiar stories in Los Angeles, and were made so in other parts of the country by the motion picture *Chinatown*. Without Owens River water the San Fernando Valley could not have been developed. The San Fernando Valley was where Harrison Gray Otis and Harry Chandler, through two interlocking syndicates, the San Fernando Mission Land Company and the Los Angeles Suburban Homes Company, happened to have bought or optioned, before the completion of the aqueduct and in some cases before the aqueduct vote, almost sixty-five thousand acres, virtually the entire valley from what is now Burbank to what is now Tarzana, at strictly dry-land prices, between $31 and $53 an acre. "Have A Contract for A Lot in Your Pocket When the Big Bonds are Voted," the advertisements read in the *Times* during the days before the initial vote on the aqueduct bonds. "Pacoima Will Feel the First Benefits of the Owens River Water and Every Purchaser Investing Now Will Reap the Fruits of his Wisdom in Gratifying Profits."

A great deal of Los Angeles as it appears today derived from this impulse to improve Chandler property. The Los Angeles Civic Center and Union Station and the curiosity known as Olvera Street (Olvera Street is part of El Pueblo de Los Angeles State Historic Park, but it was actually conceived in 1926 as the first local theme mall, the theme being "Mexican marketplace") are where they are because Harry Chandler wanted to develop the north end of downtown, where the *Times* building and many of his other downtown holdings lay. California has an aerospace industry today because Harry Chandler believed that the development of Los Angeles required that new industry be encouraged, and, in 1920, called on his friends to lend Donald Douglas $15,000 to build an experimental torpedo plane.

The same year, Harry Chandler called on his friends to build Caltech, and the year after that to build a facility (the Coliseum, near the University of Southern California) large enough to attract the 1932 Olympics. The Hollywood Bowl exists because Harry Chandler wanted it. The Los Angeles highway system exists because Harry Chandler knew that people would not buy land in his outlying subdivisions unless they could drive to them, and also because Harry Chandler sat on the board of Goodyear Tire & Rubber, which by then had Los Angeles plants. Goodyear Tire & Rubber had Los Angeles plants in the first place because Harry Chandler and his friends made an investment of $7.5 million to build them.

It was this total identification of the Chandler family's destiny with that of Los Angeles that made the *Times* so peculiar an institution, and also such a rich one. Under their corporate umbrella, the Times Mirror Company, the Chandlers now own, for all practical purposes, not only the *Times*, which for a number of years carried more full-run advertising linage than any other newspaper in the United States, but *Newsday*, *New York Newsday*, the *Baltimore Sun*, the *Hartford Courant*, the *National Journal*, nine specialized book- and educational-publishing houses, seventeen specialized magazines, the CBS affiliates in Dallas and Austin, the ABC affiliate in St. Louis, the NBC affiliate in Birmingham, a cable-television business, and a company that exists exclusively to dispose of what had been Times Mirror's timber and ranchland (this company, since it is meant to self-destruct, is described by Times Mirror as "entropic"): an empire with operating revenues for 1989 of $3,517,493,000.

The climate in which the *Times* prospered was a special one. Los Angeles had been, through its entire brief history, a boom town. People who lived there had tended to believe, and were encouraged to do so by the increasingly fat newspaper dropped at their doors every morning, that the trend would be unfailingly up. It seemed logical that the people who made business work in California should begin to desert San Francisco, which had been since the gold rush the financial center of the West, and look instead to Los Angeles, where the money increasingly was. It seemed logical that shipping should decline in San Francisco, one of the world's great natural ports, even as it flourished in Los Angeles, where a port had to be dredged, and was, at the insistence of the *Times* and Harry Chandler. It seemed logical that the wish to dredge this port should involve, since Los Angeles was originally landlocked, the annexation first of a twenty-mile corridor to the sea and then the "consolidation" with Los Angeles ("annexation" of one incorporated city by another was prohibited by state law) of two entire other cities, San Pedro and Wilmington, both of which lay on the Pacific.

The logic here was based on the declared imperative of unlimited opportunity, which in turn dictated unlimited growth.

What was construed by people in the rest of the country as accidental—the sprawl of the city, the apparent absence of a cohesive center—was in fact purposeful, the scheme itself: this would be a new kind of city, one that would seem to have no finite limits, a literal cloud on the land that would eventually touch the Tehachapi range to the north and the Mexican border to the south, the San Bernardino Mountains to the east and the Pacific to the west; not just a city finally but its own nation, The Southland. That the Chandlers had been sufficiently prescient to buy up hundreds of thousands of acres on the far reaches of the expanding cloud—300,000 acres spanning the Tehachapi, 860,000 acres in Baja California, which Harrison Gray Otis and Harry Chandler were at one point trying to get the Taft administration to annex from Mexico, thereby redefining even what might have seemed Southern California's one fixed border (the Pacific was seen locally as not a border but an opportunity, a bridge to Hawaii and on to Asia)—was only what might be expected of any provident citizen: "The best interests of Los Angeles are paramount to the *Times*," Harry Chandler wrote in 1934, and it had been, historically, the *Times* that defined what those best interests were.

The *Times* under Harrison Gray Otis was a paper in which the owners' opponents were routinely described as "thieves," "scoundrels," "blackmailers," "venal," "cowardly," "mean," "un-American," "assassinlike," "petty," "despotic," and "anarchic scum." It was said of General Otis (he had been commissioned a brigadier general when he led an expeditionary force to the Philippines during the Spanish-American War, and he was General Otis forever after, just as his houses were The Bivouac and The Outpost, the *Times* building was The Fortress, and the *Times* staff The Phalanx) that he had a remarkably even temper, that of a hungry tiger. A libel suit or judgment against the paper was seen as neither a problem nor an embarrassment but a journalistic windfall, an opportunity to reprint the offending story, intact and often. In November of 1884, after the election of Grover Cleveland to the presidency, the *Times* continued to maintain for eleven days that the president-elect was James G. Blaine, Harrison Gray Otis's candidate.

Even under Harry Chandler's son Norman, who was publisher from 1944 until 1960, the *Times* continued to exhibit a fitful willfulness. The Los Angeles for which the *Times* was at that time published was still remote from the sources of national and international power, isolated not only geographically but developmentally, a deliberately adolescent city, intent on its own growth and not much interested in the world outside. In 1960, when Norman Chandler's son Otis was named publisher of the *Times*, the paper had only one foreign correspondent, based in Paris. The city itself was run by a handful of men who worked for the banks and the old-line law firms downtown and drove home at five o'clock to Hancock Park or Pasadena or San Marino. They had lunch at the California Club or the Los Angeles Athletic Club. They held their weddings and funerals in Protestant or Catholic churches and did not, on the whole, know people who lived on the West Side, in Beverly Hills and Bel Air and Brentwood and Pacific Palisades, many of the most prominent of whom were in the entertainment business and were Jewish. As William Severns, the original general manager of the Los Angeles Music Center's operating company, put it in a recent interview with Patt Morrison of the *Times*, there was at that time a "big schism in society" between these downtown people and what he called "the movie group." The movie group, he said, "didn't even know where downtown was, except when they came downtown for a divorce." (This was in itself a cultural crossed connection, since people on the West Side generally got divorced not downtown but in Santa Monica.)

It was Norman Chandler's wife, Dorothy Buffum Chandler, called Buff, who perceived that it was in the interests of the city, and therefore of the *Times*, to draw the West Side into the power structure, and she saw the Music Center, for which she was then raising money, as a natural way to initiate this process. I once watched Mrs. Chandler, at a dinner sometime in 1964, try to talk the late Jules Stein, the founder and at that time the chairman of MCA, into contributing $25,000 toward the construction of the Music Center. Jules Stein said that he would be glad to donate any amount to Mrs. Chandler's Music Center, and would then expect Mrs. Chandler to make a matching contribution, for this was the way things got done on the West Side, to the eye clinic he was then building at the UCLA Medical Center. "I can't do that," Mrs. Chandler said, and then she leaned across the table, and demonstrated what the Chandlers had always seen as the true usefulness of owning a newspaper: "But I can give you twenty-five thousand dollars' worth of free publicity in the paper."

By the time Mrs. Chandler was through, the Music Center and one of its support groups, The Amazing Blue Ribbon, had become the common ground on which the West Side met downtown. This was not to say that all the top editors and managers at the *Times* were entirely comfortable on the West Side; many of them tended still to regard it as alien, a place where people exchanged too many social kisses and held novel, if not dangerous, ideas. "I always enjoy visiting the West Side," I recall being told by Tom Johnson, who had in 1980 become the publisher of the *Times*, when we happened to be seated next to each other at a party in Brentwood. He then took a notepad and a pen from his pocket. "I like to hear what people out here think." Nor was it to say that an occasional citizen of a more self-absorbed Los Angeles did not still surface, and even write querulous letters to the *Times*:

> Regarding "The Party Pace Picks Up During September" (by Jeannine Stein, Aug. 31): the social season in Los Angeles starts the first Friday in October when the Autumn Cotillion is held. This event, started over fifty years ago, brings together the socially prominent folks of Los Angeles who wouldn't be seen in Michael's and haven't yet decided if the opera is here to stay. By the time Cotillion comes around families are back from vacation, dove hunting season is just over and deer hunting season hasn't begun so the gentlemen of the city find no excuse not to attend. Following that comes the annual Assembly Ball and the Chevaliers du Tastevin dinner followed by the Las Madrinas Debutante Ball. If you are invited to these events you are in socially. No *nouveau riche* or publicity seekers nor social climbers need apply.

The *Times* in which this letter appeared, on September 10, 1989, was one that maintained six bureaus in Europe, five in Latin America, five in Asia, three in the Middle East, and two in Africa. It was reaching an area inhabited by between 13 and 14 million people, more than half of whom, a recent

Rand Corporation study suggests, had arrived in Los Angeles as adults, eighteen years old or over, citizens whose memories did not include the Las Madrinas Debutante Ball. In fact there is in Los Angeles no memory everyone shares, no monument everyone knows, no historical reference as meaningful as the long sweep of the ramps where the San Diego and Santa Monica freeways intersect, as the way the hard Santa Ana light strikes the palm trees against the white western wall of the Carnation Milk building on Wilshire Boulevard. Mention of "historic" sites tends usually to signal a hustle under way, for example transforming a commercial development into historic Olvera Street, or wrapping a twenty-story office tower and a four-hundred-room hotel around the historic Mann's Chinese Theater (the historic Mann's Chinese Theater was originally Grauman's Chinese, but a significant percentage of the population has no reason to remember this), a featured part of the Hollywood Redevelopment.

Californians until recently spoke of the United States beyond Colorado as "back east." If they went to New York, they went "back" to New York, a way of speaking that carried with it the suggestion of living on a distant frontier. Californians of my daughter's generation speak of going "out" to New York, a meaningful shift in the perception of one's place in the world. The Los Angeles that Norman and Buff Chandler's son Otis inherited in 1960—and, with his mother, proceeded over the next twenty years to reinvent—was, in other words, a new proposition, potentially one of the world's great cities but still unformed, outgrowing its old controlling idea, its tropistic confidence in growth, and not yet seized by a new one. It was Otis Chandler who decided that what Los Angeles needed if it was to be a world-class city was a world-class newspaper, and he set out to get one.

Partly in response to the question of what a daily newspaper could do that television could not do better, and partly in response to geography—papers on the West Coast have a three-hour advantage going to press, and a three-hour disadvantage when they come off the press—Otis Chandler, then thirty-two, decided that the *Times* should be what was sometimes called a daily magazine, a newspaper that would cover breaking news competitively, but remain willing to commit enormous resources to providing a kind of analysis and background no one else was providing. He made it clear at the outset that the paper was no longer his father's but his, antagonizing members of his own family in 1961 by running a five-part report on the John Birch Society, of which his aunt and uncle Alberta and Philip Chandler were influential members. Otis Chandler followed up the John Birch series, in case anyone had missed the point, by signing the Chandler name to a front-page editorial opposing Birch activities. "His legs bestrid the ocean, his reared arm crested the world," as the brass letters read (for no clear reason, since it is what Cleopatra says about Antony as the asps are about to arrive in the fifth act of *Antony and Cleopatra*) at the base of the turning globe in the lobby of the *Times* building. "His voice was propertied to all the tuned spheres." One reason Otis Chandler could property the voice of the *Times* to all the tuned spheres was that his *Times* continued to make more money than his father's. "The paper was published every day and they could see it," he later said about his family. "They disagreed endlessly with my editorial policies. But they never disagreed with the financial results."

In fact an unusual kind of reporting developed at the *Times*, the editorial philosophy of which was frequently said to be "run it long and run it once." The *Times* became a paper on which reporters were allowed, even encouraged, to give the reader the kind of detail that was known to everyone on the scene but rarely got filed. On the night Son of Sam was arrested in New York, according to Charles T. Powers, then in the *Times*' New York bureau, Roone Arledge was walking around Police Headquarters, "dressed as if for a touch football game, a glass of scotch in one hand, a portable two-way radio in the other, directing his network's feed to the Coast," details that told the reader pretty much all there was to know about celebrity police work. In San Salvador in the early spring of 1982, when representatives from the centrist Christian Democrats, the militarist National Conciliation Party, and the rightist ARENA were all meeting under a pito tree on Francisco ("Chachi") Guerrero's patio, Laurie Becklund of the *Times* asked Guerrero, who has since been assassinated, how people so opposed to one another could possibly work together. "We all know each other—we've known each other for years," he said. "You underestimate our *política tropical*." A few days later, when Laurie Becklund asked an ARENA leader why ARENA, then trying to close out the Christian Democrats, did not fear losing American aid, the answer she got, and filed, summed up the entire relationship between the United States and the Salvadoran right: "We believe in gringos."

This kind of detail was sometimes dismissed by reporters at other papers as "L.A. color," but really it was something different: the details gave the tone of the situation, the subtext without which the text could not be understood, and sharing this subtext with the reader was the natural tendency of reporters who, because of the nature of both the paper on which they worked and the city in which it was published, tended not to think of themselves as insiders. "Jesse don't wanna run nothing but his mouth," Mayor Marion Barry of Washington, D.C., was quoted as having said, about Jesse Jackson, early in 1990 in a piece by Bella Stumbo in the *Los Angeles Times*; there was in this piece, I was told in New York, after both the *New York Times* and the *Washington Post* had been forced to report the ensuing controversy, nothing that many *Post* and *New York Times* reporters in Washington did not already know. This was presumably true, but only the *Los Angeles Times* had printed it.

Unconventional choices were made at the *Times*. Otis Chandler had insisted that the best people in the country be courted and hired, regardless of their politics. The political cartoonist Paul Conrad was lured from the *Denver Post*, brought out for an interview, and met at the airport, per his demand, by the editor of the paper. Robert Scheer, who had a considerable reputation as a political journalist at *Ramparts* and *New Times* but no newspaper experience, was not only hired but given whatever he wanted, including the use of the executive dining room, the Picasso Room. "For the money we're paying Scheer, I should hope he'd be abrasive," William Thomas, the editor of the *Times* from 1971 until 1989, said to a network executive who called to complain that Scheer had been abrasive in an interview. The *Times* had by then abandoned traditional ideas of what newspaper reporters and editors should be paid, and was in some cases paying double the going rate. "I don't think newspapers should take a back seat to magazines, TV, or public relations," Otis Chandler had said early on. He had bought the *Times* a high-visibility Washington bureau. He had bought the *Times* a foreign staff.

By 1980, when Otis Chandler named Tom Johnson the publisher of the *Times* and created for himself the new title of editor in chief, the *Times* was carrying, in the average week, more columns of news than either the *New York Times* or the *Washington Post.* It was running long analytical background pieces from parts of the country and of the world that other papers left to the wires. Its Washington bureau, even Bob Woodward of the *Washington Post* conceded recently, was frequently beating the *Post.* Its foreign coverage, particularly from Central America and the Middle East, was, day for day, stronger than that of the national competition. "Otis was a little more specific than just indicating he wanted the *Times* to be among the top U.S. newspapers," Nick Williams, the editor of the *Times* from 1958 until 1971, said later of Otis Chandler's ascension to publisher of the *Times.* "He said, 'I want it to be the number one newspaper in the country.'" What began worrying people in Los Angeles during the fall of 1989, starting on the morning in October when the *Times* unveiled the first edition of what it referred to on billboards and television advertisements and radio spots and bus shelters and bus tails and rack cards and in-paper advertisements and even in its own house newsletter as "the new, faster-format *Los Angeles Times,*" was whether having the number one newspaper in the country was a luxury the Chandlers, and the city, could still afford.

It was hard, that fall at the *Times*, to sort out exactly what was going on. A series of shoes had already been dropped. There had been in January 1989 the installation of a new editor, someone from outside, someone whose particular depths and shallows many people had trouble sounding, someone from the East (actually he was from Tennessee, but his basic training had been under Benjamin Bradlee at the *Washington Post*, and around the *Times* he continued to be referred to, tellingly, as an Easterner), Shelby Coffey III. There had been some months later the announcement of a new approach to what had become the *Times*' Orange County problem, the problem being that a few miles to the south, in Orange County, the *Times*' zoned edition had so far been unable to unseat the *Orange County Register*, the leading paper in a market so rich that the *Register* had a few years earlier become the one paper in the United States with more full-run advertising linage than the *Times*.

The new approach to this Orange County problem seemed straightforward enough (the editor of the Orange County edition, at that time Narda Zacchino, would get twenty-nine additional reporters, an expanded plant, virtual autonomy over what appeared in the *Times* in Orange County, and would report only to Shelby Coffey), although it did involve a new "president," or business person, for Orange County, Lawrence M. Higby, whose particular skills—he was a marketing expert out of Taco Bell, Pepsi, and H. R. Haldeman's office in the Nixon White House, where he had been known as Haldeman's Haldeman—made some people uneasy. Narda Zacchino was liked and respected around the *Times* (she had more or less grown up on the paper, and was married to Robert Scheer), but Higby was an unknown quantity, and there were intimations that not everyone was entirely comfortable with these heightened stakes in Orange County. According to the *Wall Street Journal*, Tom Johnson, the publisher, said in an August 1989 talk to the Washington bureau that the decision to give Narda Zacchino and Lawrence Higby autonomy in Orange County had led to "blood all over the floor" in Los Angeles. He described the situation in Orange County as "a failure of mine," an area in which "I should have done more sooner."

Still, it was September 1989 before people outside the *Times* started noticing the blood, or even the dropped shoes, already on the floor. September was when it was announced, quite unexpectedly, that Tom Johnson, who had been Otis Chandler's own choice as publisher and had in turn picked Shelby Coffey as editor, was moving upstairs to what were described as "broader responsibilities," for example newsprint supply. The publisher's office, it was explained, would now be occupied by David Laventhol, who had spent time at the *New York Herald Tribune* and the *Washington Post*, had moved next to *Newsday* (he was editor, then publisher), had been since 1987 the president of the parent Times Mirror Company, and had achieved, mainly because he was seen to have beat the *New York Times* in Queens with *New York Newsday*, a certain reputation for knowing how to run the kind of regional war the *Los Angeles Times* wanted to run in Orange County. David Laventhol, like Shelby Coffey, was referred to around the office as an Easterner.

Then, on October 11, 1989, there was the format change, to which many of the paper's most vocal readers, a significant number of whom had been comparing the paper favorably every morning with the national edition of the *New York Times*, reacted negatively. It appeared that some readers of the *Los Angeles Times* did not want color photographs on its front page. Nor, it appeared, did these readers want News Highlights or news briefs or boxes summarizing the background of a story in three or four sentences without dependent clauses. A Laguna Niguel subscriber described himself in a letter to the editor as "heartsick." A Temple City reader characterized the changes as "beyond my belief." By the first of December even the student newspaper at Caltech, the *California Tech*, was having a little fun at the *Times*' expense, calling itself the *New, Faster Format Tech* and declaring itself dedicated to "increasing the amount of information on the front page by replacing all stories with pictures." In the lost-and-found classified section of the *Times* itself there appeared, sandwiched among pleas for lost Akitas ("Has Tattoo") and lost Saudi Arabian Airlines ID cards and lost four-carat emerald-cut diamond rings set in platinum ("sentimental value"), this notice, apparently placed by a group of the *Times*' own reporters: "*LA TIMES*: Last seen in a confused state disguised as *USA Today*. If found, please return to Times Mirror Square."

The words "*USA Today*" were heard quite a bit during the first few months of the new, faster format, as were "New Coke" and "Michael Dukakis." It was said that Shelby Coffey and David Laventhol had turned the paper over to its marketing people. It was said that the marketing people were bent on reducing the paper to its zoned editions, especially to its Orange County edition, and reducing the zoned editions to a collection of suburban shoppers. It was said that the paper was conducting a deliberate dumb-down, turning itself over to the interests and whims (less to read, more local service announcements) of the several thousand people who had taken part in the videotaped focus groups the marketing people and key editors had been running down in Orange County. A new format for a newspaper or magazine tends inevitably to suggest a perceived problem with the product, and the insistence with which this particular new format was promoted—the advertising stressed the superior disposability of the new *Times*, how easy it was, how cut down, how little time the reader need spend with it—convinced many people that the paper was determined to be less than it had been. "READ THIS," *Times* rack cards now demanded. "QUICK."

The architects of the new, faster format became, predictably, defensive, even impatient. People with doubts were increasingly seen as balky, resistant to all change, sulky dogs in the manger of progress. "Just look at this," Narda Zacchino, who as editor of the Orange County edition had been one of the central figures in the redesign, ordered me, brandishing first a copy of that morning's *USA Today* and then one of that morning's *Times*. "Do they look alike? No. They look nothing alike. I know there's been a negative response from within the paper. 'This is *USA Today*,' you hear. Well, look at it. It's not *USA Today*. But we're a newspaper. We want people to read the newspaper. I've been struggling down there for seven years, trying to get people to read the paper. And, despite the in-house criticism, we're not getting criticism from outside. Our response has been very, very good."

Shelby Coffey mentioned the redesign that Walter Bernard had done in 1977 for Henry Anatole Grunwald at *Time*. "They got scorched," he said. "They had thousands of letters, cancellations by the hundreds. I remember seeing it the first time and being jarred. In fact I thought they had lost their senses. They had gone to color. They had done the departments and the type in quite a different way. But it stood up over the years as one of the most successful, maybe *the* most successful, of the redesigns. I think you have to accept as a given that it's going to take six months or a year before people get used to this."

Around the paper, where it was understood that the format change had originally been developed in response to the needs of the Orange County edition, a certain paranoia had taken hold. People were exchanging rumors by computer mail.

People were debating whether the Orange County edition should be encouraged to run announcements of local events in column one of page one ("Tonight: Tito Puente brings his Latin Jazz All-Stars to San Juan Capistrano. . . . Puente, a giant among salsa musicians, is a particular favorite at New York's celebrated Blue Note nightclub. Time: 8 P.M. at the Coach House, 33157 Camino Capistrano. Tickets: $19.50. Information: (714) 496-8930") and still call itself the *Los Angeles Times.* People were noticing that the Orange County edition was, as far as that went, not always calling itself the *Los Angeles Times* —that some of its subscription callers were urging telephone contacts to subscribe to "the Orange County *Times.*" People were tormenting one another with various forms of the verb "to drive," as in "market-driven" and "customer-driven" and "a lot of people are calling this paper market-driven but it's not, what drives this paper is editorial" and "this paper has different forces driving it than something like *The Nation.*" (The necessity for distinguishing the *Los Angeles Times* from *The Nation* was perhaps the most arresting but far from the only straw point made to me in the course of a few days at the *Times.*)

The mood was rendered no less febrile by what began to seem an unusual number of personnel changes. During the first few days of November 1989, the *Los Angeles Herald Examiner* folded, and a visible number of its columnists and its sports and arts and entertainment writers began appearing immediately in the *Times.* A week or so later, Dennis Britton, who had been, with Shelby Coffey and two other editors, a final contender for the editorship of the *Times* (the four candidates had been asked by Tom Johnson to submit written analyses of the content of the *Times* and of the areas in which it needed strengthening), bailed out as one of the *Times*' deputy managing editors, accepting the editorship of the *Chicago Sun-Times.*

A week after that, it was announced that Anthony Day, the editor of the *Times* editorial pages since 1971, would be replaced by Thomas Plate, who had directed the partially autonomous editorial and op-ed pages for *New York Newsday* and was expected to play a role in doing something similar for Orange County. In the fever of the moment it was easy for some people to believe that the changes were all of a piece, that, for example, Anthony Day's leaving the editorial page had something to do with the new fast read, or with the fact that some people on the Times Mirror board had occasionally expressed dissatisfaction with the paper's editorial direction on certain issues, particularly its strong anti-Administration stand on Central American policy. Anthony Day was told only, he reported, that it was "time for a change," that he would be made a reporter and assigned a beat ("ideas and ideology in the modern world"), and that he would report directly to Shelby Coffey. "There was this strange, and strangely moving, party for Tony last Saturday at which Tom Johnson spoke," a friend at the *Times* wrote me not long after Day was fired. "And they sang songs to Tony—among them a version of 'Yesterday' in which the words were changed to 'Tonyday'. ('Why he had to go, we don't know, they wouldn't say')."

Part of the problem, as some people at the *Times* saw it, was that neither Shelby Coffey nor David Laventhol shared much history with anybody at the *Times*. Shelby Coffey was viewed by many people at the *Times* as virtually unfathomable. He seemed to place mysterious demands upon himself. His manner, which was essentially border Southern, was unfamiliar in Los Angeles. His wife, Mary Lee, was for many people at the *Times* equally hard to place, a delicate Southerner who looked like a lifetime Maid of Cotton but was in fact a doctor, not even a gynecologist or a pediatrician but a trauma specialist, working the emergency room at Huntington Hospital in Pasadena. "You know the golden rule of the emergency room," Mary Lee Coffey drawled the first time I met her, not long after her arrival in Los Angeles. She was wearing a white angora sweater. "Keep 'em alive till eight-oh-five."

Together, Shelby Coffey and David Laventhol, a demonstrated corporate player, suggested a new mood at the *Times*, a little leaner and maybe a little meaner, a little more market-oriented. "Since 1881, the *Los Angeles Times* has led the way with award-winning journalism," a *Times* help-wanted advertisement read around that time. "As we progress into our second century, we're positioned as one of America's largest newspapers. To help us maintain our leadership position, we're currently seeking a Promotion Writer." Some people in the newsroom began referring to the two as the First Street Gangster Crips (the Gangster Crips were a prominent Los Angeles gang, and the *Times* building was on First Street), and to their changes as drive-bys. They were repeatedly referred to as "guys whose ties are all in Washington or New York," as "people with Eastern ideas of what Los Angeles wants or deserves." Shelby Coffey's new editors were called "the Stepford Wives," and Shelby Coffey himself was called, to his face, "the Dan Quayle of journalism." (That this was said by a reporter who continued to be employed by the *Times* suggested not only the essentially tolerant nature of the paper but the extent to which Coffey appeared dedicated to the accommodation of dissent.) During the 1989 Christmas season, a blowup of his photograph, with a red hat pinned above it, appeared in one of the departments at the *Times.* "He Knows When You Are Sleeping," the legend read. "And With Whom."

This question of Coffey and Laventhol being "Easterners" was never far below the surface. "Easterner," as the word is used in Los Angeles, remains somewhat harder to translate than First Street Gangster Crip. It carries both an arrogance and a defensiveness, and has to do not exactly with geography (people who themselves came from the East will quite often dismiss other people as "Easterners") but with a virtually uncrackable complex of attitudes. An Easterner, in the local view, believes that Los Angeles begins and ends on the West Side and is about the movie business. Easterners, moreover, do not understand even the movie business: they come out in January and get taken to dinner at Spago and complain that the view is obscured by billboards, by advertisements for motion pictures, missing the point that advertisements for motion pictures are the most comforting possible view for those people who regularly get window tables at Spago. Easterners refer to Los Angeles as El Lay, as La La Land, as the Left Coast. "I suppose you're glad to be here," Easterners say to Californians when they run into them in New York. "I suppose you can always read the *Times* here," Easterners say on their January visits to Los Angeles, meaning the *New York Times.*

Easterners see the *Los Angeles Times* only rarely, and complain, when they do see it, about the length of its pieces. "They can only improve it," an editor of the *New York Times* said to me when I mentioned that the *Los Angeles Times* had undertaken some changes. He said that the paper had been in the past "unreadable." It was, he said, "all gray." I asked what he meant. "It's these stories that cover whole pages," he said. "And then the story breaks to the next page and keeps going." This was said on a day when, of eight stories on the front page of the *New York Times*, seven broke to other sections. "Who back east cares?" I was asked by someone at the *Los Angeles Times* when I said that I was writing about the changes at the paper. "If this were happening to the *New York Times*, you'd have the *Washington Post* all over it."

When people in Los Angeles talked about what was happening at the *Times*, they were talking about something harder to define, in the end, than any real or perceived or feared changes in the paper itself, which in fact was looking good. Day for day, not much about the *Times* had actually changed. There sometimes seemed fewer of the analytic national pieces that used to appear in column one. There seemed to be some increase in syndicated soft features, picked up with the columnists and arts reviewers when the *Herald Examiner* folded. But the "new, faster-format *Los Angeles Times*" (or, as early advertisements called it, the "new, fast-read *Los Angeles Times*") still carried more words every day than appear in the New Testament. It still carried in the average week more columns of news than the *New York Times* or the *Washington Post.* It still ran pieces at a length few other papers would countenance—David Shaw's January 1990 series on the coverage of the McMartin child-abuse case, for example, ran 17,000 words. The paper's editorials were just as strong under Thomas Plate as they had been under Anthony Day. Its reporters were still filing stories full of details that did not appear in other papers, for example the fact (this was from Kenneth Freed in Panama, January 1, 1990) that nearly 125 journalists, after spending less than twelve hours in Panama without leaving Howard Air Force Base, where they were advised that there was shooting on the streets of Panama City ("It is war out there," the briefing officer told them), had accepted the Southern Command's offer of a charter flight back to Miami.

The *Times* had begun, moreover, to do aggressive local coverage, not historically the paper's strong point, and also to do frequent "special reports," eight-to-fourteen-page sections, with no advertising, offering wrap-up newsmagazine coverage of, say, China, or Eastern Europe, or the October 1989 Northern California earthquake, or the state of the environment in Southern California. A week or so before Christmas 1989, Shelby Coffey initiated a daily "Moscow Edition," a six-to-eight-page selection of stories from that day's *Los Angeles Times.* This Moscow Edition, which was prepared in Los Angeles, faxed to the *Times* bureau in Moscow, and delivered by hand to some 125 Soviet officials, turned out to be sufficiently popular that the Moscow bureau received a call from the Soviet Foreign Ministry requesting that the *Times* extend its publication to weekends and even to Christmas Day.

"Shelby may be fighting more of a fight against the dumbing-down of the newspaper than we know or he can say," one *Times* editor, who had himself been wary of the changes under way but had come to believe that there had been among some members of the staff an unjustified rush to judgment, said to me. "That the *Times* is still essentially the same paper seems to me so plainly the case as to refute the word 'new' in 'the new, faster-format *Los Angeles Times*.' What small novelty there is would have received very little promotion had it begun as a routine editorial modification. But it didn't originate in editorial discussion. It originated in market research, which was why it got promoted so heavily. The *Times* needed a way to declare Orange County a new ball game, and this was it. But you can't change the paper anywhere without changing it everywhere. And once the *Times* throws the switch, a colossal amount of current seems to flow through the whole system."

In a way the uneasiness had to do with the entire difficult question of "Easterners." It was not that Shelby Coffey was an Easterner or that David Laventhol was an Easterner but that Easterners had been brought in, that there was no Chandler in the publisher's office, no one to whom the *Los Angeles Times* was intrinsically more important than, say, *Newsday*, no one who could reliably be expected to have a visceral appreciation not just of how far the *Times* had come but of how far Los Angeles itself had come, of how fragile the idea of the place was and how easily it could be lost. Los Angeles had been the most idealized of American cities, and the least accidental. Its development had proceeded not from the circumstances of geography but from sheer will, from an idea. It had been General Otis and Harry Chandler who conceived the future of Los Angeles as one of ever-expanding possibility, and had instructed the readers of the *Times* in what was needed to achieve that future. It had been Otis Chandler who articulated this vision by defining the *Times*' sphere of influence as regional, from Santa Barbara to the border and from the mountains to the sea, and who told the readers of the *Times* that this was what they wanted.

What the *Times* seemed to be telling its readers now was significantly different, and was based not on the logic of infinite opportunity proceeding from infinite growth but on the logic of minimizing risk, on corporate logic, and it was not impossible to follow that logic to a point at which what might be best for the *Times* and what might be best for Los Angeles would no longer necessarily coincide. "You talk to people in Orange County, they don't want news of Los Angeles," David Laventhol said one afternoon in late November of 1989. "We did a survey. Ask them what news they want, news from Los Angeles rates very, very low."

We were talking about his sense that Southern California was fragmenting more than it was coalescing, about what one *Times* editor had called "the aggressive disidentification with Los Angeles" of the more recent and more uniformly affluent communities in Ventura and San Diego and Orange counties. This aggressive disidentification with Los Angeles was the reason the Orange County Edition had been made autonomous.

"I spent many years in the New York market, and in many ways this is a more complex market," David Laventhol said. "The *New York Times* and some other papers were traditionally able to connect the entire New York community. It's much tougher here. If anything could bind this whole place together—anything that's important, anything beyond baseball teams—it would probably be the *Times*. But people are looking inward right now. They aren't thinking in terms of the whole region. It's partly a function of transportation, jobs, the difficulty of commuting or whatever, but it's also a function of lifestyle. People in Orange County don't like the West Side of Los Angeles. They don't like the South Side of Los Angeles.

They don't like whatever. They're lined up at the county line with their backs to Los Angeles."

Some years ago, Otis Chandler was asked how many readers would actually miss the *Times* were it to stop publishing tomorrow. "Probably less than half," Otis Chandler had said, and been so quoted in his own paper. For reasons that might not have been clear to his market-research people, he had nonetheless continued trying to make that paper the best in the country. During the 1989 Christmas season there was at the *Times*, as there had traditionally been, a party, and a Christmas toast was given, as it had traditionally been, by the publisher. In the past the publishers of the *Times* had stressed the growth of the enterprise, both achieved and anticipated. It had been a good year, David Laventhol said at the 1989 Christmas party, and he was glad it was over.

—*1990*

NEW YORK

Sentimental Journeys

WE KNOW her story, and some of us, although not all of us, which was to become one of the story's several equivocal aspects, know her name. She was a twenty-nine-year-old unmarried white woman who worked as an investment banker in the corporate finance department at Salomon Brothers in downtown Manhattan, the energy and natural resources group. She was said by one of the principals in a Texas oil-stock offering on which she had collaborated as a member of the Salomon team to have done "top-notch" work. She lived alone in an apartment on East 83rd Street, between York and East End, a sublet cooperative she was thinking about buying. She often worked late and when she got home she would change into jogging clothes and at eight-thirty or nine-thirty in the evening would go running, six or seven miles through Central Park, north on the East Drive, west on the less traveled road connecting the East and West Drives at approximately 102nd Street, and south on the West Drive. The wisdom of this was later questioned by some, by those who were accustomed to thinking of the Park as a place to avoid after dark, and defended by others, the more adroit of whom spoke of the citizen's absolute right to public access ("That park belongs to us and this time nobody is going to take it from us," Ronnie Eldridge, at the time a Democratic candidate for the City Council of New York, declared on the op-ed page of the *New York Times*), others of whom spoke of "running" as a preemptive right. "Runners have Type A controlled personalities and they don't like their schedules interrupted," one runner, a securities trader, told the *Times* to this point. "When people run is a function of their lifestyle," another runner said. "I am personally very angry," a third said. "Because women should have the right to run anytime."

For this woman in this instance these notional rights did not prevail. She was found, with her clothes torn off, not far from the 102nd Street connecting road at one-thirty on the morning of April 20, 1989. She was taken near death to Metropolitan

Hospital on East 97th Street. She had lost 75 percent of her blood. Her skull had been crushed, her left eyeball pushed back through its socket, the characteristic surface wrinkles of her brain flattened. Dirt and twigs were found in her vagina, suggesting rape. By May 2, when she first woke from coma, six black and Hispanic teenagers, four of whom had made videotaped statements concerning their roles in the attack and another of whom had described his role in an unsigned verbal statement, had been charged with her assault and rape and she had become, unwilling and unwitting, a sacrificial player in the sentimental narrative that is New York public life.

Nightmare in Central Park, the headlines and display type read. *Teen Wolfpack Beats and Rapes Wall Street Exec on Jogging Path. Central Park Horror. Wolf Pack's Prey. Female Jogger Near Death After Savage Attack by Roving Gang. Rape Rampage. Park Marauders Call It "Wilding," Street Slang for Going Berserk. Rape Suspect: "It Was Fun." Rape Suspect's Jailhouse Boast: "She Wasn't Nothing." The teenagers were back in the holding cell, the confessions gory and complete. One shouted "hit the beat" and they all started rapping to "Wild Thing." The Jogger and the Wolf Pack. An Outrage and a Prayer.* And, on the Monday morning after the attack, on the front page of the *New York Post*, with a photograph of Governor Mario Cuomo and the headline "*None of Us Is Safe*," this italic text: "A visibly shaken Governor Cuomo spoke out yesterday on the vicious Central Park rape: 'The people are angry and frightened—my mother is, my family is. To me, as a person who's lived in this city all of his life, this is the ultimate shriek of alarm.'"

Later it would be recalled that 3,254 other rapes were reported that year, including one the following week involving the near decapitation of a black woman in Fort Tryon Park and one two weeks later involving a black woman in Brooklyn who was robbed, raped, sodomized, and thrown down an air shaft of a four-story building, but the point was rhetorical, since crimes are universally understood to be news to the extent that they offer, however erroneously, a story, a lesson, a high concept. In the 1986 Central Park death of Jennifer Levin, then eighteen, at the hands of Robert Chambers, then nineteen, the "story," extrapolated more or less from thin air but left largely uncorrected, had to do not with people living wretchedly and marginally on the underside of where they wanted to be, not with the Dreiserian pursuit of "respectability" that marked the revealed details (Robert Chambers's mother was a private-duty nurse who worked twelve-hour night shifts to enroll her son in private schools and the Knickerbocker Greys), but with "preppies," and the familiar "too much too soon."

Susan Brownmiller, during a year spent monitoring newspaper coverage of rape as part of her research for *Against Our Will: Men, Women and Rape*, found, not surprisingly, that "although New York City police statistics showed that black women were more frequent victims of rape than white women, the favored victim in the tabloid headline . . . was young, white, middle class and 'attractive'." In its quite extensive coverage of rape-murders during the year 1971, according to Ms. Brownmiller, the *Daily News* published in its four-star final edition only two stories in which the victim was not described in the lead paragraph as "attractive": one of these stories involved an eight-year-old child, the other was a second-day follow-up on a first-day story that had in fact described the victim as "attractive." The *Times*, she found, covered rapes only infrequently that year, but what coverage they did "concerned victims who had some kind of middle-class status, such as 'nurse,' 'dancer' or 'teacher,' and with a favored setting of Central Park."

As a news story, "Jogger" was understood to turn on the demonstrable "difference" between the victim and her accused assailants, four of whom lived in Schomburg Plaza, a federally subsidized apartment complex at the northeast corner of Fifth Avenue and 110th Street in East Harlem, and the rest of whom lived in the projects and rehabilitated tenements just to the north and west of Schomburg Plaza. Some twenty-five teenagers were brought in for questioning; eight were held. The six who were finally indicted ranged in age from fourteen to sixteen. That none of the six had previous police records passed, in this context, for achievement; beyond that, one was recalled by his classmates to have taken pride in his expensive basketball shoes, another to have been "a follower." *I'm a smooth type of fellow, cool, calm, and mellow*, one of the six, Yusef Salaam, would say in the rap he presented as part of his statement before sentencing.

> *I'm kind of laid back, but now I'm speaking so that you know / I got used and abused and even was put on the news. . . .*
>
> *I'm not dissing them all, but the some that I called.*
>
> *They tried to dis me like I was an inch small, like a midget, a mouse, something less than a man.*

The victim, by contrast, was a leader, part of what the *Times* would describe as "the wave of young professionals who took over New York in the 1980's," one of those who were "handsome and pretty and educated and white," who, according to the *Times*, not only "believed they owned the world" but "had reason to." She was from a Pittsburgh suburb, Upper St. Clair, the daughter of a retired Westinghouse senior manager. She had been Phi Beta Kappa at Wellesley, a graduate of the Yale School of Management, a congressional intern, nominated for a Rhodes Scholarship, remembered by the chairman of her department at Wellesley as "probably one of the top four or five students of the decade." She was reported to be a vegetarian, and "fun-loving," although only "when time permitted," and also to have had (these were the *Times*' details) "concerns about the ethics of the American business world."

In other words she was wrenched, even as she hung between death and life and later between insentience and sentience, into New York's ideal sister, daughter, Bacharach bride: a young woman of conventional middle-class privilege and promise whose situation was such that many people tended to overlook the fact that the state's case against the accused was not invulnerable. The state could implicate most of the defendants in the assault and rape in their own videotaped words, but had none of the incontrovertible forensic evidence—no matching semen, no matching fingernail scrapings, no matching blood —commonly produced in this kind of case. Despite the fact that jurors in the second trial would eventually mention physical evidence as having been crucial in their bringing guilty verdicts against one defendant, Kevin Richardson, there was not actually much physical evidence at hand. Fragments of hair "similar [to] and consistent" with that of the victim were found on Kevin Richardson's clothing and underwear, but the state's own criminologist had testified that hair samples were necessarily inconclusive since, unlike fingerprints, they could not be traced to a single person. Dirt samples found on the defendants' clothing were, again, similar to dirt found in that part of the park where the attack took place, but the state's criminologist allowed that the samples were also similar to dirt found in other uncultivated areas of the park. To suggest, however, that this minimal physical evidence could open the case to an aggressive defense—to, say, the kind of defense that such celebrated New York criminal lawyers as Jack Litman and Barry Slotnick typically present—would come to be construed, during the weeks and months to come, as a further attack on the victim.

She would be Lady Courage to the *New York Post*, she would be A Profile in Courage to the *Daily News* and *New York Newsday*. She would become for Anna Quindlen in the *New York Times* the figure of "New York rising above the dirt, the New Yorker who has known the best, and the worst, and has stayed on, living somewhere in the middle." She would become for David Dinkins, the first black mayor of New York, the emblem of his apparently fragile hopes for the city itself: "I hope the city will be able to learn a lesson from this event and be inspired by the young woman who was assaulted in the case," he said. "Despite tremendous odds, she is rebuilding her life. What a human life can do, a human society can do as well." She was even then for John Gutfreund, at that time the chairman and chief executive officer of Salomon Brothers, the personification of "what makes this city so vibrant and so great," now "struck down by a side of our city that is as awful and terrifying as the creative side is wonderful." It was precisely in this conflation of victim and city, this confusion of personal woe with public distress, that the crime's "story" would be found, its lesson, its encouraging promise of narrative resolution.

One reason the victim in this case could be so readily abstracted, and her situation so readily made to stand for that of the city itself, was that she remained, as a victim of rape, unnamed in most press reports. Although the American and English press convention of not naming victims of rape (adult rape victims are named in French papers) derives from the understandable wish to protect the victim, the rationalization of this special protection rests on a number of doubtful, even magical, assumptions. The convention assumes, by providing a protection for victims of rape not afforded victims of other assaults, that rape involves a violation absent from other kinds of assault. The convention assumes that this violation is of a nature best kept secret, that the rape victim feels, and would feel still more strongly were she identified, a shame and self-loathing unique to this form of assault; in other words that she has been in an unspecified way party to her own assault, that a special contract exists between this one kind of victim and her assailant. The convention assumes, finally, that the victim would be, were this special contract revealed, the natural object of prurient interest; that the act of male penetration involves such potent mysteries that the woman so penetrated (as opposed, say, to having her face crushed with a brick or her brain penetrated with a length of pipe) is permanently marked, "different," even—especially if there is a perceived racial or social "difference" between victim and assailant, as in nineteenth-century stories featuring white women taken by Indians—"ruined."

These quite specifically masculine assumptions (women do not want to be raped, nor do they want to have their brains smashed, but very few mystify the difference between the two) tend in general to be self-fulfilling, guiding the victim to define her assault as her protectors do. "Ultimately we're doing women a disservice by separating rape from other violent crimes," Deni Elliott, the director of Dartmouth's Ethics Institute, suggested in a discussion of this custom in *Time*. "We are participating in the stigma of rape by treating victims of this crime differently," Geneva Overholser, the editor of the *Des Moines Register*, said about her decision to publish in February of 1990 a five-part piece about a rape victim who agreed to be named. "When we as a society refuse to talk openly about rape, I think we weaken our ability to deal with it." Susan Estrich, a professor of criminal law at Harvard Law School and the manager of Michael Dukakis's 1988 presidential campaign, discussed, in *Real Rape*, the conflicting emotions that followed her own 1974 rape:

> At first, being raped is something you simply don't talk about. Then it occurs to you that people whose houses are broken into or who are mugged in Central Park talk

> about it *all* the time. . . . If it isn't my fault, why am I supposed to be ashamed? If I'm not ashamed, if it wasn't "personal," why look askance when I mention it?

There were, in the 1989 Central Park attack, specific circumstances that reinforced the conviction that the victim should not be named. She had clearly been, according to the doctors who examined her at Metropolitan Hospital and to the statements made by the suspects (she herself remembered neither the attack nor anything that happened during the next six weeks), raped by one or more assailants. She had also been beaten so brutally that, fifteen months later, she could not focus her eyes or walk unaided. She had lost all sense of smell. She could not read without experiencing double vision. She was believed at the time to have permanently lost function in some areas of her brain.

Given these circumstances, the fact that neither the victim's family nor, later, the victim herself wanted her name known struck an immediate chord of sympathy, seemed a belated way to protect her as she had not been protected in Central Park. Yet there was in this case a special emotional undertow that derived in part from the deep and allusive associations and taboos attaching, in American black history, to the idea of the rape of white women. Rape remained, in the collective memory of many blacks, the very core of their victimization. Black men were accused of raping white women, even as black women were, Malcolm X wrote in *The Autobiography of Malcolm X*, "raped by the slavemaster white man until there had begun to emerge a homemade, handmade, brainwashed race that was no longer even of its true color, that no longer even knew its true family names." The very frequency of sexual contact between white men and black women increased the potency of the taboo on any such contact between black men and white women. The abolition of slavery, W. J. Cash wrote in *The Mind of the South*,

> . . . in destroying the rigid fixity of the black at the bottom of the scale, in throwing open to him at least the legal opportunity to advance, had inevitably opened up to the mind of every Southerner a vista at the end of which stood the overthrow of this taboo. If it was given to the black to advance at all, who could say (once more the

> logic of the doctrine of his inherent inferiority would not hold) that he would not one day advance the whole way and lay claim to complete equality, including, specifically, the ever crucial right of marriage?
>
> What Southerners felt, therefore, was that any assertion of any kind on the part of the Negro constituted in a perfectly real manner an attack on the Southern woman. What they saw, more or less consciously, in the conditions of Reconstruction was a passage toward a condition for her as degrading, in their view, as rape itself. And a condition, moreover, which, logic or no logic, they infallibly thought of as being as absolutely forced upon her as rape, and hence a condition for which the term "rape" stood as truly as for the *de facto* deed.

Nor was the idea of rape the only potentially treacherous undercurrent in this case. There has historically been, for American blacks, an entire complex of loaded references around the question of "naming": slave names, masters' names, African names, call me by my rightful name, nobody knows my name; stories, in which the specific gravity of naming locked directly into that of rape, of black men whipped for addressing white women by their given names. That, in this case, just such an interlocking of references could work to fuel resentments and inchoate hatreds seemed clear, and it seemed equally clear that some of what ultimately occurred—the repeated references to lynchings, the identification of the defendants with the Scottsboro boys, the insistently provocative repetition of the victim's name, the weird and self-defeating insistence that no rape had taken place and little harm been done the victim—derived momentum from this historical freight. "Years ago, if a white woman said a Black man looked at her lustfully, he could be hung higher than a magnolia tree in bloom, while a white mob watched joyfully sipping tea and eating cookies," Yusef Salaam's mother reminded readers of the *Amsterdam News*. "The first thing you do in the United States of America when a white woman is raped is round up a bunch of black youths, and I think that's what happened here," the Reverend Calvin O. Butts III of the Abyssinian Baptist Church in Harlem told the *New York Times*. "You going to arrest me now because I said the jogger's name?" Gary Byrd asked rhetorically on his WLIB show, and was quoted by Edwin Diamond in *New York* magazine:

> I mean, she's obviously a public figure, and a very mysterious one, I might add. Well, it's a funny place we live in called America, and should we be surprised that they're up to their usual tricks? It was a trick that got us here in the first place.

This reflected one of the problems with not naming this victim: she was in fact named all the time. Everyone in the courthouse, everyone who worked for a paper or a television station or who followed the case for whatever professional reason, knew her name. She was referred to by name in all court records and in all court proceedings. She was named, in the days immediately following the attack, on some local television stations. She was also routinely named—and this was part of the difficulty, part of what led to a damaging self-righteousness among those who did not name her and to an equally damaging embattlement among those who did—in Manhattan's black-owned newspapers, the *Amsterdam News* and the *City Sun*, and she was named as well on WLIB, the Manhattan radio station owned by a black partnership that included Percy Sutton and, until 1985, when he transferred his stock to his son, Mayor Dinkins.

That the victim in this case was identified on Centre Street and north of 96th Street but not in between made for a certain cognitive dissonance, especially since the names of even the juvenile suspects had been released by the police and the press before any suspect had been arraigned, let alone indicted. "The police normally withhold the names of minors who are accused of crimes," the *Times* explained (actually the police normally withhold the names of accused "juveniles," or minors under age sixteen, but not of minors sixteen or seventeen), "but officials said they made public the names of the youths charged in the attack on the woman because of the seriousness of the incident." There seemed a debatable point here, the question of whether "the seriousness of the incident" might not have in fact seemed a compelling reason to avoid any appearance of a rush to judgment by preserving the anonymity of a juvenile suspect; one of the names released by the police and published in the *Times* was of a fourteen-year-old who was ultimately not indicted.

There were, early on, certain aspects of this case that seemed not well handled by the police and prosecutors, and others that seemed not well handled by the press. It would seem to have been tactically unwise, since New York State law requires that a parent or guardian be present when children under sixteen are questioned, for police to continue the interrogation of Yusef Salaam, then fifteen, on the grounds that his Transit Authority bus pass said he was sixteen, while his mother was kept waiting outside. It would seem to have been unwise for Linda Fairstein, the assistant district attorney in charge of Manhattan sex crimes, to ignore, at the precinct house, the mother's assertion that the son was fifteen, and later to suggest, in court, that the boy's age had been unclear to her because the mother had used the word "minor."

It would also seem to have been unwise for Linda Fairstein to tell David Nocenti, the assistant U.S. Attorney who was paired with Yusef Salaam in a "Big Brother" program and who had come to the precinct house at the mother's request, that he had "no legal standing" there and that she would file a complaint with his supervisors. It would seem in this volatile a case imprudent of the police to follow their normal procedure by presenting Raymond Santana's initial statement in their own words, cop phrases that would predictably seem to some in the courtroom, as the expression of a fourteen-year-old held overnight and into the next afternoon for interrogation, unconvincing:

> On April 19, 1989, at approximately 20:30 hours, I was at the Taft Projects in the vicinity of 113th St. and Madison Avenue. I was there with numerous friends. . . . At approximately 21:00 hours, we all (myself and approximately 15 others) walked south on Madison Avenue to E. 110th Street, then walked westbound to Fifth Avenue. At Fifth Avenue and 110th Street, we met up with an additional group of approximately 15 other males, who also entered Central Park with us at that location with the intent to rob cyclists and joggers . . .

In a case in which most of the defendants had made videotaped statements admitting at least some role in the assault and rape, this less than meticulous attitude toward the gathering and dissemination of information seemed peculiar and self-defeating, the kind of pressured or unthinking standard procedure that could not only exacerbate the fears and angers and suspicions of conspiracy shared by many blacks but open what seemed, on the basis of the confessions, a conclusive case to the kind of doubt that would eventually keep juries out, in the trial of the first three defendants, ten days, and, in the trial of the next two defendants, twelve days. One of the reasons the jury in the first trial could not agree, *Manhattan Lawyer* reported in its October 1990 issue, was that one juror, Ronald Gold, remained "deeply troubled by the discrepancies between the story [Antron] McCray tells on his videotaped statement and the prosecution's scenario":

> Why did McCray place the rape at the reservoir, Gold demanded, when all evidence indicated it happened at the 102 Street crossdrive? Why did McCray say the jogger was raped where she fell, when the prosecution said she'd been dragged 300 feet into the woods first? Why did McCray talk about having to hold her arms down, if she was found bound and gagged?
>
> The debate raged for the last two days, with jurors dropping in and out of Gold's acquittal [for McCray] camp. . . .
>
> After the jurors watched McCray's video for the fifth time, Miranda [Rafael Miranda, another juror] knew it well enough to cite the time-code numbers imprinted at the bottom of the videotape as he rebuffed Gold's arguments with specific statements from McCray's own lips. [McCray, on the videotape, after admitting that he had held the victim by her left arm as her clothes were pulled off, volunteered that he had "got on top" of her, and said that he had rubbed against her without an erection "so everybody would . . . just know I did it."] The pressure on Gold was mounting. Three jurors agree that it was evident Gold, worn down perhaps by his own displays of temper as much as anything else, capitulated out of

> exhaustion. While a bitter Gold told other jurors he felt terrible about ultimately giving in, Brueland [Harold Brueland, another juror who had for a time favored acquittal for McCray] believes it was all part of the process.
>
> "I'd like to tell Ronnie someday that nervous exhaustion is an element built into the court system. They know that," Brueland says of court officials. "They know we're only going to be able to take it for so long. It's just a matter of, you know, who's got the guts to stick with it."

So fixed were the emotions provoked by this case that the idea that there could have been, for even one juror, even a moment's doubt in the state's case, let alone the kind of doubt that could be sustained over ten days, seemed, to many in the city, bewildering, almost unthinkable: the attack on the jogger had by then passed into narrative, and the narrative was about confrontation, about what Governor Cuomo had called "the ultimate shriek of alarm," about what was wrong with the city and about its solution. What was wrong with the city had been identified, and its names were Raymond Santana, Yusef Salaam, Antron McCray, Kharey Wise, Kevin Richardson, and Steve Lopez. "They never could have thought of it as they raged through Central Park, tormenting and ruining people," Bob Herbert wrote in the *News* after the verdicts came in on the first three defendants.

> There was no way it could have crossed their vicious minds. Running with the pack, they would have scoffed at the very idea. They would have laughed.
>
> And yet it happened. In the end, Yusef Salaam, Antron McCray and Raymond Santana were nailed by a woman.
>
> Elizabeth Lederer stood in the courtroom and watched Saturday night as the three were hauled off to jail. . . . At times during the trial, she looked about half the height of the long and lanky Salaam, who sneered at her from the witness stand. Salaam was apparently too dumb to realize that Lederer—this petite, soft-spoken, curly-haired prosecutor—was the jogger's avenger. . . .
>
> You could tell that her thoughts were elsewhere, that she was thinking about the jogger.
>
> You could tell that she was thinking: I did it.
>
> I did it for you.

Do this in remembrance of me: the solution, then, or so such pervasive fantasies suggested, was to partake of the symbolic body and blood of The Jogger, whose idealization was by this point complete, and was rendered, significantly, in details stressing her "difference," or superior class. The Jogger was someone who wore, according to *Newsday*, "a light gold chain around her slender neck" as well as, according to the *News*, a "modest" gold ring and "a thin sheen" of lipstick. The Jogger was someone who would not, according to the *Post*, "even dignify her alleged attackers with a glance." The Jogger was someone who spoke, according to the *News*, in accents "suited to boardrooms," accents that might therefore seem "foreign to many native New Yorkers." In her first appearance on the witness stand she had been subjected, the *Times* noted, "to questions that most people do not have to answer publicly during their lifetimes," principally about her use of a diaphragm on the Sunday preceding the attack, and had answered these questions, according to an editorial in the *News*, with an "indomitable dignity" that had taught the city a lesson "about courage and class."

This emphasis on perceived refinements of character and of manner and of taste tended to distort and to flatten, and ultimately to suggest not the actual victim of an actual crime but a fictional character of a slightly earlier period, the well-brought-up virgin who briefly graces the city with her presence and receives in turn a taste of "real life." The defendants, by contrast, were seen as incapable of appreciating these marginal distinctions, ignorant of both the norms and accoutrements of middle-class life. "Did you have jogging clothes on?" Elizabeth Lederer asked Yusef Salaam, by way of trying to discredit his statement that he had gone into the park that night only to "walk around." Did he have "jogging clothes," did he have "sports equipment," did he have "a bicycle." A pernicious nostalgia had come to permeate the case, a longing for the New York that had seemed for a while to be about "sports equipment," about getting and spending rather than about having and not having: the reason that this victim must not be named was so that she could go unrecognized, it was astonishingly said, by Jerry Nachman, the editor of the *New York Post*, and then by others who seemed to find in this a particular resonance, to Bloomingdale's.

Some New York stories involving young middle-class white women do not make it to the editorial pages, or even necessarily to the front pages. In April 1990, a young middle-class white woman named Laurie Sue Rosenthal, raised in an Orthodox Jewish household and at age twenty-nine still living with her parents in Jamaica, Queens, happened to die, according to the coroner's report from the accidental toxicity of Darvocet in combination with alcohol, in an apartment at 36 East 68th Street in Manhattan. The apartment belonged to the man she had been, according to her parents, seeing for about a year, a minor city assistant commissioner named Peter Franconeri. Peter Franconeri, who was at the time in charge of elevator and boiler inspections for the Buildings Department and married to someone else, wrapped Laurie Sue Rosenthal's body in a blanket; placed it, along with her handbag and ID, outside the building with the trash; and went to his office at 60 Hudson Street. At some point an anonymous call was made to 911. Franconeri was identified only after Laurie Sue Rosenthal's parents gave the police his beeper number, which they found in her address book. According to *Newsday*, which covered the story more extensively than the *News*, the *Post*, or the *Times*,

> Initial police reports indicated that there were no visible wounds on Rosenthal's body. But Rosenthal's mother, Ceil, said yesterday that the family was told the autopsy revealed two "unexplained bruises" on her daughter's body.
>
> Larry and Ceil Rosenthal said those findings seemed to support their suspicions that their daughter was upset because they received a call from their daughter at 3 A.M. Thursday "saying that he had beaten her up." The family reported the conversation to police.
>
> "I told her to get into a cab and get home," Larry Rosenthal said yesterday. "The next I heard was two detectives telling me terrible things."
>
> "The ME [medical examiner] said the bruises did not constitute a beating but they were going to examine them further," Ceil Rosenthal said.

"There were some minor bruises," a spokeswoman for the Office of the Chief Medical Examiner told *Newsday* a few days later, but the bruises "did not in any way contribute to her death." This is worth rerunning: A young woman calls her parents at three in the morning, "distraught." She says that she has been beaten up. A few hours later, on East 68th Street between Madison and Park avenues, a few steps from Porthault and Pratesi and Armani and Saint Laurent and the Westbury Hotel, at a time of day in this part of New York 10021 when Jim Buck's dog trainers are assembling their morning packs and Henry Kravis's Bentley is idling outside his Park Avenue apartment and the construction crews are clocking in over near the Frick at the multimillion-dollar houses under reconstruction for Bill Cosby and for the owner of The Limited, this young middle-class white woman's body, showing bruises, gets put out with the trash.

"Everybody got upside down because of who he was," an unidentified police officer later told Jim Dwyer of *Newsday*, referring to the man who put the young woman out with the trash. "If it had happened to anyone else, nothing would have come of it. A summons would have been issued and that would have been the end of it." In fact nothing did come of the death of Laurie Sue Rosenthal, which might have seemed a natural tabloid story but failed, on several levels, to catch the local imagination. For one thing she could not be trimmed into the role of the preferred tabloid victim, who is conventionally presented as fate's random choice (Laurie Sue Rosenthal had, for whatever reason, taken the Darvocet instead of a taxi home, her parents reported treatment for a previous Valium dependency, she could be presumed to have known over the course of a year that Franconeri was married and yet continued to see him); for another, she seemed not to have attended an expensive school or to have been employed in a glamour industry (no Ivy Grad, no Wall Street Exec), which made it hard to cast her as part of "what makes this city so vibrant and so great."

In August 1990, Peter Franconeri pled guilty to a misdemeanor, the unlawful removal of a body, and was sentenced by Criminal Court judge Peter Benitez to seventy-five hours of community service. This was neither surprising nor much of a story (only twenty-three lines even in *Newsday*, on page twenty-nine of the city edition), and the case's lenient resolution was for many people a kind of relief. The district attorney's office had asked for "some incarceration," the amount usually described as a "touch," but no one wanted, it was said, to crucify the guy: Peter Franconeri was somebody who knew a lot of people, understood how to live in the city, who had for example not only the apartment on East 68th Street between Madison and Park but a house in Southampton and who also understood that putting a body outside with the trash was nothing to get upside down about, if it was handled right. Such understandings may in fact have been the city's true "ultimate shriek of alarm," but it was not a shriek the city wanted to recognize.

2

Perhaps the most arresting collateral news to surface, during the first few days after the attack on the Central Park jogger, was that a significant number of New Yorkers apparently believed the city sufficiently well-ordered to incorporate Central Park into their evening fitness schedules. "Prudence" was defined, even after the attack, as "staying south of 90th Street," or having "an awareness that you need to think about planning your routes," or, in the case of one woman interviewed by the *Times*, deciding to quit her daytime job (she was a lawyer) because she was "tired of being stuck out there, running later and later at night." "I don't think there's a runner who couldn't describe the silky, gliding feeling you get running at night," an editor of *Runner's World* told the *Times*. "You see less of what's around you and you become centered on your running."

The notion that Central Park at night might be a good place to "see less of what's around you" was recent. There were two reasons why Frederick Law Olmsted and Calvert Vaux, when they devised their winning entry in the 1858 competition for a Central Park design, decided to sink the transverse roads below grade level. One reason, the most often cited, was aesthetic, a recognition on the part of the designers that the four crossings specified by the terms of the competition, at 65th, 79th, 85th, and 97th streets, would intersect the sweep of the landscape, be "at variance with those agreeable sentiments which we should wish the park to inspire." The other reason, which appears to have been equally compelling, had to do with security. The problem with grade-level crossings, Olmsted and Vaux wrote in their "Greensward" plan, would be this:

> The transverse roads will . . . have to be kept open, while the park proper will be useless for any good purpose after dusk; for experience has shown that even in London, with its admirable police arrangements, the public cannot be assured safe transit through large open spaces of ground after nightfall.
>
> These public throughfares will then require to be well-lighted at the sides, and, to restrain marauders pursued by the police from escaping into the obscurity of the park, strong fences or walls, six or eight feet high, will be necessary.

The park, in other words, was seen from its conception as intrinsically dangerous after dark, a place of "obscurity," "useless for any good purpose," a refuge only for "marauders." The parks of Europe closed at nightfall, Olmsted noted in his 1882 pamphlet *The Spoils of the Park: With a Few Leaves from the Deep-laden Note-books of "A Wholly Unpractical Man,"* "but one surface road is kept open across Hyde Park, and the superintendent of the Metropolitan Police told me that a man's chances of being garrotted or robbed were, because of the facilities for concealment to be found in the Park, greater in passing at night along this road than anywhere else in London."

In the high pitch of the initial "jogger" coverage, suggesting as it did a city overtaken by animals, this pragmatic approach to urban living gave way to a more ideal construct, one in which New York either had once been or should be "safe," and now, as in Governor Cuomo's "none of us is safe," was not. It was time, accordingly, to "take it back," time to "say no"; time, as David Dinkins would put it during his campaign for the mayoralty in the summer of 1989, to "draw the line." What the line was to be drawn against was "crime," an abstract, a free-floating specter that could be dispelled by certain acts of personal affirmation, by the kind of moral rearmament that later figured in Mayor Dinkins's plan to revitalize the city by initiating weekly "Tuesday Night Out Against Crime" rallies.

By going into the park at night, Tom Wicker wrote in the *Times*, the victim in this case had "affirmed the primacy of freedom over fear." A week after the assault, Susan Chace suggested on the op-ed page of the *Times* that readers walk into the park at night and join hands. "A woman can't run in the park at an offbeat time," she wrote. "Accept it, you say. I can't. It shouldn't be like this in New York City, in 1989, in spring." Ronnie Eldridge also suggested that readers walk into the park at night, but to light candles. "Who are we that we allow ourselves to be chased out of the most magnificent part of our city?" she asked, and also: "If we give up the park, what are we supposed to do: fall back to Columbus Avenue and plant grass?" This was interesting, suggesting as it did that the city's not inconsiderable problems could be solved by the willingness of its citizens to hold or draw some line, to "say no"; in other words that a reliance on certain magical gestures could affect the city's fate.

The insistent sentimentalization of experience, which is to say the encouragement of such reliance, is not new in New York. A preference for broad strokes, for the distortion and flattening of character and the reduction of events to narrative, has been for well over a hundred years the heart of the way the city presents itself: Lady Liberty, huddled masses, ticker-tape parades, heroes, gutters, bright lights, broken hearts, 8 million stories in the naked city; 8 million stories and all the same story, each devised to obscure not only the city's actual tensions of race and class but also, more significantly, the civic and commercial arrangements that rendered those tensions irreconcilable.

Central Park itself was such a "story," an artificial pastoral in the nineteenth-century English romantic tradition, conceived, during a decade when the population of Manhattan would increase by 58 percent, as a civic project that would allow the letting of contracts and the employment of voters on a scale rarely before undertaken in New York. Ten million cartloads of dirt would need to be shifted during the twenty years of its construction. Four to five million trees and shrubs would need to be planted, half a million cubic yards of topsoil imported, 114 miles of ceramic pipe laid.

Nor need the completion of the park mean the end of the possibilities: in 1870, once William Marcy Tweed had revised the city charter and invented his Department of Public Parks, new roads could be built whenever jobs were needed. Trees could be dug up, and replanted. Crews could be set loose to prune, to clear, to hack at will. Frederick Law Olmsted, when he objected, could be overridden, and finally eased out. "A 'delegation' from a great political organization called on me by appointment," Olmsted wrote in *The Spoils of the Park*, recalling the conditions under which he had worked:

> After introductions and handshakings, a circle was formed, and a gentleman stepped before me, and said, "We know how much pressed you must be . . . but at your convenience our association would like to have you determine what share of your patronage we can expect, and make suitable arrangements for our using it. We will take the liberty to suggest, sir, that there could be no more convenient way than that you should send us our due quota of tickets, if you will please, sir, in this form, *leaving us to fill in the name*." Here a packet of printed tickets was produced, from which I took one at random. It was a blank appointment and bore the signature of Mr. Tweed.
>
> As superintendent of the Park, I once received in six days more than seven thousand letters of advice as to appointments, nearly all from men in office. . . . I have heard a candidate for a magisterial office in the city addressing from my doorsteps a crowd of such advice-bearers, telling them that I was bound to give them employment, and suggesting plainly, that, if I was slow about it, a rope round my neck might serve to lessen my reluctance to take good counsel. I have had a dozen men force their way into my house before I had risen from bed on a Sunday morning, and some break into my drawing room in their eagerness to deliver letters of advice.

Central Park, then, for its underwriters if not for Olmsted, was about contracts and concrete and kickbacks, about pork, but the sentimentalization that worked to obscure the pork, the "story," had to do with certain dramatic contrasts, or extremes, that were believed to characterize life in this as in no other city. These "contrasts," which have since become the very spine of the New York narrative, appeared early on: Philip Hone, the mayor of New York in 1826 and 1827, spoke in 1843 of a city "overwhelmed with population, and where the two extremes of costly luxury in living, expensive establishments and improvident wastes are presented in daily and hourly contrast with squalid mixing and hapless destruction." Given this narrative, Central Park could be and ultimately would be seen the way Olmsted himself saw it, as an essay in democracy, a social experiment meant to socialize a new immigrant population and to ameliorate the perilous separation of rich and poor. It was the duty and the interest of the city's privileged class, Olmsted had suggested some years before he designed Central Park, to "get up parks, gardens, music, dancing schools, reunions which will be so attractive as to force into contact the good and the bad, the gentleman and the rowdy."

The notion that the interests of the "gentleman" and the "rowdy" might be at odds did not intrude: then as now, the preferred narrative worked to veil actual conflict, to cloud the extent to which the condition of being rich was predicated upon the continued neediness of a working class; to confirm the responsible stewardship of "the gentleman" and to forestall the possibility of a self-conscious, or politicized, proletariat. Social and economic phenomena, in this narrative, were personalized. Politics were exclusively electoral. Problems were best addressed by the emergence and election of "leaders," who could in turn inspire the individual citizen to "participate," or "make a difference." "Will you help?" Mayor Dinkins asked New Yorkers, in a September 1990 address from St. Patrick's Cathedral intended as a response to the "New York crime wave" stories then leading the news. "Do you care? Are you ready to become part of the solution?"

"Stay," Governor Cuomo urged the same New Yorkers. "Believe. Participate. Don't give up." Manhattan borough president Ruth Messinger, at the dedication of a school flagpole, mentioned the importance of "getting involved" and "participating," or "pitching in to put the shine back on the

Big Apple." In a discussion of the popular "New York" stories written between 1902 and 1910 by William Sidney Porter, or "O. Henry," William R. Taylor of the State University of New York at Stony Brook spoke of the way in which these stories, with their "focus on individuals' plights," their "absence of social or political implications" and "ideological neutrality," provided "a miraculous form of social glue":

> These sentimental accounts of relations between classes in the city have a specific historical meaning: empathy without political compassion. They reduce the scale of human suffering to what atomized individuals endure as their plucky, sad lives were recounted week after week for almost a decade . . . their sentimental reading of oppression, class differences, human suffering, and affection helped create a new language for interpreting the city's complex society, a language that began to replace the threadbare moralism that New Yorkers inherited from 19th-century readings of the city. This language localized suffering in particular moments and confined it to particular occasions; it smoothed over differences because it could be read almost the same way from either end of the social scale.

Stories in which terrible crimes are inflicted on innocent victims, offering as they do a similarly sentimental reading of class differences and human suffering, a reading that promises both resolution and retribution, have long performed as the city's endorphins, a built-in source of natural morphine working to blur the edges of real and to a great extent insoluble problems. What is singular about New York, and remains virtually incomprehensible to people who live in less rigidly organized parts of the country, is the minimal level of comfort and opportunity its citizens have come to accept. The romantic capitalist pursuit of privacy and security and individual freedom, so taken for granted nationally, plays, locally, not much role. A city where virtually every impulse has been to stifle rather than to encourage normal competition, New York works, when it does work, not on a market economy but on little deals, payoffs, accommodations, *baksheesh*, arrangements that circumvent the direct exchange of goods and services and prevent what would be, in a competitive economy, the normal ascendance of the superior product.

There were in the five boroughs in 1990 only 581 supermarkets (a supermarket, as defined by the trade magazine *Progressive Grocer*, is a market that does an annual volume of $2 million), or, assuming a population of 8 million, one supermarket for every 13,769 citizens. Groceries, costing more than they should because of this absence of competition and also because of the proliferation of payoffs required to ensure this absence of competition (produce, we have come to understand, belongs to the Gambinos, and fish to the Lucheses and the Genoveses, and a piece of the construction of the market to each of the above, but keeping the door open belongs finally to the inspector here, the inspector there), are carried home or delivered, as if in Jakarta, by pushcart.

It has historically taken, in New York as if in Mexico City, ten years to process and specify and bid and contract and construct a new school; twenty or thirty years to build or, in the cases of Bruckner Boulevard and the West Side Highway, to not quite build a highway. A recent public scandal revealed that a batch of city-ordered Pap smears had gone unread for more than a year (in the developed world the Pap smear, a test for cervical cancer, is commonly read within a few days); what did not become a public scandal, what is still accepted as the way things are, is that even Pap smears ordered by Park Avenue gynecologists can go unread for several weeks.

Such resemblances to cities of the third world are in no way casual, or based on the "color" of a polyglot population: these are all cities arranged primarily not to improve the lives of their citizens but to be labor-intensive, to accommodate, ideally at the subsistence level, since it is at the subsistence level that the work force is most apt to be captive and loyalty assured, a third-world population. In some ways New York's very attractiveness, its promises of opportunity and improved wages, its commitments as a city in the developed world, were what seemed destined to render it ultimately unworkable. Where the vitality of such cities in the less developed world had depended on their ability to guarantee low-cost labor and an absence of regulation, New York had historically depended instead on the constant welling up of new businesses, of new employers to replace those phased out, like the New York garment manufacturers who found it cheaper to make their clothes in Hong Kong or Kuala Lumpur or Taipei, by rising local costs.

It had been the old pattern of New York, supported by an expanding national economy, to lose one kind of business and gain another. It was the more recent error of New York to misconstrue this history of turnover as an indestructible resource, there to be taxed at will, there to be regulated whenever a dollar could be seen in doing so, there for the taking. By 1977, New York had lost some 600,000 jobs, most of them in manufacturing and in the kinds of small businesses that could no longer maintain their narrow profit margins inside the city. During the "recovery" years, from 1977 until 1988, most of these jobs were indeed replaced, but in a potentially perilous way: of the 500,000 new jobs created, most were in the area most vulnerable to a downturn, that of financial and business services, and many of the rest in an area not only equally vulnerable to bad times but dispiriting to the city even in good, that of tourist and restaurant services.

The demonstration that many kinds of businesses were finding New York expendable had failed to prompt real efforts to make the city more competitive. Taxes grew still more punitive, regulation more Byzantine. Forty-nine thousand new jobs were created in New York's city agencies between 1983 and 1990, even as the services provided by those agencies were widely perceived to decline. Attempts at "reform" typically tended to create more jobs: in 1988, in response to the length of time it was taking to build or repair a school, a new agency, the School Construction Authority, was formed. A New York City school, it was said, would now take only five years to build. The head of the School Construction Authority was to receive $145,000 a year and each of the three vice presidents $110,000 a year. An executive gym, with Nautilus equipment, was contemplated for the top floor of the agency's new headquarters at the International Design Center in Long Island City. Two years into this reform, the backlog on repairs to existing schools stood at 33,000 outstanding requests. "To relieve the charity of friends of the support of a half-blind and half-witted man by employing him at the public expense as an inspector of cement may not be practical with reference to the permanent firmness of a wall," Olmsted noted after his Central Park experience, "while it is perfectly so with reference to the triumph of sound doctrine at an election."

In fact the highest per capita taxes of any city in the United States (and, as anyone running a small business knows, the widest variety of taxes) provide, in New York, unless the citizen is prepared to cut a side deal here and there, only the continuing multiplication of regulations designed to benefit the contractors and agencies and unions with whom the regulators have cut their own deals. A kitchen appliance accepted throughout the rest of the United States as a basic postwar amenity, the in-sink garbage disposal unit, is for example illegal in New York. Disposals, a city employee advised me, not only encourage rats, and "bacteria," presumably in a way that bags of garbage sitting on the sidewalk do not ("Because it is," I was told when I asked how this could be), but also encourage people "to put their babies down them."

On the one hand this illustrates how a familiar urban principle, that of patronage (the more garbage there is to be collected, the more garbage collectors can be employed), can be reduced, in the bureaucratic wilderness that is any third-world city, to voodoo; on the other it reflects this particular city's underlying criminal ethic, its acceptance of graft and grift as the bedrock of every transaction. "Garbage costs are outrageous," an executive of Supermarkets General, which owns Pathmark, recently told *City Limits* about why the chains preferred to locate in the suburbs. "Every time you need to hire a contractor, it's a problem." The problem, however, is one from which not only the contractor but everyone with whom the contractor does business—a chain of direct or indirect patronage extending deep into the fabric of the city—stands to derive one or another benefit, which was one reason the death of a young middle-class white woman in the East 68th Street apartment of the assistant commissioner in charge of boiler and elevator inspections flickered so feebly on the local attention span.

It was only within the transforming narrative of "contrasts" that both the essential criminality of the city and its related absence of civility could become points of pride, evidence of "energy": if you could make it here you could make it anywhere, hello sucker, get smart. Those who did not get the deal, who bought retail, who did not know what it took to get their electrical work signed off, were dismissed as provincials, bridge-and-tunnels, out-of-towners who did not have what it took not to get taken. "Every tourist's nightmare became a reality for a Maryland couple over the weekend when the husband was beaten and robbed on Fifth Avenue in front of Trump Tower," began a story in the *New York Post* during the summer of 1990. "Where do you think we're from, Iowa?" the prosecutor who took Robert Chambers's statement said on videotape by way of indicating that he doubted Chambers's version of Jennifer Levin's death. "They go after poor people like you from out of town, they prey on the tourists," a clerk explained in the West 46th Street computer store where my husband and I had taken refuge to escape three muggers. My husband said that we lived in New York. "That's why they didn't get you," the clerk said, effortlessly incorporating this change in the data. "That's how you could move fast."

The narrative comforts us, in other words, with the assurance that the world is knowable, even flat, and New York its center, its motor, its dangerous but vital "energy." "Family in Fatal Mugging Loved New York" was the *Times* headline on a story following the September 1990 murder, in the Seventh Avenue IND station, of a twenty-two-year-old tourist from Utah. The young man, his parents, his brother, and his sister-in-law had attended the U.S. Open and were reportedly on their way to dinner at a Moroccan restaurant downtown. "New York, to them, was the greatest place in the world," a family friend from Utah was quoted as having said. Since the narrative requires that the rest of the country provide a dramatic contrast to New York, the family's hometown in Utah was characterized by the *Times* as a place where "life revolves around the orderly rhythms of Brigham Young University" and "there is only about one murder a year." The town was in fact Provo, where Gary Gilmore shot the motel manager, both in life and in *The Executioner's Song*. "She loved New York, she just loved it," a friend of the assaulted jogger told the *Times* after the attack. "I think she liked the fast pace, the competitiveness."

New York, the *Times* concluded, "invigorated" the jogger, "matched her energy level." At a time when the city lay virtually inert, when forty thousand jobs had been wiped out in the financial markets and former traders were selling shirts at Bergdorf Goodman for Men, when the rate of mortgage delinquencies had doubled, when 50 or 60 million square feet of office space remained unrented (60 million square feet of unrented office space is the equivalent of fifteen darkened World Trade Towers) and even prime commercial blocks on Madison Avenue in the Seventies were boarded up, empty; at a time when the money had dropped out of all the markets and the Europeans who had lent the city their élan and their capital during the eighties had moved on, vanished to more cheerful venues, this notion of the city's "energy" was sedative, as was the commandeering of "crime" as the city's central problem.

3

The extent to which the October 1987 crash of the New York financial markets damaged the illusions of infinite recovery and growth on which the city had operated during the 1980s had been at first hard to apprehend. "Ours is a time of New York ascendant," the New York City Commission on the Year 2000, created during the mayoralty of Edward Koch to reflect the best thinking of the city's various business and institutional establishments, had declared in its 1987 report. "The city's economy is stronger than it has been in decades, and is driven both by its own resilience and by the national economy; New York is more than ever the international capital of finance, and the gateway to the American economy."

And then, its citizens had come gradually to understand, it was not. This perception that something was "wrong" in New York had been insidious, a slow-onset illness at first noticeable only in periods of temporary remission. Losses that might have seemed someone else's problem (or even comeuppance) as the markets were in their initial 1987 free-fall, and that might have seemed more remote still as the markets regained the appearance of strength, had come imperceptibly but inexorably to alter the tone of daily life. By April of 1990, people who lived in and around New York were expressing, in interviews with the *Times*, considerable anguish and fear that they did so: "I feel very resentful that I've lost a lot of flexibility in my life," one said. "I often wonder, 'Am I crazy for coming here?'" "People feel a sense of impending doom about what may happen to them," a clinical psychologist said. People were "frustrated," "feeling absolutely desolate," "trapped," "angry," "terrified," and "on the verge of panic."

It was a panic that seemed in many ways specific to New York, and inexplicable outside it. Even later, when the troubles of New York had become a common theme, Americans from less depressed venues had difficulty comprehending the nature of those troubles, and tended to attribute them, as New Yorkers themselves had come to do, to "crime." "Escape From New York" was the headline on the front page of the *New York Post* on September 10, 1990. "Rampaging Crime Wave Has 59% of Residents Terrified. Most Would Get Out of the City, Says Time/CNN Poll." This poll appeared in the edition of *Time* dated September 17, 1990, which carried the cover legend "The Rotting of the Big Apple." "Reason: a surge of drugs and violent crime that government officials seem utterly unable to combat," the story inside explained. Columnists referred, locally, to "this sewer of a city." The *Times* ran a plaintive piece about the snatch of Elizabeth Rohatyn's Hermès handbag outside Arcadia, a restaurant on East 62nd Street that had for a while seemed the very heart of the New York everyone now missed, the New York where getting and spending could take place without undue reference to having and not having, the duty-free New York; that this had occurred to the wife of Felix Rohatyn, who was widely perceived to have saved the city from its fiscal crisis in the midseventies, seemed to many a clarion irony.

This question of crime was tricky. There were in fact eight American cities with higher homicide rates, and twelve with higher overall crime rates. Crime had long been taken for granted in the less affluent parts of the city, and had become in the midseventies, as both unemployment and the costs of maintaining property rose and what had once been functioning neighborhoods were abandoned and burned and left to whoever claimed them, endemic. "In some poor neighborhoods, crime became almost a way of life," Jim Sleeper, an editor at

Newsday and the author of *The Closest of Strangers: Liberalism and the Politics of Race in New York*, noted in his discussion of the social disintegration that occurred during this period:

> . . . a subculture of violence with complex bonds of utility and affection within families and the larger, "law-abiding" community. Struggling merchants might "fence" stolen goods, for example, thus providing quick cover and additional incentive for burglaries and robberies; the drug economy became more vigorous, reshaping criminal lifestyles and tormenting the loyalties of families and friends. A walk down even a reasonably busy street in a poor, minority neighborhood at high noon could become an unnerving journey into a landscape eerie and grim.

What seemed markedly different a decade later, what made crime a "story," was that the more privileged, and especially the more privileged white, citizens of New York had begun to feel unnerved at high noon in even their own neighborhoods. Although New York City Police Department statistics suggested that white New Yorkers were not actually in increased mortal danger (the increase in homicides between 1977 and 1989, from 1,557 to 1,903, was entirely among what the NYPD classified as Hispanic, Asian, and black victims; the number of white murder victims had steadily declined, from 361 in 1977 to 227 in 1984 and 190 in 1989), the apprehension of such danger, exacerbated by street snatches and muggings and the quite useful sense that the youth in the hooded sweatshirt with his hands jammed in his pockets might well be a predator, had become general. These more privileged New Yorkers now felt unnerved not only on the street, where the necessity for evasive strategies had become an exhausting constant, but in even the most insulated and protected apartment buildings. As the residents of such buildings, the owners of twelve- and sixteen- and twenty-four-room apartments, watched the potted ficus trees disappear from outside their doors and the graffiti appear on their limestone walls and the smashed safety glass from car windows get swept off their sidewalks, it had become increasingly easy to imagine the outcome of a confrontation between, say, the relief night doorman and six dropouts from Julia Richman High School on East 67th Street.

And yet those New Yorkers who had spoken to the *Times* in April of 1990 about their loss of flexibility, about their panic, their desolation, their anger, and their sense of impending doom, had not been talking about drugs, or crime, or any of the city's more publicized and to some extent inflated ills. These were people who did not for the most part have twelve- and sixteen-room apartments and doormen and the luxury of projected fears. These people were talking instead about an immediate fear, about money, about the vertiginous plunge in the value of their houses and apartments and condominiums, about the possibility or probability of foreclosure and loss; about, implicitly, their fears of being left, like so many they saw every day, below the line, out in the cold, on the street.

This was a climate in which many of the questions that had seized the city's attention in 1987 and 1988, for example that of whether Mortimer Zuckerman should be "allowed" to build two fifty-nine-story office towers on the site of what is now the Coliseum, seemed in retrospect wistful, the baroque concerns of better times. "There's no way anyone would make a sane judgment to go into the ground now," a vice president at Cushman and Wakefield told the *New York Observer* about the delay in the Coliseum project, which had in fact lost its projected major tenant, Salomon Brothers, shortly after Black Monday, 1987. "It would be suicide. You're better off sitting in a tub of water and opening your wrists." Such fears were, for a number of reasons, less easy to incorporate into the narrative than the fear of crime.

The imposition of a sentimental, or false, narrative on the disparate and often random experience that constitutes the life of a city or a country means, necessarily, that much of what happens in that city or country will be rendered merely illustrative, a series of set pieces, or performance opportunities. Mayor Dinkins could, in such a symbolic substitute for civic life, "break the boycott" (the Flatbush boycott organized to mobilize resentment of Korean merchants in black neighborhoods) by purchasing a few dollars' worth of produce from a Korean grocer on Church Avenue. Governor Cuomo could "declare war on crime" by calling for five thousand additional police; Mayor Dinkins could "up the ante" by calling for sixty-five hundred. "White slut comes into the park looking for the African man," a black woman could say, her voice loud but still conversational, in the corridor outside the courtroom where, during the summer of 1990, the first three defendants in the Central Park attack, Antron McCray, Yusef Salaam, and Raymond Santana, were tried on charges of attempted murder, assault, sodomy, and rape. "Boyfriend beats shit out of her, they blame it on our boys," the woman could continue, and then, referring to a young man with whom the victim had at one time split the cost of an apartment: "How about the roommate, anybody test his semen? No. He's white. They don't do it to each other."

Glances could then flicker among those reporters and producers and courtroom sketch artists and photographers and cameramen and techs and summer interns who assembled daily at 111 Centre Street. Cellular phones could be picked up, a show of indifference. Small talk could be exchanged with the marshals, a show of solidarity. The woman could then raise her voice: "White folk, all of them are devils, even those that haven't been born yet, they are *devils.* Little *demons.* I don't understand these devils, I guess they think this is *their court.*" The reporters could gaze beyond her, faces blank, no eye contact, a more correct form of hostility and also more lethal. The woman could hold her ground but avert her eyes, letting her gaze fall on another black, in this instance a black *Daily News* columnist, Bob Herbert. "You," she could say. "You are a *disgrace.* Go ahead. Line up there. Line up with the white folk. Look at them, lining up for their first-class seats while *my* people are downstairs behind *barricades* . . . kept behind barricades like *cattle* . . . not even allowed in the room to see their sons lynched . . . is that an *African* I see in that line? Or is that a *Negro.* Oh, oh, sorry, shush, white folk didn't know, he was *passing* . . ."

In a city in which grave and disrupting problems had become general—problems of not having, problems of not making it, problems that demonstrably existed, among the mad and the ill and the underequipped and the overwhelmed, with decreasing reference to color—the case of the Central Park jogger provided more than just a safe, or structured, setting in which various and sometimes only marginally related rages could be vented. "This trial," the *Daily News* announced on its editorial page one morning in July 1990, midway through the trial of the first three defendants, "is about more than the rape and brutalization of a single woman. It is about the rape and the brutalization of a city. The jogger is a symbol of all that's wrong here. And all that's right, because she is nothing less than an inspiration."

The *News* did not define the ways in which "the rape and the brutalization of the city" manifested itself, nor was definition necessary: this was a city in which the threat or the fear of brutalization had become so immediate that citizens were urged to take up their own defense, to form citizen patrols or militia, as in Beirut. This was a city in which between twenty and thirty neighborhoods had already given over their protection, which was to say the right to determine who belonged in the neighborhood and who did not and what should be done about it, to the Guardian Angels. This was a city in which a Brooklyn vigilante group, which called itself Crack Busters and was said to be trying to rid its Bedford-Stuyvesant neighborhood of drugs, would before September was out "settle an argument" by dousing with gasoline and setting on fire an abandoned van and the three homeless citizens inside. This was a city in which the *Times* would soon perceive, in the failing economy, "a bright side for the city at large," the bright side being that while there was believed to have been an increase in the number of middle-income and upper-income families who wanted to leave the city, "the slumping market is keeping many of those families in New York."

In this city rapidly vanishing into the chasm between its actual life and its preferred narratives, what people said when they talked about the case of the Central Park jogger came to seem a kind of poetry, a way of expressing, without directly stating, different but equally volatile and similarly occult visions of the same disaster. One vision, shared by those who had seized upon the attack on the jogger as an exact representation of what was wrong with the city, was of a city systematically ruined, violated, raped by its underclass. The opposing vision, shared by those who had seized upon the arrest of the defendants as an exact representation of their own victimization, was of a city in which the powerless had been systematically ruined, violated, raped by the powerful. For so long as this case held the city's febrile attention, then, it offered a narrative for the city's distress, a frame in which the actual social and economic forces wrenching the city could be personalized and ultimately obscured.

Or rather it offered two narratives, mutually exclusive. Among a number of blacks, particularly those whose experience with or distrust of the criminal justice system was such that they tended to discount the fact that five of the six defendants had to varying degrees admitted taking part in the attack, and to focus instead on the absence of any supporting forensic evidence incontrovertibly linking this victim to these defendants, the case could be read as a confirmation not only of their victimization but of the white conspiracy they saw at the heart of that victimization. For the *Amsterdam News*, which did not veer automatically to the radical analysis (a typical issue in the fall of 1990 lauded the FBI for its minority recruiting and the Harlem National Guard for its high morale and readiness to go to the Gulf), the defendants could in this light be seen as victims of "a political trial," of a "legal lynching," of a case "rigged from the very beginning" by the decision of "the white press" that "whoever was arrested and charged in this case of the attempted murder, rape and sodomy of a well-connected, bright, beautiful, and promising white woman was guilty, pure and simple."

For Alton H. Maddox, Jr., the message to be drawn from the case was that the American criminal justice system, which was under any circumstances "inherently and unabashedly racist," failed "to function equitably at any level when a Black male is accused of raping a white female." For others the message was more general, and worked to reinforce the fragile but functional mythology of a heroic black past, the narrative in which European domination could be explained as a direct and vengeful response to African superiority. "Today the white man is faced head-on with what is happening on the Black Continent, Africa," Malcolm X wrote.

> Look at the artifacts being discovered there, that are proving over and over again, how the black man had great, fine, sensitive civilizations before the white man was out of the caves. Below the Sahara, in the places where most of America's Negroes' foreparents were kidnapped, there is being unearthed some of the finest craftsmanship, sculpture and other objects, that has ever been seen by modern man. Some of these things now are on view in such places as New York City's Museum of Modern Art. Gold work of such fine tolerance and workmanship that it has no rival. Ancient objects produced by black hands . . . refined by those black hands with results that no human hand today can equal.
>
> History has been so "whitened" by the white man that even the black professors have known little more than the most ignorant black man about the talents and rich civilizations and cultures of the black man of millenniums ago . . .

"Our proud African queen," the Reverend Al Sharpton had said of Tawana Brawley's mother, Glenda Brawley: "She stepped out of anonymity, stepped out of obscurity, and walked into history." It was said in the corridors of the courthouse where Yusef Salaam was tried that he carried himself "like an African king."

"It makes no difference anymore whether the attack on Tawana happened," William Kunstler had told *New York Newsday* when the alleged rape and torture of Tawana Brawley by a varying number of white police officers seemed, as an actual prosecutable crime if not as a window on what people needed to believe, to have dematerialized. "If her story was a concoction to prevent her parents from punishing her for staying out all night, that doesn't disguise the fact that a lot of young black women are treated the way she said she was treated." The importance of whether or not the crime had occurred was, in this view, entirely resident in the crime's "description," which was defined by Stanley Diamond in *The Nation* as "a crime that did not occur" but was "described with skill and controlled hysteria by the black actors as the epitome of degradation, a repellent model of what actually happens to too many black women."

A good deal of what got said around the edges of the jogger case, in the corridors and on the call-in shows, seemed to derive exclusively from the suspicions of conspiracy increasingly entrenched among those who believe themselves powerless. A poll conducted in June of 1990 by the *New York Times* and WCBS-TV News determined that 77 percent of blacks polled believed either that it was "true" or "might possibly be true" (as opposed to "almost certainly not true") that the government of the United States "singles out and investigates black elected officials in order to discredit them in a way it doesn't do with white officials." Sixty percent believed that it was true or might possibly be true that the government "deliberately makes sure that drugs are easily available in poor black neighborhoods in order to harm black people." Twenty-nine percent believed that it was true or might possibly be true that "the virus which causes AIDS was deliberately created in a laboratory in order to infect black people." In each case, the alternative response to "true" or "might possibly be true" was "almost certainly not true," which might have seemed in itself to reflect a less than ringing belief in the absence of conspiracy. "The conspiracy to destroy Black boys is very complex and interwoven," Jawanza Kunjufu, a Chicago educational consultant, wrote in his *Countering the Conspiracy to Destroy Black Boys*, a 1982 pamphlet that has since been extended to three volumes.

> There are many contributors to the conspiracy, ranging from the very visible who are more obvious, to the less visible and silent partners who are more difficult to recognize.
>
> Those people who adhere to the doctrine of white racism, imperialism, and white male supremacy are easier to recognize. Those people who actively promote drugs and gang violence are active conspirators, and easier to identify. What makes the conspiracy more complex are those people who do not plot together to destroy Black boys, but, through their indifference, perpetuate it. This passive group of conspirators consists of parents, educators, and white liberals who deny being racists, but through their silence allow institutional racism to continue.

For those who proceeded from the conviction that there was under way a conspiracy to destroy blacks, particularly black boys, a belief in the innocence of these defendants, a conviction that even their own statements had been rigged against them or wrenched from them, followed logically. It was in the corridors and on the call-in shows that the conspiracy got sketched in, in a series of fantasy details that conflicted not only with known facts but even with each other. It was said that the prosecution was withholding evidence that the victim had gone to the park to meet a drug dealer. It was said, alternately or concurrently, that the prosecution was withholding evidence that the victim had gone to the park to take part in a satanic ritual. It was said that the forensic photographs showing her battered body were not "real" photographs, that "they," the prosecution, had "brought in some corpse for the pictures." It was said that the young woman who appeared on the witness stand and identified herself as the victim was not the "real" victim, that "they" had in this case brought in an actress.

What was being expressed in each instance was the sense that secrets must be in play, that "they," the people who had power in the courtroom, were in possession of information systematically withheld—since information itself was power—from those who did not have power. On the day the first three defendants were sentenced, C. Vernon Mason, who had formally entered the case in the penalty phase as Antron McCray's attorney, filed a brief that included the bewildering and untrue assertion that the victim's boyfriend, who had not at that time been called to testify, was black. That some whites jumped to engage this assertion on its own terms (the *Daily News* columnist Gail Collins referred to it as Mason's "slimiest argument of the hour—an announcement that the jogger had a black lover") tended only to reinforce the sense of racial estrangement that was the intended subtext of the assertion, which was without meaning or significance except in that emotional deep where whites are seen as conspiring in secret to sink blacks in misery. "Just answer me, who got addicted?" I recall one black spectator asking another as they left the courtroom. "I'll tell you who got addicted, the inner city got addicted." He had with him a pamphlet that laid out a scenario in which the government had conspired to exterminate blacks by flooding their neighborhoods with drugs, a scenario touching all the familiar points, Laos, Cambodia, the Golden Triangle, the CIA, more secrets, more poetry.

"From the beginning I have insisted that this was not a racial case," Robert Morgenthau, the Manhattan district attorney, said after the verdicts came in on the first jogger trial. He spoke of those who, in his view, wanted "to divide the races and advance their own private agendas," and of how the city was "ill-served" by those who had so "sought to exploit" this case. "We had hoped that the racial tensions surrounding the jogger trial would begin to dissipate soon after the jury arrived at a verdict," a *Post* editorial began a few days later. The editorial spoke of an "ugly claque of 'activists'," of the "divisive atmosphere" they had created, and of the anticipation with which the city's citizens had waited for "mainstream black leaders" to step forward with praise for the way in which the verdicts had brought New York "back from the brink of criminal chaos":

> Alas, in the jogger case, the wait was in vain. Instead of praise for a verdict which demonstrated that sometimes criminals are caught and punished, New Yorkers heard charlatans like the Rev. Al Sharpton claim the case was fixed. They heard that C. Vernon Mason, one of the engineers of the Tawana Brawley hoax—the attorney who thinks Mayor Dinkins wears "too many yarmulkes"—was planning to appeal the verdicts . . .

To those whose preferred view of the city was of an inherently dynamic and productive community ordered by the natural play of its conflicting elements, enriched, as in Mayor Dinkins's "gorgeous mosaic," by its very "contrasts," this case offered a number of useful elements. There was the confirmation of "crime" as the canker corroding the life of the city. There was, in the random and feral evening described by the East Harlem attackers and the clear innocence of and damage done to the Upper East Side and Wall Street victim, an eerily exact and conveniently personalized representation of what the *Daily News* had called "the rape and the brutalization of a city." Among the reporters on this case, whose own narrative conventions involved "hero cops" and "brave prosecutors" going hand to hand against "crime" (the "Secret Agony of Jogger DA," we learned in the *Post* a few days after the verdicts in the first trial, was that "Brave Prosecutor's Marriage Failed as She Put Rapists Away"), there seemed an unflagging enthusiasm for the repetition and reinforcement of these elements, and an equally unflagging resistance, even hostility, to exploring the point of view of the defendants' families and friends and personal or political allies (or, as they were called in news reports, the "supporters") who gathered daily at the other end of the corridor from the courtroom.

This seemed curious. Criminal cases are widely regarded by American reporters as windows on the city or culture in which they take place, opportunities to enter not only households but parts of the culture normally closed, and yet this was a case in which indifference to the world of the defendants extended even to the reporting of names and occupations. Yusef Salaam's mother, who happened to be young and photogenic and to have European features, was pictured so regularly that she and her son became the instantly recognizable "images" of Jogger One, but even then no one got her name quite right. For a while in the papers she was "Cheroney," or sometimes "Cheron*a*y," McEllhonor, then she became Cheroney McEllhonor Salaam. After she testified, the spelling of her first name was corrected to "Sharonne," although, since the byline on a piece she wrote for the *Amsterdam News* spelled it differently, "Sharrone," this may have been another misunderstanding. Her occupation was frequently given as "designer" (later, after her son's conviction, she went to work as a paralegal for William Kunstler), but no one seemed to take this seriously enough to say what she designed or for whom; not until after she testified, when *Newsday* reported her testimony that on the evening of her son's arrest she had arrived at the precinct house late because she was an instructor at the Parsons School of Design, did the notion of "designer" seem sufficiently concrete to suggest an actual occupation.

The Jogger One defendants were referred to repeatedly in the news columns of the *Post* as "thugs." The defendants and their families were often said by reporters to be "sneering." (The reporters, in turn, were said at the other end of the corridor to be "smirking.") "We don't have nearly so strong a question as to the guilt or innocence of the defendants as we did at Bensonhurst," a *Newsday* reporter covering the first jogger trial said to the *New York Observer*, well before the closing arguments, by way of explaining why *Newsday*'s coverage may have seemed less extensive on this trial than on the Bensonhurst trials. "There is not a big question as to what happened in Central Park that night. Some details are missing, but it's fairly clear who did what to whom."

In fact this came close to the heart of it: that it seemed, on the basis of the videotaped statements, fairly clear who had done what to whom was precisely the case's liberating aspect, the circumstance that enabled many of the city's citizens to say and think what they might otherwise have left unexpressed. Unlike other recent high visibility cases in New York, unlike Bensonhurst and unlike Howard Beach and unlike Bernhard Goetz, here was a case in which the issue not exactly of race but of an increasingly visible underclass could be confronted by the middle class, both white and black, without guilt. Here was a case that gave this middle class a way to transfer and express what had clearly become a growing and previously inadmissible rage with the city's disorder, with the entire range of ills and uneasy guilts that came to mind in a city where entire families slept in the discarded boxes in which new Sub-Zero refrigerators were delivered, at twenty-six hundred per, to more affluent families. Here was also a case, most significantly, in which even that transferred rage could be transferred still further, veiled, personalized: a case in which the city's distress could be seen to derive not precisely from its underclass but instead from certain identifiable individuals who claimed to speak for this underclass, individuals who, in Robert Morgenthau's words, "sought to exploit" this case, to "advance their own private agendas"; individuals who wished even to "divide the races."

If the city's problems could be seen as deliberate disruptions of a naturally cohesive and harmonious community, a community in which, undisrupted, "contrasts" generated a perhaps dangerous but vital "energy," then those problems were tractable, and could be addressed, like "crime," by the call for "better leadership." Considerable comfort could be obtained, given this story line, through the demonization of the Reverend Al Sharpton, whose presence on the edges of certain criminal cases that interested him had a polarizing effect that tended to reinforce the narrative. Jim Sleeper, in *The Closest of Strangers*, described one of the fifteen marches Sharpton led through Bensonhurst after the 1989 killing of an East New York sixteen-year-old, Yusuf Hawkins, who had come into Bensonhurst and been set upon, with baseball bats and ultimately with bullets, by a group of young whites.

> An August 27, 1989, *Daily News* photo of the Reverend Al Sharpton and a claque of black teenagers marching in Bensonhurst to protest Hawkins's death shows that they are not really "marching." They are stumbling along, huddled together, heads bowed under the storm of hatred breaking over them, eyes wide, hanging on to one another and to Sharpton, scared out of their wits. They, too, are innocents—or were until that day, which they will always remember. And because Sharpton is with them, his head bowed, his face showing that he knows what they're feeling, he is in the hearts of black people all over New York.
>
> Yet something is wrong with this picture. Sharpton did not invite or coordinate with Bensonhurst community leaders who wanted to join the march. Without the time for organizing which these leaders should have been given in order to rein in the punks who stood waving watermelons; without an effort by black leaders more reputable than Sharpton to recruit whites citywide and swell the march, Sharpton was assured that the punks would carry the day. At several points he even baited them by blowing kisses . . .

"I knew that Bensonhurst would clarify whether it had been a racial incident or not," Sharpton said by way of explaining, on a recent "Frontline" documentary, his strategy in Bensonhurst. "The fact that I was so controversial to Bensonhurst helped them forget that the cameras were there," he said. "So I decided to help them . . . I would throw kisses to them, and they would go nuts." *Question*, began a joke told in the aftermath of the first jogger trial. *You're in a room with Hitler, Saddam Hussein, and Al Sharpton. You have only two bullets. Who do you shoot? Answer: Al Sharpton. Twice.*

Sharpton did not exactly fit the roles New York traditionally assigns, for maximum audience comfort, to prominent blacks. He seemed in many ways a phantasm, someone whose instinct for the connections between religion and politics and show business was so innate that he had been all his life the vessel for other people's hopes and fears. He had given his first sermon at age four. He was touring with Mahalia Jackson at eleven. As a teenager, according to Robert D. McFadden, Ralph Blumenthal, M. A. Farber, E. R. Shipp, Charles Strum, and Craig Wolff, the *New York Times* reporters and editors who collaborated on *Outrage: The Story Behind the Tawana Brawley Hoax*, Sharpton was tutored first by Adam Clayton Powell, Jr. ("You got to know when to hit it and you got to know when to quit it and when it's quittin' time, don't push it," Powell told him), then by the Reverend Jesse Jackson ("Once you turn on the gas, you got to cook or burn 'em up," Jackson told him), and eventually, after obtaining a grant from Bayard Rustin and campaigning for Shirley Chisholm, by James Brown. "Once, he trailed Brown down a corridor, through a door, and, to his astonishment, onto a stage flooded with spotlights," the authors of *Outrage* reported. "He immediately went into a wiggle and dance."

It was perhaps this talent for seizing the spotlight and the moment, this fatal bent for the wiggle and the dance, that most clearly disqualified Sharpton from casting as the Good Negro, the credit to the race, the exemplary if often imagined figure whose refined manners and good grammar could be stressed and who could be seen to lay, as Jimmy Walker said of Joe Louis, "a rose on the grave of Abraham Lincoln." It was left, then, to cast Sharpton, and for Sharpton to cast himself, as the Outrageous Nigger, the familiar role—assigned sixty years ago to Father Divine and thirty years later to Adam Clayton Powell—of the essentially manageable fraud whose first concern is his own well-being. It was for example repeatedly mentioned, during the ten days the jury was out on the first jogger trial, that Sharpton had chosen to wait out the verdict not at 111 Centre Street but "in the air-conditioned comfort" of

C. Vernon Mason's office, from which he could be summoned by beeper.

Sharpton, it was frequently said by whites and also by some blacks, "represented nobody," was "self-appointed" and "self-promoting." He was an "exploiter" of blacks, someone who "did them more harm than good." It was pointed out that he had been indicted by the state of New York in June of 1989 on charges of grand larceny. (He was ultimately acquitted.) It was pointed out that *New York Newsday*, working on information that appeared to have been supplied by federal law-enforcement agencies, had in January 1988 named him as a federal informant, and that he himself admitted to having let the government tap his phone in a drug-enforcement effort. It was routinely said, most tellingly of all in a narrative based on the magical ability of "leaders" to improve the commonweal, that he was "not the right leader," "not at all the leader the black community needs." His clothes and his demeanor were ridiculed (my husband was asked by *Esquire* to do a piece predicated on interviewing Sharpton while he was having his hair processed), his motives derided, and his tactics, which were those of an extremely sophisticated player who counted being widely despised among his stronger cards, not very well understood.

Whites tended to believe, and to say, that Sharpton was "using" the racial issue—which, in the sense that all political action is based on "using" one issue or another, he clearly was. Whites also tended to see him as destructive and irresponsible, indifferent to the truth or to the sensibilities of whites—which, most notoriously in the nurturing of the Tawana Brawley case, a primal fantasy in which white men were accused of a crime Sharpton may well have known to be a fabrication, he also clearly was. What seemed not at all understood was that for Sharpton, who had no interest in making the problem appear more tractable ("The question is, do you want to 'ease' it or do you want to 'heal' it," he had said when asked if his marches had not worked against "easing tension" in Bensonhurst), the fact that blacks and whites could sometimes be shown to have divergent interests by no means suggested the need for an ameliorative solution. Such divergent interests were instead a lucky break, a ready-made organizing tool, a dramatic illustration of who had the power and who did not, who was making it and who was falling below the line; a metaphor for the sense of victimization felt not only by blacks but by all those Sharpton called "the left-out opposition." *We got the power*, the chants go on "Sharpton and Fulani in Babylon: Volume I, The Battle of New York City," a tape of the speeches of Sharpton and of Leonora Fulani, a leader of the New Alliance Party. *We are the chosen people. Out of the pain. We that can't even talk together. Have learned to walk together.*

"I'm no longer sure what I thought about Al Sharpton a year or two ago still applies," Jerry Nachman, the editor of the *New York Post*, who had frequently criticized Sharpton, told Howard Kurtz of the *Washington Post* in September of 1990. "I spent a lot of time on the street. There's a lot of anger, a lot of frustration. Rightly or wrongly, he may be articulating a great deal more of what typical attitudes are than some of us thought." Wilbert Tatum, the editor and publisher of the *Amsterdam News*, tried to explain to Kurtz how, in his view, Sharpton had been cast as "a caricature of black leadership":

> He was fat. He wore jogging suits. He wore a medallion and gold chains. And the unforgivable of unforgivables, he had processed hair. The white media, perhaps not consciously, said, "We're going to promote this guy because we can point up the ridiculousness and paucity of black leadership." Al understood precisely what they were doing, precisely. Al is probably the most brilliant tactician this country has ever produced . . .

Whites often mentioned, as a clinching argument, that Sharpton paid his demonstrators to appear; the figure usually mentioned was five dollars (by November 1990, when Sharpton was fielding demonstrators to protest the killing of a black woman alleged to have grabbed a police nightstick in the aftermath of a domestic dispute, a police source quoted in the *Post* had jumped the payment to twenty dollars), but the figure floated by a prosecutor on the jogger case was four dollars. This seemed on many levels a misunderstanding, or an estrangement, or as blacks would say a disrespect, too deep to address, but on its simplest level it served to suggest what value was placed by whites on what they thought of as black time.

In the fall of 1990, the fourth and fifth of the six defendants in the Central Park attack, Kevin Richardson and Kharey Wise, went on trial. Since this particular narrative had achieved full resolution, or catharsis, with the conviction of the first three defendants, the city's interest in the case had by then largely waned. Those "charlatans" who had sought to "exploit" the case had been whisked, until they could next prove useful, into the wings. Even the verdicts in this second trial, coinciding as they did with yet another arrest of John ("The Dapper Don") Gotti, a reliable favorite on the New York stage, did not lead the local news. It was in fact the economy itself that had come center stage in the city's new, and yet familiar, narrative work: a work in which the vital yet beleaguered city would or would not weather yet another "crisis" (the answer was a resounding yes); a work, or a dreamwork, that emphasized not only the cyclical nature of such "crises" but the regenerative power of the city's "contrasts." "With its migratory population, its diversity of cultures and institutions, and its vast resources of infrastructure, capital, and intellect, New York has been the quintessential modern city for more than a century, constantly reinventing itself," Michael Stone concluded in his *New York* magazine cover story, "Hard Times." "Though the process may be long and painful, there's no reason to believe it won't happen again."

These were points commonly made in support of a narrative that tended, with its dramatic line of "crisis" and resolution, or recovery, only to further obscure the economic and historical groundwork for the situation in which the city found itself: that long unindictable conspiracy of criminal and semicriminal civic and commercial arrangements, deals, negotiations, gimmes and getmes, graft and grift, pipe, topsoil, concrete, garbage; the conspiracy of those in the know, those with a connection, those with a rabbi at the Department of Sanitation or the Buildings Department or the School Construction Authority or Foley Square, the conspiracy of those who believed everybody got upside down because of who it was, it happened to anybody else, a summons gets issued and that's the end of it. On November 12, 1990, in its page-one analysis of the city's troubles, the *New York Times* went so far as to locate, in "public spending," not the drain on the city's vitality and resources it had historically been but "an important positive factor":

> Not in decades has so much money gone for public works in the area—airports, highways, bridges, sewers, subways and other projects. Roughly $12 billion will be spent in the metropolitan region in the current fiscal year. Such government outlays are a healthy counterforce to a 43 percent decline since 1987 in the value of new private construction, a decline related to the sharp drop in real estate prices. . . . While nearly every industry in the private sector has been reducing payrolls since spring, government hiring has risen, maintaining an annual growth rate of 20,000 people since 1987 . . .

That there might well be, in a city in which the proliferation of and increase in taxes were already driving private-sector payrolls out of town, hardly anyone left to tax for such public works and public-sector jobs was a point not too many people wished seriously to address: among the citizens of a New York come to grief on the sentimental stories told in defense of its own lazy criminality, the city's inevitability remained the given, the heart, the first and last word on which all the stories rested. We love New York, the narrative promises, because it matches our energy level.

—1990

THE LAST THING HE WANTED

This book is for Quintana
and for John.

ONE

I

SOME REAL things have happened lately. For a while we felt rich and then we didn't. For a while we thought time was money, find the time and the money comes with it. Make money for example by flying the Concorde. Moving fast. Get the big suite, the multi-line telephones, get room service on one, get the valet on two, premium service, out by nine back by one. Download all data. Uplink Prague, get some conference calls going. Sell Allied Signal, buy Cypress Minerals, work the management plays. Plug into this news cycle, get the wires raw, nod out on the noise. *Get me audio*, someone was always saying in the nod where we were. *Agence Presse is moving this story*. Somewhere in the nod we were dropping cargo. Somewhere in the nod we were losing infrastructure, losing redundant systems, losing specific gravity. Weightlessness seemed at the time the safer mode. Weightlessness seemed at the time the mode in which we could beat both the clock and affect itself, but I see now that it was not. I see now that the clock was ticking. I see now that we were experiencing not weightlessness but what is interestingly described on page 1513 of the *Merck Manual* (Fifteenth Edition) as a sustained reactive depression, a bereavement reaction to the leaving of familiar environments. I see now that the environment we were leaving was that of feeling rich. I see now that there will be no Resolution Trust to do the workout on this particular default, but I did not see it then.

Not that I shouldn't have.

There were hints all along, clues we should have registered, processed, sifted for their application to the general condition. Try the day we noticed that the banks had called in the paper on all the malls, try the day we noticed that somebody had called in the paper on all the banks. Try the day we noticed that when we pressed 800 to do some business in Los Angeles or New York we were no longer talking to Los Angeles or New York but to Orlando or Tucson or Greensboro, North Carolina. Try the day we noticed (this will touch a nerve with frequent fliers) the new necessity for changes of equipment at Denver, Raleigh-Durham, St. Louis. Try, as long as we are changing equipment in St. Louis, the unfinished but already bankrupt Gateway Airport Tower there, its boutiques boarded up, its oyster bar shuttered, no more terrycloth robes in the empty cabanas and no more amenity kits in the not quite terrazzo bathrooms: this should have alerted us, should have been processed, but we were moving fast. We were traveling light. We were younger. So was she.

2

FOR THE record this is me talking.

You know me, or think you do.

The not quite omniscient author.

No longer moving fast.

No longer traveling light.

When I resolved in 1994 to finally tell this story, register the clues I had missed ten years before, process the information before it vanished altogether, I considered reinventing myself as PAO at the embassy in question, a career foreign service officer operating under the USICA umbrella. "Lilianne Owen" was my name in that construct, a strategy I ultimately jettisoned as limiting, small-scale, an artifice to no point. *She told me later*, Lilianne Owen would have had to keep saying, and *I learned this after the fact.* As Lilianne Owen I was unconvincing even to myself. As Lilianne Owen I could not have told you half of what I knew.

I wanted to come at this straight.

I wanted to bring my own baggage and unpack it in front of you.

When I first heard this story there were elements that seemed to me questionable, details I did not trust. The facts of Elena McMahon's life did not quite hang together. They lacked coherence. Logical connections were missing, cause and effect. I wanted the connections to materialize for you as they eventually did for me. The best story I ever told was a reef dream. This is something different.

The first time Treat Morrison ever saw Elena McMahon she was sitting alone in the coffee shop at the Intercon. He had flown down from Washington on the American that landed at ten A.M. and the embassy driver had dropped him at the Intercon to leave his bag and there was this American woman, he did not think a reporter (he knew most of the reporters who covered this part of the world, the reporters stayed close to where they believed the story was, that was the beauty of operating on an island where the story had not yet appeared on the screen), an American woman wearing a white dress and reading the classified page of the local paper and sitting alone at a round table set for eight. Something about this woman had bothered him. In the first place he did not know what she was doing there. He had known she was an American because he recognized in her voice when she spoke to a waiter the slight flat drawl of the American Southwest, but the American women left on the island were embassy or the very occasional reporter, and neither would be sitting at apparent loose ends in the Intercon coffee shop. In the second place this American woman was eating, very slowly and methodically, first a bite of one and then a bite of the other, a chocolate parfait and bacon. The chocolate parfait and bacon had definitely bothered him.

At the time Treat Morrison saw Elena McMahon eating the parfait and bacon in the coffee shop at the Intercon she had been staying not at the Intercon but out on the windward side of the island, in two adjoining rooms with an efficiency kitchen at a place called the Surfrider. When she first came to the Surfrider, in July of that summer, it had been as assistant manager, hired to be in charge of booking return flights and baby-sitters and day tours (the sugar mill plus the harbor plus the island's single Palladian Revival great house) for the young Canadian families who had until recently favored the place because it was cheap and because its Olympic-length pool was deeper at no point than three feet. She had been introduced to the manager of the Surfrider by the man who ran the car-rental agency at the Intercon. Experience in the travel industry was mandatory, the manager of the Surfrider had said, and she had faked it, faked the story and the supporting letters of reference about the three years as social director on the Swedish cruise ship later reflagged (this was the inspired invention, the detail that rendered the references uncheckable) by Robert Vesco. At the time she was hired the island was still getting occasional misguided tourists, not rich tourists, not the kind who required villas with swimming pools and pink sand beaches and butlers and laundresses and multiple telephone lines and fax machines and instant access to Federal Express, but tourists nonetheless, mostly depressed young American couples with backpacks and retired day-trippers from the occasional cruise ship that still put in: those less acutely able to consider time so valuable that they would spend it only in the world's most perfect places. After the first State Department advisory the cruise ships had stopped, and after the second and more urgent advisory a week later (which coincided with the baggage handlers' strike and the withdrawal of two of the four international air carriers with routes to the island) even the backpackers had migrated to less demonstrably imperfect destinations. The Surfrider's Olympic-length pool had been drained. Whatever need there had been for an assistant manager had contracted, then evaporated. Elena McMahon had pointed this out to the manager but he had reasonably suggested that since her rooms would be empty in any case she might just as well stay on, and she had. She liked the place empty. She liked the way the shutters had started losing their slats. She liked the low clouds, the glitter on the sea, the pervasive smell of mildew and bananas. She liked to walk up the road from the parking lot and hear the voices from the Pentecostal church there. She liked to stand on the beach in front of the hotel and know that there was no solid land between her and Africa. "Tourism—Recolonialization by Any Other Name?" was the wishful topic at the noon brown-bag AID symposium the day Treat Morrison arrived at the embassy.

3

IF YOU remember 1984, which I notice fewer and fewer of us care to do, you already know some of what happened to Elena McMahon that summer. You know the context, you remember the names, *Theodore Shackley Clair George Dewey Clarridge Richard Secord Alan Fiers Felix Rodriguez aka "Max Gomez" John Hull Southern Air Lake Resources Stanford Technology Donald Gregg Aguacate Elliott Abrams Robert Owen aka "T.C." Ilopango aka "Cincinnati,"* all swimming together in the glare off the C-123 that fell from the sky into Nicaragua. Not many women got caught in this glare. There was one, the blonde, the shredder, the one who transposed the numbers of the account at the Credit Suisse (the account at the Credit Suisse into which the Sultan of Brunei was to transfer the ten million dollars, in case you have forgotten the minor plays), but she had only a bit part, day work, a broadly comic but not in the end a featured role.

Elena McMahon was different.

Elena McMahon got caught, but not in the glare.

If you wanted to see how she got caught you would probably begin with the documents.

There are documents, more than you might think.

Depositions, testimony, cable traffic, some of it not yet declassified but much in the public record.

You could pick up a thread or two in the usual libraries: Congress of course. The Foreign Policy Institute at Hopkins, the Center for Strategic and International Studies at Georgetown. The Sterling at Yale for the Brokaw correspondence. The Bancroft at Berkeley, where Treat Morrison's papers went after his death.

There are the FBI interviews, none what I would call illuminating but each offering the occasional moment (the chocolate parfait and bacon is one such moment in the transcripts of the FBI interviews), the leading detail (I found it suggestive that the subject who mentioned the parfait and bacon to the FBI was not in fact Treat Morrison), the evasion so blatant that it inadvertently billboards the very fact meant to be obscured.

There are the published transcripts of the hearings before the select committee, ten volumes, two thousand five hundred and seven pages, sixty-three days of testimony arresting not only for its reliance on hydraulic imagery (there were the conduits, there was the pipeline, there was of course the diversion) but for its collateral glimpses of life on the far frontiers of the Monroe Doctrine. There was for example the airline that operated out of St. Lucia but had its headquarters in Frankfurt (Volume VII, Chapter 4, "Implementing the Decision to Take Policy Underground") and either was or was not (conflicting testimony on this) ninety-nine percent owned by a former Air West flight attendant who either did or did not live on St. Lucia. There was for example the team of unidentified men (Volume X, Chapter 2, "Supplemental Material on the Diversion") who either did or did not (more conflicting testimony) arrive on the northern Costa Rican border to burn the bodies of the crew of the unmarked DC-3 that at the time it crashed appeared to be registered to the airline that was or was not ninety-nine percent owned by the former Sky West flight attendant who did or did not live on St. Lucia.

There is of course newspaper coverage, much of it less than fruitful: although a comprehensive database search on *McMahon, Elena* will yield, for the year in question, upwards of six hundred references in almost as many newspapers, all but a handful of them lead to the same two AP stories.

History's rough draft.

We used to say.

When we still believed that history merited a second look.

Not that this was a situation about which many people would have been willing to talk for attribution, or even on background. As someone who quite accidentally happened to be present at the embassy in question at the time in question, I myself refused a dozen or so press requests for interviews. At the time, I chose to believe that I refused such requests because they seemed to impinge on what was then my own rather delicate project, a preliminary profile of Treat Morrison for *The New York Times Magazine*, to be followed, if this exploratory drilling went as hoped, by a full-scale study of his proconsular role through six administrations, but it was a little more than that.

I refused such requests because I did not want to be drawn into discussion of whatever elements seemed questionable, whatever details seemed not to be trusted, whatever logical connections seemed to be missing between the Elena Janklow I had known in California (Catherine Janklow's mother, Wynn Janklow's wife, co-chair, committee member, arranger of centerpieces and table favors for a full calendar of benefit lunches and dinners and performances and fashion shows, originator in fact of the locally famous No Ball Ball, enabling the benevolent to send in their checks and stay home) and the Elena McMahon in the two AP stories.

I could find no reasonable excuse not to participate in the subsequent study in crisis management undertaken by the Rand Corporation on behalf of DOD/State, but I was careful: I adopted the vernacular of such studies. I talked about "conflict resolution." I talked about "incident prevention." I did provide facts, more facts even than I was asked to provide, but facts of such stupefying detail and doubtful relevance that none of the several Rand analysts engaged in the project thought to ask the one question I did not want to answer.

The question of course was what did I think had happened.

I thought she got caught in the pipeline, swept into the conduits.

I thought the water was over her head.

I thought she realized what she had been set up to do only in however many elongated seconds there were between the time she registered the presence of the man on the bluff and the time it happened.

I still think this.

I say so now only because real questions have occurred to me.

About the events in question.

At the embassy in question.

At the time in question.

You may recall the rhetoric of the time in question.

This wasn't a situation that lent itself to an MBA analysis.

This wasn't a zero-sum deal.

In a perfect world we might have perfect choices, in the real world we had real choices, and we made them, and we measured the losses against what might have been the gains.

Real world.

There was no doubt certain things happened we might have wished hadn't happened.

There was no doubt we were dealing with forces that might or might not include unpredictable elements.

Elements beyond our control.

No doubt, no argument at all.

And yet.

Still.

Consider the alternatives: trying to create a context for democracy and maybe getting your hands a little dirty in the process or just opting out, letting the other guy call it.

Add it up.

I did that.

I added it up.

Not zero-sum at all.

You could call this a reconstruction. A corrective, if you will, to the Rand study. A revisionist view of a time and a place and an incident about which, ultimately, most people preferred not to know. Real world.

4

If I could believe (as convention tells us) that character is destiny and the past prologue et cetera, I might begin the story of what happened to Elena McMahon during the summer of 1984 at some earlier point. I might begin it in, say, 1964, the year during which Elena McMahon lost her scholarship to the University of Nevada and within a week invented herself as a reporter for the Los Angeles *Herald Examiner*. I might begin it four years later, in 1968, the year during which, in the course of researching a backgrounder on the development of the oil business in southern California, Elena McMahon met Wynn Janklow in his father's office on Wilshire Boulevard and, with such single-minded efficiency that she never bothered to write the piece, reinvented herself as his wife.

Crucible events.

Revelations of character.

Absolutely, no question, but the character they reveal is that of a survivor.

Since what happened to Elena McMahon during the summer of 1984 had notably little to do with surviving, let me begin where she would begin.

The night she walked off the 1984 campaign.

You will notice that participants in disasters typically locate the "beginning" of the disaster at a point suggesting their own control over events. A plane crash retold will begin not with the pressure system over the Central Pacific that caused the instability over the Gulf that caused the wind shear at DFW but at some manageable human intersect, with for example the "funny feeling" ignored at breakfast. An account of a 6.8 earthquake will begin not at the overlap of the tectonic plates but more comfortably, at the place in London where we ordered the Spode that shattered the morning the tectonic plates shifted.

Had we just gone with the funny feeling. Had we just never ordered the Spode.

We all prefer the magical explanation.

So it was with Elena McMahon.

She had walked off the campaign the day before the California primary at one-forty in the morning Los Angeles time, she repeatedly told the DIA agent Treat Morrison flew down to take her statement, as if the exact time at which she walked off the campaign had set into inexorable motion the sequence of events that followed.

At the time she walked off the campaign she had not seen her father in some months, she told the DIA agent when he pressed her on this point.

How many months exactly, the agent had said.

I don't know exactly, she had said.

Two points. One, Elena McMahon did know exactly how many months it had been since she had last seen her father. Two, the exact number of months between the time Elena McMahon had last seen her father and the time Elena McMahon walked off the campaign was, like the exact time at which she walked off the campaign, not significant. For the record: at the time Elena McMahon walked off the 1984 campaign she had not seen her father in twenty-one months. The last time she had seen him was September 1982, either the fourteenth or the fifteenth. She could date this almost exactly because it had been either the day or the day after Bashir Gemayel was assassinated in Lebanon and at the moment the phone rang she had been sitting at her desk doing White House reaction.

In fact she could date it not almost exactly but exactly.

It had been the fifteenth. September 15, 1982.

She knew it had been the fifteenth because she had arrived in Washington on the fifteenth of August and given herself a month to find a house and put Catherine into school and get the raise that meant she was no longer a provisional hire (there again a survivor, there again that single-minded efficiency), and at the moment her father called she had just made a note to ask about the raise.

Hey, her father had said when she picked up the telephone. This was his standard way of initiating telephone contact, no name, no greeting, just *Hey*, then silence. She had outwaited the silence. I'm passing through Washington, he had said then, maybe you could meet me the next half hour or so.

I'm at work, she had said.

Some kind of coincidence, he had said, since that's where I called you.

Because she was on deadline she had told him to meet her across the street at the Madison. This had seemed a convenient neutral venue but as soon as she walked in and saw him sitting alone in the bar, drumming his fingers insistently on the small table, she knew that the Madison had not been a propitious choice. His eyes were narrowed, fixed on three men in apparently identical pin-striped suits at the next table. She recognized one of the three as White House, his name was Christopher Hormel, he was OMB but for whatever reason he had been hovering officiously around the podium during the noon briefing on Lebanon. That's not policy, that's politesse, Christopher Hormel was saying as she sat down, and then he repeated it, as if he had coined a witticism.

Just keep on shoveling it, her father had said.

Christopher Hormel had pushed back his chair and turned.

Spit it out, buddy, what's your problem, her father had said.

Daddy, she had said, an entreaty.

I have no problem, Christopher Hormel had said, and turned away.

Faggots, her father had said, his fingers roaming the little dish of nuts and toasted cereal for the remaining macadamia nut.

Actually you're wrong, she had said.

I see you're buying right into the package here, her father had said. You're very adaptable, anybody ever mention that?

She had ordered him a bourbon and water.

Say Early Times, he had corrected her. You say bourbon in these faggot bars they give you the Sweet Turkey shit or whatever it's called, then charge extra. And hey, you, pal, crack out the almonds, save the Cheerios for the queers.

When the drink came he had drained it, then hunched forward. He had a small deal going in Alexandria, he had said. He had a source for two or three hundred nines, Intratecs, lame little suckers he could pick up at seventy-five per and pass on for close to three hundred, the guy he passed them to would double his money on the street but let him, that was street, he didn't do street, never had, never would.

Wouldn't need to either.

Because things were hotting up again.

Whole lot of popping going on again.

She had signed the bill.

Hey, Ellie, give us a smile, whole lot of popping.

The next time she saw him was the day she walked off the 1984 campaign.

5

SHE HAD not planned to walk off the campaign. She had picked up the plane that morning at Newark and except for the Coke during refueling at Kansas City she had not eaten in twenty-eight hours but she had not once thought of walking away, not on the plane, not at the rally in South Central, not at the meet-and-greet at the Maravilla project, not sitting on the sidewalk in Beverly Hills waiting for the pool report on the celebrity fund-raiser (the celebrity fund-raiser at which most of the guests had turned out to be people she had known in her previous life as Elena Janklow, the celebrity fund-raiser at which in the natural course of her previous life as Elena Janklow she would have been standing under the Regal Rents party tent listening to the candidate and calculating the length of time before she could say good night and drive home to the house on the Pacific Coast Highway and sit on the deck and smoke a cigarette), not even then had she framed the thought *I could walk off this campaign.*

She had performed that day as usual.

She had filed twice.

She had filed first from the Evergreen operations office in Kansas City and she had filed the update during downtime at the Holiday Inn in Torrance. She had received and answered three queries from the desk about why she had elected not to go with a story the wires were moving about an internal poll suggesting shifts among most-likely-voters. *Re your query on last night's Sawyer-Miller poll,* she had typed in response to the most recent query. *For third time, still consider sample too small to be significant.* She had improved the hour spent sitting on the sidewalk waiting for the pool report on the celebrity fund-raiser by roughing in a draft for the Sunday analysis.

She had set aside the seductive familiarity of the celebrity fund-raiser.

The smell of jasmine.

The pool of blue jacaranda petals on the sidewalk where she sat.

The sense that under that tent nothing bad was going to happen and its corollary, the sense that under that tent nothing at all was going to happen.

That had been her old life and this was her new life and it was imperative that she keep focus.

She had kept focus.

She had maintained momentum.

It would seem to her later that nothing about the day had gone remarkably wrong but it would also seem that nothing about the day had gone remarkably right: for example, her name had been left off the manifest at Newark. There was a new Secret Service rotation and she had packed her press tags and the agent in charge had not wanted to let her on the plane. Where's the dog, the agent had said repeatedly to no one in particular. The Port Authority was supposed to have a dog here, where's the dog.

It had been seven in the morning and already hot and they had been standing on the tarmac with the piles of luggage and camera equipment. I talked to Chicago last night, she had said, trying to get the agent to look at her as she groped through her bag trying to find the tags. This was true. She had talked to Chicago the night before and she had also talked to Catherine the night before. Who she had not talked to the night before was her father. Her father had left two messages on her machine in Georgetown but she had not returned the calls. Hey, her father had said the first time he called. Then the breathing, then the click. She located something smooth and hard in her bag and thought she had the tags but it was a tin of aspirin.

We had a real life and now we don't and just because I'm your daughter I'm supposed to like it and I don't, Catherine had said to her.

Pardon my using your time but I've been trying to call your mother and that asshole she lives with refuses to put her on the line, her father had said to her machine the second time he called.

Chicago said I was on the plane, she had said to the agent.

We don't have a dog, it'll take all day to sweep this shit, the agent had said. He seemed to be directing this to a sound tech who squatted on the tarmac rummaging through his equipment.

She had touched the agent's sleeve in an effort to get him to look at her. If somebody would just check with Chicago, she had said.

The agent had retracted his arm abruptly but still had not looked at her.

Who is she, he had said. She hasn't been cleared by the campaign, what's she doing here.

The sound tech had not looked up.

Tell him you know me, she had said to the sound tech. She could not think whose tech he was but she knew that she had seen him on the plane. What she had come during the campaign to describe as her advanced age (since no one ever demurred this had become by June an embarrassing reflex, a tic that made her face flush even as she said it) made asking for help obscurely humiliating but that was not important. What was important was getting on the plane. If she was not on the plane she would not be on the campaign. The campaign had momentum, the campaign had a schedule. The schedule would automatically take her to July, August, the frigid domes with the confetti falling and the balloons floating free.

She would work out the business about Catherine later.

She could handle Catherine.

She would call her father later.

Tell him you know me, she repeated to the sound tech's back.

The sound tech extracted a mult cable from his equipment bag, straightened up and gazed at her, squinting. Then he shrugged and walked away.

I'm always on the plane, I've been on the plane since New Hampshire, she said to the agent, and then amended it: I mean on and off the plane. She could hear the note of pleading in her voice. She remembered: the tech was ABC. During Illinois she had been standing on the edge of a satellite feed and he had knocked her down pushing to get in close.

Tough titty, cunt, I'm working, he had said when she objected.

She watched him bound up the steps, two at a time, and disappear into the DC-9. The bruise where he had pushed her was still discolored two months later. She could feel sweat running down beneath her gabardine jacket and it occurred to her that if he had passed her on the way to the steps she would have tripped him. She had worn the gabardine jacket because California was always cold. If she did not find the tags she would not even get to California. The ABC tech would get to California but she would not. Tough titty, cunt, I'm working. She began to unpack her bag on the tarmac, laying out first tapes and notebooks and then an unopened package of panty hose, evidence of her sincerity, hostages to her insistence that the tags existed.

I just didn't happen to be on the plane this week, she said to the agent. And you just came on. Which is why you don't know me.

The agent adjusted his jacket so that she could see his shoulder holster.

She tried again: I had something personal, so I wasn't on the plane this week, otherwise you would know me.

This too was humiliating.

Why she had not been on the plane this week was none of the agent's business.

I had a family emergency, she heard herself add.

The agent turned away.

Wait, she said. She had located the tags in a pocket of her cosmetics bag and scrambled to catch up with the agent, leaving her tapes and notebooks and panty hose exposed on the tarmac as she offered up the metal chain, the bright oblongs of laminated plastic. The agent examined the tags and tossed them back to her, his eyes opaque. By the time she was finally allowed on the plane the camera crews had divided up the day's box lunches (there was only the roast beef left from yesterday and the vegetarian, the Knight-Ridder reporter sitting next to her said, but she hadn't missed shit because the vegetarian was just yesterday's roast beef without the roast beef) and the aisle was already slippery from the food fight and somebody had rigged the PA system to play rap tapes and in the process disconnected the galley refrigerator. Which was why, when she walked off the campaign at one-forty the next morning in the lobby of the Hyatt Wilshire in Los Angeles, she had not eaten, except for the Coke during refueling at Kansas City and the garnish of wilted alfalfa sprouts the Knight-Ridder reporter had declined to eat, in twenty-eight hours.

Later she would stress that part.

Later when she called the desk from LAX she would stress the part about not having eaten in twenty-eight hours.

She would leave out the part about her father.

Pardon my using your time but I've been trying to call your mother and that asshole she lives with refuses to put her on the line.

She would leave out the part about Catherine.

We had a real life and now we don't and just because I'm your daughter I'm supposed to like it and I don't.

She would leave out her father and she would leave out Catherine and she would also leave out the smell of jasmine and the pool of blue jacaranda petals on the sidewalk outside the celebrity fund-raiser.

Small public company going nowhere, bought it as a tax shelter, knew nothing about the oil business, she had written in her notebook on the day in 1968 when she interviewed Wynn Janklow's father. *I remember I said I wanted to take a look at our oil wells, I remember I stopped at a drugstore to buy film for my camera, little Brownie I had, I'd never seen an oil well before and I wanted to take a picture. And so we drove down to Dominguez Hills there and took a few pictures. At that point in time we were taking out oil sands from twelve to fourteen thousand feet, not enough to reveal viscosity. And today the city of Los Angeles is one of the great oil-producing areas in the world, seventeen producing fields within the city limits. Fox, Hillcrest, Pico near Doheny, Cedars, United Artists, UCLA, five hundred miles of pipeline under the city, the opposition to drilling isn't rational, it's psychiatric, whole time my son was playing ball at Beverly Hills High School there I was taking out oil from a site just off third base, he used to take girls out there, show them my rockers.*

The old man had looked up when the son entered the office.

Just ask him if he didn't, the old man said.

Beverly Hills crude, the son said, and she married him.

Pick yourself up.

Brush yourself off.

I hadn't eaten in twenty-eight hours, she would say to the desk.

Not that it mattered to the desk.

6

ON THE plane to Miami that morning she had experienced a brief panic, a sense of being stalled, becalmed, like the first few steps off a moving sidewalk. Off the campaign she would get no overnight numbers. Off the campaign she would get no spin, no counterspin, no rumors, no denials. The campaign would be en route to San Jose and her seat on the DC-9 would be empty and she was sitting by herself in this seat she had paid for herself on this Delta flight to Miami. The campaign would move on to Sacramento at noon and San Diego at one and back to Los Angeles at two and she would still be sitting in this seat she had paid for herself on this Delta flight to Miami.

This was just downtime, she told herself. This was just an overdue break. She had been pushing herself too hard, juggling too many balls, so immersed in the story she was blind to the story.

This could even be an alternate way into the story.

In the flush of this soothing interpretation she ordered a vodka and orange juice and fell asleep before it came. When she woke over what must have been Texas she could not at first remember why she was on this sedative but unfamiliar plane. *RON Press Overnites at Hyatt Wilshire*, the Los Angeles schedule had said, and the bus had finally arrived at the Hyatt Wilshire and the press arrangements had been made out of Chicago but her name was not on the list and there was no room.

Chicago fucked up, what else is new, the traveling press secretary had shrugged. So find somebody, double up, wheels up at six sharp.

She recalled a fatigue near vertigo. She recalled standing at the desk for what seemed a long time watching the apparently tireless children with whom she had crossed the country drift toward the bar and the elevator. She recalled picking up her bag and her computer case and walking out into the cold California night in her gabardine jacket and asking the doorman if he could get her a taxi to LAX. She had not called the desk until she had the boarding pass for Miami.

7

WHEN SHE arrived at the house in Sweetwater at five-thirty that afternoon the screen door was unlatched and the television was on and her father was asleep in a chair, the remote clutched in his hand, a half-finished drink and a can of jalapeño bean dip at his elbow. She had never before seen this house but it was indistinguishable from the house in Hialeah and before that the unit in Opa-Locka and for that matter the place between Houston and NASA. They were just places he rented and they all looked alike. The house in Vegas had looked different. Her mother had still been living with him when they had the house in Vegas.

Pardon my using your time but I've been trying to call your mother and that asshole she lives with refuses to put her on the line.

She would deal with that later.

She had dealt with the plane and she would deal with that.

She sat on a stool at the counter that divided the living room from the kitchen and began reading the Miami *Herald* she had picked up at the airport, very methodically, every page in order, column one to column eight, never turning ahead to the break, only occasionally glancing at the television screen. The Knight-Ridder reporter who had been sitting next to her on the plane the day before appeared to have based his file entirely on the most-likely-voters story the wires had moved. *California political insiders are predicting a dramatic last-minute shift in primary voting patterns here*, his story began, misleadingly. An American hostage who had walked out of Lebanon via Damascus said at his press conference in Wiesbaden that during captivity he had lost faith not only in the teachings of his church but in God. *Hostage Describes Test of Faith*, the headline read, again misleadingly. She considered ways in which the headline could have been made accurate (*Hostage Describes Loss of Faith? Hostage Fails Test of Faith?*), then put down the *Herald* and studied her father. He had gotten old. She had called him at Christmas and she had talked to him from Laguna last week but she had not seen him and at some point in between he had gotten old.

She was going to have to tell him again about her mother.

Pardon my using your time but I've been trying to call your mother and that asshole she lives with refuses to put her on the line.

She had told him on the telephone from Laguna but it had not gotten through, she was going to have to tell him again, he would want to talk about it.

It occurred to her suddenly that this was why she was here.

She had arrived at LAX with every intention of returning to Washington and had heard herself asking instead for a flight to Miami.

She had asked for a flight to Miami because she was going to have to tell him again about her mother.

That her mother had died was not going to change the course of his days but it would be a subject, it was something they would need to get through.

They would not need to talk about Catherine. Or rather: he would ask how Catherine was and she would say fine and then he would ask if Catherine liked school and she would say yes.

She should call Catherine. She should let Catherine know where she was.

We had a real life and now we don't and just because I'm your daughter I'm supposed to like it and I don't.

She would call Catherine later. She would call Catherine the next day.

Her father snored, a ragged apnea snore, and the remote dropped from his hand. On the television screen the graphic *Broward Closeup* appeared, over film of what seemed to be a mosque in Pompano Beach. It developed that discussion of politics had been forbidden at this mosque because many of what the reporter called Pompano Muslims came from countries at war with one another. "In Broward County at least," the reporter concluded, "Muslims who have known only war can now find peace."

This too was misleading. It occurred to her that possibly what was misleading was the concept of "news" itself, a liberating thought. She picked up the remote and pressed the mute.

"Goddamn ragheads," her father said, but did not open his eyes.

"Daddy," she said tentatively.

"Goddamn ragheads deserve to get nuked." He opened his eyes. "Kitty. Don't. Jesus Christ. Don't do that."

"It's not Kitty," she said. "It's her daughter. Your daughter."

She did not know how long she had been crying but when she groped in her bag for a tissue she found only damp wads.

"It's Elena," she said finally. "It's me."

"Ellie," her father said. "What the hell."

That would be one place to begin this story.

Elena McMahon's father getting involved with the people who wanted to make the deal with Fidel to take back the Sans Souci would have been another.

Way back. Much earlier. Call that back story.

This would have been another place to begin, also back story, just an image: a single-engine Cessna flying low, dropping a roll of toilet paper over a mangrove clearing, the paper streaming and looping as it catches on the treetops, the Cessna gaining altitude as it banks to retrace its flight path. A man, Elena McMahon's father, the man in the house in Sweetwater but much younger, retrieves the cardboard roll, its ends closed with masking tape. He cuts the masking tape with an army knife. He takes out a piece of paper. *Suspend all activity*, the paper reads. *Report without delay.*

November 22, 1963.

Dick McMahon's footnote to history.

Treat Morrison was in Indonesia the day that roll of toilet paper drifted down over the Keys.

On special assignment at the consulate in Surabaya.

They locked the consulate doors and did not open them for three days.

Treat Morrison's own footnote to history.

8

I STILL BELIEVE in history.

Let me amend that.

I still believe in history to the extent that I believe history to be made exclusively and at random by people like Dick McMahon. There are still more people like Dick McMahon around than you might think, most of them old but still doing a little business, keeping a hand in, an oar in the water, the wolf from the door. They can still line up some jeeps in Shreveport, they can still lay hands on some slots in Beaumont, they can still handle the midnight call from the fellow who needs a couple or three hundred Savage automatic rifles with telescopic sights. They may not remember all the names they used but they remember the names they did not use. They may have trouble sorting out the details of all they knew but they remember having known it.

They remember they ran some moves.

They remember they had personal knowledge of certain actions.

They remember they knew Carlos Prío, they remember they heard certain theories about his suicide. They remember they knew Johnny Roselli, they remember they heard certain theories about how he turned up in the oil drum in Biscayne Bay. They remember many situations in which certain fellows show up in the middle of the night asking for something and a couple or three days later these same identical fellows turn up in San Pedro Sula or Santo Domingo or Panama right in the goddamn thick of it.

Christ if I had a dollar for every time somebody came to me and said he was thinking about doing a move I'd be a rich man today, Elena McMahon's father said the day she was going down to where he berthed the *Kitty Rex*.

For the first two weeks at the house in Sweetwater she conserved energy by not noticing anything. That was how she put it to herself, she was conserving energy, as if attention were a fossil fuel. She drove out to Key Biscayne and let her mind go fallow, absorbing only the bleached flatness of the place, the pale aquamarine water and the gray sky and the drifts of white coral sand and the skeletons of live oak and oleander broken when the storms rolled in. One day when it rained and the wind was blowing she walked across the lowest of the causeways, overcome by a need to feel the water lapping over her sandals. By then she had already shed her clothes, pared down to essentials, concentrated her needs, wrapped up her gabardine jacket and unopened packages of panty hose and dropped them, a tacit farewell to the distractions of the temperate zone, in a Goodwill box on Eighth Street.

There's some question here what you're doing, the desk had said when she called to say she was in Miami. Siegel's been covering for you, but you understand we'll need to move someone onto this on a through-November basis.

That would be fair, she had said.

She had not yet conserved enough energy to resume thinking on a through-November basis.

At a point late each day she would focus on finding something that her father would eat, something he would not immediately set aside in favor of another drink, and she would go downtown to a place she remembered he liked and ask for containers of black beans or shrimp in garlic sauce she could reheat later.

From the Floridita, she would say when her father looked without interest at his plate.

In Havana, he would say, doubtful.

The one here, she would say. The Floridita on Flagler Street. You used to take me there.

The Floridita your mother and I knew was in Havana, he would say.

Which would lead as if on replay to his telling her again about the night at the Floridita in he believed 1958 with her mother and Carlos Prío and Fidel and one of the Murchisons. The Floridita in Havana, he would specify each time. Havana was the Floridita your mother and I knew, goddamn but we had some fun there, just ask your mother, she'll tell you.

Which would lead in the same replay mode to her telling him again that her mother was dead. On each retelling he would seem to take it in. Goddamn, he would say. Kitty's gone. He would make her repeat certain details, as if to fix the flickering fact of it.

She had not known how sick Kitty was, no.

She had not seen Kitty before she died, no.

There had been no funeral, no.

Kitty had been cremated, yes.

Kitty's last husband was named Ward, yes.

It was true that Ward used to sell pharmaceuticals, yes, but no, she would not describe it as dealing dope and no, she did not think there had been any funny business. In any case Ward was beside the point, which was this: her mother was dead.

Her father's eyes would go red then, and he would turn away.

Pretty Kitty, he would say as if to himself. Kit-Cat.

Half an hour later he would again complain that he had tried to call Kitty a night or two before and the asshole dope dealer she lived with had refused to put her on the line.

Because he couldn't, Elena would say again. Because she's dead.

Sometimes when the telephone rang in the middle of the night she would wake, and hear the front door close and a car engine turning over, her father's '72 Cadillac Seville convertible, parked on the spiky grass outside the room in which she slept. The headlights would sweep the ceiling of the room as he backed out onto the street. Most nights she would get up and open a bottle of beer and sit in bed drinking it until she fell asleep again, but one night the beer did not work and she was still awake, standing barefoot in the kitchen watching a local telethon on which a West Palm Beach resident in a sequined dress seemed to be singing gospel, when her father came in at dawn.

What the hell, her father said.

I said to Satan get thee behind me, the woman in the sequined dress was singing on the television screen.

You shouldn't be driving, Elena said.

Victory today is mine.

Right, I should take out my teeth and go to the nursing home, he said. Jesus Christ, you want to kill me too?

The woman in the sequined dress snapped her mike cord as she segued into "After You've Been There Ten Thousand Years," and Dick McMahon transferred his flickering rage to the television screen. I been there ten thousand years I still won't want to see you, honey, he shouted at the woman in the sequined dress. Because honey you are worthless, you are worse than worthless, you are trash. By the time he refocused on Elena he had softened, or forgotten. How about a drink, he said.

She got him a drink.

If you have any interest in what I'm doing, he said as she sat down at the table across from him, all I can say is it's major.

She said nothing. She had trained herself since childhood not to have any interest in what her father was doing. This had been difficult only when she had to fill out a form that asked for *Father's Occupation*. He did deals. *Does deals?* No. She had usually settled on *Investor*. If it came up in conversation she would say that her father bought and sold things, leaving open the possibility, in those parts of the country where she had lived until 1982, raw sunbelt cities riding high on land trades, that what he bought and sold was real estate. She had lost her scholarship at the University of Nevada because the administration had changed the basis for granting aid from merit to need and she had recognized that it would be a waste of time to ask her father to fill out a financial report.

Right from the top, he said. Top shelf.

She said nothing.

This one turns out the way it's supposed to turn out, he said, I'll be in a position to deal myself out, fold my hand, take the *Kitty Rex* down past Largo and stay there. Some life. Catching fish and bumming around the shallows. Not my original idea of a good time but it beats sitting here getting old.

Who exactly is running this one, she said carefully.

What do you care, he said, suddenly wary. What did you ever care who was running any of them.

I mean, she said, how did whoever is running this one happen to decide to work through you.

Why wouldn't they work through me, he said. I still got my teeth. I'm not in the nursing home yet. No thanks to you.

Dick McMahon had closed his eyes, truculent, and had not woken until she took the glass from his hand and put a cotton blanket over his legs.

What do you hear from your mother, he had said then.

9

THAT WAS the morning, June 15, a Friday, when she should have known it was time to cut and run.

She knew how to cut and run.

She had done it often enough.

Cut and run, cut her losses, just walked away.

She had just walked away from her mother for example.

See where it got her.

She had flown to Laguna as soon as she got the call but there had been no funeral. Her connection into John Wayne was delayed and by the time she arrived in the cold May twilight her mother had already been cremated. You know how Kitty felt about funerals, Ward said repeatedly. Actually I never heard her mention funerals, Elena said finally, thinking only to hear more about what her mother had said or thought, but Ward had looked at her as if wounded. She was welcome, he said, to do what she wanted with the cremains, the remains, the ashes or whatever, the cremains was what they called them, but in case she had nothing specific in mind he had already arranged with the Neptune Society. You know how Kitty felt about open ocean, he said. Open ocean was something else Elena did not recall her mother mentioning. So if it's all the same to you, Ward said, visibly relieved by her silence, I'll go ahead with the arrangements as planned.

She found herself wondering how short a time she could reasonably stay.

There would be nothing out of John Wayne but she could get a redeye out of LAX.

Straight shot up the 405.

Ward's daughter Belinda was in the bedroom, packing what she called the belongings. The belongings would go to the hospice thrift shop, Belinda said, but she knew that Kitty would want Elena to take what she wanted. Elena opened a drawer, aware of Belinda watching her.

Kitty never got tired of mentioning you, Belinda said. I'd be over here dealing with the Medicare forms or some other little detail and she'd find a way to mention you. It might be you'd just called from wherever.

The drawer seemed to be filled with turbans, snoods, shapeless head coverings of a kind Elena could not associate with her mother.

Or, Belinda said, it might be that you hadn't. I got her those for the chemo.

Elena closed the drawer.

Moved by the dim wish to preserve something of her mother from consignment to the hospice thrift shop she tried to remember objects in which her mother had set special stock, but in the end took only an ivory bracelet she remembered her mother wearing and a creased snapshot, retrieved from a carton grease-penciled OUT, of her mother and father seated in folding metal lawn chairs on either side of a portable barbecue outside the house in Las Vegas. Before she left she stood in the kitchen watching Ward demonstrate his ability to microwave one of the several dozen individual casseroles stacked in the freezer. Your mother did those just before she went down, Belinda said, raising her voice over *Jeopardy*. Kitty would have aced that, Ward said when a contestant on-screen missed a question in the Famous Travelers category. See what he does, Belinda said as if Ward could not hear. He keeps working in Kitty's name, same way Kitty used to work in yours. Two hours later Elena had been at LAX, trying to get cash from an ATM and unable to remember either her bank code or her mother's maiden name.

It might be you'd just called from wherever.

In the deep nowhere safety of the United lounge she drank two glasses of water and tried to remember her calling card number.

Or it might be that you hadn't.

Thirty-six hours after that she had been on the tarmac at Newark with the agent saying where's the dog, we don't have a dog, it'll take all day to sweep this shit.

She had cut and run from that too.

No more schedules, no more confetti, no more balloons floating free.

She had walked away from that the way she had walked away from the house on the Pacific Coast Highway. She did not think Wynn, she thought the house on the Pacific Coast Highway.

Tile floors, white walls, tennis lunches on Sunday afternoons.

Men with even tans and recent manicures, women with killer serves and bodies minutely tuned against stretch marks; always an actor or two or three, often a player just off the circuit. *The beauty part is, the Justice Department still gets its same take*, Wynn would be saying on the telephone, and then, his hand over the receiver, *Tell whoever you got in the kitchen it's time to lay on the lunch.* Nothing about those Sunday afternoons would have changed except this: Wynn's office, not Elena, would now call the caterer who laid on the lunch.

The big Stellas would still flank the door.

Wynn would still wake at night when the tide reached ebb and the sea went silent.

Goddamn what's the matter out there.

Smell of jasmine, pool of jacaranda, blue so intense you could drown in it.

We had a real life and now we don't and just because I'm your daughter I'm supposed to like it and I don't.

What exactly did you have in Malibu you don't have now, she had asked Catherine, and Catherine had walked right into it, Catherine had never even seen it coming. You could open the door in Malibu and be at the beach, Catherine said. Or the Jacuzzi. Or the pool.

Anything else, she had asked Catherine, her voice neutral.

The tennis court.

Is that all.

The three cars, Catherine said after a silence. We had three cars.

A Jacuzzi, she had said to Catherine. A pool. A tennis court. Three cars. Is that your idea of a real life?

Catherine, humiliated, outmaneuvered, had slammed down the phone.

Smell of jasmine, pool of jacaranda.

An equally indefensible idea of a real life.

She had been thinking that over when Catherine called back.

I had my father thank you very much.

She was even about to just walk away from Catherine.

She knew she was. She knew the signs. She was losing focus

on Catherine. She was losing momentum on Catherine. If she could even consider walking away from Catherine she could certainly walk away from this house in Sweetwater. That she did not was the beginning of the story as some people in Miami came to see it.

•

10

"I HAVE FREQUENTLY stated that I did not intend to set down either autobiographical notes of any kind or any version of events as I have witnessed and affected them. It has been my firm and long-held conviction that events, for better or for worse, speak for themselves, work as it were toward their own ends. After reviewing published accounts of certain of these events, however, I find my own role in them to have been misrepresented. Therefore, on this August Sunday morning, with a tropical storm due from the southeast and hard rain already falling outside these offices I am about to vacate at the Department of State in the City of Washington, District of Columbia, I have determined to set forth as concisely as possible, and in as much detail as is consistent with national security, certain actions I took in 1984 in the matter of what later became known as the lethal, as opposed to the humanitarian, resupply."

So begins the four-hundred-and-seventy-six-page transcript of the taped statement that Treat Morrison committed to the Bancroft Library at Berkeley with instructions that it be sealed to scholars until five years after his death.

Those five years have now passed.

As have, and this would have been his calculation, any lingering spasms of interest in the matter of what later became known as the lethal, as opposed to the humanitarian, resupply.

Or so it would seem.

Since, seven years after Treat Morrison's death and two years after the unsealing of the transcript, I remain the single person to have asked to see it.

MORRISON, TREAT AUSTIN, ambassador-at-large; b. San Francisco Mar. 3, 1930; s. Francis J. and Margaret (Austin) M; B.A., U. of Calif. at Berkeley, 1951; grad. National War College 1956; m. Diane Waring, Dec. 5, 1953 (dec. 1983). Commissioned 2nd lt. U.S. Army 1951, served in Korea, Germany, mil. attaché Chile 1953–54; spec. asst to commander SHAPE Paris 1955; attaché to US Mission to E.C. Brussels 1956–57

So Treat Morrison's *Who's Who* entry began.

And continued.

All the special postings enumerated, all the private-sector sojourns specified.

All there.

Right down to *Office: Dept. of State, 2201 C St., N.W., Washington, D.C. 20520.*

Without giving the slightest sense of what Treat Morrison actually did.

Which was fix things.

What was remarkable about those four hundred and seventy-six pages that Treat Morrison committed to the Bancroft Library was, as in his *Who's Who* entry, less what was said than what was not said. What was said was predictable enough, *globalism versus regionalism, full Boland, failed nations, correct interventions, multilateral approach, Directive 25, Resolution 427, criteria not followed*, nothing Treat Morrison could not have said at the Council on Foreign Relations, nothing he had not said, up there in the paneled room with the portrait of David Rockefeller and the old guys nodding off and the young guys asking pinched textbook questions and the willowy young women who worked on the staff standing in the back of the room like geishas, shuttle up and hop a flight back down with one of the corporate guys, maybe learn something for a change, you'd be surprised, they've got their own projections, their own risk analysts, no bureaucracy, no commitments to stale ideologies, none of those pinched textbook questions, they can afford to keep out there ahead of the power curve, corporate guys are light-years ahead of us.

Sometimes.

Four hundred and seventy-six pages on correct interventions and no clue that a correct intervention was for Treat Morrison an intervention in which when you run out of options you can still get your people to the airport.

Four hundred and seventy-six pages with only a veiled suggestion of Treat Morrison's rather spectacular indifference to the conventional interests and concerns of his profession, only an oblique flash of his particular maladaption, which was to be a manipulator of abstracts whose exclusive interest was in the specific. You get just the slightest hint of that maladaption in *tropical storm due from the southeast and hard rain already falling*, just the barest lapse before the sonorous recovery of *outside these offices I am about to vacate at the Department of State in the City of Washington, District of Columbia.*

No hint at all of his long half-mad gaze.

Wide spindrift gaze toward paradise, Elena McMahon said the first time she was alone with him.

He said nothing.

A poem, she said.

Still he said nothing.

Something *galleons of Carib fire*, she said, something something *the seal's wide spindrift gaze toward paradise.*

He studied her without speaking. Diane read poetry, he said then.

There had been a silence.

Diane was his wife.

Diane was dead.

Diane Morrison, 52, wife of, after a short illness, survived by, in lieu of flowers.

I wasn't thinking about the Carib fire part, Elena had said finally.

Yes you were, Treat Morrison had said.

II

WHAT WE want here is a montage, music over. *Angle on Elena.* Alone on the dock where her father berthed the *Kitty Rex.* Working loose a splinter on the planking with the toe of her sandal. Taking off her scarf and shaking out her hair, damp from the sweet heavy air of South Florida. *Cut to Barry Sedlow.* Standing in the door of the frame shack, under the sign that read RENTALS GAS BAIT BEER AMMO. Leaning against the counter. Watching Elena through the screen door as he waited for change. *Angle on the manager.* Sliding a thousand-dollar bill beneath the tray in the cash register, replacing the tray, counting out the hundreds.

No place you could not pass a hundred.

There in the sweet heavy air of South Florida.

Havana so close you could see the two-tone Impalas on the Malecón.

Goddamn but we had some fun there.

The music would give you the sweet heavy air, the music would give you Havana.

Imagine what the music was as: Barry Sedlow folded the bills into his money clip without looking at them, kicked open the screen door, and walked down the dock, a little something in the walk, a definite projection of what a woman less wary than Elena might (*might*, *could*, *would*, *did*, *wanted to*, *needed to*) mistake for sex.

Close on Elena. Watching Barry Sedlow.

"Looks like you're waiting for somebody," Barry Sedlow said.

"I think you," Elena McMahon said.

Her father had begun to run the fever during the evening of Saturday the sixteenth of June. She had known something was wrong because the drink he had made at seven remained untouched at ten, its color mottled by melted ice.

"I don't know what that foul ball expected to get out of showing up here," he said about midnight.

"What foul ball," she said.

"What's his name, Epperson, Max Epperson, the guy you were cozying up with tonight."

She said nothing.

"Come on," he said. "Cat got your tongue?"

"I don't remember seeing anyone but you tonight," she said finally.

"Epperson. Not the guy with the mickey-mouse vest. The other one."

She had framed her response carefully. "I guess neither of them made an impression on me."

"Epperson made an impression on you all right."

She had thought this over. "Listen to me," she had said then. "No one was here."

"Have it your way," he said.

She had driven to an all-night drugstore to buy a thermometer. His temperature, when she managed to take it, was 102. By morning it was 103.2, and she took him to the emergency room at Jackson Memorial. It was not the nearest hospital but it was the one she knew, a director she and Wynn knew had been shooting there, Catherine had been on spring vacation and they had taken her to visit the location. Nothing straight bourbon won't fix, her father said in the emergency room when the triage nurse asked what was wrong with him. By noon he had been admitted and she had signed the forms and heard the difference between Medicare A and B and when she got back upstairs to the room he had already tried to yank out the IV line and there was blood all over the sheets and he was crying.

"Get me out of here," he said. "Goddamnit get me out of here."

The IV nurse was on another floor and by the time she got back and got the line running again the nurse with the narcotics keys was on another floor and it was close to five before they got him sedated. By dawn his temperature had dropped below 101 but he was focused exclusively on Max Epperson. Epperson was welshing on his word. Epperson had floated a figure of three dollars per for 69s and now he was claiming the market had dropped to two per. Somebody had to talk reason to Epperson, Epperson could queer the whole deal, Epperson was off the reservation, didn't know the first thing about the business he was in.

"I'm not sure I know what business Epperson is in," she said.

"Christ, what business are they all in," her father said.

They would need more blood work before they had a diagnosis, the resident said. The resident was wearing a pink polo shirt and kept his eyes fixed on the nurses' station, as if to distance himself from the situation and from Elena. They would need a scan, an MRI, they would need something else she did not get the name of. They would of course order a psychiatric evaluation, although evidence of mental confusion would not in itself be a diagnostic criterion. Such mental confusion, if there was mental confusion, was incidental, a secondary complication. Whatever the diagnosis, it would not be uncommon to see a psychotic break with a fever this high in a patient this age.

"He's not that old," she said. This was pointlessly argumentive but she disliked the resident. "He's seventy-four."

"After retirement you have to expect a deficit."

"He's not retired either." She could not seem to stop herself. "He's quite active."

The resident shrugged.

At noon a second resident arrived to do the psychiatric evaluation. He too was wearing a polo shirt, mint green, and he too avoided Elena's eyes. She had fixed her gaze on the signs posted in the room and tried not to listen. I/O. INFECTIOUS SHARPS ONLY. "This is just a little game," the psychiatric resident said. "Can you tell me the name of the current president of the United States."

"Some game," Dick McMahon said.

"Take your time," the psychiatric resident said. "Don't let me rush you."

"Count on it."

There was a silence.

"Daddy," Elena said.

"I get the game," Dick McMahon said. "I'm supposed to say Herbert Hoover, then he puts me away in the home." His eyes narrowed. "All right. *Wheel of Fortune*. Herbert Hoover." He paused, watching the psychiatric resident. "Franklin Delano Roosevelt. Harry S Truman. Dwight David Eisenhower. John Fitzgerald Kennedy. Lyndon Baines Johnson. Richard Milhous Nixon. Gerald whatever his name was, kept tripping over his feet. Jimmy something. The Christer. Then the one now. The one the old dummy's not meant to remember. The other old dummy. Reagan."

"Really excellent, Mr. McMahon," the psychiatric resident said. "You deserve first prize."

"First prize is, you leave." Dick McMahon turned with difficulty away from the resident and closed his eyes. When he opened them again he focused on Elena. "Funny coincidence, that asshole bringing up presidents, which brings us back to Epperson." His voice was exhausted, matter-of-fact. "Because Epperson was involved in Dallas, that deal. I ever tell you that?"

Elena looked at him. His gaze was trusting, his pale-blue eyes rimmed with red. It had not before occurred to her that he might have known who was involved in Dallas. Neither did it surprise her. She supposed if she thought about it that he might have known who was involved in a lot of things, but it was too late now, the processor was unreliable. An exploration of what Dick McMahon knew could now yield only corrupted files, crossed data, lost clusters in which the spectral Max Epperson would materialize not only at the Texas Book Depository but in a room at the Lorraine Hotel in Memphis with Sirhan Sirhan and Santos Trafficante and Fidel and one of the Murchisons.

"What deal in Dallas is that, Mr. McMahon," the psychiatric resident said.

"Just a cattle deal he did in Texas." Elena guided the resident to the door. "He should sleep now. He's too tired for this."

"Don't tell me he's still here," Dick McMahon said without opening his eyes.

"He just left." Elena sat in the chair by the hospital bed and took her father's hand. "It's all right. Nobody's here."

Several times during the next few hours her father woke and asked what time it was, what day it was, each time with an edge of panic in his voice.

He had to be somewhere.

He had some things to do, some people to see.

Some people would be waiting for him to call.

These things he had to do could not wait.

These people he had to see had to be seen now.

Late in the day the sky went dark and she opened the window to feel the air beginning to move. It was only then, while the lightning forking on the horizon and the sound of thunder created a screen, a safe zone in which things could be said that would have no consequences, that Dick McMahon began to tell Elena who it was he had to see, what it was he had to do. *Tropical storm due from the southeast and hard rain already falling.* That he could not do it was obvious. That she should undertake to do it for him would have been less obvious.

12

It is hard now to call up the particular luridity of 1984. I read back over the clips and want only to give you the period verbatim, the fever of it, the counterfeit machismo of it, the extent to which it was about striking and maintaining a certain kind of sentimental pose. Many people appear to have walked around the dead center of this period with parrots on their shoulders, or monkeys. Many people appear to have chosen during this period to identify themselves as something other than what they were, as "cargo specialists" or as "aircraft brokers" or as "rose importers" or, with what came to seem baffling frequency, as "Danish journalists." This was a period during which many people appear to have known that the way to fly undetected over the Gulf coastline of the United States was low and slow, five hundred to a thousand feet, an effortless fade into the helicopter traffic off the Gulf rigs. This was a period during which many people appear to have known that the way to fly undetected over foreign coastlines was with cash, to buy a window. This was a period during which a significant minority among the population at large appears to have understood how government funds earmarked for humanitarian aid might be diverted, even as the General Accounting Office monitored the accounts, to more pressing needs.

Piece of cake, Barry Sedlow told Elena McMahon.

This was not his personal line of work but he knew guys who did it.

Pick a small retailer in any friendly, say Honduras or Costa Rica. Ask this retailer for an invoice showing a written estimate for the purchase of, say, a thousand pairs of green Lee jeans, a thousand green T-shirts, and a thousand pairs of green rubber boots. Specify that the word "estimate" not appear on the invoice. Present this invoice, bearing an estimated figure of say $25,870 but no indication that it is merely an estimate, to the agency responsible for disbursing said humanitarian aid, and ask that the $25,870 reimbursement due be transferred to your account at Citibank Panama. Instruct Citibank Panama to wire the $25,870 to one or another "broker" account, for example the account of a third-party company at the Consolidated Bank in Miami, an account the sole purpose of which is to receive the funds and make them available for whatever need presents itself.

The need, say, to make a payment to Dick McMahon.

There are people who understand this kind of transaction and there are people who do not. Those who understand it are at heart storytellers, weavers of conspiracy just to make the day come alive, and they see it in a flash, comprehend all its turns, get its possibilities. For anyone who could look at a storefront in Honduras or Costa Rica and see an opportunity to tap into the United States Treasury for $25,870, this was a period during which no information could be without interest. Every moment could be seen to connect to every other moment, every act to have logical if obscure consequences, an unbroken narrative of vivid complexity. That Elena McMahon walked into this heightened life and for a brief period lived it is what interests me about her, because she was not one of those who saw in a flash how every moment could connect.

I had thought to learn Treat Morrison's version of why she did it from the transcript of his taped statement. I had imagined that she would have told him what she would not or did not tell either the FBI or the DIA agents who spoke to her. I had imagined that Treat Morrison would have in due time set down his conclusions about whatever it was she told him.

No hint of that in those four hundred and seventy-six pages.

Instead I learned that what he referred to as "a certain incident that occurred in 1984 in connection with one of our Caribbean embassies" should not, in his opinion, have occurred.

Should not have occurred and could not have been predicted.

By what he called "any quantitative measurement."

However, he added. One caveat. *In situ* this certain incident could have been predicted.

Which went to the question, he said, of whether policy should be based on what was said or believed or wished for by people sitting in climate-controlled rooms in Washington or New York or whether policy should be based on what was seen and reported by the people who were actually on the ground.

He was constrained by classification from discussing the details of this incident and mentioned it only, he said, as a relevant illustration of the desirability of listening to the people who were actually on the ground.

No comment, as the people who were actually on the ground were trained to say if asked what they were doing or where they were staying or if they wanted a drink or even what time it was.

No comment.

Thank you.

Goodbye.

Elena McMahon had not been trained to say this, but was on the ground nonetheless.

I recently sat at dinner in Washington next to a reporter who covered the ground in question during the period in question. After a few glasses of wine he turned to me, lowered his voice, and said about this experience that nothing that had happened to him since, including the birth of his children and assignment to several more overt wars in several more overt parts of the world, had made him feel so alive as waking up on that particular ground any day in that particular period.

Until Elena McMahon woke up on that particular ground, she did not count her life as one in which anything had happened.

No comment. Thank you. Goodbye.

13

THE FIRST time she met Barry Sedlow was the day her father left the hospital. You'll be pleased to know you'll be leaving here tomorrow, the resident had said to her father, and she had followed him out to the nurses' station. "He's not ready to go home," she had said to the resident's back.

"Not to go home, no." The resident had not looked up from the chart he was studying. "Which is why you should be making whatever arrangements you prefer with the discharge coordinator."

"But you just agreed with me. He's not ready to be discharged. The arrangement I prefer is that he stay in the hospital."

"He can't stay in the hospital," the resident said, implacable. "So he will be discharged. And he's not going to be able to take care of himself."

"Exactly. That was my point." She tried for a reasonable tone. "As you say, he's not going to be able to take care of himself. Which is why I think he should stay in the hospital."

"You have the option of making an acceptable arrangement for home care with the discharge coordinator."

"Acceptable to who?"

"To the discharge coordinator."

"So it's up to the discharge coordinator whether or not he stays here?"

"No, it's up to Dr. Mertz."

"I've never met Dr. Mertz."

"Dr. Mertz is the admitting physician of record. On my recommendation, Dr. Mertz has authorized discharge."

"Then I should talk to Dr. Mertz?"

"Dr. Mertz is not on call this week."

She had tried another tack. "Look. If this has something to do with insurance, I signed papers saying I would be responsible. I'll pay for whatever his insurance won't cover."

"You will, yes. But he still won't stay here."

"Why won't he?"

"Because unless you've made an acceptable alternate arrangement," the resident said, unscrewing the top from his fountain pen and wiping the nib with a tissue, "he'll be discharged in the morning to a convalescent facility."

"You can't do that. I won't take him there."

"You won't have to. The facility sends its van."

"I didn't mean that. I meant you can't just send someone to a nursing home."

"Yes. We can. We do it all the time. Unless of course the family has made an acceptable alternate arrangement with the discharge coordinator."

There had been a silence. "How do I reach the discharge coordinator," she said then.

"I could ask her to come by the patient's room." The resident had refitted the top of his pen and placed it in the breast pocket of his polo shirt. He seemed not to know what to do with the tissue. "When she has a moment."

"Somebody took my goddamn shoes," her father had said when she walked back into the room. He was sitting on the edge of the bed buckling his belt and trying to free his arm from the hospital gown. "I can't get out of here without my goddamn shoes." She had no way of knowing whether he intended to walk out or had merely misunderstood the resident, but she had found his shoes and his shirt and arranged his jacket over his thin shoulders, then walked him out past the nurses' station into the elevator.

"You'll need a nurse," she had said tentatively when the elevator doors closed.

Her father had nodded, apparently resigned to strategic compromise.

"I'll tell the agency we need someone right away," she had said, trying to consolidate her gain. "Today."

Once more her father had nodded.

Lulled by the ease of the end run around the hospital apparat, Elena was still basking in this new tractability when, a few hours later, securely back at the house in Sweetwater, the nurse installed in front of the television set and the bed freshly made and a glass of bourbon-spiked Ensure at the ready (another strategic compromise, this one with the nurse), Dick McMahon announced that he needed his car keys and he needed them now.

"I told you," he said when she asked why. "I've got somebody to see. Somebody's waiting for me."

"I told you," he said when she asked who. "I told you the whole deal."

"You have to listen to me," she had said finally. "You're not in any condition to do anything. You're weak. You're still not thinking clearly. You'll make a mistake. You'll get hurt."

Her father had at first said nothing, his pale eyes watery and fixed on hers.

"You don't know what's going to happen," he said then. His voice was helpless, bewildered. "Goddamn, what's going to happen now."

"I just don't want you to get hurt."

"Jesus Christ," he said then, as if defeated, his head falling to one side. "I needed this deal."

She had taken his hand.

"What's going to happen now," he had repeated.

"I'll take care of it," she had said.

Which was how Elena McMahon happened, an hour later, to be standing on the dock where the *Kitty Rex* was berthed. *Looks like you're waiting for somebody*, Barry Sedlow said. *I think you*, Elena McMahon said.

The second time she was to meet Barry Sedlow he had instructed her to be in the lobby of the Omni Hotel on Biscayne Boulevard at what he called thirteen sharp. She was to sit near the entrance to the restaurant as if she were waiting to meet someone for lunch.

There would be lunch traffic in and out of the restaurant, she would not stand out.

If he happened not to show up by the time the lunch traffic thinned out she was to leave, because at that point she would stand out.

"Why might you happen not to show up," she had asked.

Barry Sedlow had written an 800 number on the back of a card reading KROME GUN CLUB and given it to her before he answered. "Could happen I won't like the look of it," he had said then.

She had arrived at one. It had been raining hard all morning and there was water everywhere, water sluicing down the black tile wall behind the lobby pool, water roiling and bubbling over the underwater spots in the pool, water standing on flat roofs and puddling around vents and driving against the six-story canted window. In the chill of the air-conditioning her clothes were damp and clammy against her skin and after a while she stood up and walked around the lobby, trying to get warm. Even the music from the merry-go-round in the mall downstairs was muted, distorted, as if she were hearing it underwater. She was standing at the railing looking down at the merry-go-round when the woman spoke to her.

The woman was holding an unfolded map.

The woman did not want to bother Elena but wondered if she knew the best way to get on I-95.

Elena told her the best way to get on I-95.

At three o'clock the restaurant had emptied out and Barry Sedlow had not appeared. From a pay phone in the lobby she dialed the 800 number Barry Sedlow had given her and found that it was a beeper. She punched in the number of the pay phone in the Omni lobby but at four o'clock, when the phone had not rung, she left.

At midnight the phone rang in the house in Sweetwater.

Elena hesitated, then picked it up.

"You stood out," Barry Sedlow said. "You let yourself be noticed."

"Noticed by who?"

He did not respond directly. "Here's what you're going to want to do."

What she was going to want to do, he said, was walk into the Pan Am Clipper Club at the Miami airport the next day at noon sharp. What she was going to want to do was go to the desk and ask for Michelle. She was going to want to tell Michelle that she was meeting Gary Barnett.

"Who exactly is Gary Barnett," she said.

"Michelle's the blonde, not the spic. Make sure it's Michelle you talk to. The spic is Adele, Adele doesn't know me."

"Gary Barnett is you?"

"Just do it my way for a change."

She had done it his way.

Gary wants you to make yourself comfortable, Michelle had said.

If I could please see your Clipper Club card, Adele had said.

Michelle had rolled her eyes. I *saw* her *card*, Michelle had said.

Elena sat down. On a corner sofa a portly man in a silk suit was talking on the telephone, his voice rising and falling, an unbroken flow of English and Spanish, now imploring, now threatening, oblivious to the announcements of flights for Guayaquil and Panama and Guatemala, oblivious to Elena, oblivious even to the woman at his side, who was thin and gray-haired and wore a cashmere cardigan and expensive walking shoes.

Mr. Lee, the man kept saying.

Then, finally: Let me ask you one question, Mr. Lee. Do we have the sugar or don't we. All right then. You tell me we have it. Then explain to me this one thing. How do we prove we have it. Because believe me, Mr. Lee, we are losing credibility with the buyer. All right. Listen. Here is the situation. We have ninety-two million dollars tied up since Thursday. This is Tuesday. Believe me, ninety-two million dollars is not small change. Is not chicken shit, Mr. Lee. The telex was supposed to be sent on Friday. I come up from San Salvador this morning to close the deal, the Sun Bank in Miami is supposed to have the telex, the Sun Bank in Miami does not have the telex. Now I ask you, Mr. Lee. Please. What am I supposed to do?

The man slammed down the phone.

The gray-haired woman took a San Salvador newspaper from her Vuitton tote and began reading it.

The man stared balefully at Elena.

Elena shifted her gaze, a hedge against the possibility that eye contact could be construed as standing out. Across the room a steward was watching *General Hospital* on the television set above the bar.

She heard the man again punching numbers into the telephone but did not look at him.

Mr. Lee, the man said.

A silence.

Elena allowed her eyes to wander. The headline on the paper the woman was reading was GOBIERNO VENDE 85% LECHE DONADA.

All right, the man said. You are not Mr. Lee. My mistake. But if you are truly the son you are also Mr. Lee. So let me speak to your father, Mr. Lee. What is this, he cannot come to the phone? I am talking to him, he tells me to call back in ten minutes. I am calling back from a pay phone in the Miami airport and he cannot take the call? What is this? Mr. Lee. Please. I am getting from you both a bunch of lies. A bunch of misinformation. Disinformation. Lies. Mr. Lee. Listen to me. It costs me maybe a million dollars to put you and your father out of business, believe me, I will spend it.

Again the phone was slammed down.

GOBIERNO VENDE 85% LECHE DONADA. The government sells eighty-five percent of donated milk. It struck Elena that her Spanish must have failed, this was too broad to be an accurate translation.

Elena did not yet know how broad a story could get.

Again the man punched in numbers. Mr. Elman. Let me tell you the situation here. I am calling from a pay phone in the Miami airport. I fly up from San Salvador today. Because today the deal was to close. Today the Sun Bank in Miami would have the telex to approve the line of credit. Today the Sun Bank in Miami does not have the telex. Today I am sitting in the Miami airport and I don't know what to do. That is the situation here. Okay, Mr. Elman. We have a little problem here, which I'm sure we can solve.

The calls continued. Mr. Lee. Mr. Elman. Mr. Gordon. Someone was in Toronto and someone else was in Los Angeles and many people were in Miami. At four o'clock Elena heard the door buzz. At the moment she allowed herself to look up she saw Barry Sedlow, without breaking stride as he walked toward her, lay an envelope on the table next to the telephone the Salvadoran was using.

"Here is my concern," the Salvadoran was saying into the telephone as he fingered the envelope. "Mr. Elman. You and I, we have *confianza*." The Salvadoran placed the envelope in an inner pocket of his silk jacket. "But what I am being fed from Mr. Lee is a bunch of disinformation."

Later in Barry Sedlow's car on the way to Hialeah she had asked who the Salvadoran was.

"What made you think he was Salvadoran," Barry Sedlow said.

She told him.

"Lot of people say they came up from San Salvador this morning, lot of people read Salvadoran papers, that doesn't make them Salvadoran."

She asked what the man was if not Salvadoran.

"I didn't say he wasn't Salvadoran," Barry Sedlow said. "Did I. You have a bad habit of jumping to conclusions." In the silence that followed he slowed to a stop at an intersection, reached inside the Dolphins warm-up jacket he was wearing and took aim at the streetlight.

One thing she had learned growing up around her father: she recognized guns.

The gun Barry Sedlow had taken from inside his warm-up jacket was a 9mm Browning with sound suppressor.

The engine was idling and the sound of the silenced shot inaudible.

The light shattered and the intersection went dark.

"Transit passenger," Barry Sedlow had said as he transferred his foot from brake to accelerator. "Already on the six-thirty back to San Sal. Not our deal." When I say that Elena was not one of those who saw how every moment could connect I mean that it did not occur to her that a transit passenger need show no visa.

Cast your mind back.

Refresh your memory if necessary: go to Nexis, go to microfiche.

Try to locate the most interesting news stories of the period in question.

Scroll past any stories that led or even made the evening news.

Move down instead until you locate the kind of two-inch wire story that tended to appear just under the page-fourteen continuation of the page-one story on congressional response to the report of the Kissinger Commission, say, or opposite the page-nineteen continuation of the page-one story about the federal court ruling upholding investigation of possible violations of the Neutrality Act.

The kind of two-inch wire story that had to do with chartered aircraft of uncertain ownership that did or did not leave one or another southern airport loaded with one or another kind of cargo.

Many manifests were eventually analyzed by those who followed such stories.

Many personnel records were eventually accessed.

Many charts were eventually drawn detailing the ways in which the spectral companies with the high-concept names (*Amalgamated Commercial Enterprises Inc., Defex S.A., Energy Resources International*) tended to interlock.

These two-inch aircraft stories were not always identical. In some stories the aircraft in question was reported not to have left one or another southern airport but to have crashed in Georgia or experienced mechanical difficulties in Texas or been seized in the Bahamas in relation to one or another narcotics investigation. Nor was the cargo in these stories always identical: inspection of the cargo revealed in some cases an unspecified number of reconditioned Soviet AK-47s, in other cases unspecified numbers of M67 fragmentation grenades, AR-15s, M-60s, RPG-7 rocket launchers, boxes of ammo, pallets of POMZ-2 fragmentation mines, British Aerospace L-9 antitank mines, Chinese Type 72A and Italian Valmara 69 antipersonnel mines.

69s.

Epperson had floated a figure of three dollars per for 69s and now he was claiming the market had dropped to two per.

I'm not sure I know what business Epperson is in.

Christ, what business are they all in.

Some people in Washington said that the flights described in these stories were not occurring, other people in Washington (more careful people in Washington, more specific people in Washington, people in Washington who did not intend to perjure themselves when the hearings rolled in) said that the flights *could not be* occurring, or *could only be* occurring, *if indeed they were* occurring, outside the range of possible knowledge.

I myself learned to be specific during this period.

I myself learned to be careful.

I myself learned the art of the conditional.

I recall asking Treat Morrison, during the course of my preliminary interviews with him at his office in Washington, *if* in fact, *to his knowledge*, anyone in the United States government *could have* knowledge that *one or more* such flights *could be* supplying arms to the so-called contra forces for the purpose of overthrowing the Sandinista government in Nicaragua.

There had been a silence.

Treat Morrison had picked up a pen and put it down.

I flattered myself that I was on the edge of something revelatory.

"To the extent that the area in question touches on the lake," Treat Morrison said, "and to the extent that the lake has been historically construed as our lake, it goes without saying that we could have an interest. However."

Again he fell silent.

I waited.

We had gotten as far as claiming the Caribbean as our lake, our sea, *mare nostrum*.

"However," Treat Morrison repeated.

I debated with myself whether I would accept an off-the-record or not-for-attribution stipulation.

"We don't track that kind of activity," Treat Morrison said then.

One of those flights that no one was tracking lifted off from Fort Lauderdale–Hollywood International Airport at one-thirty on the morning of June 26, 1984. The aircraft was a Lockheed L-100. The official documents filed by the pilot showed a crew of five, two passengers, a cargo of assorted auto parts, and the destination San José, Costa Rica.

The U.S. Customs official who certified the manifest did not elect to physically inspect the cargo.

The plane did not land in San José, Costa Rica.

The plane had no reason to land in San José, Costa Rica, because an alternative infrastructure was already in place: the eight-thousand-foot runways laid by the 46th Combat Engineers during the aftermath of the Big Pine II maneuvers were already in place. The radar sites were in place. The water purification and delivery systems were in place. "You got yourself a regular little piece of U.S.A. here," the pilot of the Lockheed L-100 said to Elena McMahon as they waited on the dry grass off the runway while the cargo was unloaded.

"Actually I'll be going right back." She felt a sudden need to distance herself from whatever was going on here. "I mean I left my car at the airport."

"Long-term parking I hope," the pilot said.

What was also in place was the deal.

We don't track that kind of activity.

No comment. Thank you. Goodbye.

TWO

I

THE PERSONA of "the writer" does not attract me. As a way of being it has its flat sides. Nor am I comfortable around the literary life: its traditional dramatic line (the romance of solitude, of interior struggle, of the lone seeker after truth) came to seem early on a trying conceit. I lost patience somewhat later with the conventions of the craft, with exposition, with transitions, with the development and revelation of "character." To this point I recall my daughter's resistance when asked, in the eighth grade at the Westlake School for Girls in Los Angeles, to write an "autobiographical" essay (*your life, age thirteen, thesis, illustration, summary, just try it, no more than two double-spaced pages neatly typed please*) on whatever event or individual or experience had "most changed" her life. I mentioned a few of the applicable perennials (trip to Europe, volunteer job in hospital, teacher she didn't like because he made her work too hard and then it turned out to be worth it), she, less facile, less careful, more sentient, mentioned the death of her best friend in fourth grade.

Yes, I said, ashamed. Better. You have it.

"Not really," she said.

Why not, I said.

"Because it didn't actually change my life. I mean I cried, I was sad, I wrote a lot about it in my diary, yes, but what changed?"

I recall explaining that "change" was merely the convention at hand: I said that while it was true that the telling of a life tended to falsify it, gave it a form it did not intrinsically possess, this was just a fact of writing things down, something we all accepted.

I realized as I was saying this that I no longer did.

I realized that I was increasingly interested only in the technical, in how to lay down the AM-2 aluminum matting for the runway, in whether or not parallel taxiways and high-speed turnoffs must be provided, in whether an eight-thousand-foot runway requires sixty thousand square yards of operational apron or only forty thousand. If the AM-2 is laid directly over laterite instead of over plastic membrane seal, how long would we have before base failure results? (How long would we *need* before base failure results was another question altogether, one I left to the Treat Morrisons of this world.) How large a base camp will a fifteen-hundred-kilowatt generator service? In the absence of high-capacity deep wells, can water be effectively treated with tactical erdlators? I give you Friedrich Wilhelm Nietzsche, 1844–1900: "When man does not have firm, calm lines on the horizon of his life—mountain and forest lines, as it were—then man's most inner will becomes agitated, preoccupied and wistful."

Tactical erdlators have been my mountain and forest lines.

This business of Elena McMahon, then, is hard for me.

This business of what "changed" her, what "motivated" her, what made her do it.

I see her standing in the dry grass off the runway, her arms bare, her sunglasses pushed up into her loose hair, her black silk shift wrinkled from the flight, and wonder what made her think a black silk shift bought off a sale rack at Bergdorf Goodman during the New York primary was the appropriate thing to wear on an unscheduled cargo flight at one-thirty in the morning out of Fort Lauderdale–Hollywood International Airport, destination San José Costa Rica but not quite.

Her sunglasses are pushed up but her eyes are shut tight.

A dog (underfed, mangy, of no remarkable size) is bursting from the open door of a concrete structure off the apron and racing toward her.

The man beside her, his head shaved, cutoff jeans slung below his navel, is singing the theme from *Bonanza* as he crouches and beckons to the dog.

We got a right to pick a little fight—
Bo-nan-za—
If anyone fights with any one of us—
He's got a fight with me—

Her eyes remain shut.

On second thought I am not sure what would be, in this context, "appropriate."

Possibly the baseball cap lent her by one of the refueling

crew. The cap was lettered NBC SPORTS, its familiar peacock logo smeared with diesel fuel.

"Actually I think somebody was supposed to meet me," she said to the pilot when the man with the shaved head had disappeared and the last pallet been unloaded and the refueling completed. Over the past dozen hours she had come to see the pilot as her partner, her backup, her protection, her single link to the day before.

"Looks like somebody didn't give you the full skinny," the pilot said.

Smell of jasmine, pool of blue jacaranda.

Coincidentally, although not really, since it was in the role of mother that I first knew Elena, Catherine Janklow was also in that eighth-grade class at the Westlake School for Girls in Los Angeles. Elena's performance as a Westlake Mom (so we were called in school bulletins) was so attentive to detail as to be impenetrable. She organized benefits for the scholarship fund, opened her house for picnics and ditch days and sleepovers, got up every Friday at four hours before dawn to deliver the Astronomy Club to remote star-watching locations in Lancaster or Latigo Canyon or the Santa Susana Mountains, and was duly repaid by the attendance of three eighth graders at her Westlake Career Day workshop on "Getting Started as a Reporter."

"You're at an age right now when it's impossible even to imagine how much your life is going to change," Elena told the three eighth graders who turned up for her Career Day workshop.

Two of the eighth graders maintained expressions of polite disbelief.

The third jabbed a finger into the air, then crossed her arms truculently across her chest.

Elena looked at the child. Her name was Melissa Simon. She was Mort Simon's daughter. Mort Simon was someone Wynn knew who had improved the year by taking a motion picture studio private and spinning off its real assets into various of his personal companies.

"Melissa."

"Excuse me," Melissa Simon said. "But I don't quite see why my life is supposed to change."

There had been a silence.

"That's an interesting point," Elena had said then.

Catherine had not attended her mother's workshop on Getting Started as a Reporter. Catherine had signed up for a workshop conducted by a Westlake Mom who happened to be a business affairs lawyer at Paramount ("Motion Picture Development—Where Do You Fit In?"), then skipped it to finish her own eighth-grade autobiographical essay on the event or individual or experience that had "most changed" her life. "What is definitely most changing my life this semester is my mother getting cancer," Catherine's autobiographical essay began, and continued for two neatly typed double-spaced pages. Catherine's mother, according to Catherine, was that semester "too tired to do anything normal" because every morning after dropping the car pool at school she had been going to UCLA for what Catherine knowledgeably described as "radiation zapping following the exsishun [*sic*] of a stage I good prognose [*sic*] breast lesion." That this was not a fact generally known does not, to me, suggest "motivation."

Treat Morrison knew it, because he recognized the scar.

Diane had had the same scar.

Look, he said when Elena fell silent. What difference does it make. You get it one way or you get it another, nobody comes through free.

She sat on the dry grass in her black silk shift and the cap lettered NBC SPORTS and watched the L-100 taxi out for takeoff and tried to think what to do next. The cargo had been loaded onto flatbed trucks. Whoever was supposed to make the payment had not appeared. She had thought at first that the man with the shaved head and the cutoff jeans was her contact but he was not. He was, he said, on his way home to Tulsa from Angola. He was, he said, just lending a little expertise while he was in this particular area.

She had not asked him how this particular area could reasonably be construed as on the way to Tulsa from Angola.

She had not asked him what expertise he was lending.

During the ten minutes she had spent trying to talk the pilot into waiting for her contact the flatbed trucks had been driven away.

She was going to need to rethink this step by step.

She was going to need to reconnoiter, reassess.

The L-100 and the zone of safety it represented were about to vanish into the cloud cover.

Fly it down, fly it back, the pilot had said. That's my contract. I get paid to drive the bus. I get paid to drive the bus when the engines are overheating. I get paid to drive the bus when the loran goes down. I don't get paid to take care of the passengers.

Her partner, her backup, her protection.

Her single link to the day before.

He had flown it down and now he was flying it back.

Per his contract.

She did not think it possible that her father would find himself in exactly this situation, yet she had done exactly what he said he had to do. She had done exactly what her father said he had to do and she had done exactly what Barry Sedlow said to do.

Just do it my way for a change.

This would very soon be all right.

She would very soon know what to do.

She felt alert, a little light-headed. She did not yet know where she was, and the clearing in which the strip had been laid down had suddenly cleared of people, but she was ready, open to information.

This should be Costa Rica.

If this was Costa Rica the first thing she needed to do was get to San José.

She did not know what she would do if she did get to San José but there would be a hotel, offices of American banks, an airport with scheduled carriers.

Through the open door of the concrete structure off the apron she could see, intermittently, someone moving, someone walking around, a man, a man with a ponytail, a man with a ponytail wearing fatigues. She kept her eyes on this door and tried to recall lessons learned in other venues, other vocations. One thing she had learned during her four-year sojourn at the *Herald Examiner* was how easy it was to get into places where no one was supposed to be. The trick was to attach oneself to service personnel, people who had no particular investment in who got in and who stayed out. She had on one occasion followed a telephone crew into a locked hangar in which an experimental stealth bomber was being readied for its first roll-out. She had on more than one occasion gotten inside a house where someone did not want to talk to her by striking up conversation with the pool man, the gardener, the dog groomer who had run a cord inside the kitchen door to plug in a dryer.

In fact she had mentioned this during the course of her Westlake Career Day workshop.

Melissa Simon had again raised her hand. She had a point she wanted to make. The point she wanted to make was that "nobody from the media could have ever gotten into those houses if the families had normal security and their public relations people were doing their job."

Which had prompted Elena to raise the Westlake Career Day stakes exponentially by suggesting, in words that either did or did not include the phrase "try living in the real world for a change," that very few families in the world outside three or four well-defined neighborhoods on the West Side of Los Angeles County had either public relations people or what one very fortunate eighth grader might call "normal security."

Which had caused Wynn Janklow, after this was reported to him the next day by three different people (Mort Simon's partner, Mort Simon's lawyer, and the young woman who was described as Mort Simon's "issues person"), to leave half his lunch at Hillcrest uneaten in order to call Elena.

"I hear you've been telling our friends' kids their parents live in a dream world."

In the first place, she said, this was not an exact quotation.

He said something else but the connection was bad.

In the second place, she said, Mort Simon was not her friend. She didn't even know Mort Simon.

Wynn was calling from his Mercedes, driving east on Pico, and had turned up Robertson before his voice faded back in.

"You want everybody in town saying you talk like a shiksa," he had said, "you're getting the job done."

"I am a shiksa," she had said.

"That's your problem, not mine," he had said.

In fact she did know Mort Simon.

Of course she knew Mort Simon.

The house in Beverly Hills where she sat on the sidewalk waiting for the pool report on the celebrity fund-raiser was as it happened Mort Simon's house. She had even seen him briefly, lifting a transparent flap of the Regal Rents tent to survey the barricade behind which the press was waiting. He had looked directly at her but such was his generalized view of the world outside his tent that he had not recognized her and she had not spoken.

"Send out some refreshments," she had heard him say to a waiter before he dropped the flap, although no refreshments ever materialized. "Like, you know, diet Pepsi, water, I'm not paying so they can tank up."

The wife and daughter no longer lived in the house. The wife and daughter had moved to a town house just inside the Beverly Hills line from Century City and the daughter had transferred from Westlake to Beverly Hills High School. Catherine had told her that.

Living in the real world.

We had a real life and now we don't.

She put that out of her mind.

Other lessons.

More recent venues.

Not long after moving to Washington she had interviewed an expert on nuclear security who had explained how easy it would be to score plutonium. The security for nuclear facilities, he said, was always contracted out. The contractors in turn hired locally and supplied their hires with minimum rounds of ammunition. Meaning, he had said, "you got multimillion-dollar state-of-the-art security systems being operated by downsized sheriff's deputies with maybe enough ammo to take down a coyote."

She remembered exactly what he said because the interview had ended up in the Sunday magazine and this had been the pull quote.

If she could think of the man with the ponytail as a downsized sheriff's deputy, a downsized sheriff's deputy lacking even a multimillion-dollar state-of-the-art security system, this would be all right.

All it would take was nerve.

All it would take was a show of belonging wherever it was she wanted to be.

She got up, brushed the grass off her legs and walked to the open door of the concrete structure off the apron. The man with the ponytail was seated at a wooden crate on which there was an electric fan, a bottle of beer and a worn deck of Bicycle cards. He drained the beer, lobbed the bottle into a metal drum, and, with two fingers held stiff, turned over a card.

"Shit," the man said, then looked up.

"You're supposed to see that I get to San José," she said. "They were supposed to have told you that."

The man turned over another card. "Who was supposed to tell me that."

This was going to require more work than the average telephone crew, pool man, dog groomer.

"If I don't get to San José they're going to be wondering why."

"Who is."

She gambled. "I think you know who."

"Give me a name."

She had not been given names. She had asked Barry Sedlow for names and he had talked about compartmentalization, cutouts, need-to-know.

You wouldn't give me their real names anyway, she had said. Just give me the names they use.

What's that supposed to mean, he had said.

The names they use like you use Gary Barnett, she had said.

I'm not authorized to give you that information, he had said. Somebody's supposed to meet you. Your need-to-know stops there.

Somebody was supposed to meet her but somebody did not meet her.

Somebody was supposed to make the payment and somebody had not made the payment.

She was aware as she watched the man turn over cards of a sudden darkening outside, then of lightning. There was a map of Costa Rica on the wall of the concrete structure, reinforcing the impression that this was Costa Rica but offering no clue as to where in Costa Rica. The overhead light flickered and went out. The electric fan fluttered to a stop. In the absence of background noise she realized that she had been hearing the whine of an overworked refrigerator, now silent.

The man with the ponytail got up, opened the refrigerator, and took another beer from its darkened interior. He did not offer one to Elena. Instead he sat down and turned over another card, whistling softly between his teeth, as if Elena were invisible.

Who is.

I think you know who.

Give me a name.

"Epperson," she said. She seized the name from the ether of the past ten days. "Max Epperson."

The man with the ponytail looked at her, then shuffled the cards and got up. "I could be overdue a night or two in Josie," the man said.

2

WHEN I am away from this I tend to elongate the time sequence, which was in fact quite short. It was early on the morning of June 26, 1984 when Elena McMahon left Fort Lauderdale–Hollywood International Airport on the L-100, and late the same morning when the L-100 landed somewhere in Costa Rica. It was close to midnight of the same day (first there had been a bridge washed out, then a two-hour stop parked outside what seemed to be a military installation) when Elena McMahon got to San José. *You're* doing nothing, the man with the ponytail had said when she asked what they were doing at the military installation. What *I'm* doing doesn't concern you.

He had gotten out of the truck.

Anyone asks, he had said, tell them you're waiting for Mr. Jones.

From the time he reappeared two hours later until they reached San José he had not spoken. He had instead sung to himself, repeated fragments of what appeared to be the same song, so inaudibly that she knew he was singing only by the periodic spasms of pounding on the steering wheel as he exhaled the words "*great balls* of fire." In San José he had driven directly to a hotel on what appeared to be a downtown side street. Free ride ends here, he had said. Seen from the unlit street the hotel had an impressive glass porte cochere and polished brass letters reading HOTEL COLONIAL but once she was inside the small lobby the promise faded. There was no air-conditioning. An industrial fluorescent light flickered overhead, casting a sickly light on the stained velour upholstery of the single chair. As she waited for the desk clerk to finish a telephone call she had begun to find it inauspicious that the man with the ponytail had brought her to this hotel without ever asking where she wanted to go (in fact she would have had no idea where to go, she had never before been in San José), just pulled directly under the porte cochere and stopped, letting the engine idle as he waited for her to get out.

Why here, she had asked.

Why not here. He had flicked his headlights off and on several times. I thought you wanted to run into people you know.

There was a pay telephone on the wall by the elevator.

She would call Barry Sedlow.

The first thing to do was get in touch with Barry Sedlow.

As she opened her bag and tried to locate the card on which he had written the 800 number for his beeper she became aware of the desk clerk watching her.

She would tell the desk clerk she needed a drugstore, a doctor, a *clínica*.

She would get out of this place.

She had seen a bus station on the way to the hotel, the bus station would be open, she could make the call from the bus station.

She did not bother to remember the directions the desk clerk gave her to the *clínica* but as it happened she passed it on her way to the bus station. That at least was good. This could be going her way. In case anyone was watching she had been walking toward the *clínica*.

The bus station was almost deserted.

The dispatcher was sleeping noisily in a metal cage above the concourse.

The public telephones in the waiting room had rotary dials and could not be used to leave a message on a beeper, which was the only number she had for Barry Sedlow. *Emergencia*, she said over and over when she managed to wake the dispatcher. She held out a ten-dollar bill and the KROME GUN CLUB card on which Barry Sedlow had written the 800 number. *La clínica. Mi padre.* The dispatcher examined the bill and the card, then dialed the number on his push-button phone and left as a callback number one of the public phones in the waiting room.

She sat on a molded plastic bench and drank a local cola, sweet and warm and flat, and waited for the phone to ring.

Don't get your balls in an uproar, Barry Sedlow said when she picked up the phone. You made the delivery, you'll get the payment. Sometimes these things take a little longer, you got a whole bureaucracy you're dealing with, they got requisitions, regulations, paperwork, special ways they have to do things, they don't just peel off cash like guys on the street. Be smart. Stay put. I'll make a few calls, get back to you. You cool?

All right, she had said finally.

By the way, he had said then. I wouldn't call your dad. I'm keeping him in the picture about where you are and what you're doing, but I wouldn't call him.

It would not have occurred to her to call her father but she asked why not.

Because it wouldn't be smart, he had said. I'll get back to you at the Colonial.

It was almost dawn, after she had gone back to the Hotel Colonial and let the desk clerk take her passport and run her credit card, after she had gone upstairs to the single room on the third floor and sat on the edge of the metal bed and abandoned the idea of sleep, before it occurred to her that during the call to Barry Sedlow she had never once mentioned the name of the hotel.

So what, Barry Sedlow said when he finally called back and she put this to him.

Big fucking deal. Where else would you be.

This second conversation with Barry Sedlow took place on the afternoon of June 28. It was the evening of July 1 when Barry Sedlow called the third time. It was the morning of July 2 when, using the commercial ticket provided her, a one-way nonexchangeable ticket to a designated destination, Elena McMahon left San José for the island where the incident occurred that should not have occurred.

Should not have occurred and could not have been predicted.

By any quantitative measurement.

3

YOU WILL have noticed that I am not giving you the name of this island.

This is deliberate, a decision on my part, and not a decision (other writers have in fact named the island, for example, the authors of the Rand study) based on classification.

The name would get in the way.

If you knew the name you might recall days or nights spent on this island en route to or in lieu of more desirable islands, the metallic taste of tinned juice in rum punches, the mosquitoes under the net at night, the rented villa where the septic tank backed up, the unpleasantness over the Jet Ski misunderstanding, the hours spent waiting in the jammed airport when the scheduled Windward Air or BIWI flights failed to materialize, the piece of needlepoint you meant to finish and instead spotted with coconut oil, the book you meant to read and distractedly set aside, the tedium of all forlorn tropical places.

The determined resistance to gravity, the uneasy reduction of the postcolonial dilemma to the Jet Ski misunderstanding.

The guilty pleasure of buckling in and clearing the ground and knowing that you will step off this plane in the developed world.

Little guessing that the pleasant life of the plantations was about to disappear, as the history of the island you dutifully bought at the airport puts it. *Paradisaical as the sight of land must have been after the long voyage from the Cape Verdes. Not to overlook the contribution made by early Jewish settlers after the construction of their historic crushed-coral synagogue, so situated as to offer a noteworthy view of Rum Cay. Signalling a resounding defeat for the Party that had spearheaded the movement toward The Independence.*

Face it.

You did not, during your sojourns on this island, want to know its history. (High points: Arawaks, hurricane, sugar, Middle Passage, the abandonment known as The Independence.) You did not, if you had planned well, have reason to frequent its major city. (Must see: that historic crushed-coral synagogue, its noteworthy view of Rum Cay.) You had no need to venture beyond the rust-stained but still daunting (school of Edward Durell Stone) facade of our embassy there. Had you discovered such need (bad planning, trouble, a lost passport), you would have found it a larger embassy than extant American interests on the island would seem to require, a relic of the period when Washington had been gripped by the notion that the emergence of independent nations on single-crop islands with annual per capita incomes in three digits offered the exact optimum conditions under which private capital could be siphoned off the Asian rim and into *mare nostrum*.

Many phantom investment schemes had been encouraged on this island. Many training sessions had been planned, many promotional tours staged. Many pilot programs had been undertaken, each cited at its inception as a flawless model of how a responsible superpower could help bring an LDC, or Lesser Developed Country, into the roster of the self-sufficient NICs, or New Industrializing Countries. On an island where most human concerns were obliterated by weather, this was an embassy in which tropical doubts had been held at bay via the mastery of acronyms.

It was still in 1984 possible to hear in this embassy about "CBMs," or Confidence Building Measures.

It was still in 1984 possible to hear about "BHN," or Basic Human Needs.

What could not be obfuscated by acronym tended to be reduced to its most cryptic diminutive. I recall hearing at this embassy a good deal about "the Del" before I learned that it referred to a formula for predicting events developed by the Rand Corporation and less jauntily known as the Delphi Method (that which should not have happened and could not have been predicted by any quantitative measurement had presumably not been predicted by employment of the Del), and I sat through an entire study group session on "Ap Tech—Uses and Misuses" before I divined that the topic at hand was something called the Appropriate Technology movement, proponents of which apparently did not believe that technology developed in the first world was appropriate for transfer to the third. I recall heated discussion on whether the introduction of data processing into the island's literacy program either could or could not be construed as Ap Tech. Tech skills are in a different basket, an economic attaché kept repeating. Tech skills are a basket-two priority. A series of political appointees, retired contributors from the intermountain West, had passed in and out of the official residence without ever finding need to master the particular dialect spoken in this embassy.

Alexander Brokaw was of course not a political appointee.

Alex Brokaw was career, with a c.v. of sensitive postings.

Alex Brokaw had arrived on this island six months before to do a specific job.

A job that entailed bringing in the pros.

Because, as Alex Brokaw often said, *if and when this switches gear into a full-scale effort, we'll be rotating troops in and out, which is good for home-front morale but not good for construction continuity. So we damn well better bring the pros in up front.*

The pros and of course the Special Forces guys.

A job that entailed establishing the presence on the island of this selected group of Americans, and discouraging the presence of all others.

Which is why Alex Brokaw mentioned to his DCM, after the incident at the embassy's Fourth of July picnic, that it might be useful to run a background on Elise Meyer, which was the name on the passport Elena McMahon was by then using.

4

WHEN I try to understand how Elena McMahon could have assimilated with no perceptible beat the logic of traveling on a passport not her own to a place she had no previous intention of going, could have accepted so readily that radical revision of who she was, could have walked into a life not her own and lived it, I consider the last time I actually saw her.

Academy Award night, 1982.

When she was still living in the house on the Pacific Coast Highway.

It was five months later when she walked out of that house and enrolled Catherine at an Episcopal boarding school in Rhode Island and got herself hired (on the basis not of her long-gone four-year career at the *Herald Examiner* but of an editorial hunch that Wynn Janklow's scrupulously bilateral campaign contributions might still buy his estranged wife some access) at the Washington *Post*.

All that happened very fast.

All that happened so fast that the first I knew of it was when I got home from France in September of 1982 and began to go through the accumulated mail and was about to discard unopened, because it looked like one or another plea in support of or opposition to one or another issue, a plain white envelope with metered postage and a Washington D.C. return address. Had I not been distracted by a phone call I would never have opened the envelope, but I was, and I did, and there it was: a handwritten note, signed *Elena*, saying that of course I already knew that she and Catherine had relocated to the East Coast but now she was settled and just getting around to sending out her address. The printed name on the change-of-address card clipped to the note was *Elena McMahon*.

"Relocated" was the word she used.

As if leaving Wynn Janklow had been a corporate transfer.

I had not already known that she and Catherine had relocated to the East Coast.

I had known nothing.

All I knew was that on Academy Award night that year Elena McMahon had still been Elena Janklow, sitting in front of a plate of untouched cassoulet at the party that was in our rather insular community at that time the single event approaching a command performance, absently twining a Mylar ribbon torn from a balloon into the rhinestone strap of her dress. I never once saw her look at the big television screens mounted at every eye line, not even at those moments when a local favorite was up for an award and the party fell momentarily silent. Nor did she observe the other core tribal custom of the evening, which was to spring up and move toward the bar as soon as the awards ended, allowing the tables to be cleared while applauding both the triumphant arrivals of the winners and the inspirational sportsmanship of the losers.

Elena never got up at all.

Elena stayed seated, idly picking apart a table decoration to remove the miniature Oscar at its center, oblivious to winners and losers alike, oblivious even to the busboys changing the tablecloth in front of her. Only when I sat down across the table did she even look up.

"I promised Catherine," she said about the miniature Oscar.

What she said next that Academy Award night was something I interpreted at the time to mean only that she was tired of the event's structural festivity, that she had been dressed up in rhinestones in broad daylight since four in the afternoon and sitting at this table since five and now she wanted to go home.

I was wrong about what she said next.

As I would be wrong later to wonder how she could so readily assimilate the logic of walking into a life not her own and living it.

What she said next that Academy Award night was this: "I can't fake this anymore."

Suggesting that she had assimilated that logic a long time before.

5

"SOMEBODY'S GOING to let you know the move they want you to make," Barry Sedlow had said the last time he called her in San José.

"When," she had said.

"By the way. I say your dad. He says hi. I'm keeping him in the picture."

Saying "hi" was not in her father's vocabulary but she let this go. "I asked when."

"Just stay put."

In the six days since her arrival in San José she had left the room at the Colonial only twice, once to buy a toothbrush and a tin of aspirin, the second time to buy a T-shirt and cotton pants so she could wash the black silk shift. She had given the maid American dollars to bring back sandwiches, coffee, once in a while a Big Mac from the McDonald's across from the bus station.

"That's what you told me the night I got here. I've *been* staying put. I need to know when."

"Hard to say. Maybe tonight." There had been a silence. "They may want you to take payment in another venue. Who knows."

"Where."

"They'll let you know where."

An hour later the envelope containing the passport and plane ticket had begun to appear, emerging at such barely perceptible speed that she was finally forced to breathe, under the locked door of her room at the Colonial.

She did not know why she had happened to look at the door at the very moment the envelope began to appear.

There had been no giveaway sound, no rustle of paper on carpet, no fumbling in the corridor.

The envelope had been clear of the door and lying motionless inside the room for a full five minutes before, still frozen, she moved to approach it. The ticket bearing the name Elise Meyer had been written by American Airlines in Miami on June 30, 1984. The passport bearing the name Elise Meyer had been issued on June 30, 1984 at the United States Passport Agency in Miami.

In the photograph affixed to this passport she was smiling.

In the photograph affixed to her own passport she was not.

She could not compare the two because her own passport was downstairs in the hotel safe, but she was quite certain that the photographs were otherwise similar.

She studied the photograph on the passport for some time before she sorted out how it could happen to be otherwise similar to the photograph on her own passport. It could happen to be otherwise similar to the photograph on her own passport because it had been taken at the same time, not long after she got to Washington, in a passport-photo place across from the paper. She had asked for extra Polaroids to use for visas. At some point recently on this campaign (whenever it was that the Secret Service had come on and started demanding photos for new credentials) she had stuck the five or six remaining prints in a pocket of her computer bag.

Why wouldn't she have.

Of course she did.

Of course her computer bag was in a closet at the house in Sweetwater.

By the way. I saw your dad. He says hi. I'm keeping him in the picture.

6

OF COURSE Dick McMahon was by then dead. Of course he had died under circumstances that would not appear in the least out of order: the notification to the nursing agency at noon on June 27 that Mr. McMahon's night shift would no longer be required; the predictable midnight emergency twelve hours later; the fortuitous and virtually simultaneous arrival at the house in Sweetwater of the very attentive young doctor; the transfer in the early morning hours of June 28 to the two-bed room at the Clearview Convalescent Lodge in South Kendall; the flurry of visits over the next thirty-six hours from the very attentive young doctor and then the certification of the death.

It would not be unusual at this facility to see a degree of agitation in a new admission.

Nor would it be unusual, given the extreme agitation of this new admission, if a decision were made to increase sedation.

Nor would it be unusual, given the continuing attempts of this extremely agitated new admission to initiate contact with the patient in the other bed, to effect the temporary transfer of the patient in the other bed to a more comfortable gurney in the staff smoking lounge.

Nor would it be unusual if such an extremely agitated and increasingly ill new admission were, the best efforts of his very attentive young doctor notwithstanding, to just go. "Just going" was how dying was characterized at the Clearview Convalescent Lodge, by both patients and staff. He's just going. He just went.

Nor would there be need for an autopsy, because whatever happened would be certified as having happened in a licensed care facility under the care of a licensed physician.

There would be nothing out of order about the certification.

Without question Dick McMahon would be gone by the time he was certified dead.

Which was, according to the records of the Clearview Convalescent Lodge in South Kendall, at 1:23 A.M. on the morning of June 30. Since certification occurred after midnight the bill submitted for reimbursement under Medicare A was for three full nights, June 28, 29 and 30. *Policyholder deceased 171.4* was the notation placed on the Medicare A billing in the space provided for Full Description of Condition at Discharge Including Diagnostic Code.

McMAHON, Richard Allen: age 74, died under care of physician June 30, 1984, at Clearview Convalescent Lodge, South Kendall. No services are scheduled.

So read the agate-type notice appearing in the vital statistics column, which was compiled daily to include those deaths and births and marriages entered into the previous day's public record, of the July 2, 1984 edition of the Miami *Herald.*

It could have been established, by anyone who cared to check the nursing agency's file on Mr. McMahon, that the June 27 call ordering the cancellation of Mr. McMahon's night shift had been placed by a woman identifying herself as Mr. McMahon's daughter.

It would remain unestablished who had placed the midnight call to the very attentive young doctor.

Because no one asked.

Because the single person who might have asked had not yet had the opportunity to read the agate-type notice appearing in the vital statistics column of the July 2, 1984 edition of the Miami *Herald.*

Because the single person who might have asked did not yet know that her father was dead.

By the way. I wouldn't call your dad. I'm keeping him in the picture about where you are and what you're doing, but I wouldn't call him.

Because it wouldn't be smart.

7

AT THE time she left San José she did not yet know that her father was dead but there were certain things she did already know. Some of what she already knew at the time she left San José she had learned before she ever got to Costa Rica, had known in fact since the afternoon the sky went dark and the lightning forked on the horizon outside Dick McMahon's room at Jackson Memorial and he began to tell her who it was he had to see and what it was he had to do. Some of what she already knew she had learned the day she brought him home from Jackson Memorial to the house in Sweetwater and managed to deflect his intention to drive down to where the *Kitty Rex* was berthed and Barry Sedlow was waiting for him. Some of what she already knew she believed to be true and some of what she already knew she believed to be delusion, but since this was a business in which truth and delusion appeared equally doubtful she was left to proceed as if even the most apparently straightforward piece of information could at any time explode.

Any piece of information was a potential fragmentation mine.

Fragmentation mines came immediately to mind because of one of the things she already knew.

This was one of the things she already knew: the shipment on the L-100 that left Fort Lauderdale–Hollywood International Airport at one-thirty on the morning of June 26 was composed exclusively of fragmentation mines, three hundred and twenty-four pallets, each pallet loaded with twelve crates, each crate containing between ten and two hundred mines depending upon their type and size. Some of these mines were antitank and some antipersonnel. There were the forty-seven-inch L-9 antitanks made by British Aerospace and there were the thirteen-inch PT-MI-BA III antitanks made by the Czechs. There were the POMZ-2 antipersonnels and there were the Chinese Type 72A antipersonnels and there were the Italian Valmara 69 antipersonnels.

69s.

Epperson had floated a figure of three dollars per for 69s and now he was claiming the market had dropped to two per.

When the pallets of 69s had finally been unloaded on the runway that morning she had been handed a hammer by the man with the shaved head and cutoff jeans and told to open a crate so that he could verify the merchandise.

Open it yourself, she had said, offering him back the hammer.

It doesn't work that way, he had said, not taking the hammer.

She had hesitated.

He had unknotted a T-shirt from his belt and pulled it over his bare chest. The T-shirt was printed with an American flag and the legend THESE COLORS DON'T RUN.

I got nowhere particular to go, he had said, so it's your call.

She had pried open the crate and indicated the contents.

He had extracted one of the small plastic devices, examined it, walked away and placed it on the ground halfway between Elena and the concrete structure. When he returned to Elena he was singing tunelessly, snatches of the theme from *Bonanza*.

He had moved back, and motioned her to do the same.

Then he had aimed a remote at the plastic device and whistled.

When she saw the dog burst from the open door of the concrete structure she had closed her eyes. The explosion had occurred between *We got a right to pick a little fight* and *Bo-nan-za*. The silence that followed was broken only by the long diminishing shriek of the dog.

"Guaranteed sixty-foot-diameter kill zone," the man who was on his way from Angola to Tulsa had said then.

Here was the second thing she already knew: this June 26 shipment was not the first such shipment her father had arranged. He had been arranging such shipments all through the spring and into the summer of 1984, a minimum of two and usually three or four a month, C-123s, Convair 440s, L-100s, whatever they sent up to be filled, rusty big bellies sitting on the back runways at Lauderdale–Hollywood and West Palm and Opa-Locka and MIA waiting to be loaded with AK-47s, M-16s, MAC-10s, C-4, whatever was on the street, whatever was out there, whatever Dick McMahon could still promote on the strength of his connections, his contacts, his fifty years of doing a little business in Miami and in Houston and in Las Vegas and in Phoenix and in the piney woods of Alabama and Georgia.

These had not been easy shipments to assemble.

He had put these shipments together on credit, on goodwill, on a shared drink here and a promise there and a tale told at the Miami Springs Holiday Inn at two in the morning, on the shared yearning among what he called "these fellows I know for a long time" for one last score.

He had called in all his markers.

He had put himself on the line, spread paper all over the Southeast, thrown the dice just this one last time, one last bet on the million-dollar payday.

The million-dollar payday that was due to come with the delivery of the June 26 shipment.

The million-dollar payday that was scheduled to occur on the runway in Costa Rica where the June 26 shipment had just been unloaded.

One million American in Citibank traveler's checks, good as gold.

Of course I have to turn around half to these fellows I know a long time who advanced me the stuff.

Which complicates the position I'm in now.

Ellie. You see the position I'm in.

Five, ten years ago I might never have gotten out on a limb this way, I paid up front and got paid up front, did it clean, that was my strict motto, do it clean, cash and carry, maybe I'm getting old, maybe I played this wrong, but hell, Ellie, think about it, when was I going to see another shot like this one.

Don't give me goddamn hindsight.

Hindsight is for shoe clerks.

Five, ten years ago, sure, I might have done it another way, but five, ten years ago we weren't in the middle of the goddamnest hot market anybody ever saw. So what can you do. Strike while the iron is hot, so you run a little risk, so you get out on a limb for a change, it's all you can do as I figure it.

So anyway.

So what.

You can see I need this deal.

You can see I'm in a position where I need to go down there and make the collection.

It was the figure that broke her heart.

The evenness of the figure.

The size of the figure.

The figure that was part of what she believed to be a delusion, the figure that had been the *bel canto* of her childhood, the figure that was now a memory, an echo, a dream, a romance, an old man's fairy tale.

The million-dollar score, the million-dollar pop, the million-dollar payday.

The pop that was already half owed to other people, the payday that was already garnisheed.

The score that was not even a score anymore.

I'm in for a unit, my father's doing two, Wynn Janklow would say to indicate investments of one and two hundred million dollars.

Million-dollar score, million-dollar payday.

She had gone her own way.

She had made her own life.

She had married a man who did not count money in millions but in units.

She had turned a deaf ear, she had turned her back.

It might be you'd just called from wherever.

In the creased snapshot she had taken from her mother's bedroom her father was holding a bottle of beer and her mother was wearing a barbecue apron printed with pitchforks and the words OUT OF THE FRYING PAN INTO THE FIRE.

Or it might be that you hadn't.

She remembered the day the snapshot was taken.

Fourth of July, she was nine or ten, a friend of her father's had brought fireworks up from the border, fat little sizzler rockets she had not liked and sparklers that made fireflies in the hot desert twilight.

Half a margarita and I'm already flying, her mother had kept saying.

This is all right, her father had kept saying. Who needs the goombahs, we got our own show right here.

We had a life and now we don't and just because I'm your daughter I'm supposed to like it and I don't.

What's going to happen now, her father had said on the day she brought him home to the house in Sweetwater. Goddamn. Ellie. What's going to happen now.

I'll take care of it, she had said.

By eight o'clock on the morning of July 2 she had already checked out of the Hotel Colonial and was in the taxi on her way to the San José airport. By eight o'clock on the morning of July 2 she did not yet know that her father's obituary had appeared in that morning's Miami *Herald*, but she did know something else.

This was the third thing she already knew.

She had asked for her passport when she checked out.

Her own passport.

The passport she had left at the desk the night she arrived.

For the authorities, for safekeeping.

The clerk was quite certain that it had been returned to her.

Por cierto, he had repeated. *Certísimo.*

The airport taxi had been waiting outside.

If you would look again, she had said. An American passport. McMahon. Elena McMahon.

The clerk had opened the safe, removed several passports, fanned them on the desk, and shrugged.

None of the passports were American.

In the mailboxes behind the clerk she could see room keys, a few messages.

The box for her room was empty.

She considered this.

The clerk raised an index finger, tapped his temple, and smiled. *Tengo la solución*, he said. Since the passport had certainly been returned to her, the passport would doubtless be found in her room. Perhaps she would be so kind as to leave an address.

I don't think so, she had said, and walked to the open door.

Buen viaje, Señora Meyer, the clerk had called as she was getting into the airport taxi.

8

When she landed on the island at one-thirty on the afternoon of July 2 the sky was dark with clouds and the runway already swamped with the rain that would fall intermittently for the next week. The Costa Rican pilot had mentioned this possibility. "A few bands of showers that will never dampen the spirit of any vacationer," was how the pilot had put it in his English-language update from the front cabin. It had occurred to Elena as she sheltered the unfamiliar passport under her T-shirt and made a run for the terminal that these bands of showers would not in fact dampen the spirit of any vacationer, since there did not seem to be any vacationer in sight.

No golf bag, no tennis racket, no sunburned child in tow.

No anxious traveler with four overstuffed tote bags and one boarding pass for the six-seater hop to the more desirable island.

There did not even seem to be any airport employee in sight.

Only the half-dozen young men, wearing the short-sleeved uniforms of what seemed to be some kind of local military police, lounging just inside the closed glass doors to the terminal.

She had stopped, rain streaming down her face, waiting for the doors to slide open automatically.

When the doors did not open she had knocked on the glass.

After what seemed a considerable length of time, once she had been joined outside the glass door by the crew from her flight, one of the men inside had detached himself from the others and inserted a key to open the door.

Thank you, she had said.

Move on, he had said.

She had moved on.

Gate after gate was unlit. The moving sidewalks were not moving, the baggage carousels were silent. Metal grilles had been lowered over the doors to the coffee bars and concessions, even the shop that promised OPEN 24 HOURS DUTY-FREE. She had steeled herself on the plane to make direct eye contact when she went through immigration but the lone immigration official had examined the passport without interest, stamped it, and handed it back to her, never meeting her eyes.

"Where you stay," he had said, pen poised to complete whatever form required this information.

She had tried to think of a plausible answer.

"You mean while I'm here," she had said, stalling. "You mean what hotel."

"Correct, correct, what hotel." He was bored, impatient. "Ramada, Royal Caribe, Intercon, what."

"Ramada," she had said.

She had gotten a taxi for the Ramada and then, once the doors were closed, told the driver that she had changed her mind and wanted to go to the Intercon. She had registered at the Intercon as Elise Meyer. As soon as she got upstairs she called Barry Sedlow's beeper and left the number of the hotel.

Twenty minutes later the telephone had rung.

She had picked it up but said nothing.

So far so good, Barry Sedlow said. You're where you should be.

She thought about this.

She had left the number of the hotel on his beeper but she had not left the number of her room.

To get through to the room he had to know how she was registered.

Had to know that the passport was in the name Elise Meyer.

She said nothing.

Just sit tight, he said. Someone's going to be in touch.

Still she said nothing.

Losing radio contact, he said. Hel-lo-oh.

There had been a silence.

Okay I get it, he had said finally. You don't want to talk, don't talk. But do yourself a favor? Relax. Go down to the pool, tip the boy to set up a chaise, get some sun, order one of those drinks with the cherries and the pineapple and the little umbrellas, you're there as a tourist, try acting like one, just tell the operator to switch your calls, don't worry about their finding you, they're going to find you all right.

She had done this. She had not spoken to Barry Sedlow but she had done what he said to do.

I do not know why (another instance of *what "changed" her, what "motivated" her, what made her do it*) but she had put down the telephone and waited for a break in the rain and then done exactly what Barry Sedlow said to do.

At four that afternoon and again at noon the next day and again at noon of the day after that, she had bought the local paper and whatever day-old American papers she could find in the coffee shop and gone down to the Intercon pool and tipped the boy to set up a chaise within range of the pool shack telephone. She had sat on the chaise under the gray sky and she had read the newspapers all the way through, one by one, beginning with the local paper and progressing to whatever Miami *Herald* or New York *Times* or *USA Today* had come in that morning. She read on the chaise at the Intercon pool about the dock strike in the Grenadines. She read on the chaise at the Intercon pool about the demonstration in Pointe-à-Pitre to protest the arrest of the leader of the independence movement. She read in a week-old *USA Today* about the effect of fish oil on infertile pandas in distant zoos. The only stories she avoided outright, there on the chaise at the Intercon pool, were those having to do with the campaign. She moved past any story having to do with the campaign. She preferred stories having to do with natural forces, stories about new evidence of reef erosion in the Maldives, say, or recently released research on the deep cold Pacific welling of El Niño.

About unusual movements of wind charted off the coast of Africa.

About controversial data predicting the probability of earthquakes measuring over 5.5 Richter.

American, the pool boy had said when she tipped him the first day with an American dollar. Whole lot of Americans coming in.

Really, she had said, by way of closing the conversation.

Good for business, he had said, by way of reopening it.

She had looked around the empty pool, the unused chaises stacked against the shack. I guess they don't swim much, she had said.

He had giggled and slapped his thigh with a towel. Do not swim much, he said finally. No.

By the third day she had herself begun noticing the Americans. Several in the coffee shop the night before, all men. Several more in the lobby, laughing together as they stood at the entrance waiting to get into an unmarked armored van.

The van had CD plates.

Swear to Christ, that deal in Chalatenango, I did something like three and a half full clips, one of the Americans had said.

Shit, another had said. You know the difference between one of them and a vampire? You drive a stake through a vampire's heart, the fucker dies.

No Americans at the pool.

Until now.

She had become aware as she was reading the local paper that one of the men she had seen waiting to get into the van with the CD plates was standing between her chaise and the pool, blocking the tiled walkway, smoking a cigarette as he surveyed the otherwise empty pool area.

His back was to her.

His warm-up jacket was lettered 25TH DIVISION TROPIC LIGHTNING.

She realized that she was reading for the third time the same follow-up on a rash of thefts and carjackings in the immediate vicinity of Cyril E. King International Airport on St. Thomas.

Excuse me, she said. Do you know what time it is.

He flicked his cigarette in the direction of the clock over the pool shack counter.

The clock read 1:10.

She put down the local paper and picked up the Miami *Herald*.

She continued reading the Miami *Herald* until she reached page sixteen of the B section.

Page sixteen of the B section of the July 2 Miami *Herald*, two days late.

> *MCMAHON, Richard Allen: age 74, died under care of physician June 30, 1984, at Clearview Convalescent Lodge, South Kendall. No services are scheduled.*

She folded the newspaper, got up from the chaise and edged her way past the American in the warm-up jacket.

Pardon me, he said. Ma'am.

Excuse me, she said.

Outside the hotel she got a taxi and told the driver to take her to the American embassy. The "little business" (as she thought of it) at the main embassy gate took ten minutes. The "kind of spooky coincidence" (as she thought of it) or "incident" (as it immediately became known) at the embassy picnic took another ten minutes. When she got back to her room at the Intercon at approximately two-thirty on the afternoon of July 4 she wrote two letters, one to Catherine and one to Wynn Janklow, which she took to an air express office to be shipped for delivery the next day in the United States. *Sweet bird*, the letter to Catherine began. She had spoken to Catherine twice from San José and again the evening she arrived on the island but the calls had been unsatisfactory and now she could not reach her.

> *Tried to call you a few minutes ago but you had signed out to go to Cape Ann with Francie and her parents—didn't know how to reach you and there are two things I need you to know right away. The first thing I need you to know is that I'm asking your father to pick you up and bring you to Malibu for a while. Just until I get back from this trip. You don't need summer credits anyway and he can probably arrange a way you can do the S.A.T. prep out there. The second thing I need you to know is I love you. Sometimes we argue about things but I think we both know I only argue because I want your life to be happy and good. Want you not to waste your time. Not to waste your talents. Not to let who you are get mixed up with anybody else's idea of who you should be.*
>
> *I love you the most. XXXXXXXX, M.*
>
> *P.S. If anyone else comes and wants to take you from school for any reason repeat* ANY REASON *do not repeat* DO NOT *go with him or her.*

The letter to Wynn Janklow was short, because she had reached him, at the house in Malibu, as soon as she got back from the embassy. She had placed the call from a pay phone in the Intercon lobby. Had he not answered the phone she would have waited in the lobby until he did, because she needed to talk to Wynn before chancing any situation (the elevator, say, or the corridor upstairs) in which she might be alone.

Any situation in which something might happen to prevent her from telling Wynn what it was she wanted him to do.

Wynn had answered the phone.

Wynn had told her that he had just walked in off a flight from Taipei.

She had told Wynn what it was she wanted him to do.

She had not mentioned the kind of spooky coincidence at the embassy picnic.

My understanding is that Dick McMahon will not be a problem, she had heard the familiar but unplaceable voice say at the embassy picnic.

The steel band that was playing Sousa marches had momentarily fallen silent and the familiar but unplaceable voice had carried across the tent.

Deek McMaa-aan was the way the familiar voice pronounced the name. *My understanding is that Deek McMaa-aan will not be a problem.*

She had not placed the voice until she saw the Salvadoran across the tent.

Here is my concern, she remembered the Salvadoran saying in the Pan Am lounge at the Miami airport as he fingered the envelope Barry Sedlow had slipped him. *We have a little problem here.*

Transit passenger, she remembered Barry Sedlow saying in the car just after he shot out the streetlight with the 9mm Browning. *Already on the six-thirty back to San Sal. Not our deal.*

The Salvadoran was the kind of spooky coincidence.

The Salvadoran was why she called Wynn.

The Salvadoran was why she tried to call Catherine.

The Salvadoran was why she wrote the letters and took them to the air express office for next-day delivery to Catherine and to Wynn.

The Salvadoran was why she went from the air express office to a local office of the Bank of America, where she obtained eleven thousand dollars in cash, the sum of the cash available on Elena McMahon's various credit cards.

The Salvadoran was why she then destroyed the cards.

My understanding is that Dick McMahon will not be a problem.

Not our deal, Barry Sedlow had said, but it was.

She wrote the letters and she arranged for Wynn to take care of Catherine and she got the eleven thousand dollars in cash and she destroyed the credit cards because she had no way of knowing what kind of problem Dick McMahon's daughter might be seen to be.

Half a generation after the fact, from where I sit at my desk in an apartment on the upper east side of Manhattan, it would be easy to conclude that Elena's actions that afternoon did not entirely make sense, easy to assume that at some point in the hour between learning her father was dead and seeing the Salvadoran she had cracked, panicked, gone feral, a trapped animal trying to hide her young and stay alert in the wild, awake in the ether, alive on the ground.

All I can tell you is what she did.

All I can tell you is that at that time in that place there was a logic to what she did.

Wynn, the second of the two letters she wrote that afternoon read.

What I couldn't tell you on the phone was that something bad is happening. I don't know what it is. So please please do this one thing for me.

P.S., the postscript read.

You have to pick her up yourself. I mean don't send Rudich.

Rudich was someone who had worked for Wynn's father and now worked for Wynn. Rudich was who did things for Wynn. Rudich had a first name but no one ever used it and she had forgotten it. Rudich was who Wynn would call if he needed somebody to fly to Wyoming to take a ranch out of escrow. Rudich was who Wynn would send if he needed somebody to deliver a contract in person the next morning in Tokyo. Rudich was probably who now called the caterer to lay on the tennis lunches.

Rudich could do anything but Rudich could not do this one thing she needed done.

Please please do this.

Love. Still. E.

9

THE LAST time I was in Los Angeles I made a point of going to see Wynn Janklow.

"Why not come by the house Sunday," he had said on the telephone. "I'm having some people, we'll talk, bring a racket."

I made an excuse to go instead to his office in Century City.

I admired, at his prompting, the photographs taken a few months before at Catherine's wedding.

"Big blowout," he said. "Under the *huppah* on the beach at sunset, I flew Bobby Short out to play during dinner, then two bands and fireworks, I'm still finding champagne glasses in the shrubbery but what the hell, great kids, both of them."

I appreciated, again at his prompting, the view of Catalina from his office windows, the clarity of the atmosphere in spite of what he referred to as "all this enviro-freak sky-is-falling shit which as God is my witness I hear even from people I call my friends."

I waited until the secretary had brought in the requisite silver tray with the requisite folded linen napkin, the requisite two bottles of Evian, the requisite Baccarat tumblers.

Only when the secretary had left the room and closed the door did I ask Wynn Janklow to try to remember what he had thought when he received first the call and one day later this letter from Elena.

He had furrowed his brow for my benefit. "That would have been, let me think, when."

Nineteen eighty-four, I said. July 1984.

Wynn Janklow swiveled his chair and gazed out the window, squinting, as if 1984 might materialize just off Catalina.

No big deal, he said then. As he remembered he had to be in New York that week anyway, he flew into Logan instead, got a car to take him down to Newport, he and Catherine had been in New York by midnight.

Big killer heat wave, he remembered.

You know the kind.

The kind where you step out of the car onto the street and

you sink into the asphalt and if you don't move fast you're methane.

He remembered he had Catherine call Elena that night, report she was scarfing Maine lobster in the Hollywood Suite at the Regency.

Great kid even then. Always a great kid.

True enough, on the money, now that I mentioned it there had been some trick about calling Elena, the hotel didn't have her registered right, you had to ask for somebody else, she had given him the name when she called and he had given the name to Catherine.

Elise Meyer, I said.

Elise Meyer, he repeated. No problem, he was glad to be able to do what Elena wanted.

He had been here and Elena had been there but no problem, they stayed on good terms, they had this great kid after all, plus they were adults, unlike some people who got separated or divorced or whatever he and Elena had always maintained a very civilized kind of relationship.

True enough, again on the money, her call had seemed maybe a little overwrought.

Fourth of July, he was just off the plane from Taipei, thinking he'd play a little tennis, work off the jet lag before he had to be in New York.

And then this call from Elena.

Whoa, hold on, he remembered saying. So something happened at the embassy, some clerk gave you the runaround, let me make a few calls, shoot a rocket up the fucker's fat ass.

You don't understand, he remembered Elena saying.

You have to be here to understand, he remembered Elena saying.

Wynn Janklow had again gazed out the window.

"End of sad story," he said.

There had been a silence.

"The sad story is what," I said finally. "You think Elena might have been right? Is that the sad story?" I tried for a neutral tone, a therapist guiding the client back. I wanted to see him confront that hour during which Elena had gone feral. "You think maybe you did have to be there to understand?"

He did not at first respond.

"Maybe you noticed this gadget I have on the wall there," he said then.

He got up and walked to an electronic Mercator projection mounted on the wall, one of those devices on which it is possible to read the time anywhere in the world by watching part of the map pass into darkness as another part emerges into daylight.

"You can watch the sun rise and set anyplace you want," he said. "Right here. Standing right here looking at this." He jabbed at the map with an index finger. "But it doesn't tell you shit about what's happening there."

He sat down behind his desk.

He picked up a paperweight, then buzzed an intercom.

"It's just a toy," he said then. "Frankly it's just something I use when I'm making calls, I look over there and I can see at a glance who's likely to be awake. Meaning I can call them."

He had again buzzed the intercom.

"And in all fairness, I have to admit, sometimes they're awake and sometimes they aren't." He had looked up with relief as the secretary opened the door. "If you could locate a few stamps for her parking ticket, Raina, I'll walk our guest downstairs."

10

OF COURSE Elena might have been right.

Of course you had to be there to understand.

Of course, had you not been there, it might have seemed a definite stretch to call what happened at the embassy Fourth of July picnic an "incident."

Of course, had you not been there, what happened at the embassy Fourth of July picnic might have suggested not an "incident" but merely that it was time to make a few calls, shoot a few rockets up a few fat asses.

"The incident" was what Alex Brokaw called it when he suggested to his DCM that it might be useful to run a background on Elise Meyer. "I'll have to excuse myself to follow up on a little incident," was what the DCM said by way of cutting short a conversation with the Brown & Root project manager who had just arrived to supervise the hardening of the perimeter around the residence. "Just crossing the t's and dotting the i's on a rather troubling incident we had here," was what the DCM said when he put through the request for the background on Elise Meyer.

This was the rather troubling incident in its entirety:

"I'm an American citizen and I need to speak to a consular officer," Elena McMahon had said when she walked into the tented area reserved for the embassy picnic.

The traditional Fourth of July picnic held by every American embassy and open to any American citizen who happens to be in the vicinity.

The Fourth of July embassy picnic that must have seemed, given a country in which any American citizen who happened to be in the vicinity happened also to be in the official or covert employ of one or another branch of the embassy, a trying tradition at best.

She needed, she had said, to replace a lost passport.

She did not want to interrupt the picnic, she had said, but she had gone to the consulate and the guard at the gate said the consulate was closed for the holiday, and she needed her passport replaced immediately.

She needed her passport replaced immediately because she needed to return to the United States immediately.

The woman had seemed, according to the consular officer who was finally located to deal with her, "a little confused," and "unable or unwilling" to accept his "offer to try to clear up the confusion."

The confusion of course was that this woman already had her passport.

Her presence inside the tented area was proof that she already had her passport.

The confusion with this woman had begun at the gate.

She had also told the marine on duty at the gate that she had lost her passport, and when he told her to return the next morning when the consular office reopened she had insisted that tomorrow would be too late, she needed to see a consular officer now.

The marine had explained that this would be impossible because all the consular officers were at the Fourth of July picnic.

The Fourth of July picnic that unfortunately she could not attend because guests were required to present an American passport.

At which point this woman had produced her passport.

And left it, as any other guest not known to the embassy would have left his or her passport, with the guard at the entrance to the tented area.

This woman had left her passport and signed the embassy guest book.

There it was, he could show it to her, her signature: *Elise Meyer.*

Here it was, the guard could and would return it to her, her passport: *Elise Meyer.*

That was the confusion.

According to the consular officer she had taken the passport and held it out, as if she were about to show or give it to him. There had been a moment of silence before she spoke. "This was just to get me in because I need to explain something," she had said, and then she had fallen silent.

She had been looking across the tent.

The steel band had stopped playing.

The woman had seemed, the consular officer reported, "very interested in some of our Salvadoran friends."

"Neat idea, by the way, the steel band," the consular officer had added, "but next year it might be appropriate to tell them, 'Rule Britannia' isn't ours."

It was at the point when the steel band struck up "Rule Britannia" that the woman had put the passport in her bag, closed the bag, and walked out of the tent and across the lawn and out the gate.

"You were about to explain something," the consular officer had said as she started to walk away.

"Forget it," she had said without turning back.

That was the reason for ordering the background.

The background that was ordered to get a line on who she was and what she was doing there.

The background that threw up the glitch.

The background that turned up flat.

No history.

The passport bearing the name Elise Meyer showed that it had been issued on June 30, 1984 at the United States Passport Agency in Miami, but the United States Passport Agency in Miami reported no record of having issued a passport in the name Elise Meyer.

That was the glitch.

II

THE YOUNG FBI agent who had flown down from the Miami office had opened the initial interview by mentioning the glitch.

She had looked puzzled.

The discrepancy, the anomaly, whatever she wanted to call it.

He was certain that she could clear this immediately.

He was sure that she would have a simple explanation for the glitch.

The anomaly.

The discrepancy.

She had offered no explanation at all.

She had merely shrugged. "At my age I don't actually find discrepancies too surprising," she had said. "You must be what? Twenty-six, twenty-seven?"

He was twenty-five.

He had decided to try another tack.

"Assuming for the moment that someone provided you with apparently inauthentic documentation," he began.

"*You're* assuming that," she said. "Naturally. Because you haven't had a whole lot of experience with the way things work. You still think things work the way they're supposed to work. *I'm* assuming something more along the lines of business as usual."

"Excuse me?"

"I guess you must work in an office where nobody ever makes a mistake," she said. "I guess where you work nobody ever hits the wrong key because they're in a rush to go on break."

"I don't see your point."

"You don't think it's possible that some low-level GS-whatever in the passport office accidentally deleted my record?"

This was in fact a distinct possibility, but he chose to ignore it. "Apparently inauthentic documentation is sometimes provided for the purpose of placing the carrier in a position where they can be blackmailed into doing something they wouldn't otherwise do."

"Is that something you learned at Quantico?"

He ignored this. "In other words," he repeated, "someone could have placed you in such a position." He paused for emphasis. "Someone could be using you."

"For what," she said.

"If there were a plot," the agent said.

"That's your invention. This whole plot business. Your movie. Not anybody else's."

The agent paused. She had agreed to the interview. She had not been uncooperative. Because she had not been uncooperative he let this pass, but what she had said was not entirely accurate. The plot to assassinate Alex Brokaw was not his invention at all. There were various theories around the embassy and also in Miami about whose invention it was, the most popular of which was that Alex Brokaw himself had engineered the report in an effort to derail a certain two-track approach then favored at State, but the existence of a plot, once it was mentioned by what the cable traffic called "a previously reliable source," had to be accepted at face value. Documentable steps had to be taken. The record at State had to duly show the formation of a crisis management team on the Caribbean desk. The paperwork had to duly show that wall maps had been requisitioned, with colored pins to indicate known players. The concertina perimeter around the embassy overflow office structures had to be duly reinforced. On the record. All AM/EMBASSY dependents and nonessential personnel had to be duly encouraged to take home leave. In triplicate. All American citizens with access to AM/EMBASSY personnel and uncleared backgrounds had to be interviewed.

Duly.

Including this one.

This one had access to AM/EMBASSY personnel by virtue of being on the island.

This one had thrown a glitch.

Something about this one's use of the phrase "your movie" bothered him but he let that go too.

"If there were a plot," he repeated, "someone could be using you."

"Those are your words."

In the silence that followed the young man had clicked his

ballpoint pen on the table. There were other things about this one that bothered him, but it was important to keep what bothered him out of this picture. It was possible they might be experiencing a syntactical problem, a misunderstanding that could be cleared up by restatement. "Why not put it in your own words," he said finally.

She fished a loose cigarette from her pocket and then, when he made the error of interpreting this as an encouraging sign, replaced the cigarette in her pocket, ignoring the match he was still fumbling to strike.

"There could be a game in there somewhere," she had said then. "And I could be in there somewhere."

"In the plot."

"In the game."

The agent said nothing.

"In whatever you want to call it," she said then. "It's your movie."

"Let's approach this from another angle," he said after a silence. "You came here from San José. Costa Rica. Yet no record exists showing you ever entered Costa Rica. So let's start there."

"You want to know how I got into Costa Rica." Her voice had again suggested cooperation.

"Exactly."

"You don't even need a passport to enter Costa Rica. An American citizen can enter Costa Rica on a tourist card. From a travel agency."

"But you didn't."

There had been another silence.

"I'm going to say something," she said then. "You're going to get it or you won't. I haven't been here long, but I've been here long enough to notice a lot of Americans here. I notice them on the street, I notice them at the hotel, I notice them all over. I don't know if they have their own passports. I don't know whose passports they have. I don't know whose passport I have. All I know is, they aren't on vacation."

Again she took the loose cigarette from her pocket and again she put it back.

"So I'd suggest you just think for a while about what they're doing here," she had said then. "And I bet you could pretty much figure how I got into Costa Rica."

Subject "Elise Meyer" acknowledges entering country in possession of apparently inauthentic documentation but provides no further information concerning either the source of said documentation or her purpose in entering said country, the agent's preliminary report read. *Recommendation: continued surveillance and investigation until such time as identity of subject can be verified, as well as subject's purpose in entering said country.*

This initial interview took place on July 10, 1984.

A second interview, during which subject and interrogator reiterated their respective points, took place on July 11, 1984.

Elena McMahon moved from the Intercon to the Surfrider on July 12.

It was August 14 when Treat Morrison flew down from Washington on the American that landed at ten A.M. and, when he stopped by the Intercon to leave his bag, happened to see her sitting by herself in the Intercon coffee shop.

Sitting by herself at the round table set for eight.

Wearing the white dress.

Eating the chocolate parfait and bacon.

When he got to the embassy later that day he learned from Alex Brokaw's DCM that the woman he had seen in the Intercon coffee shop had arrived on the island on July 2 on an apparently falsified American passport issued in the name Elise Meyer. At his request the DCM had arranged to have him briefed on the progress of the continuing FBI investigation meant to ascertain who Elise Meyer was and what she was doing there. Later it occurred to him that there would have been at that time in that embassy certain people who already knew who Elise Meyer was and what she was doing there, but it did not occur to him then.

THREE

I

I SHOULD UNDERSTAND Treat Morrison.

I studied him, I worked him up.

I researched him, I interviewed him, I listened to him, watched him.

I came to recognize his way of speaking, came to know how to read the withheld phrasing, the fast dying fall or diminuendo that would render key words barely audible, the sudden rise and overemphasis on the insignificant part of the sentence (". . . and by the *way*"), the rush or explosion of syllables jammed together (". . . and the hell it *is* . . ."), the raising of the entirely rhetorical question (". . . and . . . *should* I have regrets?"), the thoughtful acting out of the entirely rhetorical answer (head tilted up, a gaze into the middle distance, then "I . . . don't think . . . *so*"), the unconvincingly brisk reiteration: ". . . and I have *no regrets*."

No regrets.

Treat Morrison had no regrets.

Quite early in the course of these dealings with Treat Morrison I came to regard him as fundamentally dishonest. Not dishonest in the sense that he "lied," or deliberately misrepresented events as he himself construed them (he did not, he never did, he was scrupulous to a fault about reporting exactly what he believed to be true), but dishonest in the more radical sense, dishonest in that he remained incapable of seeing the thing straight. At the outset I viewed this as an idiosyncrasy or a defect of character, in either case singular, peculiar to the individual, a personal eccentricity. I came only later to see that what I viewed as personal was deep in the grain of who he was and where he came from.

Let me give you a paragraph from my notes.

Not interview notes, not raw notes, but early draft notes, notes lacking words and clauses and marked with *CH* for "check" and *TK* for "to come," meaning I didn't have it then but planned to get it, notes worked up in the attempt to get something on paper that might open a way to a lead:

Treat Austin Morrison was born in San Francisco at a time, 1930, when San Francisco was still remote, isolated, separated physically from the rest of the United States by the ranges of mountains that closed off when the heavy snows came, separated emotionally by the implacable presence of the Pacific, by the ???TK and by the ???TK and by the fogs that blew in from the Farallons every afternoon at four or five. His father held a minor city sinecure, jury commissioner in the municipal court

There this particular note toward a lead skids to an abrupt stop. Scratched in pencil after the typed words "municipal court" is a comma, then one further penciled clause:

a job he owed to his wife's well-placed relatives in the Irish wards (??CH "wards") south of Market Street.

More false starts:

The son of a parochial school teacher and a minor city official in San Francisco, Treat Austin Morrison enrolled at the University of California at Berkeley when it was still offering a free college education to any qualified California high school graduate who could scrape up the $27.50 (??CH) registration fee plus whatever little he or she could live on. The man who would later become America's man-on-the-spot in the world's hottest spots, ambassador-at-large with a top-secret portfolio, earned part of his college costs by parking cars at the elite Hotel Claremont in Oakland, the rest by

Treat Austin Morrison may have been Saturday's hero on the football field (XXX BETTER LINE TK), the University of California's own All-PAC 8 (??CH) quarterback, but Saturday night would find him back in the kitchen at the exclusive Phi Gamma Delta house, where he paid for his room and board by hashing, washing dishes and waiting table for the affluent party animals who called themselves his fraternity brothers and from whom he borrowed the textbooks he could not afford to buy. The discipline developed in those years stands him in good stead as

T.A.M. was raised an only child

T.A.M., the only son and during most of his formative years the only living child of a

T.A.M., the only son and after his older sister's suicide the only living child

There are pages of such draft notes, a thick sheaf of them, most of them uncharacteristically (for me) focused on the subject's early deprivations and childhood pluck (uncharacteristically for me because it has not been my actual experience that the child is father to the man), all of them aborted. I see now that there was a clear common thread in these failed starts, that I was trying to deal with something about Treat Morrison that continued to elude me: this was a man who was at the time I interviewed him living and working at the heart of the American political establishment. This was a man who could pick up the telephone and affect the Dow, reach the foreign minister of any one of a dozen NATO countries, the Oval Office itself. This was a man generally perceived as a mover, a shaker, a can-do guy, someone who appeared to thrive on negotiation, on dealing, on calculation and calibration and adjustment, the very stuff that defines a successful social operator. Yet this remained someone who projected nothing so much as an extreme, even resistant loneliness, an isolation so impenetrable as to seem to demand analysis, examination, a reason why.

Treat Morrison himself appeared to have no interest in examining what I am distressed to notice I was choosing to call "his formative years."

I would not hear from him about early deprivations or childhood pluck, nor would I get from him even the slightest clue that the traditional actors in the family drama (or, in the vocabulary into which I appear to have been sinking, the formative dynamic) had been in his case other than casual acquaintances.

"As far as I know she was regarded as an excellent teacher," he said about his mother. "Very well thought of, very esteemed by the sisters who ran the school." He paused, as if weighing this for fairness. "Of course she was a Catholic," he said then.

Since this afterthought was the most specific and least remote information he had so far seemed inclined to convey,

I decided to pursue it. "Then you were raised a Catholic," I began, tentatively, expecting, if not revelation, at least confirmation or correction.

What I got was zero.

What I got was Treat Morrison waiting, at bay, his fingers tented.

"Or were you," I said.

He said nothing.

"Raised a Catholic," I said.

He aligned a square crystal paperweight with the edge of his desk blotter.

"Not to say that I entirely disagreed with many of the pertinent precepts," he said then, "but as far as the whole religious business went, it just wasn't an area that particularly interested me."

"He was very well liked around the courthouse," he said about his father. "As far as I know."

"It was something that happened," he said about the death of his sister at age nineteen. "I was twelve, thirteen years old when it happened, there were the seven years between us, seven years at that age could be a lifetime, to all intents and purposes Mary Katherine was someone I barely knew."

"For all anyone knows it was an accident," he said when I tried to follow up on this subject. "She was watching the seals, the surf came up and took her, Mary Katherine never had any coordination, she was always in the emergency room, if she wasn't breaking her ankle she was dropping a bicycle on her leg or knocking herself out with a tetherball or every other damn thing."

"I guess I didn't see any useful reason to dwell on that," he said when I suggested that very few people who get accidentally taken by the surf while watching the seals happen to have mailed goodbye notes to (although not to their mother or father or brother) three former teachers at Lowell High School and a former boyfriend who had recently left to go through OCS at Fort Lewis. MISSION TEEN A HOMEFRONT CASUALTY, the headline read in the San Francisco *Chronicle* the morning after the letters began to surface. I had found it on microfiche. LOWELL GRAD WROTE FINAL DEAR JOHN. "There you see the goddamn media again," Treat Morrison said about this.

"Goddamn media was meddling even then in something they couldn't possibly begin to understand."

"Which would have been what." I recall trying for an offhand delivery. "What was it exactly that the media didn't begin to understand."

Treat Morrison said nothing for a moment. "A lot of people get some big mystical kick out of chewing over things that happened forty, forty-five years ago," he said then. "Little sad stories about being misunderstood by their mother or getting snubbed at school or whatever. I'm not saying there's anything wrong with this, I'm not saying it's self-indulgent or self-pitying or any other damn thing. I'm just saying I can't afford it. So I don't do it."

I find in my notes and taped interviews only two instances in which Treat Morrison volunteered anything about his background that could be construed as personal. The first such instance is buried deep in a taped discussion of what a two-state solution would mean to Israel. Three-quarters of the way through a sixty-minute tape, at 44:19 to be exact, Treat Morrison falls silent. When he resumes talking it is not about two-state versus one-state for Israel but about having once had some pictures framed for his mother. It seemed that his mother had broken a hip and been forced to move from her house in the Mission district to a Mercy convalescent home in Woodside. It seemed that he had stopped to see her on his way to a meeting in Saigon. It seemed that she had kept mentioning these pictures, snapshots of him and his sister at a place they used to go on the Russian River. "She'd had them stuck in a mirror, she wanted them at the new place, I thought I'd get them put in a frame, you know those frames that take four or five little pictures. So fine. But when I go to pick it up, the clerk has written on the package '*kids playing by stream.*'"

47:17. A pause on the tape.

"So that was a lesson," he says then.

Actually I knew immediately what the lesson would have been.

I had been working this row long enough to make the inductive leaps required by Treat Morrison's rather cryptic staccato.

The lesson would have been that no one else will ever view

our lives exactly as we do: someone else had looked at the snapshots and seen the two children but had failed to hear the music, had failed even to know or care that he or she was lacking the emotional score. Just as someone else could have looked at the snapshot Elena McMahon took from her mother's bedroom and seen her father holding the beer and her mother in the apron printed with pitchforks ("*man and woman at barbecue*") but never seen the fat little sizzler rockets, never seen the sparklers that made fireflies in the hot desert twilight. Never heard *half a margarita and I'm already flying*, never heard *who needs the goombahs, we got our own show right here.*

I knew all that.

The conventions of the interview nonetheless required that I ask the obvious question, follow up, encourage the subject to keep talking.

50:05. "What was the lesson," I hear myself say on the tape.

"In the first place," Treat Morrison says on the tape, "it wasn't some 'stream,' we didn't have 'streams' in California, 'streams' are what they have in England, or Vermont, it was the goddamn Russian River."

Another pause.

"In the second place we weren't 'playing.' She was eleven, for Christ's sake, I was four, what would we '*play*.' We were getting our picture taken, that's the only reason we were even together."

And then, without a beat: "Which has to kind of give you an insight into how differently an Israeli and a Palestinian might view the same little event or the same little piece of land."

That was one of Treat Morrison's two ventures into the personal.

The second such venture is also on tape, and also has to do with his mother. It seemed that he had arranged to have his mother driven to Berkeley to see him receive an honor of some sort. He did not remember what the honor had been. What the honor had been was not the point. The point was that because they would have no other time alone, he had made a reservation to take his mother to dinner at the Claremont Hotel.

"Big white gingerbread job, just as you start up into the hills," he says on the tape. "Funny thing was, I don't know if you knew this, I parked cars there as an undergraduate."

"I think I did know that." My voice on the tape.

"Well then. So." A pause, then a rush of words. "My memory of this place was of someplace very very—I mean the definition of glamour. I mean at that time for that side of the bay this place was pretty much the *ne plus ultra* of big-deal sophistication. So I take my mother there. And it still looked the same, same big lobby, same big wide corridors, except now it looked to me like a cruise ship beached in maybe 1943. I hadn't walked into the place in twenty-five years. I mean, hell, I graduated in 1951, and I swear to Christ they still have the same piano player in the lobby. Playing the same goddamn songs. 'Where or When.' 'Tenderly.' 'It Might as Well Be Spring.' Now the night I'm there with my mother it so happened it *was* spring, spring 1975 to be exact, April, goddamn Saigon closing down, and outside the hotel while my mother and I are having dinner there's this torchlight parade, march, conga line, whatever, all these kids carrying torches and chanting *Ho Ho / Ho Chi Minh.* Plus something about me personally, I frankly don't even remember what it was, that's not the point. And inside the piano player keeps pounding out 'It Might as Well Be Spring.' And I'm sitting there hoping my mother doesn't understand that the kids are outside because I'm inside. 'Mary Katherine died thirty-three years ago tomorrow,' my mother says. Real casual, you understand, never looks up from the menu. 'I believe I'll take the prime rib,' she says then. 'What will you take.' What I took was another goddamn double bourbon, bring two while you're at it."

Ho Ho / Ho Chi Minh

The war Mister Morrison / Will not win

Was what they chanted outside the Claremont that night.

Something else I found on microfiche.

The first time Treat Morrison was alone with Elena he mentioned Mary Katherine's death.

"Why did she do it," Elena said.

"I don't have an answer for that kind of tragedy," he said.

"Which kind do you have an answer for," Elena said.

Treat Morrison studied her for a moment. "I read you," he said then.

"I read you too," she said.

Of course she did, of course he did.

Of course they read each other.

Of course they knew each other, understood each other, recognized each other, took one look and got each other, had to be with each other, saw the color drain out of what they saw when they were not looking at each other.

They were the same person.

They were equally remote.

2

DREAM, THE notebook entry is headed, all in caps.

The notebook, a spiral-bound Clairefontaine with a red cover and pale-gray three-eighth-inch graph paper inside, was one kept by Elena Janklow during the months in 1981 and 1982 immediately before she left the house on the Pacific Coast Highway and once again became (at least for a while, at least provisionally) Elena McMahon.

"*I seem to have had an operation,*" Elena Janklow's account of the dream begins. Her handwriting, all but the last entries made in the same black fine-point pen. "*Unspecified but unsuccessful. I am 'sewn back up again,' but roughly, as after an autopsy. It is agreed (I have agreed to this) that there is no point in doing a careful job, I am to die, a few days hence. The day on which I am assigned to die is a Sunday, Christmas Day. Wynn and Catherine and I are in Wynn's father's apartment in New York, where the death will take place, by gas. I am concerned about how the gas will be cleared out of the apartment but no one else seems to be.*

"*It occurs to me that I must shop for Saturday night dinner, and make it special, since this will be my last day alive. I go out on 57th Street and along Sixth Avenue, very crowded and cold, in a bundled-up robe. My feet are very loosely sewn and I am afraid the stitching (basting really) will come out, also that my face is not on straight (again as in an autopsy it has been peeled down and put back up), and getting sadder and sadder.*

"*As I shop it occurs to me that maybe I could live: why must I die? I mention this to Wynn. He says then call the doctor, call Arnie Stine in California and tell him. Ask Arnie if you need to die tomorrow. I call Arnie Stine in California and he says no, if that's what I want, of course I do not need to die tomorrow. He can 'arrange it for later' if I want. I continue shopping, for Christmas dinner now as well as for Saturday night. I get a capon to roast for Christmas. I am euphoric, relieved, but still concerned that I cannot be sewn back together properly. Arnie Stine says I can be but I am afraid I will fall apart while shopping, walking on my loose feet.*

"*I am trying to be careful when I wake up.*"

It was Catherine who found the spiral-bound notebook, the summer Wynn picked her up at school and brought her first to the Hollywood Suite at the Regency and then to the house on the Pacific Coast Highway. She had been looking through the desk in the pantry for takeout menus when she found the notebook, on which her mother had printed, in Magic Marker, the word MENUS. In fact there actually were menus in the notebook, not takeout menus of course but menus Elena had made up for dinners or lunches, a dozen or more of them, with notes on quantities and recipes ("*three lbs lamb for navarin serves eight outside*"), cropping up at random among the other entries.

The peculiarity was in the other entries. They were not exactly the kind of notes a professional writer or reporter might make, but neither were they conventional "diary" notes, the confessions or private thoughts set down by a civilian. What was peculiar about these entries was that they reflected elements of both modes, the personal and the reportorial, with no apparent distinction between the two. There were scraps of what appeared to be overheard dialogue, there were lists of roses and other garden plants. There were quotes from and comments on news stories, there were scraps of remembered poetry. There were what appear to have been passing thoughts, some random, some less so. And there were of course the dreams.

"I get a little spacey when I stop smoking, probably because I get too much oxygen."

"What he's best at getting hold of is other people's money."

This much I can see without going outside: climbing Cecile Brunner roses, Henri Martin roses, Paulii roses, Chicago Peace roses, Scarlet Fire roses, blue and white amaryllis, scabiosa, Meyer lemons, star jasmine, santolina, butterfly bush, yarrow, blue lavender, delphinium, gaura, mint, lemon thyme, lemon grass, bay laurel, tarragon, basil, feverfew, artichokes. This much I can see with my eyes closed. Also: the big yellow and white poppies in the bed on the south wall.

"You may have stayed at the Savoy, but I doubt very much you stayed at the Savoy and lost sixteen thousand pounds at Annabel's."

I have eaten dinner on Super Bowl Sunday in the most expensive restaurants in Detroit, Atlanta, San Diego and Tampa Bay.

Interview in LAT with someone who just resurfaced after thirteen years underground: "I never defined myself as a fugitive. I defined myself as a human being. Human beings have things they have to deal with. Because I was Weather Underground, being a fugitive was something I had to deal with, but it wasn't a definition of me." What mean??? If a fugitive is what you are, how does it change the situation to define yourself as a "human being"?

I fled Him down the nights and down the days
I fled Him down the arches of the years

The most terrifying verse I know: merrily merrily merrily life is but a dream.

DREAM, the next two entries nonetheless begin.

I go to my mother's house in Laguna, crying. Ward's daughter Belinda is also there. Catherine has been kidnapped, I tell my mother. "I thought she came to tell you she was having Christmas dinner at Chasen's," Belinda says.

A party in a house that seems to be this one. Wynn and Catherine and I live in it but so do my mother and father. The party is in progress and I go out on the beach for a little quiet. When I come back my father is waiting at the bottom of the stairs. Catherine is either drunk or drugged, he says. He can hear her vomiting upstairs but doesn't want to intrude. I run up and notice that the upstairs has been painted. This is a little disturbing: how much time exactly has passed?

The last entry in this notebook, not a dream, was actually not one but six notes, each made in a different pen and on a different page but all apparently made in response to the daily regimen Catherine had described in her eighth-grade autobiographical essay as "radiation zapping following the exsishun [*sic*] of a stage 1 good prognose [*sic*] breast lesion":

The linear accelerator, the mevatron, the bevatron.
"Just ask for R.O., it's in the tunnel."

"A week before you finish you'll go on the mevatron to get your electrons. Now you're getting your photons."
Photons? Or "protons"???

Waiting for the beam after the technician goes and the laser light finds the place.

The sensation of vibration when the beam comes.
The stunning silent bombardment, the entire electromagnetic field rearranged.

"You don't feel anything," Arnie Stine said. "The beam doesn't feel like anything."
"Just between us nobody who hasn't been on that table has any idea what the beam feels like," the technician said.

The beam is my alpha and my omega

I finished this morning
How I feel is excluded, banished, deprived of the beam
Alcestis, back from the tunnel and half in love with death

3

OF COURSE we would not need those last six notes to know what Elena's dreams were about.

Elena's dreams were about dying.

Elena's dreams were about getting old.

Nobody here has not had (will not have) Elena's dreams.

We all know that.

The point is that Elena didn't.

The point is that Elena remained remote most of all to herself, a clandestine agent who had so successfully compartmentalized her operation as to have lost access to her own cut-outs.

The last entry in this notebook is dated *April 27, 1982.*

It would have been not quite four months later, August 1982, when Elena McMahon left Wynn Janklow.

Relocated to the East Coast, as she put it.

It would have been some three months after that, late November 1982, when she returned for the first time to California.

She had flown out from Washington on the morning flight to interview a Czech dissident then teaching at UCLA and rumored to be short-listed for a Nobel Prize in literature. She had meant to do the interview and go straight to the airport and turn in the rental car and take the next flight back, but when she left UCLA she had driven not to the airport but up the Pacific Coast Highway. Just as she would make no conscious decision to walk off the 1984 campaign, just as she would make no conscious decision to ask for a flight to Miami instead of to Washington, she had made no conscious decision to do this. She was unaware even that the decision had been made until she found herself parking the rental car in the lot outside the market where she used to shop. She had gone into the drugstore and said hello to the pharmacist and picked up a couple of surfing magazines for Catherine and a jar of aloe gel for herself, a kind she had been unable to locate in Washington. The pharmacist asked if she had been away, he hadn't seen her in a while. She said that she had been away, yes. She said the same thing to the checkout clerk in the market, where she bought corn tortillas and serrano chiles, something else she had been unable to locate in Washington.

She had been away, yes.

Always good to get back, right.

With weather this dry they were lucky to have gotten through Thanksgiving without a fire, yes.

No way she was ready to start dealing with Christmas, no.

She had sat then in the rental car in the parking lot, almost deserted at four in the afternoon. Four in the afternoon was not the time of day when women who lived here shopped. Women who lived here shopped in the morning, before tennis, after working out. If she still lived here she would not be sitting in a rental car in the parking lot at four in the afternoon. One of the high school boys who worked in the market after school was stringing Christmas lights on the board advertising the day's specials. Another was rounding up carts, jamming the carts into long trains and propelling each train into the rack with a single extended finger. By the time the last light dropped behind Point Dume the carts were all racked and the Christmas lights were blinking red and green and she had stopped crying.

"What was that about," Treat Morrison said when she mentioned this to him.

"It was about my not belonging there anymore," she said.

"Where did you ever belong," Treat Morrison said.

Let me clarify something.

When I said that Elena McMahon and Treat Morrison were equally remote I was shortcutting, jumping ahead to the core dislocation in the personality, overlooking the clearly different ways in which each had learned to deal with that dislocation.

Elena's apparently impenetrable performances in the various roles assigned her were achieved (I see now) only with considerable effort and at considerable cost. All that reinvention, all those fast walks and clean starts, all that had cost something. It had cost something to grow up watching her father come and go and do his deals without ever noticing what it was he dealt. *Father's Occupation: Investor.* It had cost something to talk to Melissa Simon on Westlake Career Day when all her attention was focused on the beam. *You don't feel anything*, Arnie Stine said. *The beam doesn't feel like anything. Just between us nobody who hasn't been on that table has any idea what the beam feels like*, the technician said. It had cost something to remember the Fourth of July her father's friend brought fireworks up from the border and to confine the picture to the fat little sizzler rockets she had not liked and the sparklers that made fireflies in the hot desert twilight.

To limit what she heard to *half a margarita and I'm already flying, who needs the goombahs, we got our own show right here.*

To keep the name of her father's friend just outside the frame of what she remembered.

Of course the name of her father's friend was Max Epperson.

You knew it was.

Treat Morrison would not have needed to forget that detail.

Treat Morrison had built an entire career on remembering the details that might turn out to be wild cards, using them, playing them, sensing the opening and pressing the advantage. Unlike Elena, he had mastered his role, internalized it, perfected the performance until it betrayed no hint of the total disinterest at its core. He knew how to talk and he knew how to listen. He was widely assumed because he refused the use of translators to have a gift for languages, but in fact he communicated with nothing more than a kind of improvisational pidgin and very attentive listening. He could listen attentively in several languages, not excluding his own. Treat Morrison could listen attentively to a discussion in Tagalog about trade relations between the United States and Asia, and Treat Morrison could listen with the same exact calibration of attentiveness to a Houston bartender explaining how when the oil boom went belly up he zeroed in on bartending as an entrée to the private service sector. Once on the shuttle I sat across the aisle from Treat Morrison and watched him spend the entire flight, National to LaGuardia, listening attentively to the stratagems employed by his seatmate in the course of commuting between his home in New Jersey and his office in Santa Ana.

"You have the Delta through Salt Lake," I heard Treat Morrison prompt when the conversation showed signs of lagging.

"Actually I prefer the American through Dallas," the seatmate said, confidence restored in the intrinsic interest of his subject.

"The American out of Newark."

"Out of Newark, sure, except Newark has the short runways, so when the weather goes, scratch Newark."

During the ride in from LaGuardia I had asked Treat Morrison how he happened to have the Delta through Salt Lake at his fingertips.

"He'd already mentioned it," Treat Morrison said. "Before we were off the ground at National. He took it last week and hit some pretty hairy turbulence over the Wasatch Range. I listen. That's my business. Listening. That's the difference between me and the Harvard guys. The Harvard guys don't listen."

I had heard before about "the Harvard guys," also about "the guys who know how not to rattle their teacups" and "the guys with the killer serves and not too much else." This was a vein in Treat Morrison that would surface only when exhaustion or a drink or two had lowered his guard, and remained the only visible suggestion of whatever it had meant to him to come out of the West and confront the established world.

This was another area he was not inclined to explore.

"What the hell, the last I heard this was still one country," was what he said when I tried to pursue it. "Unless you people in the media have new information to the contrary."

He regarded me in truculent silence for a full thirty seconds, then seemed to remember that truculent silence was not his most productive tack.

"Here's the deal," he said. "There are two kinds of people who end up in the State Department. And believe me, I am by *no means* talking about where somebody came from, I'm talking about what kind of person he is."

He hesitated.

A quick glance to assess my reaction, then the amendment: "And of course I mean what kind of person *he is or she is.* Male, female, space alien, whatever. I don't want to read some PC crap about myself in the goddamn New York *Times.* Okay. State. Two kinds of individuals end up there. There's the kind of individual who goes from post to post getting the place cards right and sending out the reminder cards on time. And there's the other kind. I'm one of the other kind."

I asked what kind that was.

"Crisis junkies," he said. "I'm in this for the buzz, take it or leave it."

This was Treat Morrison when his performance went off. When it was on he was flawless, talking as attentively as he listened, rendering opinions, offering advice, even volunteering surprisingly candid analyses of his own modus operandi. "There's a trick to inserting yourself in a certain kind of situation," he said when I once remarked on his ability to move from end game to end game without becoming inconveniently identified with any of them. "You can't go all the way with it. You have to go back and write the report or whatever, give the briefings, then move on. You go in, you pull their irons out of the fire, you get a free period, maybe six months, no more, during which you're allowed to lecture everybody who isn't up to speed on this one little problem on the frivolity of whatever other damn thing they've been doing. After that you move past it. You know who the unreported casualties of Vietnam were? Reporters and policy guys who didn't move past it."

That was another difference between Treat Morrison and Elena.

Elena inserted herself in a certain kind of situation and went all the way with it.

Elena failed to move past it.

Which is why, by the time Treat Morrison arrived on the scene, Elena had already been caught in the pipeline, swept into the conduits.

Into the game.

Into the plot.

Into the setup.

Into whatever you wanted to call it.

FOUR

I

ONE OF the many questions that several teams of congressional investigators and Rand Corporation analysts would eventually fail to resolve was why, by the time Treat Morrison arrived on the island, almost six weeks after she had learned from the Miami *Herald* that her father was dead and more than a month after she had learned from the FBI that the passport she was using had a trick built into it, Elena McMahon was still there.

She could have left.

Just gone to the airport and gotten on a plane (there were still scheduled flights, not as many as there had been but the airport was open) and left the place.

She would have known since the intitial FBI interview that the passport with the trick built into it would not be valid for reentry into the United States, but that in itself might well have seemed an argument to get off this island, go somewhere else, go anywhere else.

She had some cash, there were places she could have gone.

Just look at a map: unnumbered other islands there in the palest-blue shallows of the Caribbean, careless islands with careless immigration controls, islands with no designated role in what was going on down there.

Islands on which nothing either overt or covert was under way, islands on which the U.S. Department of State had not yet had occasion to place repeated travel advisories, islands on which the resident U.S. government officials had not yet found it necessary to send out their own dependents and nonessential personnel.

Islands on which the ranking American diplomatic officer was not said to be targeted for assassination.

Entire archipelagoes of neutral havens where an American woman of a certain appearance could have got off the plane and checked into a promising resort hotel (a promising resort hotel would be defined as one in which there were no Special Forces in the lobby, no armored unmarked vans at the main entrance) and ordered a cold drink and dialed a familiar number in Century City or Malibu and let Wynn Janklow and the concierge work out the logistics of reentry into her previous life.

Just think about it: this was not a woman who on the evidence had ever lacked the resources to just get on a plane and leave.

So why hadn't she.

The Rand analysts, I believe because they sensed the possibility of reaching an answer better left on the horizon, allowed this question to remain open, one of several "still vexing areas left to be further explored by future students of this period." The congressional investigators answered the question like the prosecutors many of them had been, resorting to one of those doubtful scenarios that tend to bypass recognizable human behavior in the rush to prove "motive." The motive on which the congressional investigators would settle in this instance was "greed": CAUGHT BY GREED, the pertinent section heading reads in their final report. Elena McMahon, they concluded, had stayed on the island because she still expected someone to walk up and hand her the million dollars she was supposed to have received on delivery of Dick McMahon's last shipment.

"Elena McMahon stayed where she was," to quote this section exactly, "because she apparently feared that if she left she would be cheated out of or would otherwise forfeit the money she believed she was owed, i.e., the payment she claimed was due her father."

But that was flat wrong.

The payment due her father was by then no longer the point.

The payment due her father had stopped being the point at the instant she read in the Miami *Herald* that her father had been certified dead at the Clearview Convalescent Lodge in South Kendall on June 30, 1984.

Which happened also to be the date on the passport with the trick built into it.

My understanding is that Dick McMahon will not be a problem.

2

"STOP TALKING to the goddamn baby-sitter," her father had said the evening she was about to leave the house in Sweetwater for Fort Lauderdale–Hollywood International Airport and the unscheduled flight that would not land in San José, Costa Rica.

She was trying to tell the nurse about her father's midnight medication.

"Ellie. I want you to listen to me."

"He won't swallow it but you can mash it up in a little brandy," she said to the nurse.

The nurse continued flicking through channels.

"Don't let any of those guys talk you into staying over down there," her father said. "You deliver the goods, you pick up the payment, you get back on the plane, you're back here tomorrow. That's my deal."

"I thought *Cheers* was on two," the nurse said.

"Get the TV critic out of here and listen to me," Dick McMahon said.

She sent the nurse to locate *Cheers* in the kitchen.

"That one's not really a nurse," Dick McMahon said. "The one in the morning, she's a nurse, but that one's a baby-sitter." He had leaned back in his chair, exhausted. "Ellie. Okay. You deliver the goods, you pick up the payment, you get back on the plane. That's my deal." Each time he said this it was as if for the first time. "Don't let any of those guys mickey-mouse you into staying over, you follow me?"

She said that she followed him.

"Anybody gives you any trouble, you just tell them."

She waited.

She could see the network of veins beneath the transparent skin of his eyelids.

Tell them what, she prompted.

"Tell them, oh *goddamn*." He was rousing himself with difficulty. "Tell them they're going to have to answer to Max Epperson. Then you call Max. Promise me you'll call Max."

She did not know whether Max Epperson was dead or alive

or a hallucination but she promised nonetheless that she would call Max.

Wherever Max might be.

"You just tell Max I'm a little under the weather," Dick McMahon said. "Tell Max I need him to look out for you. Just until I'm a hundred percent again. Just tell him I said that, you understand?"

She said that she understood.

Barry Sedlow had told her to be at Fort Lauderdale–Hollywood at midnight sharp.

She was to wait not in the terminal but at Post J, if she asked at the Butler operations office they would direct her to Post J.

At Post J there would be a locked gate onto the tarmac.

She was to wait at Post J.

Someone would unlock the gate.

By the time she was ready to leave her father was again asleep in his chair, but when she kissed his forehead he reached for her hand.

"You don't remember this but when you had your tonsils out I wouldn't let you stay in the hospital by yourself," he said. "I was afraid you'd wake up scared with nobody around. So I slept in a chair in your room."

Elena did not remember this.

All Elena remembered was that when Catherine had appendicitis she herself had slept on a gurney in Catherine's room at Cedars.

Her father's eyes were still closed.

He did not let go of her hand.

These were the next-to-last words her father spoke to her:

"You never even knew that, see. Because you were a winner, you took the whole hospital deal like a winner, you didn't wake up once."

"I did wake up," she said. "I do remember."

She wished she did.

She hoped Catherine would.

She held his hand until his breathing was even, then walked to the door.

"This payday comes in," he said when she opened the screen door, "for the first time in my life I'll have something to leave you."

"I did wake up," she repeated. "I knew you were there."

By the way.
I saw your dad.
He says hi.
I'm keeping him in the picture.

In fact I know why Elena McMahon was still on the island.

Elena McMahon was still on the island because of what she had known since the instant she read in the Miami *Herald* that her father had been certified dead in South Kendall on the same day the passport with her photograph on it was supposed to have been issued in Miami. What she had known since that instant was this:

Somebody out there was playing a different game, doing a different deal.

Not her father's deal.

A deal her father had not known about.

Her father's role in this deal he had not known about was to have been something more than just assembling the shipments, the shipments that had over the course of the spring refocused his dwindling energy, his flagging interest in staying alive. Her father's role was to have begun once he arrived on the ground to collect the million-dollar payday.

Consider her father: a half-crazy old man who had spent his life dealing merchandise that nobody would admit they wanted dealt, an old man whose interest in who used his merchandise was limited to who could pay for it, an old man whose well-documented impartiality about where his merchandise ended up could allow him to be placed on the wrong side of whatever was going to happen on this island.

Who would miss him, who would care?

Who would not believe he had done whatever it was they were going to say he had done?

An old man in a sick season.

An old man with no reputation to lose.

The shipments had just been the cheese in the trap.

She had sprung the trap and her father was dead and now she was set up to do whatever it was that he was supposed to have done.

Somebody had her lined up, somebody had her jacked in the headlights.

Had her in the scope.

Had her in the crosshairs.

What she did not know was who.

And until she knew who, until she located the line of fire, she could not involve Wynn.

She needed Wynn out of the line of fire.

She needed Wynn to take care of Catherine.

3

THE QUESTION of why Treat Morrison arrived on the island was another area in which neither Rand nor the congressional investigators did a particularly convincing job, but in this case there would have been daunting structural obstacles, entire layers of bureaucracy dedicated to the principle that self-perpetuation depended on the ability not to elucidate but to obscure. "The cooperation of those individuals and agencies who responded to our numerous requests is appreciated," the preface to the Rand study noted in this connection. "Although some other individuals and agencies did not acknowledge or respond to our requests, it is to be hoped that future assessments of this incident will benefit from their assistance and clarification."

I also knew at the time why Treat Morrison arrived on the island, but it was not an answer calculated to satisfy the Rand analysts.

Treat Morrison arrived on the island for the buzz.

The action, the play.

Treat Morrison arrived on the island because it was one more place where he could insert himself into a certain kind of situation.

Of course he had a "mission," a specific charter, and he also had a specific agenda. He always had a specific mission when he inserted himself into this kind of situation, and he also always had a specific agenda. The agenda did not necessarily coincide with the charter, but neither did it, if the insertion was smooth, necessarily conflict. "Certain people in Washington might have certain front-burner interests they want me to address, and that would be my charter," he once told me to this point, his tone that of someone explaining to a child what goes on at the office. "Typically, however, there might be some other little angle, something they maybe don't know about or think is back-burner. And I might also try to address that."

That would be his agenda.

Treat Morrison's charter in this case was to correct or clarify whatever misunderstandings or erroneous impressions might or might not have been left during the recent tour of the region undertaken by a certain senator and his senior foreign policy aide. There had then been a subsequent trip, made by only the senior foreign policy aide, who was twenty-seven years old and whose name was Mark Berquist. Various questions had been raised, by American embassy personnel in the countries involved, having to do with what the senator and Mark Berquist were doing in these countries and with whom they had been meeting and what, during such meetings, had been said or not said. These questions, which of course derived from a general suspicion that the visits may have lent encouragement if not outright support to what were usually called "unauthorized fringe elements," had languished awhile on the Caribbean and Central American desks and then, once it seemed clear that no answers would be forthcoming, had been strategically leaked out of Tegucigalpa to the ranking American reporters who covered the area.

"According to well-placed embassy sources," was the way the New York *Times* had attributed the questions.

The Los Angeles *Times* had added corroboration from "a European diplomat experienced in the region."

The Washington *Post* had relied on "knowledgeable U.S. observers."

In the brief flurry that followed, Mark Berquist defined the purpose of his trips as "strictly fact-finding," "generally focused on business and agricultural matters" but "not in any area of particular interest to you."

The senator himself said that he had made the trip only to "encourage participation in what is getting to be in our state a very active and mutually beneficial sister-city program."

The call for a hearing died before it got to subcommittee.

Which might have been the end of it had the visits from the senator and Mark Berquist not been followed, at least in the area on which Alex Brokaw's embassy reported, by certain incidents, not major but nonetheless troubling, in that they tended to legitimize the "previously reliable source" who had in late June reported the existence of a plot to assassinate Alex Brokaw.

There had been for example the two steamer trunks apparently abandoned in a windward condominium that had been rented, at the time of Mark Berquist's second visit, by a young Costa Rican woman who had since disappeared, skipped out on the weekly rent. When the owner returned he found the steamer trunks, which he moved into the hallway to be opened and discarded. The trunks sat in the breezeway for ten or twelve days before the janitor got around to opening them. According to the police report on the incident the contents of the two trunks included twenty Galil semiautomatic assault rifles, two AK-47s, seventeen silencers, three walkie-talkies, three bags of ammunition, assorted explosives and detonators and electronic devices, four bulletproof vests, and two sets of scales. According to the embassy report on the incident the presence of the scales argued for a drug connection and rendered the incident not of immediate concern. The embassy report further concluded that the absent Costa Rican tenant was not an asset of any U.S. agency known to the embassy.

That the tenant (no longer absent, since her body had been subsequently found in a ravine off the Smugglers' Cove highway) was not an asset of any U.S. agency known to the embassy was one thing Treat Morrison doubted.

A few days after the business with the steamer trunks (but before the young woman's body turned up) there had been the incident outside the Intercon, within minutes of Alex Brokaw's scheduled speech at a chamber of commerce lunch in the Intercon ballroom. There had been a small crowd, a demonstration of sorts, having to do with the question of who was responsible for the precipitous loss of the tourist business. It was the contention of the demonstrators that the United States was responsible for the precipitous loss of the tourist business. It was the contention of the embassy, and this was the point to which Alex Brokaw had intended to address his remarks, that the loss of the tourist business would be more than compensated for by the economic benefits that would accrue not only to this island but to the entire Caribbean basin were the United States Congress to approve military aid to the Nicaraguan freedom fighters for fiscal year 1985.

Economic benefits that were even now accruing.

In anticipation.

In recognition of the fact that there was already, let us be perfectly up front on this point, a presence.

A covert presence, true.

But only in anticipation of overt.

This was the subtext of the message that Alex Brokaw, alone in the back seat of his reinforced car, had been attempting to condense to an index card as his driver inched through the demonstrators outside the Intercon toward the police barricade set up at the entrance. The actual text of the message he was committing to the index card was this: *Just ask your friends the merchants of Panama what the United States Southern Command has meant to them.*

"Actually a fairly feeble demo," the driver reported having heard Alex Brokaw say at the exact instant it began to happen, first the quick burst of semiautomatic fire, then, as the police closed in, the dull pops of the tear gas canisters.

"Nothing like a little tear gas to clear out the sinuses," is what Alex Brokaw recalled saying.

According to the police report on the incident, inquiries focused on two Hondurans registered until that morning at the airport Days Inn. According to the embassy report on the incident, the two missing Hondurans could not be located for questioning but were not assets of any U.S. agency known to the embassy.

That the two missing Hondurans were not assets of any U.S. agency known to the embassy was a second thing Treat Morrison doubted.

The third thing Treat Morrison doubted was more amorphous, and had to do with the "previously reliable source" who had in late June reported the existence of a plot to assassinate Alex Brokaw. There was from the outset something about this report that had struck many people in Washington and Miami as overly convenient, beginning with the fact that it coincided with the workup sessions on legislation providing military aid to the Nicaraguan freedom fighters for fiscal year 1985. The same people in Washington and Miami tended to dismiss these recent incidents as equally convenient, further support for the theory that Alex Brokaw, in an effort to lay the foundation for a full-scale overt buildup on the island, had himself put the assassination report into play and was now lending credibility to the report with further suggestions of American personnel under siege.

"Clouding his own pond" was what Alex Brokaw was said to be doing.

The consensus that Alex Brokaw was clouding his own pond had by late July reached critical mass, as had the colliding metaphors: the way in which Alex Brokaw was said to be clouding his own pond was by "playing the Reichstag card."

The problem with clouding your own pond by playing the Reichstag card was that you would have to be fairly dense to try it, since otherwise you would know that everybody would immediately assume you were clouding your own pond by playing the Reichstag card.

That Alex Brokaw was sufficiently dense to so cloud his own pond was the third thing Treat Morrison doubted, and to locate the point at which these doubts intersected would have been part of his agenda. The other part of his agenda would have had to do with the unexpected visit he received, the evening before leaving Washington, from the senior foreign policy aide to the senator whose visit to the area had raised the original questions.

"T.M., I'll only be on your screen for fifteen minutes," Mark Berquist had said when he materialized, pink-cheeked and wearing a seersucker suit, in Treat Morrison's office after the secretaries had left. The air-conditioning was off and the windows were open and Mark Berquist's shirt had appeared to be constricting his throat. "It might be wise if we got some air."

"Mr. Berquist," Treat Morrison had said. "Why not sit down."

A barely perceptible pause. "Actually I'd prefer we took a walk," Mark Berquist had said meaningfully, his eyes scanning the bookshelves as if a listening device might reveal itself disguised as a copy of *Foreign Affairs.*

"I wouldn't presume to take up your time."

There had been a silence.

Treat Morrison had looked at his desk clock.

"You've wasted two minutes, which leaves you thirteen," Treat Morrison said.

There had been another silence, then Mark Berquist took

off his seersucker jacket and arranged it on the back of a chair. When he finally sat down he avoided looking directly at Treat Morrison.

"Let me give you a little personal background," Mark Berquist said then.

He said that he had been on the Hill for five years, ever since graduating from Villanova. At Villanova, he said, it so happened that he had been fortunate enough to know the sons of several prominent Cuban exiles, and the sons as well of two ambassadors to Washington from that general area, namely Argentina and El Salvador. It had been these friendships, he said, that ultimately led to his commitment to do his humble best to level the playing field for democracy in the area.

Treat Morrison turned his desk clock to face Mark Berquist.

"Seven," he said.

"You're aware that we have an interest there." Mark Berquist was finally meeting Treat Morrison's eyes. "A kind of situation."

"I'd get to it fast if I were you."

"It may be a situation you're not going to want to get into."

Treat Morrison at first said nothing.

"Goddamn," he said then. "I have actually never heard anyone say something like that." In fact this was not true. Treat Morrison had been hearing people say things like that his entire adult life, but none of these people had been twenty-seven-year-old staff aides on the Hill. "Call me naive, but I would have thought you'd have to be an actor to say something like that."

Treat Morrison had leaned back and clasped his hands behind his head. "Ever given any thought to doing some acting, Mr. Berquist? Going on the boards? Smell of the greasepaint, roar of the crowd?"

Mark Berquist said nothing as he stood up.

"Not all that different from politics," Treat Morrison said. He was now studying the ceiling, squinting slightly at the overhead light. "If you stop to analyze it. I assume you saw certain people down there."

Mark Berquist yanked his seersucker jacket off the back of the chair, biting off each word evenly. "It's an old boys' town here, and you're one of the old boys, so feel free to take any shot you want. I am just telling you that this is a puzzle with a lot of pieces you may not want to put together."

"One of the people I'm assuming you saw was Bob Weir."

"That's a fishing expedition," Mark Berquist said. "And I'm not biting."

Treat Morrison said nothing.

Bob Weir was the "previously reliable source" who had in late June reported the existence of the plot to assassinate Alex Brokaw.

"And just let me add one thing," Mark Berquist said. "You would be making a serious error in judgment if you were to try to crucify Bob Weir."

Treat Morrison had watched in silence as Mark Berquist jabbed his arms into the seersucker jacket in an attempt to find the sleeves.

"By the way," Treat Morrison said then. "For future reference. I'm not an old boy."

4

ACTUALLY I had met Bob Weir.

I had come across him two years before, in 1982, in San Salvador, where he was running not a restaurant but a discotheque, a dispirited place called Chez Roberto, eight tables and a sound system in a strip mall in the San Benito district. Within hours of arriving in San Salvador I had begun hearing the name Bob Weir mentioned, always guardedly: it seemed that he was an American with what was called an interesting history, an apparent gift for being in interesting places at interesting times. He happened for example to have been managing an export firm in Guatemala at the time Jacobo Arbenz was overthrown. He happened to have been managing a second export firm, in Managua, at the time the Somoza regime was overthrown. In San Salvador he was said to be particularly close to a distinctly bad actor named Colonel Álvaro García Steiner, who had received special training from the Argentinian military in domestic counterterrorism, at that time a local specialty.

In the absence of anything more constructive to do I stopped by Chez Roberto on several different evenings, hoping to talk to its proprietor. There were the usual armored Cherokee Chiefs in the parking area and the usual Salvadoran businessmen inside (I never saw anyone dancing at Chez Roberto, nor in fact did I ever see a woman) but on each of these evenings Bob Weir was said to be "out of the city" or engaged in "other business" or simply "not seeing anyone at the present time."

It was some days after my last visit to Chez Roberto when a man I did not know sat down across from me in the coffee shop at the Sheraton. He was carrying one of the small zippered leather purses that in San Salvador at that time suggested the presence of a 9mm Browning, and he was also carrying a sheaf of recent American newspapers, which he folded open on the table and began to scan, grease pencil in hand.

I continued eating my shrimp cocktail.

"I see we have the usual agitprop from your colleagues," he said, grease-penciling a story datelined San Salvador in the Miami *Herald*.

Some time passed.

I finished the shrimp cocktail and signaled for a check.

According to the clock over the cashier's desk the man had now been reading the newspapers at my table for eleven minutes.

"Maybe I misunderstood the situation," he said as I signed the check. "I was under the impression you'd been looking for Bob Weir."

I asked if he were Bob Weir.

"I could be," he said.

This pointlessly sinister encounter ended, as many such encounters in San Salvador at that time ended, inconclusively. Bob Weir said that he would be more than happy to talk to me about the country, specifically about its citizens, who were entrepreneurial to the core and wanted no part of any authoritarian imposition of order. Bob Weir also said that he would be more than happy to introduce me to some of these entrepreneurial citizens, but unfortunately the ones I mentioned, most specifically Colonel Álvaro García Steiner, were out of the city or engaged in other business or simply not seeing anyone at the present time.

Many people who ran into Bob Weir of course assumed that he was CIA.

I had no particular reason to doubt this, but neither did I have any particular reason to believe it.

All I knew for certain about Bob Weir was that when I looked at his face I did not see his face.

I saw a forensic photograph of his face.

I saw his throat cut ear to ear.

I mentioned this to a few people and we all agreed: whatever Bob Weir was playing, he was in over his head. Bob Weir was an expendable. That Bob Weir was still alive and doing business two years later, not just doing business but doing it in yet another interesting place at yet another interesting time, not just doing it in this interesting place at this interesting time but doing it as a "previously reliable source," remains evidence of how little any of us understood.

5

When Treat Morrison told me later about his unexpected visit from Mark Berquist he said that he had been a little distracted.

Otherwise, he said, he would have handled it differently.

Wouldn't have let the kid get under his skin.

Would have focused in on what the kid was actually saying.

Underneath the derring-do.

Underneath the kid talking like he was goddamn General Lansdale.

He had been a little distracted, he said, ever since Diane died.

Diane Morrison, 52, wife of, after a short illness.

Diane, he said, had been one of God's bright and beautiful creatures, and at some point during the month or two before she died he had begun having trouble focusing in, trouble concentrating.

Then of course she did die.

He had finally straightened out the shifts with the nurses and just like that, she died.

And after that of course there was certain obligatory stuff.

The usual obligatory financial and social stuff, you know what I mean.

Then nothing.

The nurses weren't there and neither was she.

And one night he came home and he didn't want dinner and he didn't want to go to bed and he just kept having another drink until it was near enough to dawn to swim a few laps and go to the office.

Hell of a bad night, obviously.

And when he got to the office that morning, he said, he realized he'd been on overload too long, it was time to get away for a few days, he'd even considered going to Rome by himself but he didn't see how he could spare the time, and the end result was that he spent about eleven months running on empty.

Eleven months being a little distracted.

As far as this visit from Mark Berquist went, in the first place the kid had caught him working late, trying to clear his desk so he could get the early flight down there, it was imperative that he get the early flight because Alex Brokaw was delaying his own weekly flight to San José in order to brief him in the secure room at the airport, so this had been a situation in which he was maybe even more distracted than usual.

You can certainly see that, he added.

I was not sure that I could.

He had not been so distracted that he neglected to enter into his office log, since the secretaries who normally kept his schedule were gone, the details of the meeting in his own painstaking hand:

> *Date: Monday August 13, 1984.*
> *Place: 2201 C Street, N.W.*
> *Time: In 7:10 P.M./out 7:27 P.M.*
> *Present: T.A.M. / Mark Berquist*
> *Subject: Unscheduled visit, B. Weir, other topics.*

"That was just clerical," Treat Morrison said when I mentioned the log entry. "That wasn't concentrating, that was just reflex, that was me covering my ass like the clerks do, if you spent any time in Washington you'd know this, you do your goddamn log on autopilot."

He was cracking the knuckles of his right hand, a tic.

"As far as I was concerned," he said, "this was just another kid from the Hill with wacko ideas that any sane person had to know wouldn't get to first base outside the goddamn District of Columbia."

He fell silent.

"Christ," he said then. "I should have taken the three or four days and gone to Rome."

Again he fell silent.

I tried to picture Treat Morrison in Rome.

In the single image that came to mind he was walking by himself on the Veneto, early evening, everybody sitting out in front of the Excelsior as if it were still 1954, everybody except Treat Morrison.

Shoulders slightly hunched, gaze straight ahead.

Walking past the Excelsior as if he had someplace to go.

"Because the point is," he said, then stopped. When he again spoke his voice was reasonable but he was again cracking the knuckles of his right hand. "The point is, if I'd gone to Rome, this meeting never had to happen. Because I would have been back on my game before this dipshit kid ever got south of Dulles."

It was he who kept circling back to this meeting with Mark Berquist, worrying it, chipping at it, trying to accommodate his failure to fully appreciate that the central piece in the puzzle he might not want to put together had been right there in his office.

Mark Berquist.

Which went to the question, as Treat Morrison would elliptically put it in the four hundred and seventy-six pages he committed to the Bancroft Library, of whether policy should be based on what was said or believed or wished for by people sitting in climate-controlled rooms in Washington or New York or whether policy should be based on what was seen and reported by the people who were actually on the ground. He had been, he kept repeating, a little distracted.

Had he not been a little distracted, he would have put it together immediately that the report of the plot to assassinate Alex Brokaw had not originated, as Alex Brokaw believed it had, with the previously reliable source who passed it to the embassy. Nor had it originated, as most people in Washington believed it had, with Alex Brokaw.

The report of the plot to assassinate Alex Brokaw had of course originated in Washington.

With Mark Berquist.

Who had passed it to the previously reliable source.

Bob Weir.

Treat Morrison had been that close to it and he had blown it.

He had not been concentrating.

Had he been concentrating, everything else would have fallen into place.

I mean Christ, he said. This isn't rocket science. This is textbook stuff. A, B, C. One two three.

If you put an assassination plot into play you follow it with an assassination attempt. If you stage an assassination attempt you put somebody out front.

A front, an assassin.

A front with a suitable background.

A front who can be silenced in the assassination attempt.

The assassination attempt which would or would not fail, depending on exactly how unauthorized the fringe elements turn out to be.

A, B, C. One two three.

Night follows day.

Not rocket science.

Had he been concentrating he would have added it up. Or so he was still telling himself.

The very last time we spoke.

6

THE RHYTHM common to plots dictates a lull, a period of suspension, a time of lying in wait, a certain number of hours or days or weeks so commonplace as to suggest that the thing might not play out, the ball might not drop. In fact the weeks between the day Elena McMahon learned that her father was dead and the day Treat Morrison arrived on the island seemed on the surface so commonplace that only a certain rigidity in her schedule might have suggested that Elena McMahon was waiting for anything at all. At exactly six-thirty, on each of the mornings before she left the Intercon, she turned on the television set in her room and watched the weather on CNN International: showers over Romania, a front over Chile, the United States reduced to a system of thunderstorms, the marine layer shallowing out over southern California, the world beyond this island turning not slowly but at an inexorable meteorological clip, an overview she found soothing.

The shallowing out of the marine layer over southern California meant that stratus over Malibu would burn off by noon.

Catherine could lie in the sun today.

At no later than ten minutes past seven on each of those mornings she put on a pair of shorts and a T-shirt and began to walk. She walked five miles, seven miles, ten, however long it took to fill two hours exactly. At no later than ten minutes past nine she had two cups of coffee and one papaya, no more. She spent the two hours between ten and noon downtown, not exactly shopping but allowing herself to be seen, establishing her presence. Her routine did not vary: at the revolving rack outside the big Rexall she would pause each day to inspect the unchanging selection of postcards. Three blocks further she would stop at the harbor, sit on the low wall above the docks and watch the loading or unloading of one or another inter-island freighter. After the Rexall and the harbor she inspected the bookstore, the pastry shop, the posters outside the municipal office. Her favorite poster showed a red circle and diagonal slash superimposed on an anopheles mosquito, but no legend to explain how the ban was to be effected.

The afternoons were at first more problematic. For a couple of days she tried sitting out by the Intercon pool, but something about the empty chaises and the unbroken summer overcast, as well as about the occasional appearance of one or another of the Americans who now seemed billeted at the Intercon in force, had made her uneasy. On the third day, in a secondhand bookstore near the medical school, she found an Italian grammar and a used textbook called *General Medicine and Infectious Diseases*, and after that spent allotted hours of each afternoon teaching herself Italian (from two to four) and (between five and seven) the principles of diagnosis and treatment.

After she moved from the Intercon to the windward side of the island she had her job, such as it was: assistant manager at the Surfrider. By the time she was hired there was already not much left to do, but at least she had a desk to arrange, a domain to survey, certain invented duties. There were the menus to be made, the flowers to be arranged. There was the daily run to the airport, in one of the Surfrider's three battered jeeps, to pick up the papers and mail and drop packages for shipment. On the windward side she had not the Intercon pool with its empty chaises but the sea itself, the oppressive low roar of the surf breaking on the reef and the abrupt stillness at ebb and full tide and the relief of the wind that came up toward dawn, banging the shutters and blowing the curtains and drying the sheets that were by then drenched with sweat.

On the windward side she also had, once the last backpacker moved on, the available and entirely undemanding companionship of the Surfrider manager, an American named Paul Schuster who had first come to the islands as a Pan American steward and had metamorphosed into a raconteur of the tropics with a ready trove of stories about people he had known (he would not say who but she would recognize the names if he told her) and curiosities he had encountered (she would not believe the readiness with which inhibition got shed under the palm trees) and places he had operated on islands up and down the Caribbean.

There had been the guesthouse on Martinique, the discotheque in Gustavia. Great spots but not his kind of spot. His kind of spot had been the ultra-exclusive all-male guesthouse on St. Lucia, total luxe, ten perfect jewel-box suites, only the crème de la crème there, he would not say who but major operators on Wall Street, the hottest-of-the-hot motion picture agents and executives, *pas de* hustlers. His kind of spot had also been Haiti, but he got scared out of Haiti when dead chickens began showing up on the gate of the place he had there, the first and for all he cared to know the only first-rate gay bathhouse in Port-au-Prince.

He might not be the smartest nelly on the block but hey, when he saw a dead chicken he knew what it meant and when he saw a hint he knew how to take it.

Pas de poulet.

Pas de voodoo.

Pas de Port-au-Prince.

Paul Schuster made frequent reference to his own and other people's homosexuality, but during the time Elena had been at the Surfrider there had been what might have seemed in retrospect a slightly off-key absence of evidence of this, no special friend, no boys who came or went, in fact no one who came or went or stayed, only the two of them, alone at meals and in the evening hours when they sat out by the drained pool and burned citronella sticks against the mosquitoes. Until the night before Treat Morrison arrived, Paul Schuster had been unflaggingly convivial, in a curiously dated style, as if he had washed up down here in the vicinity of 1952 and remained uncontaminated by the intervening decades.

"Happy hour," he would cry, materializing with a pitcher of rum punch on a porch where she was reading *General Medicine and Infectious Diseases.* "Chug-a-lug. Party time."

She would reluctantly mark her place and set aside *General Medicine and Infectious Diseases.*

Paul Schuster would again describe the scheme he had to redecorate and remarket the Surfrider as an ultra-luxe spa for European businessmen.

Top guys. Heavy hitters. Men of a certain class who may not be able to find full relaxation in Düsseldorf or wherever.

She would again say that she was not at all certain that the mood on the island at this very moment exactly lent itself to remarketing the Surfrider.

He would again ignore this.

"Here I go again," he would say. "Spilling my ideas like seed." This was a simile that never failed to please him. "Spilling my seed out where anybody in the world can lap it up. But hey, ideas are like buses, anybody can take one."

The one evening Paul Schuster was not unflaggingly convivial was that of August 13, which happened also to be the one evening he had invited a guest to dinner.

"By the way, I told Evelina we'll be three tonight," he had said when she came back from her morning trip to the airport. Evelina was the one remaining member of the kitchen staff, a dour woman who more or less stayed on because she and her grandchildren lived rent-free in a cottage behind the laundry. "I have a chum coming by, somebody you should know."

She had asked who.

"Kind of a famous restaurateur here," Paul Schuster had said.

When she came downstairs not long after seven Elena could see Paul Schuster and an older man sitting outside by the empty pool, but because the two seemed locked in intense conversation she picked up a magazine on the screened porch, where Evelina was already setting the table.

"Stop hiding in there." Paul Schuster's voice was imperious. "I want you to meet our guest."

As she walked outside the older man had half risen, the barest gesture, then sunk back into his chair, a rather ghostly apparition in espadrilles and unpressed khaki pants and a black silk shirt buttoned up to the neck.

"*Enchanté*," he had murmured, in a gravelly but clearly American accent. "Bob Weir."

"I'm frankly surprised you haven't run into Bob before," Paul Schuster said, a slight edge in his voice. "Bob makes it his business to run into everybody. That's how he could turn up here one morning and by dinner he's the best-known American on the island." Paul Schuster snapped his fingers. "He was at it before he even cleared customs. Running into people. Wouldn't you say that was the secret of your success, Bob?"

"Make your point, don't do it the hard way," Bob Weir said.

In the silence that followed, Elena had heard herself asking Bob Weir how long he had been here.

He had considered this. "A while now," he said finally.

There was another silence.

She was about to ask him about his restaurant when he suddenly spoke. "I believe I saw you at the airport this morning," he said.

She said that she was at the airport every morning.

"That's good," Bob Weir said.

This enigmatic pronouncement hung in the air between them.

She noticed that Paul Schuster was leaning slightly forward, tensed, transfixed.

"I don't know that it's *good* exactly," she said finally, trying for a little silvery laugh, a Westlake Mom tone. "It's just part of my job."

"It's good," Bob Weir said. "Because you can take Paul with you tomorrow. Paul has something to do at the airport tomorrow morning."

"Oh no I don't," Paul Schuster said. It seemed to Elena that he had physically recoiled. "Uh uh. I don't go to the airport."

"At ten." Bob Weir addressed this to Elena as if Paul Schuster had not spoken. "Paul needs to be there at ten."

"I do *not* need to be there at ten," Paul Schuster said.

"We can be there whenever you want," Elena said, conciliatory.

"Paul needs to be there at ten," Bob Weir repeated.

"Let me just lay one or two home truths on the table," Paul Schuster said to Bob Weir. "*Paul* doesn't need to be there at all. *She'll* be there if and when I tell her to be there. And believe me, there's still a big *if* in this situation, and the big *if* is *moi*." Paul Schuster snatched up the empty pitcher of rum punch. "And *if* she's there, you know who'll be there with her? Nobody. *Nul*. Period. Now let's just change the subject. We're out of punch. Get Evelina out here."

Elena stood up and started toward the porch.

"In my personal view you don't have as many home truths in your deck as you think you do," she heard Bob Weir say to Paul Schuster.

"What do I see on that porch," she heard Paul Schuster say, an accusation. "Do I see that Evelina has already set the table?"

Elena stopped. The hour at which dinner was served, meaning the hour at which Evelina would be free to go back to the cottage with her grandchildren, had become during the preceding week a minor irritation to Paul Schuster, but he had not before made an issue of it. It occurred to her that she could be witnessing some form of homosexual panic, that Bob Weir might know something that Paul Schuster did not want him to know.

"Evelina," he called. "Get out here."

Evelina had appeared, her face impassive.

"I sincerely hope you're not planning to foist dinner on us before eight-thirty exactly."

Evelina had stood there.

"And if you're about to tell me as usual the fish will dry out by eight-thirty," Paul Schuster said, "then let me cut this short. *Don't bring it out at all. Forget the fish. Pas de poisson.*"

Evelina's eyes flickered from Paul Schuster to Elena.

"Don't look to *her*," Paul Schuster said. "She just works here. She's just one of the help. Same as you used to be." Paul Schuster picked up the empty pitcher and handed it to Evelina. "If you would be good enough to refill this pitcher," he said as he started inside, "I'll call into town for the truck."

Evelina was halfway into the kitchen before she asked why the truck.

"Because I want you and your bastard brats out of here tonight," Paul Schuster said, and let the door bang behind him.

Elena closed her eyes and tried to breathe deeply enough to relax the knot in her stomach. She could hear Paul Schuster inside, singing snatches from *Carousel.* In a locked rattan cabinet in his office he kept original-cast recordings of a number of Broadway musicals, worn LPs in mildewed sleeves, so scratched by now that he rarely played them but frequently sang them, particularly the lesser-known transitions, doing all the parts.

He's dead, Nettie, what am I going to do, she heard him ask, soprano.

He seemed to be in the vicinity of his office.

Why, you're going to stay here with me, she heard him answer himself, alto. *Main thing is to keep on living, keep on caring what's going to happen.*

He seemed now to be in the kitchen.

"Paul has a genuine theatrical flair," she heard Bob Weir say.

She said nothing.

"'*Neh-ver*, no *neh-ver*, walk *ah-lone*,'" Paul Schuster was singing as he returned. He was carrying a full pitcher of punch. "All's well that ends well. We *dine* at eight-thirty."

"Maybe I should have mentioned this before," Bob Weir said. "I didn't come by to eat."

Elena said nothing.

"I've lived down here long enough to know," Paul Schuster had said. "Sometimes you have to take a strong position. Isn't that so, Elise?"

Elena said that she supposed it was so.

Paul Schuster picked up the pitcher of punch and filled his glass.

Elena said no more for me thank you.

Paul Schuster wheeled to face Elena. "Who asked you," he said.

"You're driving the cattle right through the fence," Bob Weir said to Paul Schuster.

"I think you must be stupid," Paul Schuster had said to Elena. He was standing over her, holding the pitcher of punch. "Are you stupid? Just how stupid are you? Are you stupid enough to just sit there while I do this?"

She looked up at him just in time to get the full stream of punch in her eyes.

"And since you're the one drove the cattle through it," she heard Bob Weir say to Paul Schuster, "you better goddamn well mend it."

She had gotten up, the sticky punch still running down her hair and face, her eyes stinging from the citrus, and walked into the empty hotel and up the stairs. That was the night she stood in the rusted bathtub and let the shower run over her for a full ten minutes, the drought and the empty cistern and the well going dry notwithstanding. That was also the night she called Catherine at the house in Malibu and told her that she would try to be home before school started.

"Home where," Catherine had asked, wary.

There had been a silence.

"Home wherever you are," Elena had said finally.

After she hung up she pulled a chair to the window and sat in the dark, looking out at the sea. At one point she heard raised voices downstairs, and then the sound of cars backing out the gravel driveway.

More than one car.

Two cars.

Paul Schuster was still downstairs, she could hear him.

Which meant that someone other than Bob Weir must have come by.

She told herself that Paul Schuster had been drinking and would apologize in the morning, that whatever the business about the airport had been it was something between him and Bob Weir and whoever else had arrived after she came upstairs, nothing to do with her, but when she woke in the morning she played back in her mind the sound of the raised voices. She had been listening the night before for Bob Weir's voice and she had been listening the night before for Paul Schuster's voice but only when she woke in the morning was she able to separate out a third voice.

My understanding is that Dick McMahon will not be a problem.

Transit passenger, not our deal.

It was when she separated out the voice of the Salvadoran that she understood that she would need to find someplace else to stay.

Someplace where the airport would not be an issue.

Whatever the issue was.

Someplace where the Salvadoran would not appear.

Someplace where she would not have to see Paul Schuster.

Someplace where he could not find out who she was.

At the time later that morning when Treat Morrison walked into the Intercon coffee shop and saw Elena McMahon sitting alone at the round table set for eight there remained a number of things she did not understand.

The first thing Elena McMahon did not understand was that Paul Schuster already knew who she was.

Paul Schuster had known all along who she was.

She was Dick McMahon's daughter.

She was who they had to front the deal since they did not have Dick McMahon.

Paul Schuster had known this ever since Bob Weir told him to hire her.

Told him to hire her and send her to the airport every morning.

Send her to the airport every morning to establish a pattern.

A pattern that would coincide with Alex Brokaw's weekly trips to San José.

Until now, Paul Schuster had always done what Bob Weir told him to do. The reason Paul Schuster had always done what Bob Weir told him to do (until now) was that Bob Weir had knowledge of certain minor drug deals in which Paul Schuster had been involved. This knowledge on Bob Weir's part had seemed to Paul Schuster more significant than it might have seemed because one of the federal agencies with which Bob Weir had a connection was the Drug Enforcement Administration.

However.

This knowledge was not in the end sufficiently significant to ensure that Paul Schuster would have gone to the airport with Elena McMahon on that particular morning.

And believe me, there's still a big if *in this situation, and the big* if *is* moi.

Paul Schuster might not be the smartest nelly on the block, but when he saw a hint he knew how to take it.

Pas de airport.

What had been meant to happen at the airport that morning was something else Elena McMahon did not understand.

Treat Morrison understood more.

Treat Morrison understood for example that "Bob Weir" was the name used in this part of the world by a certain individual who, were he to reenter the United States, would face outstanding charges for exporting weapons in violation of five federal statutes. Treat Morrison also understood that this certain individual, whose actual name as entered in the charges against him was Max Epperson, could not in fact, for this and other reasons, reenter the United States.

What Treat Morrison understood was a good deal more than what Elena McMahon understood, but in the end Treat Morrison still did not understand enough. Treat Morrison did not for example understand that Max Epperson, also known as "Bob Weir," had in fact reentered the United States, and quite recently.

Max Epperson had reentered the United States by the process, actually not all that uncommon, known as "going in black," making prior covert arrangement to circumvent normal immigration procedures.

First in the early spring of 1984, and a second time in June of 1984, Max Epperson had reentered the United States without passing through immigration control, entering in the first instance via a military plane that landed at Homestead AFB and in the second via a commercial flight to Grand Cayman and a United States Coast Guard vessel into the Port of Miami. The first reentry had been for the express purpose of setting up a certain deal with a longtime partner. The second reentry had been for the express purpose of confirming this deal.

Making sure that this deal would go down on schedule and as planned.

Ensuring that the execution of the deal would leave no window for variation from its intention.

Impressing the urgency of this on Dick McMahon.

Max Epperson's longtime partner.

Max Epperson's old friend.

Who needs the goombahs, we got our own show right here.

Max Epperson's backup in uncounted deals, including the ones on which he faced charges.

Somebody had to talk reason to Epperson, Dick McMahon had said to Elena the first morning at Jackson Memorial. *Epperson could queer the whole deal, Epperson was off the reservation, didn't know the first thing about the business he was in.*

It will have occurred to you that Max Epperson, in order to so reenter the United States, in order to go in black, necessarily had the cooperation of a federal agency authorized to conduct clandestine operations. As far as Treat Morrison went, it would have gone without saying that Max Epperson could have had the cooperation of a federal agency authorized to conduct clandestine operations. Max Epperson would naturally have been transformed, at the time the federal weapons charges were brought against him, into a professional informant, an asset for hire. The transformation of Max Epperson into the professional known as "Bob Weir" would have been the purpose in bringing the charges in the first place. This was an equation Treat Morrison, distracted or not distracted, could have done in his sleep. What Treat Morrison had failed to figure was the extent to which his seeing Elena McMahon in the Intercon coffee shop would modify the equation.

She would still be the front, but Alex Brokaw would no longer be the target.

I'm not sure I know what business Epperson is in, she had said to her father that morning at Jackson Memorial.

Christ, what business are they all in, her father had said to her.

FIVE

I

WHEN I look back now on what happened I see mainly fragments, flashes, a momentary phantasmagoria in which everyone focused on some different aspect and nobody at all saw the whole.

I had been down there only two days when it happened.

Treat Morrison had not wanted me to come down at all.

I had told him before he left Washington that in order to write the piece I wanted to write it would be essential to see him in action, see him *in situ*, observe him inserting himself into a certain kind of situation. He had seemed at the time to concede the efficacy of such a visit, but any such concession had been, I realized quite soon, only in principle.

Only in the abstract.

Only until he got down there.

When I called to say that I was coming down he did not exactly put me off, but neither did he offer undue encouragement.

Actually it was turning out to be kind of a fluid situation, he said on the telephone.

Actually he wasn't certain how long he'd be there.

Actually if he was there at all, he was going to be pretty much tied up.

Actually we could talk a hell of a lot more productively in Washington.

I decided to break the impasse.

At that time I happened to own a few shares of Morrison Knudsen stock, and it had recently occurred to me, when I received an annual report mentioning Morrison Knudsen's role in a new landing facility under construction on the island, that this otherwise uninteresting island to which Treat Morrison had so abruptly decamped might be about to become a new Ilopango, a new Palmerola, a staging area for the next transformation of the war we were not fighting.

I looked at the clock, then asked Treat Morrison about the landing facility.

He was silent for exactly seven seconds, the length of time it took him to calculate that I would be more effectively managed if allowed to come down than left on my own reading annual reports.

But hell, he said then. It's your ticket, it's a free country, you do what you want.

What I did not know even after I got there was that the reason he had resisted my visit was in this instance not professional but personal. Because by seven o'clock on the evening of the day he arrived, although only certain people at the embassy knew it, Treat Morrison had managed to meet the woman he had seen eight hours before in the Intercon coffee shop. Two hours after that, he knew enough about her situation to place the call to Washington that got the DIA agent down in the morning.

That was the difference between him and the Harvard guys.

He listened.

2

I HAVE NO idea what was in her mind when she told him who she was.

Which she flat-out did. Volunteered it.

She was not Elise Meyer, she was Elena McMahon.

She told him that within less than a minute after she went upstairs to his room with him that evening.

Maybe she recognized him from around Washington, maybe she thought he might recognize her from around Washington, maybe she had been feral too long, alert in the wild too long.

Maybe she just looked at him and she trusted him.

Because believe me, Elena McMahon had no particular reason, at that particular moment, to tell a perfect stranger, a perfect stranger who had *for reasons she did not know* approached her in the lobby of the Intercon, what she had not told anyone else.

I mean she had no idea in the world that had she gone to the airport at ten that morning Alex Brokaw would have been dead that night.

Of course Alex Brokaw was at the airport at ten, because he had delayed his weekly flight to San José in order to brief Treat Morrison.

Of course Alex Brokaw was still alive that night, because Dick McMahon's daughter had not been at the airport.

Of course.

We now know that, but she did not.

I mean she knew nothing.

She did not know that the Salvadoran whose voice she had most recently heard the night before trying to mediate whatever the argument had been between Paul Schuster and Bob Weir was Bob Weir's old friend from San Salvador, Colonel Álvaro García Steiner.

Deal me out, Paul Schuster had kept saying. *Just deal me out.*

You have a problem, Bob Weir had kept saying.

There is no problem, the Salvadoran had kept saying.

She did not even know that Paul Schuster had died that morning in his office at the Surfrider. According to the local police, who as it happened were now receiving the same training in counterterrorism from Colonel Álvaro García Steiner that Colonel Álvaro García Steiner had received from the Argentinians, there was no evidence that anyone else had been present in the office in the hours immediately preceding or following the death. Toxicological studies suggested an overdose of secobarbital.

It was late that first day, when he came back to the Intercon from the embassy, that Treat Morrison again noticed the woman he had seen that morning in the coffee shop.

He had been picking up his messages at the reception desk, about to go upstairs.

She had seemed to be pleading with the clerk, trying to get a room.

Nothing for you, the clerk had kept repeating. One hundred and ten percent booked.

I found a place I can move into tomorrow, she had kept repeating. I just need tonight. I just need a closet. I just need a rollaway in an office.

One hundred and ten percent booked.

Of course Treat Morrison intervened.

Of course he told the clerk to double up on one of the USG bookings, let him free up a room for her.

He had more than one reason to free up a USG room for her.

He had every reason to free up a USG room for her.

He already knew that she had arrived on the island on July 2 on an apparently falsified American passport issued in the name Elise Meyer. He had already been briefed on the progress of the continuing FBI investigation meant to ascertain who Elise Meyer was and what she was doing there. It went without saying that he would tell the clerk to free up a room for her. Just as it went without saying that he would suggest a drink in the bar while the clerk worked out the logistics.

She had ordered a Coca-Cola.

He had ordered an Early Times and soda.

She thanked him for his intervention.

She said that she had been staying in a place on the windward side and had been looking all day for a new place, but could not move into the place she wanted until the following day.

So she would be gone tomorrow.

She could promise him that.

No problem, he said.

She said nothing.

In fact she said nothing more until the drinks arrived, had seemed to retreat into herself in a way that reminded him of Diane.

Diane when she was sick.

Not Diane before.

When the drinks arrived she peeled the paper wrapping off a straw and stuck the straw between the ice cubes and, without ever lifting the glass from the table, drained half the Coca-Cola.

He watched this and found himself with nothing to say.

She looked at him.

"My father used to order Early Times," she said.

He asked if her father was alive.

There had been a silence then.

"I need to talk to you alone," she had said finally.

I told you.

I have no idea.

Maybe she told him who she was because he ordered Early Times. Maybe she looked at him and saw the fog off the Farallons, maybe he looked at her and saw the hot desert twilight. Maybe they looked at each other and knew that nothing they could do would matter as much as the slightest tremor of the earth, the blind trembling of the Pacific in its bowl, the heavy snows closing the mountain passes, the rattlers in the dry grass, the sharks cruising the deep cold water through the Golden Gate.

The seal's wide spindrift gaze toward paradise.

Oh yes.

This is a romance after all.

One more romance.

3

I RECENTLY TRIED to talk to Mark Berquist about what happened down there.

I know Mark Berquist slightly, everybody now knows Mark Berquist.

Youngest member of the youngest class ever elected to the United States Senate. The class that hit the ground running, the class that arrived on the Hill lean mean and good to go. Author of *Constitutional Coercion: Whose Rights Come First?* Maker of waves, reliable antagonist on the Sunday shows, most frequently requested speaker on the twenty-five-thousand-dollar-plus-full-expenses circuit.

Where his remarks were invariably distorted out of context by the media.

So invariably, his administrative aide advised me, that the senator was understandably wary about returning calls from the media.

"Wait just one minute," he said when I finally managed to waylay him, in the corridor outside a hearing, at a moment when the television crews who normally functioned as his protective shield had been temporarily diverted by a rumor that the President's wife had just entered the rotunda with Robert Redford. "I only speak to media on background."

I said that background was all I wanted.

I said that I was trying to get as much perspective as possible on a certain incident that had occurred in 1984.

Mark Berquist's eyes flickered suspiciously. Nineteen eighty-four had ended for him with the conclusion of that year's legislative session, and was as distant now as the Continental Congress. To bring up 1984 implied that the past had consequences, which *in situ* was not seen as a useful approach. This unspoken suggestion of consequences was in fact sufficiently unthinkable as to drive Mark Berquist to mount a broad-based defense.

"If this has anything to do with the period of the financing of the 1984 reelection campaign you can just file and forget,"

Mark Berquist said. "Since, and let me assure you that this is perfectly well documented, I didn't even move over to the executive branch until after the second inaugural."

I said that the period of the financing of the 1984 reelection campaign was not specifically the period I had in mind.

The period I had in mind was more the period of the resupply to the Nicaraguan contra forces.

"In the first place any reference to the so-called contra forces would be totally inaccurate," Mark Berquist said. "In the second place any reference to the so-called resupply would be totally inaccurate."

I suggested that both "contra" and "resupply" had become in the intervening years pretty much accepted usage for the forces and events in question.

"I would be extremely interested in seeing any literature that used either term," Mark Berquist said.

I suggested that he could see such literature by having his staff call the Government Printing Office and ask for the February 1987 *Report of the President's Special Review Board*, the November 1987 *Report of the Congressional Committees Investigating the Iran-Contra Affair*, and the August 1993 *Final Report of the Independent Counsel for Iran/Contra Matters.*

There was a silence.

"These are matters about which there has already been quite enough misrepresentation and politicalization," Mark Berquist said then. "And to which I have no intention of contributing. However. Just let me say that anyone who uses the terms you used just betrays their ignorance, really. And to call it ignorance is putting the best face on it. Because it's something worse, really."

I asked what it really was.

"The cheapest kind of political bias. That's what the media never understood." He looked down the corridor as if for his missing press escort, then at his watch. "All right, one more shot. Your best question."

"On the record," I said, only reflexively, since whether it was on the record was of no real interest to me.

"Negative. No. You agreed to the ground rules. On background only."

The reason it was of no real interest to me whether this was on the record or on background was because Mark Berquist would never in his life tell me the one thing I wanted to know.

The one thing I wanted to know from Mark Berquist was not at what point the target had stopped being Alex Brokaw. I knew at what point the target had stopped being Alex Brokaw: the target had stopped being Alex Brokaw when Elena McMahon left the Surfrider, did not go to the airport, lost her potential proximity to Alex Brokaw. The one thing I wanted to know from Mark Berquist was at what point exactly *he had known* that the target had changed from Alex Brokaw to Treat Morrison.

I asked Mark Berquist this.

One shot, best question.

Mark Berquist's answer was this: "I can see you've bought hook, line and sinker into one of those sick conspiracy fantasies that, let me assure you, have been thoroughly and totally discredited and really, I mean time and time again. And again, calling this kind of smear job sick is putting the best face on it."

More colliding metaphors.

On background only.

4

IT PLAYED OUT, when the time came, very quickly. For the last nine of the ten days he had been on the island they had been meeting at the place she had found, an anonymous locally owned motel, not a chain, the chains were by then fully booked for USG personnel, a two-story structure near the airport so unremarkable that you could have driven to the airport a dozen times a day and never noticed it was there.

The Aero Sands Beach Resort.

The Aero Sands was on a low bluff between the highway and the beach, not really a beach but a tidal flat on which some fill had been thrown to protect the eroding bluff. The bluff ended where the highway curved down to the water just south of the Aero Sands, but on the bluff a hundred or so yards north of the Aero Sands there was a small shopping center, a grocery and a liquor store and a video rental place and outlets for sports supplies and auto parts, and it was in the parking lot of this shopping center that Treat Morrison would leave his car.

He had checked all this out.

He did not want his car seen in the Aero Sands parking lot, he did not want to be seen himself entering the exposed front door of her room.

He wanted to approach the Aero Sands from where he could assess it, have ample time to pick up on any official presence, anyone who might recognize him, anything out of the ordinary.

On the first of the nine days Treat Morrison came to the Aero Sands he brought the DIA agent, who took her statement and flew directly back to Washington, airport to Aero Sands to airport, no contact with the embassy.

On the following days Treat Morrison came to the Aero Sands alone.

At a few minutes before whatever time he told her he would be there she would leave open the sliding glass back door to her room and walk across the concrete pool area behind the motel. From a certain point just past the small pool it was possible to look north and get a partial view of the path on the bluff, and she always did, hoping he might be early, but he never was. She would nod at the woman who every evening pushed both an old man in a wheelchair and a baby in a stroller around the pool. Then she would continue on, down the dozen rickety wooden steps to what passed for the beach. There in the clear, there in the open space between the water and the bluff, Elena McMahon would wait in a place where Treat Morrison could see her as he approached.

As he had told her to do.

The point was that he believed he was protecting her.

He believed this right up to the instant, at seven-twenty on the evening of the tenth day he had been on the island, a day in fact on which he had made the final arrangement to take her back to the United States with him, take her in black via DIA and get the whole goddamn situation worked out in Washington, when it happened.

After it was over, after the flight to Miami during which he had been mostly incoherent and after the surgery and after the ICU, at some point when he was alone in a private room at Jackson Memorial, Treat Morrison remembered passing the man on the bluff as he walked from the shopping center to where he could already see her on the beach.

There had been nothing out of the ordinary about seeing the man on the bluff.

Nothing at all.

Nothing about the man on the bluff to signal an official presence, nothing to suggest someone who by recognizing him could place her beyond his protection.

Nothing.

He had already been able to see her on the beach.

She had been wearing the same white dress she was wearing in the Intercon coffee shop.

She had been looking out across the tidal flat.

She had been watching the bioluminescence on the water out by the reef.

The man on the bluff had been leaning over, tying his shoe, his face obscured.

There was a full moon but the man's face had been obscured.

That the man's face had been obscured was of course something that did not occur to Treat Morrison until after the fact, by which time the man on the bluff was beside the point, since it had been immediately and incontrovertibly established, according to both the FBI and the local police, who had coincidentally been staking out the Aero Sands all that week on an unrelated drug matter, that the man on the bluff, if indeed there had been a man on the bluff, was not the would-be assassin.

The reason this had been immediately and incontrovertibly established was that the local police who had been so fortuitously on hand had managed to kill the would-be assassin right there on the beach, her white dress red with blood before her clip was even emptied.

What bothered Treat Morrison most was not just the man on the bluff.

What bothered him more, what had begun to bother him even as the anesthesiologist was telling him to count backward from one hundred, what was bothering him so much by the time he was alone in the private room at Jackson Memorial that the doctor ordered sedation added to his IV line, was that over the preceding nine days he had checked out the Aero Sands at many different times of day and night, from every possible angle and with every possible eventuality in mind, and he did not recall having at any point during that week seen the local police.

Who had been so fortuitously on hand.

Suggesting that they had not been there at all.

Suggesting that if they had been there at all they had been there only at a certain moment, only at the moment they were needed.

A conclusion that could lead nowhere, since Elena McMahon was already dead.

I mean you could add it up but where does it get you.

This was Treat Morrison's last word on the subject.

I mean it's not going to bring her back.

5

AMERICAN IMPLICATED in attempted assassination was the headline on the first AP story as it ran in the Miami *Herald*, the only paper in which I initially had occasion to see it. I recall reading it in the elevator of the hospital where Treat Morrison had finally been stabilized for the flight to Miami. It was that morning's *Herald*, impossible to come by down there except at the embassy, abandoned in the waiting room by Alex Brokaw's DCM when the helicopter arrived to take Treat Morrison to the airport.

Colonel Álvaro García Steiner had also been in the waiting room, watching warily from a sagging sofa as the local police spokesman was interviewed by a San Juan television channel.

The paper was lying on a molded plastic chair and was folded open to this story.

As I picked it up I happened to look out the window behind Colonel Álvaro García Steiner and see the helicopter, just lifting off the lawn.

I walked to the elevator and got on it and started to read the story as the elevator descended.

The elevator had stopped to pick someone up on the third floor when I hit the name of the American implicated in the attempted assassination.

Academy Award night, two and a half years before.

Was the last time I saw her.

Said to have been using the name Elise Meyer.

Embassy sources confirmed however that her actual name was Elena McMahon.

Reports that the suspected assassin had been supplying arms and other aid to the Sandinista government in Nicaragua remain unconfirmed.

Until the next day, when Bob Weir happened to find himself in a position to provide the manifests that detailed the shipments that happened to coincide with weapons recently seized in a raid against a Sandinista arms cache.

Also fortuitously.

Since the manifests confirmed the reports that the suspected assassin had been supplying arms and other aid to the Sandinista government in Nicaragua.

The reports that had been further corroborated by the discovery of Sandinista literature in two adjoining rooms at the Surfrider Hotel recently vacated by the would-be assassin.

Immediately and incontrovertibly confirmed.

Immediately and incontrovertibly corroborated.

Which of course was the burden of the second AP story.

6

IMAGINE HOW this went down.

She would have come out of the Aero Sands.

At the certain point just past the pool where it was possible to get a partial view of the path on the bluff she would have glanced up.

She would not have seen Treat Morrison.

She would have passed the woman who pushed the old man in the wheelchair and the baby in the stroller and she would have nodded at the three of them and the baby would have turned to look at her and the old man would have touched his hat and she would have reached the last of the rickety wooden steps onto the beach before she realized that there had been a man on the bluff and that she had seen the man before.

She would have not even consciously registered seeing the man on the bluff, she would have registered only that she had seen him before.

The man on the bluff with the ponytail.

The man at the landing strip in Costa Rica.

I could be overdue a night or two in Josie.

Anyone asks, tell them you're waiting for Mr. Jones.

You're *doing nothing. What* I'm *doing doesn't concern you.*

She had not registered seeing him but something about seeing him had slowed motion just perceptibly, twenty-four frames a second now reduced to twenty. The baby had turned too slowly.

As in the hour before our death.

The old man in the wheelchair had lifted his hand to his hat too slowly.

As in the hour before our death.

She did not want to look back but finally she did.

When she heard the shots.

When she saw Treat Morrison fall.

When she saw the man on the bluff turn to her.

You get it one way or you get it another, nobody comes through free.

7

AFTER THE two AP stories the story stopped, dropped into a vacuum.

No mention.

Off the screen.

That the intended political consequences never materialized was evidence, in retrospect, that Treat Morrison had not entirely lost his game.

"I mean it was just all wrong," he said to me. "It would have been just plain bad for the country."

I suggested that he had not done it for the country.

I suggested that he had done it for her.

He did not look directly at me. "It was just all wrong," he repeated.

Only once, a year or so later, did Treat Morrison almost break down.

Almost broke down in such a predictable way that I did not even bother recording what he said in my notes. I remember him talking again about being distracted and I remember him talking again about not concentrating and I recall him talking again about that dipshit kid never getting south of Dulles.

Goddamn, he kept saying.

You think you have it covered and you find out you don't have it covered worth a goddamn.

Because believe me this was just one hell of a bad outcome.

The last outcome you would have wanted.

If you'd been me in this deal.

Which of course you weren't.

So you have no real way of understanding.

I mean you could add it up but where does it get you.

I mean it's not going to bring her back.

So Treat Morrison told me.

The very last time we spoke.

8

TREAT MORRISON died four years later, at age fifty-nine, a cerebral hemorrhage on a ferry from Larnaca to Beirut. When I heard this I remembered a piece by J. Anthony Lukas in the New York *Times* about a conference, sponsored by the John F. Kennedy School of Government at Harvard, at which eight members of the Kennedy administration gathered at an old resort hotel in the Florida Keys to reassess the 1962 Cuban missile crisis.

The hotel was pink.

There was a winter storm off the Caribbean.

Theodore Sorensen swam with the dolphins. Robert McNamara expressed surprise that CINCSAC had sent out the DEFCON 2 alert instructions uncoded, in the clear, so that the Soviets would pick them up. Meetings were scheduled to leave afternoon hours for tennis doubles. Douglas Dillon and his wife and George Ball and his wife and McNamara and Arthur Schlesinger ate together by candlelight in the main dining room. Communications were received from Maxwell Taylor and Dean Rusk, too ill to attend.

When I read this piece I imagined the storm continuing.

The power failing, the tennis balls long since dead, the candles blowing out at the table in the main dining room where Douglas Dillon and his wife and George Ball and his wife and Robert McNamara and Arthur Schlesinger are sitting (not eating, no dinner has arrived, no dinner will arrive), the pale linen curtains in the main dining room blowing out, the rain on the parquet floor, the isolation, the excitement, the tropical storm.

Imperfect memories.

Time yet for a hundred indecisions.

A hundred visions and revisions.

When Treat Morrison died it occurred to me that I would like to have seen just such a reassessment of what he might have called (did in fact call) certain actions taken in 1984 in the matter of what later became known as the lethal, as opposed to the humanitarian, resupply.

Imperfect memories of the certain incident that should not have occurred and could not have been predicted.

By any quantitative measurement.

I would like to have seen such a reassessment take place at the same hotel in the Keys, the same weather, the same mangroves clattering, the same dolphins and the same tennis doubles, the same possibilities. I would like to have seen them all gathered there, old men in the tropics, old men in lime-colored pants and polo shirts and golf hats, old men at a pink hotel in a storm.

Of course Treat Morrison would have been there.

And when he went upstairs and opened the door to his room Elena McMahon would have been there.

Sitting on the balcony in her nightgown.

Watching the storm on the water.

And if you are about to say that if Elena McMahon was upstairs in this pink hotel there would have been no reason for the conference, no incident, no subject, no reason at all: *Just file and forget.*

As Mark Berquist would say.

Because of course Elena would have been there.

I want those two to have been together all their lives.

23 January 1996

CHRONOLOGY

NOTE ON THE TEXTS

NOTES

INDEX

Chronology

1934–36 Born December 5, 1934, at Mercy General Hospital in Sacramento, California, the first of two children of Eduene Jerrett and Frank Reese Didion, who married on January 1. Mother, twenty-four, worked as an assistant city librarian. Father, twenty-six, is an insurance salesman, prone to drink and dread. He often drives to Nevada to shoot craps. The family shares a house on Highland Avenue in Sacramento with Didion's maternal grandparents. She is a fifth-generation Californian: her great-great-great-grandfather on her father's side, Matthew Kilgore, left Ohio for Sacramento in 1855, and on her mother's side her great-great-great-grandmother, Nancy Hardin Cornwall, came west from Arkansas in 1846.

1937–46 In November 1937, father joins the National Guard. Brother Jim is born in December 1939; the following year, the family moves into a home of their own at 2211 U Street. Mother gives her a Big Five tablet so she can "amuse [her]self"; she begins to visit the public library's Ella K. McClatchy branch. On December 7, 1941, Japanese bombers attack Pearl Harbor, in Hawaii, and the United States enters World War II. Father is sent by the Army Air Corps to Fort Lewis in Tacoma, Washington, then to Duke University in Durham, North Carolina, and finally to Peterson Field in Colorado Springs. The family travels to accompany him. In Colorado Springs, suffers her first migraine; she is eight years old. Learns from an issue of *Vogue* about the magazine's Prix de Paris essay contest for college seniors; her mother says she "could win when I got old enough." In late 1943, the family returns to Sacramento after father is reassigned to Detroit. Attends the Arden School in Sacramento.

1947–48 Reads Ernest Hemingway's *A Farewell to Arms* and retypes the first paragraph to get inside the language and see what makes it work. At her eighth-grade graduation in June 1948, delivers a speech on California heritage. "They who came to California," she declares, "were not the self-satisfied, happy and content people, but the adventurous, the restless, and the daring. They were different even from those who settled in other western states." Family moves to Walnut Avenue in Sacramento, and father buys land for development. That summer, on a family vacation, walks into the Pacific, wanting "to know what it would feel like"; back home, she is fascinated by Sacramento's river culture. In the fall, begins freshman year at C.K. McClatchy Senior High School.

1949–52 Becomes a member of the Mañana Society, a sorority sponsored by the Sacramento school district to promote civic and cultural values; her initiation takes place in the Governor's Mansion, where her friend Nina Warren's father, Earl—later chief justice of the United States Supreme Court—is in his second term as chief executive. An indifferent student, she enjoys acting, both in school productions and at a local repertory house. Reads *Moby-Dick* and *An American Tragedy*, and the work of Henry James. The family moves into a "big dark Victorian" three-bedroom house at 500 Hawthorn Street. In 1950, she learns to drive in an Army jeep her father has bought for her and takes friends to Lake Tahoe on weekend trips. Becomes a member of the Student Council and the Press Club and works on the school newspaper, *The Prospector*, and the yearbook. Takes an after-school job with the society page of *The Sacramento Union*. In April 1952, is rejected by Stanford University, her college of choice. Takes classes at Sacramento Junior College in the fall.

1953 Begins at the University of California at Berkeley in the spring, pledging Delta (Tri-Delt) and living in the sorority house on Warring Street. Among her sorority sisters is Barbara Brown, daughter of future California governor Edmund Gerald (Pat) Brown, Sr. Joins staff of student newspaper *The Daily Californian* her first semester. Coedits a special fashion edition with friend Peggy LaViolette; attempts to interview poet W. H. Auden for the paper but, as she later recalls, "was so absolutely terrified that I couldn't think of any questions." Father is sent to Letterman Army Hospital at the Presidio in San Francisco for observation and treatment of drinking and emotional withdrawal. Visits him on weekends with her mother; they have lunch and watch pickup baseball games.

1954 Leaving sorority life, moves into a house at 2520 Ridge Road, which she shares with three other undergraduate women. In the fall is admitted to Mark Schorer's sought-after creative writing workshop, for which she writes short stories. ("He gave me a sense of what writing was about, what it was for," she later remembers.)

1955 Takes a literature class with Schorer. Is selected by *Mademoiselle* magazine to participate in their summer guest editor program, becoming guest editor in fiction. (Prior participants include Sylvia Plath, who was managing guest editor in 1953.) Arrives in Manhattan in May, staying at the Barbizon Hotel for Women; others in her cohort include Gael Greene and Janet Burroway. On June 14, interviews Jean Stafford for the magazine. Returns to Sacramento by train in July, visiting Boston, Quebec, and Chicago en route. Takes a job for the rest of the summer at *The Sacramento Union*, composing wedding notices. Turns down offer to become society editor. In August, her Stafford piece comes out, her first publication in a national venue. Studies Henry James in a class taught by Henry Nash Smith, who praises her "truly remarkable abilities as a critic." Enters the Prix de Paris writing competition, administered by *Vogue*.

1956–58 Becomes editor of *The Occident*, the UC Berkeley student literary magazine, and publishes her first short story, "Sunset," there. Makes the second round of the Prix de Paris competition, and submits a profile of California residential architect William Wilson Wurster as her final contest entry; on May 15, 1956, is awarded first prize. Choosing a $1,000 cash prize over a two-week trip to Paris, she is also offered a job at *Vogue* in New York for $45 a week. Over the summer, travels from Sacramento to Berkeley each week to complete a Milton course required for graduation. In the fall, moves to New York, where she lives on East 79th Street. At first, writes only promotional copy, on a schedule that allows her to submit to other magazines. Rents a third-floor walkup at 1215 Park Avenue for $130 a month. Meets Noel Parmentel and becomes involved with him; he becomes her guide to literary New York. Learns concision from editor Allene Talmey, who edits her captions with a ruthless efficiency. Begins working on a novel, at first titled *Harvest Home* and then *In the Night Season*, which will eventually be published as *Run River*. In 1958, Parmentel introduces her to John Gregory Dunne, soon to be a writer at *Time*.

1959–62 In the summer of 1959, gives notice at *Vogue* to become college editor at *Mademoiselle*, but decides to stay after *Vogue* editor Jessica Daves offers a new job as feature associate, writing articles at a higher salary. On November 1, begins writing the "People Are Talking About" column, contributing unsigned pieces to the magazine. Continues to freelance for other publications, including *Mademoiselle*, and begins an association with the *National Review*, writing book and film reviews. In the evenings works on her novel, hanging its pages on her living room wall. Publishes her first signed piece in *Vogue* in June 1961, "Jealousy: Is It a Curable Illness?" Moves to 41 East 75th Street. Breaks up with Parmentel and becomes involved with Dunne. Submits pages of the novel as a partial manuscript; a dozen publishers turn it down. At Parmentel's instigation, submits to Ivan Obolensky, who offers an advance of $1,000 but insists she change the title to *Run River*. The money allows her to take a two-month leave from *Vogue* to complete the book. In June 1962, she flies to California; votes for Joe Shell over Richard M. Nixon in the Republican gubernatorial primary because Nixon is insufficiently conservative.

1963 *Run River* is published on April 26. Reviews are brief and mixed, and sales are disappointing. Dunne grows increasingly dissatisfied at *Time*, where, by order of top editors—who support United States military efforts—he has been told to sanitize reports from Vietnam. In the fall, he and Didion become engaged.

1964 Marries Dunne on January 30 at the mission church at San Juan Bautista. Back in New York, begins to write a film column for *Vogue*, but feels overwhelmed by the city. Her anxiety becomes debilitating; as she describes the episode in her 1967 essay "Goodbye to All That," it is hard to leave the house. In April, decides with Dunne to leave New York for Los Angeles on a temporary basis—six or seven months. In June, they rent the Hardin Gatehouse, a four-bedroom home on two acres at 5500 Palos Verdes Drive South, on the Palos Verdes Peninsula in Portuguese Bend. Rent is $500 a month. Aided by Dunne's brother Dominick, a producer, they meet with television executives hoping to write scripts, and sell a story idea to the anthology series *Chrysler Theatre* for $1,000. *Vogue* cancels her film column; she writes short stories, publishing "Coming Home" in *The Saturday Evening Post* on July 11. With Dunne, proposes a film treatment of his project *Show Me a Hero* to agents at William Morris; attends screenings and reads screenplays. Supports Barry Goldwater in the 1964 presidential election, won in a landslide by Lyndon Baines Johnson.

1965 Travels to Mexico for *The Saturday Evening Post*, where John Wayne is working on *The Sons of Katie Elder*. The resulting piece, "John Wayne: A Love Story," offers a template to which she will return, framing her reporting through a personal, even autobiographical, lens. On August 11, Marquette Frye, a twenty-one-year-old African American man, is stopped in the South Los Angeles community of Watts by California Highway Patrol officer Lee Minikus. An altercation ensues, triggering the Watts Riots, which cause 34 deaths and more than 1,000 injuries before they end on August 16. "For days," Didion will write in her 1967 essay "Los Angeles Notebook," "one could drive the Harbor Freeway and see the city on fire, just as we had always known it would be in the end."

1966 Meets Blake Watson, a physician at St. John's Hospital in Santa Monica, who facilitates the private adoption of a baby girl, born on March 3. Didion and Dunne name her Quintana Roo, after the Mexican state on the Yucatan Peninsula. They bring the child home on March 6, cancelling a planned trip to Saigon for *The Saturday Evening Post* after realizing that they cannot take a baby to a war. On May 1, they are evicted from their house in Portuguese Bend and take up temporary residence at 155 Fifth Anita Drive in West Los Angeles, home of Sara Mankiewicz, widow of screenwriter

Herman J. Mankiewicz. Six days later, Didion publishes her most ambitious piece of early journalism, "Some Dreamers of the Golden Dream"—originally titled "How Can I Tell Them There's Nothing Left?" —in *The Saturday Evening Post.* In June, Quintana is christened in Brentwood, at St. Martin of Tours Catholic Church. The couple meets Henry Robbins, an editor at Farrar, Straus & Giroux, who will be influential in both of their careers. Leaving Quintana with her grandparents in Sacramento, they travel to the Central Valley town of Delano to report on César Chávez and the National Farm Workers' strike against grape growers for *The Saturday Evening Post.* In August, they visit Hawaii, the subject of Didion's "Letter from Paradise, 21 19′ N., 157 52′ W." Back in Los Angeles, they move into a crumbling mansion at 7406 Franklin Avenue in Hollywood, at a rent of $400 a month.

1967 On January 14, the Human Be-In takes place at the Polo Fields in San Francisco's Golden Gate Park; more than 20,000 people come to hear Timothy Leary, Allen Ginsberg, Gary Snyder, and bands including the Grateful Dead, Jefferson Airplane, and Big Brother and the Holding Company. The event is widely regarded as introducing the hippie movement to the national consciousness. Didion meets Paul Hawken, a Haight-Ashbury insider who offers her access to the community. She travels to the Bay Area in the spring and summer, staying in Berkeley. On June 3, she publishes her first of more than twenty "Points West" columns in *The Saturday Evening Post*, alternating with Dunne. On July 12, she signs a two-book deal with Henry Robbins for a nonfiction book about "the LSD life in California" and a novel called *Maria Talking* (later published as *Play It As It Lays*). The contract stipulates an advance of $6,000 per title. "Slouching Towards Bethlehem," gathering her impressions of Haight-Ashbury life, appears as the *Post*'s cover story on September 23. Decides she can't expand the essay and instead begins to gather and revise pieces for a collection of her previously published nonfiction.

1968 In the spring, visits California First Lady Nancy Reagan in Sacramento for *The Saturday Evening Post*; the resulting story, "Pretty Nancy," is the first of many she will write about the Reagans. On April 4, the Reverend Martin Luther King, Jr., is shot and killed in Memphis, Tennessee. *Slouching Towards Bethlehem* is published on May 10; Dan Wakefield in *The New York Times*, among many laudatory reviewers, calls it "a rich display of some of the best prose written today in this country." *Time* sends Julian Wasser to photograph Didion; the ensuing sessions, which feature her smoking, with her Corvette Stingray, become the first iconic images of her. On June 5, Senator Robert F. Kennedy is shot in the kitchen of the Ambassador Hotel on Wilshire Boulevard after winning the California Democratic presidential primary; he dies the following day. Didion checks herself into the outpatient psychiatric clinic at St. John's Hospital for vertigo, nausea, and extreme alienation; this, she will later write in "The White Album," "does not now seem to me an inappropriate response to the summer of 1968." In August, Richard M. Nixon is nominated as the Republican candidate for president at the party's convention in Miami Beach. Three weeks later, amidst a police riot against student protesters in Chicago, Vice President Hubert H. Humphrey is nominated by the Democrats. In November, Nixon wins the presidency. Didion, Dunne, and Dunne's brother Dominick acquire the rights to James Mills's 1966 novel *The Panic in Needle Park*, with the couple attached as screenwriters. Didion is named one of the *Los Angeles Times*'s Women of the Year.

1969 Publishes "The Revolution Game," her final piece in *The Saturday Evening Post*, on January 25; the magazine suspends publication in February. On August 9, while swimming in her sister-in-law's Beverly Hills pool, learns of the killings of actress Sharon Tate, hairdresser Jay Sebring, and three others at Tate's Benedict Canyon home. "There were twenty dead, no, twelve, ten, eighteen," she will write of the rumors that swirled through the community. "Black masses were imagined, and bad trips blamed." The next night, supermarket executive Leno LaBianca and his wife Rosemary are murdered in their house at 3301 Waverly Drive. The killers, who won't be arrested until December, are members of the Manson Family, a loose tribe of outcasts, led by a charismatic ex-convict named Charles Manson, who have hung around the countercultural fringes of the entertainment industry since 1968. On November 14, finishes a draft of her second novel, *Play It As It Lays.* She is offered a column by *Life* magazine. Her first piece, written from Hawaii (where she has gone with her family) and later collected in *The White Album* under the title "In the Islands," causes a stir for its revelation that she and Dunne are "on this island in the middle of the Pacific in lieu of filing for divorce."

1970 In January, preproduction begins on *The Panic in Needle Park*, with Dominick Dunne producing and Jerry Schatzberg directing, starring Al Pacino and Kitty Winn. *Play It As It Lays* is published on July 27 to rapturous reviews. It furthers Didion's investigation into fragmentation and narrative breakdown, operating as a series of vignettes separated by white space, like cinematic jump cuts, to tell the story of Maria Wyeth, an actress recovering from a breakdown as she unravels in late 1960s Los Angeles. That summer, she meets Linda Kasabian, a participant in the Tate-LaBianca murders who has chosen to cooperate with prosecuting attorneys in return for a promise of immunity. The *Los Angeles Times* reports in August that Didion is writing a book about her, but the project rapidly unravels. Accompanied by Dunne, spends a month traveling in the South to research a piece for *Life.* Although the article is never finished, the notes will be published in 2017 as part of *South and West.* In October, filming of *The Panic in Needle Park* begins, after six weeks of rehearsal, in Manhattan; shooting wraps on December 22.

1971–72 In January 1971, *Play It As It Lays* is nominated for a National Book Award. Moves with Dunne to 33428 Pacific Coast Highway in Malibu; they hire Harrison Ford, then a carpenter and contractor, to handle renovations. In May, *The Panic in Needle Park* premieres at Cannes. Reviews are mixed, but Kitty Winn is named Best Actress of the Festival. The film cements Didion and Dunne's place at the center of the Hollywood intelligentsia. They are offered projects: a remake of *Tender Is the Night*, a sequel to *The Graduate.* They ultimately settle on an adaptation of *Play It As It Lays*, directed by Frank Perry and produced by Dominick Dunne. It comes out October 19, 1972, starring Tuesday Weld as Maria; she is nominated for a Golden Globe. Didion is diagnosed with multiple sclerosis, the cause of her temporary blindness years before.

1973 In the spring, Henry Robbins is made editor-in-chief of Farrar, Straus & Giroux and offers Didion a $60,000 advance for her next essay collection. Not long afterward, he has a heart attack; he leaves FSG to become executive editor at Simon & Schuster. Didion wants him to remain her editor, offering to return the first half of her advance. Meets Robert Silvers, editor of *The New York Review of Books*, and writes her first piece for him ("Hollywood: Having Fun," published on March 22). During the summer, with Dunne, attends the Cartagena Film Festival in Colombia. From Cartagena, they travel to Bogotá, then back to Los Angeles, stopping to refuel in Panama. The trip inspires her essay "In Bogotá" and her novel *A Book of Common Prayer*, the first of many works on the subject of Latin America and its relationship to the United States. In the fall, begins working with Dunne on *Rainbow Road*, a screenplay loosely adapting *A Star Is Born* (1937/1954) for the rock era; they spend three weeks on the road with rock bands, including Led Zeppelin and Uriah Heep. Dunne envisions James Taylor and Carly Simon in the leading roles.

1974 In May, receives a $210,000 combined advance for her next novel (*A Book of Common Prayer*) and essay collection (*The White Album*), Henry Robbins at Simon & Schuster outbidding others in an auction arranged by her agent, Lois Wallace. In August, with Dunne, submits the third and final draft of *Rainbow Road*, in which Barbra Streisand has taken an interest; they withdraw from the project, receiving $125,000 and 10 percent of future grosses. Other writers will later revise their screenplay, which is retitled *A Star Is Born*.

1975–76 Spends a month at UC Berkeley in the spring of 1975 as a Regents' Lecturer, teaching a class and working on *A Book of Common Prayer*. On April 20, while she is at Berkeley, Saigon falls to the Viet Cong and the People's Army of Vietnam. Three weeks later, delivers a talk titled "Why I Write" to a standing-room-only crowd: "I write entirely to find out what I'm thinking, what I'm looking at, what I see and what it means. What I want and what I fear." On September 18, heiress turned Symbionese Liberation Army revolutionary Patricia Hearst is arrested in San Francisco; *Rolling Stone* editor Jann Wenner asks Didion to cover her trial. After briefly attending the trial, however, she backs away from Hearst as subject, writing about her only in a 1982 essay, "Girl of the Golden West." (She will later publish fourteen pages of her *Rolling Stone* notes in *South and West.*) On December 8, 1976, *A Star Is Born* comes out, to lackluster reviews.

1977–78 *A Book of Common Prayer*—Didion's third novel, set in the fictional Latin American country of Boca Grande —is published on March 1, 1977. She takes eleven-year-old Quintana with her on a national book tour. Dunne publishes his novel *True Confessions*, which becomes a New York Times best seller. They visit London in November; the following July, they move from Malibu to 202 Chadbourne Avenue in Brentwood Park, the family's last address in Los Angeles. Three months later, the Agoura fire jumps the Pacific Coast Highway and burns to within 125 feet of their former Malibu property.

1979–80 Didion's second essay collection, *The White Album*, is published on June 19, 1979; it gathers and extends the nonfiction she has published since *Slouching Towards Bethlehem*, and is widely and glowingly reviewed. ("Essentially," Jerzy Kozinski writes in the *Los Angeles Times*, "*The White Album* is about our American mythologies, both private and collective, and realities both private and collective. Joan Didion is once again our quintessential essayist.") On July 31, Henry Robbins dies of a heart attack on a platform of the Union Square subway station in Manhattan. He is fifty-one years old. In an October *Nation* article titled "Joan Didion: Only Disconnect," Barbara Grizzuti Harrison questions Didion's increasingly high reputation and mocks her style, describing her as "neurasthenic Cher." In June 1980, reviews V. S. Naipaul's recent work in *The New York Review of Books*, whose editor, Robert Silvers, encourages her to write more overtly about politics.

1981–83 With Dunne, works on a screen adaptation of his novel *True Confessions.* Directed by Ulu Grosbard and starring Robert De Niro and Robert Duvall, the film premieres at the Venice Film Festival in September 1981 to considerable acclaim. On June 15, 1982, the couple travels to El Salvador, where they spend just under two weeks; in mid-July, she sends her first report on the trip to *The New York Review of Books.* On October 30, Dominick Dunne's daughter Dominique is strangled by her boyfriend. She dies on November 4. The same day, *The New York Review of Books* publishes the first of three installments of *Salvador.* It is released in book form in March 1983.

1984 *Democracy*, Didion's fourth novel, is published by Simon & Schuster on April 1. A metafiction of sorts, the novel is narrated by a character named Joan Didion, who seems to be reporting on the narrative rather than creating it. Writing in *The New York Times*, Mary McCarthy praises the book's "technical mastery and on-target social observation" but criticizes its "knowingness" and "depthlessness."

1985–86 In November 1985, reads from her work at Bennington College in Vermont, where Quintana is a sophomore, and speaks at a PEN writers' conference in New York. Spends time in Miami the following spring, researching her next book.

1987–88 Publishes *Miami*, her fourth book of nonfiction, on October 1, 1987. The book connects the politics of the 1960s with those of the 1980s—the Kennedy Assassination to the Iran-Contra scandal. Dunne learns he is "a candidate for a catastrophic cardiovascular event" and undergoes an angiogram and an angioplasty. He views this new lease on life as a chance to change things up and pushes for the couple to move to New York. In early 1988, they sell their house in Brentwood Park and buy an apartment at 30 East 71st Street in Manhattan. Didion begins to write the "Letter from Los Angeles" for *The New Yorker* and continues to write about politics for *The New York Review of Books.* (Many of these pieces will be collected in her third book of essays, *After Henry.*) During the summer of 1988, she covers the Jesse Jackson campaign and the Democratic Convention in Atlanta.

1989–91 On April 19, 1989, a twenty-eight-year-old woman named Trisha Meili is raped and beaten while jogging in Central Park, and five young men of color are arrested and charged. Didion's account, published in the January 17, 1991, issue of *The New York Review of Books* under the title "Sentimental Journeys," is a ruthless dissection of this constructed narrative. "It is precisely in this conflation of victim and city, this confusion of personal woe with public distress," she writes, "that the crime's 'story' would be found." On December 25, 1990, Dunne faints at Honolulu International Airport. Back in New York, he has open-heart surgery to insert a plastic valve. The couple continues to write scripts, beginning a project based on the life and death of anchorwoman Jessica Savitch. It will eventually be released as *Up Close & Personal*, with Robert Redford and Michelle Pfeiffer. In early 1991, tries to get out of her Simon & Schuster contract, but the company refuses to let her go. Later in the year, participates in a celebrity ad campaign for the Gap; is photographed by Annie Leibovitz with Quintana, wearing matching black turtlenecks. Donates her papers to the Bancroft Library at UC Berkeley.

1992–93 On May 1, 1992, third collection of essays, *After Henry*, is published. The title is an homage to Henry Robbins. The book gathers twelve pieces, including "Sentimental Journeys" and "Girl of the Golden West." Several pieces deal with presidential politics, signaling a new direction, one she will explore throughout the decade. Supports Jerry Brown for president, although she does not register to vote. In July, covers the Democratic National Convention at Madison Square Garden in New York. In December, Frank Reese Didion dies in Monterey at eighty-four. In March 1993, addresses the Charter Day ceremony at the University of California, Berkeley.

1994–98 In June 1994, O.J. Simpson is arrested for murdering his wife, Nicole, and Ronald Goldman after a slow-speed police chase. His trial, which extends into the following year, captivates the nation. Dunne covers it for *The New York Review of Books*. In March 1996, *Up Close & Personal* is released, the last script by Didion and Dunne to be produced. On August 27, Didion's fifth novel, *The Last Thing He Wanted*, is published. Registers to vote to support President Bill Clinton's reelection. In January 1997, Dominick Dunne's ex-wife Lenny dies at sixty-four. In 1998, reports on Clinton's impeachment for *The New York Review of Books*. In October, Quintana is contacted by her birth sister, and meets her biological family for the first time.

1999–2000 Contributes essays on religion in American political life to *The New York Review of Books*, and a profile of Martha Stewart to *The New Yorker*.

2001 On May 15, Eduene Jerrett Didion dies in California, two weeks before her ninety-first birthday. "The preceding afternoon," her daughter writes, "I had talked to her on the telephone from New York and she had hung up midsentence, a way of saying goodbye so characteristic of her . . . that it did not occur to me until morning, when my brother called, that in this one last instance she had been just too frail to keep the connection." On September 11, two hijacked airliners hit the World Trade Center towers in lower Manhattan, destroying them. Another strikes the Pentagon, and a fourth crashes in a field in Pennsylvania, after a passenger revolt. The same day, *Political Fictions*, Didion's fourth book of essays, is published. It collects her political writing from the previous decade and zeroes in on what has become a key theme: that public life is a matter of narrative rather than policy. This represents not just a degradation of the discourse but also another way that "we tell ourselves stories in order to live."

2002 On November 13, gives the Robert B. Silvers Lecture at the New York Public Library; published in *The New York Review of Books* the following January as "Fixed Opinions, or The Hinge of History" and in book form in May as *Fixed Ideas: America Since 9.11*, it argues that the Bush administration has used the events of 9/11 "to stake new ground in old domestic wars."

2003 In June, Dunne has a pacemaker installed, but his health continues to fail. On July 26, Quintana marries Gerry Michael, a Manhattan bartender, in a ceremony at New York's Cathedral of Saint John the Divine. On September 23, publishes *Where I Was From*, her long-anticipated California book, in which she takes apart the myths—the narratives—on which she was raised. "Actually," she will later tell an interviewer, "I started that book several years before my mother and father died. I was unable to get very far with it. Once my mother and father died, I immediately picked it up again after twenty years, and I realized that it had been impossible to write while my mother and father were alive because I didn't want to present a version of California that they would not recognize." On Christmas Day, Quintana is taken to Beth Israel North Hospital in Manhattan. She is admitted to the ICU and diagnosed with pneumonia in both lungs and septic shock. She is put in an induced coma. On December 30, after visiting her at the hospital, Dunne suffers a heart attack and dies. "*Life changes fast*," his wife will write. ". . . *Life changes in the instant. . . . You sit down to dinner and life as you know it ends.*" He is seventy-one.

2004 On January 22, Quintana is released from the hospital. Three days later, she is admitted to Columbia-Presbyterian Hospital in Manhattan with pulmonary embolisms. On March 23, a memorial service for Dunne is held at the Cathedral of Saint John the Divine. Speakers include his wife, daughter, and brother, as well as Calvin Trillin and Susanna Moore. On March 25, Quintana collapses at Los Angeles International Airport and undergoes emergency neurosurgery at UCLA Medical Center in Westwood. Didion flies to California, staying at the Beverly Wilshire Hotel. On April 30, Quintana is transferred to the Rusk Institute at New York University Hospital. She remains there until July. In October, Didion begins to write *The Year of Magical Thinking*, a memoir of her season of grief. She finishes the manuscript at the end of the year.

2005 Writes on "The Case of Teresa Schiavo" for *The New York Review of Books* of June 9. On August 26, Quintana dies of acute pancreatitis at New York–Presbyterian/Weill Cornell Medical Center. On October 11, *The Year of Magical Thinking* is published, and, despite her loss, Didion embarks on a national tour. Following *Where I Was From*, the book cements a new role for her as memoirist, excavating personal narratives as well as public ones. It sells more than 200,000 copies in hardcover, the biggest numbers of her career. In

October, producer Scott Rudin approaches her about developing the memoir as a play. On November 16, *The Year of Magical Thinking* receives the National Book Award for nonfiction.

2006–7 In January, Didion agrees to the stage adaptation of *The Year of Magical Thinking*, and meets with Rudin and director David Hare. In the spring, Vanessa Redgrave agrees to portray Didion. In the fall, writes a lengthy takedown of Dick Cheney; it appears as the cover story of *The New York Review of Books* on October 5. On March 29, 2007, *The Year of Magical Thinking* premieres at the Booth Theatre on Broadway for a limited run of 144 performances. The play—a one-woman show—diverges from, and expands upon, the book by engaging with Quintana in more detail, functioning as a bridge between the memoir and *Blue Nights.* In an interview, Didion calls the process one of "maintaining movement. And also maintaining a version of things that I could live with. That was very strong with the play. Because as I said in *Blue Nights*, watching that play on 45th Street at night was one moment during the day when Quintana did not necessarily die." In November, she is honored for Distinguished Service to American Letters at the National Book Awards.

2008–10 Reads from her work at Dartmouth College in October 2008 and meets with students. The next year, on August 26, Dominick Dunne dies of bladder cancer at the age of eighty-three.

2011 In the spring, receives an honorary Doctor of Letters from Yale University. On November 4, her memoir *Blue Nights* is published; the book addresses her own aging, as well as her daughter's life and death. "I hadn't dealt with Quintana," she will tell an interviewer. "I had dealt with her to some extent in the play, but the play had, from my point of view, a whole other way of preserving myself, at a distance. Yet, part of the point is that you never work it out."

2012–16 Cancels a planned trip to California after fracturing a kneecap, but is able to travel to Hartford on June 28, 2012, to speak at the Mark Twain House and Museum. On July 3, 2013, is awarded the National Humanities Medal at the White House, by President Barack

Obama. In January 2015 appears in an advertising campaign for the designer Céline, wearing a black pullover and oversized dark glasses.

2017 On March 7, publishes *South and West*, a book of nonfiction gathering material from two early, unfinished pieces: her journey through the South in 1970 and her notes on Patty Hearst for *Rolling Stone*. The book occasions a number of wide-ranging career retrospectives. On October 11, Netflix releases the documentary *Joan Didion: The Center Will Not Hold*, directed by her nephew, Griffin Dunne, the son of Dominick and Lenny.

2018–19 An adaptation of her novel *The Last Thing He Wanted* begins filming in June 2018. Directed by Dee Rees and starring Anne Hathaway and Ben Affleck, it is scheduled for release the following fall.

Note on the Texts

This volume contains all of Joan Didion's books of the 1980s and 1990s: her novels *Democracy* (1984) and *The Last Thing He Wanted* (1996), and her nonfiction collections *Salvador* (1983), *Miami* (1987), and *After Henry* (1992). All of these works have appeared in numerous printings and editions since their initial publication, both in the United States and elsewhere, but Didion has not sought to correct or revise them, and the texts included here have been taken from first printings.

Salvador. Didion flew to El Salvador on June 15, 1982, accompanied by her husband, John Gregory Dunne, and by Christopher Dickey, Central American bureau chief for *The Washington Post.* The idea that she should write about that country's civil war came from Robert Silvers, editor of *The New York Review of Books.* Returning to the United States on June 28, she immediately began to expand her notes, and by mid-July she had sent an initial draft of the book to Dickey, for his suggestions.

Salvador was first published in three installments ("In El Salvador," "In El Salvador: Soluciones," and "El Salvador: Illusions") in *The New York Review of Books*, on November 4, November 18, and December 2, 1982. It was then published by Simon & Schuster in New York, on March 1, 1983. Several new printings and editions of *Salvador* have appeared since, in New York, Toronto, and London, and in 2006 the book was included in *We Tell Ourselves Stories in Order to Live: Collected Nonfiction*, published in the Everyman's Library series, but Didion is not known to have revised her work on any of these occasions. The text of *Salvador* in the present volume is that of the 1983 Simon & Schuster first printing.

Democracy. Didion referred to her fourth novel, *Democracy*, by the title *Angel Visits* in her early notes, now at the Bancroft Library at Berkeley. She understood the phrase to mean "a pleasant interlude of short duration" in "nineteenth-century usage" and intended the novel to be "a study in provincial manners," but over the course of numerous drafts and approximately four years of writing and revision, both her plans and her title changed.

The first edition of the novel, published by Simon & Schuster on April 2, 1984, was followed in the same year by a Canadian printing

(Toronto: Lester & Orpen Dennys) and newly typeset U.S. paperback and British editions, the former from Pocket Books in New York and the latter from Pavanne in London. Several further editions and printings have appeared in subsequent years, but Didion is not known to have revised her work. The text of *Democracy* in the present volume is that of the 1984 Simon & Schuster first printing.

Miami. As in the case of *Salvador*, Didion's *Miami* was first published in *The New York Review of Books*; its four installments ("Miami," "Miami: 'La Lucha'," "Miami: Exiles," and "Washington in Miami") appeared on May 28, June 11, June 25, and July 16, 1987. Simon & Schuster published *Miami* on September 16, 1987. None of the many subsequent printings and editions of the book is known to have been altered by the author. The text of *Miami* presented in this volume is that of the 1987 Simon & Schuster first printing.

After Henry. First published by Simon & Schuster on April 14, 1992, *After Henry* gathered items that Didion had originally written for magazines, the earliest in 1979 and the most recent in 1991. A part of one essay, "Pacific Distances," had appeared in 1978 in a keepsake volume published by the Friends of the Bancroft Library at Berkeley, *Telling Stories*, as part of the title piece "Telling Stories." In most cases, Didion expanded, revised, and/or retitled her magazine contributions. In the case of "Pacific Distances," she combined and then added to three previously published pieces.

The following is a list of the magazine items from which *After Henry* was assembled:

After Henry. *New West*, September 10, 1979 (as "A Death in the Family").

In the Realm of the Fisher King. *The New York Review of Books*, December 21, 1989 (as "Life at Court").

Inside Baseball. *The New York Review of Books*, October 27, 1988.

Shooters Inc. *The New York Review of Books*, December 22, 1988 (as "'Shooters, Inc.'").

Girl of the Golden West. *The New York Review of Books*, March 18, 1982 (as "Sentimental Education").

Pacific Distances. *The New Yorker*, September 4, 1989 (as "Letter from Los Angeles"); *New West*, November 5, 1979 (as "Nuclear Blue").

Los Angeles Days. *The New Yorker*, September 5, 1988 (as "Letter from Los Angeles").

Down at City Hall. *The New Yorker*, April 24, 1989 (as "Letter from Los Angeles").

L.A. *Noir. The New Yorker*, September 4, 1989 (as "Letter from Los Angeles").

Fire Season. *The New Yorker*. September 4, 1989 (as "Letter from Los Angeles").

Times Mirror Square. *The New Yorker*, February 26, 1990 (as "Letter from Los Angeles").

Sentimental Journeys. *The New York Review of Books*, January 17, 1991 (as "New York: Sentimental Journeys").

After Henry has been reprinted on several occasions without textual alteration since its first publication, and some of its contents appear in other Didion collections, including *Political Fictions* (New York: Alfred A. Knopf, 2001) and *We Tell Ourselves Stories in Order to Live* (New York: Everyman's Library, 2006). The text of *After Henry* in the present volume is that of the 1992 Simon & Schuster first printing.

The Last Thing He Wanted. In a later interview, Didion explained that she had aimed to build "a very, very tight plot" in *The Last Thing He Wanted*; at the end, "everything would fall into place" without her designs having been apparent to the reader. In order to achieve this effect, and "to keep the plot in mind," she wrote the novel quickly and intently, finishing it in "about three months."

Alfred A. Knopf published *The Last Thing He Wanted* on August 16, 1996. None of the multiple subsequent printings and editions of the novel is known to reflect her involvement. The text presented here is that of the 1996 Knopf first printing.

This volume presents the texts of the original printings chosen for inclusion here, but it does not attempt to reproduce features of their design and layout. The texts are presented without change, except for the correction of typographical errors. Spelling, punctuation, and capitalization are often expressive features and they are not altered, even when inconsistent or irregular. The following is a list of errors corrected, cited by page and line number: 8.24, faced; 19.18, even immature"; 176.16, paradisical; 260.36, condominum; 280.30, Eight; 425.23, "We're; 473.8–29, fraction; 591.23, Yusuf; 595.17, Yusuf.

Notes

In the notes below, the reference numbers denote page and line of this volume (the line count includes chapter headings but not blank lines). For further information about Didion's life and works, and references to other studies, see Tracy Daugherty, *The Last Love Song: A Biography of Joan Didion* (New York: St. Martin's Press, 2015); Sharon Felton, ed., *The Critical Response to Joan Didion* (Westport, Conn.: Greenwood Publishing, 1993); Ellen G. Friedman, ed., *Joan Didion: Essays & Conversations* (Princeton, NJ: Ontario Review Press, 1984); Mark Royden Winchell, *Joan Didion* (Boston: Twayne, 1980).

SALVADOR

3.2–4 *Robert Silvers . . . Christopher Dickey*] Silvers (1929–2017) edited *The New York Review of Books* from 1963 until his death; Dickey (1951–2020), the author of *With the Contras: A Reporter in the Wilds of Nicaragua* (1986), among other books, was Central American bureau chief for *The Washington Post* in 1982 and accompanied Didion and her husband during their travels in El Salvador.

7.6 the Molina and Romero regimes] Arturo Armando Molina (b. 1927) served as president of El Salvador from July 1972 to July 1977; he was succeeded by Carlos Humberto Romero (1924–2017), who led the country until October 1979, when he was deposed in a military coup.

7.8 *Costa del Sol*] A famous tourist region in southern Spain.

14.5–6 *desaparecidos*] Individuals forcibly "disappeared" and presumably murdered.

14.23 Duarte government's] José Napoleón Duarte (1925–1990) served as El Salvador's president from June 1984 to June 1989.

18.28 Bailey bridges] Portable, prefabricated bridges developed during the Second World War.

18.28–29 Elliott Abrams] Abrams (b. 1948) served as U.S. assistant secretary of state for human rights and humanitarian affairs from 1981 to 1985, and as assistant secretary of state for inter-American affairs from 1985 to 1989.

22.12 *campesinos*] Peasant farmers.

22.38 Halazone tablets] Used to disinfect untreated drinking water.

23.29–30 *noche obscura*] Dark night: a reference to the "dark night of the soul" described in an untitled late sixteenth-century poem and subsequent treatise (the *Declaración*) by Spanish mystic St. John of the Cross (1542–1591).

26.28 TVA] The Tennessee Valley Authority.

28.17 *cuartel*] Barracks.

29.10 Escuela Militar] El Salvador's principal military academy, founded in the mid-nineteenth century and located in San Salvador.

32.28–29 *Apocalypse Now . . . Bananas*] A 1979 war film directed by Francis Ford Coppola, and a 1971 comedy directed by Woody Allen set in the fictional banana republic of San Marcos.

43.33 *minifundismo . . . latifundismo*] Smallholdings of small farms in support of the Latin American system of large landed estates.

45.25 Bohemian Club] A private San Francisco men's club, established in 1872.

45.31 Chris Evert Lloyd] American tennis champion, born in 1954.

47.12–13 the Majano coup] Colonel Adolfo Arnoldo Majano (b. 1938) and other military officers led a coup against President Carlos Romero (1924–2017) on October 15, 1979, with the support of the United States.

49.2 *mestizos*] People of mixed European and Native American ancestry.

49.28 San Juan Bautista] Saint John the Baptist.

52.28 *Guernica*] A large and widely acclaimed oil on canvas by Pablo Picasso (1881–1973), painted in response to the 1937 bombing of the Basque town of Guernica by German and Italian fascist forces during the Spanish Civil War.

53.28–29 *Pudd'nhead Wilson . . . Wild Palms*] Works by Mark Twain (Samuel Clemens, 1835–1910), Ambrose Bierce (1842–c. 1914), and William Faulkner (1897–1962).

53.33 *The Old Patagonian Express.*] A 1979 travel narrative.

54.26 White Warriors Union] The Union de Guerreros Blancos (UGB), an alliance of rightist "death squads" formed in 1977 and responsible for anti-Jesuit violence.

56.14 A-37Bs] Attack aircraft produced by Cessna beginning in 1967.

57.27 Benning] Military cadets and others from El Salvador often trained at the School of the Americas at Fort Benning, Georgia, during the 1970s and 1980s.

66.30 SENATOR ZORINSKY] Edward Zorinsky (1928–1987), a Nebraska Democrat who served as chairman of the Senate Subcommittee on Western Hemisphere Affairs.

67.23 Operation Pineapple] Also known as Operation Piña, a plot that led to the assassination of Archbishop Óscar Romero in San Salvador on March 24, 1980; its details were discovered in a confiscated diary in May, and suggested the involvement of ARENA party leader Roberto D'Aubuisson (1943–1992) in the crime, for which no one was ultimately prosecuted.

69.24 CD plates] Vehicle registration plates indicating diplomatic status, "CD" an abbreviation for "Corps Diplomatique."

DEMOCRACY

77.16 Schofield] Schofield Barracks, a U.S. Army installation on the Hawaiian island of Oahu. Opened in 1908, it is home to the 25th Infantry Division.

77.24 Swiss Family Robinson] *The Swiss Family Robinson*, an 1812 novel by Johann David Wyss (1743–1818), about a family shipwrecked in the East Indies.

77.30 Johnston] Also known as Johnston Atoll or Kalami Atoll, an uninhabited U.S. territory in the North Pacific that from 1934 to 2004 was under the control of the U.S. military. A series of nuclear tests took place there from April to August 1958.

79.32 Tan Son Nhut] International airport located in Saigon, South Vietnam (now Ho Chi Minh City).

80.6 *Welbeck Street.*] A street in London's West End.

80.7 Trollope] Anthony Trollope (1815–1882), a British author and civil servant who wrote forty-seven novels and many other books evoking the social and domestic life of Victorian England.

80.9–16 these lines . . . foreign song.] See Wallace Stevens's "Of Mere Being," first published in his *Opus Posthumous* (1957).

81.18 Tropical Belt Coal Company] A fictional company, established by Europeans in Indonesia, in the 1915 novel *Victory* by Joseph Conrad (1857–1924).

82.11 Tristan da Cunha] A small volcanic island and British Overseas Territory in the South Atlantic, inhabited by fewer than three hundred people.

82.37 Outrigger Canoe Club] Private club in Honolulu, founded in 1908 on Waikiki Beach, on the present-day site of the Royal Hawaiian Hotel.

83.2 *Lurline*] One of four ocean liners built by the Mason Line for travel between San Francisco and Honolulu. The ship made its first voyage in 1932.

84.13 Kaneohe] Kaneohe Yacht Club, founded in 1924 on Kaneohe Bay, on the windward side of the Hawaiian island of Oahu.

84.13 Nuannu] Central valley of the Hawaiian island of Oahu, stretching from Honolulu Harbor to Nu'uanu Pali, an area of the Ko'olau mountains with a panoramic view of the island's windward coast.

85.38 Patou] Jean Patou (1887–1936), French fashion designer and perfumer.

87.20 *Aloha oe*] Hawaiian phrase meaning "farewell to thee," and title of the 1878 popular song written by the Hawaiian princess Lili'uokalani (1838–1917), who would be the last monarch of the Hawaiian Islands, before being overthrown on January 17, 1893.

87.24 Pacific Club] Exclusive club in downtown Honolulu, founded in 1851.

87.37 Long Binh and Cam Ranh Bay] Locations of American military bases during the Vietnam War. Long Binh, located northeast of Saigon, was the largest U.S. Army installation in the country, with as many as 60,000 personnel. It was attacked by the Viet Cong in 1967, and again in 1969 during the Tet Offensive. Cam Ranh Bay, a deepwater bay on the South China Sea, was used by various branches of the American military, including the Army, Navy, and Air Force. It was a key port of entry for American military personnel in Vietnam, and the site of the Army's 6th Convalescent Center.

87.39 the Royal in Rabat] Golf club in Rabat, the capital city of Morocco. Its course was designed by English American golf club architect Robert Trent Jones (1906–2000).

88.12 Punahou School] Private college preparatory school in Honolulu, Hawaii, founded in 1841.

88.31 Alexander Young Hotel] Hotel opened in 1903 in Honolulu by Alexander Young (1833–1910), designed by George W. Percy (1847–1900); the building was demolished in 1981.

89.19 John Huston] An American film director and actor, Huston (1906–1987) is most widely remembered for *The Maltese Falcon* (1941), *The Treasure of the Sierra Madre* (1948), *The African Queen* (1951), and *Under the Volcano* (1984).

91.22–23 Chubby Checker] Checker's version of "The Twist," recorded in 1960, became a number-one hit, setting off a national dance craze; he was born Ernest Evans in 1941.

93.5–6 Dong Kingman] Dong Kingman (1911–2000) was a Chinese American painter and watercolorist.

93.12 Clipper Clubs] Members-only airport lounges operated by Pan American World Airways before it sold off many of its international routes and declared bankruptcy in 1991.

94.22 FN-FALs] Battle rifles first offered for sale in 1953 by the Belgian arms manufacturer FN Herstal; the initials "FAL" stand for "fusil automatique léger," or "light automatic rifle." They fire 7.62-millimeter cartridges and have been used by both national militaries and insurgent forces around the world.

94.27–28 Phantoms] Manufactured by McDonnell-Douglas, the F-4 Phantom II is a long-range two-seat fighter-bomber introduced in 1961, and subsequently a staple of the arsenals of the U.S. Marine Corps, Navy, and Air Force. It was widely used by American forces throughout the Vietnam War.

96.13 Garuda] The flagship airline of Indonesia.

99.24 Da Nang] Fifth largest city in Vietnam and the location during the Vietnam War of the Da Nang Air Base, the busiest air base in the world. On August 13, 1972, the base was the site of the final American ground combat operations of the war. The city fell to North Vietnamese forces in 1975.

99.34–35 The Mamas and the Papas . . . Dream of Me] 1931 American pop song, with music by Fabian Andre (1910–1960) and Wilbur Schwandt (1904–1998) and lyrics by Gus Kahn (1886–1941). The Mamas & the Papas recording was featured on the group's 1968 album *The Papas & the Mamas*, with lead vocals by Cass Elliot (1941–1974).

100.12 Arvin] Nickname for the Army of the Republic of Vietnam (ARVN), the South Vietnamese military force from 1955 to 1975.

102.17 the Dalton School] Private college preparatory school on the Upper East Side of Manhattan, founded in 1919.

103.1 Canton jars] Hand-painted ceramic jars from Canton, China.

104.25 Gridiron Dinner] Annual dinner of the Gridiron Club and Foundation, a journalistic organization founded in Washington, D.C., in 1885. In the years since it opened, every U.S. president with the exception of Grover Cleveland has spoken at the dinner, which has the tradition of being archly satirical in tone.

107.8 Parke-Bernet] American auction house on the Upper East Side of Manhattan, founded in 1937.

109.24–25 Pré Catelan] A three-star gourmet restaurant in the Bois de Boulogne, Paris, established in 1856.

111.7 Minnesota Multiphasic Personality Inventory] Standardized test of adult personality and pathology, developed in 1943 by Starke R. Hathaway (1903–1984) and J. C. McKinley (1891–1950) of the University of Minnesota.

115.2 Mineo's murder] Salvatore Mineo (1939–1976), an American actor, was stabbed and killed in the carport of his West Hollywood apartment building on February 12, 1976, after returning home from a rehearsal. Police treated the case as having "homosexual motivation." In 1979, Lionel Ray Williams was convicted of the killing; he did not know Mineo.

118.14 Henry Adams] Adams (1838–1918) was among the most prominent American writers of the late nineteenth and early twentieth centuries, author of the novel *Democracy* (1880) and the autobiography *The Education of Henry Adams*, published posthumously in 1918.

119.2–9 Apologies . . . we burned.] Didion quotes from "Loveliest of trees . . . ," a section of *A Shropshire Lad* (1896) by A. E Housman (1859–1936), "New Hampshire" by T. S. Eliot (1888–1965), first published in 1934, and "Calmly We Walk through This April's Day" by Delmore Schwartz (1913–1966), collected in *Summer Knowledge: New and Selected Poems, 1938–1958* (1959).

119.37 the DAO] The Defense Attaché Office, a division of the United States Department of Defense that existed from 1973 to 1975 to administer U.S. military responsibilities following the 1973 cease-fire in Vietnam.

127.21 Aramco] Nickname for the Saudi Arabian Oil Company, founded in 1933.

131.27 Wahiawa] Community in Honolulu County, Hawaii, that is home to Schofield Barracks, as well as other military installations.

133.25 Luchow's] Landmark lower Manhattan restaurant, opened in 1882 by August Luchow (1856–1923); it remained in operation until 1984.

133.26 Mabel Mercer] Mercer (1900–1984) was an influential British cabaret singer who spent much of her career in New York.

133.33 *suprêmes de volaille à l'estragon*] Chicken Supreme with tarragon sauce.

134.20 CODEL] Abbreviation for a congressional delegation traveling overseas.

135.26 Bahasa Indonesian] Standardized version of Indonesian, adapted from Malay after Indonesia was granted independence in 1949, by nationalists seeking a language that would unify the country's diverse constituencies.

138.22 Surabaya] The second largest city in Indonesia, with a population of three million, and the capital of East Java province.

138.24 *Straits Times*] English-language daily newspaper published in Singapore since 1845.

138.26 Solo] Colloquial name for the city of Surakarta on the Indonesian island of Java.

140.11 Puncak] A mountain pass and popular resort area on the Indonesian island of Java.

140.13 Bogor] City in Indonesia's West Java province, nicknamed the "Rain City." It has a population of more than a million people.

145.33 Kahala District] Exclusive neighborhood in Honolulu, Hawaii, known for its beachfront real estate.

151.20 the 442nd] The 442nd Infantry Regiment, which during World War II was made up of second-generation Japanese American, or Nisei, soldiers. The regiment was established in 1943 and fought mostly in Europe. It was deactivated in 1946.

151.23 D.S.C.] The Distinguished Service Cross is the U.S. Army's second-highest military honor, awarded for extraordinary heroism.

151.26 Arno Line] German military defense line in northern Italy, beginning at the Arno River and extending through Florence and Pisa to the Adriatic. The line was overrun by Allied troops during the Battle of the Arno Line in July and August 1944.

152.4 merc] Shorthand slang for "mercenary."

158.19 *kapu*] Traditional Hawaiian code of conduct, involving a system of social obligations and taboos. It was dismantled in 1819 by King Liholiho at the urging of his stepmother, Queen Ka'ahumanu. The word is used in this context to mean something that is off-limits, out of bounds.

167.34–35 "The Darktown Strutter's Ball"] Song written in 1917 by Shelton Brooks (1886–1975), now considered a standard. It has been performed and recorded by artists including Bing Crosby (1903–1977), Alberta Hunter (1895–1984), Fats Waller (1904–1943), and Chick Webb (1905–1939).

176.33–39 *I should worry . . . millionaire.*] American jump rope chant.

178.33 Lunalilo Freeway] Located on the island of Oahu, the Lunalilo Freeway (also known as Interstate H-1, or the Queen Liliʻuokalani Freeway) is the oldest and most heavily trafficked freeway in Hawaii. It extends for twenty-seven miles, from Daniel K. Inouye International Airport through downtown Honolulu.

183.31 G-2] The Grumman Gulfstream II aircraft is a twin-engine business jet introduced in 1966. It has a seating capacity of nineteen and a range of four thousand miles.

186.11 citron pressé] Also known as French lemonade, a beverage made of lemon juice, sugar, and chilled water, served separately and mixed to taste in the glass.

194.27 Cholon] Neighborhood in Saigon (now Ho Chi Minh City) on the west bank of the Saigon River, that is considered to be the largest Chinatown in the world.

197.38 Air America] American airline established in 1946 and run covertly by the CIA from 1950 to 1976; it provided supplies and support for undercover operations during the Vietnam War.

198.38 Iguassú Falls] A set of waterfalls on the Iguassu River, on the border between Argentina and Brazil. They are the largest waterfalls in the world.

199.27 Dalat] Vietnamese city that is the capital of Lâm Đồng province. The city is nearly a mile above sea level and has a population of approximately 425,000.

200.1 Kolekole Pass] Hiking trail in the Wai'anae Mountains of Oahu. It is located on the grounds of the Schofield Barracks.

208.6 Tiger Ops] Operations conducted by so-called Tiger teams, a group of experts and consultants who test the vulnerability of an organization's assets and security.

208.10 AID] The Agency for International Development, an independent U.S. aid agency that gives development assistance for civilian projects around the world.

208.11 USIA] The United States Information Agency, created within the State Department in 1953 to "understand, inform and influence foreign publics in promotion of the national interest, and to broaden the dialogue between Americans and U.S. institutions, and their counterparts abroad." The agency existed until 1999.

209.20–21 the Cercle Sportif] Le Cercle Sportif Saigonnais, an athletic club founded in 1902 that during the 1950s and 1960s became a central hub of influence for the Vietnamese and foreign elite in Saigon.

211.30 Pleiku] City in the central highlands of Vietnam and capital of Gia Lai province. It has a population of approximately 458,000.

216.8 Nakhon Phanom] Nakhon Phanom Royal Thai Navy Base is a military airfield that was used during the Vietnam War by the U.S. Air Force to fly covert missions into Vietnam and Laos.

220.2 Chasen's] Restaurant in West Hollywood, California, opened in 1936, famous for its chili and its celebrity clientele. Regular customers, including Frank Sinatra (1915–1998), Alfred Hitchcock (1899–1980), and Ronald Reagan (1911–2004), had booths named in their honor. The restaurant closed in 1995.

223.35 "Golden Triangle"] A mountainous region surrounding the point at which the borders of Thailand, Myanmar, and Laos converge, known for opium production and trafficking.

224.20 Livermore . . . Brookhaven] The Lawrence Livermore National Laboratory in northern California was founded in 1952 by Ernest O. Lawrence and Edward Teller. It is part of the Department of Energy's Nuclear National Security Administration. The Los Alamos National Laboratory, outside Santa Fe, New Mexico, was established in 1942, and was home to the Manhattan Project, which led to the development of the first atomic bombs. Brookhaven National Laboratory was created in 1947 on Long Island, New York, to specialize in nuclear physics and national security.

228.3 Kwajalein] An island in the Republic of the Marshall Islands, designated as an American "trust territory" in 1944. Since then, the island has been under the control of the U.S. military, and was a command center for Operation Crossroads, which coordinated the U.S. nuclear tests at Bikini Atoll in 1946.

229.14 Clark] U.S. Air Force base on the Philippine island of Luzon, a major staging area for American forces during the Vietnam War; it was transferred to Philippine control in 1991.

MIAMI

241.33 Arthur M. Schlesinger, Jr.] Historian (1917–2007) who served as special advisor to President John F. Kennedy from 1961 to 1963.

242.5 José Martí] Martí (1853–1895), a writer and advocate for Cuban independence, spent much of the last decade of his life in exile in the United States.

242.9 the 26 Julio] Movimiento 26 de Julio, a guerrilla organization central to the Cuban revolution; it was named after the date of Fidel Castro's unsuccessful first attack on the Batista regime on July 26, 1953.

242.10 Fulgencio Batista] Batista (1901–1973) served as elected president of Cuba from 1940 to 1944, and as military dictator from 1952 to 1959, when he was overthrown.

243.26 Jeane Kirkpatrick] American diplomat (1926–2006) who in 1986 was a fellow at the American Enterprise Institute and former U.S. ambassador to the United Nations.

243.33–34 the Martyrs of Girón monument] A monument to those who died during the attempted invasion of Cuba at the Bay of Pigs.

244.15–16 Claude Pepper] Pepper (1900–1989), a Democrat, represented his Miami-area district in Congress from 1963 until his death.

245.15 the Mariel exodus] From April to October 1980, approximately 125,000 Cubans emigrated to the United States by sea, from the port of Mariel.

245.35 *barbudos*] Bearded revolutionaries.

247.6 *quince*] *Quinceañera*, the celebration of a girl's fifteenth birthday.

252.35 Hetty Green's son] Green (1934–1916), sometimes described as "the richest woman in America," had one son, Edward Green (1868–1936), a businessman and noted philatelist.

257.38–39 Dr. Josef Mengele] Mengele (1911–1979), a Nazi war criminal notorious for his medical experiments at Auschwitz, escaped to South America in 1949 and eluded capture; his remains were posthumously identified in 1985.

259.11 Mariels] Also referred to as Marielitos, Cubans who arrived in the United States as part of the Mariel boatlift of 1980.

272.3 the Adolfo . . . collection] Adolfo Sardiña, known professionally as Adolfo and born in Cárdenas, Cuba, in 1933, emigrated to New York in 1948.

272.19 Paula Hawkins] Hawkins (1927–2009), a Republican, was one of Florida's U.S. senators from 1981 to 1987.

276.34 Refrescos Cawy] A soda company founded in Cuba in 1948 and relaunched in Miami in 1962.

276.35 *guayaberas*] Lightweight men's shirts worn untucked, with two rows of closely sewn vertical pleats in front and back.

277.12 *botánicas*] Stores offering medicinal herbs and religious goods and services.

282.22–23 the Torch of Friendship monument] Monument in downtown Miami, dedicated in 1960 and celebrating U.S.–Latin American friendship.

285.1–3 Voltaire . . . say it'] The quotation, often attributed to Voltaire, first appeared in *The Friends of Voltaire* (1906) by S. G. Tallentyre, a pseudonym of Beatrice Evelyn Hall (1868–1956).

285.3 Wendell Willkie] Willkie (1892–1944) was the 1940 Republican presidential nominee.

285.31 Ring] A reference to *Der Ring des Nibelungen*, an epic cycle of operas by Richard Wagner (1813–1883) that includes *Das Rheingold* (1869), *Die Walküre* (1870), *Siegfried* (1876), and *Götterdämmerung* (1876).

293.3 Allen Dulles] Dulles (1893–1969) served as director of the Central Intelligence Agency from February 1953 until November 1961, when he was forced to resign in the wake of the failed Bay of Pigs invasion.

293.17 *A Thousand Days*] *A Thousand Days: John F. Kennedy in the White House*, a 1965 history by Arthur M. Schlesinger, Jr. (1917–2007), who had served as special assistant to Kennedy.

294.28 Radio Martí] U.S. government radio station established to provide an alternative to Cuban state media and to hasten the fall of Fidel Castro; it began broadcasting from Washington on May 20, 1985, and continues to operate from Miami.

296.16 OCS] Officer Candidate School, an intensive course for potential U.S. Army officers, offered at Fort Benning, Georgia.

300.9 the Tower Commission report] Report published in February 1987 in the wake of the Iran–Contra affair; it concluded that U.S. officials illegally sold arms to Iran in order to fund the Nicaraguan Contras.

300.10 Manucher Ghorbanifar] Iranian arms dealer (b. 1945) and former intelligence agent involved in the Iran–Contra affair as a go-between.

300.11 SAVAK] The Iranian intelligence and secret police agency during the reign of Mohammad Reza Pahlavi, founded in 1957 and abolished in the wake of the Islamic revolution of 1979.

300.12 Michael Ledeen] Ledeen (b. 1941) was involved in the Iran–Contra affair as a staff consultant to National Security Advisor Robert McFarlane.

300.18 Walt Whitman Rostow] Rostow (1916–2003) served as President Johnson's national security advisor, from 1966 to 1969.

300.29 the INS] The U.S. Immigration and Naturalization Service.

302.29 Raúl] Raúl Castro (b. 1931), brother to Fidel and first secretary of the Communist Party of Cuba beginning in 2011.

307.13 LA VERDAD ES NUESTROS] The Truth is Ours.

309.3 the Segundo Frente del Escambray] An anti-Batista guerrilla group principally active in the Escambray mountains; its leader, Eloy Menoyo (1934–2012), and other members left Cuba for Miami in 1961.

313.5–6 Capitán Dreyfus] Alfred Dreyfus (1859–1935), a French artillery officer wrongfully convicted of treason in 1894 and finally exonerated in 1906 after a divisive and widely publicized series of judicial and political scandals known as "l'affaire Dreyfus."

316.15 *Somos Cubanos*] *We Are Cubans.*

317.2 Meyer Lansky] American mobster (1902–1983) with interests in casinos in numerous countries including Cuba, where he oversaw the gambling industry in close association with the Batista regime.

317.19 Venceremos Brigade] Established in 1969 by members of Students for a Democratic Society, an organization sponsoring annual trips to Cuba; *brigadistas* work with Cubans and study the Cuban revolution.

318.19 *Vanidades*] Women's fashion magazine published in Havana from 1937 until 1960; it was subsequently produced in New York and, beginning in 1966, in Miami.

318.20 Casa Moneo] Spanish and Latin American food and specialty goods store in New York, in business from 1929 to 1988.

320.3 the case of the poet, Heberto Padilla] Padilla (1932–2000), who initially supported the Cuban revolution, was imprisoned in March 1971 for his 1968 collection *Fuera del juego.*

323.28 *Mauvaise Conduite*] 1984 documentary, released in the United States as *Improper Conduct.*

324.24 "Falangist . . . Nasserite."] The Falange, an extreme nationalist Spanish political party founded in 1933 and adopted by General Franco in 1937, rejected both capitalism and communism; Gamal Abdel Nasser (1918–1970), as president of Egypt from 1956 to 1970, evolved a political ideology combining elements of Arab nationalism, socialism, and Cold War nonalignment.

339.31 Eugene Hasenfus] Hasenfus (b. 1941) survived the October 5, 1986, crash of a cargo plane carrying weapons to the Nicaraguan Contras after it was shot down by the Sandinista government. His presence on board led to a congressional investigation into the role of the CIA and the Reagan administration in illegal arms shipments.

345.40–346.2 what Hannah Arendt . . . imaginary world."] See Arendt's *The Origins of Totalitarianism* (1951).

354.37–40 Wayne Newton . . . Lasorda] Newton (b. 1942), a singer and entertainer, was known for his Las Vegas shows; Shields (b. 1965) was a model and actress; de la Renta (1932–2014) a fashion designer; Crespi (b. 1951) a fashion designer and former model; Lasorda (b. 1927) a former baseball player and manager of the Los Angeles Dodgers from 1976 to 1996.

356.32–33 Blair House] A complex of buildings in Washington, D.C., used as the President's guest house.

357.4 Patrick Buchanan] American journalist (b. 1938) who served as communications director in the Reagan White House, from February 1985 to March 1987.

357.5–6 Morton Kondracke] America journalist and political commentator, born in 1939.

363.26 the Roldós Doctrine and the Rio Treaty] In 1980, Ecuadoran president Jaime Roldós Aguilera (1940–1981) signed a charter of conduct with Colombia, Peru, and Venezuela, which asserted that international human rights concerns may justify violations of national sovereignty. The Inter-American Treaty of Reciprocal Assistance or Rio Treaty, signed in 1947 by the United States, Mexico, and most Caribbean, Central American, and South American nations, holds that an attack on one signatory nation will be considered an attack on all.

364.29 Faith Ryan Whittlesey] Whittlesey (1939–2018), a former member of the Pennsylvania House of Representatives, served as director of the White House office of public liaison from March 1983 to March 1985, after which she was appointed U.S. ambassador to Switzerland.

365.39–40 the Machel government] Samora Machel (1933–1986) led Mozambique from its independence in 1975 until his 1986 death in a plane crash.

366.17–18 the Kissinger Commission] Former U.S. secretary of state and national security adviser Henry Kissinger (b. 1923) chaired a National Bipartisan Commission on Central America, appointed by the Reagan administration in July 1983; its January 1984 report supported administration policies.

367.5 Jonas Savimbi] Savimbi (1934–2002), a Chinese-trained guerrilla leader and politician who fought for Angolan independence as cofounder of UNITA (União Nacional para a Independência Total de Angola), received military assistance from the United States and South Africa during the subsequent Angolan Civil War, a U.S.-Soviet proxy war.

367.17 FDN] Fuerza Democrática Nicaragüense, an anti-Sandinista guerrilla group established in Guatemala City in August 1981.

374.29 the Warren Commission] Commission ordered by President Johnson in November 1963 to investigate the assassination of President Kennedy, chaired by Earl Warren (1891–1974), chief justice of the Supreme Court; it presented its findings in September 1964.

375.1 Johnny Roselli] Roselli (1905–1976), who represented the interests of the Chicago mafia in Los Angeles and Las Vegas and who was reportedly involved in CIA efforts to assassinate Fidel Castro in 1960, was found dead near Miami in August 1976, his body stuffed into an oil drum and dumped at sea.

375.39 Dick Goodwin] Richard N. Goodwin (1931–2018) served as an advisor and speechwriter to President Kennedy.

AFTER HENRY

393.2 Bret Easton Ellis] Ellis (b. 1964), a novelist, is the author of *Less Than Zero* (1985) and *American Psycho* (1991), among other books.

397.4 My husband . . . his first.] See *Delano: The Story of the California Grape Strike* (1967), by John Gregory Dunne (1932–2003).

397.29 the Daisy] A members-only Los Angeles nightclub, established in 1962.

398.10–11 "Childhood . . . Edna St. Vincent Millay] See "Childhood Is the Kingdom Where Nobody Dies," from *Collected Poems* (1939).

398.15 the Stanislaus] A central California river, tributary to the San Joaquin.

399.14–19 a poem by Delmore Schwartz . . . *sister.*] See "Time's Declaration" in Schwartz's *Summer Knowledge: New and Selected Poems, 1938–1958* (1959).

405.1 *In the Realm of the Fisher King*] When it was first published (as "Life at Court," *The New York Review of Books*, December 21, 1989), this essay was presented as a review of the following books: *What I Saw at the Revolution: A Political Life in the Reagan Era*, by Peggy Noonan; *Jean Howard's Hollywood: A Photo Memoir*, photographs by Jean Howard, text by James Watters; *My Turn: The Memoirs of Nancy Reagan*, by Nancy Reagan, with William Novak; *At Reagan's Side*, by Helene von Damm; *Behind the Scenes*, by Michael K. Deaver, with Mickey Herskowitz; and *Speaking My Mind: Selected Speeches*, by Ronald Reagan.

406.2 the Brezhnev Doctrine] Soviet foreign policy announced in the wake of its 1968 occupation of Czechoslovakia, prohibiting individual Eastern Bloc nations from abandoning communism or liberalizing.

406.19–20 Vachel Lindsay . . . silver Zion"] See Lindsay's poem "Bryan! Bryan! Bryan! Bryan!" first published in 1919 and subtitled "A Rhyme in the American Language, Being Impressions of a Sixteen-Year-Old in 1896."

407.2–3 what Annie Hall's grandmother . . . Woody Allen."] In his 1977 romantic comedy *Annie Hall*, Allen (b. 1935) visits his girlfriend's family for Easter dinner; at one point he turns to the camera and says, "the old lady at the end of the table is a classic Jew-hater."

407.7–8 Larry Speakes] Speakes (1939–2014) served as acting White House press secretary from 1981 to 1987.

407.23 Richard John Neuhaus] Neuhaus (1936–2009), a minister and author, had written *Time Toward Home: The American Experiment as Revelation* (1975), *Unsecular America* (1986), and other books.

407.25–27 Michael Novak . . . value-free."] Novak (1933–2017), a Catholic philosopher, was the author of *The Spirit of Democratic Capitalism* (1982).

407.27–28 George Gilder . . . free market.] Gilder's best-selling *Wealth and Poverty* (1981) argued for the practical and moral superiority of free market capitalism.

407.29–30 Jean-François Revel . . . perish] Revel (1924–2006), a French journalist, published *How Democracies Perish* in 1983.

407.38–408.2 Macedo's new monograph . . . Tribe's] Stephen Macedo (b. 1957) and Laurence Tribe (b. 1941); the former published *The New Right v. The Constitution* in 1986.

408.5 PROF] Professional Office System, an IBM communications software package introduced in 1981 and used by the White House and other government agencies.

408.14 John Ford] Ford (1894–1973) directed Westerns, including *The Searchers* (1956) and *The Man Who Shot Liberty Valance* (1962).

408.25 Laffer curves] Theoretical models of the relationship between tax rates and tax revenue, originally circulated by economist Arthur Laffer (b. 1940) during the Ford administration and used during the Reagan administration as a rationale for tax cuts.

408.36 Jack Wheeler] Wheeler (1944–2010), who served in various executive positions at the Securities and Exchange Commission from 1978 to 1986, was described by one source in a 1986 *Washington Post* profile as "the Indiana Jones of the right" for his efforts to support Cold War "freedom fighters."

408.38 Grover Norquist] Norquist (b. 1956), a founder in 1985 of Americans for Tax Reform, traveled widely in the 1980s in support of anti-Soviet guerrilla forces.

409.24 Le Cirque] A French restaurant in midtown Manhattan established in 1974 and described when it closed in 2018 as "a showplace for the era's excess and glamour."

409.29 the California Club] A private Los Angeles social club, founded in 1888.

409.37–410.5 William Wilson . . . Bloomingdale] Wilson (1914–2009), Jorgensen (1898–1999), Dart (1907–1984), and Bloomingdale (1916–1982), all wealthy businessmen, were friends and advisors of President Reagan before his move to Washington, D.C.

410.36 David Jones] Jones (1936–2014), who moved his business from New York to Hollywood in 1963, was Nancy Reagan's longtime florist.

411.2 Chasen's] See note 220.2.

411.15 the Joseph Cottens'] Actor Joseph Cotten (1905–1994) and his first wife, born Lenore Kipp (1904–1960).

411.16 Jennifer Jones] American actress (1919–2009), winner of a 1943 Academy Award for her role in *The Song of Bernadette.*

413.23–25 James Baker . . . Donald Regan] Baker (b. 1930), Meese (b. 1931), and Deaver (1938–2007) served respectively as White House chief of staff, counselor, and deputy chief of staff, from the beginning of President Reagan's first term until 1985. Regan (1918–2003) replaced Baker in February 1985.

414.3–4 Galanoist] See note 459.5.

414.26 Jerry Zipkin] Zipkin (1914–1995), a socialite and longtime friend of Nancy Reagan.

415.6 Ben Bradlee] Bradlee (1921–2014) served as executive editor of *The Washington Post* from 1968 to 1991.

415.9 Katharine Graham] Graham (1917–2001) was publisher of *The Washington Post* from 1963 to 1991.

415.16 Tony Orlando] American singer and songwriter (b. 1944), most widely known as a member of the group Tony Orlando and Dawn, which hosted a television variety show from 1974 to 1977.

416.19 the visit to Bitburg] President Reagan visited the Kolmeshöhe military cemetery in Bitburg, West Germany, on May 5, 1985, provoking controversy because the cemetery contained the graves of Waffen-SS troops; a stop at the site of the Bergen-Belsen concentration camp was added belatedly to his itinerary in an attempt to assuage his critics.

416.23 David Stockman] Stockman (b. 1946), one of the principal early spokesmen for President Reagan's economic policies, served as director of the Office of Management and Budget from 1981 to 1985; his influence within the administration was diminished after he made excessively candid remarks in a December 1981 *Atlantic Monthly* article by William Greider, "The Education of David Stockman."

417.23–24 McFarlane . . . Irish passports] In September 1986, former national security advisor Robert McFarlane (b. 1937) traveled to Iran with others on a secret diplomatic mission; his party carried a Bible signed by President Reagan, a key-shaped cake to signify reopened relations with Iran, and military equipment.

417.32 SDI] The Strategic Defense Initiative, dubbed "Star Wars" by its critics after it was introduced by President Reagan in a March 1983 address to the nation, envisioned a space-based shield against intercontinental ballistic missiles.

418.7–8 Jim Wright's district] Wright (1922–2015), a Texas Democrat, served as House majority leader from 1977 to 1987.

418.35 Shane-like] See *Shane*, a 1953 Western directed by George Stevens (1904–1975).

420.25 Tom Hayden] Hayden (1939–2016), who came to prominence for his activism against the Vietnam War, served in the California State Assembly from 1982 to 1992.

421.12 Brinkley] David Brinkley (1920–2003) hosted *This Week with David Brinkley*, a Sunday morning interview and commentary program focused on politics, from November 1981 until November 1996.

421.20 Jack Kemp] Kemp (1935–2009), who served in the House of Representatives from 1971 to 1989, ran unsuccessfully for the Republican presidential nomination in 1988.

425.40 "the best and the brightest."] *The Best and the Brightest* (1972), by David Halberstam (1934–2007), describes the failures of Vietnam policymaking, by technocratic experts, in the Kennedy and Johnson administrations.

428.17 Mr. Dole's] Bob Dole (b. 1923), who served as U.S. senator from Kansas from 1969 to 1996, ran unsuccessfully for the 1988 Republican presidential nomination, as he had in 1980; he later won the nomination but was defeated by the incumbent President Clinton in the 1996 presidential election.

429.24 Elizabeth Drew] American political journalist (b. 1935) who served as *The New Yorker*'s Washington correspondent from 1973 to 1992.

432.36–37 "Coming to America,"] Also known as "America," a 1980 song by Neil Diamond (b. 1941), used as Dukakis's campaign theme.

433.5–8 the one-on-one . . . Theodore H. White] See White's *The Making of the President 1960* (1961), *The Making of the President 1964* (1965), *The Making of the President 1968* (1969), and *The Making of the President 1972* (1973).

433.18 Bruce Babbitt] Babbitt (b. 1938), who served as governor of Arizona from 1978 to 1987, ran in the 1988 Democratic presidential primary.

439.11 Michael Harrington . . . Richard Viguerie] Harrington (1928–1989) was the author of *The Other America: Poverty in the United States* (1962) among other books and a cofounder of the Democratic Socialists of America; Viguerie (b. 1933), author of *The New Right: We're Ready to Lead* (1981) and other books, was a pioneer of political direct mail.

440.29 Dukakis's "snowblower,"] In a video shown before Dukakis's speech at the 1988 Democratic National Convention, his cousin Olympia Dukakis wheeled his twenty-five-year-old snowblower out of his garage, presenting it as evidence of his frugality.

441.16 David Garth] Garth (1930–2014), a political consultant, worked for then-Senator Albert Gore in his effort to win the 1988 Democratic presidential primary elections.

441.24 Robert S. Strauss] Strauss (1918–2014), who served as chairman of the Democratic National Committee from 1972 to 1977, has been described as a Washington "insider's insider."

442.17–18 Tom Bradley . . . Andy Young] Bradley (1917–1998) was mayor of Los Angeles from 1973 to 1993, and Young (b. 1932) mayor of Atlanta from 1982 to 1990.

444.8 Charles Manatt . . . Emerson] Manatt (1936–2011), a lawyer, chaired the Democratic National Committee from 1981 to 1985; Emerson (b. 1954) was deputy campaign manager for Gary Hart during the 1988 Democratic presidential primary season.

444.9–10 John Van de Kamp . . . Shrum] Van de Kamp (1936–2017) was attorney general of California from 1983 to 1991; McCarthy (1930–2007) was lieutenant governor of California from 1983 to 1995; Shrum (b. 1943), who founded a political consultancy firm in 1986, worked on Congressman Dick Gephardt's 1988 presidential campaign and for Michael Dukakis after Gephardt withdrew.

445.21 David Ferrie and Jack Martin] Ferrie (1918–1967), a former pilot, and Martin (b. 1915), a private investigator, have both been alleged to have been involved in a conspiracy to assassinate President Kennedy.

447.10–11 David Ben-Gurion's tomb] Ben-Gurion (1886–1973), Israel's first prime minister, is buried near the kibbutz at Sde Boker where he spent his retirement.

448.15 Gemayel] Amine Gemayel (b. 1942), who served as president of Lebanon, after the assassination of his brother Bachir (1947–1982), from 1982 to 1988.

448.16–17 David Gergen] Gergen (b. 1942) served as White House communications director from June 1981 to January 1984.

454.10 "Tania"] The nom de guerre Patricia Hearst adopted after joining the Symbionese Liberation Army.

456.25–27 Kevin Starr . . . Californian aesthetic."] See Starr's *Americans and the California Dream, 1850–1915* (1973), chapter 6.

457.2 Julia Morgan] Morgan (1872–1957), a California architect, was the principal designer of the Hearst Castle at San Simeon.

459.2 Jack Scott] Scott (1942–2000), author of *The Athletic Revolution* (1971), drove Hearst from California to New Jersey with his parents after other SLA members were killed by police in May 1974.

459.5 Galanos] James Galanos (1924–2016), American fashion designer.

461.4 Grossinger's] A Catskills resort hotel.

462.22 Cesar Chavez] Chávez (1927–1993), a cofounder of the National Farm Workers Association, led the Delano grape strike of 1965–70.

463.12 LACSA and TACA] The national airlines of Costa Rica and El Salvador.

463.14 *¡No más barata!*] *None cheaper!*

465.31–32 Djuna Barnes] American writer and illustrator (1892–1982) most often remembered for her novel *Nightwood* (1936), a lesbian classic.

466.36 E. H. Gombrich] A prominent art historian (1909–2001), born in Austria and naturalized in the United Kingdom in 1937.

468.6–8 Jane Alpert . . . Ed Janss] Alpert (b. 1947), a left-wing terrorist arrested in 1969 for her role in a number of New York City bombings, jumped bail and eluded capture until 1974, and in 1975 refused to testify in the trial of one of her co-conspirators; Cleaver (1935–1998), a leader of the Black Panther Party and author of *Soul on Ice* (1968), returned to the United States in 1975 after seven years abroad; Ellsberg (b. 1931) was tried for espionage in 1973 for releasing the *Pentagon Papers*; Alexander (1925–2005), a journalist, appeared on *60 Minutes* beginning in 1975; Feiffer (b. 1929), a cartoonist for *The Village Voice*, published *Feiffer on Nixon: The Cartoon Presidency* in 1974; novelist Gold (b. 1924) published *Swiftie the Magician* the same year; Caen (1916–1997) was a columnist for the *San Francisco Chronicle*; Edwin Janss, Jr. (1914–1989), heir to and executive of a California real estate and investment firm, made President Nixon's "enemies list" for his opposition to the Vietnam War, and in the early 1970s held exhibitions and published collections of his underwater photographs.

468.15 Céline] Louis-Ferdinand Céline (1894–1961), a French writer, is most often remembered for his novel *Voyage au bout de la nuit* (*Journey to the End of the Night*, 1932), and for his pro-fascist pamphleteering during World War II.

472.5 Robert Oppenheimer . . . Alamogordo.] On July 16, 1945, a device nicknamed "The Gadget" was detonated at the Alamogordo Bombing and Gunnery Range near Socorro, New Mexico, in the first-ever nuclear weapons test; Oppenheimer (1904–1967) led the Los Alamos Laboratory, which developed the device.

472.37 Glenn Seaborg's] Seaborg (1912–1999), a professor at the University of California at Berkeley, was awarded the 1951 Nobel Prize in Chemistry for his discovery of numerous transuranium elements.

474.14 Bohemian Grove] A private campground in Monte Rio, California, belonging to the exclusive, all-male Bohemian Club of San Francisco and the site of an annual summer gathering of prominent businessmen and politicians.

476.18 sig-alert] Notice of a traffic disruption, named after its inventor Loyd Sigmon (1909–2004), the "father of L.A. traffic reporting."

481.29 *haole*] Hawaiian term, generally derogatory, for non-Hawaiians, especially those of European ancestry.

490.11–12 Marvin Davis, to Kenny Rogers] Davis (1925–2004) was a petroleum entrepreneur and real estate developer, Rogers (1928–2020) a singer and songwriter.

490.27 Merv Griffin's] Griffin (1925–2007) hosted *The Merv Griffin Show*, a television talk show, from 1965 to 1986.

490.30 Pickfair . . . Pia Zadora] Zadora (b. 1953), an actress and singer, married businessman Meshulam Riklis in 1977; their mansion was originally built in the 1920s for Mary Pickford and Douglas Fairbanks, thus "Pickfair."

494.31 Hillcrest] A Los Angeles country club.

497.38 the Thalberg Award] The Irving G. Thalberg Memorial Award, given periodically to film producers beginning in 1937.

499.24 *The Last Tycoon*] An unfinished novel by F. Scott Fitzgerald (1896–1940), published posthumously in 1941.

506.16–17 Andrew Young] See note 442.17–18.

514.13 Schenley] Schenley Industries, a New York–based liquor importer and producer.

518.7 the California Club] See note 409.29.

520.30 Gloria Molina . . . Mike Woo] Molina (b. 1948) was elected to the Los Angeles City Council in 1987, Alatorre (b. 1943) and Woo (b. 1951) in 1985.

523.11 Tiny Tim, Frank Fontaine] Tiny Tim (born Herbert Khaury, 1932–1996), a musician, is most often remembered for his comic falsetto-and-ukulele rendition of "Tiptoe through the Tulips," and Fontaine (1920–1978), a comedian, for his guest appearances on television variety shows in the 1950s and 1960s.

525.15 the McMartin child-abuse case] In March 1984, Virginia McMartin (1907–1995), founder of a preschool in Manhattan Beach, California, was arrested with six others and charged with child sexual abuse. There were two trials in their case, among the longest and most expensive in U.S. history, involving hundreds of children and allegations of satanic ritualism; the second came to an end in July 1990, and all charges were dropped.

526.33 William Morris] A Hollywood talent agency.

528.11 Carlos Lehder] Colombian cocaine smuggler (b. 1949) and cofounder of the Medellín cartel, extradited to the United States in 1987 and sentenced to life imprisonment.

533.26–28 "Beautiful country . . . Robinson Jeffers poem] See Jeffers's "Apology for Bad Dreams," first published in *New Masses* in May 1926.

537.27 Donald Douglas] Aviation engineer (1892–1981) and founder in 1921 of Douglas Aircraft Company, based in Santa Monica.

543.28 Son of Sam] David Berkowitz (b. 1953), a New York serial killer; he was arrested on August 10, 1977.

543.30 Roone Arledge] A broadcasting executive (1931–2002), president of ABC Sports from 1968 to 1986 and of ABC News from 1977 to 1988.

543.38–39 Francisco ("Chachi") Guerrero's] Guerrero (1925–1989), a conservative landowner, had served as chief justice of El Salvador's Supreme Court and ran unsuccessfully for president in 1984; he died by assassination.

546.15 H. R. Haldeman's] Haldeman (1926–1993) served as chief of staff in the Nixon White House from January 1969 to April 1973.

547.32–33 "New Coke"] A reformulated version of Coca-Cola, introduced on April 23, 1985, and withdrawn, after failing among consumers, on July 11.

550.23 Maid of Cotton] A beauty pageant sponsored by the National Cotton Council and other industry groups and held in Memphis and later Dallas from 1939 to 1993.

559.2–4 her story . . . her name.] See Trisha Meili, *I Am the Central Park Jogger*, published in 2003.

562.24 Bacharach bride] Probably a reference to Bachrach Studios, a national portrait photography firm founded in Baltimore in 1868 and still in operation, or to its then-principal Fabian Bachrach (1917–2010).

566.26–27 the Scottsboro boys] Nine young African American men, wrongly convicted of raping two white women in Alabama in 1931; their case became a cause célèbre and was appealed twice to the United States Supreme Court.

567.22–23 Percy Sutton] Sutton (1920–2009), who served as Manhattan borough president from 1966 to 1977 and who ran unsuccessfully for New York City mayor in 1977, cofounded Inner City Broadcasting in 1970; it acquired WLIB in 1972.

573.10 Jim Buck's dog trainers] Buck (1931–2013) established Jim Buck's School for Dogs in the early 1960s.

573.11 Henry Kravis's] Kravis (b. 1944) is a businessman and investor.

577.2 William Marcy Tweed] Tweed (1823–1878) led the New York Democratic political patronage organization known as Tammany Hall from 1858 to 1871.

583.37–38 Gary Gilmore . . . *The Executioner's Song*.] Norman Mailer's *The Executioner's Song* (1976) is a true crime novel about Gary Gilmore (1940–1977), who was executed for murder in January 1977.

590.30 Alton H. Maddox, Jr.] Maddox (b. 1945), a trial lawyer, represented several of the defendants in the Central Park jogger case.

590.38–591.18 "Today the white . . . millenniums ago . . .] See *The Autobiography of Malcolm X* (1965), chapter 11.

591.26 William Kunstler] Kunstler (1919–1995) famously defended radical groups including the Black Panther Party, the Catonsville Nine, and the Weather Underground.

596.16 Howard Beach] On December 20, 1986, in Howard Beach, Queens, four African American men were beaten by a larger group of whites after their car broke down; one, Michael Griffith, was hit by a car and killed as he tried to escape.

596.16–17 Bernhard Goetz] Goetz (b. 1947) shot four African American men on a New York City subway on December 22, 1984, after they threatened him; his trial was widely polarizing.

598.10 Mahalia Jackson] American gospel singer (1911–1972).

598.15 Adam Clayton Powell, Jr.] Powell (1908–1972), a clergyman, was elected to the House of Representatives from Harlem in 1945 and served until 1971.

598.20 Bayard Rustin] Civil rights organizer (1912–1987).

598.21 Shirley Chisholm] Chisholm (1924–2005), who served in the House of Representatives for New York from 1969 to 1983, sought the 1972 Democratic presidential nomination, the first woman to do so.

598.21 James Brown] Singer and songwriter (1933–2006), known as the "godfather of soul."

598.31–32 as Jimmy Walker said . . . Lincoln."] Walker (1881–1946), the mayor of New York, made the remark after Louis (1914–1981) donated his winnings from a January 9, 1942, heavyweight prizefight to the Navy Relief Society.

598.35 Father Divine] African American spiritual leader (c. 1876–1965) and self-proclaimed reincarnation of Jesus Christ.

THE LAST THING HE WANTED

607.12 *Agence Presse*] Agence France Presse is the world's oldest news organization and based in Paris. It was founded in 1835.

607.20–21 the *Merck Manual*] *The Merck Manual of Diagnosis and Therapy*, a medical textbook first published in 1899 and continuously in print since, in revised editions.

617.3 DIA] Defense Intelligence Agency, an arm of the U.S. Department of Defense dedicated to military intelligence.

609.10 PAO] Public Affairs Officer, a U.S. Defense Department official responsible for public relations.

609.11 USICA] The United States International Communications Agency, active from 1953 to 1999 and dedicated to the practice of public diplomacy.

610.32 Robert Vesco] Vesco (1935–2007), an American financier, contributed secretly to President Nixon's 1972 reelection campaign, and fled the United States for Costa Rica in 1973 while under investigation by the Securities and Exchange Commission for securities fraud.

612.5 *Theodore Shackley*] A longtime CIA officer who retired in 1979, Shackley (1927–2002) met with several individuals involved in the Iran–Contra affair in 1984 and 1985, but denied his involvement in an arms-for-hostages swap.

612.5 *Clair George*] George (1930–2011) was deputy director of operations for the Central Intelligence Agency from 1984 to 1987. He was subsequently found guilty of lying to congressional investigators about the agency's involvement in the Iran–Contra affair, and was pardoned by President George H. W. Bush in 1992.

612.5–6 *Dewey Clarridge*] Duane "Dewey" Clarridge (1932–2016), a Central Intelligence Agency senior operations officer, was pardoned in 1992 by President George H. W. Bush for his involvement in the Iran–Contra affair.

612.6 *Richard Secord*] Secord (b. 1932), an Air Force major general known for decades of work in covert operations, pled guilty in 1989 to one count of lying to Congress about his role in the Iran–Contra affair.

612.6 *Alan Fiers*] As head of the CIA's Central American Task Force beginning in 1984, Fiers (b. 1939) was responsible for coordinating support for the Nicaraguan Contras. He was pardoned by President George H. W. Bush in 1992 for his role in concealing the agency's efforts from Congress.

612.6–7 *Felix Rodriguez aka "Max Gomez"*] A retired CIA operations officer who had participated in the 1961 Bay of Pigs invasion of Cuba and the 1967 capture and assassination of Ernesto "Che" Guevara (1928–1967) in Bolivia, Rodríguez (b. 1941) assisted Lieutenant Colonel Oliver North (b. 1943) in supplying arms to the Nicaraguan Contras, working from Ilopango air base outside San Salvador, where he was known by the pseudonym "Max Gomez."

612.7 *John Hull*] Hull (1920–2017), an American expatriate, helped supply the Contras with weapons and other supplies from an airstrip on his ranch in Costa Rica, near the Nicaraguan border. In 1988, the Costa Rican government arrested him on charges of drug trafficking, but he fled the country while on bail.

612.7 *Southern Air*] Southern Air Transport, a Miami-based cargo airline established by the CIA and active from 1947 to 1998. During the 1980s, the airline flew shipments of weapons bound for Iran and for the Nicaraguan Contras.

612.7 *Lake Resources*] A company founded by Iranian American businessman Albert Hakim (1936–2003), used to shelter and launder money during the Iran–Contra affair.

612.7–8 *Stanford Technology*] Stanford Technology Trading Group International, a shell company established to launder money during the Iran–Contra affair.

612.8 *Donald Gregg*] Gregg (b. 1927), who served as national security advisor to Vice President George H. W. Bush, is alleged to have had knowledge of illegal arms shipments to the Nicaraguan Contras, but evidence was insufficient to charge him with any crime.

612.8 *Aguacate*] Location of an American air base in Honduras known as "the Farm" and used for launch and recovery during the Iran–Contra affair.

612.8 *Elliott Abrams*] Abrams (b. 1948), who was appointed assistant secretary of state for inter-American affairs in 1985, lied to Congress in 1986 about the State Department's support for the Nicaraguan Contras. He later cooperated with investigators in exchange for a reduced sentence, and in 1992 received a presidential pardon.

612.8–9 *Robert Owen aka "T.C."*] In 1987, Owen (b. 1953) testified before Congress that as a courier for Lieutenant Colonel Oliver North (b. 1943), he carried cash and munitions lists between the U.S. and Central America as part of an illegal scheme to arm the Nicaraguan Contras. "T.C." stood for "The Courier."

612.9 *Ilopango aka "Cincinnati,"*] Military airfield in El Salvador into which Southern Air Transport flew arms for the Nicaraguan Contras.

612.10 the C-123 . . . Nicaragua] On October 5, 1986, a flight delivering weapons to the Contras was shot down by the Nicaraguan government, and one of its American crew, Eugene Hasenfus (see note 339.31), was taken prisoner. The incident exposed the illegal supply operation to further scrutiny.

617.22–23 Bashir Gemayel] Gemayel (1947–1982), elected president of Lebanon on August 23, 1982, was assassinated before he could take office, in a bomb attack on September 14, 1982.

618.36 nines, Intratecs] Nines is shorthand for 9mm semi-automatic handguns. Intratec is an American subsidiary of Swedish munitions company Interdynamic AB, known for the TEC-9 line of semi-automatic handguns.

624.25 *Hillcrest*] See note 494.31.

628.10–11 Sans Souci] Nightclub on the outskirts of Havana, owned by Florida-based mob boss Santo Trafficante, Jr. (1914–1987); it closed after Fidel Castro (1926–2016) came to power on December 31, 1958.

629.20 Carlos Prío] Carlos Prío Socarrás (1903–1977), president of Cuba from 1948 to 1952, when he was overthrown in a military coup led by his successor, Fulgencio Batista (1901–1973). He committed suicide at age seventy-four in Miami Beach, where he had been living in exile.

630.34 the Murchisons] Influential and politically conservative Texas oil family that founded the Southern Union Company. They were alleged, without proof, to have been involved in the assassination of President Kennedy on November 22, 1963.

639.6 *Wide spindrift . . . paradise*] From the poem "Voyages" by Hart Crane (1899–1932), collected in his first book, *White Buildings* (1926).

643.21–22 Texas Book Depository] Warehouse building in Dallas, Texas, from a sixth-floor window of which Lee Harvey Oswald (1939–1963) fired the shots that killed President Kennedy on November 22, 1963.

643.22 Lorraine Hotel] Motel in Memphis, Tennessee, where the Reverend Martin Luther King, Jr. (1929–1968), was shot and killed by James Earl Ray (1928–1998) on April 4, 1968.

643.23 Sirhan Sirhan] On June 5, 1968, Sirhan (b. 1944), a Palestinian resident of California, shot Senator Robert Francis Kennedy (1925–1968) in the kitchen of the Ambassador Hotel in Los Angeles; Kennedy died the next day.

643.23 Santos Trafficante] Trafficante, Jr. (1914–1987), a Florida-based mob boss, is alleged to have participated in a conspiracy to assassinate President Kennedy.

655.1 Kissinger Commission] See note 366.17–18.

665.38 *Herald Examiner*] Afternoon newspaper published in Los Angeles from 1903 to 1989; it was part of the Hearst news syndicate.

674.3 Edward Durell Stone] Stone (1902–1978), an American modernist architect, was responsible for the design of the U.S. Embassy in New Delhi, India, completed in 1959, and the Kennedy Center in Washington, D.C., completed in 1971.

674.30 the Rand Corporation] Global policy center, headquartered in Santa Monica, California; it was established in 1948 by Douglas Aircraft to facilitate research and analysis for the United States military.

689.16 Pointe-à-Pitre] City on the island of Guadeloupe, a French protectorate in the Lesser Antilles; it has a population of approximately 171,000.

690.6 Chalatenango] Municipality in El Salvador with a population of approximately twenty-one thousand.

690.19–20 25TH DIVISION TROPIC LIGHTNING] U.S. Army division based at Schofield Barracks on the Hawaiian island of Oahu. The division was initially activated in 1941.

697.12 DCM] Deputy Chief of Mission, the second in command at an embassy or diplomatic mission.

697.15 Brown & Root] Brown & Root Industrial Services, a company specializing in industrial maintenance, engineering, and construction, and based in Baton Rouge, Louisiana.

716.30–32 *Cecile Brunner roses . . . Scarlet Fire roses*] Light pink Cecile Brunner roses were first grown in France in 1881 by Joseph Pernet-Ducher (1859–1928). Henri Martin roses were introduced in Australia in 1855 and later named for the historian Henri Martin (1810–1883), one of the creators of the Statue of Liberty. Paulii roses, white hybrid tea roses, were developed by the American horticultural firm Jackson and Perkins. Chicago Peace roses, hybrid tea roses, were brought to America in 1956 by Star Roses & Plants. Single-flower Scarlet Fire roses were introduced in 1952 by the German nursery Kordes.

735.10 Galil semiautomatic assault rifles] Military weapons introduced in 1973 by the Israeli arms company Israel Military Industries, and used in Nicaragua, El Salvador, Lebanon, Somalia, Iraq, Afghanistan, and other wars and conflicts around the globe.

737.9 Reichstag] The German parliament building, burned in a fire on February 27, 1933. German chancellor Adolf Hitler (1889–1945) used the fire as a pretext to turn against the Communists, initiating the shift to authoritarianism that led to the development of the Third Reich. Despite the arrest and execution of Dutch Communist Marinus van der Lubbe (1909–1934) for arson, it is widely believed that the Nazis set the fire.

743.36 the Excelsior] Luxury hotel on the Via Veneto in Rome, opened in 1906.

747.39 Gustavia] Capital of the French Caribbean island of Saint Barthélemy.

759.32 Palmerola] Air base in Honduras, also known as Soto Cano Air Base, opened in 1940 and used by the United States military as a launching area for operations in Central America during the 1980s.

762.22 USG] United States government.

774.12 Theodore Sorensen] Sorensen (1928–2010) was one of President Kennedy's speechwriters and a close advisor during the Cuban Missile Crisis.

774.12–13 Robert McNamara . . . CINCSAC] McNamara (1916–2009) was U.S. secretary of defense from 1961 to 1968. The first commander-in-chief of the Strategic Air Command or CINCSAC during his tenure was General Thomas S. Power (1905–1970), who took office in 1957. Power was succeeded by General John Dale Ryan (1915–1983) in 1964, and Ryan by General Joseph J. Nazarro (1913–1990) in 1967.

774.16–17 Douglas Dillon . . . George Ball] Dillon (1909–2003) served as secretary of the treasury from 1961 to 1965, and Ball (1909–1994) as under secretary of state from 1961 to 1966.

774.19–20 Maxwell Taylor and Dean Rusk] Taylor (1901–1987) served as chairman of the Joint Chiefs of Staff from 1962 to 1964, and Rusk (1909–1994) as secretary of state from 1961 to 1968.

774.30–31 *Time yet . . . revisions.*] From the poem "The Love Song of J. Alfred Prufrock" by T. S. Eliot (1888–1965), first published in the journal *Poetry* in 1915.

Index

THE LIBRARY OF AMERICA SERIES

Library of America fosters appreciation of America's literary heritage by publishing, and keeping permanently in print, authoritative editions of America's best and most significant writing. An independent nonprofit organization, it was founded in 1979 with seed funding from the National Endowment for the Humanities and the Ford Foundation.

1. Herman Melville: Typee, Omoo, Mardi
2. Nathaniel Hawthorne: Tales & Sketches
3. Walt Whitman: Poetry & Prose
4. Harriet Beecher Stowe: Three Novels
5. Mark Twain: Mississippi Writings
6. Jack London: Novels & Stories
7. Jack London: Novels & Social Writings
8. William Dean Howells: Novels 1875–1886
9. Herman Melville: Redburn, White-Jacket, Moby-Dick
10. Nathaniel Hawthorne: Collected Novels

11 & 12. Francis Parkman: France and England in North America

13. Henry James: Novels 1871–1880
14. Henry Adams: Novels, Mont Saint Michel, The Education
15. Ralph Waldo Emerson: Essays & Lectures
16. Washington Irving: History, Tales & Sketches
17. Thomas Jefferson: Writings
18. Stephen Crane: Prose & Poetry
19. Edgar Allan Poe: Poetry & Tales
20. Edgar Allan Poe: Essays & Reviews
21. Mark Twain: The Innocents Abroad, Roughing It

22 & 23. Henry James: Literary Criticism

24. Herman Melville: Pierre, Israel Potter, The Confidence-Man, Tales & Billy Budd
25. William Faulkner: Novels 1930–1935

26 & 27. James Fenimore Cooper: The Leatherstocking Tales

28. Henry David Thoreau: A Week, Walden, The Maine Woods, Cape Cod
29. Henry James: Novels 1881–1886
30. Edith Wharton: Novels

31 & 32. Henry Adams: History of the U.S. during the Administrations of Jefferson & Madison

33. Frank Norris: Novels & Essays
34. W.E.B. Du Bois: Writings
35. Willa Cather: Early Novels & Stories
36. Theodore Dreiser: Sister Carrie, Jennie Gerhardt, Twelve Men
37. Benjamin Franklin: Writings (2 vols.)
38. William James: Writings 1902–1910
39. Flannery O'Connor: Collected Works

40, 41, & 42. Eugene O'Neill: Complete Plays

43. Henry James: Novels 1886–1890
44. William Dean Howells: Novels 1886–1888

45 & 46. Abraham Lincoln: Speeches & Writings

47. Edith Wharton: Novellas & Other Writings
48. William Faulkner: Novels 1936–1940
49. Willa Cather: Later Novels
50. Ulysses S. Grant: Memoirs & Selected Letters
51. William Tecumseh Sherman: Memoirs
52. Washington Irving: Bracebridge Hall, Tales of a Traveller, The Alhambra
53. Francis Parkman: The Oregon Trail, The Conspiracy of Pontiac
54. James Fenimore Cooper: Sea Tales

55 & 56. Richard Wright: Works

57. Willa Cather: Stories, Poems, & Other Writings
58. William James: Writings 1878–1899
59. Sinclair Lewis: Main Street & Babbitt

60 & 61. Mark Twain: Collected Tales, Sketches, Speeches, & Essays

62 & 63. The Debate on the Constitution

64 & 65. Henry James: Collected Travel Writings

66 & 67. American Poetry: The Nineteenth Century

68. Frederick Douglass: Autobiographies
69. Sarah Orne Jewett: Novels & Stories
70. Ralph Waldo Emerson: Collected Poems & Translations
71. Mark Twain: Historical Romances
72. John Steinbeck: Novels & Stories 1932–1937
73. William Faulkner: Novels 1942–1954

74 & 75. Zora Neale Hurston: Novels, Stories, & Other Writings

76. Thomas Paine: Collected Writings

77 & 78. Reporting World War II: American Journalism

79 & 80. Raymond Chandler: Novels, Stories, & Other Writings

81. Robert Frost: Collected Poems, Prose, & Plays
82 & 83. Henry James: Complete Stories 1892–1910
84. William Bartram: Travels & Other Writings
85. John Dos Passos: U.S.A.
86. John Steinbeck: The Grapes of Wrath & Other Writings 1936–1941
87, 88, & 89. Vladimir Nabokov: Novels & Other Writings
90. James Thurber: Writings & Drawings
91. George Washington: Writings
92. John Muir: Nature Writings
93. Nathanael West: Novels & Other Writings
94 & 95. Crime Novels: American Noir of the 1930s, 40s, & 50s
96. Wallace Stevens: Collected Poetry & Prose
97. James Baldwin: Early Novels & Stories
98. James Baldwin: Collected Essays
99 & 100. Gertrude Stein: Writings
101 & 102. Eudora Welty: Novels, Stories, & Other Writings
103. Charles Brockden Brown: Three Gothic Novels
104 & 105. Reporting Vietnam: American Journalism
106 & 107. Henry James: Complete Stories 1874–1891
108. American Sermons
109. James Madison: Writings
110. Dashiell Hammett: Complete Novels
111. Henry James: Complete Stories 1864–1874
112. William Faulkner: Novels 1957–1962
113. John James Audubon: Writings & Drawings
114. Slave Narratives
115 & 116. American Poetry: The Twentieth Century
117. F. Scott Fitzgerald: Novels & Stories 1920–1922
118. Henry Wadsworth Longfellow: Poems & Other Writings
119 & 120. Tennessee Williams: Collected Plays
121 & 122. Edith Wharton: Collected Stories
123. The American Revolution: Writings from the War of Independence
124. Henry David Thoreau: Collected Essays & Poems
125. Dashiell Hammett: Crime Stories & Other Writings
126 & 127. Dawn Powell: Novels
128. Carson McCullers: Complete Novels
129. Alexander Hamilton: Writings
130. Mark Twain: The Gilded Age & Later Novels
131. Charles W. Chesnutt: Stories, Novels, & Essays
132. John Steinbeck: Novels 1942–1952
133. Sinclair Lewis: Arrowsmith, Elmer Gantry, Dodsworth
134 & 135. Paul Bowles: Novels, Stories, & Other Writings
136. Kate Chopin: Complete Novels & Stories
137 & 138. Reporting Civil Rights: American Journalism
139. Henry James: Novels 1896–1899
140. Theodore Dreiser: An American Tragedy
141. Saul Bellow: Novels 1944–1953
142. John Dos Passos: Novels 1920–1925
143. John Dos Passos: Travel Books & Other Writings
144. Ezra Pound: Poems & Translations
145. James Weldon Johnson: Writings
146. Washington Irving: Three Western Narratives
147. Alexis de Tocqueville: Democracy in America
148. James T. Farrell: Studs Lonigan Trilogy
149, 150, & 151. Isaac Bashevis Singer: Collected Stories
152. Kaufman & Co.: Broadway Comedies
153. Theodore Roosevelt: Rough Riders, An Autobiography
154. Theodore Roosevelt: Letters & Speeches
155. H. P. Lovecraft: Tales
156. Louisa May Alcott: Little Women, Little Men, Jo's Boys
157. Philip Roth: Novels & Stories 1959–1962
158. Philip Roth: Novels 1967–1972
159. James Agee: Let Us Now Praise Famous Men, A Death in the Family, Shorter Fiction
160. James Agee: Film Writing & Selected Journalism
161. Richard Henry Dana Jr.: Two Years Before the Mast & Other Voyages
162. Henry James: Novels 1901–1902
163. Arthur Miller: Plays 1944–1961
164. William Faulkner: Novels 1926–1929
165. Philip Roth: Novels 1973–1977
166 & 167. American Speeches: Political Oratory
168. Hart Crane: Complete Poems & Selected Letters

169. Saul Bellow: Novels 1956–1964
170. John Steinbeck: Travels with Charley & Later Novels
171. Capt. John Smith: Writings with Other Narratives
172. Thornton Wilder: Collected Plays & Writings on Theater
173. Philip K. Dick: Four Novels of the 1960s
174. Jack Kerouac: Road Novels 1957–1960
175. Philip Roth: Zuckerman Bound
176 & 177. Edmund Wilson: Literary Essays & Reviews
178. American Poetry: The 17th & 18th Centuries
179. William Maxwell: Early Novels & Stories
180. Elizabeth Bishop: Poems, Prose, & Letters
181. A. J. Liebling: World War II Writings
182. American Earth: Environmental Writing Since Thoreau
183. Philip K. Dick: Five Novels of the 1960s & 70s
184. William Maxwell: Later Novels & Stories
185. Philip Roth: Novels & Other Narratives 1986–1991
186. Katherine Anne Porter: Collected Stories & Other Writings
187. John Ashbery: Collected Poems 1956–1987
188 & 189. John Cheever: Complete Novels & Collected Stories
190. Lafcadio Hearn: American Writings
191. A. J. Liebling: The Sweet Science & Other Writings
192. The Lincoln Anthology
193. Philip K. Dick: VALIS & Later Novels
194. Thornton Wilder: The Bridge of San Luis Rey & Other Novels 1926–1948
195. Raymond Carver: Collected Stories
196 & 197. American Fantastic Tales
198. John Marshall: Writings
199. The Mark Twain Anthology
200. Mark Twain: A Tramp Abroad, Following the Equator, Other Travels
201 & 202. Ralph Waldo Emerson: Selected Journals
203. The American Stage: Writing on Theater
204. Shirley Jackson: Novels & Stories
205. Philip Roth: Novels 1993–1995
206 & 207. H. L. Mencken: Prejudices
208. John Kenneth Galbraith: The Affluent Society & Other Writings 1952–1967
209. Saul Bellow: Novels 1970–1982
210 & 211. Lynd Ward: Six Novels in Woodcuts
212. The Civil War: The First Year
213 & 214. John Adams: Revolutionary Writings
215. Henry James: Novels 1903–1911
216. Kurt Vonnegut: Novels & Stories 1963–1973
217 & 218. Harlem Renaissance Novels
219. Ambrose Bierce: The Devil's Dictionary, Tales, & Memoirs
220. Philip Roth: The American Trilogy 1997–2000
221. The Civil War: The Second Year
222. Barbara W. Tuchman: The Guns of August, The Proud Tower
223. Arthur Miller: Plays 1964–1982
224. Thornton Wilder: The Eighth Day, Theophilus North, Autobiographical Writings
225. David Goodis: Five Noir Novels of the 1940s & 50s
226. Kurt Vonnegut: Novels & Stories 1950–1962
227 & 228. American Science Fiction: Nine Novels of the 1950s
229 & 230. Laura Ingalls Wilder: The Little House Books
231. Jack Kerouac: Collected Poems
232. The War of 1812
233. American Antislavery Writings
234. The Civil War: The Third Year
235. Sherwood Anderson: Collected Stories
236. Philip Roth: Novels 2001–2007
237. Philip Roth: Nemeses
238. Aldo Leopold: A Sand County Almanac & Other Writings
239. May Swenson: Collected Poems
240 & 241. W. S. Merwin: Collected Poems
242 & 243. John Updike: Collected Stories
244. Ring Lardner: Stories & Other Writings
245. Jonathan Edwards: Writings from the Great Awakening
246. Susan Sontag: Essays of the 1960s & 70s
247. William Wells Brown: Clotel & Other Writings
248 & 249. Bernard Malamud: Novels & Stories of the 1940s, 50s, & 60s
250. The Civil War: The Final Year
251. Shakespeare in America

252. Kurt Vonnegut: Novels 1976–1985
253 & 254. American Musicals 1927–1969
255. Elmore Leonard: Four Novels of the 1970s
256. Louisa May Alcott: Work, Eight Cousins, Rose in Bloom, Stories & Other Writings
257. H. L. Mencken: The Days Trilogy
258. Virgil Thomson: Music Chronicles 1940–1954
259. Art in America 1945–1970
260. Saul Bellow: Novels 1984–2000
261. Arthur Miller: Plays 1987–2004
262. Jack Kerouac: Visions of Cody, Visions of Gerard, Big Sur
263. Reinhold Niebuhr: Major Works on Religion & Politics
264. Ross Macdonald: Four Novels of the 1950s
265 & 266. The American Revolution: Writings from the Pamphlet Debate
267. Elmore Leonard: Four Novels of the 1980s
268 & 269. Women Crime Writers: Suspense Novels of the 1940s & 50s
270. Frederick Law Olmsted: Writings on Landscape, Culture, & Society
271. Edith Wharton: Four Novels of the 1920s
272. James Baldwin: Later Novels
273. Kurt Vonnegut: Novels 1987–1997
274. Henry James: Autobiographies
275. Abigail Adams: Letters
276. John Adams: Writings from the New Nation 1784–1826
277. Virgil Thomson: The State of Music & Other Writings
278. War No More: American Antiwar & Peace Writing
279. Ross Macdonald: Three Novels of the Early 1960s
280. Elmore Leonard: Four Later Novels
281. Ursula K. Le Guin: The Complete Orsinia
282. John O'Hara: Stories
283. The Unknown Kerouac: Rare, Unpublished & Newly Translated Writings
284. Albert Murray: Collected Essays & Memoirs
285 & 286. Loren Eiseley: Collected Essays on Evolution, Nature, & the Cosmos
287. Carson McCullers: Stories, Plays & Other Writings
288. Jane Bowles: Collected Writings
289. World War I and America: Told by the Americans Who Lived It
290 & 291. Mary McCarthy: The Complete Fiction
292. Susan Sontag: Later Essays
293 & 294. John Quincy Adams: Diaries
295. Ross Macdonald: Four Later Novels
296 & 297. Ursula K. Le Guin: The Hainish Novels & Stories
298 & 299. Peter Taylor: The Complete Stories
300. Philip Roth: Why Write? Collected Nonfiction 1960–2014
301. John Ashbery: Collected Poems 1991–2000
302. Wendell Berry: Port William Novels & Stories: The Civil War to World War II
303. Reconstruction: Voices from America's First Great Struggle for Racial Equality
304. Albert Murray: Collected Novels & Poems
305 & 306. Norman Mailer: The Sixties
307. Rachel Carson: Silent Spring & Other Writings on the Environment
308. Elmore Leonard: Westerns
309 & 310. Madeleine L'Engle: The Kairos Novels
311. John Updike: Novels 1959–1965
312. James Fenimore Cooper: Two Novels of the American Revolution
313. John O'Hara: Four Novels of the 1930s
314. Ann Petry: The Street, The Narrows
315. Ursula K. Le Guin: Always Coming Home
316 & 317. Wendell Berry: Collected Essays
318. Cornelius Ryan: The Longest Day, A Bridge Too Far
319. Booth Tarkington: Novels & Stories
320. Herman Melville: Complete Poems
321 & 322. American Science Fiction: Eight Classic Novels of the 1960s
323. Frances Hodgson Burnett: The Secret Garden, A Little Princess, Little Lord Fauntleroy
324. Jean Stafford: Complete Novels
325. Joan Didion: The 1960s & 70s
326. John Updike: Novels 1968–1975
327. Constance Fenimore Woolson: Collected Stories
328. Robert Stone: Dog Soldiers, Flag for Sunrise, Outerbridge Reach
329. Jonathan Schell: The Fate of the Earth, The Abolition, The Unconquerable World
330. Richard Hofstadter: Anti-Intellectualism in American Life, The Paranoid Style in American Politics, Uncollected Essays 1956–1965

This book is set in 10 point ITC Galliard Pro, a face designed for digital composition by Matthew Carter and based on the sixteenth-century face Granjon. The paper is acid-free lightweight opaque that will not turn yellow or brittle with age. The binding is sewn, which allows the book to open easily and lie flat. The binding board is covered in Brillianta, a woven rayon cloth made by Van Heek–Scholco Textielfabrieken, Holland.

Composition by Dianna Logan, Clearmont, MO.

Printing and binding by LSC Communications, Crawfordsville, IN.

Designed by Bruce Campbell.

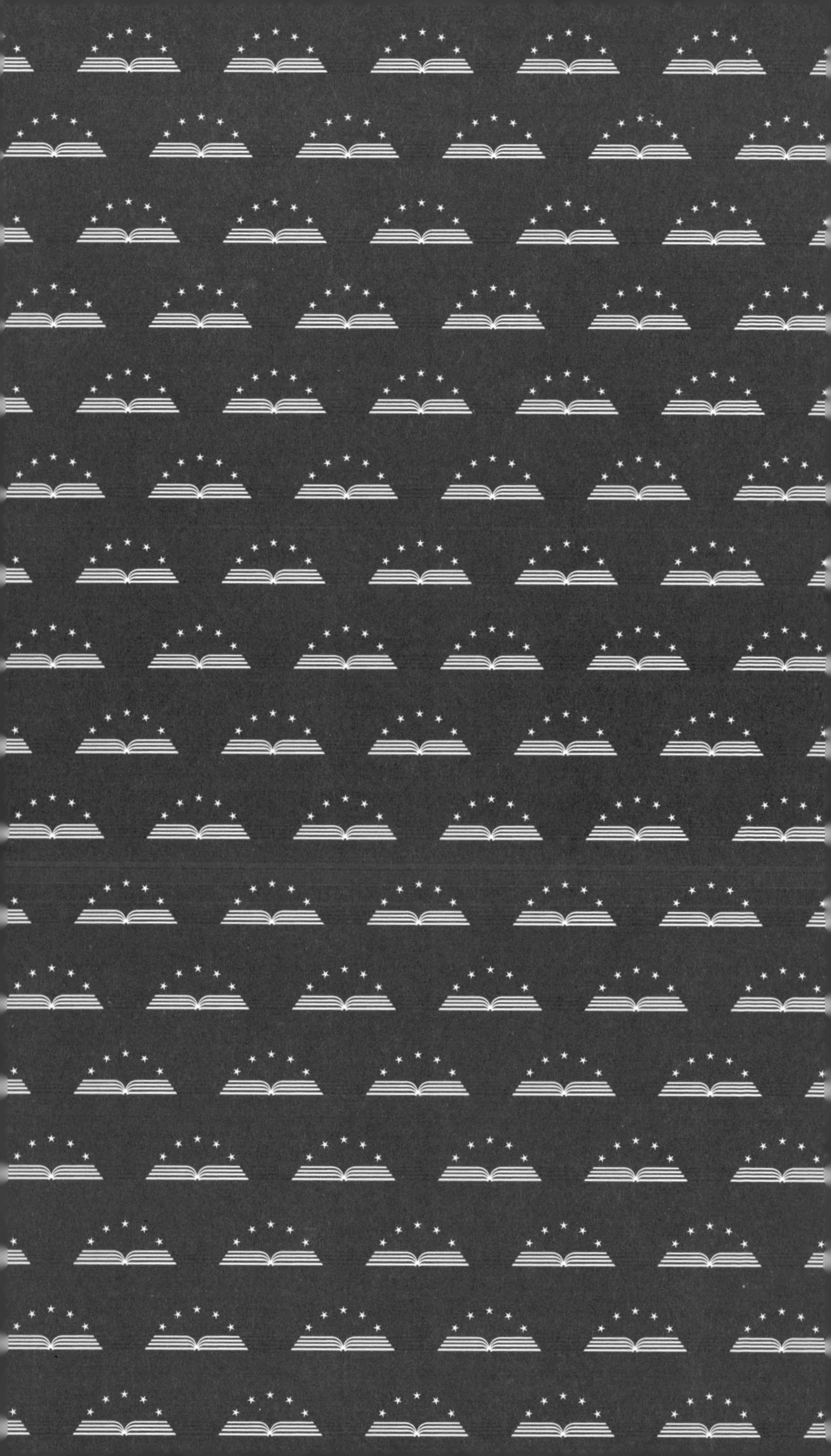